TICK

A NOVEL

J. Higgs
Dec 2022

JEFFREY HIGGS

ISBN 978-1-63874-674-4 (paperback)
ISBN 978-1-63874-675-1 (digital)

Christian Faith Publishing
832 Park Avenue
Meadville, PA 16335
www.christianfaithpublishing.com

This is a work of fiction. Unless otherwise indicated, all the names, characters, businesses, places, events, and incidents in this book are either the product of the author's imagination or used in a fictitious manner. Any resemblance to actual persons, living or dead, or actual events is purely coincidental.

Printed in the United States of America

To my family and friends
Thank you for your love and support. Life
would be a lonely journey without you.

Acknowledgments

The idea for writing *Tick* came after a particularly grueling trip to South America, assisting in developing a new mine near Arequipa, Peru. On the flight down to Peru, I read a novel that failed miserably to keep me entertained. I believed that I was capable of writing a book that was better than the novel I had just finished. But that was a lesson to be learned.

The day before my scheduled return to Utah, I spent hours walking along the oceanfront boardwalk in Miraflores, where I developed the basic concept and plotline for *Tick*. As it turned out, it became my most challenging endeavor.

In many ways, writing *Tick* has been a blessing. It has enabled me to recount some of my adventures growing up in Peru. In a small way, I hope this novel honors my parents, Will and Leah Higgs, now passed, who left friends and family behind in Utah in the '50s to carve out a living at twelve thousand feet in an isolated mining camp in the Peruvian Andes. My parents and the people they worked and socialized with—engineers, technicians, teachers, doctors, nurses, and housekeeping staff—were quite remarkable people, each in their own right: intelligent, adventuresome, committed, fun-loving, warm and giving, providing a wide range of attributes to draw upon for several of the book's main characters.

Writing the novel also allowed me to honor my grandparents from Utah, Myrtle and Horace Higgs, and Hattie and Milo Baxter. Like the character, Tick, my Depression-era grandparents were stoical, rarely complaining about the hand life had dealt them and continually generous with their time and resources. The small house I have described in the book as the Thomas family residence is an accurate description of the Higgs's home in Bountiful, Utah.

In many ways, I evoked the positive role models in my life to describe my main characters, but I soon discovered that writing a book involves a lot more than character development. For one thing, it is helpful to know how to write so that your thoughts are understandable to your readers! This fact brings me to thank the love of my life, Kathryn, my gifted wife of fifty years, whose efforts on *Tick* have been extraordinary. My sharp gal could instantly determine where my thoughts needed clarification and would spend hours working on a single sentence to get just the right wording. I especially appreciate her help editing many of the dialogs between women, not my strongest suit.

Of course, many other individuals contributed to *Tick*, some directly and others indirectly. I want those individuals to know that while I may not have precisely reflected their expertise or beliefs, they have all been profoundly helpful. I will start with my immediate family:

My attorney son, Andrew, was a tremendous help both in the legal confrontation segment between Susan Messener of Child Protective Services at the hospital and the trial scene later in the book. The time and effort he spent on the legal issues to improve the storyline is much appreciated.

Christopher Higgs, my firstborn, was sensitive to the moral tone of the book, inspiring edits more in line with our mutual Christian faith. He also urged me to beef up the book's tension between the good and evil characters. Christopher's wife, Jenny Higgs, was my final editor, and I appreciate the time and effort she put into improving the book.

Val Higgs, my sister, was the first person to read the complete *Tick* draft and later the final version. She read them nonstop, providing edits, and was very supportive of the effort.

Profound gratitude goes to my "critical care" readers, good friends who spent long hours reading the manuscript and recommending edits.

Included are Rich and Ellen Broggi, whose help in the editing process was tremendous and whose thoughtful and trustworthy review of the Christian message contained in the novel was invaluable.

Phil and Barb Schwin became *Ticks*'s first-time fans after listening to the early chapters while we were on a road trip to Southern Utah. We received their "thumbs-up" after reading the completed manuscript months later. The Schwins' enthusiastic reaction to the story early on was just the boost I needed to continue writing.

Peggy Sommer, a dear friend with a nursing background, poured over the book, determined to make the hospital scenes sound more realistic.

Others graciously read the book carefully, marking edits and making suggestions, proving again that no matter how hard you work on something, there is always room for improvement: this list includes Carole Cottam, Sue Ellen Wilcox, Rusty Dunbar, Claire Cassella, Karen Charnholm, and my friends at Pilates (spurred on by Eveline Rosa)—Jan Logan, Jan Thomas, Sharon Web, and Carma Barnhart.

There are others, people who have influenced the direction of the book; such as Dr. Michael Matlak and Dr. James Wilkens. I would shamelessly ask them questions and then use the information in the book. I hope I got it right. Included in this category are two people that have had a profound impact on the book, two people who at the time of this writing have never read it, Pastor David Jensen and Charlie Huebner. Both men are excellent Christian teachers, and I hope *Tick* accurately expresses their beliefs.

There have also been professionals involved in this effort. Ryan Bronson edited the first version of the book, instructing me on the essential elements of writing. We also have the Christian Faith Publishing professionals who have cleaned up the final version text and made this book possible.

Finally, we have Rio Urano, my talented artist and friend who did the beautiful cover design.

Writing *Tick* has been a valuable journey for me. As a book about good versus evil, God's Sovereignty, and man's free will, it has helped clarify my faith in God and the importance of family.

He shall cover you with His feathers, and under His wings you shall take refuge. (Psalm 91:4)

Fall Days in the Mountains

God's indescribable creativity was on full display that October afternoon. The autumn sunlight was perfect for showcasing the beauty of the Uinta's high peaks, some extending up over 13,000 feet, towered above hundreds of ponds and lakes glistening in the glacial valleys below. The fall leaves in aspen groves danced in the cold wind, resplendent in a red, orange, green, and yellow kaleidoscope. They captured the light from the setting sun and softened a terrain dominated by the rock buttresses above.

The protruding ledge eight hundred feet above the boulder-strewn stream was a perfect vantage point for observing the area's grandeur and a horizon silhouetted by Kings Peak, the highest mountain in Utah. Below, a stream, a flashing rivulet of light, emptied into a small lake surrounded by aspen, and, above, the sky was a pale blue, marked with clouds tinged by rays from the afternoon sun. The only anomaly was a slowly fading white line jutting out from a silver comet, heading west.

The picture-perfect scenery offered no hope nor peace of mind to the shivering twelve-year-old girl huddled under a lone, stunted pine tree. Not even the unlikely presence of the tree itself, thriving well above the tree line in a cold, moistureless environment, could lead her to believe that she too could overcome impossible odds and survive. She couldn't even find solace in her keen imagination, her default escape mechanism, now blunted by grief, pain, and exhaustion. On this day, the plane overhead with its silver contrail would not be carrying a mother and daughter away to some great and happy adventure.

Two days earlier, Timothy Bird had taunted her as he squatted like a deranged guerilla on the slope above, throwing rocks over the edge of the cliff, beyond angry that he could not reach nor see her beneath the branches of the pine tree. She hated his voice, sharp and penetrating, conveying nothing but refined cruelty.

In the past, she would have retaliated, her sharp wit and agile tongue capable of hurling back equally scathing language. Yet now, when she could speak without fear of immediate retribution, her tongue remained still. She hadn't spoken for over a year. In her mind, words and pain had formed a permanent association.

"You had so much potential." The sarcasm in Timothy's voice as he shouted down to the girl was thinly veiled, as was his frustration. "I wanted to separate you from your mother years ago, but then who would have cooked for me? She was a helluva cook, but she was pathetic and weak, just like you. Your loser mom completely contaminated you with her brainless, two-thousand-year-old feel-good religion. Oh, and about your dear mother, whom you so nobly deserted—she put up a good fight, which is more than I can say for her cowardly pup. She even got in a few licks before I cut her to pieces."

Logic and experience told her that her mother, Alissa, was dead, but her heart struggled to accept the notion. Her gut wanted revenge.

"Yeah, she would be proud of your big escape, cleverly trapped on a ledge. What a genius! You now have two options: jump off the cliff and splatter the few brains you have or stay on the ledge and die of hunger and thirst. It's your choice, cookie. Either way, the crows will peck your eyes out, and nobody will ever find your smelly little corpse."

Days before in open rebellion, the girl had taken a stance that would have predictably resulted in Timothy killing her. Her mother thwarted these actions exchanging her life and, in the girl's tortured mind, her soul for those of her daughter. With her back pressed against the trunk of the tree, the girl knew she had to stay alive somehow. She needed to hurt him, to make him pay.

All of it was her fault.

"Of course, I could go back to the ranch, get a rope, and pull you up. I might skin you alive then. Call it a transformative make-over, something to improve on your pitiful looks. Who knows? I might change my mind, but I'll be back in a few days. You can think about it while I'm gone."

Her mother had told her that someday they would be free, that good would win out over evil. But as the years passed, their situation became more precarious, and it was intolerable during the past year. Her mother recently even talked of an angel with fiery wings coming to save them. It was an image that the girl, with her hardened, practical mind, found it difficult to believe.

Despite her considerable skills in concealment, Timothy had relentlessly tracked her across the mountains; traces of blood and drag marks from the shackle on her ankle left telltale marks revealing her path. He finally cornered her on a slope next to a cliff, and fear and desperation forced her to take a desperate gamble—a running leap from the cliff's brink to a lonely pine tree, a span of at least eight feet. Unable to hold on to a branch, she crashed down through the tree's limbs, landing hard on the ledge below and breaking her arm.

She was out of his reach but trapped.

Athletically gifted and fearless when it came to heights, she hoped to find some way down to the valley below. However, the cliff walls were without handholds and impassible, and her left arm was now a useless, dangling, painful impediment. She held no hope of rescue.

In her mind, the world was full of Timothies. Faint recollections from the past, her mother's tales of a different life, and a God who loved them were now just that—dreams and stories.

Mom's God had deserted them, she thought. *There had been no escape. No rescue. No angel.*

Perhaps when he returned, she could kill him by luring him down to the ledge and then pushing him over the cliff. She could watch him twist and cry out as he fell, see the fear in his mocking eyes, and hopefully hear his bones shattering on the sheer hardness of the rocks below. Then, she could climb the rope to freedom.

Reality set in. She was weak, and Timothy was massive, strong, and cautious. Anger, a product of the powerless, gave way to grief, and for the first time in years, she allowed herself to cry.

Hiking

Brad Hughes felt tired as he started to climb the last few switchbacks through a boulder-laden slope leading up to the ridge's top. It was an exhilarating, heart-pounding physical exhaustion that revitalized him rather than the numbing fatigue that had been with him the past four years since he lost his wife, Catherine, to heart disease. The hike was good for him. Being out in the mountains, away from work and the endless bombardment of e-mails, meetings, and phone calls had cleared his head. This venture was long overdue.

By any measure, at age fifty-eight, Hughes was successful, own-ing and operating many gravel and limestone operations in the inter-mountain region surrounding Salt Lake City. He was a miner, sup-plying the primary construction materials for projects in that area: crushed rock mixed in with concrete for foundations and sidewalks, base material for roadbeds, and pulverized limestone used as a filler in asphalt roofs and as a main source of calcium for egg-laying hens.

The location of his operations was ideal, having significant, cost-saving transportation advantages over the competition. Over the years, Brad had carefully assembled a knowledgeable, ethical management team that ran his debt-free operations. Truth be known, the company would thrive even without his guidance.

He had raised three successful boys, all of whom, unfortunately, lived out of state. Ben, his oldest son, and his wife, Becky, lived in New Orleans with their three children: ten-year-old Kaitlin and the five-year-old twins, Jerome and Jonathan. Brian and his wife, Natalie, resided in Irvine, California, with their two-year-old, Lizzy. The youngest, David, a recent graduate of the Colorado School of Mines, was unmarried and currently working on a mining development project in Chile.

Brad dimly recognized that his current role related to his family was to serve as an example for a moral life, to be an encouraging and loving grandfather, and high on his list, to teach the grandchildren to be good skiers. As for his sons, Brad respected and supported their desire to make their own decisions and put their families first. His days of raising a family were over. Invisible boundaries dictated that he be a provider of advice or help only when asked and occasionally be a source of vacation funds.

He scarcely dated since his wife's death, regretting not having lived in the moment when he was younger, leaving so much of the burden of raising a family on his wife.

Unable to find a woman with Catherine's charm and grace and not wanting to hurt the feelings of women with whom he was unwilling to commit, he found it best to remain sociable, but remote. Most of his time was spent working, visiting his family, or serving on the boards of several charities that he supported.

Resting to catch his breath in the thin mountain air, Brad took in the grandeur that surrounded him. Four days ago he had awakened in the night, feeling a compulsion to get away. The next morning, Brad uncharacteristically canceled a sales meeting and headed to the sporting goods store to purchase camping equipment. When he informed his sons of his plan to take off unaccompanied into the wilderness, they tried to dissuade him, offering to come out and climb with him as soon as schedules would permit, and inviting him to come to visit the grandchildren. Brad rejected their requests. He had spent most of his adult life planning vacations around his family, always available for them, but this time, he wanted to be alone. For the first time since he could remember, he would set out on a solitary adventure.

Athletic and an excellent snow skier, Brad was by no means an experienced outdoorsman. He had taken the boys to a few campgrounds in past years that were nothing more than well-defined plots of land in the forest with close-by public restrooms. That was a far cry from a five-day companionless outing in the Uinta Mountain High Wilderness Area. Nevertheless, he planned his excursion carefully.

Brad's childhood spent in isolated mining camps, along with frequent ski outings, had given him an appreciation for challenging terrain, bad weather, and the many curve balls nature could throw. He went first-class, buying the best and lightest tent and sleeping bag combination, along with a stove and sufficient food to last the week. From his possessions, he took layered clothing that was suitable for any weather, some 8 mm. climbing rope, a six-shot .38 Special revolver, and an emergency medical kit. He planned out exactly where he was going, mapped out a route, and instructed his secretary, Whitney Heldar, to arrange a search party if he was not back in ten days.

It was now the third day of his hike, and Brad found himself in a desolate area, inexplicably drawn by the image of Catherine's profile high on a ridge, displayed by the motley-colored strata and shadows on a rock face. This impulsive "look-see" was a two-hour deviation from his planned route, and many miles beyond the short outing he had planned for the day.

The elevation began to take its toll as he made his way up a talus slope with a cliff to his right, and on a particularly tricky section of the mountain, he paused and carefully examined his surroundings. He was alone, standing on the edge of a thirty-some-foot slope of broken and fine weathered rock. There was a cliff with a barely visible treetop at the base of the fractured rock, the tree extending up just above the slope's edge.

The wind's keening was the only sound that Brad heard until a sudden shift in wind direction carried another unexpected, muffled, and vaguely recognizable noise over the cliff's edge, rising up the slope and reaching his ears. Taking a step closer to the edge, Brad leaned toward the sound below, compelled to know what it was and feeling inexplicably summoned by it.

Pausing once again, he wondered if the noise was a natural anomaly. *But what if it wasn't?*

Feeling driven to know, he removed a rope from his backpack and, after tying it to a large boulder, started down the slope. When he reached the bottom, still grasping the rope, he leaned out over the edge of the cliff and finally discovered the source of the sound that had provoked him into taking such a foolhardy risk.

It was a young girl, and she was crying. Wearing light cotton clothes and huddled under the tree, the girl had drawn her legs up into a ball, tucking her head between her knees. Blackened blood stained the fabric of her shorts. Brad immediately called out to her, but to his amazement, she scuttled like a startled crab around the trunk of the tree, disappearing from view.

He repeatedly called out to her, but his appeals went unanswered. She remained silent, hiding behind the tree.

The ledge was about fifteen feet down with a sheer wall—it was a prison with no escape. Although the day's deviation led to the girl's discovery, Brad was far from the main trail, and he knew that a rescue attempt gone awry could leave them both stranded. His cell phone wasn't a present option—he hadn't had reception for hours—and shouting for help would be pointless.

The more he thought about it, in fact, the riskier it looked. Even if he could rappel down to the girl, he would still need to pull them both back up the wall and the slope. He wasn't sure his arthritic shoulder was strong enough to hold up. Years ago, he had suffered a shoulder injury playing football and never fully recovered his left arm's strength. Even worse, his rope wasn't long enough to reach down to the ledge from where he had tied it near the top of the slope. He would have to climb back up the hill, untie his rope, slide down the hill to a stone outcrop above the ledge, and then retie the rope.

If that weren't enough, climbing the slope without a rope with the girl on his back would be risky. The hill was quite steep and covered with loose soil and rock.

Sighing, he reluctantly realized that he had no choice. If he left the girl, she would face the night exposed to the elements with only what little food and water he had left and the shirt on his back to keep her warm. He had left most of his supplies back at his base camp, which was now a good six-hour hike away. Even if he threw down what supplies he had, he could not be sure she was strong enough to take advantage of them. He had to take the risk.

Climbing back up the slope, Brad retrieved his rope and then carefully planned his descent and the subsequent climb up from the ledge. He tied a series of knots in the rope at about one-foot intervals and cut foot holes in the bottom of his backpack. He then slid prudently down the loose rock to the outcropping above the ledge.

Upon reaching the bottom of the slope, he lassoed the rope around the stone outcropping, tying the one knot stuck in his mind from his youth: the king of knots, the bowline. He had memorized the mnemonic used to teach the knot to children: "Up through the rabbit hole, round the big tree, down through the rabbit hole, and off goes he."

Brad had never been an advocate of the saying, "No good deed goes unpunished," but after the first few minutes of the rescue, he was a believer. The problems started about midway down the descent to the ledge. Upon spotting him, the girl emerged from her hiding place and moved toward the edge of the cliff. Panicked that she could fall to her death, Brad waved at her to move away from the cliff's edge, swung sideways, and lost his grip on the rope. As he fell to the ledge, a sharp, protruding rock lacerated his calf.

Angry with himself for his clumsiness, he awkwardly stood up and took stock of the situation. And there she was, standing some fifteen feet away. Her face was a shifting display of exhaustion, disdain at his mishap, and startlingly, crazed fury and open defiance. She looked to be about twelve or thirteen years old. Her hair was dirty, matted, and full of leaves, and a terrible wound ran from her cheekbone down toward her mouth. Dark, congealed blood marked the injury and trailed down her neck. Her left arm, bandaged with a torn, dirty piece of cloth from her clothing, hung limply at her side.

Brad moved toward the girl but stopped when she edged even closer to the cliff, the two of them locked in a foolish dance. The impasse, lasting only a few seconds, went on for what seemed to Brad like hours.

And then, ever so carefully, he spoke, "If I move back, will you please move away from the cliff? You are scaring me half to death."

The girl did not respond, so he stepped back to the far edge of the ledge. Slowly, the girl edged her way back from the edge and squatted on the ground behind a hip-high boulder. She had an angry, now calculating expression on her face. As he watched her, Brad couldn't help but feel somewhat helpless and confused; he assumed that rescuers were appreciated, welcomed, and cooperated with, but this was turning into a fiasco. She looked as though she wanted to kill him.

The standoff continued with Brad reassuringly talking to the girl, and the girl, in turn, maintaining her defiant, aggressive stance. Suddenly, her expression softened, and she stood up. Her eyes shifted to the horizon gazing at the sun, which was now low in the sky. She gave a slight, almost imperceptible nod and invited Brad to come closer. With the unimaginable vulnerability of an injured child bringing out his most protective instincts, he slowly walked toward her, circling her position, careful to keep between the girl and the edge of the cliff, lured by what he thought was a gesture of trust.

The attack was sudden and premeditated. Brad never knew what alerted him, perhaps some primal instinct, but the girl pounced just as he came into striking distance. Grasping a large rock she had hidden behind the boulder, the girl swung at his head, and as his hands went up in self-defense, she drove her shoulder into him in a desperate attempt to push him over the ledge. Only his high school and college years in the trenches as a middle linebacker saved him as he instinctively crouched, lowering his center of gravity. He drove forward into the onrushing girl, taking the blow of the rock on his shoulder. Wrapping his arms around her, he tackled a wisp of air compared with the two-hundred-and-fifty-pound fullbacks he contended with in the past.

Thoughts of an easy outcome were quickly dispelled—a whistle didn't blow, and the play didn't come to a halt. Brad had the girl tucked up against him, but it didn't deter her attack. Somehow she managed to rain blows on his back, simultaneously twisting her body with the intent to bash in his skull. When that strategy failed, she tried to knee him in the groin, and then, like a pit bull, she sank her teeth into his left shoulder.

Brad fought back, his every move designed to subdue the girl without injuring her. With his right hand, he pushed her head back. With his left arm, he took hold of her right arm, twisting it behind her and pulling her tightly against him, successfully restraining her movement. The struggle was strangely silent because the girl did not scream or cry out; the only sounds were her heavy breathing and her feet slipping on the rock as she now tried to push them both over the cliff's edge. In control of the situation, Brad repeatedly tried to calm the girl.

"Please don't fight me! I am here to help you! I promise I won't hurt you." His words had no impact on the determined girl.

Finally, in desperation, he looked upward.

Please, God, I need your help to get control of this child. I promise I will take care of her.

As quickly as the fight started, it ended, and for a second, Brad thought he had lost the girl to exhaustion, perhaps even death. In reality, her attention had shifted. Brad felt a chill, as if a cloud had blocked the sun. He then heard an unearthly scream as an enormous eagle flared out just above his back. The eagle, angry that its well-hidden perch atop the tree had been compromised, swooped past from behind him, and he could feel the air pushing down from its outstretched wings. Then, just as suddenly as it had appeared, the eagle vanished across the ridge.

The girl stopped struggling, becoming limp in his arms as the stone she had been holding fell from her hand, rolled over the cliff and, with a sharp, echoing crack, joined the broken and shattered rocks below. Baffled by her attack and fighting to regain his composure, Brad relaxed his grip on the girl and held her at arm's length, examining her as you would a dangerous animal. Any anger he felt was dispelled when he looked into her eyes, eyes that were now inquisitively staring back at him as if he had somehow transformed into another creature. Despite being bloodshot and framed by dark circles, the startling uniqueness of her eyes struck him: black pupils and incandescent green irises, a streak of amber running through her right iris—the most unusual eyes he had ever seen.

"It's all right. It's gone now," Brad reassured. "I think we startled that eagle as much as it did us! I'm not here to hurt you either, only to get you off this mountain to safety."

Waiting for a response but not receiving one, he continued, "I need to move you to a safer location."

Unable to elicit a response, he carefully lifted the girl and carried her to the back of the ledge, setting her down gently as far away from the edge of the cliff as possible. She quietly lay there exhausted, her eyes focused on his face. She was fighting to stay alert and seemingly not in pain. Thinking she might be going into shock, Brad took advantage of the slope to elevate her legs above her head and then, kneeling over her, examined her wounds. Brad had seen his share of industrial and recreational accidents, ranging from mangled hands to badly scraped knees and chins, but nothing in his experience came close to the nature and extent of the child's injuries. Someone had brutalized her.

In addition to having what appeared to be a knife wound, the girl's left forearm was swollen, perhaps broken. She had a profound wound down her cheek, a bloody laceration running across her right shoulder and extending down to her lower back, and smaller abrasions seemingly everywhere. She had a shackle around her left ankle. Under closer examination, the ankle looked deformed.

Disgusted with the inadequacy of his first-aid kit and his lack of emergency training, Brad forged ahead. He fashioned a crude splint for her arm from branches and tore his T-shirt into strips to bandage the cuts on her cheek and forearm. Brad decided to leave the large wound on her shoulder and back alone because it had clotted into the fabric of her shirt. Cleaning those wounds, he thought, might do more harm than good. Finally, using what was left of the T-shirt, he bandaged the wound on his leg.

Counting on the trapped heat from his body to warm her tiny frame, Brad removed his extra-large fleece jacket and zipped her up in it. The jacket covered her below her knees. The sun ducked behind a cloud, and the autumn mountain air chilled him as he sat there, evaluating his next steps. He had to get both of them up and out of their rocky prison. Then they would need to hike to his camp: some sixteen miles down the ridge. The sun was low in the sky, and they would already be facing most of the hike in the dark.

Before getting started, he wanted to get fluid into her and, if possible, some food. She eagerly started drinking when he held the valve of his knapsack water bag to her parched lips. He remembered reading that one shouldn't let a dehydrated person drink too much or too fast. Brad wasn't sure what constituted "fast," so he decided to err on the side of caution, forcing her to drink slowly. Food was a bigger problem; he only had a few chewy nutrition bars that he thought might be difficult for her to eat, given the wound on her cheek.

Using a stone, he pulverized the bars into a coarse powder, making it possible for the girl to swallow without chewing. A real meal would have to wait until they got back to the campsite.

When he finished with the high-priority items and the girl was somewhat settled, Brad tried to get her to communicate. "Can you talk to me? Do you understand English? What's your name?" No response. "*Hablas Español?*" Again, she just looked at him.

"Okay, I'm praying that you understand English because I need some information to help get us off this mountain. Can you at least nod your head and let me know if you understand what I am saying?"

When her head bobbed up and down, a huge weight was lifted off his back. "That's a start," he replied. "Now tell me… Are you running away from somebody?" She nodded yes. "Do they know where you are? Are we in danger from them?" Again, she nodded. "If that's the case, we had better get going. I have cut leg holes in the bottom of my knapsack, and I want you to roll on your side so I can get you into it. I'm pretty sure you are small enough to fit. Then we are out of here, and I am going to get you to safety."

The girl looked at him skeptically, disbelief in her eyes, but once again, her head nodded in affirmation.

Brad's plan was a success. He easily managed to roll her on her side, put her legs through the holes in the knapsack, and then pull it up around her back and chest. Then, lying on his side next to her, he drew the straps of the backpack over his shoulders. Rolling over on his knees, he stood up.

"I don't know if you have it in you, but if you can, I need you to put your right arm around my neck and hold on tight while I climb this rope." The girl obliged, tightening her right arm around his neck. Her left arm, now in a sling, was pressed against his back.

Brad grabbed the rope and began walking up the steep rock face. The knots in the rope provided him the leverage to use his legs for most of the heavy lifting. The girl was light, well-balanced in the knapsack, and holding on to him tightly.

After reaching the cliff's top and now on his hands and knees, he started climbing up the slope.

It didn't take long for Brad to realize that they were in big trouble. It was like climbing a steep hill in heavy snow, his hiking boots slipping backward in the loose rock with each step he took.

Feeling desperate, Brad managed to take out his hunting knife and, turning the blade sideways, used it as a pickaxe, thrusting it into the rocky ground and pulling them up the steeper parts of the slope. Still, without the efforts of the girl, he doubted whether they would have made it. Anytime he fell, started to twist sideways, or slid back on the slope, she would thrust her feet out and dig her worn sneakers into the ground for extra traction.

At the top of the slope in the thin air, his heart pounding, exhausted, Brad struggled to his feet, panting, now feeling the weight of the girl. She never panicked, and he knew that she had played an essential role in getting them up the slope. When he finally caught his breath, he asked, "Do you need to get down? Would you like some water?" But he quickly remembered that the girl wasn't much of a talker. "If yes, tap my head once. If no, tap it twice… No rocks, please!"

The girl quickly tapped his head twice, so Brad began to limp his way down the mountainside. They were at least four hours from the main trail, and his leg was aching with every step. His mind raced with thoughts on what he should do and in what order when he finally got her to his campsite. He needed to get her warm, he thought, get something hot into her system—perhaps oatmeal—clean her wounds and cover them with antibiotic cream.

Then it hit him. First and foremost, he had to keep the girl safe. Whoever had done this to her was still out there and possibly close by. He wondered if she was a runaway from a fanatical polygamous colony, where young women were raised from birth to serve their prophet, told what to think, how to dress, and whom to marry: women who were raised to believe the outside world was evil, to be kept at a distance. Dissent resulted in ex-communication and separation from the group, from their families, and, in their minds, from God. The prophets always controlled access to heaven. But, if that was the case, it didn't look like she had bought into the program.

If the assailants were armed, there was little he could do, he thought. He had his pistol, but it might not do much good if faced with an adversary armed with a shotgun or rifle. Worse, his camp was out in the open. Anyone going down the trail would spot it immediately.

Not accustomed to the sensation of fear, and realizing he could be walking into an ambush, Brad reacted by turning off his flashlight. He then picked his way down the mountain, sticking to the trees and avoiding the main trail. He was now in a constant state of vigilance.

Brad's decision cost time and effort, and they did not arrive at the campsite until well past midnight. Amazingly, the girl had slept for most of the journey, waking only at her rescuer's request to drink more water.

Day 2

Arriving at the campsite, Brad retrieved his sleeping bag, wrapped the girl in it, and carried her to a nearby boulder field that he had explored the day before. It wasn't much of a campsite—small, with no view and a long walk to water—but at least it was hidden and somewhat defensible, with only one natural access point.

"Look, I don't want to be out in the open tonight, and I think this place is well hidden. I am going to go back and pick up my equipment. Are you going to be all right if I leave you for a few minutes?"

The girl gave him an affirmative head nod, and he set out.

Returning to his camp, he broke down the tent and gathered the rest of his camping equipment, all the while doing his best to eliminate any signs of his recent residency in the area. He then set up the new camp at the boulder field on level ground the size of a postage stamp, surrounded by towering rock.

Confident that they were hidden from view, Brad heated water on a camp stove and made some oatmeal, which, thankfully, the girl could eat. He then boiled a pot of water, removed the fleece he had lent her, and started a process that he had dreaded for the entire journey down the mountain—dealing with her horrific injuries. The cleaning and caring procedure would be the same for each wound: clean the laceration as best he could, apply antibiotic ointment, and bandage.

The wound across her shoulder and back was especially challenging to clean. Brad was concerned about embarrassing the young girl in any manner or aggravating a possibly broken left arm. He placed her on her right side and cut away the back of her shift, carefully trimming around the fabric that had penetrated the wound. He soaked the remaining fabric with warm water and gently pulled the fibers out of the injury. The lesion was deep, with torn flesh in some areas reaching down into the muscle. It was a long wound that, like a snake, wrapped around her body.

His stomach churning and chills going down his legs, Brad tried his best not to hurt the child as he wrapped her in makeshift bandages. The girl, who now resembled a miniature Frankenstein, had been astonishingly brave, never crying out once throughout the process, only silently flinching during the worst parts. Finally finished, Brad pulled his fleece shirt over her and zipped the patient into the sleeping bag.

Exhausted, Brad lay down next to the silent girl in the corner of the tent, hoping to catch some sleep. For hours he lay awake, still in his hiking clothes, rocks digging into his side, having given up his mattress to the girl. She was restless, tossing and turning as if in flight. It was, by every account, a miserable night.

Dawn broke with a heavy mist and intermittent rainfall. Thunder reverberated between the boulders of their little fortress. Not liking the idea of exposing the girl to the weather and worried about being seen in the daylight by her captors, Brad made plans to hike out at nightfall. He spent the morning waiting for the girl to wake up, and when she finally opened her eyes, he fashioned a potty using a cooking pot lined with a plastic bag. Placing the pot next to her, Brad explained what it was for and then left the tent to give her some privacy.

When he returned to the tent, he retrieved the makeshift chamber pot and was relieved to see that she could use it; although, the color of her urine indicated that she was dehydrated.

Obviously in pain, her movements slow and careful, Brad gave her three pulverized ibuprofen capsules before preparing a hot oatmeal breakfast with torn up biscuits and jelly. When she finished eating, he used a wet, warm washcloth to clean the blood on her face and neck. He also washed her feet and around the wounds on her back.

In the light of day, Brad could now see healed-over lash marks on her lower back, small round burns on her feet, and scars on both forearms. Angry and disgusted, he zipped her back up in the sleeping bag and, as a final task, rinsed the blood out of her matted hair with warm water, carefully avoiding the laceration on the side of her head. He gently dried and combed out her short blond hair before she fell back asleep.

Brad's adrenaline rush faded, and after pulling on two layers of clothing and making a mattress from pine straw, he crawled over to his corner of the tent, his pistol and knife under the shirt he was using as a pillow. Sheets of rain hammered against the side of the tent. The air was cold, humid, and musky. Sleep was hard to come by. Images of her wounds darkened his mind, accented by lightning strikes and earth-shaking booms of thunder. She would be scarred for life, he thought.

What kind of monster would do such a thing?

He awoke in the afternoon, feeling a hot breath against his cheek. As his eyes adjusted to the dim light in the tent, he became aware of the girl pushed up beside him, holding the blade of his multi-plier tool inches away from his throat. Her eyes were questioning, uncertain, and fearful.

Brad gathered his thoughts. "Little girl, whoever you are, God did not put me on this mountain to hurt you. You're angry and frightened—with every reason to feel that way, I'm sure, but I'm not the bad guy here. If you use that knife on me now, you'll be on your own, and good luck, but take the knife down now, and I will do everything in my power to keep you safe. I'm too tired to fight with you, so you choose."

The girl pulled back, and as Brad put out his hand, she resignedly handed him the tool, flinching as he took it as if expecting a blow, and watching closely as Brad carefully folded the blade into the handle.

26

"Where is the case?" he asked. The girl reached behind her and handed it to him. Then he put the tool back into the case and, holding it in the palm of his hand, extended it to the girl.

"Here, you can keep it. I'm going to trust you with it. If I ever do anything to harm you, feel free to use it on me. But if you do take it, you must agree to trust me and do what I say, at least until I get you off this mountain. Do you understand me?"

The girl's eyes showed approval, and she nodded her head.

"Good. Just don't cut yourself, please. Say, do you need to use the pot again?" The girl nodded her head, so Brad handed her his makeshift potty and left the tent, stepping outside into a slight drizzle of rain. When he returned, he was satisfied to see that she seemed hydrated.

At this point, Brad decided to make a bold gamble—a high-risk act of faith. "Look, child, we need more water, but it will take me about fifteen minutes to fetch it. Have you ever handled a pistol?" The girl nodded. "In that case, I am going to leave my pistol with you for your protection. If I run into your friends, I will convince them I am just a hiker and lead them away from here."

Brad took the pistol from his holster and casually handed it to the girl. "This is a six-shot .38 Special revolver. I like it because it's easy to use. Just pull back the hammer and fire." He then watched as the girl unexpectedly opened the cylinder, confirming that the weapon was loaded. Brad smiled. "I'm trusting you. We have to work together."

As he approached the campsite with the water, Brad prayed that the strange little rescue wouldn't shoot him. Calling out as he came around the boulders, he found the girl where he had left her at the entrance to the tent, gun in hand. Walking over to her and doing his best to pretend that nothing was out of the ordinary, he set the water down and asked for the gun. To his great relief, the girl didn't hesitate to hand it back to him. He then prepared two packages of ramen noodles and opened a can of Vienna sausages that they shared.

"You need to get more rest," he said. "We have a long hike tonight, but I promise you, tomorrow we will be off this mountain."

Brad watched as the girl settled down, shaking his head with skeptical respect as she took the multi-tool out of its case and extended the knife blade, placing it under the knapsack that she was using as a pillow. As he lay down next to her, he took his pistol out of its holster and placed it between them. He turned to the girl and winked.

"The gun is mine, but if something happens to me, you should take it and protect yourself."

The girl gave him a quick nod, and he thought he saw a smile. "I guess we'll be taking care of each other," he said. Brad closed his eyes and fell asleep. It was four in the afternoon.

Some six hours later, Brad awakened hungry. He pulled a light meal together as quietly as possible, careful not to rattle any pans, using a penlight to see. He roused the child and let her eat while he hurriedly prepared for the trip down the mountain. She watched his every move as he grabbed his brand-new, top-of-the-line winter shirt and cut off the sleeves, making them into knee-highs to cover her legs. He finalized his fashion statement with his heavy woolen socks for her feet. He helped her back into his hooded fleece jacket and, after guiding her into the knapsack, covered her with a makeshift poncho made by cutting away the tent door flap, a hole in its center for her head.

She was as well protected as he could make her, and he trusted that she would stay warm and dry, even if it rained heavily during the night. With his rescued and well-cared-for passenger on his back, he abandoned the tent, leaving the bulk of his equipment on the mountain. He carried only the girl and whatever clothing, food, and water they might need for the night's hike.

Using a walking stick to steady himself, Brad started limping down the mountain, his injured calf muscle throbbing. Knowing he was in for a nine-to ten-hour hike before he could expect any help, his goal was to get into cell phone range sometime in the early morning.

As Brad painfully hiked through the night, the girl slept soundly, her head resting on his shoulder, drops of drool falling from the corner of her mouth chilling the back of his neck.

Brad was drained when dawn finally broke. The light slowly revealed the surrounding landscape, and the high peaks of the Uintas were shrouded in mist. It was a beautiful morning.

He continued down the mountain, always looking behind him, periodically checking for a cell signal. At 10:00 a.m., the bars on his phone told him he finally had reception.

Rescue

Surveying the area, Brad spotted an open meadow where a chopper could land safely. He then determined the site coordinates using the GPS on his iPhone. Not wanting to be out in the open while waiting for help and still wary of the girl's captors, Brad carried the child to a wooded area on a knoll to the east of the meadow, a sanctuary with good cover and visibility. Once the girl was comfortable, he dialed 911.

A female voice came on the line, "911, what is your emergency?"

"I have a medical emergency, and I am requesting an immediate helicopter extraction at the following coordinates in the Uinta Mountains."

After repeating the coordinates twice and confirming that the operator had them down correctly, Brad continued, "The injured party looks to be around twelve or thirteen years old, female, very thin, with several serious lacerations and possibly a broken arm. I strongly recommend law enforcement accompany the medical team. Someone has tortured the girl, and the perpetrators may still be in the area."

"You said tortured? That's a serious statement. Please understand, sir, that hoax calls are punishable by law."

"I'm aware of that, madam, but *tortured* is precisely what I mean, and I couldn't be more serious in telling you that the rescue team must be accompanied by law enforcement. The child has indicated that someone is chasing her, and her wounds are unmistakably man-made. She has a shackle locked around her ankle, and whoever has worked her over may be nearby. I have to assume they are armed and dangerous."

Brad gave the operator his name and address and was told to hold for the operator's supervisor. After some moments, a male's voice was on the line.

"Where exactly did you find the child, and how would you describe her current condition?" the man asked.

"I found the girl yesterday trapped on a ledge in the mountains about sixteen miles from our current location. Along with many other wounds, she was suffering from exposure and dehydration. I carried her down to get cell phone coverage. She has been able to drink and eat. I would say her condition at this point is critical but stable. Oh, she also has a shackle around her left ankle. She may have a broken arm, and she has deep lacerations on her back, arm, and cheek. Look, if you need confirmation of my identity, you can call my secretary, Tammy Heldar, at—"

The supervisor interrupted, "Mr. Hughes? Mr. Brad Hughes of Hughes Industries?"

"That's correct," responded Brad.

"We will have an airlift with police personnel on board as soon as possible."

"Thank you. When the airlift arrives at the coordinates, there's a meadow large enough to land in, but your pilots may not see me. We are hiding in a grove of trees to the east of the meadow. I'll come out with the girl once they arrive. Please hurry."

Brad spent the next fifteen minutes on his cell phone, answering more detailed questions about the girl's condition, particulars on where and how he had found her, and if he was armed. Finally, the conversation ended. Help was on the way.

Having seen several movies where ringing phones prove to be disastrous, Brad set his phone to vibrate. He then covered the girl with his jacket.

"Hang in there," he whispered. "We're going to be off this mountain soon, and you're going to be okay."

The girl nodded.

Over the next two hours, Brad received several text messages assuring him that the rescue was in progress. For Brad, the time seemed to pass quickly. The girl fell asleep in his arms, with her thin body draped across his chest, her head tucked under his chin. The slight rising and falling of her chest reassured him that she was alive, and he even heard occasional snoring. The sun was bright with its rays passing through the branches, keeping them relatively warm and inducing feelings of safety and tranquility.

For the first time since finding the girl, Brad could relax a bit. He fought to resist the sun-induced drowsiness and did his best to remain motionless while keeping his attention focused on the meadow below; they weren't out of the woods yet.

The distinctive sound of helicopter rotors was a relief. Brad woke the girl, carefully picked her up, and began walking toward the landing site. He watched as the Life Flight Agusta 109 K2 helicopter settled onto the meadow, and four well-armed men wearing dark uniforms emerged. Two men took defensive positions around the chopper, and the other two jogged directly toward Brad.

A clipped conversation took place at the edge of the meadow led by a short, stocky man with powerful musculature.

"Mr. Hughes, my name is Nate Hoger. I'm the deputy chief of the Special Operations Bureau in Salt Lake City." He extended his arms as if to take the girl who was now fully alert. She stiffened in Brad's arms, and the officer redirected his attention to the girl.

"Hello there. What's your name?"

"She doesn't speak," Brad answered. Hoger took another step closer. The girl's reaction was swift, drawing away as she angrily kicked out in disapproval. Both men took a quick step back, and Brad begrudgingly shook his head.

"I think you are frightening her! I can take her."

Hoger lowered his arms and smiled reassuringly at the girl. "It's okay. Nobody is going to make you do anything you don't want to do." He then turned to Brad. "I'm sorry, but I am going to have to take your pistol and knife. I can't allow you to board the chopper with any weapons." Looking back at the girl, spotting the multi-plier tool now in her hand, he added, "I will need to take that as well." The girl pulled back but gave it up as Brad took it from her hand.

After taking the weapons, Hoger smiled again at the distrustful girl. "Let's get you on board and out of here. You're going to like riding in a helicopter."

Brad followed Hoger toward the chopper, with the other officer in tow. "Given your security concerns, I asked the medical personnel to remain on board—they will assess and manage the girl's injuries until we get her to the hospital."

Reaching the helicopter, Hoger and a crewmember assisted Brad with the high step into the aircraft, and Brad placed the girl on a stretcher in the cabin. All the while, he held her hand and spoke loudly so that she could hear him over the noise of the engines. "These people are here to help you. You're going to be okay now."

Hoger signaled one of his men closely guarding the aircraft to step up into the helicopter. "Mr. Hughes, this is Officer Mitchel. He and the other two officers will stay behind to begin a search of the area."

Mitchel stepped forward and shook Brad's hand. He then opened a map and asked Brad to confirm where he had found the girl. Brad was able to recount the route and verified the information he had previously communicated to 911 personnel.

Hoger took Mitchel aside and barked out some instructions before giving a hand signal to the pilot. Mitchel jumped down from the chopper just as it began to power up into the air.

Nate Hoger had been in law enforcement for over twenty-five years following a stint as a Navy SEAL, where he had served with distinction. A fair-minded man with a compassionate side to his nature, he was by no means soft, demanding commitment, professionalism, and dedication from the men who served under him. Hoger had seen it all over the years: bodies ripped apart by explosive devices and every kind of wound an explosion, gun, or knife could inflict on flesh. But as the medical team worked to evaluate the young girl's condition and rebandage her injuries, the deputy chief was stunned. The rusty shackle on the girl's ankle appalled him, and when they unveiled the cut on her forearm, he was quick to spot old scars—

scars that looked like defensive knife wounds. Could the girl have been involved in knife fights?

Experience and years in law enforcement had made Nate Hoger a suspicious man, and until proven otherwise, Brad Hughes was a suspect. Hoger shifted his attention to Brad, who had declined any medical check over for himself and hovered over the child. Hoger saw an exhausted man in his late fifties with grizzled stubble. The man looked fit, was about six-foot-one, weighed around 190 pounds, with brown eyes surrounded by dark circles. His left shoe and torn pant leg were bloody due to some injury.

He also noted that Brad's attention was focused entirely on the child and that he spoke loudly and reassuringly while the trauma team placed an oxygen mask over her face and inserted an IV. The girl appeared to trust him, her eyes riveted on his face, seemingly ignoring the medics working on her. Brad asked the medics to explain each procedure and the rationale behind it.

No, Hoger thought, *Mr. Hughes isn't involved in any wrongdoing.* His eyes shifted focus to the girl's makeshift outfit and the heap of bloody shirt bandages on the floor of the helicopter.

As improbable as Hughes's story was, finding the girl on the ledge, getting her up a slope, backpacking her off the mountain, then hiking at night without a flashlight, why would a person inflict this kind of punishment on the child and then ruin a good thermal shirt, a tent, and his backpack for her well-being?

Nevertheless, Hoger knew he would have to do a complete background check on this man and keep him under surveillance until the full story came to light.

The helicopter touched down on the Children's Hospital landing pad, and a waiting team of doctors, nurses, and attendants unloaded the girl's gurney. As the medics rushed the child toward the emergency entrance, Hoger pulled Brad aside to speak to him, separating the girl from Brad for the first time since their confrontation on the high mountain ledge.

Then, all hell broke loose.

A Dangerous Little Girl?

No one saw it coming. During the flight, the girl had been cooperative and showed no sign of stress while being unloaded from the chopper. But when separated from Brad, her reaction was ferocious. Somehow, she had managed to remove the restraint straps holding her down. Rising, she attempted to jump off the gurney, only to be forcibly restrained by an orderly. She grabbed the orderly's finger and bent it backward viciously, driving him to his knees in pain. Without hesitation, she rolled off the gurney, tearing off the monitors and the IV from her arm, and sprinted toward Brad.

The medical team scrambled to catch her, a medic blocking her path, crouching, his arms outstretched. Barely breaking her stride, the girl thrust a stiff arm to his face, her right elbow locked, her hips rotating and all of her leg and core strength behind the blow. Dazed, the medic crumbled to the pavement with a broken nose. Brad turned around just as the girl ran into his arms.

Kneeling on the concrete helipad, Brad sheltered the girl. He was once again stunned by the girl's violent behavior. After a helicopter rescue and with dozens of people caring for her, he assumed she would feel protected and safe by now. Did something specific happen to trigger this explosion, or is this a matter for a neurologist to determine?

The disheveled girl hid in Brad's arms, her eyes focused on the medical personnel who were covertly watching as they tended to their wounded. In turn, the team cast furtive glances in her direction and at each other, shocked by such a violent attack.

A nurse quickly took charge of the situation. "Hey, mister, either you carry her down to the emergency room, or I call security! We need to get this girl off the helipad and downstairs…now!"

Brad picked up the girl and, following the nurse, along with Hoger, entered an elevator.

Another procession trailed prudently behind. The injured orderly holding his finger, and the medic, his head tilted back, pressed gauze against his nose. Along with a nurse, they headed for the staircase.

His back against the corner of the elevator, Hoger studied the girl, his thoughts focused on what he had just witnessed. Her injuries were horrific, he knew, yet she still managed to cut down two grown men like a reaper cutting through grain. The blow she delivered was textbook, with all her weight and strength behind it; it wasn't the flaying of a twelve- or thirteen-year-old girl, and Hoger strongly suspected that the girl had received self-defense training *and a lot of it*. From the shackle on her ankle, he surmised that she had been a prisoner, somehow enslaved.

Why would anyone take the time to train her in combat techniques?

As the elevator started its descent, Hoger caught the girl's eyes, and he was surprised to see that she was sizing him up. It was the defiant, calculating look of a warrior. He had seen it in combat situations when someone planned to go down fighting, searching for any advantage. In this case, he expected something different, perhaps a guilty, fearful look of a child expecting punishment for her actions, but this was a look of contempt. The girl had gauged that he represented her greatest threat, and she was determined to let him know that she wasn't going to be intimidated by him.

As the group left the elevator, Nate Hoger's eyes remained focused on the girl, and as Brad carried her down the hallway, her eyes fearlessly remained locked on the deputy. He felt compassion for her and wondered what could spawn such anger and hostility in a young girl, yet he admired her grit and courage. Still, he was thankful he had taken the multi-plier tool away from her.

In the emergency room, a medical team began evaluating the girl's condition, which involved a round of x-rays and an extensive physical exam. A picture quickly emerged, and it wasn't pretty. In addition to the fresh injuries Brad discovered in the mountains, the girl had two broken ribs and a broken left arm. The open wounds on her back and her cheek required meticulously thorough cleaning to prevent the risk of infection.

Not surprisingly, they discovered many older injuries that had healed over; the most serious was a previously broken bone in her ankle that had healed improperly. Other older injuries included a fractured collarbone, broken fingers and ribs, and scars on both her arms that appeared to be old knife wounds. She also had round burn scars on the bottoms of her feet.

The shackle on her ankle was the final insult. Made on a hand forge, it was old and rusty and surprisingly heavy—perhaps something one might see in a medieval prison or a slave market. It belonged in a museum, not on the ankle of a child. They called in maintenance to cut it off with a grinder, and the manacle was immediately turned over to Hoger's team—the first piece of physical evidence.

Considering her overall condition, the severity of the flesh wounds and other injuries needing treatment, the child would need to be hospitalized. But one thing was clear—the distrustful girl would have nothing to do with the doctors unless Brad was right there holding her hand, reassuring her, and explaining what the doctors planned to do. Just before they added a sedative into her IV, Brad leaned over and whispered, "The doctors are going to help you relax now so that you don't feel anything while they treat your injuries. You'll wake up before you know it. I trust these doctors, and I'll be right here with you the whole time. I won't leave you."

Two of the hospital's finest doctors—Dr. Weinstein, a plastic surgeon, and Dr. Brackford, an orthopedic surgeon—were on call in the trauma unit and began their treatment on the young patient. Then Brad was ushered into another examination room, where a doctor evaluated the wound on his calf. The tear required sutures, easily performed with the benefit of a local anesthetic.

Knowing Brad and the girl were in good hands, Officer Hoger returned to the station to coordinate and devote more resources to the search on the mountain. Before leaving the hospital, he prudently stationed an officer to guard the girl and Brad.

"I don't want Mr. Hughes talking to anybody until I can interview him," Hoger said to the officer. "Ask him to stay in the waiting room and tell him if he uses his phone, he mustn't say a word to anyone about the girl or her rescue. Tell him that I will be back to see him shortly. Oh, and offer to get him something from the cafeteria. He's probably quite hungry."

An hour later, Hoger returned to interview Brad, anxiously pacing in a small waiting room. A police officer stood outside the room. Hoger was an experienced interrogator. He knew that his best chance to find cracks in Brad's story would be while Brad was still tired and a bit disoriented.

"Take a seat, Mr. Hughes."

Brad complied, and Hoger took a seat directly across from him. He removed a recording device from his pocket, turned it on, and set it on the armrest of his chair.

"This is just a formality, Mr. Hughes. We don't suspect you as having any involvement in the girl's injuries, but I'll need your statement."

Brad, not the least bit concerned, replied in the affirmative, and the interview began with Hoger reading Brad his Miranda warning.

Hoger first congratulated Brad on the rescue and praised his descent from the mountain. He then carefully listened as Brad went through a complete recounting of the story.

Brad was truthful, mostly. He downplayed the girl's attack on the ledge and omitted that she had held a knife to his neck at the campsite. He didn't want to explain the eagle's role in the events or his actions, including giving the child a loaded pistol. They would all think he was crazy.

There was another factor, one that was more important to Brad. Somewhere along the way, the girl had gotten under his skin. He liked her, and the last thing he wanted to do was brand her as being psychotic. She had already displayed a penchant for violence, and he didn't want to add fuel to the fire. He was hopeful that, once she realized the staff was looking out for her best interests, she would come around for them, just as she did for him.

As the interview trudged on, Hoger asked Brad in a friendly manner to repeat parts of the story that aroused his curiosity. Why did he go hiking? Did he hike often? What drew him to climb up the ridge? Why did the girl fight so hard not to be separated from him? Did he know the girl? Why did she trust him so much?

Not one to lose his patience, Brad was visibly becoming irritated as Hoger repeatedly asked questions about his relationship with the girl and his deviation from his planned route.

"I don't have a clue why she likes me," he said. "Perhaps it's because I am the first person who has ever tried to help her. As for the rest, if you lay it out logically, the odds of my being on that spot in the mountains yesterday were a million to one. I saw what I saw. I don't blame you for being suspicious, but all I can do at this point is to repeat myself. I have told you everything I know."

Hoger turned off the recorder. Neither man was appeased, but neither of them harbored any particular animosity either. The tension broke when Hoger unexpectedly reached into his pocket to retrieve a vibrating cell phone. His bearing stiffened as he listened to the voice on the other end, and as he walked toward the doorway, he rattled off a stream of instructions barely audible to Brad's ears.

"Mobilize everybody. Make sure every exit to the area is blocked off—nobody gets out until I say so. And call the FBI… We need to set up a meeting as soon as possible."

Hoger shut off his phone and came back into the room.

"You were right, Mr. Hughes. Someone was after the girl. I have to go."

"What happened?" Brad asked. "Did you find the people who did this?"

Hoger gave Brad a sideways look as he retrieved his recorder. "Events are still unfolding. At this point, I'm not at liberty to say."

Brad stood up and moved in front of Hoger, blocking his path to the door.

"Bull! I warned you that there was trouble up there. I've sat here for the past hour, doing my best to cooperate with you. I'm not an idiot. I know when I'm being interrogated, and you know I had nothing to do with this. I deserve some answers."

Hoger felt a surge of anger that abated as he sized Brad up, seeing determination and exhaustion on his face. He then took a slow, deep breath. It would all be in the news that evening, and he was beginning to respect the man—so he answered him.

"Three of my men are down. Two of them are still out in the open—presumed dead—and a third is bleeding out in a ravine. We are pulling together a team to go in. Whoever these people are, they're damn good. That's all we know. But do me a favor, Mr. Hughes, keep it to yourself."

Brad was suddenly at a loss for words, so he nodded and moved aside.

Just as Hoger reached the door, a young nurse ran into the room.

"The girl is wide-awake, Mr. Hughes. Could you please come with me now? We have a problem."

Brad quickly limped down the hallway, accompanied by Hoger and the two officers. It was a chaotic scene, as the girl struggled with a determined group of nurses, each trying to hold her down and keep her from reinjuring herself. Brad pushed his way into the melee, lowered his face to hers, and calmly began to talk her down. The wild-eyed little girl gained control of herself and settled back onto the bed, her eyes fixated on Brad. And just like that, the drama ended.

Hoger turned to Brad. "It looks like everything is under control. Probably a good idea for you to stick around here for a while, okay?"

Brad nodded, and Hoger took one last look at the girl before leaving the room, but not before Brenda Martin, the head nurse, said, "Okay, everybody, the show is over," she announced. "Only essential people in the room. We need to see if the child has reinjured herself, and please get Dr. Weinstein back down here."

Glancing toward Brad, Nurse Martin said, "You seem to be the only one who can keep her calm. Do you mind sticking around until we can get this under control?"

"It's not a problem, I'll stay," Brad replied.

"There's a room with two beds available on the floor," the nurse said. "It certainly looks like you could use some rest."

A while later, they placed Brad and the girl in the room guarded by a police officer. Exhausted by the events of the past two days, Brad fell asleep instantly. The girl fought to stay awake, keeping her eyes on Brad, but eventually, fatigue won out over resolve.

In an empty patient room, a few of the hospital personnel stood to watch the breaking news on the television, a report describing a massive police mobilization in the Uintas. Two officers had been shot and killed, and a third officer wounded in critical condition had been airlifted to the hospital.

When the night shift came on, the evening passed uneventfully, and the enigmatic patients slept soundly.

Please Stay Awhile

The next morning the girl dashed Brad's expectations of a quick exit from the hospital.

Mistakenly thinking that his injured roommate was still asleep, Brad left the room to use his phone out of her earshot. Moments later, the panicky, exhausted girl was by his side, clinging to him with all that was left in her. Nurses and security attempted to return her to the room, only to have the girl kick out at them. With insight that came from somewhere outside of himself, Brad picked the child up and carried her back to the room where he sat by her bedside, holding her hand.

After a lengthy internal consultation, the doctors asked Brad to remain at the hospital for a few days until the girl's condition was stable. He had planned to be in the mountains for a few more days, and he had no immediate commitments, so this was not a major inconvenience. The doctors also decided to move the girl to a room adjacent to the nurses' station, where she and Brad would be under twenty-four-hour observation. If Brad needed any support, help was only a few feet away.

It wasn't easy. So far, nobody had a clue who the child was, and all Brad could get out of the girl were head nods. He didn't like not knowing her name (at least when he addressed her). "Hey, you" was out of the question, and "sweetie" or "honey" were words he was uncomfortable using, sounding overly familiar and most definitely not a good fit given her personality.

His dilemma unexpectedly resolved itself when the song "I've Got You Under My Skin" came up on his iPhone that he had placed on her bedside table while helping a nurse dress her wounds. As soon as it started to play, the girl grabbed the phone and put it up to her ear. She then closed her eyes and listened, wholly absorbed in the song.

Brad leaned in and jokingly told the girl, "I can relate to that song! You have definitely gotten under my skin. Maybe I should call you Tick."

The nurse chimed in. "We did find a deer tick under her arm, you know."

Brad turned back toward the girl with a look of humorous anticipation, but to his surprise, she vigorously nodded her head in agreement.

Just like that, the name stuck.

The police finally allowed Brad to contact his family and colleagues, with the condition that all information be limited to letting them know that he was safely off the mountain. There could be no mention of his role in Tick's rescue, nor knowledge of her existence, and talking to the press was not an option.

Brad was more than happy to accommodate the police—he distrusted the press and public media. At least as they related to his mining operations, past experiences taught him that hidden ambitions, sensationalism, and bias often took precedence over truth when it came to news reporting.

Mainly, he didn't feel like a hero—he was quite content to remain anonymous.

The FBI requested permission to enter and search Brad's home, computers, and cell phone. He reluctantly agreed to the request and provided the necessary passwords, stipulating that his attorney must accompany and document the investigation. It worked out for Brad as the FBI was kind enough to bring his iPad, clothing, and shaving kit back to the hospital.

Two days later, the attorney called to report that the search was complete. As expected, the investigation went smoothly, aside from an officer's comment about Brad's affection for John Wayne westerns. Brad would later learn that the investigation had been far more thorough than he was led to believe. Among other things, the FBI had interviewed his customers and business associates, explaining that they were investigating everybody who had been in those mountains during the past week.

Days later, Hoger filled Brad in on the details of what had happened to his men on the mountain. When Brad's call came into 911, he had set into motion a collaborative, well-rehearsed, but rarely put into practice rescue effort between Life Flight and the Salt Lake City Sheriff's Department—an emergency requiring both law enforcement and rescue personnel. The three men Hoger selected to accompany him all had military backgrounds and were skilled mountaineers.

Apparently, the assailant had arrived at the opposite side of the ridge just before the officers, and realizing he was sure to be spotted, the assailant elected to ambush the officers. Even though following protocol—the officers had been spread out—the ambush was successful. The assailant let loose with a semi automatic AR-15, immediately killing two of the agents.

The one survivor, Thomas Redford, had been lucky—hit, but able to roll himself into a depression. The girl's kidnapper, unable to get a clean shot without being exposed to Redford's gunfire, chose to retreat. Redford later testified that he never got a good look at the shooter, but thought only one was involved.

It was a hard conversation. Officer Burkes Mitchel had served with Hoger in the Navy, and Hoger was a godfather to one of Mitchel's boys. He had been the one who advised his widow of the tragedy.

Brad spent most of his time sitting in a chair next to Tick's bed. Aware of his presence, she rested comfortably, but she became uncooperative without Brad's cajoling whenever the doctors or nurses attempted to examine her. Her behavior was a real problem for Brad who had to remain at her bedside whenever she was awake. To pass the time, he read aloud Louis L'Amour novels on his iPad, with Tick's eyes fixed on his face and following his every move, more interested in him than his stories.

When Tick slept—some twelve hours per day—Brad followed the fruitless search underway in the Uintas for the killer of the two agents, aware that the FBI and local police had no leads save one: they were waiting to talk to the one eyewitness.

Although she had yet to mutter a word, by day six, the doctors felt Tick was strong enough for authorities to attempt a limited interview. That morning, Nate Hoger, accompanied by Brenda Thomas, walked into the young patient's room. Not surprisingly, Brad was eager to get an update on the search.

"I'm so sorry about your men. I watched the funeral procession on my iPhone. What a tragedy," Brad said. "Have you made any progress?"

"Unfortunately, no," replied Hoger. "Nothing. Whoever he is, he has disappeared without a trace, although we have done our best to block off the area. We have dogs out searching, but they haven't picked up any trails. Right now, this girl is our only lead."

"Nate, we found a nickname for her. It's Tick. She has gotten under all of our skin."

Hoger laughed. "What does she have to say about that?"

"She likes it," Brad said. "But she still hasn't said a word since I found her."

Looking over at Tick, Brad saw her intently reading an article from *Nature* magazine. Her focus on the pages seemed quite convincing. One would never have suspected that she was wholly engaged in the men's conversation, but Brad knew better. She never missed anything.

"We have some maps and aerial photos that we'd like to show her," said Hoger. "We're hoping she can let us know how many people we are dealing with and where to find them."

Brad helped Tick into a wheelchair and wheeled her down to a small hospital conference room. As he entered the room, he discovered the gathered group to be surprisingly large. It included seven local law enforcement officers and FBI agents, all seated around a large conference table that accommodated several maps and aerial photographs.

Tick sat stiffly in her chair as Brad wheeled her to the head of the table next to nurse Thomas, and he took a seat on Tick's opposite side. Tick, for her part, seemed a bit uneasy but not frightened. She reacted to the crowd suspiciously, examining each participant's face while continually glancing over at Brad, trying to read his reactions and looking for guidance.

The meeting began with a forest ranger questioning Brad about his route and where he had deviated from his original plans. Brad traced his route, and the ranger then showed Tick a satellite image of the area, pointing to the spot where she was found and asking if she knew how she got there. Using her finger, the girl traced a line to a heavily wooded area about twenty miles to the north.

The area was private property immediately adjacent to the Uinta-Wasatch-Cache National Forest, separated from the park by cliffs and almost impassable terrain.

The ranger shook his head. "That's not right. She couldn't have covered that terrain in her condition."

Tick sat up rigidly and quickly leaned forward to snatch a pen off the table. Over and over, she circled the heavily wooded area on the map. Then, after a cold stare directed at the ranger, she stretched out and seized a nearby notepad off the table.

"*I'm not a liar!*" she wrote. "*This is where my mother and I lived. Please find her!*"

She took a moment to pass a look of desperation toward Brad and the group, then circled the area again, and wrote, "*It's all rigged with bombs!*"

Brad, amazed that she wrote something and relieved that she was finally communicating, turned to her and whispered, "What's your real name? What's your mother's name?"

Tick leaned back in the wheelchair and closed her eyes for a moment. She took a deep breath, deliberately calming herself. She tensed and then relaxed her muscles, all the while preparing to respond. Then she opened her eyes and, poker-faced, scanned the people sitting around the table.

"*Esther Morgan,*" she wrote. "*My mother's name is Alissa, but call me Tick.*"

"Esther? That's a beautiful name," Brad said. "Where are you from? Have you always lived in the mountains? Who is your father?"

"*Los Angeles. I don't have a father,*" she wrote.

"Do you have any family we can contact…grandparents, aunts, uncles?"

She shook her head no.

"This is important, Esther… The police have to know who held you captive and who killed their men. They need you to help in identifying them."

"*Timothy Bird. He went to the University of Washington. He kidnapped us. And don't call me Esther—that's private. I want you to call me Tick.*"

Brad was taken aback by her response but chalked it up as just another one of her mysteries. "Okay, Tick it is."

One of the FBI officers abruptly interrupted. "So, Tick, is Timothy Bird the only person on the mountain or are there others?"

The girl wrote, "*Only Timothy. Everyone else is dead.*"

"How many people? How were they killed?"

Tick looked at Brad questioningly for direction. "It's all right. You can answer him," Brad said.

"*Twelve people. Mostly in fights.*"

The agent spoke up sternly, "I see knife wounds on your arms. Were you involved in these fights? Did you kill anyone?"

Brad quickly rose from his chair and leaned in toward the officer. "What kind of question is that? You people told me that you needed help tracking down the killers, and I believe she has done just that. The child is exhausted, battered, and trying to help you, and now…now, you have the gall to interrogate her?" Brad turned to the group. "This interview is over—until I retain a lawyer for Tick, you'll need to back off."

The agent stood up. "You know, Mr. Hughes, we need to get to the bottom of this sooner rather than later. This girl is our only lead. We know what she is capable of."

Brad had already heard enough and started to wheel Tick from the room, but Nate Hoger blocked their exit and addressed the group.

"Mr. Hughes is right. We were out of line there. At this point, we will confine our questions to tactical matters. Mr. Hughes, with your permission, I'd like to ask Tick just a few more questions."

Brad glanced at Tick for approval and then, after receiving the nod, pushed her back to the table. He could see that the aggressive FBI agent was visibly annoyed, and an underlying tension now washed over the room.

Turning to Tick, Hoger continued. "I apologize. We have all been up for days. Mr. Hughes understandably wants to protect you. You don't have to answer any questions without his okay."

Tick agreed with a glare.

"Tick, our number one goal right now is to find your mother, and I think you can help us. Can you tell us if this Timothy is well-armed?"

Her written answer left the group thunderstruck:

—*A Remington 700 XCR Tactical 338 Lapua*
—*A Colt Defensive AR 15 LT 6720-R Quad Rail*
   Magpul LT
—*A Glock 21 .45 ACP*

Tick wanted to continue working on the list, but Hoger stopped her. "That's enough. I think we can safely assume that he's well-armed. Tick, can you tell us what Timothy looks like? About how tall do you think he is, and what color are his eyes? Does he have any distinguishing marks, like a scar, maybe?"

The girl quickly wrote, "*About 6'4", dark brown hair with some gray, a scar over his left eye, blue eyes.*"

Then, uncharacteristically, she continued, providing additional information.

"He has lots of disguises. When he goes out, he always looks different—even ancient. He can fool you, and he is very strong and fit."

"Does he have any hiding places?"

"Just the ranch... Maybe Mexico. He talked about it once." She wrote hurriedly, again pointing to the wooded area on the map.

Sensing Tick's growing fatigue, Hoger asked one final question, "You wrote to watch out for bombs, what did you mean?"

Once again, Tick looked up at Brad for his approval.

Brad said, "It's all right. Would it be easier to show them in a drawing?"

If there had been any remaining doubt about Tick's acuity, she put to rest with what followed. The group watched in amazement as, now struggling with exhaustion, she drew out a detailed sketch of a ranch house backed up against a ridge and a tunnel leading to an elaborate cave complex with explosive charges planted in multiple locations. She knew about the triggering mechanisms, conveying that they were sophisticated apparatuses that included beams of light along with pressure sensors.

As she completed the drawing, Brad noticed that Tick's hands were shaking. "Okay, that's it. She's had enough for now. I'm taking her back to her room. She might be up to meeting with you again tomorrow."

Hoger replied first, thanking the girl for her help; the entire team was voicing their appreciation. Hoger then asked Tick if they could send a sketch artist over the next day to work with her on Timothy's sketch.

⁓⬨⁓

After visiting hours were over that evening, the ward at its quietest, Nate Hoger, Brenda Thomas, and a handful of law enforcement and hospital administrators entered Tick's room. She had finally fallen asleep, and Brad, worried about being away from his business for such an extended period, sat in a chair reading an audit report.

Hoger, dressed in his field gear, spoke first. "Brad, sorry to bother you so late. You may remember Jenny Dresder from our meeting this morning. She is one of the agents helping us coordinate the search for Timothy Bird. She has some information for you."

"Of course," replied Brad, thinking back to his confrontation at the meeting. "I hope you understand that I am doing my best to cooperate with you, Officer Hoger. Your agent's questions were quite leading, and I felt Tick should have legal representation under that circumstance. She needs someone to have her back. For some reason, she trusts me."

Agent Dresder replied, "Actually, I think her safety is all of our concern. You were right in putting a halt to that line of questioning. She shouldn't have been asked to testify against herself. But that's not why I'm here. From what we have learned today, Tick is a target, and if you stay on with her, you may become one as well."

Brad was a good listener, but this bit of news immediately sharpened his attention on the agent.

"After we met with Tick, we put out a nationwide inquiry on Timothy Bird. Our Seattle department got back to us, instructing us to provide Tick with twenty-four-hour protection. Timothy Bird is a suspected serial killer and possibly part of a larger group. For your and Tick's security, we will be transferring you to a different wing in the hospital, a wing scheduled for renovation. It's a more secure location. That, of course, depends on your willingness to stay with her."

Brad viewed the FBI's stipulations and their underlying intentions warily. The investigation was still in its infancy, and he knew that he might even be a person of interest. The smart thing would be to exit the scene right now, but then he would never know if they treated her fairly. And then there was that promise he had made. He felt compelled to stay.

"We will be posting a guard at your door twenty-four hours a day," Dresder said. "There will be another guard at the entrance to the wing. I'm afraid you won't have any privacy. The room will be under constant surveillance, and we will be monitoring all communication you have to the outside—nobody must learn about your involvement with Tick. Agent Steve Brewer will be flying in from Seattle shortly. Hopefully, when he arrives, he will be able to provide you with more detail about Bird."

Dresder explained to Brad that she didn't expect him to remain with Tick for more than a week or so. "We know that asking you to stay on as Tick's pro tem guardian is unusual, but given her attachment to you and her fragility…we plan to transfer Tick into a protective custody program once the doctors give the okay."

The next day, Brad helped Tick into her wheelchair. With Brenda Martin and an agent, he pushed her across a covered bridge to an older, recently vacated facility known as the Walker Building.

"We shut this wing of the hospital down just two weeks ago when we were finally able to occupy our new facilities," Nurse Martin said. "It's a wonderful building, and renovation is scheduled to start as soon the architects finalize some structural issues to bring the building up to new earthquake standards. When the renovation is complete, we will almost double the number of beds."

Looking out of the windows on the walkway, Brad realized he had seen the building before. It was an older three-story brick structure with tall windows, beautiful timber and plaster cornices, and a cupola on top. His company had funded a portion of the building's renovation, which was a product of early Utah architecture and well worth preserving.

"You and Tick will be in my favorite room in the hospital," Nurse Martin said. "It's a large corner room with a balcony and a wonderful view of the mountains. We call it The Palace. The doctors have been using it to crash when they are on call because it's right across the bridge from the new operating suite. That will have to stop now, of course, because the police are sealing the floor off. There will be a private nurse on duty at all times at the station just outside your door, so if you need anything, just let the nurse know. Don't be shy about it. It's their job to take care of you. I will also be checking in on you periodically."

Her description of the room proved accurate—a bright, cheery room that was more than large enough to accommodate two beds with a privacy screen. The room felt homey, painted in a light taupe, scenic pictures of Utah decorating the walls, a small dining table, an enormous padded chair with an ottoman in the corner between two large windows, and a door leading to the balcony.

The staff had gone out of its way to make the occupants comfortable: a vase of fresh flowers, an excellent selection of books and magazines, two board games, and, sitting on Tick's bed, a folded towel in the shape of an elephant. Their room was an oasis, a spot of life in an otherwise lifeless, empty building. Once bursting with activity, the other rooms were now empty dark spaces waiting to be stripped down to their studs, revitalized, and given new life with life-saving equipment, doctors, nurses, and finally, children.

The next few days were uneventful but far from restful. Brad found himself isolated in the company of a very bright girl who became hyper-alert as she gained strength. She was a child who now wouldn't sleep but desperately needed to rest—a child who, despite Brad's efforts to entertain and divert her, had now become focused on the search for her mother.

Tick simply would not shut down, and consequently, her weight loss was becoming a concern.

She continued to be uncooperative with others, demanding Brad's complete attention and insisting that he participate in everything that took place, including medical consultations, cleaning or dressing her wounds, physical therapy, and meals. On one occasion, when Brad left the room to talk to a doctor, Tick bolted out of bed and followed him into the hallway as FBI agents scrambled after her.

The most challenging issue, at least from the kitchen staff's perspective, was her unequivocal distaste for hospital food, or as Tick, ever so graciously, wrote on her slate, "*Pig slop prepared by amateurs.*" She refused to eat standard hospital fare. Brad and a nutritionist would spend hours coming up with food she would eat. More weight loss was not an option.

Adding to Tick's anxiety was the absence of information about her mother and the ongoing search at the ranch and surrounding property—it was all she could think about. Nate Hoger hadn't visited in days; Brad felt cut off. Worse, negative information had leaked about Tick. The story circulating was that a troubled girl had escaped captivity from the mountain compound, naming Timothy Bird as her alleged kidnapper. The story included mention of an unidentified camper who found and rescued the girl.

Brad found himself more and more involved in decisions concerning Tick's care. He was good with people—a natural leader—and the authorities and hospital staff seemed happy to accept the status quo, no one wanting to rock the boat while Tick healed. Law enforcement was now engrossed in what had become one of the largest manhunts in recent history. This effort included learning everything possible about Alissa and her daughter, Esther.

Tick's inability or unwillingness to speak confounded Brad because no physical abnormalities were causing the problem. The speech specialist brought in to examine her diagnosed the issue as "agnogenic." When Brad asked for the definition of the word, the doctor arrogantly replied, "You know, agnogenic, idiopathic…a condition having no known cause."

Brad, put off by the doctor's high-mindedness, thought a more honest response would have been "I don't have a clue." Regardless of whether Tick's issue was agnogenic, idiopathic, or the Devil's work, she was quickly learning how to manipulate her mode of communication and take advantage of her unique status as a kidnap victim. She gained a remarkable degree of control over her care, and if she didn't want to communicate with someone, she simply put down her slate.

Tick, it turned out, was a huge pain in the ass.

After the police interview, Brad allowed Tick to use his iPad and showed her how to open applications. She quickly made an extraordinary effort to learn how to type, practicing on an application Brad purchased and had downloaded for her. He had always been amazed at how quickly the grandchildren picked up things on their computers; Tick was no exception to that rule.

For a twelve-year-old rescued from years of captivity, she was a capable writer with an extraordinary vocabulary and the ability to set forth her ideas and opinions clearly. She had an astonishing awareness of people and things and no fear of communicating what she thought. She would write reviews of the hospital staff, sometimes critical commentary, particularly if a staff member angered her or, in her opinion, did something wrong. Brad, not a judgmental man, began seeing some things through her eyes in a new light. Tick's acerbic stream of commentary revealed an entirely new view of the hospital landscape.

Reflecting on the girls' insight, he thought, *Now I know how the inventor of the telescope must have felt when he first looked at the stars through the magnifying lens.* Her candor made him uncomfortable, and it came to a head when her condemnation spilled out on a young staff psychologist.

With only a few years' experience under her belt, the young psychologist was an idealist, doing her best to help children at the hospital. At one point, after watching Tick write on the slate, she asked Brad to let her read the commentary.

Brad reluctantly handed over the slate, and Tick's words nearly brought the doctor to tears.

"*Does she think that talking slowly in a wearisome monotone makes her sound superior? She is treating me like an ignorant child—all her questions are insipid. She is beyond naïve! Of course I didn't like having my feet burned! Tell her to go back to the primal soup she came from!*"

Dismissal was always non-negotiable because Tick would become uncooperative when asked to work with someone she found wanting. But after the humiliated psychologist left the room, Brad's patience with Tick came to an end.

"Look, I expect you to share your feelings," Brad said in a tightly controlled voice. "God knows you have the right to express yourself, but you don't have the right to tear people down the way you do. There is an amazing book called The Bible, Tick. It's God's word, and it teaches us to encourage people. You need to use your words to help people, not to hurt them."

She looked into his eyes, her face expressionless. It was an effective strategy for Tick because it was easy for her to hold someone captive with just a look, but Brad was not about to be put off by her guile.

"That young doctor was trying to help you, Tick. You could have expressed your feelings in a thousand more positive ways. For example, 'I wish she would talk to me like I'm an adult' or 'I wish she would interact with me on a more mature level.' We are all God's creations and valuable. Do you understand? The primal soup comment was entirely uncalled for."

Pausing, he felt a pang of regret and a sense of uncertainty. Perhaps he had gone too far. Tick needed all the support she could get. He observed her reaction as she sat there, tablet in hand, looking at him, her expression tight and unyielding, bringing back memories of the few times he had disciplined his boys when they were young. Catherine took the disciplinarian role, allowing her husband to enjoy a calm house when he returned from a long day at the office or from a business trip. Whenever the boys received discipline from their father, they were pretty tough, taking their punishment somewhat nonchalantly. His boys weren't overly sensitive.

He had never disciplined a girl, let alone a girl in her condition. He wondered if Tick would reject him now, leaving her without an ally or comforter. Would she cry? Would she sulk? Would she rebel? Had he crushed her spirit? He had no insight into her possible reaction.

Tick's response was completely unexpected. She picked up the slate and wrote, *"I know! I know! Proverbs 21:23."*

Brad scrambled for his iPhone to look up the Biblical reference: "Those who guard their mouths and their tongues keep themselves from calamity."

Brad shook his head. He suddenly realized just how little he knew about the girl and that she had depths he didn't appreciate.

"Who taught you that verse? I guess I'm not the only one who thinks you need to watch what you say. You do need to stop and think before you express your thoughts. Words can be very hurtful."

Frustrated and losing count of how many punishing encounters had taken place between Tick and those assigned to her care, Brad feared that her abusive conduct and defiant behavior would ultimately alienate her from everyone at the hospital. The doctors and nurses occasionally faced and capably handled unruly or difficult children, but Tick was a different story. She was threatening peoples' feelings of self-worth, and indeed, her harsh, insightful judgments hit home. Brad winced as he imagined her in a different, less tolerant facility.

Her real influence came from the fact that the staff respected her opinions. It was not just that she was so strangely dynamic for someone her age, nor was it her unique status as a key player in a national, unfolding story. Tick was exceptionally bright and keenly aware, and her criticisms of hospital staff personnel always contained a hard kernel of truth. The only person she never found fault with was Brad. The FBI wanted her out of Utah and at an undisclosed location. Their inevitable separation might only be days away. He wouldn't be there for her over the long run, and she would need a lot of help.

Unfortunately, she wasn't making many friends.

CHAPTER

Reading Time

Reading time in the evenings had become an important ritual; the time Brad spent reading was therapeutic for Tick. It helped her relax. Brad, racking his brain to come up with a good book for Tick, settled on *Anne of Green Gables* by L. M. Montgomery. He chose the book because it portrayed a young girl with a fiery spirit who, like Tick, lost her family and faced a new and uncertain future—a child who bucked the system but matured into a fine, successful young woman loved by all. This book radiated optimism and traditional values, and Brad hoped the story would capture her interest and give her hope.

Following along with studied enthusiasm, Tick would often comment on her slate, using biblical references, sometimes-obscure Old Testament passages, provoking Brad to dig into his Bible so that he could connect with her thinking. A typical example was when Anne Shirley, the main character, was unfairly accused of stealing a broach. She was later found innocent and won a place in her new family's home. Tick turned her slate toward Brad: *"Amos 5:24."*

Brad looked up the passage attributed to the Old Testament (760 BC) prophet: a fiery, fearless, and honest shepherd from southern Israel who chastised the northern Israelites for living under a pious veneer of religion, worshiping idols and oppressing the poor.

"But let justice roll on like a river, righteousness like a never failing stream."

Finishing reading the passage, Brad carefully examined his new companion.

Where did she come up with that? he wondered.

Well into the book, they were interrupted by a knock on the hospital room door. When Brad opened the door, Nate Hoger, who was standing next to a heavyset older man dressed in a suit, greeted him. After the two men entered the room, Hoger was the first to speak.

"Good evening, Brad. Hello there, Tick… You're looking much better since I last saw you." Hoger felt uncharacteristically unsettled, wishing he could be anywhere but in that room on that day.

"This is Steve Brewer of the FBI's Seattle Department. Steve is a special agent who has investigated Timothy Bird in the past. I had wanted you to meet with Steve earlier, but the investigation up at the ranch has kept all of us busy."

The men shook hands, and Hoger continued, "If you have been following the news, you probably know that we found the ranch site exactly where Tick said it would be. Just as she told us, it is rigged with explosives, which is proving to be a major challenge for the bomb squad. They are using a drone to survey the complex and taking pictures, but that's taking some time."

As Hoger spoke, Brad fixed his eyes on Tick. He watched as she hurriedly wrote on her slate and looked up at Hoger anxiously, signaling for him to come over to the bed. Hoger knew what she would be asking and dreaded providing the response.

Hoger's demeanor had already telegraphed the answer—it was a body language people with family members in the military would recognize. But Brad knew Tick would need confirmation.

"Do you have any information on my mother?"

Hoger was slow to answer, his stomach churning. He was mentally reviewing the autopsy report, and he couldn't bring himself to meet Tick's eyes.

"I'm so sorry, Tick. She didn't make it. It might help you to know that we think she died quickly and painlessly from a knife wound."

Tick gave him a hard, angry look, grabbed her slate, and scribbled "*Liar!*" before throwing it at Nate's feet.

Nate stood awkwardly, frozen without saying a word. Brad's focus centered on Tick, who had turned over in her bed, her back to the three men. It occurred to Brad that she hadn't been harboring any real hope that her mother was alive. Instead, she had been concerned about *how* she died.

What kind of world has she been living in? he thought. And the look on her face, no tears, no glimpse of devastation or confusion; it was a stoic look of a person resigned to her fate and utterly alone. He had never felt so sorry for anyone in his life.

Finally, Nate signaled the men to the doorway.

"We have uncovered a cemetery and are processing several bodies," Hoger said. "The mother's body is one of six we have recovered so far. We have been able to confirm an ID. Her DNA is a match with Tick's. Sorry it took so long, but the lab tests take a while, and we wanted to be certain."

"I understand."

"Another reason we're here is to update you on the hunt for Timothy Bird. Steve has been on his tail for years but hasn't been able to secure enough convicting evidence to charge him. He is astute and extremely dangerous, perhaps one of the nation's most prolific serial killers."

Looking over at Tick, Hoger lowered his voice some more to make sure Tick couldn't hear.

"People who cross Bird have accidents, and Tick is the first witness directly linking him to any of his victims. We believe that Bird, and possibly others, may be planning to come after her."

Steve Brewer then addressed Brad. "And if he finds out who rescued her, you and possibly even your family may be in danger as well. From what I can determine, just about everybody who has crossed him in the past has ended up dead. Your name cannot be linked to the rescue. We will release a false statement from her rescuer, who has returned to his home back east, explicitly requesting his anonymity. We need your full cooperation in this, even to the point your family shouldn't be told anything about what's happened. You never know what might turn up on social media, and if anyone can make a connection, it's Bird. You could be putting your entire family in danger if he learns anything of your involvement."

Brewer added, "Who knows about the rescue?"

"As far as I know, only the emergency personnel, the hospital staff, my lawyer, and Whitney Heldar, my administrative assistant. I didn't talk to any of my associates about the hike, and right now they all believe I'm on a trip to South America. Whitney is notoriously protective of my privacy. You don't need to worry about her. I set up a cover story as soon as you asked me to stay over at the hospital. I didn't want to be bothered by phone calls."

"Okay, that's good," said Brewer. "Be careful to keep it that way. We have a list of everybody who knows anything about your involvement in Tick's rescue, and we have talked to all of them. Fortunately, the group is relatively small, but as much as we would like to, we can't control conversations. We have also scrubbed your name from any admission documents here at the hospital or in reports to government agencies, so we are hopeful that, with your cooperation, we can keep your involvement with Tick private."

Hoger chimed in. "As soon as the doctors clear Tick to travel and we get organized, we will be taking her to an undisclosed location. She will then enter into a witness protection program. We would like you to remain with her until then, if possible."

"Of course, I will text my office and family. I will tell them I have extended my vacation."

"Great. We have some arrangements to make concerning Tick's long-term care, but hopefully, everything will be in place by the time she is ready to be moved. An agent from Child Protective Services will be getting in touch with you to help with the transition."

"Are you sure she doesn't have any living family?" Brad asked.

"We have a fairly comprehensive history on her mother, Alissa Morgan," said Brewer. "She was raised in an orphanage in Virginia. Tick's father is unknown, but we have learned that Alissa moved to California shortly after becoming pregnant, withholding the father's identity. His name is not on the birth certificate."

"How old is Tick?"

"She is twelve, turning thirteen next April. The first, to be exact."

"How do you think they ended up at the ranch?" Brad asked.

"Well, they both lived in California until they went missing over seven years ago. As you know, Tick says that they were kidnapped. The facts are in line with Tick's story. They just disappeared overnight. Alissa was working at a prestigious restaurant. Apparently, she was a fabulous cook, and she was well-liked by everybody."

Brad turned his attention toward Hoger. "Do you have any leads on Bird?"

"No, he's a chameleon. He could be anywhere by now, but I will keep you posted. We are going to find him," Hoger added a look of determination in his eyes.

The men shook Brad's hand and said their goodbyes to Tick.

It would be yet another sleepless night for Brad, worrying about the little bundle huddled under her blanket and thinking about what the future held in store for her.

The next morning, Brad found an entirely different girl on his hands. Tick was a puddle, a deflated balloon. The adrenaline and fierce determination that had held her together through her ordeal were all but consumed. Her body and mind were giving way to the injuries and setbacks she had endured, and a deep depression was setting in. She just wanted to sleep and to be left alone. She rejected going on walks or to physical therapy and didn't even want Brad to read to her.

When he wasn't urging Tick to exercise or eat, Brad spent most of his time sitting in the chair, merely looking at her. He would listen as the air-conditioner clicked on and off, the sound of the air coursing through the vents, the squeaking of shoes as nurses and law enforcement went up and down the hall.

He had never sat idly like this. In the past, he was distracted with work, family, sports, TV, or books. Now, quietly sitting there with the girl, his mind adjusted to the absence of constant stimulation, and his thoughts became more and more introspective. Occasionally, he would pick up the Bible and try to understand how to connect his faith to his situation.

Tick's appearance fascinated him. She looked like a wild range horse that had been caught in a barbed-wire fence. She was a long-limbed, sinewy amalgamation of lacerated skin, bones, and muscles with several bright-white bandages contrasting her tanned skin. Her hair was short and blonde, and she wore a red cap to keep her head warm. Her slim fingers, some knobby, were calloused with neglected nails; these were not the fingers of your usual twelve-year-old.

Then there was an exotic look about her, so different from his family's Irish-English lineage. Her face was symmetrical, with aristocratic features and cute elfish ear. When she was awake, her beautiful green eyes streaked with amber radiated awareness and intelligence. Her tanned skin suggested she was perhaps Latin American or Spanish in descent.

Brad's first experience with Tick's night terrors shook him to his core. The beginning signs of each episode started when her sleep became disturbed and increasingly restless. Then the incident would rapidly escalate to wide-eyed shouting, yelling, and thrashing about, with Brad unable to calm her or wake her up.

It was during those nights that Brad learned she could speak. Tick clearly articulated random words, but never remembered the episode in the morning.

During the next several days, Tick's depression lifted, and life became more predictable. In the mornings, Brad would wake up around 5:30 a.m., shower, shave, and dress. The nurses helped Tick shower and dress for breakfast at 7:00 a.m., followed by doctors' rounds at 8:30. Then, Brad, Tick, and the guards who accompanied them would take long walks up and down the deserted wing, their footsteps echoing along the hallways with Tick setting a demanding pace and balking when Brad called it quits.

Tick would rest until noon when they brought in lunch. An hour of physical rehab would follow. Around three o'clock, they would read—Tick's quietest time of the day. The two pampered prisoners would huddle up in a remarkably comfortable recliner placed near the corner windows, books in hand, and milkshakes on the side tables. Sometimes a chocolate sundae with sprinkles and a cherry, Tick's favorite novelty, was brought in. After another walk, they ate dinner, followed by board or card games, and more reading. Lights out for Tick was 9:00 p.m.

The only breaks in the routine were visits by Nate Hoger (who had started calling Brad "Mr. Mom") and Steve Brewer, who had Tick go through books of photographs to identify people.

Three of the sessions were particularly difficult.

The first was a visit from Nate Hoger, who took the time to inform Brad about a recent development at the ranch house. The event would make the local news that night and national headlines the next morning: a massive explosion had occurred at the site. Tick's drawing had proven to be spot-on, as verified by the crack bomb squad brought in from Washington. The ranch and cavern complex was a deadly trap, crisscrossed with laser triggers linked to what proved to be barrels of ANFO, the same explosives that Timothy McVeigh and Terry Nichols used to destroy the Federal Building in Oklahoma City.

The experts had meticulously explored the ranch and cave complex using a small camera-equipped drone that they had passed through several holes drilled into the walls of the ranch house. Each day, the remote-controlled drone was flown deeper into the complex, taking numerous pictures as it carefully traversed a course designed to avoid the triggers Tick had pointed out in her drawing.

The images showed a ranch-style house backed up to a rocky ridge with a tunnel leading to a cave. The house was spacious, with eight bedrooms, a large living room, and an expansive view of a narrow glacial valley. It had a study and a sizeable, well-equipped kitchen.

The cave had one large chamber featuring a large boxing type ring and several adjoining smaller caverns, transformed into holding pens. These cells were separated from the main cavern by iron bars set in the floor and ceiling, with sturdy small iron doors allowing access.

The largest of these quarters had a small stream, just a rivulet, running through the back corner. In this area, there was a bucket with a warped toilet seat resting on top. The orderly room held a bed, made up with military precision, a warped wardrobe, a bureau with pale-blue chipped paint, a kerosene lamp, and a child's dress and undergarments neatly hanging from a makeshift clothesline.

Whether it was operator error or a mechanical malfunction with the drone, something had gone horribly wrong. Early that morning, the drone had triggered a massive explosion, bringing down the entire ridge. The blast front rocketed out of the cave's mouth, tearing the ranch house to pieces, dust, and debris mushrooming into the sky. The bomb squad's trailer proved to be inadequate, a massive boulder crashed through the vehicle, killing one man and severely injuring two others.

Brad knew the authorities would soon be placing greater pressure on Tick to fill in the gaps regarding the events at the ranch, and three days after the explosion, Steve Brewer came to The Palace with two agents. They showed Tick a lineup of pictures, including Timothy Bird's likeness. She bristled, identifying him immediately, her index finger smashing down on his image as if grinding him into the table. She remained agitated for hours after the interview.

An even more difficult session ensued later that week when they showed Tick images of a father and son who had gone missing in the Uintas close to a year before, followed by pictures of a rodeo queen from Evanston, Wyoming, who had gone missing months later. Tick carefully held and studied each image, her face wooden. The missing girl, a champion rider sitting on a magnificent horse, had won a barrel race at some rodeo and was holding up a blue ribbon, her dust-covered face jubilant. The picture of the boy and father was taken at a lake in the Uintas: The boy looked ridiculously joyful, holding up an eleven-inch brook trout beautifully colored with red and yellow spots.

Tick wrote in her tablet, "*They're all dead—made to fight in Timothy's arena—Janet Herrington killed the girl—Timothy killed the boy and his father.*" She then turned away, frozen and unwilling to continue the session.

Tick couldn't sleep that night, tossing and turning and continuously adjusting her pillow, pulling her blanket on, then off. Brad stayed up with her, but he was unable to distract or comfort her.

Sickened by the unfolding shocks of Tick's captivity, Brad had mixed emotions. He was worn out by her demanding nature and impatient to return to his work. He was dreading the upcoming visit by Social Services and his forthcoming separation from the girl.

Incredibly, he realized that he was really going to miss her.

Vindication

Steve Brewer sat alone at the Lucky H Bar and Grille in the Little America Hotel in Salt Lake City. He was a happy man. The hotel was a beautifully remodeled, upscale hotel with all the amenities, his room spacious and tastefully decorated. The bed was exceptionally comfortable, so much so that Steve pulled the bedding away from a corner end to take note of the manufacturer's label.

Salt Lake City, Utah's capital city, nestled in the rugged Wasatch Mountains, was nothing less than impressive. His trips to the crime site were like being on vacation; the fresh, crisp mountain air, striking terrain, and vibrant fall colors were marvelous.

But the one factor contributing the most to his well-being was that, after nearly a decade, he finally had a witness who could provide airtight evidence linking Timothy Bird to numerous murders.

When the waitress came to take his order, he asked for a gin and tonic, a sixteen-ounce steak, a baked potato with all the fixings, and creamed spinach. If his wife had been sitting with him, she would have cast a disapproving eye, emitting sounds of disapproval. Admittedly, he had avoided stepping on his bathroom scale for quite some time now. Still, he was not in denial over his noticeable potbelly and thinning hair—he accepted the unavoidable aging process.

It just so happened that on this night he felt like celebrating. He was only two years away from mandatory retirement, and the past five years of his career were disappointing. Brewer was marking time, sidelined, out of the loop.

It all started nine years earlier when he investigated the murder of Jessica Milford, a psychology professor at the University of Washington. It had been a particularly gruesome murder. According to the coroner, her death came slowly—painfully. She was brutally tortured. When death finally came, it was a blessing.

During Brewer's investigation, Timothy Bird's name was mentioned as a former student who might harm the professor. Brewer met with Milford's daughter, Jill, who described an incident where she found her mother frantically pacing in the garden, wringing her hands, completely distraught.

Urging her mother to tell her what was wrong, Jessica explained that she believed a PhD student in behavioral sciences, Timothy Bird, was an evil man who should be in jail. She claimed that he was responsible for the suicide of one of her students. According to Jill, her mother felt that the university covered up the incident by merely having Timothy Bird expelled.

Despite her mother's refusal to provide further details, Jill believed that she was never the same again. "She became fearful, nervous, and started drinking. She used to say, half-jokingly, 'There must be a God because Satan exists and the universe needs balance.'"

Days after obtaining a warrant for the university's files on Bird, Brewer was annoyed when, after stalling the inquiry, the university reluctantly admitted that all records covering the grounds of Bird's expulsion had disappeared. Brewer then began interviewing faculty members, staff, and past students; the interviews fell on opposite ends of the opinion spectrum.

Some remembered Timothy in glowing, exuberant, almost god-like terms: brilliant, articulate, charismatic, and a deep thinker—all combined in a six-foot-four athletic frame. Then there were murky, cautious, evasive statements. As one undergraduate teacher put it, "He was very bright and quite popular, as I remember, but..." She turned away and looked down at the floor. Then, in a small, timid voice, she added, "It's foolish, I know, but I felt like he was always sizing me up for something menacing. He never did anything overtly, but I was always uneasy around him. I'm just being silly. I didn't have that much to do with him."

Interviews with faculty and fellow students in the behavioral sciences doctoral program with Bird were particularly disturbing. There were ten postgraduate students and four faculty members who worked closely with Timothy. Of that group, two faculty members and four students had died within four years of Timothy's expulsion, an astonishing mortality rate. Coincidently, the two dead faculty members had led the investigation leading to Timothy's expulsion. The remaining faculty and fellow students in the program denied having any meaningful recollection of Timothy Bird—collective amnesia?

Convinced that he was on to something, Brewer learned that Linda Cummings, the girl who had committed suicide, was enrolled in the behavioral sciences program along with Bird. Linda committed suicide two months before Jessica Milford's breakdown.

For Brewer, it was routine police work to locate Linda's roommate, Susan Ricker, who was now living in Coos Bay, Oregon. He called Susan and requested an interview, and after some hesitation, she agreed to meet with him on a Saturday. Hoping to take in some scenery, Brewer left early, driving south on Highway 15 to where it intersected with Highway 20, then west to the coast where he followed Highway 101 from Newport to Coos Bay, one of the most scenic drives in the country.

Finding Susan Ricker's house was not easy. A rusty mailbox at the entrance of a long, narrow driveway cut through dense forest was the only identifying marker. Not sure what he would find at the end of the pine needle-covered driveway, Brewer was pleasantly surprised when he drove into an open area with a well-kept, spacious lawn. There, he spotted a neat bungalow, and a garden with swings and a slide at the side of the house. Brewer knocked on the door before introducing himself to an attractive, petite brunette. Susan offered him a seat on the deck, and after pouring two glasses of iced tea, she told him her story about Linda.

"Linda was from a farming family in Nebraska. We started rooming together at U-Dub after she responded to an ad I placed on a bulletin board. For the first year, everything was great. She was neat, considerate, and very conscientious about sharing chores and expenses at the apartment. Then, in the middle of the second year, it all fell apart when she started dating Timothy Bird."

Pausing, she looked up at the trees swaying back and forth in a light breeze, her eyes moistening. Then she looked back at Brewer with a resolute expression.

"I didn't trust him from the first time I met him," she continued. "He could have dated any girl on the campus, but for some reason, he pursued Linda, and he did it with a vengeance, sending her flowers, taking her to expensive restaurants, even flying her up to Vancouver to see a play. It's not that she wasn't attractive—she was. But she was naïve, without a trace of guile, and he was handsome, sophisticated, and oh so charming."

Susan explained that the couple had been dating for about three months when Linda came home one night, all excited.

"She told me that Timothy had invited her to join a secret society with a weird name. I remember it was called the Epilektoi. When I asked her what it was and who was in the society, she told me she had been sworn to secrecy. All I ever learned is that it means 'the chosen ones.' It refers to a group of elite Greek warriors, but that's about all I know about it."

Susan explained that, for the next two to three months, Linda spent more and more time away from the apartment, coming in late and missing classes. Then she started using drugs.

"I would find all kinds of drug paraphernalia around the apartment. Linda started acting crazy, talking about how most people are just sheep, senselessly walking in circles, waiting to be told what to do, mindlessly following the crowd. I tried everything to help her— calling her family, talking to her advisor, Professor Milford—but we couldn't get anywhere with her. She wouldn't even meet with her parents when they flew out to visit her. She was lost. When she started stealing from me to pay for her drugs, I asked her to leave the apartment. Three months later, she was dead."

After the memorial service for Linda at the university, Susan said something horrible happened.

"Timothy Bird and his friends attended the service, and on my way out, I heard them laughing in the hall around the corner from me. Then I heard Timothy Bird brag to one of his friends, 'You owe me five hundred dollars, and I should get a bonus. I got her to off herself in less than a year.' Petrified that they might see me, I hid in a broom closet until I knew they had left. I told Professor Milford what happened, and she promised she would look into it." Susan then nervously added, "I read about what happened to Professor Milford in the paper. Do you think Timothy had anything to do with it? You know, I could never testify against Bird. I have two children."

Brewer left the meeting convinced that he was after the right man but wondering if he would ever find anybody with the courage to testify against him.

Brewer then launched an investigation into Timothy Bird's past, drawing on every resource he could muster. He learned that Bird was the only child of Beth and Jason Bird, a wealthy Seattle couple who had died years earlier when their car plunged over a cliff on the Coast Highway. The crash was ruled an accident, but when Brewer and his agents revisited the case, pictures of the wrecked vehicle showed what appeared to be faint traces of paint from another car on the left fender. It was inconclusive evidence at best. Regardless of what happened, their deaths left Timothy Bird a very wealthy man, with assets totaling well over $40 million.

Jason and Beth Bird inherited their fortune from Beth's father, a timber baron, and the couple traveled between homes in Greece, Florida, and Seattle. Their only child, Timothy, was cared for by a succession of nannies provided through a local Seattle service. Sweet-talking a secretary at the agency, Brewer persuaded her to open the archives, and she provided him with a list of nannies who had cared for Timothy. Using the record, he was able to interview five of them—the others were deceased.

Brewer repeatedly heard the same story: The child was cold, disobedient, cunning, and manipulative. His parents refused to discipline Timothy, and nannies, unable to cope with the child, would resign in frustration.

Brewer hired an actuary to examine the group's mortality rate—fellow students, faculty members, and nannies. Consistent among the professors and students in Timothy's doctoral program, the group seemed to have exceptionally high mortality rates—actually, as a group, 17 percent higher than usual.

The most telling information he learned about Timothy Bird occurred by happenstance while on vacation in Greece. Seizing the opportunity to learn more about the Birds, Brewer visited the island of Mykonos, where the Birds had once owned a home. At the house, he spoke with a local gardener who had tended the grounds for many years. The gardener referred him to Kupia Petras, an older woman who had cared for Timothy as a child.

Brewer found Kupia in a modest house being cared for by her daughter. When shown a picture of Timothy, she recognized him immediately, her expressions startled and frightened. Crossing herself, Kupia told the translator that he was the son of the devil, reliving the day the Birds' two dachshunds had gone missing. While looking for them, she came upon Timothy, hidden away in a ravine behind the house. The animals were muzzled, tied down, and Timothy was methodically skinning them alive. She said he had looked at her indifferently and unconcerned, as though he were making mud pies, and then he smiled. She ran away and told no one of the incident.

"I am an old lady now—not so afraid of death," she said. "But please, tell no one of this conversation. If he finds out, he will kill me like the dogs!"

Returning to the US, Brewer's investigations went downhill. All of the deaths had been ruled accidental, and for those that looked suspicious, Timothy had airtight alibis. After countless investigations, and expenditures, the Bureau lost confidence in Brewer and his judgment, and Professor Milford's death remained unsolved. In all that time, Brewer and Bird never exchanged words; Bird's lawyers did all the talking. But Brewer would always remember the cold, mocking eyes and arrogant swagger as Bird left the interviews.

Brewer's greatest humiliation had come when he entered a conference room with his fellow agents where someone had written on the blackboard, "Brewer needs to take up a new sport. Bird hunting isn't his bag."

And now, here he was in Salt Lake City, drinking a gin and tonic, anticipating a great meal. His Bird hunting days weren't over after all.

The explosion at the site had been a huge setback, but they had a treasure trove of images taken of the ranch and surrounding property. They also had found thirteen bodies in the mountains directly linked to Timothy Bird, and best of all, a witness, Esther Morgan, who could identify him.

If Nate Hoger was right, Tick wouldn't be afraid to testify. All they had to do was keep her alive.

Child Protective Service

It had been two weeks since Tick's rescue, and Brad and the doctors were pleased with her progress. Her wounds were healing well, no signs of infection, and her fever was gone. Finally, she seemed rested; moreover, the battery of medical tests she had endured all came in negative.

She was a strong girl, well on the road to recovery.

Notwithstanding a pronounced limp caused by her deformed left ankle, she recovered her strength. Tick always pushed herself to the extreme, determined to take longer and longer walks—first in the hallways, then around the grounds, soon it was off into the adjacent neighborhood, and sometimes to the local ice cream shop. Her guards and a nurse would discreetly accompany them, finding the outings a welcome respite from the empty, ghostly halls they frequented. At times, it was challenging to match the girl's pace.

The cause of the ankle injury was one of the few tidbits of information Brad had been able to pry from Tick. She wrote that after what she called "the troubles" started, Timothy forced her to wear a ball and chain when she worked outside. She was in the garden when Timothy called her to come into the house. When she replied that she was busy, he grabbed the chain, yanked her off her feet, and dragged her into the house. That's when the ankle broke, and it had not healed properly. Shocked by how coolly she had related the story—as if it was not a big deal—the account had left Brad stunned and questioning what "the troubles" were, and what constituted a big deal in her mind?

Tick, wide-eyed and taking in all the sights outside of the hospital, was especially fascinated seeing children playing at a park, riding their bikes, or just passing by on the sidewalk. A boy whizzing by on a board with wheels one day prompted Tick to ask a dozen questions about what it was. Brad stopped himself from offering to give Tick his son's forgotten skateboard tucked somewhere in the garage, remembering her messed-up ankle.

Tick's suspicious, sometimes moody nature remained practically unchanged, although improving. She was adjusting to the hospital routine and the medical team that consistently worked with her. The group included Dr. Weinstein and Dr. Brackford, and nurses Brenda Martin, Leslie Thomas, and Abigail Jones.

If an outside specialist—for example, an eye doctor—needed to see her, Brad, a nurse, and a guard would accompany Tick to the specialist's office. She was typically cooperative and rarely complained, even if the procedure was uncomfortable. Although quite wary of her guards, she grew to accept them—often sharing her candy with them on their walks.

The specialists with whom she refused to cooperate were psychologists and psychiatrists; she refused even to acknowledge their presence. At one point, she wrote to Brad on her tablet, "*They're just useless manipulators—trying to get into my head.*"

The hospital library proved to be a treasure trove, and if Brad hadn't put his foot down, she would read well into the night. When it came to issues that impacted her health, Brad was quite firm with her: when to go to bed, what to eat, and when to stop walking or exercising. He recognized that Tick hadn't learned to govern herself, and she carried practically everything to the extreme.

She studied everyone she came in contact with, learning their names and remembering every detail they had revealed about themselves. At her core, she was an exceptionally observant, bright, and engaging girl who seemed to thrive despite her circumstances and the hospital's unnaturally protective environment.

When Susan Messener of Child Protective Services entered Tick's room, Brad was carefully cleaning the wound area on her cheek. Abigail Jones was standing by supervising his efforts. Concentrating on the task at hand, Brad hadn't noticed the presence of a stranger in the room. Messener's strident words directed at Ms. Jones startled him. "Excuse me, nurse, what in the world is going on here? Why aren't you performing your duties? This man isn't even related to the child, but you're letting him clean that wound?"

Susan Messener was in her element; a manipulative woman, she had a knack of charming her supervisors and using others to get ahead, all the while verbally abusing her coworkers. Her rise to power had been swift, often at the expense of her peers. A master of political correctness, Susan was skilled at bringing her colleagues' faults to their supervisors' attention, making the case of defending the integrity of the organization and representing herself as a valiant warrior for children in need.

The director of Child Protective Services had given Ms. Messener the file on Esther Morgan, instructing her to facilitate the girl's transfer into FBI protective custody. The case was a godsend to Messener. Finally, a high-profile case where she could demonstrate her skills and gain the recognition she deserved, the recognition that could leapfrog her into the public eye and a possible promotion.

In Esther's file, she had read that the girl had established a unique bond with the man who had rescued her, a man whose name and residence was not included in the record to protect his anonymity. It merely referred to him as "Mr. X." The medical staff and hospital administrators had granted him family status, requesting that Mr. X remain with the girl until she healed and was able to accept and bond with others. "The hospital is convinced that, without Mr. X, Esther might harm herself or others," the file read. It also described the violent episode that left two employees injured when the girl first arrived at the hospital.

Messener gleaned from the report that the girl's relationship with her rescuer was problematic for the FBI. Concerned about Esther's security, the Bureau wanted her out of Utah as soon as possible. She was a key witness against a serial killer and possibly an accomplice to the crimes committed at the ranch. Esther had information that the FBI needed to know, and her rescuer, the report noted, had blocked a full interrogation of the girl.

This case was Ms. Messener's chance to make her mark, and she entered the room prepared to take full advantage of it.

Physically pushing Abigale Jones aside, she spoke to Tick in a syrupy voice.

"So, you are Esther Morgan, the brave girl I have heard so much about. You and I are going to be best friends." Messener then elbowed her way in front of Brad, sat on the edge of the bed, and reached out and took Tick's hand with an inappropriate familiarity.

Taken by surprise, Brad did his best to prevent Tick's inevitable reaction, but he was too late. Enraged, Tick slapped Messener's hand away hard before retreating to the far side of the bed. She grabbed Brad's iPad and started typing furiously, the scar on her face turning curiously purple-red.

"*Who said she could touch me! She is a horrible, ugly creature. Timothy would cut out her tongue, make her cook it, and eat it for dinner. Tell her to go away right now!*" Brad read what she had written just as Messener snatched the tablet out his hands.

After reading the note, Messener stood up, towering over the bed, her face red with anger. Hissing at the girl, spittle coming out of her mouth, she said, "Don't you dare threaten me, young lady. I read your file, and I know with whom I'm dealing. You'll be making a big mistake if you cross me, and don't you even think about touching me again. Do you understand? You are already in enough trouble."

"Enough!" said Brad, placing himself between Messener and Tick, calmly taking the iPad out of Messener's hands. "That's my tablet, and you have no business reading a private communication between Tick and me. Who do you think you are anyway, coming in here and talking to this girl like that?"

Looking at the note again, shaking his head, he added in a conciliatory tone, "She can be difficult with strangers, especially if they don't bother to get to know her first, but I don't think she was trying to threaten you. She has been through a lot. Did I hear you say that you read a file on her? She likes to be called Tick."

Brad's words only added fuel to the fire, and Messener's response was venomous.

"Don't you tell me what to call her! Nothing said or done between you and Esther is private, and I know a threat when I hear one. I am also aware that the FBI is concerned with your manipulation of Esther… I agree with their suspicions. You may think that you're quite the hero, but all you have done is exploit the vulnerability of a young child to fuel your ego. She is my responsibility now, and your little games are over. You need to get out of the way now and let the professionals do their job!"

Brad wanted to strangle the woman on the spot, but he controlled his temper.

"I'm sorry you feel that way. Tick's confidence in me is mystifying, but I feel honored that such a special child trusts me. Since you read the file, I'm sure you also read that I was specifically asked by her doctors to stay on until she is cleared to leave. I am not going anywhere without talking to them first."

Realizing that Brad wasn't about to back down, Messener left the room and went directly to the office of Sam Evans, the hospital director, where Mr. Evans's secretary told her that he was away at a board meeting. She then demanded to see Vince Dogart, the assistant director. Upon entering his office, she introduced herself as the senior director of Child Protective Services in charge of Esther Morgan.

"Mr. Dogart, do you realize you have a non-family adult male in a room with a young girl? Do you have any idea of the ethics violations your hospital is engaged in?"

Startled, Dogart drew back into his chair, completely confused. Dogart, a CPA, was an excellent administrator able to account for every capital expenditure the hospital had made over the past decade. The one thing Dogart couldn't handle, however, was one-to-one confrontations.

Having just returned from a three-week vacation, he replied, "No, I was not aware of that. What do you mean by a 'non-family' male?"

Sensing weakness, Messener replied, "Just that, you have a non-staff, non-family male taking care of the girl who was found on the mountain."

Exploiting the information she had taken from Esther's file, she continued, "The FBI doesn't even support the hospital's sanction of this arrangement. The man has interfered with their investigation. For all you know, this guy could be a pedophile. Have you even checked him out?"

Shrinking back, Dogart replied, "I don't think our staff would allow a pedophile in a child's room."

"You don't think? You don't think!" Messener leaned in over Dogart's desk and then took on a sharp and severe tone. "How is that going to look to the attorney general and the press? I want him off the premises immediately."

Just as Dogart started to protest, Messener grabbed his phone. "Who do you want me to call first, the press or perhaps our staff attorney to start proceedings? The child could be in danger. The man is unstable and physically threatened me. You are breaking every rule in the book. I want him gone—now!"

Vince Dogart capitulated, and moments later, he, Messener, and two staff security officers consulted with the FBI security detail in Tick's room hallway.

There was a spirited discussion, but the FBI team finally, and reluctantly, nodded their heads in agreement. Then the officers, along with the security team, walked into Brad and Tick's room.

Brenda Martin, who had received an SOS from her duty nurse, arrived at the scene just as Messener marched into the room and said, "Sir, you are no longer authorized to be with this child, and I must insist that you leave the premises immediately. Your possessions will be boxed up and returned to you. You are to leave your iPad, but you can take your phone."

Tick immediately became distressed and sat up in her bed, attempting to catch Brad's eyes. Brad could not respond to her, his back to Tick as security officers forcefully escorted him out the door, followed by Brenda, who was pleading his case.

Brad was as outraged and angry as he had ever been in his life, desperate to get back to Tick, knowing she would freak out, and wondering who could help him get back to her. He had previously helped raise millions for the hospital, and now he was being escorted out like a criminal.

The entourage walked down the empty hallway, crossed the bridge to the new building, then down another hall leading to the grand staircase. After descending the stairs to the marble portico on the main floor, the officers released Brad. Tick's FBI guards, who had become quite fond of Brad, paused to shake his hand and wish him well, incredulous at the turn of events. Walking across the portico to the door and realizing he didn't even have a ride home, Brad's attention focused on his cell phone.

Shouts from down the hall grabbed his attention. There she was, sprinting down the second-floor hallway, running parallel to guardrails that led to the sweeping marble staircase, two hospital security personnel, and Brenda Martin in her wake.

Tick was on the loose.

One of the FBI escorts, who had walked back up the stairs, positioned himself in a kneeling position between Tick and Brad in an attempt to corral the sprinting girl.

If she hadn't known the agent, Tick likely would have used her cast as a weapon, knocking him out of the way. Instead, she chose to leap over him, jumping impossibly high in the air. If he had stayed down, he might have been able to grab a leg and bring her down. Instead, he tried to stand up and catch her.

Tick's foot hit the agent's shoulder, and she pushed off just as he tried to stand up. The net effect was to launch the girl high in the air over the railing. The agent managed to grab a foot but only succeeded in flipping her upside down. Her trajectory reached its apex, and gravity had its way. She rapidly accelerated headfirst toward the gold-veined marble floor below.

Brad had anticipated the worst and was sprinting across the foyer. He fully extended to catch her just before she hit the floor, cradling her head and spine, but failing to protect her hips and legs, which hit hard, bouncing off the stone surface.

Bones and soft flesh were no match for unyielding marble, and Brad and Tick slid headfirst into the base of the marble stairs. Brad somehow managed to pull Tick under him, shielding her with his head and shoulder as they smashed into the unyielding riser.

For a moment, all motion in the lobby stopped. People stood in shock over the events they had just witnessed.

Then the great institution shot into gear, its newest mission to save Brad and Tick's lives.

Who Will Clean Up This Mess?

Dr. Mattie Barnes sipped hot chocolate at her cabin at Georgetown Lake, Montana, reviewing her paper on post-surgery childcare before its submission to the *Journal of the American Medical Association.* Barnes had spent over four years working on the manuscript and was taking an extended vacation to finish the final edits.

Mattie had made it clear to all her associates that she needed some uninterrupted time alone, and that her light caseload was to be covered by an associate MD. She was surprised when a call came in on her private line, a line strictly reserved for emergencies. Something serious must have occurred.

Born and raised in Bozeman, Montana, Mattie was the daughter of a telephone lineman. At the age of eighteen, she had a life-changing experience while snowmobiling with her father, older brother, and high school boyfriend near the Big Sky ski resort.

It had been a cloudless spring day. The sun was out as they snowmobiled around in short sleeves, happy to be outdoors. Mattie had fallen back about a quarter-mile when suddenly, roaring down a chute into the run-out zone, an eighty-mile-per-hour billowing white mass of snow and ice snatched up her father, brother, and boyfriend like leaves in a hurricane. Mattie just managed to miss the brunt of the avalanche, veering her snowmobile into a grove of trees. Blinded, trapped in a frosty cloud, she hid helplessly behind her sled, wondering what had happened to all the men in her life.

She did everything by the book. She switched her rescue transceiver from transmitting to receive mode, searched the target areas herself for signals from their backcountry transmitters, probed with a pole she carried on her snowmobile.

Mattie's efforts proved to be fruitless. They all died. Her brother, the last member she was able to locate, was smashed up against a tree. He died in her arms.

Blaming herself for surviving when the men who meant the most to her had all perished, Mattie channeled all the energy of her pain and guilt into her studies, honoring her loved ones the best way she knew how. Her mother, a sensible, strong woman, was initially relieved that her daughter would react by focusing on her studies. But that soon turned into genuine concern as her brilliant, exuberant, and fun-loving daughter became one-dimensional before her eyes.

After graduating at the top of her class from Stanford University with a major in biological science, Mattie dedicated herself to medicine, earning a medical degree and additional qualifications in psychiatry, as well as attaining the highest scores on the Utah State medical licensing board exam. She practiced child psychiatry for two years, but then, driven to help critically ill children, took a step back. She spent the next seven years in residency and fellowship training in pediatric critical care.

Seventeen years after entering college, Dr. Barnes's award-winning career had been meteoric, leading to her current position as director of the Intensive Care Unit at the SLC Children's Hospital. Now in her early fifties, she coordinated a superb team of pediatric critical care specialists, using cutting-edge medicines and treatments with one of the most successful outcome rates in the nation. Mattie was a miracle worker, running the PICU with an iron hand, her life dedicated to one task—saving children's lives.

Mattie set down her laptop and answered her phone. She immediately recognized the voice on the other end of the line. It was Sam Evans, the director of the Children's Hospital—an associate and a close friend.

"Hi, Sam, how are you doing? I thought you were at the board meeting."

Sam was in no mood for small talk. He immediately came to the point. "We have a problem, Mattie. I need you to come in."

"Come on, Sam." Mattie's words now came slower, the enunciation, sharp, distinct. "You know I need this time away. Everything is covered. How could you possibly need my help? What happened?"

"Are you aware of the girl that was found on the mountain a few weeks ago?"

"Vaguely," replied Mattie. "I understand they rescued a young child in the mountains, and shortly after that, someone killed two policemen. It's in all the news. I received a text from Laura saying that they opened a wing in the Walker Building and would be placing the girl in The Palace for security reasons. Laura tells me her injuries are serious but not life-threatening."

"Well, this is highly confidential, but the child in question had been kidnapped and brutalized by her captor. The man who rescued her is Brad Hughes, a prominent businessman in the valley. You may even know him. He has been involved in several fundraising campaigns. Anyway, he was hiking in the Uintas when he found Esther— that's the girl's name. She was airlifted to Children's with significant injuries and suffering from exposure. You know," Sam continued, "I'm equipped to deal with the presence of law enforcement agents and irritating news reporters hanging around the hospital hounding me for information, but caring for Esther medically has been a major headache from the start. She has formed a bond with Mr. Hughes, an attachment which is disabling for her and for us. Whenever we try to separate her from Hughes, she becomes seriously disruptive, actually militant, completely hindering any attempt made by staff to treat her injuries. So, in a nutshell, Mattie, I bent the hospital's 'family only' policy on extended and overnight visitation. Mr. Hughes has been staying with Esther in The Palace under FBI protection, which he is willing to do until she is stabilized and transferred into CPS's hands."

Mattie could hear the frustration in her friend's voice. "Good heavens, Sam. This child sounds like an inspiration for a TV movie. Do you think this extreme bonding behavior is consequential to being rescued by Mr. Hughes, or could there be more to it?"

Mattie was well-acquainted with the Stockholm syndrome and was thinking of children she had worked with in the past who had strongly bonded to individuals who harassed, beat, and abused them.

"Well…"

"I mean… Is he interfering with her care in any way?"

"No," Sam replied. "By all accounts, he has been a tremendous help with Esther's care. As far as his background is concerned, he has been painstakingly vetted and cleared by the FBI. Mr. Hughes isn't the problem. Dr. Weinstein and Dr. Brackford have both asked that he stay on, and Brenda Thomas has backed them up."

"I see." Mattie knew that if Brenda was okay with the arrangement, then it had to be all right. "So what's your concern now?"

"As of today, Esther is in critical condition," replied Sam. "It's a long story, but she escaped from the ward, ran down the hall, and accidentally fell from the second floor down into the central foyer. Mr. Hughes, who was leaving the building, somehow managed to catch her, but both of them were injured. The girl is in surgery with a pelvic fracture, internal injuries, and a broken femur. She also rebroke her arm. Doctors Brackford, Peters, and Stobel are in OR with her now. Mr. Hughes has a dislocated shoulder and a concussion."

"Are you kidding me?" Mattie sat down hard on the bench by her phone, shaking her head in disbelief. "What injuries was she recovering from before this fall?"

"The girl came to us in terrible shape, Mattie. She was suffering from exposure, broken ribs, a brutal whiplash down her back, a deep cheek laceration, a broken and slashed arm, and a head laceration."

Outright puzzled over how such a calamity could have taken place at Children's Hospital, Mattie continued to hunt for answers.

"None of this makes any sense, Sam. First, you said the girl was recovering in The Palace with Mr. Hughes, the person she couldn't be without, staying there with her along with FBI agents. Now you're telling me that she has fallen over a railing, was caught by Mr. Hughes but critically injured, and is now in surgery? I'm sorry, but something is missing here… Lots of things are missing from this picture. How could this have happened?"

"Well, Mattie, that's a fair question. We're still trying to figure it all out, but from my understanding, CPS assigned a caseworker to facilitate Esther's custody transfer to the FBI, who planned to put her in a witness protection program. The CPS caseworker had an altercation with Mr. Hughes and ordered his removal from the hospital. Esther panicked, attacked the caseworker, ran down the hallway, and accidentally fell over the railing. Mr. Hughes was leaving the lobby and somehow managed to break her fall. We have an incident review meeting at 5:00 p.m. to go over all the details, and I'm hoping you can be there."

"She attacked the caseworker?" asked Mattie.

"Um, Brenda thinks she was provoked, but I still don't have the full story. Brenda had just left the room and there are no eyewitness accounts of what happened. I expect to be getting the surveillance video any minute. Hopefully, it will answer some questions, but I can tell you that Esther broke the woman's finger and knocked her out. For that matter, she did the same thing to two orderlies when they were offloading her at the helipad a few weeks ago. Both times were in reaction to being separated from Mr. Hughes. It's hard to believe an injured, scrawny girl could pack such a wallop."

"Actually, I think it's beyond bizarre," Mattie exclaimed.

"Mattie, we have our hands full here. The girl is difficult, but cooperative when she understands what is going on—provided Mr. Hughes is with her. Everyone thinks she is highly intelligent, and even though she's mute, she communicates at a very high level using a slate or iPad. The fact is everything was going along quite well until the CPS woman showed up. They tell me the caseworker was heavy-handed, and the staff is fuming about what happened."

"What are we up against?"

"Aside from Esther's critical condition, the Feds are afraid of losing their star witness to the crimes on the mountain, and the caseworker, Susan Messener, is currently consulting with her lawyer and has threatened to sue the hospital. She contends that the child is psychotic, should have been sedated and put in the psych ward, and that the hospital was negligent in both the girl's care and in allowing Mr. Hughes to stay with her. She has accused Mr. Hughes of threatening and physically assaulting her. Our attorney, Andrew Therber, has already stepped in to protect our interests. Hopefully, he will be able to manage any legal ramifications from today's fiasco."

Mattie's mind was awash with questions and concerns about Esther. "You and Andrew will have to contend with the legal problems. That's your bailiwick. My concern is for Esther. What's her last name? What do you know about her?"

"Her last name is Morgan," Sam replied. "She lived with her mother, Alissa, in Los Angeles before they went missing about seven years ago. The mother was one of the victims found in the mountains last week, murdered about the time the girl made her escape. The FBI tells me that Esther has no remaining family. We will follow the Children's Hospital's orphan protocol."

Mattie knew what that meant. Under the hospital's orphan protocol, the court gives the director of the Pediatric Care Unit temporary custody when family members of a child cannot be located or are otherwise incapable of providing guardianship.

"Again, Mattie, all of this is strictly confidential. You can't even let people know you're working on the case. Your assistant is in the loop, though, so you can talk to her."

Mattie couldn't have been more eager to get going. "All right, if I hurry, I can make it by four. See you then, Sam."

Mattie threw a change of clothes into an overnight bag and closed down the cabin. The manuscript that she had been so focused on less than an hour earlier remained unfinished.

Hoping to gather more information before jumping on I-15 toward Salt Lake City, Mattie dialed Laura Shelby, her assistant for the past three-plus years.

"Mattie, thank God you called. This place is a disaster area," the tension in Laura's voice was evident. "I guess you know about Tick?"

"Tick?" replied Mattie.

"Oh, sorry, Esther Morgan, the kidnap victim," Laura replied. "Tick is the nickname we have all been using for her."

Mattie replied, "Yes, I did hear about Esther Morgan and her fall at the hospital. She's been going by Tick?"

"Yeah, an aide found one small tick on her," Laura replied, "but it's mostly about a song... Anyway, before you ask, we ran a preliminary antibody test for Lyme disease—negative results, but that's the least of our worries."

"So what are we dealing with now?" asked Mattie.

"They're still working on her—Doctors Brackford, Peters, and Stobel attending. They're performing a catheter embolization as we speak to control internal bleeding in her pelvic cavity. The only reason she's still alive is that she fell only yards from the ER and was on the table in OR within minutes of hitting the marble floor in the foyer.

Mattie responded sarcastically, "Some girls have all the luck."

"You're right, it's surreal. The bleeding is coming from a fractured left femur as well as a pelvic fracture."

"Yes, I'm aware of the fractures," Mattie interjected, "and I'm anxious to get the report on the extent of those breaks and how they plan to treat them. The poor child!"

"Oh, and if all of that isn't enough to take in, the FBI's concern with Esther's security here at the hospital has intensified. They're insisting that she remain isolated in The Palace, so we've begun liberating some of the medical equipment set aside for the new ICU."

Mattie instructed, "Set up the room as a critical care unit, but she is not leaving the ICU until I say so. When do they expect her from OR?"

"If she survives, she should be in the ICU within the hour. Mattie, it's paramount that Mr. Hughes is with her when she wakes up. The last time she came out of anesthesia, he was waiting outside the room, and it took four nurses to hold her down. In her critical condition, we can't take a chance that she'll react so violently. Hughes has to be right there when she wakes up."

Mattie took a deep breath. The inclusion of Mr. Hughes in the mix was unprecedented, and the idea would take some getting used to.

"Tell me some more about Mr. Hughes and this extraordinary bond that Esther has with him."

"You'd have to see it to believe it," said Laura. "She won't have anything to do with anybody if he isn't right there with her. But he seems like a nice guy, and he's been great with her."

Mattie continued, "So you're confident that he is good for the girl?"

"Yes! I don't think we can manage without him. She is quite a handful."

Mattie thought for a moment before responding. "Okay, he should be close by when Esther wakes up, I guess, but until I understand why she is pathologically bonded to the man, let's keep him on a short leash."

Mattie was far from being a judgmental person, but until she had a chance to meet with Mr. Hughes, the jury was out. She continued her list of instructions for Laura.

"As for The Palace, get maintenance up to the wing to check out all the equipment, the power supply—everything. When they've done that, I want to see a written checklist. It's an old room with state-of-the-art equipment coming in. Equipment failure is not an option. Work up a staffing schedule for my review—senior people who have already worked with Esther. I guess you know confidentiality is a big issue, so the FBI will need to see the list."

"Got it."

"Two more things: find out what you can about Ms. Messener and the Hughes situation, and call me back while I am on the road. I want to get all the information I can before the five o'clock incident review meeting."

Then Mattie asked her final question, one that knotted her insides because she was sure she already knew the answer. "Has she been molested?"

"No" Laura replied. "They examined her in the ER when she first came. It's probably the only thing that hasn't happened to her."

"That's good," Mattie replied, relief audible in her voice. "I will see you soon."

Laura was incredibly capable. With degrees in journalism and business administration, she was a genius at digging up information. She seemed to have an almost global network of informants. And given the fact that some of the children requiring emergency care had been victims of abuse, Laura had several sources at CPS.

It was of little surprise to Mattie, then, that her phone rang about an hour later, just as she approached Pocatello, Idaho.

"I spoke to some of Susan Messener's staff," Laura said, "as well as a few acquaintances of mine. They didn't hesitate to share their opinion. From what they tell me, she is a backstabber and a self-righteous bully who intimidates her staff. One caseworker told me that she keeps most of the children under her supervision on Ritalin, prescribed by her favorite physician, Dr. Pelzer."

Laura knew that Mattie thought methylphenidate, better know as Ritalin, while a highly beneficial drug for controlling symptoms of attention deficit hyperactivity disorder, was too often prescribed as a default drug to treat common behavioral problems.

"I also talked to Brenda, who witnessed Ms. Messener slap the child hard during the confrontation—right over the wound on her cheek."

"Was that before or after Esther broke her finger and knocked her out?"

"Before... Brenda is furious!"

"What about Mr. Hughes?"

Laura laughed. "A boy scout. He is well off. He owns his own business, has a well-regarded family and an excellent reputation for being an honest and fair man. His company is a major donor to the hospital. His wife died of heart failure a few years back, and he lives on his own—at least, that's what Brenda tells me. The FBI insists that his identity be kept strictly confidential."

"When was the last update out of OR?"

"Thirty minutes ago. Tick... I mean, Esther is in the ICU, and she's stable. Thank God."

"Okay, make sure to have the medical report and all her charts available when I get in. I want to review her case before I go into the incident review meeting. What about Mr. Hughes? What's his status?"

"Concussion and a right shoulder separation," Laura replied. "We moved him to a room right across from Esther. You made Dr. Brackford's day. He was quite relieved that Mr. Hughes would be present when the girl wakes up. By the way, one thing you won't like is that the FBI has set up a temporary partition at the end of the hall and posted a guard outside."

"You have got to be kidding me!"

"No, they are quite concerned about her security."

"Okay, get to work in the Palace. I don't want that kind of distraction to impact our work."

Laura hung up the phone and immediately started in on the tasks Mattie had assigned.

A product of self-indulgent, liberal parents, Laura had grown up in a chaotic environment. Both of her parents were hippie artists, and when not looking for inspiration in a bottle or drugs, they looked for it in the latest art colony or exotic locale. Having some talent, they always found work—mosaic restoration in Spain, exotic wall finishes for wealthy clients in Connecticut, or running an art gallery in Oakland, California. Nights were spent with a claptrap accumulation of fellow progressive sophisticates, stoned on what they deemed to be the best weed currently grown. Laura, like a dinghy attached to the mother ship, was constantly being tossed side-to-side in her parents' choppy wake.

Her mother was a less-than-worthless source of valuable information for a daughter's questions and concerns about boys, relationships, or love. When a stoned artist friend of Laura's father came on to her sexually, Laura, confused and shaken, went to her mother about it and received an unsympathetic, curt lesson on safe sex. The man continued as a family friend, leaving Laura vulnerable to the predator.

Smart as a whip, Laura pulled together a brilliant essay about her unconventional life, winning a full scholarship to UCLA School of Journalism and graduating with honors, including an additional degree in business administration.

Having worked numerous jobs on campus, she left school debt-free but broke, without any expectations of help from outside parties; her irresponsible parents died in a car accident in Costa Rica during her sophomore year. They had left her nothing, and she used her entire savings to fly their bodies back to California for burial.

Graduating cum laude had not helped Laura pave a smoother path to meaningful employment. Her appearance—blue streaks in her hair, a nose ring, and an enormous dragon tattoo on her back, mostly covered up—prevented her from passing employer scrutiny tests. Further, her defense mechanisms had made her guarded and hard to get to know.

Laura met Mattie nearly three years ago on a flight from Chicago to Salt Lake City. She had just wrapped up a disappointing job interview with a public relations firm—"Your grades are excellent, but we are looking for someone with more experience." Frustrated and suspecting her nontraditional appearance—not her lack of experience—had cost her the position, she found herself on an early-morning flight to Utah, where a friend had connections at a local restaurant. Laura decided she could waitress and learn how to ski while continuing her job search.

As the plane reached its cruising altitude, Laura reached under the seat for her backpack and pulled out her résumé. "Lots of good you did me," she grumbled as she reviewed her life's accomplishments, looking for a cause to be rejected other than her blue streaks and nose ring.

"Tough day?" the elegantly attired woman sitting next to her asked.

"You have no idea."

"Tell me about it. It can't be all that bad."

As the plane touched down in Salt Lake City, Laura realized that she had provided her seatmate with a thorough and personal rundown of her background. She had disclosed her course load at college, her GPA, scholarship awards, volunteer work with disadvantaged children in the Bay Area, and even down to her hippie family and life experiences, but the stranger had revealed nothing of herself. Mattie had expertly unearthed the five Ws—who, what, where, when, and why. Laura, a journalism major, had learned nothing about her seatmate.

As they rose to leave the plane, Mattie reached into her purse and pulled out a business card and seven one-hundred-dollar bills.

"I need a new administrative assistant, and I think you would be perfect for the position. If you take the job, you will be on probation for six months. Believe me, I will let you go if you don't contribute. The starting salary will be $3,500 a month. I'll expect to see you at the office at 6:00 a.m. sharp, starting tomorrow."

Mattie handed Laura the money. "Here's an advance. Spend the money on hotel charges, and buy an appropriate outfit for a hospital office. Please lose the nose ring, and frankly, lose the blue hair. If you accept my offer, then I'll expect a positive, professional attitude. If you don't think you can cut it, keep the money and buy a new snowboard."

Mattie smiled, shook Laura's hand, and walked off the plane.

Laura spent most of that evening on her computer researching the Children's Hospital and, more specifically, reading everything published by or about Dr. Mattie Barnes. She was at the hospital at five o'clock the next morning only to find that Mattie had already arrived and was hard at work reviewing case files.

Laura immersed herself willingly and capably into the job. At the end of the six-month trial, her monthly paycheck increased by five hundred dollars, helping to pay the rent for a furnished apartment in an upscale neighborhood close to the hospital.

Her job was challenging, a combination of IT, scheduling, budgeting, and the favorite aspect of her work, facilitating the patient-parent critical care experience under the most trying, emotional circumstances. Her working relationship with Mattie transcended normal work relationships. Mattie never missed the slightest inconsistency or mistake, demanding perfection. Laura regarded her boss as a brilliant doctor who knew what was in the best interests of her patients, and she accepted her workload without question. Laura kept the department running smoothly, doing her best to take as much of the administrative load off Mattie's back as possible.

The most disquieting part of the relationship for Laura was not work-related, however. Mattie often questioned Laura about her personal life, expressing her opinions about how she spent her free time and with whom she spent it. On one occasion, Mattie explicitly told her not to date a staff physician, a man who Laura learned had questionable morals. In Laura's mind, Mattie's questions and sentiments were more the purview of a concerned parent, rather than an administrator.

Without question, Mattie and Laura had formed an unusual bond. Still, one thing was sure. When Mattie arrived at the hospital, a complete report on Esther's medical condition would be waiting for her, along with a progress report on the converted Palace.

That is, if Tick were still alive.

Sworn Testimony

Mattie arrived at the hospital forty minutes before the scheduled 5:00 p.m. review meeting, allowing her just enough time to go over the day's events with Laura, confer with Tick's surgeons, and check on her new patient.

Laura met Mattie at the hospital entrance in time to alert her boss about the invasion of FBI security officers on the second floor, and the pair quickly made their way to the elevator. The intensive care units—critical care, trauma, burn, and post-op surgical—were located on the second floor, all under the leadership of Dr. Mattie Barnes.

When the elevator door opened and the women stepped out, a burly security guard posted in the elevator vestibule at the ICU entrance examined their ID badges and offered a restrained nod as they walked past him. Upon entering the ICU unit, all eyes were on Mattie as she walked up to the staff's support station. No one could detect a trace of annoyance in her gait or on her face. She was, as always, calm, collected, focused, and professional.

Mattie's composure during life and death situations in the ICU was predictable and highly valued by her staff. Still, Laura knew Mattie was more than a little irritated by FBI security guards' presence, disrupting the second floor's evenness. God help the officer who interfered in any way with the care these children required.

Laura believed that Mattie's calm demeanor over the officer's intrusion was a ruse, applying a wise old military axiom to keep your powder dry. Mattie was fully prepared to blast the invaders should they in any way interfere with the efficiency of the ICU.

At the support station, Mattie spoke briefly to one of the RNs before walking down the hall toward Unit 3, the room that housed Tick. There, seated in front of a barricade of freestanding privacy screens and effectively closing off the east end of the area that accommodated two rooms and a family support lounge, sat another security guard. The guard, in his midthirties, immediately stood up as Mattie approached.

"I'm Dr. Barnes, the medical director of this intensive care facility. I will require frequent and unrestricted access through this partition to treat my patient—day or night."

"Yes, Dr. Barnes, of course," responded the guard. "I know who you are. You will have clear and unrestricted access at all times."

Passing through the screens, Mattie caught her first glimpse of the man whom she surmised to be Mr. Hughes, a forceful looking man standing in the doorway of his room with his head wrapped in a bandage, his arm in a sling, and a stern expression on his face. Mattie gave him a nod and a cursory smile as she turned into Tick's room, where Dr. Brackford, the orthopedic surgeon, and Dr. Stobel, the vascular surgeon, met her.

Pulling back a warming blanket from the unconscious girl, Mattie was amazed at how well Tick's figure conformed to the actions attributed to her. She was a thin, sinewy girl with well-defined muscles attached to long limbs. Even in her injured state, she projected real athleticism. Pinned down by external fixators and white from loss of blood, Tick was swathed in bandages and bruised and battered. Still, she somehow radiated a strong life force, but it was akin to an immobilized dazed bird teetering between life and death after smashing into a window. Tick's survival was anything but certain.

Mattie forcibly pushed the girl's appearance out of her mind as she and the surgeons conferred about her condition. The doctors were most concerned about the problematic bleeding in her pelvic cavity, and they presented their recommendations for her ongoing care and treatment. Given Tick's weakened condition, loss of blood, and femur and pelvic fractures, the surgical team had elected to treat her with external fixation, anchoring her bones with pins attached to metal frames penetrating through her skin. These devices would be in place until x-rays confirmed bone restoration—possibly a two-week process. She would then be in a body cast for another ten to twelve weeks, followed by months of physical therapy.

As they continued discussing Tick's case, the unit secretary entered the room and reminded the doctors that they were late for a meeting in the main conference room. Mattie would have to examine Tick after the meeting.

Brad hadn't moved from the doorway across the hall as Mattie rushed out through the partition. He had hoped to get in a few words, but before he could open his mouth, she was gone.

At the nursing station, Mattie stopped to speak with Leslie Thomas, an RN who had cared for Tick in The Palace.

"I presume the gentleman in Unit 2 is Mr. Hughes?"

"Yes."

"Let's get him into bed. He should be lying down, and tell him not to worry about Esther. Everything looks quite positive so far. I will meet with him and give him an update on her condition later this evening. Also, I don't expect Esther to wake up before I get back from the meeting, but if she does start to wake up, go ahead and move Mr. Hughes into the room with her. I want her kept as calm as possible."

Mattie and Dr. Brackford took the stairway and hurried up two flights. Mattie paused before entering the conference room to catch her breath and to collect herself. She then followed Dr. Brackford into the room, which was surprisingly packed.

At the end and along one side of the large oval conference table sat Sam Evans and Vince Dogart from administration, along with Andrew Therber, the hospital attorney. Dr. Weinstein, Dr. Brackford, Abigail Jones (the nurse who had been on duty), and Brenda Martin were coworkers who filled the rest of the chairs on that same side.

Unfamiliar faces, those of FBI and law enforcement personnel, filled most of the seats on the opposite side of the table. Next to one of the officers, Mattie spotted Diane Mansfield, director of Child Protective Services, a woman she had worked with on several cases. Beside, Ms. Mansfield sat a large woman who Mattie assumed was Susan Messener. Next to her sat a bearded man who introduced himself as Kenneth Enloe, Susan Messener's attorney.

Messener's left hand held an ice pack to her cheek. Her right elbow was resting on the table with her elevated hand, highlighting a heavily bandaged middle finger stranded in the air. As Mattie took the empty seat at the head of the table opposite from Sam, it took all the self-control she could muster not to laugh at the apparent hand gesture that perfectly expressed Messener's intentions, both for the hospital and Mr. Hughes.

Following introductions, Agent Jenny Dresder explained why law enforcement was present in the meeting. "Our men are responsible for Esther Morgan's security, as well as the security of this entire hospital floor, and we are here to determine what happened earlier today."

Dresder then gave the floor to Sam Evans, who was acting as chair for the meeting.

"I want to thank you all for making this meeting on such short notice. As Agent Dresder stated, we need to ascertain what happened here today, and we have many serious issues that require resolution. Initially, I would like to thank Ms. Messener for attending. She was under no obligation to do so.

"I also want to thank Mr. Enloe for his attendance, but rest assured, it is our goal to avoid any litigation. Mr. Enloe, I understand you have a prepared statement that you'd like to read, so let's start there."

Messener's attorney cleared his throat.

"Ms. Messener entered the room to find nurse Abigail Jones sitting in a chair indifferently watching Mr. Hughes cleaning the wounds on Esther Morgan's face. As this looked like a gross dereliction of her nursing duties, Ms. Messener rightfully questioned her idleness. Mrs. Jones used the excuse that the nursing staff allowed Mr. Hughes to clean Miss Morgan's wounds because Miss Morgan would only allow Mr. Hughes, Dr. Weinstein, and Dr. Brackford to touch her face. Not satisfied with her unprofessional conduct, my client admonished Mrs. Jones and asked to speak to her supervisor, nurse Brenda Martin. After Mrs. Jones left the room, Esther Morgan handed my client a vicious note, a note you have in evidence, a document implying my client should have her tongue cut off. Instead of supporting my client, Mr. Hughes became angry and forcibly snatched the tablet from her hands. He then violently shoved her, telling her that the tablet was his property, saying, 'Who do you think you are? Stay out of our business!'"

Enloe continued, "Frightened by Hughes's violent actions and wanting to avoid further confrontation, my client immediately left the room and spoke with Vince Dogart in administration. Acting in his capacity as vice president to the Children's Hospital, Mr. Dogart took the correct course of action and had Mr. Hughes removed from the room.

"Following Mr. Hughes's departure from the room, Esther Morgan started to follow him. My client, knowing she was dealing with a dangerous girl, was put in the position of having to restrain her. Miss Morgan reacted violently, striking my client hard across the chest, and then continued to assault my client. Nurse Martin, who was present but did nothing to prevent the attack, provided no support. In fear and self-defense, my client tried to restrain Miss Morgan. Living up to her documented reputation for extreme violence, Miss Morgan then broke my client's finger and knocked her out, resulting in a traumatic brain injury.

"The actions and negligence of this hospital have caused serious injuries to my client. Esther Morgan is a danger to herself and others, and despite knowledge of her dangerous propensities, this hospital failed to provide my client with even the minimal degree of care and protection. My client was recklessly exposed to a known risk which resulted in terrible injuries."

With an arrogant twist of his head, he added, "We will pursue legal action against the hospital and Mr. Hughes. I have already drafted the complaint."

Enloe passed around neatly stapled copies of the complaint to the attendees. "This complaint lays out my client's case and includes a signed declaration from my client attesting to the facts of her attack. As you can see, given her substantial physical injuries, my client will be unable to perform her duties with CPS for the foreseeable future. She has also incurred tremendous emotional and psychological injuries as a result of this vicious assault. She will be receiving extensive psychological counseling to deal with the extreme trauma this assault has caused. Also, and given this hospital's willful disregard for my client's safety, we will also be pursuing punitive damages.

"However, should the hospital choose to avoid litigation, as well as the possibility of punitive damages, my client is requesting a total of $10 million. This offer is good for the next twenty-four hours. At twenty-four hours and one minute, I will file my client's complaint."

The room fell silent. From Mattie's perspective, the incident review hearing had suddenly and drastically turned into a declaration of war by Messener's attorney, a man relishing the impact his statements had on those in the room. However, Sam Evans appeared unsuitably calm, drumming his fingers on the table and looking vacantly out of the window closest to him.

Incident review meetings at the Children's Hospital were rituals taken very seriously. Daily, this hospital performed state-of-the-art medical procedures, using high-tech, specialized equipment, dispensing research-based pharmaceuticals. Whenever there was a negative outcome, reviews were structured to determine the truth, improve and correct treatment guidelines, and move forward without personal animosity or hostilities. But this meeting had nothing to do with the complexities of state-of-the-art medicine and the doctors who practiced it; instead, it was an exceedingly harsh indictment of negligence by Children's Hospital that could result in firings, not to mention diminished funds from all-important donors.

Mattie looked to Sam, a consistently strong, effective, and supportive administrator, to respond to Mr. Enloe's statements, but he remained silent. His face was blank, impassive.

Even stranger, when either nurse—Brenda Martin or Abigail Jones—started to speak in protest of Messener's account of events, Sam Evans had cut them off—silencing two critical witnesses.

Now, confused and angry, Mattie spoke up, determined to protect both her staff and a severely injured child.

"I am sorry for your injuries, Ms. Messener. Esther has behaved unpredictably when she has felt threatened, but you must bear in mind that she has been kidnapped, severely beaten, and has just lost her mother. She has suffered from unimaginable physical and emotional trauma, and her 'outbursts' are understandable. As the CPS representative assigned to her care, you would indeed have been privy to all information regarding her history and behavior. You were undoubtedly aware of her potential for violence, and I assume you are trained to deal with—"

Messener interrupted, rising to her feet in anger.

"It's clear to me, Dr. Barnes, that you are more interested in covering up your staff's negligent actions than actually doing anything about them. However, I will put a spotlight on this farce. I will be bringing charges against this hospital, against your department, as well as against Esther's so-called rescuer—and I assume you would have been trained to deal with that!"

Her attorney rose as well. "My client is correct. This situation is a travesty, and we will see you in court."

As Messener started toward the door, Andrew Therber, the hospital's attorney, spoke up in a subdued voice.

"Ms. Messener, hold up, please. You have made serious charges against the hospital and Mr. Hughes. Are you willing to stand by your testimony?"

"I most certainly am," replied Messener.

"Haven't you been listening?" her attorney added.

"Yes, Mr. Enloe," replied Therber. "I have indeed. I've also reviewed the declaration your client signed for your proposed complaint, and I note that she signed it under penalty of perjury. If you don't mind, please take your seats and have your client look through it one more time, and then let me know if you have any additions or changes you wish to make."

Taking the document in hand, Messener glanced at it before tossing it back to Therber. "Everything that is in that declaration is correct. No changes are needed."

A peculiar smile sprouted on Therber's face. He turned, nodding to Agent Dresder, who picked up a remote and aimed it at a television monitor tucked into the back corner of the room.

"Why don't you take a seat, Ms. Messener? You're going to want to see this video, courtesy of our FBI friends."

Agent Dresder turned to the flat-screen TV. Addressing the group, she began, "The FBI also shared many of the concerns Ms. Messener has expressed about the advisability of having Mr. Hughes in the room with the patient, particularly given the severity of the circumstances and our lack of knowledge of either individual. For that reason, both Mr. Hughes and Esther Morgan have been under twenty-four-hour a day audio and video surveillance since being moved into the new facility, a.k.a. The Palace."

Messener sat rigidly in her seat, a nerve causing her eyelid to twitch uncontrollably.

Mr. Enloe puffed up and aggressively admonished the group, spitting out the words.

"What you're looking at here is illegal! Patient confidentiality is sacrosanct. You had no right to violate my client's or Miss Morgan's privacy. We were not informed about any surveillance."

"Oh, yes," replied agent Dresder. "We were careful to obtain a warrant for our actions. The court order is in the file on Esther Morgan provided to CPS. You both should have been aware of it."

"I think we should start the video," continued Agent Dresder, focusing on Messener. "Perhaps when you entered the room."

The audio and video clarity was stunning. The video showed the initial benign confrontation between Brad and Messener and the subsequent conversations and actions leading up to Brad's expulsion from the room. At that point, Agent Dresder ran the video in slow motion, frame by frame.

Mattie felt her hands clench in a tight ball. Her nails were digging into her palms as she watched Esther try to rise from the bed and saw Messener move to block Tick from leaving the room. Then Messener struck, grabbing the top of Tick's shoulder with her left hand and pinching her meaty fingers down hard on the muscle just below the girl's neck, her other hand clamping down on Esther's right wrist, cruelly twisting it back. Then, as the girl gasped in pain, Messener pushed her hard, back down onto the bed.

Tick's reaction looked like a rehearsed dance routine. Bounding to her feet, she folded her left arm into her body and then, rotating her shoulder, threw the cast on her forearm toward Messener's exposed neck. The blow most likely would have crushed her larynx, but at the last second, Tick pulled her punch, leaving Messener untouched, and Tick off balance. Messener angrily struck Tick across her cheek—a vicious slap that threw her head back as if a mule had kicked her, knocking her back on the bed.

As the scene continued to unfold, frame-by-frame, Mattie's heart tightened as Tick, rocked by the blow, closed her eyes and lowered her head as if in prayer. Then came the final indignation. The hefty woman grabbed the child's chin, cupped it, and wrenched Tick's head upward, forcing eye contact with her.

As their eyes met, it was as if time stopped, fear noticeably unfolding on Messener's face. Tick's eyes were strangely calm, narrowed, calculating, and fixed as she grabbed the middle finger on the hand that held her chin. She drove her shoulder into the large woman's gut, pushed forward, and stood up, finally snapping the finger as she would a small twig, twisting it forward, and driving the woman to her knees. She released the finger and pulled her fist back for a right cross that landed flush across the woman's face, knocking her out. Tick ran for the door, easily dodging past the guard.

Tick's last camera view showed her sprinting down the hall in blue pajamas, decorated with pink cartoon cheetahs. Dr. Brackford broke the stunned silence in the conference room with an excited outcry, as if watching his team intercept a pass in the end zone to win the Super Bowl. It didn't take him long to realize that he had forgotten himself, so he quickly sat down with a reddened face.

Dresder stopped the tape, and every eye turned on Messener.

"You see," Messener cried. "The child is dangerous. She could have killed me!"

"But she didn't," replied Dresder. "She pulled her punch, even after you abused her. They tell me that her shoulder suffered bruising where you grabbed it, and many of her facial sutures needed repair.

As for your sworn testimony, it seems to be quite different from tapes of the actual event. It is our opinion that Mr. Hughes behaved properly under the circumstances, and Esther's actions were strictly in self-defense. Ms. Messener, you need to consult with Mr. Enloe. You are in serious trouble."

Enloe sat motionless, trying to control his facial expressions. He half-heartedly stated that his client had been set up as he stood up and led Ms. Messener from the room.

Before the meeting broke up, the participants were sworn to secrecy. As she stood up to leave, Messener's boss, Diane Mansfield, looked over at Mattie. "I'm sorry, Dr. Barnes. I will see to it that Susan Messener never works for CPS again."

Mattie gave Mansfield a sympathetic nod of understanding, then turned and addressed her colleagues, her thoughts now turning to new challenges. "Brenda, Dr. Brackford, would you mind staying behind for a few minutes? I have a lot of catching up to do on what has happened here, especially Esther Morgan's security issues. Perhaps it would be helpful if Agents Hoger and Dresder remain as well." Receiving positive affirmations, she turned to Sam Evans, who was now at the door. "Sam, could I talk to you and Andrew in private for a minute?" Evans, knowing what was coming, was quick to reply, "That's fine, Mattie. We can talk in the vestibule at the end of the hall."

Reaching the vestibule, Mattie asked—in just above a whisper, but over-enunciating each word slowly and with a clarity that Sam recognized as her style when she was agitated—"Was all this drama necessary? Why couldn't you have just taken that despicable woman outside and arranged an accident or, at the very least, have her arrested for child abuse? You should have filled me in before the meeting. I felt completely off balance in there."

Andrew Therber was the first to reply, "He acted on my request, Dr. Barnes. Ms. Messener planned to involve this hospital, your department, Mr. Hughes, and who knows how many others in a lawsuit that would have dragged on for no telling how long. But once she provided us with her signed declaration, which completely contradicts the surveillance video, it put us in a position to stop any litigation. Further, she most likely will now be facing charges of assault and lying to the police and FBI."

Mattie coolly replied, "Okay, I understand, but it might have been nice if you had let me in on your little surprise. I came close to breaking the rest of the fingers on her hand!"

"Sorry, Mattie," replied Sam. "There wasn't time. When the FBI finally released those tapes to us, you were still on the road, and we barely finished looking at them before the meeting started. As it turned out, your righteous indignation added more fuel to the fire. You might have been out of the loop, but you were helpful."

Mattie let out a sarcastic laugh.

"You're making me feel downright worthwhile, Sammy. Now, how about you do something worthwhile, too? I still need to determine if Mr. Hughes stays or goes, and I want to see the videos of his interactions with Esther before today's incident."

"Of course," Sam replied. "Agent Dresder has them. Andrew, will you go back with Mattie and make sure Dresder gives Mattie what she needs?"

Minutes later, Mattie and the group were scrolling through films of the days before the accident. Her staff, Hoger, and Dresder answered questions and filled her in on all the events that had transpired, including the security issues related to Tick's case.

Mattie made up her mind within minutes of watching the film. Hughes, frequently utterly exasperated with the demanding child, patiently responded to her every legitimate need, overriding her only when her demands were unreasonable. He always treated the girl with respect, explaining in detail why things needed to be done his or the staff's way. Hughes did everything in his power to keep her on an even keel, reading to her, walking with her, coaxing her to eat, gently teasing her when she was unreasonable, and icing her damaged ankle after long walks. He treated Esther as though she were his very own daughter, and Mattie instantly felt less apprehensive about his remaining in the hospital, but the jury was still out.

After fast-forwarding through two days' worth of video, Mattie said, "That's enough. He stays. I have to go now, but I'd like a copy of all the video to review in detail later."

Agent Dresder handed her backup disks with instructions that they be kept in the hospital safe when not being reviewed by Dr. Barnes, to be checked in and out only with an agent present.

As Hoger and Dresder rose to leave, Dresder handed Mattie a separate disk. "You and your team might want to look at this video as well. It's from the security camera in the lobby."

Mattie took the disk and rose from her chair. As Hoger and Dresder walked to the door, Hoger, a short, commanding officer, pulled Mattie aside.

"Dr. Barnes, I wouldn't underestimate Tick. There are people in this world who are capable of killing someone with just about any ordinary object you might find in a room. I think the girl may be in that category. If she hadn't pulled the punch, that woman would be history."

Mattie replied, "I'm not sure what you saw, but all I saw was a girl reacting to yet another beating. Just what do you suggest? Would you like me to put her in restraints?"

"Don't get me wrong," replied Hoger. "I like Tick. There is something exceptional about her." There was a trace of admiration in his voice. "She is very knowledgeable about weaponry, and I believe she has been trained in hand-to-hand combat. Those look like defensive knife wounds on her arms." Pausing, he added, "She showed restraint, and that's something to work with, right? Anyway, treat her fairly and listen to Hughes. He's a good man, and he has a way with her—a tick-whisperer." He allowed himself one quick laugh before adding, no longer amused, "I still wouldn't advise backing her into a corner."

Mattie looked at Hoger questionably. "Do you think that Esther is going to be much of a threat in external fixators and a body cast? She will be immobilized for at least ten weeks, and then she'll face months of rehabilitation. I doubt she'll be a threat to anyone for a long time."

"Well, they tell me you're a miracle worker. If you are half as good as they say you are, she'll be up and at it in no time."

Mattie was a bit taken aback. "From your mouth to God's ears. Now, I do need to meet with my staff."

"Of course… Oh, one last thing, remember, Esther wants to be called Tick."

Adjourning to a smaller conference room, the team reviewed Tick's status, this time in greater detail. The doctors and nurses examined the different scans, along with the complete surgical report. They had a critically injured child on their hands. Still, there was some good news, most of it coming from Dr. Brackford who said that her fractures were all in alignment and immobilized. The fractures appeared to offer the prospect of very positive outcomes for healing normally. Barring infection and sepsis, Tick should regain her full physicality.

Fortunately, she had been given immediate care in one of the best trauma centers in the nation, and the surgical team had worked brilliantly. Brad was in far better condition, with a dislocated shoulder and a bad concussion. He would be under observation for the concussion, in a sling for the shoulder, and experience some discomfort in the coming weeks. All in all, he appeared to be in good shape.

Finally, Mattie and her team began to watch the security tape showing Tick's fall.

It was a short clip, showing a side view of the door leading outside the hospital, spanning across the foyer and the lower part of the staircase. It showed Brad turning and sprinting, then diving, fully extended, with outstretched arms that reached Tick by only inches before she hit the floor headfirst. He managed to catch and cradle her head with one hand—with his other hand, he shielded her lower back, absorbing the bulk of the impact on his elbows and forearms, protecting her head and spine. But he was unable to defend her hip, leg, and broken arm, all of which slammed onto the hard marble floor. As they slid toward the stairwell, Brad managed to pull Tick under him, hunching his shoulders to protect her from the impact.

Mattie and the team watched the film at least three times in slow motion. Later, Dr. Brackford would say he saw it in his dreams for months. He could almost feel the bones breaking, and it wasn't something he wanted to remember.

Mattie agreed with everyone that it was a miracle Tick had survived such a horrific accident, crediting Brad with saving the child's life for a second time. The FBI had the surveillance memory disk removed from the machine and placed in a sealed bag to go into the hospital safe, preventing the video from becoming a sensation on YouTube if it got into the wrong hands. They allowed Mattie to keep the surveillance disk showing Brad's interaction with Tick, as she was determined to learn as much as she could about the girl and her rescuer.

First Impressions

Leaving the conference room, Dr. Barnes took the stairs down to the second floor, this time with grave concerns about her decision to place Esther in the ICU unit. Had she placed the other children in the ICU in some danger?

She had just learned details about Timothy Bird from Nate Hoger. The FBI and other law enforcement agencies' intense search was ongoing, and placing armed guards in a children's hospital indicated a threat too horrible to imagine. By the time she took the last step on the stairway, Mattie was clear about the need to isolate Tick from the other children. She would have Tick transferred back to The Palace as soon as possible.

Controlling her uneasiness, she walked with the nurses on duty from room to room, carefully reviewing every child's chart under her care. Then, entering each room, she made a point to personally connect with each child—a hug, a smile, a laugh, a teasing comment, and a brief conversation. The children's anxious parents received her undivided attention—information, reassurances, and support.

Finally, Mattie came to the partition at the end of the hall, and after clearing security, she walked directly toward Brad's room. As she approached the door, the nurse on duty, Leslie Thomas, caught her eye.

"Watch out." Nurse Thomas mouthed the words, shaking her head and pointing toward Brad's room.

Exasperated by his clouded recollection of the day's disastrous events, Brad was worried about Tick, and he had been pacing like a tiger in a cage, largely ignoring the nurse's instructions to stay in bed.

He remembered being escorted out of Tick's room by the police. But he had only a vague recollection of running toward her falling body or how, moments later, he found himself in a neck brace strapped on a stretcher with his head wrapped in bandages. Then, there was an excursion through a CT scanner and a nurse telling him to hold his breath and remain still. The attending emergency room doctor informed him that he had dislocated his shoulder, had suffered a concussion, and needed some sutures in his forehead. None of this surprised Brad. His shoulder was killing him, he had a terrible headache, and he vomited at one point.

His shoulder was maneuvered back into place, and they sutured his forehead and placed him in a room under supervised care. A nurse checked in on him hourly, evaluating his condition as it related to his concussion.

But that wasn't the worst of it. Nobody would tell him anything about Tick's condition. Some bull about "patient confidentiality."

It wasn't until three o'clock when Brenda Martin told Brad that Tick was in the OR and that the ICU director had given the okay to move him to an empty room across from where Tick would be taken. They wanted him nearby to keep her calm if she woke up. Brenda, who had been Brad's friend and confidant at The Palace, was particularly anxious and worried. She was hesitant to provide Brad with any further details until after discussing Tick's condition with Mattie.

From the doorway of his new room in the ICU, Brad caught a glimpse of medical personnel rolling a stretcher into the room across the hall. Anxious to know if Tick was out of surgery, Brad started toward her room, only to be stopped by one of the nurses who ushered him back to bed.

Later, a tall, slender woman walked down the hall with an unmistakable air of authority, followed by other staff members. She met Brad's eyes and nodded her head before vanishing into Tick's room. Some forty-five minutes later, she hurriedly left the room with

Dr. Brackford but glanced over at Brad while relaying instructions to an accompanying nurse before vanishing down the hallway.

And now she was back.

Standing up as she entered his room, Brad felt a sudden surge of dizziness, losing his balance and grasping the end of the bed to avoid falling to the floor for the second time that day. Seeing the man struggling to stand, Mattie hurried to his side to steady him.

"Mr. Hughes, your doctor has ordered you to stay in bed for a good reason. You have a concussion, and another fall could be dangerous."

Attempting to concentrate on what he had just heard, Brad mumbled, "Okay, I get it." Then, quickly shifting his mental gears to more pressing concerns, he continued, "Can you please tell me how Tick is doing? I've been kept in the dark, and I want to know how she's doing."

Mattie was slow to reply. "If you get back in bed, then I'm quite prepared to fill you in."

Brad sat down on the bed with a frustrated expression on his face, impatient to hear the news.

"Esther is sleeping now," Mattie said. "She has fractured her pelvis and femur, and her left arm was fractured again."

Brad sighed and looked to the ceiling.

"More concerning to us, however, is that she lost a great amount of blood. The pelvic cavity contains major arteries, veins, muscles, and nerves. Her pelvic fracture was quite traumatic. At this time, she is stable, and her prognosis is favorable. We see no evidence of nerve damage. Dr. Brackford is optimistic about a full recovery from her fractures, and I concur."

Then she took a breath. "If you hadn't been so quick to react by breaking her fall, I am certain she would be dead or paralyzed for life."

"So what is your position here… Are you a doctor?" Brad asked.

"Oh, I apologize, Mr. Hughes. Yes, I'm Dr. Barnes. I am taking over as Esther's attending physician. I understand that she has a very close relationship with you and doesn't cope well if you're not nearby."

Brad did not respond.

"So I'm hopeful that you'd be willing to... Would it be possible for you to continue here with Esther until her condition is more favorable...for possibly a couple more weeks? I think she needs you right now."

Brad only glared at Mattie.

"Of course, Mr. Hughes, it is completely up to you. For now, we could certainly use your help to keep her calm and quiet when she wakes up, probably early tomorrow morning. You realize, Mr. Hughes, that's the only reason you are here in my unit. Ordinarily, you would be home in your bed."

Mattie stood quietly, watching him process the information. His face was expressionless, but his eyes were much more alert, and his pupils dilated as if confronting a threat.

"You haven't made it clear to me why you have become her attending physician," Brad finally replied in a firm, level voice. "Tick has received excellent care from her doctors here, and she was starting to trust them. Tick doesn't respond well to strangers. Are you able to give her better care than what she was getting? Why the change?" Brad didn't wait for her to answer. "Also, what happens when Child Protective Services comes in to browbeat her again, or worse, throw her into a psych ward? Or what if the FBI decides to haul her away for an interrogation? Do I get tossed out on my ear again? I mean, is anybody here genuinely interested in her welfare?"

Mattie, biting her tongue, politely responded. "I understand your concern, Mr. Hughes. For the record, I am a licensed, board-certified physician in pediatric critical care and psychiatry. I serve as the director of this hospital's PICU unit, and I have spent most of my career working with children. The hospital and FBI have pledged to provide the necessary resources for Esther's care, and I can promise you that she will get the best treatment Children's Hospital has to offer."

She continued, "I have authorized power of attorney over Esther's care under a special arrangement with Family Court. Her case may become more complicated. The FBI wants to take her into protective custody at some point. I don't have a crystal ball to know when they plan to do this or what legal challenges Esther might face, but I can assure you that nothing happens until I say so. I will not release her from my care until she has safely recovered. Further, I will do everything in my power to protect the child's future welfare. That said, I would like you to get some rest right now and allow me to spend some time with Esther. When I finish, I will answer any additional questions you might have, and I will take you over to see her. As for you, you must get some rest. Okay?"

Brad's reaction was predictable and reminded Mattie why she enjoyed working with children.

"I'm fine," he said. "You need to worry about Tick... And it's Tick, not Esther."

Mattie pulled back the sheets on his bed and, in a no-nonsense voice, ordered him to lie down. Brad complied, and Mattie then excused herself and headed across the hall to finish her examination of Tick. She entered Tick's room to find the attending nurse standing alone by her patient's bedside. Mattie began her evaluation looking for slap marks invoked by Susan Messener and was quick to spot finger-shaped bruises extending from the top of the bandages. She felt a renewed surge of anger toward the CPS woman, and those feelings grew more pronounced when she spotted deep angry bruising on Tick's shoulder where she had been squeezed, obviously very hard. Mattie ordered the attending nurse to fetch a camera. She wanted to make sure they had a record of Messener's abusive actions.

A small red cap had been placed on Tick's head to prevent heat loss. Her face was thin and bandaged, but the bandages did not conceal her features. She was a beautiful girl with a perfectly balanced face, high forehead, and a pretty, well-proportioned nose. Mattie removed the cap to get a better look at her head, noticing the girl's almost elfish ears cutely extending out from her short blond hair.

One of Tick's hands was resting outside of the blanket, and as Mattie lifted it to continue her assessment, she scrutinized the girl's hands. Her long and delicate fingers were now heavily calloused and damaged. A number of the digits appeared to have older, unset fractures. The knuckles on her right hand were swollen from the blow dished out to Messener. When the attending nurse returned with the camera, Mattie asked her to bring her an ice pack.

The examination took well over an hour as Mattie carefully studied Tick's chart, confirming every annotation against the reality facing her. When the examination was complete, she sat back and studied Tick's face, processing all the information she had received about the girl and mentally reviewing the security tapes she had seen. All of it was incongruous with the girl she saw lying on the bed.

Sam Evans was right, she thought. Tick was a scrawny little thing who packed a big wallop. What Sam had failed to tell her was that the girl looked like an angel, an angel just fallen from the sky.

"You have been with us less than two weeks," she spoke softly as if a loud noise might exacerbate the injuries. "In that time, you have completely turned this hospital upside down. I can't wait for us to get to know each other."

Mattie stood up and pulled the blanket over Tick again. "You haven't had it easy, have you, little girl?" She leaned over her and kissed Tick's forehead. "You're going to be okay. I can feel that God is watching over you, sweet pea. Don't lose heart. This will all be a distant memory someday. God is with you, and you have more people supporting you than you know."

Mattie headed back across the hall only to find Brad pacing back and forth again, anxiously waiting to get an update on Tick's condition.

"How is she?" he asked.

"Well, her injuries are critical, but her vitals are all good. We have used external fixators to stabilize her fractures. It looks quite medieval, so don't despair when you see her. As I said earlier, your girl likely won't wake up until early tomorrow, but I'm guessing you'd like to see her now, right?"

Then, without waiting for an answer, she took Brad's elbow and slowly led him across the hall into Tick's room. With caution, Brad took the seat next to Tick's bed, looking at her in disbelief. He struggled to take it all in. Strange steel cages surrounded her limbs. Pins penetrated her body, and she lay there with a tube inserted down her throat. He couldn't help but think that she had escaped from one level of hell only to fall into another.

He gently brushed Tick's forehead, and with tears in his eyes, leaned in close to her.

"I'm back, Tick." His speech was soft but deliberate. "It will take a stick of dynamite to take me away from you. I'm going to make sure that you get the best care possible. You are going to be just fine."

Convinced that Tick seemed more relaxed at the sound of Brad's voice and reluctant to break the spell, Mattie stepped quietly away from the private visit, feeling strangely moved by this pair.

No sooner had she left the room when Brad's expletive bellowed into the hallway. Mattie rushed into the room to see Brad rise out of his chair. He turned to Mattie with rage on his face.

"Who in the hell slapped her? Look! You can see finger marks over the top of the bandages!"

Mattie, gesturing to Brad to lower his voice, whispered her reply. "We know all about it, Mr. Hughes. Ms. Messener will be facing serious charges and will never go near another child in this hospital or, hopefully, any other child ever again."

His anger flared like a bolt of lightning. Mattie had rarely seen such rage in a man's face. His eyes were blazing, his fists balled up. Then, as quickly as it surfaced, the wrath disappeared behind a stony face.

Mattie's heart was pounding. "See the ice pack there on her hand, Mr. Hughes? If it's any consolation, she defended herself quite effectively. Not only did she break Messener's finger, but she knocked her out."

Brad did not respond, turning again to Tick, but the quiet moment was gone. Mattie felt suddenly drained.

"It's late," she said. "I need to get something to eat, and you need to lie down. Let's get you back to your room. If by some happenstance, she begins to stir, a nurse will come to get you. She must see your face when she opens her eyes. I plan on remaining here at the hospital tonight as well."

As they walked back to Brad's room, he asked, "So you have temporary legal custody?"

"That's right. I have a special arrangement with Family Court to gain temporary guardianship of a sick or injured child when there are no family members and where care decisions are required."

"And it's up to you if I'm allowed to stay here in the hospital while she recovers?"

"Well, my staff supports you, and they tell me that Esther will go to extraordinary lengths to keep you nearby. We must keep her quiet and immobilized in the coming days."

"So you will decide if I stay or go, and what is to become of Tick?"

"I am not Mrs. Messener, Mr. Hughes. I understand your concern, and I want you here for as long as it takes," Mattie replied, looking away and gazing down at her watch.

Brad touched Mattie's elbow to get her to turn and face him. The physical touch, the intensity of his eyes, and the force of his conviction were authoritative. Mattie felt a flash of anger.

"Listen to me, Dr. Barnes. I will do everything in my power to help Tick—"

Mattie interrupted, now entirely focused. "Tick? Are you the one who gave her that name?"

Brad replied, softening his stance, "Yes, and that is what she prefers us to call her... As I was saying, there isn't much I wouldn't do to help Tick, but I should have some say in her care. She needs to be protected. I can't... I won't allow a repeat of what happened here today."

"We will be watching out for Tick's welfare, and I can assure you that we will provide the best of care," Mattie replied.

"I need more assurance than that," Brad countered in a demanding voice. "Are you willing to put yourself in a position where you have some oversight and accountability for your actions? Can you arrange for me to have an equal share in her custody? I don't want her to end up a throwaway. I have already let her down once... I'm not about to let that happen again. I don't want everybody to turn and walk away from her when this is over."

Mattie had heard enough. "Mr. Hughes, you are in my house, and if you choose to stay, you must play by my rules. There is no way to provide joint custody, and even if there were, I wouldn't agree to it. You are just going to have to trust me. I truly am sorry for what happened here today, but Tick needs your help now to survive. I can only imagine the sacrifices you are making for this girl. I know that we are asking a lot—"

"What did happen here today?" Brad interrupted. "Did you have custody over her when all this happened?"

A bit startled, and with a confused expression on her face, Mattie replied, "Yes, technically, I have custody over any orphan in Children's. Orphaned children needed to have an advocate, and that was my role, but I was out on vacation."

"Who is in charge when you are gone?" he asked in an interrogative tone.

Mattie, not used to being on the defensive, replied guardedly, "Sam Evans and then her attending physician, Dr. Brackford. Evans was in a board meeting, and Dr. Brackford was in surgery. The CPS woman overstretched her authority. It was an accident."

"Accidents don't just happen," replied Brad. "Like an unreported close call, there is always a chain of events, where, with some thought, preventative steps should have been taken to avoid future accidents. It looks to me like you didn't have clear guidelines in place."

He could be right, she thought, but Mattie wasn't about to sit there to be lectured like one of his employees.

"We will get to the bottom of what happened today, and I can assure you it won't happen again. Technically, you could check out of here tomorrow, so to answer my question: Are you staying or going?"

Not allowing him to answer, she continued, "And as far as questioning my or this hospital's oversight and accountability, let me say this, Children's Hospital does an exceptional, world-renowned job treating the children in its care. After that, our job is to pass them back to their parents or into the system. I suspect it will be the same for you, as well, Mr. Hughes. At some point, you will go back to running your company, and Tick will become a distant memory."

Mattie realized her comment had hit home from the hurt expression on his face. Perhaps she had gone too far.

Brad was quick to regain his composure, however, replying firmly, "Of course I will stay with her, but understand this... I am going to use every resource I have to see that Tick not only gets the best treatment, but also that she is protected."

"Then we agree, Mr. Hughes. You'll stay on for a while longer, and we will both do our very best to take care of Tick, regardless of who is in charge."

Brad extended his hand, "Okay, then... For the long run."

Mattie, irritated with the man and still a bit shaken by the anger she had seen in his eyes a few moments earlier, didn't want to ask him what "for the long run" meant. She extended her hand nonetheless, only to have it grasped firmly, her fingers disappearing in his encompassing grip. She felt vulnerable as if somehow she was being trapped, somehow being changed.

Feeling uncomfortable, Mattie pointed to a leather toiletry kit with the initials "BH" on the flap. "I see someone has dropped off your kit. You might want to take a shower and shave before Tick wakes up. You'll feel better, and she should see you freshened up. I will have a nurse show you the way to the shower, and I'll have a meal sent up. Please get some rest, Mr. Hughes."

In a deliberate attempt to level the playing field a bit, Brad asked one final question.

"By the way, do I have to call you Dr. Barnes?" Brad asked. "Given the circumstances, shouldn't we be on a first-name basis?"

Mattie responded with a preoccupied expression on her face. "Yes, you can call me by my first name—Mattie."

"Well, Mattie, if you want to succeed with Tick, you have to be honest with her. Don't sugarcoat anything or talk down to her. She's amazingly bright and perceptive, and she can't stand any deception. She studies people, and she can be very judgmental. Also, she thinks about every word you say to her."

"Thank you. I've heard similar comments about Tick from several other sources, but I appreciate your confirming it."

Brad persisted. "Also, you have to stand up to her. She can come on strong, and I promise you, she *will* test you. You can't take it personally."

Mattie offered a terse, professional opinion. "Yes, Mr. Hughes… Brad, it's quite normal for abused children to act out in kind. I am fully acquainted with this behavior, and I would never take it personally."

Brad shook his head. "No, that's not what I mean. Tick is not a mean or spiteful child. She is just unusually insightful for her age, testing and challenging everyone before allowing a person into her space. She is quite extraordinary. You will see."

Mattie left the room annoyed and exasperated, yet satisfied with her decision to enlist Brad's support.

I don't have to like the man, she thought. What was essential to Mattie was his evident devotion to Tick. She could sense that he would do anything for her.

Brad, for his part, was somewhat amused about Mattie's subtle hints about his grubby appearance. She reminded him of his beloved Catherine, who often assessed his appearance. And like Catherine, Dr. Barnes seemed fair, intelligent, and thoughtful. She also must be an extraordinary doctor, he thought, given her position in such a well-known and respected hospital. He felt a sense of relief that she was now in charge of Tick's care.

He wasn't upset about the prospect of being stuck in a hospital room, even for months if it came to that. The past weeks had enforced a lesson he had learned from experience—life throws out all kinds of challenges. While one should never be fatalistic and placidly accept difficult circumstances, some situations required the maturity and wisdom to let go of the control one never had in the first place.

Catherine was dead, and nothing was going to bring her back. Tick was drowning and needed someone to tread water with her, helping get her back to shore. It wasn't in his makeup to leave her floundering. Hopefully, they would get the girl squared away quickly, and he could return to his normal life.

Brad doubted that Mattie had a good understanding of what was going on in Tick's world outside the hospital. She was not only in real danger from Timothy Bird and possibly others connected to Bird, but also from law enforcement. Tick had become a player in a far larger game consisting of one of the more publicized, if not prominent, criminal investigations in US history. As a faithful Christian, Brad took the promise he made to God to take care of the girl very seriously. It was hard for him not to think that he had failed her miserably earlier in the day. And, in fact, Tick was in worse shape than when he found her on the cliff.

Brad had been admittedly disingenuous with Mattie by bluffing with his offer to share custody of Tick. He knew that there was no likelihood of gaining joint custody, but that wasn't his real motivation. Brad only wanted some say in Tick's care. He believed that he was the most reliable advocate she had, and at the end of the day, Brad thought he had made some progress with the girl's new doctor.

Remembering his displeasure at being escorted out of the hospital before Tick's tumble, Brad didn't honestly know if he would be able to put this foundling and her plight behind him forever. Mattie had questioned out loud what he had privately been asking himself all along. Besides providing some anonymous financial support, could he continue to help Tick despite the formidable complications she presented? He never felt so emotionally confounded in his life.

His head was throbbing, and he was unable to get comfortable with his arm in a sling. As he lay on the bed, a course of action began to formulate in his mind. He would have his secretary draft an announcement for his signature, a statement that would relieve him of day-to-day operations as CEO. It was time for his VP, Bill Fairmont, a good man, to take the reins. Fairmont had earned the chance to run the company. Truth be known, Brad had been prepared to lose Fairmont to another outfit for a while now. Brad would remain on as chairman of the board and take an indefinite leave of absence for personal reasons.

He would need to have his attorney draft up the paperwork. There was another more pressing issue; he needed to develop a strategy to protect Tick.

After showering and eating a few bites of a noodle casserole that had turned cold on the tray, Brad went to bed. His last thoughts before drifting into a well-deserved sleep were of Dr. Barnes-Mattie. She was a beautiful woman, he thought, fairly tall with a nice figure, intelligent, a fighter, dark eyes, fair skin, auburn hair pulled back in a neat bun, and graceful hands with long fingers.

In his mind, she was one of the most attractive women he had come across in years.

Just before her six o'clock cell phone alarm sounded, Mattie, woke up on her office couch. She had sufficient time to shower, dress, blend a protein shake and get to the small ICU conference room where she would receive an update on all the patients before the nursing staff's 7:00 a.m. shift change.

The update went as expected. Tick's vitals had remained stable throughout the night, and Mattie was relaxed as she made her way into Tick's room at the end of the hallway. She greeted the attending nurse and Brad who was sitting at the far end of the room.

When he saw her, he stood up immediately. He was neatly dressed and clean-shaven, but he looked tired and anxious. Mattie strolled over to Tick's bed and looked her over carefully, studying the monitors and searching for signs of consciousness. Brad commented on how pale Tick looked as he began pacing the floor. Mattie suspected that it was going to be a long day.

Within minutes, Tick began to stir. Brad stood as close to one side of her bed as he could without getting in the way of the nurse and Dr. Barnes. He began talking to her calmly, steadily, hoping that she would recognize his voice, praying that she wouldn't panic upon waking up in this strange room, hurting, terrified, and immobilized by metal devices.

Then, her eyelids fluttering but not yet opened, Tick groaned as Mattie and the team removed her breathing tube. When they pulled the end of the tubing from her throat, she coughed and hoarsely called out for her mother as she opened her eyes.

"Mommy?"

Brad quickly moved in and reached for her swollen hand, assuring her that he was right there with her. He then turned his head away for a brief moment, prayerfully expressing joy and relief.

"She spoke!" he exclaimed. "I can't believe it."

After responding to Mattie's simple verbal commands with wobbly nods and shakes of her head, not words, Tick focused her blurry eyes on Brad. She pointed to the bandage on his head and the sling on his arm, and she appeared somewhat distraught as she stretched out her good arm for him. Brad hurried to grab the iPad sitting on the table next to Tick's bed. He held it near her hand, and she grabbed the stylus, scribbling, "*You're hurt! How? Was it my fault?*"

Reading the pad over Brad's shoulder, Mattie was astonished by Tick's urgent concern for someone else before bewailing her disastrous situation. Brad assured Tick that he was fine, explaining how they had both been injured. Laughing, he asked her to pack a parachute the next time she went flying.

"I'm too old to be making diving catches!"

He assured Tick that she had done nothing wrong, that an "incompetent, mean and stupid person was to blame." Tick became more and more alert to her surroundings, but she was not yet fully aware of her physical state. Then she noticed the tall, thin woman wearing a white jacket standing at the end of her bed.

Looking toward Brad, Tick took wrote on her tablet. "*Woman there, staring at me... Tell her to stop.*"

Brad signaled Mattie to come closer. "This is Dr. Mattie Barnes. She's your new doctor."

Mattie couldn't remember seeing such unusually beautiful eyes, eyes that suddenly narrowed as they focused on Mattie, radiating a world of mistrust that was disturbing to see in a child so drained and fragile.

"Hello, Esther," Mattie said, smiling. "I hope you didn't think I was rude for staring, but I was noticing your beautiful eyes and was trying to decide what color they are. Brad tells me you like to be called Tick. Do you want me to use that name or Esther?"

Tick looked away from Mattie and wrote on her tablet before turning it toward Brad to read.

"Only my mother can call me Esther, and she's dead. I don't want her for my doctor. I want Dr. Brackford!"

Brad was determined to do his best to get Mattie off to a good start with Tick. "Tick, you may be interested to know that Dr. Barnes is in charge of the entire team here at Children's Hospital. Dr. Brackford works for her. She's the best of the best, and she has spent her life treating sick and wounded children and making them well. She is your main doctor now, but Dr. Brackford will help her, and you will still see him as well. We're fortunate to have Dr. Barnes on our team now, Tick. She is a good person, and she'll do everything to help you get healthy again."

Tick gave Mattie another sideways look and proceeded to write *Matthew 7:15* on her pad. She handed it to Brad and closed her eyes.

Brad reached for his cell phone, once again stumped by a biblical reference, but it was Mattie who responded, her voice firm but gentle. "I know that verse. 'Watch out for false prophets. They come to you in sheep's clothing, but inwardly they are ferocious wolves.'"

Brad had heard the verse many times, but nonetheless, he was impressed with Mattie.

"Tick, I'm not a wolf in sheep's clothing. I'm a doctor who only wants you to get better, but I understand why you might not trust me. I watched a video of what went on between you and the woman who slapped you yesterday in your room. What she did was very wrong. She is in serious trouble. She will never be allowed in this hospital again. You won't see her ever again. Nobody is blaming you for defending yourself, Tick, and that includes me, so please give me a chance to prove that I'm not here to hurt you."

Mattie leaned in a bit closer. "Brad has told me that you like people to be direct with you and that I should always be honest with you. I think it is important that you know what has happened to you and how we plan to treat you. But I can't talk to you if you won't open your eyes and look at me. If you'd like, I can come back later."

Tick's eyes flashed open, and she glared at Mattie in anticipation. Mattie presented her patient with facts and information regarding her injuries, surgery, and details of her care and treatment. She went through everything with Tick, including treatment options, possible complications, and the long-term prognosis.

Mattie would often stop to ask, "Are you following me? Do you want more detail?" Tick would invariably nod her head yes.

When she finished, Mattie spoke to the elephant in the room. "We know you are capable of speech, Tick. Brad and I heard you calling out for your mother as you were coming out of the anesthesia. We need to get you talking again. It's not something to worry about now, but we will be working on it."

Tick's face turned white, tears falling from her now-closed eyes. It was a sore subject, and Mattie mentally kicked herself for bringing the topic up, but she was relieved that her patient seemed composed.

Of course, that lasted only a few hours. That afternoon when Brenda Martin entered the room, Tick managed to grab a glass of water from the bed table and hurl it at the nurse, pointing her finger toward the door. Brad was caught off-guard. Brenda had been their favorite nurse by far, and she was wonderfully supportive to both he and Tick from the beginning.

She was one of the good guys, he thought.

Tick's explanation for the incident was less than forthcoming, writing only "*traitor*" on the pad before dozing off. Later that night, when Mattie returned to find Tick fast asleep, Brad disclosed the incident and how baffled he was by her outburst. "Tick liked Brenda... They were good buddies. I don't know what has changed or why she's calling her a traitor."

"Brenda came into the room just after Ms. Messener had you escorted out. Tick must hold Brenda partially responsible for what happened. Brenda is devastated. I found her crying at the nurse's station."

Observing Tick and Brad's interaction with the staff, Mattie determined that the hospital records noting Tick's behavior and conduct were entirely accurate. Namely, Tick was not cooperative with anyone without Brad's involvement. Mattie did not believe in labeling children, but she quickly reached two general conclusions about Tick: the first being if it came down to "fight or flight," Tick would always choose to fight. The second was more nuanced. Most of Tick's reactions were thought out and strategically useful to her, a means to the end she desired: Brad's constant presence. Tick was a thinker and a planner.

It also became apparent to Mattie that Tick had become attached to select members of her nursing staff, a group she had apparently winnowed down at the beginning of her stay: Abigail Jones, Leslie Thomas and Beverly Lee. Mattie found it ironic that Tick had managed to limit her care team to three of the best nurses in the ICU. Knowing the staffing problems Tick had created in the past, losing nurses once again to the child's care would be a significant staffing headache.

The girl had a genius for disrupting the normal flow at the hospital.

The next morning as they changed Tick's bandages, Mattie saw the lash marks on Tick's back for the first time. The injuries were terrible, now being kept open to prevent infection, but Mattie could see they were deep, extending down into the muscle. Other old wounds had left extensive scarring. All the damage on her back appeared to have been produced by a bullwhip. Cosmetic surgery could help in the future, but Tick would be scarred for life.

Equally concerning to Mattie was Tick's growing awareness of her injuries and limitations. She showed signs of depression and wouldn't help the staff regulate her level of pain, suffering needlessly and fibbing, "*I'm not in pain. I'm fine.*"

Concerned about the presence of law enforcement in the ICU and the impact on her other patients, Mattie planned to transfer Brad and Tick back over to the other wing as soon as Tick's health would allow it. She spent a hectic afternoon reviewing work being done at The Palace and meeting with Tick's security detail. On a positive note, The Palace's makeover was complete; the room had been sterilized and was now fully operational. The maintenance staff had even been able to hook Tick's monitors into the ICU center. An on-site nurse and central monitoring could now see her vital signs around the clock.

Security was still a significant concern. Nate Hoger, who had cautioned Mattie about Tick days earlier, was busy setting up the provisions. He ordered armed officers placed at the deserted hall entrance, and access to the floor was now only possible if a guard or nurse buzzed in the person.

Mattie asked Hoger for more information about Mr. Hughes, and Hoger volunteered that Brad had cleanly passed an extensive background check. As Hoger put it, "I wouldn't have any trouble trusting him with my daughter."

Hoger explained that everything about Brad's encounter with Tick checked out except his statement about seeing his deceased wife's face on the side of the mountain, which lured him to leave the main trail and climb the ridge where he found Tick.

"His story was so implausible that it nearly led to our taking him in for questioning," Hoger said. "As it turned out, I had one of my men duplicate the path Brad claimed to have made, following the same timeline. Amazingly, the light and shadows on the ridge painted a clear profile of a woman. We were lucky to get a picture of it because it's not always apparent, depending on the position of the sun."

Mattie also requested that Laura be permitted to research Tick's past before the kidnapping. The FBI denied her request; the ongoing investigation was sensitive—they didn't want the confusion of two parties asking acquaintances the same questions. They also did not want to establish any links between California and Utah, fearing Timothy might take advantage of any contacts. Hoger did ask Mattie to provide a list of questions for his field agents and promised her a report when it became available.

That afternoon, Mattie met with Judge Thornton of Family Court and Diane Mansfield of Child Protective Services. They reviewed the incident at the hospital in detail, and sure enough, Brad was right. There were holes in the Orphan Protocol. Without clearing it with Dr. Barnes or the designated hospital staff, CPS could come in and visit with an orphan child. The CPS guidelines stipulating permissible actions before the discharge of a child from the hospital were ambiguous.

It was a dated agreement. The lines of authority were not clear. There had only been three cases in fifteen years of practice where the Orphan Protocol had taken effect. The groups had respected each other, and the outcome had always been quite positive, with family friends ultimately taking responsibility for the children. In this case, the protocol broke down.

Mattie requested and received changes to the agreement. Once the Orphan Protocol was invoked, the hospital would be in complete control of the child until Mattie or an appropriate authority deemed the child out of danger and ready to be discharged. CPS could not even visit the child without hospital consent and would need to be accompanied by an attending physician. When the child was out of danger, the court, the hospital, and CPS would convene a meeting to develop a strategy to meet the child's needs.

As the meeting concluded, Judge Thornton asked Mattie to stay behind.

"How is the girl doing?" he asked.

"She is still in critical condition. It is very much touch and go."

"I see you have decided to keep Mr. Hughes involved."

"Yes," replied Mattie. "He is amazingly supportive of her and seems to be the only person she trusts. He wanted a shared custody agreement, but I told him that it would be impossible."

"That was a good call, Mattie. I could never dilute your authority. You will have to remain in charge. I am sure you can make Mr. Hughes understand the reasons for our decision."

Then, reaching into a drawer on his desk, Thornton pulled out a newspaper. The feature article titled *Utah Death Ranch*. It described the discovery of thirteen corpses, and it linked the site to the rescue of a twelve-year-old girl in the Uintas, where two policemen had been murdered.

The article reported that this same girl had recently been injured in a fall while trying to flee FBI agents at the hospital. The article described the girl as violent, attacking, and injuring several hospital personnel and a CPS caseworker. It also speculated that the girl might have been involved in the actual killings on the mountain.

They had branded Tick as being a coconspirator to a serial killer.

"Given the danger this girl is in, I think it best that we patch her up and turn her over to the FBI. She belongs either in a witness protection program or possibly in detention. They tell me there is evidence linking her to some of the murders."

Mattie glumly replied, "I understand your concern, Judge. But if we don't look out for Esther, who will?"

"I don't know, but I'm sure that once she's back on her feet, she'll be better off in the hands of the FBI," replied Thornton. "I suspect they will work out an immunity agreement if she cooperates. Mr. Hughes has already made a good start on it."

"What do you mean?" asked Mattie.

"You don't know?" replied Thornton. "Mr. Hughes set up a quarter-million-dollar scholarship fund for her college education. I received the papers yesterday. He set the trust up a week ago. The girl has a guaranteed college education if she wants it, or if she fails to take advantage of college, she receives the money on her twenty-ninth birthday. Mr. Hughes has also set up a provisional hundred-and-fifty-thousand-dollar fund for her counseling and legal defense if required."

Mattie was stunned. The man she had been so frustrated with had not only been proven right about the inadequacy of the Orphan Protocol, but he had just extended extraordinary generosity to a child he barely knew. She didn't know what to make of it.

⁓ↈↈↈↈↈ⁓

It was late when Mattie returned to the hospital, unsure of her feelings toward Brad and upset that her new patient was in so much trouble. Could Tick be a killer? How would Brad react if she was? Was Brad just another wealthy executive used to getting his way or was there much more to him?

Mattie went straight up to Tick's room, avoiding Brad by claiming that she was in a hurry and that there wasn't time for a visit.

She studied the sleeping girl. "Who are you?" she whispered to herself. "What have you done? What have they done to you?"

Frustrated, faced with conflicting thoughts about both Brad and Tick, displeased with the entire situation, barely speaking to Brad, Mattie left the room.

Healing?

Had it been three or four days since the fall? Brad wondered, looking down at his watch. He had lost all track of time. It was late, close to midnight, as he stood next to Tick's bedside. He had never felt so drained nor so exhausted.

Tick wasn't doing well. She was withdrawn, in pain, closed off, and had sunk into a deep depression. She refused to eat, was losing weight once again, and nothing Brad said or did seemed to help.

They were hastily transferred back into The Palace just two days after her fall and surgery. Brad assumed that the parents of critically ill children found it disquieting to have Esther Morgan, along with armed guards, on their floor—possibly a genuine threat to everyone's safety. He wondered if the news stories speculating that Tick had participated in the Death Ranch killings were behind their central units' banishment.

Did the hospital administration wish to hide Tick and the whole ugly matter away, out of sight, out of mind?

The hospital staff had transformed the large Palace room to accommodate sophisticated monitoring equipment and a large electric bed, a room that no longer resembled the warm and inviting sanctuary it had previously been. Now, anything that could harbor a germ—wall art, cheerful fabric at the windows, colorful bedspreads—all of that was gone, leaving a purely antiseptic and unwelcoming space behind.

They placed Brad's bed with a privacy screen in the farthest corner of the room. Thankfully, Laura had done her best to make his area slightly less austere. He was grateful to see a small bedside table with a reading lamp on it.

A supply of sterile hospital scrubs, masks, and shoe covers was boxed and stored in a closet. Mattie had instructed Brad to wear these garments when he was around Esther—which was most of the time.

When Mattie finally entered the room late that evening, she went directly to Tick's bedside to examine her and study the monitors. After scribbling a few notes on her chart, she turned to leave the room but not before Brad approached her to ask about Tick's condition.

Elbowing Brad out of her way, Mattie mumbled, "Not as well as I would like."

Brad grabbed her by the arm. Mattie glared down at her arm and then back up at Brad, who immediately realized that as desperate as he was for information, grabbing her was a mistake.

"Excuse me, Dr. Barnes! I'm sorry." He couldn't hide his perturbation with Mattie. "But I didn't quite catch that. Could you be civil and answer my question in a voice that a person can actually hear?"

Mattie's demeanor shifted. "My apologies, Mr. Hughes. Tick's vitals are stable, but she isn't recovering as quickly as I was expecting. Rest assured that I am on top of it and will keep you posted. There is something else. You were right. The Orphan Protocol was flawed. The hospital didn't have clear lines of authority. Part of what happened here is my responsibility."

She stood there staring at him, feeling guilty that she had somehow failed Tick, as well as feeling embarrassed about the prospect of getting a lecture from a relative stranger who now thought less of her.

"That's very good to know," Brad countered, "but what's that got to do with why you have been avoiding me?"

"Well, I assumed that you were angry with me," Mattie said, "that I was somehow responsible."

"For Pete's sake," Brad replied. "What are the odds of all this happening again? Of course, I'm not angry with you. I'm the one who has let this child down."

Mattie's thoughts careened to her childhood. *For Pete's sake…* It was a phrase her father had used when he was completely exasperated by her behavior, and hearing those words struck an endearing note that instantly put her at ease.

Her concerns shifting, Mattie composed herself and set her file down on Brad's bedside table.

"Why—" Mattie asked the question only to be interrupted by Brad.

"Look, Mattie," Brad cut in, "I was fed up and angry with Tick's condition, with the whole scenario and how powerless I have been… you can't believe I would hold you responsible."

Mattie squared her shoulders, looking Brad in the eye. "No, that's not what I was about to ask you. Why would you give a quarter of a million dollars and set up a defense fund for a child you hardly know?"

"Where did you hear that?"

"At Family Court. We were reviewing the incident, and Judge Thornton brought it up."

Brad shook his head and sighed. "I'm a parent, Dr. Barnes… I know what it takes to raise and educate a child, and she has no one. Let's just say that I believe it was the right thing to do."

Mattie took notice of Brad's halting explanation. *He looks so uncomfortable*, she thought to herself. *What's bothering him? He doesn't look well.*

She continued, "There are thousands of deserving orphans out there, Mr. Hughes. Why give her that much?"

Brad looked away, and Mattie realized the question was none of her business and was quick to change the subject.

She asked, "Why do you feel you have let her down? By all accounts, you have had the best intentions for her."

"I promised her that I would protect her, Dr. Barnes, and just look at her."

Knowing that Brad wasn't looking for sympathy, Mattie changed the subject. "Tell me about Tick. What's she like? What makes her so special to you?"

"There's not much to tell," replied Brad, sitting down in his chair. "I hardly know her since she doesn't talk and hasn't communicated much about herself or what happened on the mountain."

"Oh, please!" Mattie protested. "Can't you do better than that? You have been stuck like glue with her for over two weeks. You have set her up with a small fortune! Don't tell me you haven't formed some opinions."

"Well, you're right. I have, lots of them. For starters, Tick's survival skills in the wild are beyond belief for someone her age. How she managed to escape Bird in her condition—hiking out in harsh terrain and then surviving two nights on the ledge of a cliff bleeding and with a broken arm is nothing short of miraculous. Do you know that she made a hand drill and managed to start a fire? She even built a little debris hut under the tree."

"What is a debris hut?"

"It's a survival shelter. You dig a little pit, create a floor with leaves or any kind of loose bits, then you build an A-frame out of branches and cover the whole thing with more leaves and branches. It was freezing up on that mountain, and Tick was only wearing light clothing. Most children her age would have frozen to death."

"So she is trained in survival skills?"

"Someone had to teach her those skills, but being trained is completely different than actually pulling it off under harsh conditions, especially given her horrendous injuries."

"What about her knowledge of martial arts? Hoger believes she is highly skilled. The newspapers are reporting that there was a fighting ring in a cave. The papers are speculating that she and Alissa were part of Timothy Bird's organization and that Tick could be involved."

Brad had read the same articles on his iPhone and was furious about how they characterized Tick. "They can speculate all they want, but making her into a twelve-year-old complicit member of Timothy Bird's organization is absurd. One look at her little body covered with old scars and new wounds tells an entirely different story."

Looking at Tick, he continued, "She hasn't divulged much information yet, but I guess that after Bird kidnapped her, he was the one who trained and taught her survival skills. I suspect that he was also the one who brutalized her for some sick reason. Keep in mind, Tick's mother was present as a major influence on her daughter. Someone spent a lot of time teaching her from the Bible, and I doubt it was Bird. It's amazing how much scripture Tick can quote."

Brad paused in thought. "It's possible that Bird was training her the same way a pit bull is trained for dogfights, only to be put back in a cage after the fight is over. That wouldn't make her the criminal! The FBI could write a book on what they don't know about the girl. They should focus on the fact that she saved a lot of lives when she informed them about the bombs Bird had planted in the cave."

"Do you think she has killed anyone?"

Brad frowned at Mattie with a stab of suspicion. "Is this being recorded?"

"No," replied Mattie. "I have an audio/video kill switch when I am in the room. It was one of the conditions I requested when I took the case to protect patient-doctor confidentiality. This conversation will never leave the room."

"Well, the truth is, I know she has been in some knife fights. Her scars are proof of that, but no, I feel sure that she has not killed anybody."

"What makes you so sure about that?"

"Because she communicated that information to me in writing, and I believe her. She admits to fighting, but she said that she never killed anyone. Tick was beginning to trust me enough to open up about the ranch when that horror from CPS came in. Mark my words, Tick is no killer. There are many qualities that I admire about her: she has depth, grit, and courage, just to name a few... I could go on. Once you get to know her, you'll understand what I am saying. There is something extraordinary about her."

"What does your family think of all this?"

"I haven't told them anything yet. With Timothy Bird on the loose and probably other vipers involved, I don't want my family knowing anything of my involvement. As far as they know, I'm in South America right now."

For the first time that night, he laughed. "It's been a complete pain in the rear keeping my fictitious itinerary straight and choosing Internet pictures of my invented locations to send the boys. Obviously, there were no selfies. Taking an extended trip of a lifetime to practice my Spanish and see places like Machu Picchu was the only story I could come up with. I think I'll be taking a long cruise next—one that sails around the world in early November and doesn't end until…well…until it ends!"

Smiling, he reflected, "I only wish it were true. Anyway, I told my staff that I am taking an indefinite leave of absence, and I appointed another president to run my company."

Mattie seriously questioned why this man would cut himself off so completely from his previous life, a man who was so calmly running his life off the rails.

"So, Brad… What do you think is Tick's biggest issue, aside from her obvious injuries?"

Brad looked down at Tick and began to well up. "Getting over the loss of her mother. She hasn't shared a lot about her, but she must have adored her. I will never forget the expression on her face when they confirmed Alissa was dead. It was total desolation. Tick thinks about her mother fairly constantly, I think. I can see it in her eyes—and when she does, it's like the life goes out of her for a moment. Then she pulls herself together, distracting herself by reading and learning something new. She never laughs and rarely smiles. For some reason, she blames herself for her mother's death."

"That can be an emotional black hole," Mattie commented.

"Then, blast it all if another nightmare named Messener showed up at her bedside… Why should Tick believe that anyone in the world would protect her? Why should she trust me or anybody else for that matter? It's no wonder she's depressed. It breaks my heart."

Mattie felt her chest tighten, and her eyes stung. She knew it was best to end the visit. On her way out, she placed her hand on Brad's shoulder and reminded him that children are resilient and that, in time, Tick's grief will ebb, but she wondered if what she was saying was true.

Brad thanked her, and Mattie left him to his thoughts as she retreated to her routine, making the rounds on the children's ward, reading charts, talking to the nightshift nurses, interns and doctors. But something was different. Painful memories buried under decades of work resurfaced, bobbing up and down like a fisherman's float. She remembered how she felt after the avalanche—paralyzed by grief over the irreplaceable loss of her father, brother, and boyfriend, and wondering how she could ever make it right.

CHAPTER

Breakthrough

The early season snowstorm caught everyone off-guard, including the Utah Department of Transportation snow removal crews. The falling flakes were heavy with moisture, not Utah's famous light powder.

Mattie's windshield wipers barely managed to provide sufficient visibility as she maneuvered her Jeep through unplowed streets, each tire grappling for traction. Making matters worse, she couldn't shake the nightmare she had about Tick the night before. The child alone on the ledge, her lifeless body covered with snow, her face white, her green eyes unresponsive, staring at the sky, blank—just like her brother, father, and boyfriend back in Montana.

Mattie hated winter days.

Tick's depression was getting worse. It had been a week since her surgery, and she had become increasingly apathetic. Her appetite was scarcely existent, and she seemed to be going downhill.

Arriving at the hospital shortly after 7:00 a.m., Mattie went straight up to The Palace. Brad was sitting in his chair by the window, peering out at the falling snow when she walked in. She greeted the nurse on duty with a cup of coffee and a doughnut and then instructed her to go on break.

Adding to Mattie's concern for Tick and weighing on her mind, she noticed that Brad didn't look well the previous evening, his face flushed, his eyes pinched. She walked straight over to him, placing her hand on his forehead.

"How long have you felt feverish?" she asked.

Brad hesitated and glanced over at Tick, who was now awake. "I haven't felt great for several days. My right shoulder has been giving me some trouble."

"Your right shoulder?" Mattie inquired, pulling back his shirt and seeing a bandage that didn't begin to cover the angry, red, and swollen area around it. "What is this?"

"Just something I got on the mountain. I've been putting antibiotic cream on it, and I hoped it was getting better."

As Mattie removed the bandage, she began to launch a barrage of demanding questions: "Why are there teeth marks on your shoulder? How did this happen? Why isn't this wound on your chart?"

Mattie folded her arms in an impatient stance, waiting for answers.

"It's not a big deal," replied Brad. "I never brought it up because it was nothing. Tick was terrified that I was out to harm her when I first met her on the mountain, and in self-defense, she bit me. It was a pretty normal reaction. I have been treating it myself."

"Oh, I can see that, Mr. Hughes—and a great job you've done, too. A bad bite like this from a human introduces all sorts of harmful bacteria, and you've developed quite an infection as a result."

Mattie examined the nasty wound for another minute, lost in thought.

That wildcat wasn't afraid. She was trying to rip his shoulder off.

"Tick, I can't treat this wound in the room. I need to take him to another area for a few minutes to take care of it properly. I promise I will have him right back to you. Okay?"

Tick's face revealed concern and a flash of embarrassment, but Brad quickly reassured her. "Take it easy. I'll be fine. I will be right back." She nodded her head in agreement and gave Brad a half-hearted wave.

Mattie signaled Nurse Beverly Lee to come into the room, explaining that she and Brad would be over at the main hospital for about thirty minutes.

Beverly, one of the nurses who worked with Tick, liked her young patient, finding her brave, clever, and remarkably perceptive.

She felt flattered that Tick seemed to like her, but since Tick's fall, none of the nurses, not even Dr. Barnes herself, had attempted to watch over Tick without Brad in the room. Aware of Tick's reputation for freaking out when separated from Brad, Beverly was a bit anxious.

But the unexpected happened—Tick remained in control of herself, first closing her eyes and breathing deeply, then asking Beverly for some ice water before settling back onto her pillow.

Brad and Mattie made their way down the long, empty hallway, past the guard and over to the emergency room. Brad trailed a few feet behind her, feeling an intense sensation of déjà vu, having experienced Mattie's silent treatment before. He supposed that she wasn't happy that he kept the bite and the facts of the bite to himself—yet another deception.

From Mattie's perspective as a doctor, she probably feels that my not reporting Tick's bite prevents her from acquiring an accurate picture of the girl.

Brad would argue that he had the liberty and moral obligation to make that judgment call to protect Tick. If Mattie didn't understand, then it was too darn bad. Still, he didn't like crossing Mattie, and he just wished the bite had healed without any problems. He worried that Mattie would think less of Tick because of it.

Entering the exam room, Mattie pointed to a hospital gown, ordered him to put it on, and left the room while he changed. She returned, pulled on sterile gloves, and began to examine his back and shoulder. His back was scratched in addition to the bite wound, scabs breaking away from nearly healed wounds.

How did these injuries happen, and why aren't these noted on his chart? Mattie wondered. *Didn't the ER check his shoulder when they treated his injuries days ago?*

She suspected that Brad was responsible, glibly hiding and explaining away everything.

"What exactly happened up there on the mountain, Mr. Hughes?"

Brad grunted a reply, trying not to cry out as she cleaned the bite wound. "I told you, she didn't know what my intentions were, and we had a bit of a scuffle. It took some time to gain her trust." *Thank you, God, for that eagle,* he reflected gratefully. "This conversation must remain on a patient-doctor basis and kept confidential. I don't want another Messener-type situation where Tick is condemned unfairly, messing up her life more than it already is. Agreed?"

Mattie nodded her head stiffly and continued to clean, pack, and bandage the wound. Then she started in again. "This happened close to a month ago. How have you been treating the wound?"

"When I arrived at the hospital, I secretly commandeered some bandages and disinfectant, and everything seemed fine for a couple of days. When it started to throb, I took some amoxicillin. That helped for a while, but last week, it started to bother me again."

"Just where did you come up with an amoxicillin prescription?" she asked.

"Well, since I regularly travel overseas to visit my company's mining operation in South America, I learned to carry an antibiotic in my travel kit."

"I see," Mattie's voice was now terse, "and when did you intend to do something about this?"

"I didn't think I would be here this long, Dr. Barnes. I suppose I would have gone to an InstaCare to have it treated."

And what would you have told them, she wondered, now exasperated. *Perhaps an encounter with a small vampire? And why do you think I would ever consider causing Tick harm by disclosing confidential information about her?*

She asked him if he recently had any contact with Tick without wearing gloves. He assured her that he hadn't, always washing his hands and putting on gloves before going near her. Mattie examined the wound on his leg as well, the one injury, other than those resulting from Tick's fall, that was on his chart, and ordered him to get dressed before leaving the room.

As they walked back down the hallway, Mattie advised Brad not to get close to Esther until his infection cleared up.

"How long has it been since your last physical?"

Brad's answer, "I don't know… A couple of years, I guess—I'm fine," only inflamed Mattie's irritation with him, thinking that his macho-style answer sounded childish.

When the testy pair got back to the room, Tick sat up and wrote a note on her tablet, handing it, for the first time, directly to Mattie. *"Is he going to be all right?"*

Since her fall, Tick rarely communicated directly with anyone except Brad, so Mattie was pleased to take the pad. Seeing the palpable apprehension in Tick's eyes, the irritability Mattie felt toward Brad drained away. She focused on reassuring Tick.

"He's going to be fine. Nothing to worry about…really! The antibiotics that I will prescribe will clear it right up."

Mattie gave her patient a sideways smile and then, in a low whisper, teased, "I think you may have had a good reason to bite him. I only wish you had bitten him on his rear end… That way, he would have flinched every time he sat down, and I would have spotted a problem earlier."

Taking a step back from Tick's bed, Mattie spoke up so Brad could hear, "Tomorrow we're going to find out what else he's hiding. I'll be back tonight to check on both of you."

Tick handed her the tablet again. *"I'm not a biter. I wasn't thinking straight. I thought Timothy Bird had sent Brad. I'm sorry."*

As she left the room, Mattie felt regretful. She had never considered Brad as her patient. This was a Children's Hospital, but he undoubtedly was a patient by default, and she had seriously overlooked his care. He was so darn macho, projecting health and athleticism, the kind of guy who wouldn't think of a bite wound and a few scratches and bruises as a big deal. At the nurses' station, she prescribed a different antibiotic while awaiting his culture results and then arranged for him to have a complete physical in the morning. Things were going to change for Mr. Hughes.

Driving home that evening on now cleared streets, Mattie overlooked her rule about not taking her work home. Years ago, she learned that doctors who carried their patients back home in their heads often burned out; treating critically ill children was a passion Mattie didn't want to lose. Many of her cases were difficult, and not all patients survived catastrophic illness or injury. Still, knowing how to cope and compartmentalize her profession's sobering realities did not stop her from worrying about Tick's prospects for recovery. Despite every indication that her fractures were healing, Tick's overall condition was declining. The truth was Mattie had become unwittingly fond of both Tick and Brad.

Thinking about Brad's bruising and bite marks from their skirmish on the cliff, Mattie marveled at the exceptional degree of genuine caring Brad and Tick now demonstrated for each other. They were so genuinely guarded and protective of each other.

Brad had family and a life to go back to when his role with this mysterious girl came to an end, but Mattie knew he would never be the same if something were to happen to Tick. And Tick? Psychological trauma had left her speechless, and she seemed to be losing her resolve to live. What did she have to live for? What was important to her?

Before bed, Mattie boiled some water for a cup of herbal tea. As the tea steeped, Mattie's thoughts juggled around different approaches to take with Tick to encourage her to fight for her life. She sipped her tea and let out a tired sigh, remembering one of her favorite verses, the last spoken words *in Gone with the Wind*: "Tomorrow is another day."

It was nearly daybreak when Mattie opened her eyes from a restless sleep with a solid understanding that Tick's recuperation would depend as much on building a trusting, positive personal relationship with her as it would providing her with the best medical care.

One thing was clear: reaching the distrustful girl would require an unconventional approach. A plan began to develop—a way to help pull Tick off yet another ledge.

Another storm rocked the valley that morning, but Mattie arrived at the hospital feeling more confident and anxious to put her new strategy into play. Little did Brad know that he was about to undergo the physical exam of his lifetime.

Entering Tick and Brad's room, Mattie's no-nonsense, cheery manner set Brad back on his heels. He had spent the night gearing up to defend Tick's actions, but after seeing Mattie's friendly expression, he decided to keep quiet and play it by ear.

Mattie was pleased. She could see that Brad was much improved. His fever was down, and the antibiotic was working.

"Good morning, Tick. Good morning, Mr. Hughes. We've lots to accomplish today, so let's get started."

Tick was passively staring at the ceiling.

Banking on Tick's concern and curiosity about Brad, Mattie initiated her new strategy.

"Today," Mattie began looking at Tick, "Brad is going to get a complete head-to-toe physical. Normally, medical tests are patient confidential, but"—she turned her attention back to Brad—"I am sure you have nothing to hide." Brad mumbled something about feeling shanghaied, but reluctantly agreed, and the process began.

Mattie proceeded through the standard list of health history questions, reading them out loud: past surgeries, medications, allergies, injuries, current health status, etc.

Page two of the form, the Personal Habits, provided Mattie with the opportunity to appeal to Tick's alleged bold, curious, and mettlesome nature.

"Do you smoke, drink, or do drugs?"

"Does an occasional glass of wine count?"

"So you drink. Have you ever been intoxicated or stoned?"

Brad's head shot up, and he replied, his tone now defensive. "Seriously, is that question on the form? Yes, I may have had a bit too much to drink at times in the past. You know, back in college, but I have never used drugs."

"Do you think that Tick would have found your drinking appropriate?"

"Probably not, I was a little immature… Hey, give me a break! That was a thousand years ago!"

Turning to Tick, Mattie added, "Tick, do you think we should believe him?"

Tick shrugged, offering something that looked vaguely similar to a little smile.

"What is your level of fitness?"

"It's good, I think."

"You look slightly overweight to me."

"Really? I meet all the weight criteria for my age group."

"What do you think, Tick? Does he look on the heavy side to you? Maybe you should encourage him to exercise, perhaps during your physical therapy sessions."

Mattie continued, "Now, about your eating habits?"

"I watch what I eat."

"Really? I watched you scarf down two bags of chips the other day and pop M&Ms into your mouth. Empty calories, Brad, snacks loaded with saturated fat. Not a good example for Tick."

"I like M&Ms, and so does Tick. Aren't you being a little harsh?"

Tick was altogether alert, her eyes darting back and forth between Brad and Mattie.

"Do you suffer from uncontrollable twitches, or do you ever laugh at inappropriate times?"

"No," Brad replied, "but I think I may start twitching from these absurd questions."

"Your concussion may have affected your ability to reason normally. Have you noticed any change in your thinking? Namely, are you having difficulty processing information?"

"No, not at all! I am still entirely on top of things. The concussion hasn't affected my reasoning in any way... Jeez."

Mattie kept her game face on. "Interesting. I was concerned that you might have lost a step or two in that area."

Brad looked completely confused until he realized that Tick had become more attentive than she had been in many days. At that moment, he understood Mattie's real purpose for the exam, so he began to play along.

"Well, I *have* been keeping company with doctors quite a lot lately, so my IQ is sure to have dropped a few points." He winked at Tick, and she replied with a decided snicker. By then, she had managed to slide over to the side of her bed, fully engaged in the conversation, seemingly not wanting to miss anything.

A tech brought in a portable EKG and hooked Brad up to several leads while Mattie explained the procedure in detail to Tick, including all the technical aspects. A lab technician then pulled Brad aside to obtain several blood samples and a urine specimen for a comprehensive health profile.

Completing the exam, Mattie left the room, promising to return with the lab reports later in the day.

That afternoon, Mattie went over the test results with Brad and Tick, explaining what all the numbers and abbreviations meant, highlighting Brad's scores for each test with a yellow marker. Mattie noticed and appreciated the close attention Tick paid to all the test results. The child asked questions that many interns would have glossed over.

Then came an outcome to a question with a hidden agenda, an outcome that reinforced Mattie's notion that Tick's affection and curiosity, as it related to Brad, was the key to Tick's recovery—an outcome that also gave Mattie a measure of payback for Brad's failure to tell her about the bite wound. It was a question Mattie asked with a glint in her eye.

"Brad, I have looked over your medical history, and there is no record of your ever having a colonoscopy. Do you realize you should have started regular screening at the age of fifty? You are eight years overdue for one!"

When this topic came up, it was not a discussion Brad wanted to have, particularly in front of Tick, and he did his best to shut it down. But Tick, busy researching on her iPad, suddenly inserted herself in the conversation with a hastily written note.

"*This is an essential exam,*" she wrote. "*It says here that you can prevent colon cancer through screening that detects and removes precancerous polyps,*" Turning to Mattie, Tick continued writing. "*Set it up. I'll be okay without him.*" She scowled at Brad and then printed in bold lettering: "***I will make sure he goes.***"

Brad grudgingly nodded his head in agreement, and Mattie tried not to cheer out triumphantly.

"I will schedule the appointment for you at the university hospital, Mr. Hughes. No sense in putting it off."

Shifting her full attention to Tick, Mattie said, "You don't need to worry about him, Tick. He's in excellent health, and when he gets into a good exercise program, you'll be calling him Superman. Now, however, I have an even more important patient to check on, and that's you."

Mattie performed her standard examinations of Tick before saying goodbye and leaving the room.

Mattie's in a good mood, Brad noticed, watching as she left the room. *I wonder what she has planned.*

That night, at home in her kitchen, Mattie flipped through one of her many cookbooks, the one that contained the best breakfast recipes. Getting Tick to eat more had become a priority, but her distaste for hospital food had become legendary. She scratched "*BELCH!*" on her iPad every time her food tray appeared, usually adding "*Smells like dog food*" or something along those lines. Occasionally, she would request something like Oreo cookies and milk, or graham crackers, but she sniffed at those items, too, if they didn't measure up in some way: "*Those taste stale*" or "*That brand is revolting.*" She was not particularly popular with the hospital cooks.

Boosting Tick's desire to eat was an essential component of the new game plan, but the little gourmand would not eat food that didn't smell delicious, look appetizing, taste amazing, and hospital food did none of those things for Tick. Never one to run from a challenge, Mattie chose the recipes she would prepare, scanned them on her printer, and arranged them on the kitchen counter. "Game on, Julia Child! Here I come, Martha Stewart!"

The next day, Mattie strolled into the room just before breakfast and asked Brad to clear off his bedside table and move it close to Tick's bed. Tick was wide-awake. She and the nurse, Beverly, watched

Mattie open a large picnic basket. From its contents, she set the table with a fine linen cloth, expertly folded linen napkins, sterling silver flatware, hand-blown glassware, and a small but beautiful cut glass vase.

Mattie left the room momentarily, leaving everyone marveling. She soon returned with her assistant, Laura, who helped her carry in several parcels. For Tick, Laura placed an elegant hand-painted tray with an Audubon bird design on top of her over-bed table, and then put a beautiful place setting on the tray, complete with a rose vase. Mattie added some water to the two vases and dropped a yellow rose in each.

"Anyone hungry for breakfast? I prepared everything myself in my kitchen with my own hands, especially for both of you, and I hope you are going to enjoy it as much as I enjoyed cooking it."

Brad pulled out a chair for Mattie, and on Mattie's cue, Laura and Beverly brought in omelets, homemade blueberry muffins, creamery butter, and raspberry jam served on white porcelain. Setting a plate down on each placemat and filling their glasses with freshly squeezed orange juice, Laura chimed in with "Bon appétit!" as she and Beverly left the room.

Brad took his seat after seeing that Tick was comfortably situated in front of her tray table, wide-eyed and all. Meanwhile, Mattie poured an aromatic blend of coffee, first into Brad's cup, and then into her own.

"This looks and *smells* amazing, Mattie!" pronounced Brad. "I can't believe the effort you made for us. I hardly know what to say or how to thank you."

"It was my pleasure, Brad. Would you mind saying grace?"

Brad offered a thoughtful prayer of thanks, and Mattie said, "Let's eat!"

Mattie began the conversation by asking Brad about his childhood.

"Where did you grow up, Mr. Hughes?"

"Well, I was born in Montana, but my father accepted a position as the superintendent of a gold, silver, and copper mine in Peru,

South America, when I was just one-year-old. My sister was three. We grew up in a mining camp at 12,000 feet."

"Can you show us on a map the location of the mining camp?"

"Sure." Brad took out his iPad and located the camp using Google Earth, revealing the very house he had grown up in.

As Mattie had hoped, Tick followed the conversation closely. Every so often, Mattie would interrupt the conversation and say something like, "Excuse me, Tick, I'll wait to ask Brad another question while you eat some more of that omelet." After Tick ate a few more bites, the conversation would resume.

After an hour of genial and interesting conversation, Tick had eaten her first substantial breakfast since her dive into the foyer. She had also participated in the discussion, writing question after question. Mattie's strategy had worked.

Eventually, the difficult work of getting Tick to reveal facts about her own life—her mother, their abduction, Timothy Bird, the ranch, and the cause for her unwillingness to speak—would have to begin in earnest. Now was not the time.

Mattie headed back to her office to consider a strategy for Tick.

Cooking meals regularly for her would be taxing, but the key to her recovery. If I wake up an hour earlier, prepare two good meals, we can eat breakfast together at 6:00 a.m. and then bring lunch at 1:30 p.m. She should be hungry by then. I'll have the hospital serve a lighter meal for dinner to help her sleep.

That night, she drove home with a plan—eggs benedict in the morning and then a Michelin three-star lasagna with garlic bread for tomorrow's lunch.

Storytime

As Mattie had hoped, Tick took a lively interest in learning about Brad, and he proved to have an endless supply of colorful stories about his life growing up in a mining camp in South America. Brad could entertain Tick for hours, describing his menagerie of exotic animals and horses, expeditions to the Peruvian jungle, hunting trips, mining accidents, and landslides.

By the end of the first week, Tick's weight was up a bit, and her reputed curiosity about life seemed to be returning. Each day, Mattie would show up with either something she had prepared in her kitchen or boxes of food from her favorite restaurants. Brad would entertain Tick with his stories, and Mattie would interrupt to remind Tick to eat while she listened.

Feeling encouraged by Tick's turnaround in mood and weight gain, Brad purposefully recounted his stories only at mealtimes. One meal story Brad shared about the *jala pato* made Mattie completely uncomfortable. Still, Tick couldn't have been more fascinated, so Mattie didn't cut it off.

The story was about Peruvian natives from isolated villages who gathered periodically for festivals. For this occasion, each community provided a live duck decked out in a handmade, elaborately deco-rated costume. One by one, the villagers' tied ducks by their feet and hung them upside down on a goalpost crossbar, just high enough so that a rider on horseback would have to stretch out from the saddle to reach the duck's neck.

Drunken cowboys fueled by chicha, a corn beer, put on quite a show for the crowd. The men, barely able to stay in the saddle, rode their horses at full gallop toward the duck, standing tall in their stirrups, attempting to grab and pull the duck's head off. Catching a swaying ducks head was not an easy undertaking, and most riders found themselves flat on their backs, gazing up at the duck, responding amusingly to the crowd's loud laughter.

When one of the single riders was eventually triumphant, he would present the duck head to the pretty young woman he was courting from his village or to a beautiful girl from another village who had caught his eye. This unusual gift was a very macho way of expressing his interest in her. As was customary with this rather grisly sport, the men who were successful in capturing duck heads were responsible for providing the beer for the next year's event. It was a costly arrangement for these poor villagers, but the expense was never a deterrent.

Mattie groaned during the story. She could hardly stand the thought of these helpless ducks hanging upside down, victims of animal cruelty. Tick's reaction, on the other hand, was surprisingly pragmatic. One of her responsibilities at the death ranch was tending a sizable flock of chickens, something Brad and Mattie would later learn about her, and she seemed to have little concern about headless ducks.

Tick's questions and comments were erudite, unemotional. "*What did they do with the dead ducks?*" she wrote.

"Glad you asked, Tick," Brad replied. "They were plucked, dressed, and added to the *pachamanca*, a Peruvian earth oven and an age-old cooking tradition."

"*Slow roasting, I bet,*" Tick wrote. "*Great method.*"

"Nothing like it, you're right."

"*Well,*" Tick jotted, now looking at Mattie with one of her patented, defiant gazes, a look Brad would have corrected if Tick were in better shape. "*I'd like to ride in a jala pato. It looks like fun! And anyway, how do you think those isolated Indians manage to keep a diverse, resilient gene pool going? If it weren't for those ducks, three-eyed villagers would not be an uncommon sight."*

This last comment only added to Mattie's certainty that Tick's brain fired at a more aware, advanced level than most adult brains could muster, but she was too tired to get into an anthropological debate.

These special meals were demanding for Mattie, swallowing up time to herself after long hours filled with her ICU patient-care challenges. By day's end, she felt beat. Still, even after they upgraded Tick's condition from critical to fair, and from fair to good, Mattie felt compelled to continue her unorthodox treatment protocol. Tick was physically immobilized, isolated, and not allowed to participate in the many activities the hospital provided to entertain children—distractions that allowed the kids to escape from their often-painful realities.

In Tick's reality, she was still a prisoner, only now locked away in a different setting. The comparison didn't escape the girl, as Mattie was soon to learn.

The security detail on duty when Tick fell had been lobbying to apologize to Tick, a visit Mattie would supervise.

Tick was polite, pointing to herself with a half-smile as she wrote, "*James 1:12.*"

Mattie read the verse out loud to the guards. "Blessed is the one who perseveres under trial because, having stood the test, that person will receive the crown of life that the Lord has promised to those who love him."

Mattie knew that James wrote those words to encourage early Christians not to be afraid to stand up for their beliefs, even in light of inevitable persecution, not so different from what went on in some university classrooms.

From a medical standpoint, seeing that passage on the slate was an encouraging sign to Mattie, who believed Tick would go on fighting. Mattie thought Tick's Christian faith was foundational to her character, but her knowledge of scripture was, at times, misguided and deceptive. Tick was adept at quoting Bible verses and referring to scripture, sometimes to suit her own needs, not always conveying

Gospel truths, sometimes to hide her pain, and sometimes to be used as a club.

When Tick handed one of the agents her slate, he read her words out loud to the other guards, *"God commands me to love you and to forgive you, but I will never trust you! I know the real reason you guys are here, and it has little to do with my welfare. I'm just being used as a pawn in your attempt to catch Timothy Bird. I may like you, and I appreciate your apology, but the truth is, you have made me your prisoner, just like I was with him, and I don't want to associate with you until you free me. I will pray for you."*

It was a harsh censure of decent men who had just been roundly snubbed by their charge. Still, Mattie felt gratified to hear a candid expression of Tick's emotional state rather than having to figure her out through biblical quotations.

Except for Nate Hoger, Tick stuck to her word, refusing to talk to or even acknowledge FBI authorities. Brad thought Hoger was the exception because she trusted and liked him. Mattie held a more skeptical opinion of the relationship, questioning Tick's motives and suspecting that she was instinctively following Machiavelli's maxim to "keep your friends close and your enemies closer."

When Mattie first took on the case, she didn't know what to expect. In addition to Tick's culture shock and genuine threats from Timothy Bird and law enforcement, Mattie anticipated that Tick was suffering from post-traumatic stress disorder. Some extreme trauma had left her speechless, and Mattie felt that Tick's attachment to Brad would prove to be fear-based—early assumptions that were quickly dispelled.

Tick was an enigma, far more resilient than Mattie could ever have imagined. As Tick grew stronger and locked those green eyes on her when she walked into the room with meals, Mattie felt growing feelings of both apprehension and curiosity.

It was becoming clear to Mattie that Tick had spent most of her life compelled to conceal her thoughts, intelligence, and emotions from her abusive captor. More than likely, Tick was an expert at deception, and there was no reason to believe that those learned, practiced, or deceptive behaviors had changed since her escape.

Still, Mattie thought that underneath the disguise, a disguise Tick wore to survive years of a threatening existence, there was a grief-stricken, depressed, anxious, guilty, and furious little girl. No doubt, Tick had resisted every inch of her journey, her exceptional intelligence enabling her to survive, but now being put to use to cover up her painful past, both from others and, more importantly, from herself.

Mattie learned more and more about Tick during mealtimes— little snippets of information from a very cautious girl started to paint a larger, more complex picture. Tick had hunted, using both a bow and rifle. She had killed and dressed several deer, as well as a bear. One could surmise that she had a strong relationship with her kidnapper, at least before the "troubles" had started, and she had participated in several hunts. She liked to cook and asked hundreds of questions about pachamancas and Peruvian cuisine, and she was a voracious reader with a comprehensive knowledge from many books.

After her fall, Tick stopped communicating anything personal about herself or her relationship with her captors. She was even careful with Brad. Still, in unguarded moments, glimpses of her life at the ranch continued to slip out.

Catching Tick reading a book about Rome, Mattie asked Tick what other books she had read on the subject.

Tick wrote out a short but impressive list of historical literature: Cunliffe's *Rome and Her Empire*, Gibbon's *The Decline and Fall of the Roman Empire*, Shotter's *Nero*.

"*Timothy didn't want me to read,*" Tick wrote, "*and I don't know what you mean by free time. I worked or trained. He said I didn't need an education, but my mom would steal books from his library and hide them. We read them at night or when he was away, and then we snuck them back, except for the Bible, which wasn't his. We found that in the drawer of a used bureau they brought in for us. Mom said that God made sure I had His word to study and hold on to. I learned to be a fast reader, and I wouldn't talk about what I read, so we never got caught.*"

Mattie didn't believe everything the girl wrote. *Tick is too knowledgeable to have picked up everything she knew on the sly. She has been extensively homeschooled, but why would she lie?*

The days passed with a suitable variety of things for Tick to do, and as concerns about Tick's survival and weight gain faded in the rear-view mirror, Mattie felt emboldened to start pushing her. In Mattie's estimation, her patient was recovering beautifully, at least physically. The external fixators were gone, and she was now safely protected in a bright pink cast. She was gaining weight, not experiencing pain, seemingly content with her situation, and reading book after book.

Getting Tick to open up about her life during her seven-year captivity at the ranch was not going to be easy, but perhaps it was time to start challenging her.

For Brad, the time spent in The Palace in support of Mattie's new approach with Tick was both enjoyable and stressful in equal measure. He genuinely enjoyed Mattie's visits and always looked forward to her thoughtfully prepared and delicious meals. He was also grateful for Nate Hoger's visits. He was the one outsider Mattie allowed into The Palace, at Brad's request. Poker night became Tick's favorite, a game Tick instantly mastered, raking up piles of winnings—cotton swabs—to the men's amazement.

Tick was healing, and Brad was starting to feel like he could breathe again. But one question continued to weigh heavily on him: what will his role ultimately become with this child?

When Brad prayed at night, he asked for guidance to make the right decisions for Tick's future. Slowly, reluctantly, he came to understand that his future was also in play. It had been altered high on a ledge in the Uintas.

CHAPTER

16

Fleeting Fame

FBI agent Steve Brewer sat at his desk with arms crossed, looking out at Puget Sound. A rainstorm pounded the inlet, with raindrops making craters in the churning water and thudding against the windows of his Seattle office, seemingly mocking him for his failures. It was as if his mood dictated the weather.

Agent Brewer was not a happy man. He had obsessed about catching Timothy Bird and watching the subsequent prosecution and conviction: at worst, imprisoned for life, and at best, strapped down on his back with chemicals dripping into his veins, a justified execution in response to multiple murders.

However, dreams of vindication proved to be fleeting. Reviewing it all in his mind, Brewer agonized, *How could a case, which had appeared to be so promising just a month ago, become such an unmitigated disaster?*

First, there had been the deaths of Hoger's men on the mountain, then the fiasco at the hospital, where one of his agents had, in essence, launched his only witness, a twelve-year-old child, over a one-story-high balcony.

Fortunately, Esther—Tick, or whatever they wanted to call her, is off the critical list, but her doctors are not allowing any contact with the girl.

If that wasn't enough, the explosion at the crime site, heard for many miles away, virtually obliterated most of the evidence they might have found. Adding to the catastrophe, a member of the FBI bomb squad had been killed, and two others were severely injured. The death toll on the mountain continued to go up.

Washington was on the defensive; the press had been insatiable in their quest to find out more about what was now called The Utah Death Ranch. The toll was terrible: three officers killed, two permanently crippled, and the remains of thirteen bodies found in a hidden burial ground nestled in a small depression next to the cliff.

As the bodies were exhumed and identified through DNA and dental records, families with missing loved ones were informed, each body bringing a new cycle of grief and anger. Their loved ones were gone, murdered in a macabre hellhole. The Intermountain West had one funeral after another, families were torn apart, and Timothy Bird—now the most wanted man in the country—had utterly disappeared.

The only survivor of the Death Ranch was in protective custody, and she had, by default, become the focus of attention. Unsubstantiated rumors, most likely leaked by the CPS woman, had branded Tick as a potential killer. Stories circulated about Tick's attacks on hospital staff. The press began speculating that she might have participated in criminal activities at the ranch; after all, she had mainly grown up there. It also looked as though she had been trying to flee law enforcement when she fell over the balcony railing at the hospital, a fall that several people had witnessed.

Family Court issued a gag order that prevented hospital personnel or those who had recent contact with Tick from discussing or disclosing any information about her or specifics of her current situation at the hospital.

Brewer felt trapped. Lives were at stake. Timothy Bird remained at large, and Tick was in grave danger from him, if not from a larger organization. To protect Tick and Brad, a freeze on information was in place: a blackout that even shielded Messener's abusive actions. It was an information void that the press and distraught families had rushed in to fill.

The Bittner family—having just buried Thornton Bittner and his son, David—wanted justice for the murders, holding press briefings and inflaming the public against Tick, speculating that she may have participated in the killings. Everybody seemed to be weighing in with an opinion on how to handle the girl. Was she a victim or a perpetrator?

Either way, she was the only person, other than Timothy Bird himself, who knew the truth, and she wasn't talking.

Nate Hoger, serving as Salt Lake City's police spokesman, had risen to Tick's defense during live televised press briefings. He reminded the media and the public that Esther Morgan was just a twelve-year-old girl who, along with her mother, had been kidnapped and held hostage for seven years. The child had cooperated fully in an initial interview, which provided valuable information that had doubtlessly saved many lives, even though lives were lost in an explosion. He reminded the public that Esther's mother died at the ranch and that there was no substance to claims that her attempt to flee the hospital had any criminal intent.

A disturbing fact kept from the public was not in Tick's favor; technicians had found Tick's DNA from blood splatters on David Bittner's and Janet Herrington's clothing and their blood on Tick's shoes. During those initial interviews, Tick had claimed that most of the victims died in orchestrated fights.

Had she fought them? Was she involved? Had she killed?

Brewer had recently become aware of inquires made by Justin Simons, Mr. Hughes's attorney, about the possibility of adopting Tick—exploratory inquiries directed at Family Court. Brad Hughes was a good man, and nobody questioned the sincerity behind his investigations. Nevertheless, the Bureau now wanted Esther Morgan out of Utah and under their control in the worst way. What if Timothy Bird found and eliminated her, killing federal agents, hospital staff, or patients in the process? What if Hughes adopted her, and they were both tracked down and killed?

Other questions were more self-serving. If Hughes adopted Tick, would he persuade the girl to cooperate in the ongoing investigation? He had shown a marked protective, independent streak in Tick's first interview. He was not a man afraid to face down authorities.

Tick had allies and supporters: her nurses and doctors, Nate Hoger and agents on the ground in Salt Lake City, and one notable big shot back East, Ruth Evers, the head of the FBI's National Center for the Analysis of Violent Crime.

Ruth Evers was an unexpected wild card who threw her hat into the opinion ring. Highly respected, a genius in criminal profiling, and now actively involved in the case, Evers had taken an uncharacteristic interest in Tick, demanding to know every facet of her care. She had made it clear in meetings that it would be disastrous to try to force Tick to do anything against her will. If Hughes wanted to adopt her, and if she wanted to stay with him, the FBI needed to make it possible, whatever the risks.

Nonetheless, it didn't appear that anyone in Washington wanted to hear a word about the girl's condition, let alone her emotional attachment to Brad. It was highly unlikely that Brad would be allowed to adopt Tick.

Even with Evers's backing, Brewer didn't see a future for Tick with Brad. She had become the most convenient solution to unsolved crimes that were fast becoming an aggravating political issue used by opponents of the current administration that appointed the FBI director. Justifiably, the mayor of Salt Lake City and the police chief were also feeling the heat from locals concerned for their safety.

There were even problems at the hospital. Tick's residence in The Palace was delaying construction on the building's renovation project. Contractors had scheduled the crews to begin, but the workers were now sitting idle. Her protection called for six men on permanent guard duty and placed additional demands on doctors and nurses at the hospital. The cost of her care was staggering.

Brewer had grown to admire Tick's fight and determination and feared what her future held and how she might react after Dr. Barnes and Brad Hughes lost control of her care. He knew arrangements were being made in Washington DC to place Tick in a private psychiatric hospital for children. He knew her well enough to know the move would be disastrous. Those plans were unalterable, and Tick's days in Utah were numbered.

Feeling disgusted, Brewer stood up and walked over to the umbrella stand next to the door to his office. He put on his rain gear and headed out the door. He needed a beer.

Decision Time

It was four in the afternoon when Mattie's phone alerted her to a text message. For the past two days, she had been at a ski resort in Deer Valley at the hospital's annual management retreat, and she was in her room getting ready for the event's closing banquet.

"I need to speak to you first thing when you come in tomorrow, if possible. Thx."

Brad rarely texted her, and Mattie was quick to respond. *"Everything OK???"*

"Let's talk tomorrow. Have a good time at dinner."

It was still dark outside when Mattie awoke and had breakfast. She was somewhat concerned about Brad's request. Was there a problem? Typically, if something about Tick's status had changed, someone from her staff would have contacted her.

Tick's fixators were a thing of the past; she was now in a standard lower body cast formed in pink-colored plaster. Her physical progress was outstanding, beyond all expectations, and both Tick and Brad looked and felt quite well the last time Mattie was with them.

Now back at the hospital, Mattie found Brad standing next to the door, waiting. As she approached the door, he stepped out into the hallway.

"Mattie, my situation here as Tick's guardian isn't working for me anymore."

Mattie's stomach tightened. It was too soon. Tick wasn't ready to be separated from Brad. Keeping her alive, helping her regain her strength, and working to build her trust and a stable working relationship had been Mattie's primary focus. She hadn't explicitly begun to prepare Tick for Brad's eventual departure. The dread she felt with the thought of Tick losing Brad took her by surprise.

Mattie tried to remain calm. "I would prefer if you don't leave just yet. She's so much stronger now, and I'm confident she'll be able to go on without you eventually...soon. I know what a sacrifice this has been for you, but we are so close—"

Brad cut her off. "Hold on, Mattie, you didn't let me finish... I don't want to *leave* Tick. I've decided to *adopt* her and get her out of this hospital!"

Mattie dropped her hold on Brad's arm and looked at him in disbelief, her breath caught in her chest while he cleared his throat to speak more clearly.

Brad added, "Over the last several weeks, I've thought of little else except Tick's future, especially her long-term living arrangements, and I'm ready to adopt her."

Mattie's stunned expression became distinctly dubious, signaling that serious questioning was about to commence, but Brad continued to speak straight away, not wanting to give Mattie an opening.

"I won't pretend that I'm not concerned about my decision. Nobody knows the reality of Tick's situation better than I do or sees the hurdles she has to overcome. What have the last seven years done to her, enduring some kind of hell, then losing her mother in such an unspeakable manner? It's a miracle she has survived such enormous odds. I believe—as impossible as it is to explain—that I am expected to take care of her, to raise her as my own... And that's just what I plan to do."

Expressionless, Mattie began testing. "And who's expecting you to take on this responsibility? You're referring to God, right?"

Brad was silent.

Mattie continued, "I don't think piety is a solid foundation for adopting Esther, Brad. Are you telling me that you're feeling a sacred *duty* to adopt her, that you would feel guilty if you didn't take her in?"

As much as Brad had grown to like and admire Mattie, he realized what a powerful adversary she could become. Without her professional support, adopting Tick would not be likely. The answers to her questions were crucial, and he was aware that her line of questioning held an intellectually superior tone, indicating that *Dr.* Barnes, not Mattie, was waiting for his answer. He was not about to be intimidated.

"Duty? Guilt? Is that a trick question, Mattie… Dr. Barnes? I'm guessing that those words are currently being used by the mental health industry to describe ignorance or confused thinking. If that's the case, then no, I don't feel either one of those. If duty and guilt are still notions that drive people to do the right thing, yes, I would say that both duty and guilt have played a role in my decision. As for personal faith, I believe that God is deliberate, that his hand has been all over my involvement with Tick from the beginning. Does that sound pious to you?"

Mattie crossed her arms and shifted her weight to look down at the floor, somewhat surprised by Brad's transparency. Although Brad did say grace before every meal, they had never had any discussion concerning his personal beliefs. Inwardly, she was pleased because she shared similar beliefs in a living God and recognized that Tick did as well, but her training as a psychiatrist pushed her to continue questioning him.

"No, not so much pious—maybe just a bit too noble." Then, looking straight up into Brad's eyes, Mattie said, "Please don't push me for what I think about this, Brad. It's not what I think, but what you think that matters here."

"You're right," Brad said, "and believe me, my motives to adopt Tick are considerably more selfish than noble. The fact is I have grown so close to Tick that I can't bear the thought of not having her in my life. She is the smartest kid I have ever known. I like her spunk, her amazing courage, the way she thinks, her ethics, her awareness of everyone and everything around her, how she devours books, learning about the world, and always questioning everything. I love the way she throws herself at every endeavor, and I like that I'm important to her."

Challenging Mattie now, he asserted, "The truth is, I like her for all the same reasons that you admire her, and don't try telling me that she isn't your favorite patient."

Mattie started to protest Brad's accusation but held her tongue, knowing he was right. From the moment Sam Evans told her the background story behind Tick's fall, Mattie had inexplicably been drawn to the child.

Brad continued, "I already think of her as my daughter, and selfishly, I don't think I could spend the rest of my life worrying about her, wondering what has become of her, or thinking that she hated me for abandoning her—so there's the guilt part. Then, with everything in the papers about the Death Ranch and Tick's possible involvement, and the fact that a killer may attempt to track her down, not to mention her scars and her muteness, what chance is there of adoption into a normal family? There's no way I will allow her to be institutionalized."

By now, Mattie and Brad were standing only inches apart, both leaning against the wall for support.

"I'm not too old to raise another kid, Mattie, and I'll be able to provide Tick with a good home and everything she needs: a family, brothers, and family who will care for her if something happens to me. With any luck, I'll see her through college while I'm still in good health. After that, who knows? The point is, I can give her a good start and a sense of belonging. I'll be someone who will always have her back, someone who will be there for her."

Mattie, feeling more confident in Brad's position than she was ready to express, turned to face Brad again and continued examining.

"I think you may have gotten ahead of yourself with this idea, Brad. Jumping into a permanent commitment with Tick at this point is chancy. Let's be honest, we don't know what she has done in the past or what she may be capable of doing in the future. I don't know the cause for her mutism, and in my opinion, she may not speak for quite some time, if ever. I cannot assure her emotional recovery."

Brad started to open his mouth to dispute, but Mattie cut him off.

"And on top of that, she has problems that could seriously disrupt your life. What about the FBI and their ongoing investigation? And what about all the security assigned to her because she is the only living witness to Timothy Bird's crimes. Have you thought about what you would be getting yourself into?"

Brad was quick to reply. "Tick will speak again and recover, but if she doesn't, I can live with it. If I felt the least bit threatened by her or felt she posed a threat to my family, I wouldn't hesitate to leave this hospital without her and put all of this behind me. I trust Tick with my life, but Timothy Bird is a different story. He's out there somewhere, and until they catch him... Well, that's a genuine concern. He can never know about me and use my connection with her to track her down."

"What about your family, your sons, their wives, and your grandchildren?" Mattie asked. "What have you told them?"

"Nothing but lies. All three boys texted me last night, wanting to join me as soon as I return from my extended vacation. They know something fishy is going on, but they don't know what or how to get a straight story out of me. I've never been deceptive with them, so I know that they're baffled and probably quite worried by now."

He has hidden everything from them, Mattie realized. *He has dropped out of their lives without any explanation. I wonder if he understands the pressure he has put on them.*

"You haven't told them about Tick or what you've gone through since you found her?"

"For their protection, I haven't. The boys knew I was hiking up in the Uintas when Bird killed Hoger's men, so they started calling and texting me to make sure I was okay. I told them that I was hiking in a completely different part of the range, that I only learned that there had been some trouble when I was stopped by law enforcement when I left the park.

"I forgot that I had sent Brian my hiking itinerary. So when the story became front-page news and included detailed maps showing where the encounters took place, Brian figured out that I would have been right in the middle of the action. I told him I had taken a different hike, which made me seem inexplicably irresponsible.

"Then, after Tick's fall at the hospital, I told the boys that I was resigning the presidency of my company and taking an extended vacation to South America. I explained that I missed their mother very much, but after four years, it was time for me to get on with my life. The other day, I told them I was staying in a Tarma hotel, a small town in Central Peru. Wouldn't you know they checked online and discovered that the hotel is closed for renovations.

"I'm pretty sure they think that I'm having a midlife crisis, or maybe they think I've found a lady friend whom I'm keeping secret."

"So," replied Mattie, "what do you plan to do?"

Brad replied thoughtfully, "I hate to do it, but I plan to adopt Tick first, then tell the family and let the chips fall. I have made my mind up, and bringing them in on the decision when I have no intention of listening to their counsel would be disrespectful. I raised good kids, and I trust that they will come to understand and approve of my decision. If someone discloses Tick's identity before they capture Bird, then I may have to go into hiding with her. That would be a hardship, but my boys have each other and their own families now."

Mattie asked Brad how long he had been thinking about adopting Tick and if he had said anything to her about it.

"I've been thinking about adopting her for quite a while, even before the CPS woman came to call, but I began discussing it in earnest with my attorney a few weeks ago. And no, I haven't said a word about this to Tick. I didn't want to involve her until I was sure how to proceed."

Mattie looked at him drolly. "Were you in contact with your attorney the day you had your colonoscopy?" she asked.

"I don't know," replied Brad, taking out his phone to look for any text message he might have sent to his attorney that day.

"Here's one I sent that day. Why do you ask?"

"Because on the day of your procedure, Leslie mentioned that she saw Tick looking at your phone. She was hiding it behind a book. Later that day, Abigail told me that Tick had been asking questions about adoption. Isn't that a coincidence? Did you leave your phone in the room when you went out?"

"But that's impossible," Brad replied. "My iPhone is password protected."

Mattie gave a wry smile, and Brad peered into Tick's room to look at her. He groaned, remembering that he had left his phone on her tray table when he left for the procedure.

"So she cracked it! I wonder what she has been thinking all of this time!"

"Actually," replied Mattie, "I think she has been in good spirits. She knows you better than you think she does." Then, looking over at Tick, she added, "I'm pretty sure she has been listening in on this conversation as well. Don't you think you should let her know what you are planning?"

Brad glanced over at Tick just in time to catch her head disappear behind a book.

Walking over to her bed, Mattie said, "Okay, you can quit faking it. Brad has something important he wants to discuss with you." Then, in a whisper, she added, "I think you already know what it's about."

Tick immediately sat up as Brad slowly pulled up a chair to her bed.

Brad had thought about how he would broach the subject of adoption with Tick and concluded that he would flounder if he didn't keep it simple and to the point. Catherine had always let him off the hook whenever he struggled to say something endearing to her. "That's all right, my darling," she'd say. "Still waters run deep. I know how you feel."

"Tick, what would you think if I set in motion adoption procedures? Adopting you means that you would become my daughter legally and become a member of my family forever. As your adoptive father, I would become responsible for you until you reach adulthood. I need to know if this is something you want, but for my part, I think gaining a daughter like you would be a great honor."

Tick picked up her slate and, as seriously as he had ever seen her, wrote out the words, "*Why do you want to adopt me? I am nothing but trouble.*"

Brad sat back in the chair, feeling anger for the man who had caused her so much pain.

"That's something Timothy Bird might have said to you. You may not know what a wonderful, amazing girl you are, but I do, and you are a long way from being 'nothing but trouble.' Your mother must have been so proud of you, and my biggest regret is that you will never meet Catherine. She would have loved you just as I do. You have to believe there is nothing that would make me happier.

"*But what will we do about Timothy?*" Tick wrote.

"He's just a man, Tick. It's a big world, and he will have no idea where to find you. The entire country is trying to track him down. They will catch him sooner or later."

Then, with a tone of certainty, Brad said, "If he does find us, we will put him down. Look, Tick, you can't worry about all the things that might happen. We have to trust in God, live each day as it comes, and live worthwhile lives. You know what the Bible says, 'Who of you by worrying can add a single hour to your life?'"

Tick started to cry and then reached out, tightly hugging Brad. "I guess that means yes," Brad said, shifting his eyes toward Mattie as Tick joyously nodded her head up and down in agreement.

Mattie was beaming. "Well, I know you two will make a perfect pair. I will talk to Judge Thornton in the morning. I promise I will give him my strongest recommendation in favor of the adoption."

As they sat back, enjoying the moment, Brad picked up Tick's slate and wrote two lines of characters and numbers on it. He then returned the tablet to her and explained, "In case you missed it, these are the passwords to my iPad and home computer. You know the password to my phone. In the future, ask me if you want anything. I know you had to hide things from Timothy, but if we are going to be together, there can't be any deception between us, capisce?"

Tick, her face reddening, didn't protest, and Mattie rescued her from feeling embarrassed.

"What about your sons? When do you plan on telling them?"

"I think I'll talk to them as soon as the documents are in place. They are going to be in for quite a nice surprise." He turned to Tick and added, "I can't wait for them to meet you. They are wonderful boys with great families. You will be part of us."

Tick, who had been reading something on her iPad, looked over at Brad, and nodded.

"What are you looking at?" asked Mattie. Then, looking down at the pad, she read and began to laugh. "*Capisce* is an Italian word that means, *Do you understand?*"

It was time for Mattie to make her rounds, and as Brad escorted her out of the room, he asked, "Do you think I will be good for her? I need to hear it from you."

Mattie smiled, shaking her head. "You don't get it, do you? This is what she wanted all along. You're going to do just fine. I will do everything I can to help you."

Mattie would soon discover, however, that everything isn't always enough.

CHAPTER

18

The Last Stand

True to her word, Mattie, Esther Morgan's court-appointed guardian pro tem, called Judge Thornton later that same day to discuss Brad Hughes's wish to adopt the girl and express her full support for the adoption. Judge Thornton was not surprised by her call. Brad's attorney had already petitioned the court.

Thornton did not seem overly eager to discuss the matter over the phone. The judge, typically a friendly and talkative man, was curt and sounded rushed. He requested that Mattie join him for an early morning meeting in his conference room two days hence.

When Mattie hung up the phone, her instincts told her that something wasn't right. Nevertheless, she had a pleasant dinner with Brad and Tick that evening, filling them in on her day, but she kept her apprehension about Thornton and the impending meeting to herself.

On the morning of the meeting, Mattie woke up with a knot in her stomach. After taking a sip or two of tea, she drove to the courthouse. As she entered the conference room, she was surprised to see Dr. Sheri Hertz, a highly qualified therapist and Children's Court consultant, who Judge Thornton often engaged as his advisor. In the past, Mattie had worked with Dr. Hertz and surmised Hertz's mission was to familiarize herself with Esther Morgan's case. Also present was a man whom she had never met—Dr. Gifford Palmer. Dr. Palmer was a university professor out of Boston who had published several books on child development and served as a consultant for the FBI.

After they exchanged introductions and pleasantries, Judge Thornton got down to the business at hand.

"Mattie, it's my understanding that as Esther Morgan's temporary guardian, you are recommending that we place the child with Mr. Hughes. I respect you too much to be evasive, so I will get straight to the point of this meeting, which is to inform you that I have denied Mr. Hughes's petition for Esther's adoption. The court recognizes and is grateful for the help Mr. Hughes has provided during Miss Morgan's hospitalization. We hope that he will feel good knowing how valuable his assistance has been, and while his willingness to adopt Miss Morgan is admirable, the child's best interest is not possible in his care. Specifically, he is not in a position to provide the girl with the secured environment she requires. The court feels that for her safety, she needs to leave Utah."

Mattie's eyes hardened, shifting between Thornton, Palmer, and Hertz, looking for non-verbal clues as Thornton continued speaking.

"This court is asking Mr. Hughes to discontinue his association with Miss Morgan, leave the hospital, and return to his place of residence today. I'm sure that he is anxious to resume his normal life anyway. After this meeting, I will contact Hughes's attorney to advise him of my decision. Starting today, Dr. Palmer and Dr. Hertz will be helping you transition Miss Morgan into FBI custodianship. We all agree that given time and a pleasant environment, she will adjust to this change, and most importantly, her identity and her safety will be protected."

Judge Thornton let his words sink in for a moment. Mattie's heart felt as if it would pound right through her chest.

"We're asking you to remain in charge of her care, Mattie, until her transfer to an undisclosed facility. I expect your cooperation and hope you can assist in explaining the impending changes to your young patient. The plan is to transfer Miss Morgan within forty-eight hours."

A jolt of adrenaline rushed through Mattie as she squared her shoulders and responded in a calm and professional voice.

"With all due respect, Judge Thornton, I find this ruling misdirected and rash on several accounts. Am I allowed the opportunity to express my objections?"

"This is an informal gathering, Mattie. Say your piece."

"First of all, as Esther Morgan's primary physician, her legal guardian, and the only person besides Mr. Hughes who has built a genuine relationship with her, I want to know why you didn't consult me before today? It makes little sense to me and begs the question of how you reached the clinical determination that Esther will successfully adjust to a new environment. At this point in her recovery, I believe you're on very shaky ground."

Judge Thornton was quick to reply. "I'm sorry, Mattie, the FBI has been planning Miss Morgan's custody transfer for some time, and you knew her stay at Children's Hospital would be short. Mr. Hughes's petition to adopt caught us all by surprise, and we felt it necessary to formalize and expedite the process of her transfer. Your wish to be consulted about Miss Morgan's transfer into a more protected environment never occurred to me. I do apologize for the oversight."

Before Mattie could reply, Dr. Palmer interrupted. "Back in Washington, we have been reviewing the FBI's daily reports on Miss Morgan for some time, Dr. Barnes. Because of your outstanding work, she has made an extraordinary comeback from her accident. Everything we have studied suggests that she is cooperating with your staff and that she is remarkably resilient. We are confident that she will be able to adjust to her new life."

"Excuse me, Dr. Palmer. Have you ever met Esther? Have you ever set foot in Children's Hospital? What makes you think studying her from Washington DC has given you the confidence that she will adjust to being torn from the man who has become the center of her life, a man who is essentially the only person in the world whom she trusts? You've made this decision based on her getting along with my nurses. Do you realize that Esther chose them herself? She derails people she doesn't trust, and I promise you, she won't trust any of you if you take her away from Brad. Haven't you seen the tapes? Remarkably resilient? Yes, she is resilient but fed up with a life dictated by others. Your Honor, please, can I understand that Esther's future life is being derailed by inference and Pollyannaish assumptions? What reliable evidence can Dr. Palmer offer to support his decision?"

Judge Thornton looked over at both Hertz and Palmer and gestured for one of them to reply to Dr. Barnes's question.

"Well," Dr. Palmer began, "I'm free to name two sources that helped support my findings. First, the security camera operating in Esther's room for over a month allowed me to observe videos showing a considerable variety of situations where someone could study Miss Morgan's general demeanor. Secondly, I have read through the daily reports sent to headquarters by the agents on duty at the hospital, and I've recounted what they observed each day during her recovery. I believe these resources were sufficient in evaluating Miss Morgan's current psychological state concerning separating her from Mr. Hughes and transferring her to a different facility."

Listening to the man justify his superficial assessment, Mattie felt nothing but disdain for him. She shuddered, knowing that Tick was being victimized once again, first by Timothy Bird, then by CPS, and now the FBI, whose interests came before Tick's. In Mattie's mind, Palmer was just a puppet with an outstretched hand waiting for a paycheck.

"I hardly know where to begin, Dr. Palmer. I find your evaluation of Esther a distressingly inept video-view of this child's true picture. Logic tells me that since you're a consultant for the FBI and contractually obligated to support their agenda, you have a fundamental bias. I won't bother attempting to debug your thinking. You should understand any cooperation that you receive from me will be to assist my patient, not you. As I am still Esther's legal guardian as well as her primary physician, I need a full description of the facility, as you've called it, where she is being transferred. I'd like the name of this place. Is it a full-care hospital? Who's the administrator? Esther's fractures are weeks away from being healed, so—"

"Mattie," Judge Thornton broke in, "you're unhappy with my decision, but I'll ask you to give Dr. Palmer the professional courtesy he deserves and allow him time to answer your questions."

"Thank you, Judge," Palmer responded, "but Dr. Barnes's reaction is understandable, considering her reputation for being a fierce advocate for children's rights."

Turning to Mattie, Palmer said, "Esther's circumstances are complex, and the FBI has determined that if Timothy Bird locates her, he will try to eliminate her. I am in no position to argue with the United States' premier crime-fighting force, and I am not at liberty to divulge any information about her future location. Still, I can assure you that she will be safe and protected from Bird."

"And once they remove her cast and she attempts to escape to be with Mr. Hughes, what then?" countered Mattie.

"That won't happen, Dr. Barnes. She will be in a very secure facility."

"So you plan to imprison her!" Mattie responded, her voice lowering.

"Of course not," Palmer replied. "She will be safe and secure until the time when we place her with a family vetted by the Bureau."

"I see," said Mattie, "and just who will make the determination when Esther is ready, or if she's even willing to be placed with this vetted family, assuming you can find one eager to accept and care for her?"

"I will be working with her caregivers and will make that determination. We have already approached some suitable FBI agents willing to consider fostering her. We are committed to placing Esther in a good home eventually, but in the meantime, she needs to cooperate with law enforcement concerning the ongoing investigation."

Mattie was now visibly upset. "And if she doesn't like or cooperate with you, the caregivers, or law enforcement—and if she won't accept the foster parents you've chosen—what then?"

Palmer flushed. "Dr. Barnes, those are "what if" scenarios I am quite prepared to resolve. I have worked with many children with positive results, and I am confident this situation will all work out in time."

Yes, in time, Mattie thought. *You will probably write another book that no one, let alone college students, should read.*

Mattie rose out of her chair, circled it, and planted both hands on its back. "Am I to believe that you agree with this arrangement, Judge? You are placing Esther in this man's care before she has even healed, and you are doing so without my support—without Mr. Hughes's support nor counsel. Palmer can take her away, lock her up in a room somewhere, and leave her there until she cooperates with investigators. Then, if she passes his requirements, they will attempt to find foster parents for her? She faces institutionalization and questionable foster care, for what? To remove her from Brad, a reputable, good man, who saved her life twice? A man who stood by her throughout her ordeal, who loves her, and who now wants to adopt her. I've never heard of anything so twisted!"

Silence filled the room momentarily, broken by Judge Thornton, who asked Dr. Palmer and Dr. Hertz to leave the room.

As they exited, Mattie immediately approached the Judge. "Your Honor, please reconsider your decision to hand Esther over to the FBI. She is simply not going to stand for it. She just lost her mother, and now you're taking her away from the one person she can trust. Separating her from Brad Hughes will be disastrous."

"Mattie," Thornton began saying soothingly, "my nine-year-old granddaughter won't go anywhere without her Jelly Cat, a threadbare stuffed animal she has carried around since she was old enough to walk. Lord help the person who attempts to separate the two of them! I certainly understand little girls' natural capacity to form attachments, but they get over them. Esther will form new bonds in time."

"Are you seriously comparing Esther to your granddaughter, Judge? Esther has lived with a sadist for seven years. She has been trained to fight for her life like some pit bull. Her mother was murdered, and she has no other family. From her perspective, Brad Hughes is her whole life now. I believe she lives just for him. By taking him away from her, you are jeopardizing not only all the progress we've made but risking her very life."

Thornton slapped his hand down on his table, his voice rising. "Placing her very life in danger? You're suggesting that this twelve-year-old girl who may hold her breath and pound her fists when she doesn't get her way should intimidate me? No, Mattie, nothing in Dr. Palmer's carefully investigated report leads me to believe that

Miss Morgan cannot adjust to being separated from Mr. Hughes in time."

Judge Thornton softened his tone, his voice becoming almost upbeat. "I read in Palmer's report that Esther got along very well without Hughes when he was out for most of the day undergoing a medical procedure. The important issues before me, Mattie, cannot be dismissed because of this child's challenging personality and behavior. Can I overlook what the FBI is saying? There is a serial killer on the loose, and we all agree that Esther's safety is definitely at risk where she is now. Other people are at risk as well, including you and your staff, and while you may be willing to accept that risk, I am not. The authorities want her out of Timothy Bird's reach. There have been too many deaths in this sad story already. It can't continue, we can't run the risk of more. Can't you see the problems here?"

Mattie retorted, "I see that Esther is being used as a pawn in the FBI's hunt for Timothy Bird because when and if they catch him, they'll need a witness to his crimes. I also see that the press is on a witch hunt by suggesting that Esther is an accomplice to killings at the ranch without proof. What I see, Judge, is that compared with the publicized matters presented to you, the wishes of a good man who wants to give Esther a home, a family, and a chance for a normal life carries no weight."

Pausing, she added, "When you place a child into somebody's custody, your job is to safeguard that child's long-term welfare. You're not doing that for Esther by allowing the FBI to take control of her life. As far as her short-term welfare is concerned, pulling her away from caretakers who have had the all-consuming job of caring for her in her body cast is irresponsible and, quite frankly, negligent."

Mattie reached into her pocket, pulled out her iPhone, and began scrolling. When she found the picture she was looking for, she handed the phone to Thornton. "This is Esther, taken yesterday. She'll be in that hip spica cast for another three weeks if all goes well. There's a YouTube video I want you to see before I leave that illustrates the care these casted patients require: the hygiene, the bathing, and the toileting, just to name a few. Brad has helped out with her mobility and keeping her entertained and happy."

Thornton handed the phone back to Mattie and, shaking his head, said, "I don't need to see the video, Mattie. Seeing that picture gives me a good idea of the amount of care Esther requires. No doubt about it. Whose idea was it to put her in that pink cast, by the way?"

"Hers," Mattie said. "Pink is her favorite color."

Judge Thornton rose. "I have always enjoyed our association over the years, Dr. Barnes. You are a brilliant and highly respected doctor, but I must overrule you in this case. For me, it all comes down to the child's safety. I'm sorry we don't see eye-to-eye on this."

He gathered up the paperwork spread out on the table. "I have heard about the sacrifices you have made as Esther's doctor and guardian—how you prepare meals for her and how you sacrifice what little free time you have to keep her occupied with all sorts of activities. You have made a tremendous effort for her benefit, but I think that it's time for you to take a step back."

Incensed, Mattie responded, "Are you suggesting that I have lost perspective? If your granddaughter were under my care, would you want me to take a step back if you thought I was making too much of an effort to save her life? I do whatever I can do—including, who knows, tracking down a little girl's Jelly Cat if doing that would make a difference in her recovery."

"I'm sorry, Mattie," Thornton said. "I seem to have forgotten that your kind of dedication still exists. We live in a cynical world. Please accept my apology."

"On one condition, Judge Thornton," Mattie replied. "I need you to agree to allow Esther to recover in The Palace without Mr. Hughes until she is out of her body cast. Call it a trial run in familiar surroundings. If they take her out of state now and her health deteriorates to the point she is no longer useful to the FBI, if she fails to cooperate with the FBI, if she becomes violent, or injures herself, who will admit to making a mistake in thinking that this plan would work? Who will look bad if this plan is a bust? Who will take the heat?

"No matter what happens, you won't be able to step in once you sign the papers discharging your authority. One thing I'm sure of, the events surrounding the Death Ranch survivor won't remain hidden.

If you knew Brad Hughes, you'd know that he'll stop at nothing to follow Esther's footsteps, and that trail will begin right here in your courthouse."

"You're probably right about Hughes if his dedication to this child is any indication," replied Thornton. Then he paused and sat back down in his chair. "Damn it, Mattie. I'd be responsible for jeopardizing a lot of lives if there's a violent confrontation at Children's Hospital, and having her there three more weeks is just asking for too much. I'll allow one more week, God help us, but that's it. We'll meet here in seven days to finalize this and get it behind us."

"Okay," Mattie said, "but I must ask that we do this without sedating Esther. She has been doing beautifully without any sedatives. I won't allow them now. The very idea of Palmer pumping her full of drugs so that his warped opinions can't be challenged would constitute a criminal act."

Judge Thornton's head was pounding now, and he relented. "Agreed. One week, no sedatives, but I expect you to make the transition as positive as possible. I also want you to let Mr. Hughes know how indebted the state is for Esther's help. He really is a hero. His sacrifices have been extraordinary. Of course, you will be in charge until Esther's transfer. You have worked miracles with her, and I'm sorry this has turned out to be so difficult."

"Continuing with the case is not possible for me now," replied Mattie. "Tick will think that I am a party to your decision… She'll never forgive me. She would become furious every time I walked into the room, and attempting to placate her will only make things worse. I'll ask Dr. Brackford to cover for me for this week. He put Tick back together after her fall. He admires her courage and spirit, so he'll do this for me—and for her."

Then, letting an audible sigh fill the room, Mattie said, "This is your decision, Judge Thornton, not mine."

With that, Mattie stood to leave, saying, "Remember, one week and no drugs."

The judge felt a need to mollify Mattie. He had tremendous respect for her, and coming up against her left him feeling uncomfortable.

"Agreed," he said. "One week, no drugs. Good luck to us all!"

As Mattie left the room, Thornton dropped his aching head into his hands, knowing that Dr. Mattie Barnes knew what she was talking about.

By all rights, he thought, *Esther should remain with Hughes.*

But what if there was more bloodshed? He was up for reelection in two years, and if something happened, he feared his opponent would see to it that his career was over. The attorney general, who also faced reelection, shared the same concerns. It was better to take the safer course. Keep Esther protected and get her out of Utah.

Leaving the courthouse, Mattie went to her car and immediately called Brad. When he didn't answer, she voice texted, "*I'm on my way with bad news, Brad. They have denied Tick's adoption. You have been ordered to leave the hospital today. Prepare Tick now and ask her to read Isaiah 41:10. We are going to fight this, so please contact your lawyer ASAP. And stay positive.*"

She then called Laura and gave her instructions to find Brad to make sure he read the text she had just sent.

Sitting in her car, Mattie opened up her Bible app to read the Isaiah verse she learned during her darkest days years ago: "So do not fear, for I am with you; do not be dismayed, for I am your God. I will strengthen you and help you; I will uphold you with my righteous right hand."

Dr. Hertz and Dr. Palmer had arrived at the hospital and were in Tick's room before Mattie walked in. Laura had already come and gone. Brad and Tick's faces were dark and expressionless. Brad's old, weathered black Bible rested next to Tick; it stood out in sharp contrast to the crisp, white sheets on her bed. Palmer, a rotund man with a goatee, did not acknowledge Mattie's entrance but continued talking to Brad, saying something about the excellent care Tick would soon be receiving elsewhere. Dr. Hertz looked quite uneasy as she stood awkwardly just inside the room.

As Palmer blathered on, Brad took a step toward him. Palmer reacted by taking a couple of defensive skip-steps closer to Tick. Mattie's heart stopped as she turned to Tick, who had the same look on her face as in the moments before snapping the CPS woman's finger and then knocking her out. Tick's eyes were slowly narrowing—an unwavering, calculating, threatening glare.

Mattie had previously forced herself to watch the video of that incident several times, hoping to defuse the anxiety she felt as she viewed the attack, unable to reconcile the violence with the girl she had come to know so well. Yet what she had witnessed was real. There was another side to Tick, a side capable of extreme violence.

Convinced that Tick was about to defend Brad in an aggressive outburst—Palmer was standing just within her striking range—Mattie rushed to Tick's bedside, pushed Palmer out of the way, and hugged Tick tightly as she began whispering into her ear. Then, as Tick's body softened in Mattie's arms, she turned her attention to Brad.

Good Lord, Mattie thought, *he's ready to blow up, too!*

Brad's fists were balled up, and he looked ready to pounce on Dr. Palmer, who was tactlessly lecturing the room on the importance of "cooperative behavior for the child's sake."

Mattie had to call out Brad's name three times before he finally drew his attention away from Palmer. He walked over to Mattie, and she pulled him away from earshot. She spoke imploringly under her breath.

"Brad, listen to me now. This guy will report any uncooperative or hostile behavior to the Feds. They will happily sink any hope you have of adopting Tick. If there's a chance for you and Tick to be together, then you need to be as compliant and cooperative as possible."

Quickly shelving the antagonism he felt for Palmer, Brad turned to Tick, focusing his full attention on her. Sitting next to her on the bed, he held her hands, touched his forehead to hers, whispering, "I don't know how this is all going to play out, but I promise that I will never stop fighting for you to become my daughter. No matter what, I will always be there for you. Trust that God is in charge and put your faith in Him. Please promise not to do anything foolish. Cooperate with Dr. Palmer even though you don't feel like it, and behave yourself. Know that I love you. You are an amazing, beautiful girl and a blessing in my life. We'll be together someday, so don't worry, okay?"

Tick was surprisingly calm. *"Don't worry,"* she wrote. *"I know what to do. I'll be fine. I love you, too. Don't eat junk food while we're apart! C U soon.*

Brad got up to leave, but not before giving her a peck on her cheek. He was glad to see that her scar wasn't inflamed, just light pink.

Brad's heart was pounding as he called for a taxi and then gathered up his few belongings, Mattie beside him, assuring him that Laura would gather up anything he left behind. She also promised to tell the staff and everyone who had been so good to him for all these weeks how much he appreciated everything and that he would be in touch. After giving Tick another hug and then saying something privately to Palmer while shaking his hand, Brad left the room, passing a miserable-looking Dr. Hertz on the way out.

Mattie and Brad made the walk to the hospital lobby in silence, submersed in their thoughts: *What did Tick mean about knowing what to do?* thought Brad. *What was she going to do?*

For her part, Mattie simply didn't know what to say. At that moment, she knew that she only wanted to be with Brad.

They sat on a bench outside and waited for the taxi. Mattie filled Brad in on what had transpired at the courthouse and her struggle to get Thornton to agree to give Tick another week at the hospital. When Brad asked Mattie what she had whispered to Tick just before they left her room, the cab pulled up, and his question went unanswered as they stood and walked to the curb.

"I'm sorry, Brad," Mattie said. "The FBI has a lot more clout than I do. I wish I could have changed Thornton's mind."

"You have nothing to be sorry about, Mattie. You have been amazing throughout all of this. Tick wouldn't be alive today if you weren't there for her. It's not possible to thank you enough for everything you have done for both Tick and me. What happened today is not your fault, and it isn't over."

Before Brad got into the cab, he turned and asked Mattie if she would check on Tick once more before she went home.

"I'm not going back over," said Mattie. "I can't be in the same room with that man—and it will confuse Tick. I promise I will keep close track of everything that's going on with her. Trust me with this."

Brad was puzzled, even a bit hurt. How could she leave Tick now? He didn't reply, signaling the driver to get moving.

Mattie walked over to the bench, sat down again, and looked up at the cloudy sky. She closed her eyes and said a silent prayer. She had made a snap decision, a decision that could haunt her the rest of her life, but the wheels were in motion now. Staying at the hospital and being near Tick could only hurt the outcome. She had to put some distance between them, even if Brad, Laura, or any of her staff couldn't understand.

Making her way up to Sam Evans's office, she entered without knocking.

"Sam, they're taking Tick in a week. The FBI's miserable excuse for a childhood specialist will be taking guardianship."

Looking up from his desk, Sam replied, "I know. I just talked to Judge Thornton. It's unfortunate, and I don't agree with his decision, but it's out of our control, Mattie. I understand that you negotiated for the additional week before her transfer. Do you plan to just camp out at The Palace until they take her?"

"No, quite the opposite. I plan on driving up to the cabin and staying for the week. I still have more to do on my paper, and to tell you the truth, I refuse to be anywhere near Palmer. I just came in to let you know I will arrange for Dr. Brackford to cover for me."

Evans couldn't have been more surprised by Mattie's announcement.

"Are you seriously letting Palmer drive you away from your work with Tick? That's not like you. Are you sure this is what you want to do?"

Mattie headed for the door. "Sam, it's not something I want to do. It's something I have to do. Trust me."

Capitulation

Mattie felt an urgency to get to her cabin quickly, and she drove with one eye on the speedometer and the other looking out for police. She pulled into the carport, dashed into the house, and immediately sat down at her computer, where she logged in to the hospital's Electronic Health Records site.

After checking Tick's vitals' latest charting—her blood pressure, temperature, heart rate, and oxygen saturation—Mattie texted Laura to let her know that she was at the cabin and accessing EHR. She also asked her to keep close tabs on Tick. Laura didn't need instruction on how to do her job when Mattie was away. Laura understood her role was to be a second set of eyes, be aware of what was happening with all of the patients and staff, and call whenever something came up that needed Mattie's attention.

But for once, Laura didn't understand what was going on. In light of the disturbing events at The Palace—namely Brad's departure and Tick now in the hands of total strangers—Mattie's sudden departure to the cabin was mystifying, out of character.

Perhaps Mattie just needs to clear her head and escape from a situation she has little control over, she thought, as she put her confusion aside and concentrated on her work.

Laura first called Mattie late that evening.

"I just left The Palace. Tick is asleep. Brenda says that, after you left, she turned away from all of her nurses, Dr. Brackford, and the FBI caseworkers. She wouldn't budge to be taken to therapy and didn't even ask to go to the bathroom. Tick hasn't eaten or taken a sip of water since noon. Palmer insists that she will come around, but Brenda says the staff isn't happy to see Tick in this state and that they're quite worried about her. Brackford indicated to me that he's on board to cover any medical issues until her transfer but that her problematic reaction to Hughes's departure is a development that's not in his orb. He whispered that he thought Dr. Palmer was a 'lightweight.'"

"Who is on the night shift," asked Mattie?

"Abigail... Brackford is on call."

"Okay, would you please connect me with Abigail? Thanks."

Abigail came on the line.

"Hi, Mattie. I'm glad it's you."

"I understand you have all had a rough day with Tick," Mattie said. "Tell me what's going on."

"Tick completely shut down on us today. She hasn't swallowed a thing. She refused to get out of bed for assistance to the toilet, so Brenda had us put her on bed pads." Mattie could sense the frustration in Abigail's voice. "The worst part of the day was when Palmer tried to engage with her. He got nowhere. Leslie said that he talked to her as though she were five years old, clueless about who he was trying to cajole. Tick wouldn't even look at him. It's hard to believe that she didn't tell him off, but she didn't react at all. She just turned away. It was sad. Will you be in tomorrow, Mattie?"

"No," replied Mattie, "but if Tick is asleep, wake her up and tell her that you just spoke to me on the phone and that I said she is to start drinking water—immediately. Tell her that if she doesn't, Dr. Brackford will have to hook her up to an IV."

"I'll wake her up right now," Abigail said. "What about solids?"

"Missing a few meals isn't going to hurt her," replied Mattie. "I'm not so worried about that right now, but her hydration is crucial. I'll keep my eye on her vitals from home, and if I see anything concerning, I'll give Dr. Brackford a call, but I'm sure he's on top of everything."

"Of course, but it's not the same without you or Brad here with Tick—"

"I have to run now, Abby," Mattie said, cutting off her nurse, "but I want you to text me about the water."

Fifteen minutes later, a text came in, "She's drinking... Eight ounces so far."

Early the next morning, before she was out of bed, the familiar ding announcing a new text interrupted her thoughts. This time, it was Dr. Brackford: "Tick looks pale and continues her unresponsiveness to the nursing staff. Are you sure I can't persuade you to come in?"

The text surprised Mattie. She had talked to Dr. Brackford the night before and made it quite clear that she wouldn't be coming in for the duration. He had to be worried. Her response to his new text was short and to the point. "No, I won't be coming in. I am counting on you!"

Mattie walked into her study to read the latest input of Tick's vitals. Satisfied that the readouts were within normal ranges, she poured herself a cup of coffee and sat at her window, contemplatively examining a snow-covered aspen tree.

Later that afternoon, Tick's vitals showed an increased heart rate and decreased blood pressure, so Mattie called Laura.

"Laura, I need you to check on Tick's water intake. Tell Brenda that I want the duty nurses to watch her swallow the water personally. Also have them draw blood for electrolyte levels, and have the lab run it STAT. Make sure when they take the sample, they stick the mock label on the tube."

Tick had been given a false name and room designation, and Mattie was having trouble keeping up with all the deception.

God, she thought, *all the effort to keep Tick's whereabouts hidden is driving me crazy.*

It wasn't an hour later when Laura called back. "The lab ran her levels. Tick is borderline critical for dehydration. Brackford was notified and is in with Tick, now starting an IV. Are you sure you won't be coming in?"

Mattie's response was quick and pointed. "Is she fighting with the staff? Has she been violent in any way?"

"No," replied Laura, puzzled by her boss's hesitancy to check on Tick herself. "Just non-cooperative, like a slab of meat lying on the bed."

"Well, at least she's not giving Palmer an excuse to insist that you sedate her," said Mattie.

"True, but Palmer is talking about petitioning the court to allow forced feedings if she doesn't start eating soon."

"Judge Thornton won't move on that before speaking to me first. For now, have the night shift text me when they start the third IV bag. She should be good by then. Thanks, Laura."

"Mattie," Laura interjected, "Tick always responds to you. Everyone thinks—"

"Listen to me, Laura… For all intents and purposes, Dr. Brackford is Tick's attending doctor for another few days. Please leave it at that for now. I'll talk to you later."

Not more than half an hour later, Mattie's phone rang again. Laura was on the line. "Mattie, she pulled out her IV. It's back in, and she is in wrist cuff restraints overnight. We need you here!"

Mattie's voice was steely. "So I'm hearing that the line is back in, and the fluids are now flowing. Right?"

"Yeah." Laura sighed, sounding frustrated. "But not before Dr. Brackford told Palmer what he thought of this whole shameful business, and then ordered him to leave the room while he worked on Tick."

"Is she fighting the restraints?" asked Mattie.

"No, she was just lying there, and I think she may be asleep now."

"Well, then, it seems the crisis is over, but make sure to remove those cuffs as soon as Tick wakes up so she can communicate anything she needs on her pad. Try to get some sleep now, Laura, and thanks for your help today. Tomorrow, I don't want you to get involved over at The Palace at all, and you don't need to call me with updates. Dr. Brackford and Tick's nurses can handle whatever comes up."

Mattie reminded Laura about the discharged patient files piling up on her desk.

"Really, Mattie, those charts were brought over from billing, remember? You need to match up treatments with the new government billing codes. I can't work on them without your input."

"You're right, I forgot. Sorry. I'll get to those next week."

"So if you're going to be at the cabin until next week, you won't get to say goodbye to Tick?" Laura's tone was accusatory. "And you've asked me not to be involved anymore? What is going on, Mattie? I know how you feel about Tick. Brad's gone, you're not here, and she's over there without any—"

"I know, Laura. You are going to have to trust me. Of all people, you know how much I care about Tick. Her situation breaks my heart, and Brad's, and yours, and all of her nurses. Tick has gotten under all our skin—but we no longer have a say in her life, so we must give her up to a much higher authority, and I don't mean the FBI."

"So we pray for a miracle or divine intervention?" Laura's question was both sarcastic and rhetorical.

"That's right, my friend," Mattie said. "God works in mysterious ways."

"So I'll go ahead and do what I can on the files, Mattie. You know where I am if you need anything. Good night."

"Good night, Laura," Mattie said, regretful that she couldn't confide in her assistant and friend.

In the late afternoon of the third day since walking out of Tick's room with Brad, Mattie received a phone call from Judge Thornton.

"Good afternoon, Mattie. This is Judge Thornton calling."

"Good afternoon, Judge."

"I'm calling to discuss Miss Morgan," Thornton replied, recalling their heated exchange four days earlier and knowing he was about to eat a copious helping of crow.

Mattie, who had just returned to the cabin after snowshoeing on a nearby trail, was sitting at her kitchen counter, sipping tomato soup, and mindlessly flipping through a medical journal. "Okay, Judge. What about her?"

"Mattie, your Miss Morgan is making life as miserable as possible for everybody involved at the hospital."

"Is that so, Judge? I can't imagine why."

"Okay, please put your sarcasm aside. We are in trouble with Tick, and I need your guidance."

"But, Judge, I told you I would not be acting as Tick's primary care physician during her final week at Children's Hospital. Dr. Brackford is covering for me until you sign Tick over to Dr. Palmer."

"That's my problem, Mattie. Esther's disruptions at the hospital are forcing me to make some decisions today."

"I'm not sure what you're talking about, Judge. My assistant mentioned that Tick became dehydrated, but I know that Dr. Brackford and my staff are now hydrating her intravenously. Aside from a child not eating or drinking, I'm not aware of any other 'disturbances,' as you put it."

"I'm referring to this morning's events. You haven't heard?"

Trusting that, despite last night's instructions, Laura would have called if there had been a life-or-death emergency, Mattie braced herself anyway for what she was about to hear. "What happened?"

"Oh my, Mattie," Thornton began, "according to Sheri Hertz, who has been keeping me posted every day, quite a bit went down today. First thing this morning, Esther's nurse removed her wrist cuffs, as ordered by Dr. Brackford, and she wrote on her slate that she was hungry, asking for a large glass of milk, some orange juice, and some oatmeal.

"After they brought the tray in, she poured the entire concoction down her cast. It's a real mess, Mattie. Then, she wrote a long message on her notepad and flung it across the room. Dr. Palmer faxed a copy for me to read."

"What did she write?" asked Mattie.

"Let's see…

"'*Palmer: I've seen you endlessly preening, and I feel sorry for you. What is missing in your ego that makes you spend so much time looking in a mirror? If you want to look presentable, to be taken seriously, you should shave that ridiculous goatee and look upward, not inward. You are a pathetic excuse for a child development expert without question, and you will never know me, understand me, or break me. Go back to Boston and leave me alone.*

"'*Dr. Hertz: You seem like a nice woman, but you are not strong enough for all of this and really should just go home to your children. You're not going to like how this conflict is going to play out. You should leave!*

"'*Mr. Brewer: You must feel like such a complete loser because Timothy has been one step ahead of you all of these years. Stay on your toes anyway—he* **WILL** *come after you. Perhaps you should disappear. Too bad, you will never learn what happened at the ranch now, but that, of course, has been your decision.*

"'*And Hoger—I thought you were my friend.*

"'*To the FBI—I would have cooperated with you because I hate Timothy Bird more than any of you can imagine. Now, because you made Brad leave, I will never help you. I'm not afraid to die, and when I do, I'm going to get special permission from God to haunt all of you. And by the way, after you bury me, you are all going to have a lot of explaining to do—Brad and Mattie will stop at nothing to expose you.*"

"'She ended the note with Psalm 56:4, *"In God, whose word I praise—In God I trust and am not afraid. What can mere mortals do to me?"*'"

Judge Thornton paused for a moment before speaking again. "So, Mattie, there you have it—along with plans to haunt us."

"I wouldn't put it past her," replied Mattie, feeling a surge of pride. "But you said this happened this morning? What's happened since?"

"Well, they tell me that Esther's nurses did the best job they could to clean her up, but her cast is completely ruined and will soon become a health hazard. She has barely moved in her bed since this morning. Your nursing staff and Dr. Brackford have declined to recast Esther for fear she might injure herself in the process, adamantly refusing Palmer's request to sedate her. Sam Evans is fully supporting their position. He has already called me twice this week to ask me to reconsider my position, but his call today was quite blistering."

"I see." Mattie concealed her delight.

"There's more," Thornton continued. "The Salt Lake Deputy Chief Nate Hoger visited Esther yesterday. After he saw her, he called to inform me that if I didn't allow Brad back to take care of her, he would petition the upper courts to charge the FBI with child abuse. He also said that if Esther was harmed while in FBI custody, he would bring criminal charges, and that he would name me as the presiding judge in the case."

The trepidation in Judge Thornton's voice gave Mattie a glimmer of hope.

"Now, I think I know the answer to this question, Mattie, but is there anything you could do at this point to turn this ship around before it hits the rocks?"

Mattie, thinking about how she should respond, grasped the arm of her chair.

"My coming in won't change a thing," replied Mattie. "It might be difficult for you to imagine, but nothing short of drugging her out of her mind will alter the course she has taken. Tick knows what she is doing, and I believe she's capable of finishing what she has started."

"Go on, Mattie," urged the judge. "You're the child psychiatrist here. Explain to me again what you believe she's thinking."

"In no uncertain terms, Judge, this is what I know. Tick lives in a world that has taken her childhood, her mother, and has now taken the man she views as her father—Brad Hughes. Her view is black or white, and she has very fixed notions of right or wrong. She feels she has nothing to lose except her life, and she is determined to control how that happens. This is her last stand, Judge Thornton. It's her way to protest her painfully unfair life."

Judge Thornton felt drained but convinced.

"Mattie, I've heard enough. I'm feeling compelled to overturn my decision to grant guardianship to Dr. Palmer and the FBI. I know Washington is willing to capitulate. I spoke to one of their top dogs, Special Agent Ruth Evers, earlier, and she told me to approve Mr. Hughes's petition for Esther Morgan's adoption. I thought it essential to speak to you once more before making my final decision."

Audibly clearing his throat, Thornton continued sheepishly. "Mattie, I hope you understand that I am duty-bound to consider all aspects in a child custody case, and this was a particularly complex situation."

"I understand," Mattie replied, "and I agree that we have all been tested about doing the right thing for this child, but I want you to know that you have come to the only decision that gives her a chance for a happy life, so thank you."

"I will have the Morgan-Hughes adoption papers drawn up and ready early tomorrow. Let's get this one behind us."

Mattie enthusiastically replied, "I'll drive back into town tonight. I'll give Mr. Hughes a call right now and arrange to meet him at the hospital in the morning. He's going to be ecstatic! One last thing, Your Honor, I have a favor—really, a request."

"Yes, of course. What is it?"

"Could you meet us at the hospital with the adoption papers and bring your robes? Brad and I will meet you in the main foyer. How about seven? I'd like the adoption to be as formal and official as it can be, considering the circumstances. For Tick's sake, especially, but for Brad's as well, they will appreciate your presence more than you can know, and the sooner we get them together, the better."

Mattie had always been tactful and timely about taking advantage of her opportunities.

"I will be there at 7:00 a.m. sharp with the papers," Judge Thornton said, "and in my robes."

Mattie was so excited that she could barely keep ahold of the phone to call Brad. When he answered, Mattie was only able to say "Hello" before he interrupted.

"Mattie, I'm so glad you called, but I can't talk to you right now. I just got a call from Senator Buckwald in Washington, and he's willing to meet with a top FBI official and me in the morning. I can still catch the 8:30 flight if I leave now. It's amazing. They were stonewalling me, but—"

Mattie, practically bursting, shouted, "Cancel the flight! We did it, Brad! You're getting your girl! Judge Thornton is drawing up the adoption papers, and he will meet us at the hospital tomorrow morning at seven. She's yours!"

Mattie's news hit him like a tidal wave. Brad tossed his overnight bag clear across the room, shouted his thanks to God, and began firing off one question after another for Mattie. Mattie put him on speakerphone, recounting the highlights of her conversation with Thornton, and scrambled around the cabin to close it up.

Five hours later, Mattie arrived at her apartment near the hospital and fell into bed. She didn't get to sleep right away, but she slept soundly for the first time in many days once she did. On the other hand, Brad could hardly sleep a wink; his thoughts about adopting Tick could not crowd out his feelings for Catherine, the boys, and their families. He missed them all more than ever, and he wished they were all together. He prayed that they would approve of what he was about to do. While he believed that prayers are answered according to God's will, he still felt apprehensive. He had put a lot at risk, and it would be a difficult adjustment for his family.

Both Brad and Mattie arrived at the hospital well before Judge Thornton, giving Mattie plenty of time to catch up with Laura and bring her up-to-date with the adoption news. She asked Laura to arrange for the use of the small conference room and to notify Sam Evans that they were waiting to meet Judge Thornton in the foyer. As they sat together, Mattie had just enough time to answer most of Brad's unanswered questions, and while they were chatting, Brad realized that Tick wasn't the only one he had developed feelings for since taking off for a hike in the Uintas.

Judge Thornton arrived right on time, carrying a small valise. Laura greeted him at the entrance, and the two walked into the foyer, where Mattie and Brad were waiting impatiently. Thornton offered a hug to Mattie and shook Brad's hand heartily. "This is a fine day to sign some important papers. Are you ready?"

Laura ushered the threesome into a conference room and handed the judge his case. He opened it and pulled out papers, his robe, and a gift bag. He then began to speak in a more somber tone. "Mr. Hughes, it is this court's understanding that you wish to adopt Esther Morgan. Is that correct?"

Brad was quick to nod his head. "It is."

"If this is your intention, you must realize that you are taking on what this court considers to be a sacred trust: the ongoing care and nurturing of a child."

"I understand."

"Further, you do realize that she will be your responsibility until she comes of age at eighteen? I think the commitment is for your lifetime."

"Yes, I understand the commitment, one that I am happy to make for Tick."

The judge added, "You realize that after today you are taking on significant security risks. Even with the best security provisions, both her life and your life will be in danger until Timothy Bird is dead or behind bars."

Brad replied, "I have given that situation a great deal of thought, and I am more than willing to take on any risks that are involved. If necessary, I will sell my business, and we will enter a witness protection program."

"I certainly hope it will never come to that. Deputy Chief Hoger and the FBI assure me there has been no record of your name in the press, and we have expunged both your name and Esther's name from all hospital records. She will be as safe here in Utah under a different name as she would be anywhere. Also, no one outside Mattie's carefully chosen staff, and the medevac team knows what she looks like. Bird is on every wanted poster in the state—every lawman is quite anxious to find him.

"This adoption proceeding will not be publicized, and the case files will be sealed to the public. Deputy Chief Hoger tells me you are well aware of the necessity to keep pictures of Tick out of the press or social media sites. Federal agents are in the process of developing an iron-clad cover story for the media, as well as using a stand-in girl in place of Tick during the media-covered transfer of Esther Morgan out of state in an FBI jet. An agent in charge of that activity will fill you in on all the details."

"Okay, I'll wait to hear something about that."

"Well, everything is in order," Judge Thornton said. "I see no reason not to proceed with the adoption."

Judge Thornton passed the adoption papers to Brad and directed him to read through the few pages. "I understand that Laura is a notary public, so she can witness and put the seal on the document. We're ready to make this legal and effective immediately, but I want the signing to take place in front of Miss Morgan."

Brad hurriedly reviewed the papers to sign.

"I'm sorry that I didn't make the right decision for Tick from the beginning," Judge Thornton confessed. "I should have listened to Dr. Barnes. I wish you and Tick the best of luck."

"Thank you, Judge Thornton," replied Brad.

Mattie, now anxious to reunite Tick and Brad, pulled on Brad's sleeve.

"Let's go see that daughter of yours! Your Honor, would you mind putting your robes on now? You are about to make a little girl very happy!"

Laura held his robes up for the judge to get into and then grabbed his case before the three of them proceeded to walk to The Palace.

Reaching The Palace wing, Mattie spotted Brenda Martin working at a table outside Tick's room. Still unfairly exiled by Tick after the Messener affair, Brenda continued as head nurse, coming in for an hour every day to supervise and check with the nurses. When Brenda saw the trio coming, she leaped off her chair, close to tears.

"Thank God you're here."

Abigail Jones, who was attending the nursing station, joined them, and the group walked over to Tick's door in animated conversation.

When they stopped at the door, Mattie asked the judge, Laura, Brenda, and Abigail to remain outside for a few minutes. As she and Brad entered the room, the odor of sour, rancid milk hit their nostrils. They found themselves in a dark and lifeless space.

Dr. Sheri Hertz was seated in the corner, her eyes fixed on the floor and looking haggard. Seeing Mattie and Brad, she rose and awkwardly approached Mattie.

"I'm so sorry, Mattie. You were right."

Mattie didn't acknowledge her words. She was looking at Tick, who lay there with cuff restraints and an IV slowly dripping fluid into her arm. She faced the wall, her hair uncombed and dirty, her nightgown wrinkled and twisted around her torso, both arms pinned down.

This pathetic-looking child was a stark contrast to the neat, energetic girl she had left just four days before. Brad approached her quietly, placing his hand on her shoulder gingerly, as if touching a sleeping baby. Then, he whispered, "You're safe now, Tick. I'm here," and he reached over to unfasten the cuff around her wrist.

The contrast in the rooms energy was immediate. Everything seemed to vibrate the very second Tick realized who was standing over her. She came alive, every muscle in her body jumping with movement. They were soon hugging each other while Mattie opened the curtains and windows to air out the room. Tick pointed to her tablet, and Brad retrieved it. She excitedly wrote something down. He read the message and said, "I know, Tick, I know... He is watching out for both of us!"

Mattie removed Tick's IV, cleaned her up, and combed her hair. Then, she turned to Dr. Hertz, "Let's give Mr. Hughes and Tick a moment to talk alone."

In the hallway outside, Dr. Sheri Hertz cornered Mattie and Judge Thornton.

"It's all happened just the way you said it would. I would never have believed it. When you and Mr. Hughes left, Tick gave Dr. Palmer a fierce look one can't imagine. It was like she was looking forward to a challenge she knew she would win. I didn't think a child was capable of such an expression. Honestly, I was afraid she was going to look at me that way. I felt like a grasshopper hopping around on a frying pan, and I knew it wasn't going to work out from the first day. Tick didn't move a muscle, refused to go to physical therapy. She wouldn't be taken to the bathroom refused to eat. It was awful.

"We thought she was drinking water, but then we discovered what she had been doing... How can a child have that kind of willpower? How she must have suffered! Then, she poured that milk and oatmeal down her cast and wrote all those messages. Anyway, Dr.

Palmer gave up last night and went back to Boston. To his credit, he called Washington before he left and told them that agent Evers was right, that we didn't have a chance in hell of succeeding on any level by taking such a strong-willed girl into protective custody. He was afraid to take responsibility for her safety."

Finally, she asked nervously, "Do you think that having her restrained hurt her?"

Mattie sighed. "No, she's been through far worse than that. Losing Brad Hughes was killing her, not the restraints, but Judge Thornton here is about to change that."

Mattie softly grasped Judge Thornton's elbow. "Your Honor, I think it's time you met Tick."

Mattie and Judge Thornton walked into the room with Laura in tow.

As they walked in, Tick put her arm around Brad, and pulling herself up to sit, she looked in amazement at the man wearing flowing black robes with gold braid adorning the neckline and trailing down the front. He looked striking and very important.

"Tick, my name is Judge Thornton. I am the Family Court Justice for the third district in the State of Utah, and I am happy to meet you at last. I am here this morning on official court business to tell you that I have granted Mr. Hughes's petition to adopt you as his daughter. Now, I must confirm if becoming Brad Hughes's daughter forever, from this day forward, is what you want to happen. If you do, please respond by nodding your head to signify yes."

All eyes fell on Tick, whose head was already decisively nodding up and down. Large tears glistened in the corners of her eyes.

"Tick, having you as my daughter is my highest honor. Your mother must be so proud of you," Brad said as he hastily signed the documents. "I can't wait to get you home."

After Laura notarized and stamped the two signed copies—one to remain in the court's safe and the other copy for Brad—the judge said, "Mr. Hughes is now officially your father and legally responsible for your care and upbringing. You are his daughter now."

Tick grabbed her tablet and, erasing the message she had written to Brad earlier, rapidly wrote, *Judge, I forgive you for taking the best person in the world away from me and for allowing that creepy Palmer in my room. After all, we all make mistakes."*

Her expression was sincere, forthright, and Judge Thornton felt humbled. "You're so right, Tick. Thank you for your understanding. I feel honored to meet the young lady and her new father, who, in such a short period of time, have amassed a small army of loyal and, let me say, adoring friends and supporters. Dr. Barnes told me in no uncertain terms that nothing should prevent you from becoming Tick Hughes. Both Agent Hoger and Agent Dresder of the Salt Lake City FBI called me to say that I had gotten it all wrong. By the way, you are wrong about Chief Hoger. He was ready to see me in jail if I didn't send Dr. Palmer packing. Dr. Hertz, my consultant, called me every day, insisting that I had made a huge mistake, and all the doctors and nurses who work with you wanted you to be with Mr. Hughes."

Tick put her hand up to initiate a high-five with her dad as the judge continued speaking to her.

"Today's adoption is final and binding and is not conditional upon your assisting the police in capturing Timothy Bird. However, there are issues we must address. I read the comment you wrote yesterday concerning helping the FBI capture Timothy Bird. For your sake and for the sake of everyone he hurt, I am counting on you to help us bring him to justice very soon."

Thornton directed his next comment toward Brad. "The FBI has drafted a Grant of Immunity Agreement for Tick in exchange for her cooperation. This agreement protects her from any possible prosecution surrounding crimes committed at the ranch. Many families have lost loved ones, and we must help them find closure. We also need to find the people who are responsible and make them pay for their crimes."

Pausing, he looked at Tick, who was listening carefully. "There is another issue that concerns me, and that is the number of people you have assaulted since you arrived at the hospital. Dr. Barnes tells me you have only acted in self-defense, or your notion of self-defense, and after reviewing the facts, I agree with her. Still, you have injured three people quite seriously. These violent attacks cannot continue and cannot be tolerated.

"Fortunately, the staff at the hospital will not be pressing charges, but let me be clear: I don't ever want to see you in my court on an assault charge. I know you are a self-defense expert, but you must learn restraint in using your skills. I hope we both can start on a new foot and count on each other as friends."

Tick sat there quietly, looking him in the eye. With a serious demeanor, she erased her tablet and wrote, "*I meant what I said in the note. I don't like hurting people, and I'm sorry I did. I'm not like Timothy Bird, and I want to be your friend, too. Thank you, Judge.*"

"Thank you, Tick. You are an exceptional young lady."

Before the judge left the room, he opened his case, took out the gift bag, handing it to Tick. Tick tore off the ribbon in childish delight, opened the bag extracting a bright pink stuffed animal—a cat. The tag around its paw read: THE ORIGINAL JELLY CAT.

Tick hadn't seen a stuffed toy since she was five. "*Thank you very much!*" she wrote. "*She's wonderful! I'll love her forever.*"

The judge winked at Mattie as he left the room, and Mattie followed him. "Thank you for coming down, Your Honor. That was perfect. It was just what she needed."

"No, thank you," he replied. "I needed to be reminded of how drastically the decisions I make in my courtroom can affect lives. I should have met with Tick before making my decision. I hope you will accept my apology."

"Of course."

After escorting the judge to the door, Mattie went back into the room to find Brad scouring through the adoption papers with Tick. Then, he carefully placed the document in his briefcase, saying, "We'll get this framed, okay?"

Mattie was now all business, and she asked Brad to step aside while she carefully examined Tick from head to toe. For the most part, Tick was in pretty fair shape, although the cast needed to be replaced.

Leaning over Tick, she whispered words in her ear that left no room for dissent. "Okay, what you did was very brave. It worked, but you can never do anything like that again, do you understand? That was a once-in-a-lifetime performance. The play is over—forever! Until I can check you out of this hospital, you need to cooperate fully with everyone. I want you to eat, drink, sleep, exercise, roll over, bark, and comb your hair exactly as I tell you. Do we understand each other?"

Tick looked up at Mattie with a devilish twinkle in her eye, and without any argument, she nodded her head and wrote "*Woof-woof*" in large letters on her slate.

Tick spent the next few hours having her stinky cast removed. After a bath and x-rays, Dr. Brackford put her into a new cast. Her bones were healing nicely, so the new cast was less confining with less bulk. Late in the afternoon, she ate every bite of her favorite take-out hamburger with fries and a chocolate milkshake. Exhausted, Tick asked Brad to help her get settled into her bed for the night.

It had been a long four days.

You Have a Daughter

Around eleven that evening, Mattie made her way down the Walker Building's deserted hall on her way to The Palace. It had been a stressful day for her—a car had run an intersection, hitting a school bus, and seven children were now in the emergency room. Five of the children had relatively minor injuries, an assortment of scrapes, cuts, and bruises, but Terry Parker, age thirteen, was in an induced coma with a serious brain injury, and eight-year-old Torrance Small had a broken back. Emily Johnson, the driver of the car, had been killed. Mattie was bone-tired, but she wanted to check on Tick before heading home.

Leslie Thomas was on duty at the nursing station and rose to greet her, but Mattie was the first to speak. "How is Tick doing? How did the recasting go?"

Leslie, a wiry, wisp of a woman in her late forties, was one of Mattie's most capable nurses, often taking an extra shift at The Palace to help out with Tick's care.

"She's sound asleep," Leslie replied. "She finally conked out around five this afternoon. The recasting went well, but it was a tiring ordeal for her, and she was running on fumes to begin with."

Leslie paused. "When I asked her how she was feeling, she wrote, 'Victorious! They came, they saw, I conquered.' What do you think she meant by that?"

Hearing this, Mattie had to hide her exasperation with Tick's lack of self-restraint when expressing her feelings. Her pronouncement "I conquered" brought to mind the Japanese adage—*The nail that sticks out will be hammered down*—and making audacious statements was a matter that needed to be discussed with her very soon.

At least she didn't offend the judge with her cheek, Mattie thought.

"She is a fighter, Leslie," Mattie said. "What we know about Tick is extremely sketchy, but we do know she's a fighter."

"But I didn't see it that way at the time, Mattie. I saw her deliberately giving up on life because Brad was gone, and she couldn't accept the plans Palmer had laid out for her. There were no angry tantrums or outbursts. She was shutting down, beginning to fade, ignoring everyone and everything around her. She had me convinced that the FBI had shattered her will to live. It was alarming."

"Yes, in light of Tick's past aggressiveness, I can understand how you would feel that way, but I can assure you that what you were witnessing was not submission—just the opposite. Her survival instincts are powerful, Leslie. This episode was just another fight for her life—and she won, didn't she?"

"Oh, Mattie, of course, you're right. I must be a bit slow. Attempting to starve herself was a strategy that she cooked up. Am I the last to get it? Oh, never mind. Thank goodness the court cried uncle before it was too late. You know her. She wouldn't have stopped!"

Then, without thinking about how critical it would sound, Leslie asked, "Where were you? You and Brad are the only ones who can control her behavior. We needed you."

Mattie understood the subtle scolding for her absence during Tick's ordeal, but the reminder that Tick had seriously risked her life to be "victorious" felt like a punch in the stomach.

After an awkward silence, Mattie was able to throw out a casual answer. "My presence would have only created more problems. Anyway, how is Mr. Hughes doing?"

"Why don't you ask him? He's in there with Tick now. He is so excited. It's kind of cute. He is acting just like a new father. He had a lot of questions about today's exam and x-rays. I let Dr. Brackford know, so he came by earlier and filled him in."

Mattie quickly responded, "Brad can be persistent."

"I heard about the bus accident," Leslie said inquiringly. "I understand we have two in the ICU. I can fill in tomorrow if you need some extra help."

Mattie sighed as she started for The Palace door. "I appreciate that, thanks. I'll let Laura know that you're available. Tomorrow will be busy. Two burn victims from Wyoming are also being flown in early in the morning."

Walking into the room, she acknowledged Brad who got up to greet her. Mattie walked over to Tick's bed and examined her chart. Tick was fast asleep. Jelly Cat, her gift from Judge Thornton, peeked out from under the blanket next to her head.

Somewhere inside of Tick, prayed Mattie, *an ordinary twelve-year-old girl is trying to get out.*

"She's been asleep for hours," Brad whispered. "She ate a hamburger, and then she crashed. I haven't seen her this tired in a long time." Pointing to the pink cat ears poking out from the covers, he chuckled. "I can't believe how much she took to that stuffed animal. She held on to it all afternoon. She calls it Jelly."

"I guess Christmas came early for both of you today. How are you holding up?"

"All in all, I'm nervous but thrilled," replied Brad, "and I know I have you to thank for this day."

"Not me, Brad," Mattie said, shaking her head. Then, she pointed to the sleeping girl.

Yawning, she groaned, "So sorry, it's late. I'm exhausted, and weather permitting, an air ambulance will be arriving in the morning carrying patients. I'll come by tomorrow to check on both of you. We can have a better visit then."

Mattie left the room, but just as she reached the hallway, Brad caught up to her. "Mattie, hold up."

Just outside the door, Brad stopped and looked back nervously into the room.

"She's fine, Brad... She's sound asleep. Don't be a worrywart."

Brad nodded his head in agreement. "I suppose she's trained me. You know how undone she can become, and I don't want her to wake up and think I've gone again."

The stress and tension of the past five days finally showed on Mattie's face. "For Pete's sake, Brad, she's sound asleep. She has Jelly tucked up next to her, and she's just won the biggest prize of all— you! Do you honestly believe at this point that she would be worried about us walking down the hall together? You can't possibly be that naïve."

"Ouch, Mattie, that hurt." He was only moderately offended. "When it comes to Tick, I'm not naïve, just frequently clueless. There is a difference. Am I right to detect a note of disapproval?"

"I think you seriously underestimate her, Brad," said Mattie. "She is an extraordinarily clever girl, as you know, but your daughter is as manipulative as she is tenacious. I'm sure it's what kept her and her mother alive for all those years."

Pausing to reflect, she added, "Before today, she was determined to convince everyone, mainly you, that she couldn't or wouldn't exist without you, and this effectively fueled the adoption. Now that you have committed to her, she'll feel safe to put you on a much longer leash. You shouldn't feel hurt if she begins to pull away from you a bit now."

Put off by the direction the conversation was taking, Brad fired back. "You're making her sound like a real witch, Mattie."

"Not at all, Brad," Mattie answered. "Her love and devotion to you are genuine, just coming from a warped point of reference. Distancing herself from you a little bit now would be a normal reaction to feeling secure enough to explore life on her terms, and she needs a chance to do that. I like Tick enormously, you must know that, and I admire her as much as anyone I have ever known, child or adult—but our focus has been on keeping her alive, and we are still, as you just admitted, clueless about what's going on in her head. I can tell you this, she has mental wounds that run as deep as those scars on her back. Because there's no timetable for conquering all the horrible side effects of abuse, she'll require your forbearance, a really good therapist, and frequent confirmation that life—and most people, for that matter—are good. The good news is that you have something essential going for you."

"What's that?" Brad asked.

"Tick completely, unquestionably adores you. That's just another one of her mysteries."

"There's no making sense of it, I agree," Brad said. "The connection formed between us on a ledge had its origin from a much higher elevation, literally and figuratively."

Mattie gathered her thoughts. "You are very good at disarming my left-brain thinking, and I honor your belief that you and Tick were brought together by divine design. But you must realize that besides the emotional fracture that is preventing her from speaking, your daughter comes with other genuine, down-to-earth issues."

"What's on the top of your list right now?" Brad half-heartedly inquired.

"The fact that Tick carries everything to the extreme is definitely on my list. She can be dangerously impetuous, as you have witnessed yourself several times, and becoming critically dehydrated this week was life-threatening."

"Extremely foolish," agreed Brad.

"I must say," marveled Mattie, "pouring milk, orange juice, and oatmeal down her cast was quite creative. And oh, that note was awesome—aspects of carrot-and-stick strategy with some basic insolence and irrationality thrown in. What a colossal tizzy she created..."

Getting back to the moment, Mattie asked Brad, "Was there something you wanted to talk to me about earlier?"

Brad could not remember his reason for speaking to her, so he decided to broach a different subject.

"Do you remember when we were waiting for my cab, and I asked you what you were whispering in Tick's ear?"

"I don't remember that, Brad," Mattie said, shaking her head and digging into her coat pocket to retrieve a note that she began reading.

"What Tick did," Brad continued, "or I should say, how she reacted to being handed over to Palmer, was too calm and so immediate. She even told me not to worry—that she knew what to do.

My hunch is that you gave her a short, whispered lesson on passive resistance, or maybe you reminded her of the book we read about Gandhi. I don't know for sure, but something tells me..."

Mattie turned away, her face flushed.

Searching for words, Brad reached over and grabbed her by the hand. "Mattie, I know not to pry into confidential conversations between you and Tick, so I won't push you to share what you said, but I meant what I said about having you to thank for the adoption going through. There's no way I can thank you enough."

"It's all in a day's work, Brad." It was all Mattie could muster in her reply.

"Well, I hope the adoption doesn't change our partnership regarding Tick's care," persisted Brad.

"You're her father now, so it changes things quite dramatically," replied Mattie.

"That's not what I mean. I can't do this without your help. I'm counting on you to continue working with us—with Tick. You know she won't work with another psychiatrist. She won't allow anyone else to get into her head. Remember Mattie, we shook on the deal, and isn't a handshake a contract we should honor?"

Mattie's hand felt like it was burning in his grip, and she remembered the first time she met Brad—his firm handshake, his emphasis on the words "for the long term," and the feeling that she was somehow trapped. Had that thought materialized?

Mattie gently pulled her hand away. "Yes, I plan on working with Tick until she is willing to work with another competent psychiatrist. Nothing will change while she remains in the hospital, and once we discharge her, we can schedule weekly visits. Meanwhile, you have a lot to think about, and most importantly, it's time to inform your family where you've been all these weeks and what you have done."

Brad suddenly became more reserved. "Concerning my family, I am going to ask Laura to set up a teleconference tomorrow with my sons and their wives. I was hoping to use the empty conference room at the end of the hall. I plan to tell them everything that's happened since that day in the mountains and then bring Tick in and introduce her to them. Would you consider joining me when they first meet Tick? I could use your support and may need help answering questions about her condition."

"Of course, if you think I can be of help, but it will have to be later in the afternoon—any time after two. Also, just how much help will you want to answer questions about her condition, and yours for that matter, if it comes up? We do have laws in place to protect patient confidentiality."

"You're the doctor, Mattie. Tell them anything they need to know. Be open with them."

"Well then, you are going to need to sign a release allowing me to speak openly. I will have Laura get the forms for your signature. And, Brad, I do have to run now, but I'll drop by in the morning. I'll plan on having dinner with you tomorrow. What would the two of you like as a celebratory dinner?"

"Surprise us. We'll love anything you prepare."

"Done."

Mattie headed down the hall, then paused as Brad hurried after her. "Mattie... Since I've gotten to know you, I've become convinced that exceptionally bright, perceptive, determined, and slightly manipulative little girls like Tick can grow up to be the very best our world has to offer."

Mattie's face was frozen, uncertain. She looked at him intently in the darkened hallway, her hands on her hips. After a moment, and without a word, she turned toward the door and left the building.

Brad strolled back to Tick's room, thinking about his new daughter and her relationship with a doctor who sacrificed so much for her.

When he thought of the games and weird little rules Tick had devised during her time with Mattie, Brad fantasized about turning the girl upside down and shaking her, hoping that, like balls in a pinball machine, Tick's thoughts would somehow find the correct pathways.

Mattie was the only person who could get Tick to begin writing about her captivity, no matter how disturbing. Still, she stiffened melodramatically if Mattie ever approached her with a hug. Tick took every opportunity to compare another doctor's performance to Mattie's, singing her praises to the heavens. But when Mattie was present, Tick would behave almost indifferently toward her, except when she found fault with something Mattie had said or done. On those rare occasions, Tick would quickly correct her with great enthusiasm.

In many ways, however, the patient and her doctor got along beautifully and worked well together. The deep reddening Brad had seen on Mattie's face that night had provided the answer he had suspected. Mattie had unquestionably whispered some sort of instructions into Tick's ear, likely telling her what she could do that would give her some chance, however slim, of being adopted by Brad.

Most importantly, Tick and Mattie could identify with each other in subtle ways, and they established their own set of guidelines and understandings that Brad was not privy to.

As Brad entered Tick's room, his gaze turned directly toward the girl who was now his daughter; he couldn't take his eyes off her. She looked like an angel, aside from the trace of drool on her cheek—just like on the mountain.

The challenges that she presented seemed insignificant; he had come so close to losing her. Brad thanked God that her latest trial had left her uninjured, and he was greatly relieved to be in control of her care. He spent much of the night just watching her breathe, recollecting how Catherine would spend hour after hour watching and studying the breathing of each of their babies. Brad wondered why he never once sat up with her back then. Why hadn't he shared her fear that the baby's breathing might somehow stop? Why hadn't he appreciated just how valuable life was. He felt regretful.

"I'm sorry, Catherine. I get it now."

Other random thoughts began traversing through his mind, and he sat in his chair, making plans. Earlier that day, the FBI had texted him with a request to meet with Tick the next morning, and he had replied that they could have thirty minutes, tops. Tick was still exhausted. Then, there was Alissa's burial to plan. Perhaps he could have her buried next to Catherine.

Would Tick be okay with that?

Addressing the security of his home was imperative. He knew a contractor out of Idaho, who specialized in building fortified rooms. He could get the job done in a hurry.

He wasn't feeling particularly stressed, sitting there, watching Tick. He had faced numerous challenges and setbacks in the past, and somehow he had weathered them all. He wasn't one to second-guess or worry about a decision, but there were aspects of his decision to adopt Tick that would require some parental know-how—things that he was either unaccustomed to handling or just rusty from so many years in an empty nest. Fortunately, running a successful business required the ability to recruit excellent help. He wasn't worried, but his mind was in full swing: *Was Mattie correct in suggesting that Tick had powered the adoption?* Only a short time ago, he would no more have thought of adopting a child than jumping off the ledge on which he had found her. He enjoyed thinking about his life with Tick in it, but he knew there would be times that would try his soul. She did have a way of getting what she wanted.

Then, there was his family. He needed to make a list of talking points. He had to sell them on the idea of having a new sister while also helping them understand that his feelings toward them hadn't changed.

And finally, there was Mattie. The indomitable, ever so wise, professional, and beautiful Dr. Mattie Barnes—a woman with an established career and a mind and a life of her own. How was he going to keep her in his life? He wasn't about to let her walk away.

Fortunately, Brad had always been able to table his thoughts when he needed to sleep, and tomorrow was going to be a big day, so he got into bed. As he lay in bed, his attention shifted to the sound of air cursing through the hospital vents, an occasional squeak of rubber shoes on the tile in the hallway, his daughter's soft breathing. Then he fell asleep.

Fatherhood Day One

Following the adoption, Brad's morning began just after 8:00 a.m., when Mattie and Dr. Brackford came by to discuss their strategy for Tick's continued medical care. Mattie feeling confident that the best possible scenario for Tick's life had happened, greeted Tick and Brad with a smile.

"Good morning, Miss Hughes," she said as she scanned Tick's chart. "I see our beautiful patient had a great night."

Dr. Brackford handed Tick a large envelope that contained several greeting cards and notes of congratulations from her little band of caregivers. Inside the card signed by Laura was something that Tick couldn't identify.

"Oh, that's a gift certificate to Macy's department store, Tick!" Mattie said with excitement. "Use this instead of cash to pay for something you want to buy for yourself."

Tapping the side of her cast, Tick gave her shoulders a little shrug, and Brad spoke up interpreting her gesture. "When will the cast come off, Dr. Brackford?"

"Brad, your daughter has five to six weeks to go before we remove her cast, but at that point, we would like to proceed with her ankle surgery. I know we talked about doing the surgery later in the year. Still, by limiting her mobility while her ankle heals in a cast, we're also giving those older fractures and internal injuries more healing time. From what I have seen, restricting Tick's activity level when there's no cast to tie her down could be challenging."

Turning to Tick and poking her shoulder, Brackford continued, "I wish I had one ounce of the determination and drive you put into your physical therapy, young lady. You're a dynamo, but your body is trying to recover from all it has been through, and you need to give it that chance!"

Before Brad could comment, Mattie spoke up. "That ankle has to be repaired, Brad. Why wait?"

She turned her attention to Tick. "Tick, wouldn't you like to put the ankle surgery behind you?"

Mattie was pleased to see a confirming nod from her patient.

"Well, I hear you, and I'm sure that's the wisest course to take, Mattie," Brad said. Then he lowered his head in hesitation and sighed. "Give me strength."

"How long will this surgery postpone taking Tick home?" Brad asked Dr. Brackford.

"In Tick's case, it will mean tacking on an additional fourteen days or so of precautionary care and rehabilitation. The FBI will be picking up the tab."

Mattie immediately piped up. "And, Brad, this may work to your advantage while you're getting the house ready for her homecoming."

Mattie's well-timed remark redirected Brad's thoughts from a dreaded extended stay at the hospital to concerns about his house.

Unquestionably impressive in its size and appearance, the Hughes' home had even been featured in a home décor magazine. Stunningly decorated to reflect Catherine's elegant taste, the house contained an eclectic collection of furnishings and art that filled the rooms—a stylish accumulation of pieces that Brad and Catherine had inherited from their parents, comingled with newer purchases.

With Tick's impending homecoming, Brad thought he should call Catherine's good friend Cynthia, an interior decorator, to discuss making the house feel less formal and more welcoming. He also wanted to convert one of the large guest bedroom suites on the east wing into a suitable bedroom for a soon-to-be teenager.

More importantly, however, major security system renovations on the grounds and within the house had to be made. Mattie was right. These projects could begin and hopefully be completed before Tick came home.

Also on his mind was alerting Ana Canasa, his Peruvian housekeeper, that big changes were about to occur in the Hughes household. Ana had worked for the Hughes for over twenty-five years, helping Catherine keep the house in good order while keeping a sharp eye on the boys and supervising them whenever their mother was out of the house with her volunteer work or social activities. Since Catherine's death, Ana functionally ran the house.

But Ana was well into her sixties now; keeping house for a self-sufficient widower for the past four years was not particularly demanding and, at most, predictable. Brad was anxious to tell Ana that he had adopted a twelve-year-old girl, and he needed to know how she felt about taking on the additional work his adopted daughter would require. If she felt up to the challenge, and perhaps even excited about reviving her previous role as a duenna or super nanny, Brad wondered how long it would take for Ana to get Tick under her thumb or, maybe in this case, vice versa. However, he had no doubts that the two of them would get along in time—providing that Ana was willing to remain on board for the ride.

"Okay, Dr. Brackford, schedule the surgery, whenever you say. Turning to his daughter he added, "Tick, we'll just have to make the best of it for a bit longer."

Mattie smiled and speaking in a silly exaggerated English accent began teasing Tick and Brad. "You know how much we all adore having you two here with us, and we shall do our utmost to make the coming weeks nothing but fun, fun, and more fun…for both of you. We have to run now, but I shall be back this evening." Mattie left the room laughing good-naturedly, and Dr. Brackford gave Tick a big thumbs up before he was off to make his rounds.

About an hour later, Nate Hoger stopped by to talk with Brad, joined by agents Steve Brewer and Jenny Dresden. Hoger and his crew offered congratulations, expressing genuine happiness about the adoption.

Then agent Brewer delivered the news.

"We have an agreement concerning immunity from prosecution for Tick. We would like you to review it and get it back to us signed. It shields Tick from prosecution if she cooperates with our investigation... Perhaps we should discuss it outside."

Brad was quick to reply. "No, if you have something to discuss that concerns Tick, then she needs to be part of the conversation."

Hesitantly, Brewer continued, "Well, this information isn't good. We tested the blood on the clothes and shoes that Tick was wearing when you found her, and in addition to her blood, we found DNA that matches Janet Herrington's and David Bittner's. We also found traces of Tick's DNA on their clothing." He turned his gaze toward Tick. "I'm sorry, Tick... I'm hoping you'll have an explanation for this."

Brad looked over at Tick, whose face looked set in stone before he responded testily. "You must be joking! Isn't Janet Herrington one of Timothy's acolytes out of Seattle? Do you think a matchup between an adult killer and a twelve-year-old kidnap victim is going to result in a conviction of the child? And as for her blood on the boy's clothing, for all you know, she might have had a cut that dripped on his clothes when she brought him food, one of her many chores there. Perhaps he had wounds. Even if she did fight the boy, it could have been in self-defense. Why assume that he was the victim rather than the other way around?"

Brad liked Hoger and his cohorts just fine but implicating Tick in killings before knowing any of the facts made them appear inept.

"Do you have anything else on my daughter?"

Brewer diffidently replied, "Brad, you're missing the point here." He then purposefully turned to face Tick. "By cooperating in our investigation and giving truthful answers to all of the questions we plan to ask you, Tick, you will be granted complete protection from prosecution in any state or federal court, no matter how or what happened at the ranch. It means you will never be charged with any wrongdoing on your part while you were at the ranch."

He redirected his attention to Brad. "Tick is a minor who has faced impossible odds. We all want Tick to get a fresh start, but we need her detailed account of what went on at the ranch. When we capture Timothy Bird, we need your daughter to testify in court about the crimes he committed there. Her testimony will be essential. The victims' families deserve as much closure as Tick can provide, and we want Timothy Bird put away for good."

The scar on Tick's face had turned red, and she had tears in her eyes.

"What do you say, sweetheart?" said Brad. "This is completely your decision, and you don't have to make it right now."

Tick was quick to respond by writing on her tablet. *Sign their papers, please. I want you to."*

Despite Tick's plea, Brad was never one to sign anything without giving it a thorough read-through. "We will look them over. Give me another day."

The look of relief on Agent Brewer's face was noticeable. "Thank you, Tick. We won't begin interviewing you until Dr. Barnes and your father agrees to it."

"There are other issues we need to discuss," said Brewer, turning his attention to Brad. "Protecting your anonymity and whereabouts from Bird is our next order of business. We have been very fortunate so far because the press has never linked your name to Esther Morgan, either as her rescuer or as her guardian. The people who know your name and your involvement are limited to your lawyer and secretary, the top hospital administrators, several doctors, nurses, Judge Thornton and his court stenographer, and personnel who took your 911 call. We will talk to all of them again.

"The only person outside this group is Susan Messener, who, as you know, is no longer employed by the Children's Protection Service and who we consider someone to watch. For now, I would like you to look over this list of people who know about your connection with Tick, and if you can think of anyone else who we need to include, you must tell us."

Brad scanned over the list. "No, it looks complete. Messener is the only person on this list who would probably go out of her way to disclose everything she knows about us—you know our history with her. I can't be 100 percent sure that Messener didn't hear my name or learn that I live in Utah. Still, I think it's unlikely."

Agent Dresden spoke up quickly, "Messener has signed a confidentiality agreement. In exchange, she is no longer subject to prosecution by the federal or state government for child endangerment and abuse. Dropping a criminal complaint against her requires that all knowledge of Esther Morgan and the child's circumstances be kept completely confidential. Messener can never speak about the episode at the hospital. If any evidence comes to light indicating that she has failed to comply with the agreement, she will face charges. Essentially, it's a gag order with teeth, but that's as far as we can legally go with the woman."

"Putting her on a slow boat to China isn't an option then?" Brad mused.

"It won't be necessary to shanghai her," dismissed Brewer. "The matter of Tick's anonymity and keeping you both safe has been a top priority the minute we learned about Bird. I think we have come up with a solid plan to conceal Tick's identity effectively. Messener does not know your name or that you have adopted Tick."

"Let's hear the plan," Brad said, taking a seat beside Tick's bed.

"We plan to stage a fake transfer of Esther to an undisclosed location out of state. One of our female agents, who happens to be very small, will serve as Tick's double. Moreover, we'll arrange for a handful of local paper and television reporters to be there to witness and photograph Esther Morgan leaving the hospital in an ambulance and then taken to an FBI transport airplane. Children's Hospital will also issue its own press release."

Brewer went on to explain how Brad and Tick would surreptitiously be removed from the hospital and moved to a nearby military base. Arrangements would be made for Tick's care to be provided by a scaled-down medical team from Children's Hospital.

"While you're at the base," Brewer said, "we want you to let your friends and associates know—anyone you see regularly—that you've returned from your travels. Go to your office. Let people know that you're back in town. After a week, you will let your office know that you've just received a call from a lawyer in Pensacola, Florida—

close family friends have been killed in a serious car accident, and you will be catching the next flight out. Meanwhile, our office will plant an accident report in the local paper, naming George and Mary Hartman as the fatalities, and their daughter, Tick Hartman, as being injured in the crash. Newspapers around the Pensacola area will print the parent's obituary a couple of days later. Both articles will make a point that the Hartmans have no surviving relatives and that Tick is an orphan."

"And how am I connected to this family?" Brad asked, feeling thrown by how weird his life had become.

"The cover story forms around the close friendship you and Catherine built with George and Mary Helen Hartman when you all lived in Mobile, Alabama, years ago. When Tick was born, you and Catherine agreed to be the child's godparents, understanding that the Hartmans had no living relatives. In their will, they named you as Tick's guardian. Keep your explanations simple. The documentation will back you up.

"We will go over all of this with you many times until you have locked it in your brain."

Brad interrupted, "Is this story even plausible? Did you come up with this sad story yourself?"

"Well, who could believe Tick's *real* story?" Brewer said defensively, and not waiting for a reply, he continued, "Ruth Evers, the head of the National Center for the Analysis of Violent Crime in Quantico, Virginia, is behind the story. She is now heading up this case. She was openly opposed to the bureau's decision to separate you from Tick and get her out of Utah, voicing her opinion to anyone who would listen."

Pausing, he added, "Evers knew that the bureau's plan, headed up by Dr. Palmer, would never work and that Tick would never accept it, but they overruled her. This is the back-up plan she and her team have been working on for weeks, convinced that you and Tick would need a cover story to remain in Utah."

"Forgive my cynicism, Steve. I appreciate all the effort that went into this plan for our sake. Don't mind me."

Brad listened as Brewer continued. "We have a draft of the Hartman obituary for you. Tick will need to memorize your cover story as well. You must always produce the same explanations."

Brad read the obituary. It described the Hartmans as Christian missionaries working throughout the South, but it provided no specific religious affiliation. It was purposely vague, written so that it would be difficult for anyone to check out the story's veracity. And should Tick ever be questioned about being raised by missionaries, her impressive knowledge of the Bible would be quite persuasive and proof enough.

"It seems you have covered most of the bases, Steve. Let's call it quits for today. My head feels like it's going to explode, and I still have quite a bit to do before it gets too late."

"Sure, Brad, I understand, but there is one more thing we need to discuss. I understand that you will be speaking to your family tonight, so I suggest you let them know that you're home, safe and sound. Don't tell them about Tick yet. Just allow the cover story to fall into place."

Brad abruptly cut Brewer off at this point, voicing his objection to being told what he should say to his sons. "Sorry, Steve. Where my sons are concerned, I'll deal with them as I choose, and that's not negotiable. I'm planning on telling them what's really been going on here."

Brewer protested, "Do you realize the risk you would be taking by telling them about Tick, Brad? If word of Tick's identity gets out, then the two of you will be forced into a formal witness protection program. That means cutting your ties with your entire family and everyone you know. Please reconsider."

Before Brad could respond, Nate Hoger spoke up, "Listen, Steve, we're dealing with family dynamics here. It's a good guess that these boys aren't stupid. They're going to sense something's not right. Look, his sons know about the rescue. They also know her rescue occurred near the route their dad was taking that day. The boys haven't heard from Brad since the day of that rescue because, oh, right, he took off to South America. They're smart kids, they know their dad and figure he's lying to them, and they will get to the truth sooner or later."

"You're right, Nate," Brad said. "They already know I've been lying to them, and it stops today."

"Tell you what," Nate added, "I'll prepare a briefing report for your sons, Brad, and begin working with them as soon as you have spoken to them. I will make sure that they understand the importance of security."

Brad gave Hoger an appreciative nod.

Brewer continued, "One final thing, at Dr. Barnes's request, we will be providing her with several files related to this investigation, and she has permission to share the files with you. They include Tick's school records and confidential information on Timothy Bird. We hope that these reports will be useful information as you and Dr. Barnes help Tick sort through her years at the ranch, and that Tick will be forthcoming with any information that can help us."

"Of course," said Brad. "We have every reason to help you."

Finally, around noon, the agents departed. The focus shifted to getting some lunch before setting up the audio-visual conference that Brad's secretary and Laura had arranged with Brad's family later that afternoon.

For the first time since his life-altering encounter with Tick on a Uinta mountain ledge, Brad sat in front of his computer and began to gather his thoughts. He wanted to summarize his experience and create a timeline that he could refer to as he spoke to his children. As was his custom when preparing for any talk with time-related information, Brad started with the dates. Then, he added bullet points that might be pertinent to any discussion he might want to include.

Oct 5:	*Decided to go on a hike*
	Had to cancel sales meeting on the sixth
	Told boys of hiking plans
Oct 6:	*Started the hike*
Oct 9:	*Found Tick on the ledge*
Oct 11:	*Helicopter rescue—transferred to hospital*

Brad stopped for a moment and peered over at Tick. "Tick, do you remember what day we held the first interview with the FBI? Was it on the sixteenth or seventeenth of October?"

Tick looked up from a book she was reading and wrote, "*The 17ᵗʰ.*"

Oct 25:   *CPS / Tick's fall*

Brad would never forget that day.

Oct 28:   Transferred from the Critical Care Unit
back to The Palace.

"What day did they put you in the cast? Do you remember?"

Exasperated, and without looking up from her book, Tick rolled her eyes and wrote, "*Nov 8.*"

Nov 14:   Decided to adopt Tick
Problems with FBI
Hunger strike
Nov 21:   Adoption approved

With a grin on his face, Brad badgered Tick once again. "Do you remember the date the adoption went through?"

Tick's eyes jumped from her book, and upon seeing he was laughing at her, she grinned back, writing, "*Stop asking me stupid questions. Can't you see I'm trying to read!*"

Forty-five days, he thought. *If I include the day I found her, I've been with her for forty-five days, and I now have a daughter, who, in addition to trying to kill me, talks back and rolls her eyes at me. Unbelievable!*

Brad chuckled to himself and then got back to work.

Looking ahead, Brad wouldn't get Tick home until January. She would be in her cast at the FBI safe house for at least five weeks, possibly six. Then there would be another two weeks in the hospital for her ankle surgery and following that, home—but facing as much as six months of physical therapy.

She probably won't be squared away until midsummer of next year, Brad thought.

Nov 23:	*Move to safe house, set up a false FBI story*
Dec 9–11:	*We should probably plan for Alissa's funeral*
	Need to give boys a heads-up
Dec 21–29:	*The body cast should come off*
Late December:	*Back for ankle surgery?*
Mid-Jan:	*Home, finally*
Physical therapy:	*Six months? June/July*

Brad figured that he had four important undertakings to tackle:

- First, he had to tell his children about Tick. He would be facing that hurdle later in the afternoon.
- Next, he had to schedule the FBI's anxiously anticipated interview with Tick. It would be good to get that over with as soon as possible—possibly even in the coming week.
- Then, he had to talk to Ana and call his contractor.
- Finally, he needed to plan a meaningful, Christian burial for Tick's mother. He would need to talk to Mattie.

Glancing over at Tick immersed in her book, he said, "We are going to get you home before the New Year, and by next July, you'll be fully operational."

"*Oh?*" wrote Tick. "*I will be up and running long before that.*"

No wonder Mattie and Brackford want to keep you in a hospital, thought Brad.

You Have a Sister

Laura prearranged the multi-party visual conference with Brad's three sons and the two daughters-in-law, coordinating schedules within three time zones. She set up the meeting for 3:00 p.m. Mountain Standard Time. Because Mattie had patients to care for during the early afternoon, she asked Laura to deliver a new outfit for Tick—a light blue skirt with a crisp white blouse that Mattie had purchased the day before. It would be up to Laura to dress Tick and have her ready to meet five Hughes family members through the magic of split-screen viewing.

Hours later, when she had finished her rounds shortly before the scheduled call, Mattie crossed over to The Palace to find Tick ready and looking as pretty as a picture. Her short blond hair and the white-collar of the blouse framed her delicate features and gorgeous eyes.

"You look just beautiful," Mattie said honestly. "They are going to love you."

Brad was there, quietly reviewing notes he had made in preparation for the meeting. He planned to talk to his family, first by himself to tell his story, and then introduce Deputy Chief Nate Hoger and Agent Steve Brewer. They would handle covering the security implications of Tick's adoption and go over the planned cover story. With the preliminaries over, he would bring Tick in and introduce her to the family. He knew this would be the most important presentation he had ever made in his life, and he was nervous.

"It's nearly time, Mattie. I'm going to go and get situated in the conference room. Laura texted me and said everything was ready to get started." He then gave Tick a thumbs-up. "I'll be back to get you soon, sweetheart. Today is a wonderful day for the Hughes family!"

Mattie walked with Brad from The Palace to the old conference room down the hall, doing her best to bolster this man who was about to face what could amount to a firing squad.

"Take a few deep breaths now, Brad. You could always make it easy on yourself right out of the gate by telling your family that you'd like the opportunity to speak first without interruption. Then, once you've finished revealing the truth about where you have been all these weeks, the hard part is over, like ripping the sticky Band-Aid off fast."

It was good to hear Brad laugh at that, so Mattie felt safe to give him another bit of counseling.

"Carefully listen to what each of them has to say before responding. Don't assume that your kids will eagerly leap into the new family picture you have created. Remember that you have been with Tick every day for weeks, and your decision to adopt her didn't exactly happen overnight. The truth is, you left your sons way behind when you took off on your hike in the mountains, and it's going to take time for them to catch up to you."

Stopping at the conference room door, Brad answered, "The boys' mother had an extremely kind and forgiving nature. I think this would be the perfect time to see those same qualities shine through."

With a consoling pat on his back, Mattie said, "Be patient, don't push, and don't get upset if the boys' reaction is less than ecstatic. From what you've told me, your sons are fine young men, and they will want what's best for you."

"They are, but I just don't know what to expect when they meet Tick. I'm counting on you to step in if you sense the conversation starts heading downhill. I don't want Tick hurt by anything said today. Also, as we discussed, be completely open about Tick's medical issues, and if it works for you, let them know that they can call you later if they have any questions. I think they might feel freer to talk to you than to me about concerns they might have about their new sister. I've hidden enough from them."

"Of course, I'm fine with that," assured Mattie. "Our attorney, Andrew Therber, is okay with the release forms you executed. I'm free to speak openly."

Brad stepped into the conference room and closed the door. Mattie, believing that the exact opposite of love is indifference, speculated he was in for a grilling if his family cared for him as much he cared for them. She wondered how long round one would last and prayed for a good outcome.

Meanwhile, she had a job to do: keeping Tick as calm and relaxed as possible under very intimidating circumstances. She wanted Tick to understand that her dad had some fence-mending to do and that the family would need some time to process the idea of having a new adopted sister.

She would explain that change was often difficult for people, and a less than enthusiastic response would be perfectly normal and not a reflection on her. Fortunately, Tick was quite capable of being dispassionately analytical. If Mattie could prepare her for the conference call as a case study, Tick might be more inclined to observe the process more objectively rather than being caught up in it.

Tick, Laura, and Mattie spent the time coming up with various ways to distract themselves from going crazy until Brad returned. Mattie watched Tick shuffle cards like she was a Las Vegas dealer. Impressed but not intimidated, Laura was the veteran blackjack player, declaring herself the Texas Hold 'Em poker champ. When Brad walked back into The Palace, three distinctly nervous expressions greeted him, so he quickly raised both thumbs, smiled broadly, and said, "Come on, Tick! Let's take a ride down the hall!"

Tick asked to stop in the bathroom first, and while Laura helped her, Brad and Mattie had a moment to talk.

"Good to see you're still in one piece," Mattie said. "How did it go?"

"We're going to get through this," Brad replied. "My sons are all good, well-meaning men. But as you said, they need time to process what they've just learned."

Mattie could see the strain behind his game face. "I take it you disclosed everything that has taken place from the beginning?"

"Well…an accurate summary, I'd say, not so much on all the details. Becky and Natalie thought I had been hiding a serious illness from the family, and they have all been anxious about me. Ben, Brian, and David had all decided that I wasn't hiding a health issue. They figured that I had become involved with another woman and didn't want them to know about it."

"How prophetic." Mattie chuckled.

"They weren't too far off the mark," Brad admitted. "Anyway, after telling the boys what happened on my hike and where I've been since October, they battered me with questions, and honestly, I don't have answers for much of it… There are still so many unknowns out there for all of us, especially the threat of Timothy Bird."

Brad took a step closer to Mattie and lowered his voice, careful that no one should overhear.

"Having Hoger and Brewer speak to them hasn't made this whole situation easier. What they said about Bird was disquieting for the family to hear, of course, but keeping the truth from them and the FBI's plan to protect us is not an option."

"Do you think this is all too much for them to handle, Brad?"

"Well, let's face it, I've just launched them all into the twilight zone. Hoger tried to reassure Becky and Natalie that the chance of Timothy Bird harming their families was close to zero, but they are all understandably concerned for their kids. The important thing right now is that everyone understands the cover story and the need to keep Tick's real identity secret, even from their children and extended family members."

Mattie nodded in agreement.

"Here's something worth recapping. After I told them about my hike, all three boys said that they're proud of me for rescuing Tick. When he compared my hiking plan's coordinates with the reported rescue location, Brian wondered if I could be the unidentified hiker. When my texts from South America didn't mention rescuing a young girl, he dropped the notion."

"And where do they stand as far as the adoption goes?" Mattie whispered. "They all questioned why I adopted her," Brad responded. "My youngest, David, said that I didn't give such an important matter enough time or thought, and he wanted to know what makes me think that I am up to or prepared to raise a twelve-year-old girl."

Brad winked at Tick as she exited the bathroom with Laura, and then he quietly whispered to Mattie, "I'm not so sure of that myself… Let's go, Tick. They're waiting and eager to meet you!"

Mattie and Brad wheeled Tick into the conference room. Brad was nervous but inordinately proud of his girl and couldn't wait for his kids to meet her. He wanted Tick to feel genuinely welcomed by her new family.

Mattie took her seat, slightly off to the side, but close enough to see the monitor. The screen was divided into four boxes, with Brad's three sons and their wives getting their first glimpse of Tick as she and Brad settled into view.

The Hughes boys were all handsome, obviously related, taking after their father with similar eyes and stature. Both daughters-in-law were pretty, stylish-looking young women, and all five locked their eyes on Tick as she came into view—a stranger who their father had just claimed as his daughter. From the expressions on their faces, they were surprised by Tick's looks.

Natalie, Brian's wife, a Mississippi farm girl, spoke up first with nervous enthusiasm, "Hello, Tick! Welcome to the Hughes tribe. Goodness, Dad must have been hiking high in the mountains close to God to find you! Sweetie, you might be the prettiest little girl I have ever seen. Dad didn't mention how extraordinarily beautiful you are. Just that you are better than sunshine."

Brad laughed, thankful for Natalie's welcoming exuberance. "She's pretty inside *and* out," he responded. "So," Brad began, "I think introductions are in order."

Brad reached for the pencil on the desk and began pointing out and naming each family member, all the while speaking quietly to Tick.

"That's Ben, my oldest, and his wife, Becky. This is my middle son, Brian, and his wife, Natalie, and that's David in this box by himself. He used to be my youngest, but now you are."

Taking Tick's hand in his and lifting their hands together, Brad said, "Family, I am thrilled and so proud to introduce Tick Esther Hughes. Tick became one of the family yesterday in an adoption ceremony at the hospital. The Honorable Judge Thornton presided. Tick, these are your brothers and their wives, your two sisters-in-law."

Tick smiled, hearing the chorus of responsive voices saying hello to her.

Looking over at Mattie, Brad continued, "This is Dr. Mattie Barnes, who has been responsible for Tick's care as well as for treating my minor injuries. Mattie is a specialist in pediatric critical care with matching skills in child psychiatry. Mattie saved Tick's life, healed our injuries, cooked special meals for us, and has kept both of us under her thumb and on track over these past weeks. She is a great friend to us. Nobody could have taken better care of us. She has agreed to remain as Tick's primary care doctor, at least for the short term."

A choir of friendly greetings filled the room again, and Mattie politely acknowledged both couples and David. She then sat back, watching as the boys and their wives began to address Tick. It was a good beginning; the family, wanting to get to know the girl, shared information about themselves—where they lived, what they did, and all about their children. Mattie observed that no family member expressed any misgivings about Tick's newly adopted status, the group treading lightly and helping to make her feel at ease. Mattie could see that this family was, unquestionably, a remarkably sensitive, classy bunch. Knowing Brad, she had suspected as much all along.

"Guys, as I mentioned to you, Tick is not able to speak. Her doctors believe this is a temporary condition, but for the time being, she uses computers to communicate, and she's a wiz on them, so I'll just let her say hello to all of you."

Realizing that it was now her turn to speak, Tick's expression became fixed on the computer keyboard as she began rapidly typing out a message, one that astonished the family:

Thank you so much for this gathering and for being so nice to me. I enjoyed hearing about your lives and what your kids are up to, and I feel honored to be part of your family.

I promise I won't be a burden to your father. I promise I will carry my weight with household chores and responsibilities. I will study and work hard to become financially independent and pay back any money spent on my care, and I never expect or desire to inherit anything.

Brad interrupted, "Hold on, Tick. Give me a minute here, guys, will you?" He then turned to Tick, speaking softly. "Hey, my beautiful girl, you're doing great, and I'm so proud of you, but I need to speak just to you for a minute before we go on with the others." Tick nodded her head as Brad reached over to turn her chair enough to face him.

"I understand why thinking of me as your father and figuring out what that should mean might take some time for you to sort out, but I'm asking you to trust me again and begin imagining your life now as the beginning of a new story. I want you to lose the notion that I would ever think of you as a burden. You need to remove all thoughts of having to earn your keep or pay me back. The blessing I have received from God that allowed me to adopt you as my daughter is all and everything I could ask for."

Tick responded by nervously running her fingers through her hair as Brad continued talking to her, unaware that the microphone was still on and his family, now transfixed, were listening to every word he said.

"Your only, and I mean your only, job for now and years to come will be going to school and doing your best there. Other than that, I want you to enjoy your life, to explore the things that interest you, and to develop your God-given talents and abilities. Hopefully, this will take you to college and beyond, but we'll take that one step at a time."

The awkward silence that followed ended when David Hughes broke in with a whoop.

"Wow, Tick, you just got Lecture 101, and you have only been in our family for a day! I have to say, though, he cut you some real slack. He never told me to enjoy my life and have fun. Maybe it's because you're a girl?"

Brian and Ben chimed in, clearly amused, "That's because you never concentrated on very much except girls and goofing off, David!"

As the boys and their wives stumbled over themselves trying to assure Tick that the last thing on their minds was the division of their dad's assets, and promising that there would never be an issue over "stuff," as they put it, Mattie was struggling not to laugh out loud. She finally stepped in to end the meeting.

"Okay, okay. I have a very worn-out patient here who has had quite a week. I have a few more things to add before we wrap this up for tonight. Repeating what your dad has probably already told you, Tick will be in her present cast for another five to six weeks. She faces ankle surgery as soon as her body cast comes off. The bones in her ankle need resetting from a previous break. Then there is a lot of rehabilitation to face, muscles to rebuild. I've told Tick that she can expect to be fully rehabilitated in six or seven months if, of course, she doesn't overdo. This little gal doesn't always know when to stop."

Tick didn't appreciate looking irresponsible in front of the family, but she sat still, consciously avoiding an angry-looking glance in Mattie's direction.

"I'm sure all of you have enough to think about to keep you up all night. Since I suspect you would like more time to talk with your dad and Tick, I suggest you set up another conference call, and if you have any questions for me, please give my assistant, Laura, a call, and she'll set up a good time for us to talk."

Brad also said his goodbyes. "I hope you all understand now why I have only been responding to your calls with bogus text messages, but please feel free to call me at any time now, okay? I love you all more than I can say, and thank you for being so great with Tick. We'll talk tomorrow."

In unison, Brad's sons said, "Okay, Dad. We love you too."

Brad, Mattie, and Tick left the room and began their trek down the hall toward the Palace.

"So, Mattie, how do you think it went?"

"Better than anyone could expect, Brad. You've just handed them the biggest surprise of their lives, but all three sons and your two daughters-in-law reacted thoughtfully and maturely. I'm very impressed. Tick, you must have felt terrified meeting your new family like that, but you did so well. I'm proud of you. Your new family is pretty special, so be patient and give them a chance to get to know their new sister. I know they're going to love you."

Tick showed no emotion as they wheeled her back to the room. Arriving, she wrote another note and handed it to Brad, "*I thought a lot about what to say to your family. The Bible is filled with stories of lives destroyed through covetousness and anger over possessions and money, cheating on their inheritances. I don't want anything besides what you have already done for me, and I don't want to cause problems.*"

"Tick, you are my daughter, not my financial advisor," Brad said with exasperation. "It's my money, and if I want to spend it on you, then that's my business, not yours. Understand?"

Not willing to give up, Tick wrote something for Mattie to read, "*What do you think?*"

Mattie wrote back in letters large enough for Brad to read: "Ephesians 6:1."

Brad laughed as he looked at Mattie. "That's one of your know-your-scriptures games that I can answer. 'Children, obey your parents in the Lord, for this is right.' It's great advice!" he exclaimed, watching Tick fix her eyes on Mattie in a way that suggested the subject of Brad's earthly possessions wasn't over.

Then, just as Mattie was leaving, Tick signaled her over, away from Brad. "*That wasn't fair,*" she wrote. "*I can honor him, but that doesn't mean he will always be right. Money is always an issue, and I don't want to be the cause of any strife or cause any trouble.*"

Mattie thought to herself, *Darling, you've managed to redefine the word trouble at this hospital…*

Then, she spoke very quietly, "You're right. As the years pass, your dad won't always be correct, but he will always have your back and act in what he feels is your best interest. As for your concern about family members ever resenting sharing their inheritance, I think you underestimate them. You may have overlooked an even bigger issue going on in their heads right now: I suspect that Brad's sons love their dad very much, so their biggest concern, whether they can verbalize it or not, might be the fear that you've replaced them. They may be worried about losing some of their dad's affection, not his money. They've been asked to share their father with you, and that's a big deal."

Tick scribbled again. *"What can I do about that?"*

"Really nothing, Tick," replied Mattie. "Your father is a fair, loving man and sensitive to what is going on. If there are any insecure or hurt feelings, he will smooth things over, but the boys know that their dad loves them. Your role is now just to be Tick Hughes. When the family is visiting and all get together, be friendly and helpful, play with the grandchildren, and don't contribute to or add unnecessary drama. Just be yourself. As far as being supported financially by your father, that's what fathers do. They provide and protect. That's an age-old tradition, kiddo. And after all, it's only money. We both know God doesn't put much stock in that."

Mattie returned a few hours later to cook a celebratory dinner. Every aspect of the meal was picture-perfect as usual. Sneaking a bottle of wine into The Palace was breaking the no-alcohol policy at the hospital. Still, since Mattie had already stretched a career's worth of rules for Brad and Tick, she rationalized that enjoying one glass of wine with Brad was pardonable.

She also had a large, beautifully wrapped box for Tick. Aside from Jelly Cat, it was the first gift-wrapped present Tick had received since she was five years old. Tick didn't tear into the wrapping but disassembled it as though it was beyond precious, carefully folding ribbon and wrapping as though she was planning on preserving it all forever. She prudently opened the box's lid and examined the contents. Carefully folded nestled three new outfits—two casual outfits and a dressy pink shift. There was a colorful pair of gym shoes, and a stylish pair of black ballet flats lined the bottom of the box.

Tick simply didn't know how to react. She wrote Mattie a hasty thank you, then spent the evening dreamily examining her new clothing. Mattie could see how happy she was.

Mattie left early that night. She was tired and feeling generally anxious, but not about the Hughes family. Her ward was full of struggling children, and the most pressing case was a young boy who had developed complications following a heart valve replacement. She spent the next morning and into the afternoon in the ward, not dropping by her office until about one o'clock.

Laura reported that Ben Hughes, Brad's oldest son, had called requesting a conference call. "I told him that you wouldn't be available to take a call until five."

"That should work," Mattie consented. "I have some paperwork to do now, but then I'll run home and pull a meal together for Tick and Brad and be back before five o'clock."

Precisely at five, Mattie's phone rang. Ben, Becky, Brian, Natalie, and David Hughes were all on the line politely saying their hellos.

Ben spoke out first. "We appreciate that you are taking the time to talk to us, Dr. Barnes, and we hope this time is convenient for you."

"It is," Mattie replied. "Have you all spent more time talking to your father?"

"Not yet," Ben said. "We wanted to talk to you first. Dad isn't much on details. If he thinks we're pushing too hard, then he's apt to pull rank and close the conversation down. Dad can be quite stubborn."

Mattie chuckled. "I've noticed that side of him."

Ben replied, "That's why we've called you, Dr. Barnes. We still have so many questions. This whole thing feels surreal."

"Of course it would, Ben. You have just learned some staggering facts about where your father has been all these weeks: the circumstance that landed him here at Children's Hospital in the first place and what has occurred since then. I'm sure your heads are spinning. I'm also certain that adopting a child who has introduced a fair amount of turmoil into your dad's life dumbfounds you. I may not be able to answer all of your questions about Tick. Your father has more experience with her than I do. But rest assured, if there is something I can't answer for you, I will encourage your dad to provide the necessary details."

Ben then asked, "What happened to Dad over there at the hospital? He mentioned he had been injured. Is he all right?"

"A few weeks after your father rescued Tick, the FBI decided to separate him from Tick and to move Tick into protective custody. Tick was running after your father when she fell over a staircase. Your dad saved her life by breaking her fall, but he dislocated his shoulder and suffered a concussion in the process. He has fully recovered from his injuries, and I can assure you that his thinking is as clear now as it was before the accident."

"But," Brian broke in, "the papers reported that the girl… Tick…fell as she was attempting to escape the hospital. That she attacked a CPS worker."

"Don't believe everything you read, Brian," Mattie replied. "Tick's actions were entirely innocent. I'm not allowed to talk about it because the matter is in litigation, but you will eventually learn what happened."

Ben continued, "What about Tick, can you tell us more about her injuries?"

"Tick's condition as a result of her fall was grave. Her injuries were much more severe than your dad's. She sustained a difficult to repair pelvic shear, along with a badly broken femur and a fractured arm. The injuries extended to internal organs and blood vessels. The good news is that she is recovering much faster than all of us on her medical team anticipated. I would say that her overall condition is good. I will also say that the outlook for her full recovery is favorable.

"Just to make it clear, your father has saved Tick's life twice. His actions and the many sacrifices he has made have been extraordinary. Has your father told you anything?"

"Not much at all," answered Ben. "He just told us that he found Tick on a ledge and that she took a fall in the hospital. As I said, he doesn't go into details."

"I assumed he had told you more than that. But in all fairness, the FBI kept your dad isolated and restricted his communications with the outside world. You should know, he bucked the authorities hard for the okay to even tell you the truth of where he's been."

Uncomfortable with how defensive of Brad her comment sounded, Mattie quickly added, "Nevertheless, he owes you a better picture of these past weeks. He may need a bit more time to do that, guys. The stories are quite remarkable and will help you understand why he did what he did. They're not my stories to tell, but I can assure you, you should all be quite proud of him."

"About Tick's inability to speak, is that a permanent condition? Dad doesn't think so."

"We have not found any physical cause for her inability to speak, Ben. She enunciates words when she is dreaming, indicating a psychological response mechanism to trauma is in play. That's all I know at this point, but it's most certainly not related to any mental deficiency. We haven't tested her yet, but Tick's IQ may well be in the genius range. She's that intelligent."

"Last night, you told us that Dad needs our support. Can you be more specific? In what ways does he need us?"

"Again, your dad will have to talk with you about what he needs or expects from his family. Of course, his desire to raise a well-adjusted, happy individual will have a better chance of happening if Tick's family—you guys—is *there* for both of them. Show up for family gatherings as often as your lives allow, and behave as you normally do when you are together. Tick has led a very harsh, isolated life since her abduction seven years ago. She has no experience in a normal family environment and has just lost her mother. Simplistic as it sounds, accepting her as an important member of your family is the first step in developing a relationship. Of course, the history you build with anyone is not always a fifty-fifty proposition. You may have to give more than you get for a while."

Ben, laughing, said, "Becky and I have noticed that. We have three kids."

Then Natalie, Brian's wife, spoke up, "I can't begin to comprehend what this poor little girl has had to endure, and my heart just aches to know what a horrible existence she's been living, but what are we to think about all the bad things we've read about her?

Could she have killed people at that ranch? And what about how she attacked those folks at the hospital? I'm sorry that I feel so unsure about her, but I'm kind of worried that our kids might not be safe around her if she has a violent temper."

Mattie paused. She knew that her growing commitment to Tick could not overshadow an honest, responsible reply.

"Tick is extremely loyal, and her devotion to your dad is what binds her. Her aggressive behavior, when she has felt threatened, suggests something similar to wolf pack mentality. She protects and wants to be with her own. The fact that you are all part of Brad's pack, to use that analogy, means that her loyalty and devotion will extend to you as well. I have observed Tick closely for many weeks under many trying conditions, and I am convinced that she would never physically hurt any of you. If anything, she may be overprotective."

A silence intruded at the end of the line when Ben spoke. "Comparing Tick to a wolf is rather troubling, Dr. Barnes. Are you saying she could be violent toward others?"

Mattie reluctantly replied, "Yes, if she feels threatened. Tick has begun adjusting to her new world and has shown remarkable restraint on at least one occasion. However, she still exhibits visible signs of aggression through her body language, and she's a long way from being submissive. In practical terms, if one of your children is being bullied, at this point, I believe she would intervene, perhaps to an extreme. You should know that the authorities suspect she is very skilled in the martial arts. We plan to reintroduce her to the world in a controlled setting carefully, and that would include the support of a loving family."

David was finally motivated to respond. "Man, it sounds like Dad adopted the Hulk's daughter. Does she turn green too?"

"Be nice," the oldest brother chided. "Weren't you the one who threw all those seniors in the pool just because they hazed you for being a little squirt freshman? And I remember that you got us all mixed up in the fights that followed."

"Oh, yeah, but remember that they threw me in first!"

Ben's wife Becky interrupted tentatively. "She's very intense. She studied us. We all felt it. It was a bit unnerving."

Mattie was amused at the notion and allowed herself a laugh. "I can assure you she was very nervous. She's just an expert at hiding it. Tick is extremely alert and exceptionally observant—those are survival traits that served her well in captivity. Everybody who has worked with her has felt as though they were under her microscope. It's all about gaining her trust. But once won, you will find there's this extremely enchanting girl who surprises you with her energetic, exuberant, and inquisitive mind."

"But you've only known her for a short time," said Becky. "How can you have any confidence she won't be difficult...drugs, alcohol, who knows, she could end up being a delinquent?"

"Don't misunderstand me, but I don't have confidence that *your* children won't develop a substance abuse problem or engage in risky behavior at some point in their lives. Even children raised in wonderful, loving homes can fall victim to these problems. Likewise, Tick's traumatic years should not determine her destiny. But it's safe to say that your father will never ignore unacceptable behavior, as you probably may well know, and will get all the help Tick needs to become a fully functioning, successful adult."

Natalie jumped in. "So it sounds like you think Tick could turn out to be a normal girl? That makes me feel better."

Mattie paused. "Well, I'm not sure what you mean by 'normal.' Tick is a one-of-a-kind, remarkable survivor, and I believe that, down the road, she will make the Hughes family very proud. Her physical and emotional recovery will not happen overnight, however. She remains very guarded about her life at the ranch, so, through intensive therapy, some painful ground will have to be covered before those wounds heal. Having a family that is continually supportive will give her the best chance of having a *normal*, healthy life."

"Why do you think my single, fifty-eight-year-old father would make such a radical decision to adopt a twelve-year-old girl with so much baggage?" David spoke up in a critical voice. "I mean, nobody could accuse my dad of being your typical wealthy old fart out to impress the townsfolk by driving too fast in a Porsche, but should we be concerned that he is going through some kind of emotional crisis of his own?"

"That's not a simple question, so there's no simple answer. Is your father bipolar or functioning under some psychotic episode? No. We know he doesn't have a brain tumor because he had an MRI of his head after the accident. So the question remains, why? Again, I suggest that you ask him. And you should take some time and think about the personality traits your dad possesses as well as his faith in God. I think you'll come up with some answers of your own."

Brian, the oldest and most grounded of the three sons, said, "Our father is nobody's fool, and I trust that he knows exactly what he is doing and why. Hey, David, you need to back off and give Dad and Tick some consideration."

"She certainly adores your father, David," Mattie added, "and your father has frequently told me that there is something extraordinary about Tick. I share his feelings. She is brave and wise beyond her years, and it's been a joy getting to know her."

"She certainly is a beautiful girl," commented Natalie. "Her eyes are spectacular. She's terribly thin. Will the scar on her face fade?"

"Yes, the scar is already fading, and I agree, she is a stunning girl. As I said before, she's gaining weight. I know you all still have many questions, but I urge you to discuss your concerns with your father. I'll be on the floor tomorrow if you need to speak to me, but I want you all to relax and keep your minds open for positive thoughts."

Before she could hang up, Becky asked her final question. "You care for her, don't you?"

"I'd like to think I care about all my patients," Mattie responded.

"That's not what I mean."

"I know...and the answer is yes, I do."

After saying their goodbyes, Mattie hung up the phone feeling distinctly and uncomfortably sad. Brad's family would come to terms with the adoption and start to accept, if not rally around, Tick. As a physician, this was the time to feel genuine satisfaction—to feel a mission-accomplished wave of relief—and then move on to the next patient needing her care.

I should be happy, Mattie thought to herself, not willing to give any power to feelings of emptiness and loss.

Pulling away from her desk, the memory of seeing her grandmother's house years after its sale entered her mind. She remembered standing in the once-formal living room, where friends and family had gathered for special occasions, where fancy hors d'oeuvres were passed on silver platters and white wine poured into crystal stemmed glasses.

Now, sporting equipment, basketballs, hockey sticks, helmets, team jerseys, and dirty socks littered the carpeted floor.

She remembered feeling heartsick as she stood in the current owner's dining room, a room where a mahogany dining table, a china cabinet, and buffet once filled the space. It was a room where beautiful and costly wallpaper had hung, where sterling silver serving pieces and crystal glassware sparkled in the light from a picture window draped in silk.

Now, an enormous train trestle, complete with a paper-mache mountain range, stood on an oversized plywood tabletop in the center of the room, and holes cut through the living and dining room walls allowed a model train the freedom to make inappropriate trips around the house.

Mattie prided herself for unemotional, almost stoical behavior, but remembering how different the house looked underscored the sadness of missing her family and moments lost in time when she had been so happy. A different family was now making their memories. Grandmother's house had become a fun and lively home for this family. With or without one's consent, life goes on, Mattie knew. Somewhere along the line, family life had left her behind.

Get a grip on yourself, Dr. Barnes, Mattie scolded under her breath, looking blankly out the window.

Turning Tick over to her new family, it seemed, was not going to be so easy for her.

Can the FBI Be Trusted?

Shutting down his thoughts in an attempt to sleep that night was impossible for Brad. He knew his alarm clock would sound off at 3:00 a.m., heralding immense changes to his and Tick's lives. Also troubling was his family's reaction to recent cover-story indoctrination sessions with the FBI—a family that was now all too aware of the threat Timothy Bird represented: information that had not gone over particularly well with the wives. Other changes were in store; he and Tick were about to be transferred to another location to allow enough time for the cover story to fall into place. He didn't like The Palace, but he would miss Mattie and her staff.

The FBI fabrication began with Brad's return to his Salt Lake office from Peru, only to be called away again for another bogus trip, this time to Florida. He would return with and, subsequently, adopt an injured and orphaned daughter of friends killed in a car crash. The story played over and over in Brad's mind, but he couldn't improve on it.

At 4:00 a.m., he would make his way down a Walker building stairway to be picked up by Agent Jenny Dresder, who would drive him to a safe house on a military base.

Tick's path to be reunited with Brad was more involved. The plan was to load Tick onto an ambulance later that morning and transport her to the Salt Lake City International Airport. There, a twin-turboprop King Air 200 ambulance was waiting to ostensibly fly Esther Morgan somewhere back East, away from Utah to a new life far away.

Fortunately, Judge Thornton had granted Tick the opportunity to lead an entirely different life—she would never board that plane. Houdini's magic would take place at a selected airport hangar hidden from prying eyes by corrugated steel walls. A very slight female FBI agent, fitted with a fake pink cast encompassing her hips and left leg, her face hidden from public view by a headscarf, would transmute into Tick. The decoy would be wheeled in a chair from the hangar and loaded onto the plane. A carefully planned leak to select individuals would alert the press of Esther Morgan's transfer: reporters from behind a fence taking career-enhancing, exclusive pictures of the lone Death Ranch survivor as she boarded the plane.

The plan was to reunite Brad and Tick at the military base later that afternoon after the fake Esther departed—Hoger driving Tick to the base in a nondescript panel van. They would stay at the base until it was time to remove Tick's body cast, some five to six weeks down the road. At that point, Tick Hughes, the injured car wreck survivor from Florida and newly adopted daughter of Brad Hughes, would be admitted into the Children's Hospital orthopedic ward to undergo her badly needed ankle surgery.

When the alarm clock began beeping, Brad got out of bed, dressed, and then whispered goodbye to Tick, who was wide-awake and watching Brad intently. Reluctant to leave his daughter, he gave her a hug and his signature thumbs-up. Reaching the staircase, he stopped and thanked the security guard for the many considerations he and his compatriots had made over the past weeks. Nonetheless, Brad wasn't entirely comfortable about leaving his daughter in the hands of the FBI—too much water had flowed under that bridge. However, knowing that Nate Hoger would be driving the van from the airport to the safe house was reassuring. Nate had become a trusted friend.

As Brad left the building, his breath condensing in the cold November night air, he saw headlights blink on and off from a nearby parked car. As planned, FBI agent Jenny Dresder was there waiting for him.

"Good Morning, Brad," Dresder chirped. "Are you ready for your vacation to begin?"

"I'm not certain if weeks in an army barracks qualifies as a vacation, Agent Dresder," Brad replied, "but I am happy to leave this place. I could use a change of scenery. Thanks for the early morning ride."

Dresder didn't say a word as she drove on Foothill Boulevard toward the freeway entrance. Unexpectedly, she merged onto I-80 east toward Park City—away from Hill Air Force Base, located some forty miles north on I-15.

"Hey, you've taken the wrong exit, agent," Brad quickly spoke up, feeling alarmed. "Was there a change in plans?"

Smiling, Dresder responded, "No worries, Brad. Ruth Evers, the head of profiling at Quantico, is in charge of the case now, and she has implemented some changes to the plan. Good changes, Brad. Don't panic! You and Tick will be tucked away in Deer Valley."

Forty minutes later, Dresder turned into an exclusive, gated community of multi-million dollar homes and the carport of a remarkably built house high on a ridge adjacent to a ski slope. It was the second home of a wealthy couple from Washington D.C., a home nestled in a cluster of similar vacation homes where owners rarely saw each other because they infrequently occupied their homes at the same time. A man, his disabled daughter, and the comings and goings of caregivers would never be noticed by these elite, occasional residents who were mainly concerned about the skiing conditions and whether or not to eat at a restaurant or to have their meal catered and delivered to the house.

Tucked away behind pine trees and the home's façade of massive logs and enormous tinted windows, Tick and Brad would live very comfortably and in complete privacy, able to take in breathtaking views of the mountains. The three-level house was the picture of rustic elegance. The living area held massive, custom-made oak furniture, large leather sofas, comfortable chairs slipcovered in soft linens, beautifully appointed accessories, and oriental rugs. A gourmet kitchen led into the dining area, where built-in glass front china cabinets displayed an impressive array of crystal, silver, and porcelain serving pieces. Above the oak dining table hung an enormous chandelier created out of deer antlers. The first floor spread out under impossibly high ceilings trussed with wooden beams. Electronic controls effortlessly controlled everything: the temperature, fans, drapes and shades, music, and enormous TV screens.

The top floor held the bedrooms, bathrooms, and a large sleeping porch with a domed ceiling that impressively opened to the night sky.

There was a large dressing area with a steam room and shower, where skis, poles, boots, and baskets full of hats, goggles, gloves, and a variety of sunscreens were stored on the lower level. That level also housed a home theater, a wine cellar, and a complete gym with an indoor exercise pool—Tick could exercise to her heart's content—although swimming was out of the question until her cast was removed.

Wheelchair access within such a spacious home would not be an issue, and the estate's elevator could transport Tick to all three floors. An elevator door in the garage would give Tick easy and private access into the house.

"Who is paying for this?" asked Brad. He knew that renting such a world-class home during ski season would cost a fortune.

"I'm not exactly sure," replied Dresder, "but I understand that Judge Thornton knows the owners, and I overheard Evers saying that the FBI will be picking up the tab for Tick's nursing care. No question about it, you are getting the VIP treatment. I think you and Tick have won the hearts of the bureau chiefs."

Brad nodded ruefully. "Or maybe they just want to soften us up before they officially interrogate Tick." Brad was careful to say this under his breath because he liked the place.

Meanwhile, Hoger waited impatiently in the hangar with the Esther Morgan impersonator strapped in a specialized wheelchair. The agent complained nonstop about how uncomfortable and restrictive the cast felt and how exposed and vulnerable she felt. Hoger thought about how many life-threatening, excruciating injuries, procedures, and ungainly castings Tick had endured. Never once had he heard the young girl complain about her discomfort since being found on the mountain—not one time.

Tick is a soldier's soldier, a warrior, he thought. *The exact opposite of this whiny agent.*

Hoger flinched, thinking about what Tick had written to him after being separated from Brad. Her words, "*Hoger, I thought you were my friend,*" stung when Jenny Dresder read Tick's notepad commentary to him days after the Messener catastrophe. Not wanting Tick to spurn him, he went to the hospital the morning after the adoption, determined to clear up any misunderstanding she had.

When he walked into the room that day, Tick looked up at him and, smiling, wrote on her tablet. "*Did you tell the judge that you were going to arrest him for child abuse?*"

Relieved to know that he might be off the hook, Hoger replied, "I want you to know, young lady, that I consider you to be my friend, and that means a lot to me."

Tick looked at him with an exasperated expression and started writing on her pad while Nate continued to plead his case. "I spoke to Judge Thornton days before you wrote that note to me. I want you to know…"

He stopped talking to read the slate that Tick held up and was wiggling vigorously to catch his attention: "*Fiddlesticks! I was never really upset with you. I just wanted to motivate you! By the way, will you drive me from the hanger to the safe house?*"

Give me a break! Nate thought to himself. *You just wanted to motivate me! Explaining myself to this audacious twelve-year-old…am I a sap or what?*

Choosing to leave it alone, he kept his thoughts to himself, congratulated her on becoming Miss Hughes, and said he would consider it a privilege to be her chauffer: just another fan in a long line of people to fall under Tick's spell.

The ambulance arrived, the switch was made, and Hoger greeted the little imp with a smile and a high-five. As the van left the hangar and started up I-80, Tick, securely perched in her wheelchair, didn't show a trace of nervousness. She acted as though the stealthy transfer from ambulance to the windowless van was an ordinary happening.

She pushed from her mind the last ride she had taken in a van, a ride taken at age five—a ride when she had soiled her school clothes, a ride taken tied to her mother, each of them facing years of captivity, abuse, and probable death.

Tick drummed in harmony with the beat of a song on her iPad, seemingly unaffected by her separation from Brad. Catching Nate's eyes in the rearview mirror, Tick smiled and winked at him.

She can be so damn cute and cheeky, he thought. With his attention quickly back on the road, he realized that Brad Hughes had found a real treasure on that mountain.

Forty minutes later, Tick and Nate pulled into the driveway of the safe house. At the entrance to the garage, Brad was anxiously waiting to greet Tick with a hug. Nate and Brad then lowered her wheelchair from the van and into the elevator, where agent Dresder was waiting on the first floor. Then, they all toured the house together.

"*It's like being in paradise,*" Tick wrote as Brad wheeled her from room to room, marveling at the accommodations, the artwork, and the views from the massive windows.

Minutes later, Laura arrived, her car loaded down with medical supplies for Tick's care. Hoger and Dresder stayed long enough to help unload the car and then took off. Laura spent the balance of the day, helping Tick get settled before heading to the local grocery store.

Mattie arrived around dinnertime with takeout Chinese food.

At six o'clock, Mattie, Laura, Brad, and Tick turned on the evening news. The lead story described Esther Morgan's transfer into protective custody that day to "an undisclosed location near the East Coast."

Included in the broadcast were comments made by an FBI spokesman, informing the gathered reporters that Esther Morgan was recovering from her injuries and was now fit to travel. He told the reporters that Esther Morgan was being held blameless for events on the mountain and episodes at the hospital and said that Miss Morgan would be placed with a family at an undisclosed location. He commented that it would be possible for Esther to get a fresh start, free from public scrutiny.

For Brad, hearing the spokesman's statement that Tick would be getting a fresh start was music to his ears. He had returned the FBI's conditions-of-immunity document days ago unsigned, including some major revisions. From the tone of the spokesman on TV, the FBI had capitulated.

After dinner, Laura and Tick settled in to watch a movie. Meanwhile, Brad and Mattie began discussing two important undertakings that had been weighing on Brad's mind. First, he needed to plan a meaningful memorial service and interment for Tick's mother. According to Mattie, Tick would never find closure or fully heal emotionally without taking this step. Alissa's body was in a Salt Lake City morgue, and she deserved a proper Christian burial as soon as possible. Secondly, he needed to arrange Tick's interview with the FBI.

Mattie volunteered Laura's assistance to help plan the funeral, reminding Brad that, because Laura had established a trusting relationship with Tick, their friendship might enable Tick to be more open about what she would like for her mother.

"If you help her with the arrangements, she will feel free to express her ideas," Mattie told Laura. "This needs to be her goodbye, not ours."

The FBI interview was an equally pressing concern; those arrangements needed a quick resolution. The victims' families were impatient to know what had happened at the ranch, and Tick's testimony would be critical to their understanding. Timothy Bird and possibly others were still at large. Perhaps Tick's information could help with their capture. The case was getting colder by the day, and even though Tick was willing and ready to cooperate with the FBI, the interview would likely be quite traumatic for her.

Despite being housed safely away with Brad now in a beautiful home near a swanky ski resort, the interview would take Tick back to the ranch. Undoubtedly, she would have to relive much of her pain-filled life and the monster, Timothy Bird. Perhaps her recollections would take her back to a bloodstained arena, probably back to the run for her life, most certainly to memories of the mother whom she adored and had left behind.

The interview would not be easy for her.

FBI Interview (Terror Tales)

Brad scheduled the FBI interview for November 27, just four days after Tick and Brad's transfer to the Deer Valley house. The interview team would consist of five people, three of whom Tick knew and trusted—Hoger, Brewer, and Dresder, and two additional agents just in from Washington DC.

Brad and Mattie set the ground rules: questions had to be germane, specific to the ongoing investigation. Issues that pushed Tick beyond her comfort zone, such as those involving her relationship with her mother, were off-limits. Tick's responses were strictly voluntary, and if Tick became overly distressed, the meeting would be terminated.

With Brad's input, Mattie carefully planned the details for the interview, with Tick's well-being of utmost consideration. It would take place in the living room at the Deer Valley safe house. Tick would communicate on her iPad linked to a large Samsung HD TV on the wall. The agents could read Tick's response to each question as she typed it out on her keypad, and the agency would provide Brad a copy of the recorded interview.

Nate Hoger and the FBI agents arrived at 9:00 a.m. in a black Cadillac Escalade. As they stepped out of the elevator, Brad greeted his three acquaintances: Nate Hoger, Steve Brewer, and Jenny Dresder. Agent Brewer introduced Brad, Mattie, and Tick to the Washington newcomers Butch Parker and his superior, Agent Ruth Evers, the most senior FBI profiler at the National Center for the Analysis of Violent Crime located in Quantico, Virginia.

The FBI inner circle had grown larger on this faltering case, and the two high-powered newcomers were total strangers to Brad and Tick. Could they be trusted? Would they try to impugn Tick's reputation or use her as a scapegoat? Their approach with Tick would reveal much, but Brad began taking mental notes, while Mattie, a skilled observer, began sizing them up without being too obvious. Sooner or later, they would show their true colors.

Butch Parker was a tall, gray-haired man in his late fifties. Parker had been in law enforcement all of his life, active in many of the FBI's highest-profile investigations. Parker was a tireless worker, a professional, but a cynic, trusting few people. When Evers was promoted over him five years ago, it was a blow to his ego at first, but he had come to enjoy working with his new boss. *Once in a while, although rarely in Washington, the system got it right.* He would take a bullet for her now.

Ruth Evers was a star within the FBI's inner circle, with an uncanny feeling for people and their motivations. She had spent countless hours studying the tapes of Tick and Brad. Upon learning the agency's plans to separate the two, Evers had gone to the mat in opposition to the senior officer overseeing the case. Following the hospital's fiasco, she had won the battle and was now in charge of the Bird case, but not without bruised feelings within the agency.

Evers was convinced Tick was the key to the case, and she was rarely wrong. It was a supposition that Nate Hoger, clearly impressed by the child warrior, had reinforced for Ruth on the ride up to Deer Valley that morning.

Parker focused his attention away from Brad and Mattie to the pretty blonde-haired girl in a pink body cast, who had confidently wheeled herself over to the elevator to check out the arrivals.

So this is Tick, Parker acknowledged with a jolt.

He had seen tapes of her, but in the flesh, she reminded him of the animation character Ester from *The Heroic Legend of Arslan*, a show he had enjoyed watching with his grandson years back. With her short, tousled blonde hair, large green- and caramel-colored eyes under a notable set of dark eyelashes, Tick looked like Ester come to life. He wondered if she resembled the character's personality: tough and stubborn, brash and hotheaded, but well-mannered and kind.

Tick's cast was much more cumbersome than Parker had anticipated, extending down one leg and up above her waistline to her lower chest. Hoger had told him that she could stand herself up and cook. Still, he wouldn't wish that kind of restraint on anybody.

Ruth Evers also fixed her eyes on the young girl. Every other juvenile she had interviewed under remotely similar circumstances would have hung back—shy, uncertain, and fearful. This one, who had just wheeled herself into the center of the group was different.

Tick carefully examined the newcomers, her face neutral and expressionless as she politely extended her hand to Agent Parker. Someone had trained the child in good manners, but for all the noticeable bravado, Agent Evers spotted the dark circles under Tick's striking eyes—eyes that met hers directly and fearlessly, eyes that were both challenging and questioning.

Evers, wearing a well-tailored navy pantsuit, was a tall, slender, distinguished-looking woman in her early fifties, with an engaging smile and dark, penetrating eyes. She did her best to defuse the wary look in the girl's eyes.

"Hello, Tick," she said, extending her arm for a handshake. Then, getting straight to the heart of the contention Tick would have with the FBI, she confessed, "I understand why you might think of us as incompetent troublemakers. The Bureau got it completely wrong by thinking that it knew what was in your best interest. I want you to know how much I regret the suffering we put you and your father through. But, Tick, please believe that we're not all clueless. You and Brad rightfully belong together, and in the future, I promise you can count on nothing but support from my team."

Disarmed but still skeptical, Tick nodded her head but was quickly let off the hook by Mattie. "Why don't we think about getting comfortable right now? Tick has made some fresh biscuits this morning. How about tea, coffee, biscuits, and homemade jam?"

"Mr. Hoger knows the way to the kitchen," she added with a slight chuckle.

Nate led the way, patting his stomach and amusingly licking his lips. The kitchen became Tick's domain on the first day of her arrival at the house, turning her caregivers into sous-chefs. By any culinary standards, she was an impressive baker, and Nate had gained a few pounds eating the perfections she presented every time he was at the safe house checking on the Hughes.

Walking into the kitchen and smelling the freshly baked biscuits, Ruth Evers felt lifted.

Cooperation and support, not force, will win the day with Tick and Brad, she thought.

From the start, even before Tick's rebellion at the hospital, she realized that Tick and Brad would refuse to be either manipulated or separated. Proven right, and now in charge of the investigation, Evers was more convicted than ever that this duo would cooperate to the best of their abilities if treated with courtesy and respect.

Her first test as the supervisor was deliberating over Tick's one-sided immunity agreement. The legal department had been apoplectic when they received Brad's draft weeks ago. "It's not a blanket immunity agreement. It's a bomb shelter!" It imposed unlimited immunity for Tick when or if she agreed to talk to the FBI. Further, if they granted an interview, Tick could tell the agents to drop off the face of the earth at any point in the conversation with no repercussions. If the Bureau signed the contract, then the agency would have no leverage, pure and simple.

Evers took no time issuing an order. "Sign the darn thing and get it back to them pronto, as in today. I see no good alternative. I'm not going to force her into our custody again, that's for damn sure. We've already propelled her off a balcony and then stuck to our guns just to watch the girl come close to starving herself to death. Our misguided intervention was disastrous and an embarrassment to the Bureau."

If Tick cooperated now, many unanswered questions about the Death Ranch and Timothy Bird could be laid to rest.

There was, however, a wild card in the deck: Dr. Barnes. Hughes had insisted that she be at the meeting and, despite the doctor's hospitality, Evers rightly deduced that if Barnes felt Tick's well-being was being affected, she and Parker would be on their way back to Washington DC with nothing.

The group settled into the living room with coffee mugs and plates of biscuits and jam in hand. As planned, Tick, in her customized wheelchair, sat between Mattie and Brad. The agents casually took seats around the room in chairs and couches. Lowered blinds kept the bright morning sun from shining through the enormous east-facing picture windows. Burning logs in the fireplace brightened the room with flickering light and helped create a warm and relaxed atmosphere.

"If you're all comfortable, I would like to get this meeting started," Brad said, pointing to a small pile of folders in front of him. "Against counsel's advice, it's Tick's wish to provide you with as much information about Timothy Bird as she can remember. I've spent the past few days working with her on the information contained in the folders I'll be handing out. Tick has a remarkable memory, as most of you are aware. In each folder, you will find a comprehensive timeline of events, beginning with Tick and Alissa's kidnapping.

"For the victims captured and later killed, Tick has provided names, descriptions, and dates. There is information here about Timothy Bird's followers, along with dates recounting when they came to the compound and when they were away for extended periods. Finally, Tick has provided information showing locations where she thinks Timothy Bird could be hiding."

Brad's face became serious. "Understand, these are the memories of a child under extreme duress... while I've learned not to underestimate Tick's power of recall, we can't and shouldn't assume everything she says is going to be 100 percent accurate. I won't allow you to hang her out to dry over inconsistencies in her testimony. She is only twelve and has been through a hell we can hardly imagine."

The agents all nodded in agreement, and Brad continued.

"As my lawyer insists, before we begin, I want confirmation that you understand the immunity agreement in its entirety. It stipulates that we have met all of your requirements and that Tick is free from any prosecution. She makes no warranties concerning the veracity of her testimony, as I've already mentioned. There are no conditions attached to this immunity, and if she decides not to cooperate, or if her testimony is ever contradicted… Well, you will just have to live with it. Further, her testimony is provided on a need-to-know basis only, and is not to become public."

"We understand," said Evers, who then turned her attention to Tick. "You are under no obligation to testify today, but if you do so, anything you say or reveal will be kept confidential, with no repercussions."

Now more relaxed, Brad replied, "Okay then… Let's get this over with." Then he quickly handed out the folders. "Dr. Barnes, Tick, and I will be in the next room to give you a chance to review her testimony. Please let us know when you are ready to start."

While the officers studied the material, Brad, Mattie, and Tick sat by one of the den windows in silence, looking at the mountains and watching the skiers make their way down the slope. Thirty minutes passed, then forty-five before Nate walked in.

"Okay, we're ready to get started." The group headed back to the living room, and the recorded interview began. Tick was poised to start typing. Brad and Mattie sat beside her.

Steve Brewer, the principal FBI field agent on the case from Seattle, took the lead, elaborating on the role of the two FBI profilers from Quantico. He pointed out the severity of the case and the attention it was receiving.

"Normally, services provided by the profilers' group include major case management advice, threat assessment, and strategies for investigation, interviewing, or prosecution. Given the severity and scope of this investigation—and the incident that triggered Tick's fall—Agents Ruth Evers and Butch Parker are now running the show. I will be reporting to them."

Turning to Tick, Brewer continued, "Tick, are you okay to begin?"

Receiving a confirming nod, he opened. "I'll be asking most of the questions, Tick, but my colleagues may ask questions as well. To start, I want to commend you on the information you and your father have provided for us today. The briefing document is remarkable. I wish more witnesses could provide such a useful record of events, which leads me to my first question: How sure are you that the dates you have provided are accurate?"

Confidently, Tick typed, *"I'm very sure. I have no trouble connecting dates with events. I first met you on October 21. You were wearing a dark-blue jacket. You told me that my mother was dead."*

Looking at his pocket calendar, sighing, Brewer replied, "You're exactly right. That was a difficult first meeting for me, as well. I'm so sorry I had to deliver such upsetting news."

The room was silent, with only the crackling of the fire to break the stillness.

He continued, "Could you explain how you came up with the map indicating a possible location for Timothy Bird's whereabouts?"

"I overheard Timothy talking about his ranch in Mexico a few times with Janet Herrington, his girlfriend, but he never was specific about the location. It's big—over one thousand acres in an isolated location from what they were saying about it. About two years ago, I was cleaning, and I heard Timothy talking to Janet about a deep layer of ash that had fallen all over the property from an eruption of El Popo back on January 23, 2001. I recently looked up El Popo on the Internet, and it is the nickname for Popocatepetl, a volcano forty-three miles southeast of Mexico City. I looked up the prevailing winds for that day. The ranch is likely located south of the volcano."

Amazed with her response, Steve exclaimed, "That's amazingly astute of you, Tick, and extremely useful information. Thank you."

Turning to Jenny Dresder, Steve directed her to follow up on Tick's information ASAP.

"Now, will you take me back to the day that Timothy Bird took you and your mother? Do you remember that day?"

Tick's reply began to scroll spontaneously across the large TV screen.

> *Momma and I always ate breakfast with Papa and Grandma—that's what I called Mr. and Mrs. Fowler. We lived with them in Sherman Oaks, California. Before it was time for me to leave for school that day, Papa and I discussed the upcoming*

*weeks' football games. We always watched the games
together. Papa would ask me what teams to bet on,
and then he made wagers with his friends using my
tips. He said I was his piggy bank.*

Tick paused before continuing.

*I know they're both dead now. I read their
obituaries on Dad's iPad at the hospital. They were
pretty old even then. They weren't my real grandparents, but they were very good to us, and Momma and
I loved them. They took me everywhere with them,
and they loved buying me little things. Momma
would tell them to stop spoiling me, but they did it
anyway. They said it made them happy.*

*That morning, Momma was driving me to
school. A large gray van was stopped in the middle
of the road just around the corner from where we
lived. Timothy was standing outside the van, waving at Momma to stop. He came to her window and
said that he had run out of gas and asked if we
would drive his girlfriend, Janet Herrington, to the
gas station around the corner, and he would stay
with the van until she came back with a gas can.*

*My momma knew him. He had eaten at her
restaurant many times, so she said she'd be glad to
help. When Janet got into the car next to Momma,
she didn't say a word or even look at me in the back
seat, but she held a gun up near Momma's face and
said that she would pull the trigger and then kill me
if Momma didn't do what she said. She told Momma
to drive, and when we stopped at the park where
Momma took me to play, Timothy was there. He was
leaning on the van smiling and waving to us.*

*Mamma started yelling at Timothy, "What's
going on! Why are you doing this? I don't have any-*

thing you want..." She begged them not to take me, but Timothy just grabbed my momma by the hair and pulled her out of our car. I bit Janet's arm when she was getting me out of my car seat, and she slapped me hard in the face. I remember Timothy tying me up with a rope that was attached to the wall in the back of the van—and I remember he gave me a shot in my arm. I remember hearing Momma's voice somewhere near me, telling me not to be afraid. We were in that van for a very long time. I remember being cold and having an accident because I had to go...

Mattie mumbled something inaudible, looked at Tick, and then over at Brad, whose face was set in stone.

Steve pressed on. "What happened when they let you out of the van?"

Bart Madison and Marjory Perkins untied all the ropes and let us out. They made us take off our clothes because they said we smelled bad, and they sprayed us with freezing water from a hose. I remember that Marjory threw our clothes to Momma, along with a couple of old blankets, and then they started pushing us to walk until they locked us in our chamber room.

"Just to confirm, was that room in the cave?"

Yes. The cave was in the ridge behind the house. There were five of those chamber rooms in there with barred doors. Our chamber was the largest one and had a little stream running through it. Momma washed our clothes in that stream. We lived there for seven years. We called it Morgan's Grotto.

"And what do you remember about being in that cave at the beginning?"

> *At the very beginning, they gave Momma a flashlight and a bag of granola bars before they left us alone in there. Momma didn't use the flashlight very much because she didn't want the batteries to run out.*

"It must have been so frightening for both of you," Mattie said.

> *I don't remember feeling scared. Momma and I pretended we were in a cave with a friendly dragon. She kept me warm by bundling me up next to her, sang songs, told me stories, and she talked about Jesus. She said we never had to be afraid, that He would never leave us. That's what I remember the most, listening to my momma and feeling safe with her next to me.*

"Can you remember when they came back for you?" asked Brewer.

> *They came back two days later.*

"How could you know it was two days?" asked Butch Parker.

> *Because Momma asked, and Timothy told her. She also wore a wristwatch.*

"When did they let you out?"

> *They let Momma out, but not me. Timothy told Momma that she was there to cook their meals and to keep the big house clean. He threatened to kill her useless whelp if she turned out to be a dis-*

appointment in the kitchen or if she wasn't a hard worker. She also had to take orders from Marjory Perkins. I stayed there by myself during the day before Momma talked them into letting me out to help her with her chores.

Brewer asked, incredulously, "Tick, you're saying that you were left alone in the cave all day with just a flashlight?"

Marjory brought us a gas lantern, but when she came to get Momma to cook and clean, I was alone.

Tick's answers came fast and read as matter-of-fact replies.
"Did Timothy Bird or any other person ever come to see you when your mother wasn't with you?" Brewer continued.

No.

Mattie felt relieved by Tick's reply but also sickened by the thought of Tick being left alone in that cave when she was just five years old. "Can you remember what you did when you were by yourself, or how you spent the time when your mom was gone?"

That's when 'thinking school' began.

Tick had a big smile on her face as she was typing.

That's what Momma called it, but I think it's called homeschooling. If Momma were with us today, she would love to tell you all about The Alissa Morgan Thinking School for The Gifted and Talented. I made it through the eleventh grade.

This response brought genuine laughter to the group, temporary relief from Tick's gut-wrenching testimony.

"A thinking school!" Hoger exclaimed. "Please tell us more about that."

> *In the morning, when Momma was gone, before I started working with her in the house, I had to put on my "just pretend" thinking cap and make up a story to tell her when she came back at lunchtime. When I was still at level 1, she would tell me what she wanted me to think about, like a story about what a fairy princess's house and garden might look like, or if the color green could talk, what would it say? When Momma came back with something for us to eat, I would tell her my story, and we would talk and talk about it. Momma gave me my afternoon topic to work on before Marjory came again to get Momma to cook their dinner. Those evening stories were harder for me to think about when I was younger."*

Mattie asked Tick why they seemed harder.

> *The morning subjects were about describing, defining, and telling about things and objects in the world, but the evening stories had to do with ideas and feelings…about good vs. evil and about what is "truth." If my stories didn't end with positive or hopeful messages, then mom would make me retell the ending.*

"Well, I know what you mean, Tick," Mattie said. "It's much easier to examine things that you can see or touch—not like feelings or ideas."

> *But Momma was a good teacher. She taught me that with God's help, the two things I can con-*

trol are my thoughts and attitude, like the apostle Paul when the Romans imprisoned him.

"And you were her gifted and talented pupil," Brad added. "Who is Bart Madison?" asked Brewer.

He was Timothy's friend at one time, except Timothy doesn't have friends. In his late fifties, Madison stands about five feet nine inches, wears thick glasses, and has a narrow face. He looks like a rat. Bart didn't live at the ranch, but he was over there a lot. He is evil, and he loves torturing people.

If you find him, I hope you kill him but do it slowly, just let him rot in jail. I know Jesus said to turn the other cheek, but I don't believe killing a monster is wrong. David killed Goliath. The only reason Madison didn't torture me to death was that Timothy told him that he had better not impair me.

Butch Parker glanced over at Ruth Evers, who didn't acknowledge him; the young witness in front of her transfixed her.

Madison wasn't at the ranch the whole time Momma and I were there. He lived somewhere else, and later on, Timothy didn't allow him in the house. When I was ten, he kidnapped two teenage girls, the Hopkins sisters. Their car ran out of gas, and Madison stopped to offer them a ride to a gas station. He brought them to the compound, instead, to torture them. When we could hear screaming in the night, Momma would sing hymns to muffle the sounds, but I could still hear the screams.

I heard Timothy and Madison fighting the next day. Timothy told him not to come back to the ranch, that he despised pedophiles. He told Bart that he had no use for a stupid, self-indulgent pervert.

Brad made eye contact with Mattie, subtly tapping his cheek, indicating to look over at Tick. Her scar was turning red, indicating her mood had changed from unemotional to tense.

"Let's go back to your earlier captivity, Tick. You were allowed to work with your mother. Is that correct?" asked Brewer, not aware of any change in Tick's disposition.

> Yes, they began to trust my momma enough that they allowed me out of the cave to do different chores, from cleaning bathrooms to tending the chickens. Since Momma never trusted them to treat me well, she leaned on God's word for her help. She made me commit to memory and insisted that I practice Philippians 2:14–16: "Do everything without complaining and arguing so that no one can criticize you. Live clean, innocent lives as children of God, shining like bright lights in a world full of crooked and perverse people." I learned not to complain.

As Mattie read Tick's words, she was getting an enhanced picture of the kind of relationships and dynamics that existed on that ranch, and she guessed that Alissa's wise guidance stemming from her faith protected them both, probably for years.

"So cleaning and looking after the chickens kept you busy all day?" Brewer asked.

> When I was about six years old, Timothy started training me every day.

"What brought that about?"

> I would watch Timothy and Janet practice sparring, and pretty soon, I could imitate their moves. It made them laugh. One day, Timothy caught me looking through a book on his desk.

When he came after me, I kicked him hard in the groin. He couldn't even move for a minute, but then he knocked me across the room. They started letting me train with them the next day.

"How did they train you?"

Timothy is a certified martial art and Krav Maga instructor. He taught me to fight, and fight hard to win—to use a stapler, a knife, a gun, anything in a room. Later, before the troubles started, he taught me to shoot and hunt.

Mattie spoke up. "How did you like being trained to fight like that?"

Tick looked over at Mattie with a sheepish expression on her face.

The truth is, I loved it. Timothy, Janet, and I would train for hours. She and Timothy taught me everything I know about fighting, hunting for deer and pheasants, and survival skills.

Showing no bravado but merely stating her opinion, Tick wrote,

I am especially good at fighting, I think. I mean seriously good, or so they told me. Timothy said I had a talent for mayhem and would be his 401K-retirement plan.

Brad grunted, receiving, in turn, a sharp look from Mattie.

"But you're here now, testifying against him. What changed?" Brewer asked.

When Janet killed Tammy Rockford, the scales finally fell from my eyes, and everything became

clear to me. I understood what it says in Ephesians
6:13. "Therefore put on the full armor of God, so
that when the day of evil comes, you may be able to
stand your ground, and after you have done every-
thing, to stand." So that's what I did.

Brad recalled that Tammy Rockford, the young rodeo star, was one of the last victims killed at the ranch, missing for just over a year. He guessed that Tick and Alissa's "troubles" started then. He gave Tick a supportive squeeze, and Mattie asked her to take a minute to drink some water.

Steve Brewer continued, now concentrating on the victims. "Your report shows that the first victim you are aware of was a woman from Nevada. What happened to her?"

They called her whore. Momma said that
her name was Angela and that Timothy and Bart
Madison picked her up in Nevada. They brought
her to the ranch and isolated her for a long time in
the inner cave where she couldn't hear or see any-
thing. When Timothy let Angela out, Momma and
I were working in the garden, and this woman was
screaming and rubbing her eyes because the light
was blinding her. She cursed at Timothy, saying she
had dark powers and would cast a death spell on
him and Bart if they didn't let her go.
Timothy laughed at her, tied her up, and told
her that there was only one thing to do with a witch.
He and Bart Madison dug a hole, pounded a stake
into it, and piled wood around it. After they tied
Angela to the post and lit the wood, Timothy told
everyone to stay and watch the witch burn. Momma
covered my ears and shielded my eyes for most of it,
but I heard and saw enough to tell you that it was
horrible. I heard Bart laughing loudly, and I could
see Timothy and Janet standing with their arms

crossed, watching as if it meant nothing to them. Marjory Perkins acted like a crazy animal running around the fire, shouting "Kill the witch." That's what I remember.

The room fell into unbearable silence until Brewer spoke again. "We know that her full name was Angela Parsons, Tick. Now, is there anything else about the Hopkins sisters that you could tell us?" Brewer asked.

Timothy made Momma and me bury them.

Mattie sighed. *Is there any outrage Tick hadn't endured?*
"What about Tom Ford, the Nevada rancher, and John Harbor, the truck driver, who were killed two years after Angela disappeared. What happened to them?"

Timothy had been practicing hard on his self-defense skills, and he wanted to test his competency on people. He and Janet drove out to Nevada and brought back the rancher. I can't say where they met him, and I don't know if he agreed to come to the ranch under false pretenses or if they abducted him, but what happened to Mr. Ford was pathetic. He wasn't nearly as big as Timothy, and from the moment he stepped into the ring, I knew that the man was in big trouble. His stance was completely wrong, and he wasn't holding his knife correctly. Timothy was strutting around the ring, acting like some sort of super gladiator, but he only looked foolish. There was no contest, but even so, Timothy killed Mr. Ford.

About a month and a half later, he and Janet captured John Harbor when his truck broke down. Timothy decided that he would use his martial arts training and kill him with his bare hands. Timothy was bigger than Mr. Harbor, but he almost lost the fight. Mr. Harbor was a powerful man, and he must have had a lot of training. Harbor never gave up, no matter how hard Timothy hit him. Timothy cheated and ended up killing him with the knife he had hidden under his jeans. He was nothing but a murdering coward.

Parker glanced over at Evers, their eyes conveying shared knowledge. Mr. Harbor had been a Marine and had served two tours of duty in Iraq. He was a self-defense expert and had served as a trainer during his final years in the military. Timothy Bird had picked the wrong opponent.

After the fight, I pointed my finger at Timothy and called him a cheater. That's when he kicked me hard in the ribs, as he had done twice before. Mattie and Dr. Brackford told me that a number of my ribs show signs of having been broken.

"You have mentioned Tammy Rockford, the teenager from Wyoming. The timeline indicates she was killed a year ago. What happened?" asked Brewer.

Timothy kidnapped Tammy just for Janet to fight. He said he wanted Janet to taste innocent blood because she needed to be toughened up. He said she was becoming too soft.

For the first time, Tick began losing her composure, her eyes filling with tears.

"Do you want to stop now?" asked Brad.

No, I don't. I couldn't remember ever seeing anyone as pretty as Tammy was. Even as frightened and confused as she was, she was so beautiful, so innocent. Tammy attempted to fight for her life, but she didn't have a chance. Mercifully, Janet killed her within a few minutes, and I think she felt ashamed for doing it. Momma was devastated and cried for a week. I never saw her smile after that day. She would pray every night, asking God to find a way out for the two of us.

With tears running down her cheeks, Tick continued.

Momma acted very differently after that. Instead of keeping quiet, she started telling Timothy and Janet what she thought of them. She told them both that they would be going straight to hell. Timothy told her he was getting tired of her holy harping, and even if she were a great cook and housekeeper, there would be consequences for her bad attitude.

"Your mom was right. He will be going straight to hell, hopefully soon," Brad said.

Looking out of the window with obvious pain in her eyes, Tick continued typing.

Everything changed after Janet killed Tammy. Timothy began watching our every move... Momma and I still did our chores, but Timothy locked a heavy metal shackle around my ankle one day. He told me that no rats would be leaving his ship alive. He attached a ball and a chain that was so heavy to drag. Momma would beg Timothy to take it off me, but he ignored her. I didn't hear Timothy calling me one day, so he grabbed the chain and began dragging me to the house. Momma was next to me, screaming at him to stop. She tried so hard to protect me. Timothy yelled back at her, "I told you there'd be consequences." When Timothy and Momma saw that my ankle had broken, he turned to my momma like a wild man, hitting her, screaming that she was to blame.

Tick's whole body seemed to be shaking, and she was typing so furiously that the keyboard nearly toppled off the tabletop.

Suddenly, all the overhead lights in the room went on, and Mattie, standing with her hand on the light switch, turned to the group. "Okay, that's enough. We need to call it a day," Mattie said.

Tick's response was instantaneous, her words flashing on the screen in bold type:

No, Mattie, I want to finish today. I'm okay. Why does everybody think they can tell me what to do?

Tick furiously rose out of her chair as Mattie spun on her heels to face her. Tick had an inflexible expression on her face, and the two of them locked eyes, ignoring the rest of the group. Brad was now standing and watching the tense exchange. The time seemed to stretch into minutes before Tick's expression turned from anger to submission. She mouthed the word—*okay*.

Mattie's gaze on Tick was steady, but her expression of authority softened as she walked closer to the exhausted child, took her hand, and, in a voice full of compassion, said, "That's my girl."

Then, Mattie suggested they break for lunch. "Tick has made a wonderful casserole for everyone," she said. "I'm insisting that she rests for a while, but if she feels up to it later, we can resume around three o'clock."

Walking behind Tick's wheelchair, and nodding for Brad to follow, Mattie wheeled Tick into her bedroom suite. Emerging moments later, Mattie went to the kitchen, put the casserole in the oven, and made Tick a sandwich. Thirty minutes later, Tick had fallen asleep with Brad sitting by her bedside, and Mattie returned to join the group in the dining room.

After eating a lunch that one agent described as "off-the-chart delicious," Mattie invited the group to tour the rest of the house while excusing herself to check on Tick and bring Brad some food. The agents scattered, each with their personal opinions about Tick's revelations, exploring rooms and answering emails and phone calls. The delay wasn't a problem for Evers. She and Parker had flown in on a government jet, standing by for them at the airport. They could stay as late as necessary.

Ruth Evers found an inviting rocking chair in the sunroom. She sat alone, struggling to give her mind a break from Tick's testimony.

Mattie was right about that casserole, she thought. *It was the best chicken curry dish I've ever put in my mouth. Tick must have learned how to cook from her mother. That poor woman, may she rest in peace. She raised such a remarkable child. What had Timothy Bird meant by saying that Tick was his 401k-retirement plan? Whatever he was planning to do with her, thank God she is out of his clutches—so is Alissa. We must do everything possible to prevent Bird from finding Tick before we get to him, but there's no question that Tick is the key to catching that psychopath and his associates. I must ask Tick for that recipe before I leave.*

Seeing Mattie enter the room, Evers looked up and acknowledged her presence with a smile, saying, "Hello, Dr. Barnes." Mattie poured herself a glass of Merlot and joined Evers in another rocking chair that faced the ski slopes and surrounding mountains. Mattie swirled the red liquid around the goblet studying the sun's rays through the legs of the wine rolling down the inside of her glass.

"I hope we haven't disrupted your schedule too much today, Agent Evers. For all of her grit, Tick is still much weaker than she realizes."

"Not in the slightest, Doctor," Evers replied in a soft drawl. "I could sit here forever, looking out at this beautiful scenery."

Evers changed the subject. "We are completely in your debt, Doctor. You helped pull Tick through the nearly fatal injuries she sustained when she fell at the hospital. The Bureau messed up from the start, as I suspect you concur. As for Tick, well, I have to say she is the most mature girl I have ever met. Her comments revealed such unexpected wisdom, especially coming from someone so young—

and all with the grounding and understanding to support her positions. Extraordinary!"

Evers stood and crossed the room to pour herself a glass of water. Peering out at the snow-capped mountains, she let out a laugh and said, "As a parent to wonderfully average kids, I can see how Tick's superior intelligence could present unique challenges that are not in my wheelhouse. But as a highly respected child psychiatrist and pediatrician, your record of resolving complex cases is well-known."

Pausing, Evers looked at Mattie intently. "She took an immense risk, becoming so dehydrated, and then starving herself. How far do you think she would have gone? When would you have stepped in again if we hadn't backed down?"

Mattie felt a surge of anger. *What a two-faced snake-in-the-grass agent you are*, she thought, a reaction quickly replaced by guilt when she realized that Evers had guessed at the truth. Mixed emotions were covered over rapidly by Mattie's professionalism and icy calm demeanor that had seen her through other challenging situations.

Ruth Evers had just asked the questions Mattie had asked herself many times, questions with unsatisfactory answers. But she would be damned if she would try to explain herself to Evers. She would be second-guessing herself privately for a long time, she knew.

Mattie collected her thoughts before responding. "Well, thank God, your questions are academic at this point, Agent Evers, so I would prefer not to speculate. What I can say is that I am quite certain we made the correct decision. While Brad and Tick's relationship is quite complicated, and I have never recommended placement with a single man his age, there are many reasons I am certain it will work out."

Then Mattie took on a firmer tone. "And I would never take credit for pulling her through after her horrifying fall. I have an excellent medical team, but without Brad, she wouldn't be here. Brad is the one who props her up. You will get everything you need from her today. It will be accurate, truthful, and brilliant for a child her age—for that matter, any age—but an emotional component is still buried deep within her. She needs time and space to heal, and you should give it to her."

Then, almost as if talking to herself, Mattie said, "Thank God she will be out of this cast soon. She is a physical creature, and being wrapped in a stiff cocoon is understandably driving her crazy."

Evers was hoping that Mattie would be willing to discuss the extremes Tick was capable of taking, but instead, Mattie had only proved that Brad wasn't the only person ready to cross any line to protect the girl. Evers could see that Mattie also underestimated her influence over Tick, as evidenced by the stare-down that took place earlier in the living room.

Evers put her private thoughts aside. She had more questions.

"I understand that as soon as you remove Tick's cast, she faces ankle surgery. That seems so harsh and contradicts what you just said about her being out of a cast soon. Why doesn't she get some time off to enjoy life before she is incapacitated after another surgery?"

Mattie took a quick sip of wine. "Do you know how many books Tick has read about skiing since she arrived here at this house?" she asked.

"No. Why?" Evers was curious to know what that had to do with the ankle surgery.

"Three books, not counting a massive pile of ski magazines. If I cut Tick's body cast off this afternoon, she would make a beeline downstairs to grab some boots, skis, and head for the lifts."

"So you think she's reckless?" Ruth asked.

Mattie, realizing that overstating a point with this FBI woman was a mistake, answered her quickly. "I was making a point about her mindset, Agent Evers. Tick is a highly motivated twelve-year-old child *warrior* with a brain wired to compete and win."

"I'm learning that about her," Evers said.

"So putting her repaired ankle in a cast will keep her under our thumbs for another few weeks while allowing her body additional time to heal. Besides, I want her to start socializing with kids her age. My wards at Children's Hospital are full of kids recovering from all sorts of illnesses and injuries. A few now face long-term handicaps, and I think Tick might be good for them and vice versa. She hasn't been with other children for a very long time."

"Well, please don't hesitate to call me if you can think of anything I could do to help with Tick's recovery," Ruth said, hoping that Dr. Barnes wouldn't doubt her sincerity.

"There actually is something. I would like to see Tick's kindergarten school record, teacher comments, and any pre-school records that you might have. Then I want to see all the information you have gathered on Tick's mother, Alissa Morgan. I would like to see that complete case file, including the records of interviews with the people who knew and worked with Alissa. It would also be helpful to know more about Timothy Bird. Any information you can share would be tremendously helpful in my work with Tick."

"I will see to it as soon as I return, Dr. Barnes."

The two women lapsed into silence, each watching the group of beginner skiers move down the slope, one instructor in the front, one in the rear, the procession undulating like a snake with slow, cautious snowplow turns. Turn after turn, the snake made its way down the mountain.

After a long nap, around three in the afternoon, Tick returned to the living room, and the meeting resumed. Brewer, unenthusiastically, asked the first question. "Seven months after Tammy Rockford disappeared, Thornton Bittner and his son, David, went missing while on a hike in the Uintas. Do you know what happened to them?"

They got lost in a storm and ended up at the ranch. Timothy invited the Bittners in, but they ended up as captives, and he spent weeks brainwashing them. Timothy was programming David to fight me. He told David that he would have to fight me to the death if he wanted to live. Momma tried to stop the fight, but Timothy wouldn't listen to her.

"What happened in the fight?" Steve questioned, apprehensive about the answer but wanting to get to the truth. "Before you respond, Tick, remember that you have complete immunity from prosecution."

Tick's answer came, her facial scar crimson.

> *I know that. It wasn't my choice to fight David. Timothy threw me in the ring with him without a weapon. He had given David a knife, though. Before the starting bell rang, David came after me, spitting mad with so much hate in his eyes. He slashed my arm, screaming that he was going to gut me like the smelly fish I was.*

Pointing to a long scar on her arm, she continued with a disgusted expression.

> *It was nothing for me to take his knife away from him. He was a pathetic fighter and no match for me, so I just toyed with him for a few minutes and cut him with lots of little nicks. I slashed his forehead enough so blood would get into his eyes, and he couldn't see to fight anymore, but I didn't kill him. I quit and left the ring because it was over, but Timothy was furious with me. He tied me to the post and whipped me with his old bullwhip.*

Tick took a moment to look at the fireplace in reflection, then continued.

> *Timothy killed David by hitting him with a shovel in front of his father. He had Janet film it, and they played the video every night for days on a screen set up in front of Mr. Bittner's cage.*

Evers looked over at Butch Parker. Tick's story rang true. The Bittner boy's body had remained remarkably intact in the cold, rocky burial site. A massive blow to the back of his head had killed him, shattering his skull. It was a blow that no eleven- or twelve-year-old girl, even one as strong as Tick, could have delivered. There were little nicks on his arms and legs and a long superficial cut just above his eyebrows, but they were not life-threatening injuries.

Brad, who had been observing Tick, felt a chill run up his legs. There was something not right about her testimony.

She may be telling the truth, but there's something else, he thought. *There's more to this story than she's saying.*

"What happened to Mr. Bittner?" Brewer asked.

> *Timothy forced Mr. Bittner into the ring to fight. He was an accountant, for pity's sake, and had no idea how to defend himself, but Timothy dragged it out for a long time and finally killed the poor man.*

"Could you give us a better picture of your association with Timothy Bird during your captivity?"

> *Association?*

"Well, like a relationship, or some sort of bond," Brewer clarified.

> *You really should ask Dr. Barnes, the psychiatrist in the room, to tell you what she thinks about any association, relationship, or bond that I had with a total psycho! I can tell you that I didn't fully understand our slave standing with Timothy when I was younger, years before the troubles began, but we were always closely watched and in jeopardy of being beaten or worse. Timothy used the close relationship between mother and me to control us. When I was older and allowed some freedom to explore around the ranch property, it was never without Janet or Timothy threatening that mom would pay the price if I dared to run away. I remember wondering*

why they thought I would run away and leave my mother. After all, where would I go without her?

Hesitating, her face flushed, she added,

For so long, I wanted to fit in. I wanted them to like me—to be like them. Later, when I understood how evil they were and began disobeying Timothy, he said I had become a dangerous liability.

An anguished expression fell on her face.

I should have killed them all when I had the chance. I should have somehow figured out how to do it. Then, Momma, Tammy, and all the others would still be alive. I failed everybody.

She stopped typing. The room went silent. The entire group realized that this twelve-year-old girl meant every word of regret for not killing the people who shattered so many lives.

Then she resumed.

After the troubles started, we were always locked up and treated like slaves. Timothy would beat us for the slightest offense.

Brewer resumed the questioning, focusing on Timothy's acolytes.

"Who was Marjory Perkins?"

She was a student at the college Timothy had attended. She had dark hair, stood about 5'2" with brown eyes and was very heavy. Marjory followed Timothy to Wyoming and was in charge of housekeeping. She was mean, bossy, and smelled icky. She treated us like dirt.

"On your list of dates, you show Marjory Perkins dying eight months after you arrived. How did she die?"

> *From the day we were taken, my momma made it clear that no matter what was ahead for us, God was present, and we were accountable to Him for our every thought, word, and deed. She reminded me every day that if we were going to survive, we could never act as if God does not exist.*

Taking another opportunity to quote scripture, Tick typed,

> *"Since God chose you to be the holy people whom he loves, you must clothe yourselves with tenderhearted mercy, kindness, humility, gentleness, and patience." (Col 3:12)*
>
> *With Marjory Perkins, no amount of kindness worked. She despised my mother, even though Momma did everything Marjory ordered her to do without complaining. She prayed for Marjory's heart to soften, but the woman became more and more hateful, especially whenever she saw Timothy talking to Mom or when he complimented her excellent cooking.*
>
> *On the Monday after Easter, Mom and I were in the kitchen when Timothy came in to say how much he enjoyed the leg of lamb she had served for dinner, hoping that there were some leftovers. Marjory seemed to come out of nowhere and slapped my momma hard across her face, yelling at Timothy for speaking to a kitchen slave and demanding that he take care of her and her brat as he had promised he would do. Marjory said she would leave him if he didn't get rid of us. Before he stormed out of the kitchen, Timothy told Marjory that if she wanted*

us dead that badly, then she would have to dig the grave herself.

Momma told Marjory that she should get away fast and escape, suspecting she was in danger, but Marjory only laughed and mocked her. She said she would throw the lamb bone and all the leftovers on top of us when we were dead in our grave.

Momma and I spent the rest of the night in the cave, holding hands, reciting our favorite Bible verses. We came up with all sorts of memories that made us laugh, like the day the rooster attacked Timothy and how he couldn't get away fast enough before being pecked and scratched and then falling face down into a muddy puddle.

When he came to get us in the morning, he tied our hands behind our backs. Momma begged him not to hurt me, but he didn't say a word. Then he forced us at gunpoint to walk to the grave Marjory had been digging where they buried people. Mom began saying the Lord's Prayer out loud. She looked at me with such a calm look. I knew we were about to die.

Marjory and Madison were standing there, and when Timothy raised his gun and put it to Momma's head, Marjory said, "Lights out, Alissa!," but Timothy turned, shot Marjory in both legs, and pushed her into the grave. He untied us and told Momma to bury Marjory. Momma said she wouldn't do that and pleaded with him to pull Marjory out.

Timothy called Momma a holy fool and slapped her so hard that she fell. Bart Madison began burying Marjory, who was screaming and crying in the grave. He was covering her with dirt, laughing as he shoveled. I was kneeling beside my

mother when Timothy yanked us up and ordered us
to get back to our cave.

Tick stopped typing and put her hands in her lap for a moment. No one spoke. After a moment, she typed, *"Do any of you know Proverbs 11:17 and 16:29?"* Not waiting for a reply, she typed out the scriptures:

> *"You do yourself a favor when you are kind. If you are cruel, you only hurt yourself."*
> *"Violent people deceive their friends and lead them to disaster."*
> *Momma had a strong feeling that Marjory was doomed and needed to escape from Timothy. She was right. Marjory should have run like a deer, but she was way too fat.*

Brewer sighed, sickened from this nightmare of gruesome memories he was pulling out of this young victim, but he had a job to do. "Tell us about Janet Herrington."
Tick suddenly looked sad and took a deep breath.

> *Janet also went to the university with Timothy and was a national karate champion. She was tall, pretty, fast, and very strong. I thought she was Timothy's girlfriend, but it turned out he was just using her like he used everybody else. Momma said she was a good person who had lost her way.*

"What happened to Janet Herrington, Tick? Could you tell us how she died?"
Tick's face was white, and she typed out her response slowly, the words appearing across the screen in halting spurts.

> *After the troubles started, Timothy began look-*
> *ing for reasons and ways to hurt us. The day came*

when he said that he had finally had enough of me because I had become useless to him. He ordered Janet to fight me. She didn't want to, but he told her that if she didn't, she would be next. He expected a knife fight to the death between us.

She was fast and strong, and her arms were so long. I couldn't get inside her guard, and I knew I was going to lose. I did manage to cut her a few times on her arms and once on her side. Then she cut my face, I pretended to give up, and when she looked over at Timothy, I dove under her and cut her hamstring. She couldn't move. It would have been only a matter of time before I could kill her.

A flash of pain appeared on Tick's face, a recollection of a bitter battle against a stronger foe, but she also expressed pride in the words she typed out.

She was finished. I had won!

With a sigh, her face now downcast, she continued,

As she lay there, she was crying, looking at Timothy, asking him to stop the fight, but he wouldn't. He ordered me to kill her. I refused, and he flogged me with the new whip he had built. He killed Janet.

Brad looked at Tick, privately unnerved. For the second time in the interview, Brad sensed that something wasn't right about Tick's story. She wasn't telling the whole truth. When she wrote about the fight with the Bittner boy, he had misgivings. Now, her account about the fight with Janet didn't add up.

Oh, dear Lord, did she kill Janet? But that doesn't make sense. Why would Timothy whip her if she had obeyed him and killed her? The image of seeing Tick's shredded back on the mountain flashed into his mind, and he shuddered. *She didn't kill Janet,* he told himself over and over. *She has never killed anyone.* But whatever was bothering Brad, he couldn't put his finger on it.

Steve Brewer and the other agents fell silent. Ruth Evers asked the next question. "Tick, do you know if there are other people involved with Timothy?"

Tick nodded her head, then wrote,

> *Yes, but I can't tell you anything about them. Timothy would be away, sometimes for weeks, and Janet told my momma that he was meeting with friends. Sometimes we were locked in our chamber room for a few days at a time, and we knew he had visitors. One time, when we were sleeping, a bright light woke us up. I heard Timothy talking to a strange man in a foreign language. I remember the next day how hard Timothy slapped Janet when she mentioned the name Kask. He told her never to talk business around Momma or me. It's all in your report.*

"Thank you for that, Tick," Ruth said. "I'm sorry to get back to this, but could you tell us what happened after Timothy flogged you when you wouldn't kill Janet?

> *When Timothy stopped whipping me, Momma told him she was taking me into the ranch house to care for my wounds. He started to follow us, but we made it to the library before he reached us. It all happened so fast. Momma locked the big door and said that this was the day she had been praying for, that we would both be free. She picked up the small table under the window facing the mountains and began slamming it hard against the glass until it shattered into a million pieces. She told me to head for the mountains—to run as fast as I could and not*

to look back, to trust that God would guide my foot-
steps. I think she pushed me through that window
because I don't remember getting out myself. I didn't
want to leave her. Her voice sounded so strange, not
like her voice at all. I was confused, and all I could
hear was "Run! Run!" so I began running as soon as
I hit the ground.

Brad reached over and placed his hand gently on the back of Tick's neck. "I'm right here, my girl, look at me. Are you doing okay? Do we need to stop?"

Tick looked over at her father, then resolutely shook her head to indicate that she would continue.

I knew he would come after me… He's a first-
rate tracker. I left a trail of blood, and I began drag-
ging my foot. When he found me, I jumped off the
hill's side into the tree on the ledge below. He didn't
have a rope, so he couldn't get to me without jump-
ing himself. I prayed that he wouldn't jump.

Tick's face looked pale and drawn, so Brad called for one last question.

"Okay, Tick," Ruth said. "I know this has been hard on you, and you must be exhausted. You have helped us a great deal today, but I need to know more about Bart Madison. Can you tell us anything else about him?"

Tick's typing had slowed. She was clearly at the end of her rope, but the words continued scrolling across the screen.

I can't tell you very much. Bart stopped com-
ing to the ranch a long time ago, but some months
ago, I heard Timothy yelling at him over the phone,
calling him scum and saying that he better not ever
show up at the ranch because he would end up
as chicken feed. When he hung up, he told Janet

that Bart Madison had kidnapped another girl in Atlanta, a twelve-year-old and that he was taking her to his house.

Instantly, there was a buzz of talking among the agents. Evers had to put her hand up to silence the group before she could continue. "Tick, do you remember the date of that call or anything else about it?"

August 29. I also remember Timothy telling Janet that he hoped Bart would gig himself to death gigging flounder during one of those jubilees he always talked about.

Brad interrupted. "I know what a jubilee is. It's an unusual occurrence that happens in Mobile Bay, Alabama. It's when flounder, shrimp, crabs, and other marine life are forced to the shore by deoxygenated water welling up from the bottom of the bay. People who live anywhere near the shore leave their homes with gigging poles, nets, and buckets and end up taking home heaps of fresh, easy-to-catch, and free seafood. It's a huge deal in Mobile."

The agents began texting their compatriots in Atlanta. Within minutes, Evers spoke up, "Tick got it right… A twelve-year-old girl was reported missing on August 29 in Atlanta. Tick, would you be willing to work with a sketch artist tomorrow? We would like a sketch of Bart Madison. It would help us catch him."

Tick didn't hesitate to answer, her fingers pounding the keyboard.

Yes, I can do that. I want you to find him as soon as you can. Bart wanted to take me to his house when we were captured, but Timothy said no. He wouldn't get good meals if his new cook didn't have her kid with her. Madison always acted hateful toward my mom.

Then, in bold script, she typed: ***"Find them! Kill him! Kill them both!"***

Seeing Tick visibly shaking, Brad quickly stood, turned on the lights, and said, "Okay, that's it... Enough. We're finished."

Brad leaned over Tick and whispered in her ear, "You have done an amazing job for them today, and I'm very proud of you, but we are finished for today."

The agents, feeling somewhat ashamed of the ordeal they had put the girl through, gathered around Tick to express their appreciation for her help.

Ruth Evers promised Tick that they would capture Timothy Bird and Madison, but her department would make every effort to protect Tick's identity and the Hughes family until that day. She handed Tick her card with her private number written on the back and asked Tick to keep in touch—to call her for any reason at any time. Hoger hugged Tick, saying he had never felt as proud of anybody as he did of her today. Parker and Brewer told her she was amazing, perhaps the best witness in all their years working in law enforcement.

Then came something unexpected. Evers reached into her briefcase and pulled out an eight-by-twelve framed picture. It was a snapshot of Tick and Alissa taken near a pier in California. In the image, the sun was setting halfway behind the ocean, and Tick was beaming, her head thrown back, blond hair covering half her face, looking up at her mother. Another smaller worn picture was wedged in the corner of the frame. It was of a beautiful young woman standing next to a fountain with her arm wrapped around a handsome young man.

"I think this belongs to you, Tick," Evers said. "It was found at the Fowlers and has been in an evidence file all these years. Your mother was beautiful, just like you."

Tick took the picture and quickly wheeled herself away, embarrassed by her tears.

After the agents left, Brad, Mattie, and Tick worked quietly together in the kitchen, preparing a simple no-fuss dinner. Brad found an easy-listening music channel. The songs, softly airing through hidden speakers, helped soothe their frayed nerves.

After eating, they halfheartedly played some scrabble until Leslie Thomas, Tick's night nurse, arrived to help her get ready for bed. Mattie asked Leslie to stay with Tick during the night.

"This has been a tough day for her," Mattie said. "Tonight may be difficult for her as well. I have to go home, and I'd prefer that she not be alone."

Driving on I-80 through Parley's Canyon is challenging at any time of the year, but it's a horrible trip in the winter. The six-lane freeway is unnervingly curvy and steep, conveying cars, trucks, semis, and all types of recreational vehicles barreling down too fast toward the Salt Lake Valley below. Mattie fought to concentrate on the road rather than on what Brad had said to her just moments earlier. He had told her that there were two exchanges in the interview when he felt Tick was either lying or omitting facts. The first was when she described David Bittner's death, and the second was the fight with Janet Herrington. Mattie hadn't spotted any deception, but Brad could read Tick like a book.

Despite the unnerving stories Mattie had heard Tick tell the group that day, she wondered if Tick could be keeping the worst of it from them.

Ruth Evers tightened her seatbelt even before the captain came on the loudspeaker. Flying at a cruising altitude of thirty-nine thousand feet, the plane had suddenly shuddered as it hit turbulence over the Rocky Mountains. Evers looked over at Butch Parker. He was busy reviewing a video he had made of the interview, showing Tick's written responses on the TV screen.

"Well, what do you think?" she asked.

"Her answers were staggering and extremely disturbing," he replied. "She tied a lot of ends together for us today, though. Her story is consistent with all the evidence we've accumulated so far, but I'm not sure I buy into Tick as a victim. That's one smart, resilient girl and a fighter—hardly the victim type. In my opinion, she was closer to Timothy than she is letting on."

"Your takeaway surprises me, Butch. I'm inclined to believe that what we learned today from a child kidnapped by a sadist when she was five years old clears her of any intentional wrongdoing. How can you seriously think otherwise? Haven't you seen the pictures of her back?"

Parker shook his head, turning his screen toward Evers and pointing to the transcript.

Find them! Kill him. Kill them both!... Two fights to the death... Make it slow!... Made little cuts all over him... She should have run like a deer, but then she was way too fat... I should have killed them all...

"Are those the words from a normal, harmless twelve-year-old, Ruth?"

"What in the heck is wrong with you today? We both know she isn't normal! How could she be?"

Taking a moment to cool down, Evers spoke up again. "I would like a written account of your general impressions about Tick's demeanor by Friday, Butch. If your comments include the fact that she teared up several times, communicated remorse, sadness, and feelings of guilt, then I'll know we were in the same room today."

Parker smiled as he started in on his new task. He liked challenging Evers. He enjoyed knowing where she stood on things.

Evers put her seat back to rest and review mental images of Tick, Brad, and Mattie Barnes. A hospital video capturing Dr. Barnes leaning over Tick and saying something in her ear came into her thoughts—*Thank God it had all worked out.*

Evers realized that Dr. Barnes was right about Tick needing time to heal. But a feeling of helplessness and despair for the girl struck her. Tick's childhood was over; life had shown her little mercy.

A Time to Rest

What have they done with her? Where is she?

Tick was clutching the framed picture of her mother when Brad walked in to say good night. He reassured her that her mother's body was resting at the funeral home and that they would discuss plans for the funeral service in the morning.

It was approaching two months since they recovered Alissa's body from the ranch, but arranging and holding a funeral that Tick was well enough to attend had not been possible until now.

While Brad and Mattie had not discussed details for a memorial service with Tick, the groundwork for Alissa's funeral was underway. Brad was able to secure a burial plot next to his late wife, Catherine, and had set aside Sunday, December 11, for the service. The boys and their wives were aware of the arrangements and had already started making travel plans.

Laura agreed to plan a small reception at the Deer Valley house, following the service. Mattie was convinced that Tick's muteness and underlying emotional issues hinged around undisclosed events related to her mother, so she advised that Tick be allowed to plan most of the funeral service with as little help as possible from anyone. Composing an outward expression of love for her mother could help ease whatever guilt she carried. Brad was more than willing to help, but Mattie voiced her opinion that he could inadvertently dominate the preparations. She asked Laura, however, to stand by for whatever assistance Tick might need.

Mattie and Laura arrived in Deer Valley in time to join Tick and Brad at the breakfast table, where Laura snatched one of Tick's blueberry muffins. Brad began clearing the table and then initiated the conversation about Alissa's funeral.

"Tick, last night, I mentioned that we would discuss funeral arrangements for your mother this morning. Mattie, Laura, and I would like you to go over some initial plans that we have made, and—"

Tick suddenly slammed her fist on the table and grabbed her writing tablet. *"She is MY mother, you know! Why would you consider planning Momma's funeral without me?"*

Tick glowered up at Brad. Her scar was ablaze.

Brad responded carefully. "Take it easy, young lady. Just calm down. There's no cause for an outburst, and you're welcome to go to your room until you've recovered your self-control. Am I making myself clear?"

With visible, near-comedic effort, Tick shaped a look resembling contrition to replace her furious-looking face. Her fists opened, and she placed her hands in her lap, regaining composure.

Brad continued, "For starters, you have been in the hospital forever, it seems. Then let's not forget the daunting complications we faced blocking your adoption—not to mention all the time it has taken to prepare for the FBI interview. We want your mother's funeral to be exactly how you want it to be, but when has there been a good time to work this out with you? Opening up this discussion is hard for you, but it has to be done, you know that. Mattie, Laura, and I are only trying to help make planning easier for you."

"Nothing about this is easy," Tick wrote, seeming embarrassed by her outburst, *"but you're right, there hasn't been any time for Momma. What are these plans you've made?"*

"Okay, so that's what we want you to consider now," Brad said evenly. "I chose a burial spot next to Catherine's gravesite with a beautiful view of the mountains."

Pausing, Brad added, "But, Tick, if you would prefer a different location, it's okay to change that idea and make other arrangements. Also Mattie has asked Laura to assist you as you plan this out, if you'd like."

Taking her cue, Laura opened her portfolio, doing her best to feel okay about helping Tick plan Alissa's funeral. Tick had gotten under Laura's skin, too, but not always in a good way. Laura was convinced that in the history of Children's Hospital, no patient had ever received as much dedicated care and attention as Tick, thanks to top-notch hospital staff—to say nothing of the security detail posted at the hospital for her safety.

But Laura hadn't seen for herself any indication that Tick felt grateful. Tick was difficult, demanding, and still swallowed up every bit of Mattie's free time without batting an eye. If Laura had been honest with Mattie about helping with the funeral, she might have declined, not wanting to take flak from a twelve-year-old know-it-all. She was still steaming over the last time she and Tick were together, watching a movie and snacking on peanut butter crackers—

"I'm so curious about that dragon tattoo on your back," Tick had written on her iPad. *"It's not completely horrible to look at—the artist had talent—but I think it was stupid of you to ruin perfectly good skin with ink that is costly and painful to remove! What if you don't like it in a few years when your taste has changed? What if you get fat and the dragon morphs into something hideous, and when you get old, and your skin is wrinkly and saggy, what is that dragon going to look like then? Did you do it for attention or to be a nonconformist? Or was it just drunken impulsiveness? I can never get rid of my scars, and I despise them! It seems such a pity to mess up your beautiful God-given skin like that on purpose!"*

"You are such a colossal jackass!" Laura reacted, immediately remorseful for her choice of words, but not for telling Tick off. "Are you seriously that insensitive?" Tick only turned to look directly in Laura's eyes, seemingly probing for answers inside Laura's head, but there was no sign of remorse, no words of regret as she resumed watching the movie.

That was days ago. Now, putting hurt feelings aside after privately admitting that she seriously regretted getting a tattoo for all the reasons Tick had cited, Laura braced herself to help with the funeral arrangements. She understood that Tick had her demons and would do her best not to take Tick's insults personally. It came as no surprise, then, that Tick was a little slave driver, demanding that everything be perfect for her mother's service. No detail was too minor. Laura found herself bringing in samples of casket linings, florist catalogs, handfuls of instrumental Christian music CDs, and paper and typestyle samples to choose from for the service program.

Picking the headstone tested every nerve Laura had. Tick demanded to see pictures of what may well have been every granite sample in Utah before selecting. When Laura mentioned Tick's fussiness and unrealistic expectations, Mattie cut her off.

"Please just bear with it, Laura. Her mother's funeral is the most important thing she has ever done in her entire life. Keep your time working with her under two hours, or else she'll make herself—and you—sick belaboring every detail.

Too late, Laura mused. *I'm already sick of it.*

Four days later, Tick and Laura presented their plans to Brad, and they carefully went through every detail of the service and internment. Ideas for the headstone included an engraved angel with widespread wings. The inscription text to read: ALISSA MORGAN—A DEDICATED SERVANT TO OUR LORD—AN ANGEL WHO DESERVED BETTER.

Once Brad read the epitaph, he gave Laura the go-ahead to call the engraver, but Tick interrupted. *"No, Mattie needs to see it first."* Laura agreed.

That night, Mattie read the purposed inscription for the headstone. "Tick, don't you think something a little more life-affirming, perhaps something that expresses her virtues, would honor her more? The rest of the preparations are superb."

Tick spent that night working on it and finally came up with the inscription: ALISSA MORGAN—A BELIEVER AND LOVING MOTHER WHO PUT THE LORD AND HER DAUGHTER ABOVE HERSELF.

It worked for Mattie, but the tone of the message reinforced the recurring refrain. *Why the tone of guilt? What had Tick done that could be more painful than what she had already communicated to the FBI?*

Then came the issue of a viewing. Tick wanted to see her mother once again, but Brad balked at the idea. He had never liked viewings. A body looked empty and waxy once the soul had departed. He found no solace whenever he had viewed someone in a casket. He wished to remember his friends and family as they had been in life. He worried if seeing her mother in a casket would be too much for Tick to bear, but he felt bound to comply with her wishes.

Surprisingly, when Brad asked Tick to write a short eulogy for her mom, she adamantly declined, writing that she couldn't do it. Brad urged her to at least write something, some sweet memory that she could share, but she wouldn't budge. Brad ended up offering to write the eulogy himself, and Tick readily accepted.

Later that night, Brad shared his frustration with Mattie.

"It's hard for me to understand why, knowing how much she adored her mother, she won't write down anything about the person who meant the most to her in the world, a mother who was her world."

"Yes, but it's her mother in their world, not ours," Mattie countered. "The root of your daughter's speechlessness is buried somewhere in that world, Brad, and if I can't dig that up, she may never talk."

For Brad, Mattie's disclosure was hard to hear.

If managing everything going on inside their Deer Valley sanctuary wasn't enough, Brad began making daily trips to his office—the starting point in putting Tick's cover story into place. After a week, he would tell his colleagues that a car accident in Florida killed old friends. He was the godfather to their only daughter.

Weeks later, he would return to the office with news that he had adopted the deceased friends' child, a young, severely injured girl. They would be staying in Deer Valley while she recuperated.

Back at Brad's home, contractors were hard at work, transforming the house into a near fortress. Ruth Evers and her team had developed a psychological and behavioral profile of Timothy Bird and determined that he would make every effort to find Tick. His star captive had not only escaped from him and was alive to reveal information about him, but she had exposed his carefully constructed, now destroyed domain. He would be seeking vengeance, likely wanting to take his revenge "up close and personal." He would want to capture her with plans to dispense a painful death rather than just shooting her dead or hiring a killer to take her out. It was a matter of sick, evil, and unbridled pride.

Adding to this threat and now surfacing were troubling indications of a splinter organization behind Bird. *Both Tick and the FBI were convinced that this threat was real.*

In response to the threat, Brad had contractors crawling all over the house. In addition to having a sophisticated security system installed, Brad had the entire second floor of the house converted into a safe room.

The main hallway leading to the bedrooms was being closed off with a heavy-duty security door. Bedroom doors were being reinforced and would close and lock automatically upon entry or exit. A facial recognition scanner would control access to the hallway door and rooms. Construction was underway to reinforce the interior walls and replace the windows with bulletproof glass. A TV monitor that showed activity throughout the property, both inside and outside, was being installed. Finally, a gun safe had been delivered and was ready to be installed.

Although the FBI would foot some of the bills, the expedited renovation was costing Brad a fortune, but they would have protection from a home invasion.

There was, regrettably, a type of home invasion that Brad would have to live with—the invasion of his privacy. Cameras were scattered around the property and linked into an FBI monitoring system. Cameras could be temporarily disabled for privacy; however, changing control settings required complicated and lengthy security codes. His easygoing lifestyle would be a thing of the past.

Brad was also working on another project—the first real gift he would give his new daughter. Tick had been attempting to sketch a picture of her mother using the images Evers had given her.

Displeased with each attempt and becoming more and more frustrated, she crumpled sketch after sketch, creating a pile of paper on the sunroom floor.

Brad's ingenious idea occurred during breakfast while reading an article in the local paper. The report focused on Madame Akiko Amori, a renowned portrait painter from New York whose work included many world leaders' portraits. Amori, a graduate of Yale University, was vacationing in Park City and lecturing at the Kimball Art Center. Brad left the house an hour later, saying he had an errand to run at the office.

Two days later, a gray-haired, stoop-shouldered Asian woman with a strong Brooklyn accent showed up at the house armed with an easel, a camera, and a box full of paints and charcoal. Her mission was to sketch a portrait of Alissa for Tick and possibly teach something about portrait art to her new young patron.

Madame Amori was quite the character, talking nonstop while she worked. She expressed her opinions on everything from plastic surgeons that transform naturally aging faces into dreadful-looking clowns to marijuana's effectiveness to relax taut facial muscles. She was happy to share her uninhibited life experiences, including three husbands and numerous love affairs. The woman never stopped talking, fascinating Tick, who wrote out lots of questions about life in New York City.

Brad could hardly ignore Amori's somewhat unrestrained, PG-rated chatter, but he would discuss her provocative lifestyle with Tick later. The main thing was that the woman was a genius at her craft, having both the ability and desire to impart her knowledge to Tick. She liked Tick, and Tick liked her.

Amori found in Tick a tireless student who challenged her every view, but who also remembered her every instruction and practiced to improve her skills.

The days Tick spent with her new mentor were a pleasant reprieve from arranging her mother's funeral, now only days away. She became utterly immersed in her artwork, producing drawing after drawing and eagerly anticipating the next session with Madame Amori. Brad had contracted seven sessions that often extended late into the night, and he couldn't remember a time when Tick was happier.

On the other hand, Brad had to field some difficult discussions with Amori that stretched even Brad's capacity to invent new stories. She explained to Brad how, in portrait painting, knowing something about the subject was essential. Her best art came from painting people with depth and character, people she got to know and understand.

"Tick knows every nuance, expression, and thought of her mother," Madame Amori said, "but she doesn't know anything about her father, the young man in the picture. She won't even acknowledge him as her father, but it's obvious he is. She shares so many of his features. But, oh, how she loved her mother! It must be a heartbreaking loss for her."

Brad's reply came haltingly slow, frequently clearing his throat. "Her father spent much of Tick's life as a traveling missionary. Her mother had to remain in Florida caring for elderly relatives. Tick saw him rarely and carries some resentment."

Amori didn't press him on the issue and seemed to accept his explanation, but Brad started to realize just how hard it would be to create a new identity for Tick.

Nevertheless, he would have to go over this new story with Tick. She, at least, would remember his lies, even if he didn't.

Amori returned to New York, leaving Tick with new skills and several beautiful sketches of her mother. Upon leaving, she told Brad, "Your daughter is remarkable, and she has an eye for it all: color, line, shape, light, and shadow, texture…all of it. And she certainly isn't afraid of work."

Reflectively, she added, "But her real strength lies elsewhere. She sees people in a bright light. The rest of us see only shadows filtered by our self-centeredness. She will become a celebrated artist if she continues, although I know she has other talents and interests. She's too young to settle on one thing at this point, but I have loved having her as a student. She knows where to find me whenever she needs me."

Life at the Deer Valley house was a welcome mix of activities and peacefulness as the countdown continued toward Tick's liberation from the fiberglass cast—her pink prison. The Deer Valley house was never without a friendly caregiver or visitor: Abigail Jones, Leslie Thomas, Beverly Lee, Laura Shelby, Dr. Brackford, Dr. Barnes, Nate Hoger, and Jenny Dresder. There were dinner get-togethers, movies, poker, Trivial Pursuit nights, and cooking lessons. There were sunrises, sunsets, stormy days, and sunny days to appreciate and countless skiers of every ability for Tick to watch and critique as they made their way down the slope, skiing past the picture windows in the den. Tick enjoyed poking fun at skiers who looked uncoordinated or those who fell on the path in her view, but her real commentary centered on reckless skiers who endangered others. Thankfully, they were unaware of her stakeout behind tinted windows.

Brad, now able to get online with his family, relished knowing how everyone was getting along and listening to their exploits, especially those of the grandchildren. He made an effort to include Tick during these online visits, and the family was starting to accept their silent adopted sister typing on a keyboard—a sister who answered their questions in precise, erudite sentences.

Brad began feeling genuine confidence in Tick's future.

"She's doing so well, Mattie," he expressed after spending an unusually full and enjoyable day with Tick. "I think we've underestimated her ability and resolve to leave her past behind her."

Mattie looked at him as if he had grown a third eye, then gently replied, "I don't want to burst your bubble, Brad... Her time here has been a blessing, but understand, this is an artificial environment, not the real world. Everyone who enters this house knows her—they are all seasoned professionals, the cream of the crop in their field—and for that matter, they all truly care about her. Don't be misled by a few good days. She still isn't talking, and she still has a long way to go."

Mattie placed her hand on Brad's shoulder. "You're in for a lot more turmoil, Geronimo, but she's a survivor and a believer. Both you and the Lord have her back. Our role is to pinpoint and clear a path for her to find a way out."

CHAPTER

26

Reports

Dr. Barnes made the rounds on the ever-changing number of critically ill children and, as was her custom, swung by Laura's office with a deluge of instructions.

Laura's greeting was less than enthusiastic.

"Morning, Mattie. I assume Brad and Tick enjoyed the meal you prepared last night? I suppose Tick is still up all night drawing?"

Noting Laura's disapproving undertone, Mattie chose to respond in a distinctly upbeat way.

"Good morning, Laura! Yes, Brad and Tick enjoyed the meal and asked me to thank you for doing all the shopping. And before I forget, Brad has a gift for you and me. He reserved box seat tickets for us at the Eccles Theater to see the upcoming performance of *Phantom of the Opera*. He thinks we need a break. As for Tick and her late-night artwork, Brad will be cracking down on that. She needs her sleep."

"Well, it was nice of him to think of us," Laura said as she lifted a box containing several files.

"Here, this is for you. An FBI agent dropped it off earlier. He asked me to remind you that its contents are strictly confidential, and they want it back when you are finished with your review, tomorrow to be precise. They didn't seem very pleased about giving it to you." Laura handed Mattie the box. "Also I was at the meat market and picked up some halibut for your dinner at the Hughes's. I knew you'd

287

be over there cooking again tonight. Anyway, it's in the common room fridge."

"That's brilliant, Laura! You saved me a lot of time today. Thank you, thank you, thank you!" Mindful that Laura did not favor the unconventional approach or amount of time she was dedicating to Tick, Mattie reached into her purse and pulled out a beautifully inlaid hexagon box. "This is for you, my friend. It's a Chinese puzzle box, and there's something for you hidden inside the secret compartment. I'm sure you'll figure out how to open it up, but it's a challenging creation—confounding. It will require time and a lot of critical thinking to solve, but I think you'll find it worth the effort."

Laura cradled the box in her hands, turning it over, examining it all around, and giving it a little shake, "Oh, Mattie, it's exquisite! Thank you so much, but I don't understand. My birthday isn't for months."

"I know, Laura," Mattie said, laughing. "My calendar app reminds me of that every year... No, dear heart, let's say this is just a token of appreciation, in part, for all you do to help me with the Hughes's—mainly Tick, of course. I have solicited your assistance beyond your normal job responsibilities, and I know my involvement puzzles you."

Laura turned her attention to the box without saying a word before breaking the silence. "So, a complex puzzle that takes time and critical thinking to open, with something hidden inside. Hmm, I think that there's more behind this gift than your appreciation, Dr. Barnes."

"Is that what you think?" Mattie said with a smile and a telling nod.

"Yes, that's exactly what I think, Laura said, amused. "And I get it! How dense would I be if I didn't catch on to an analogy so superbly handed to me?"

"You're hardly dense, my girl, just not accustomed to me functioning outside my usual ICU box."

"You're right. I missed your 'Psychiatrist Is In' sign."

"You're funny! Anyway, I wish you good luck working on that puzzle," Mattie said, tapping the box and wondering how long it would take Laura to unlock the compartment that held a delicate gold and diamond cross. "Let's get back to work!"

"Thanks, Mattie. I'll be praying for you and your green-eyed puzzle. Speaking of puzzles, by the way, you played that well!"

Mattie paused, now puzzled. "What do you mean?"

"The adoption, going to the cabin, deserting Tick. None of it made any sense at the time. I have been giving it all a lot of thought."

Mattie laughed. "Methinks you suffer from an overactive imagination. I just couldn't be in the room with Palmer."

Laura sarcastically replied, "I understand. He was much too tough for you."

***

Mattie retreated to her desk and examined the cardboard box and its files, her thoughts on the information it might contain. Tick had shut down after the FBI interview, becoming testy if she or Brad even hinted at a clarification. It was clear that Tick felt she had contributed enough and would not be forthcoming with additional information.

Yet there was still so much more to learn about her. Mattie was determined to zero in on critical issues of particular interest, hoping that information in the report would provide illumination.

Opening the package, she found the first folder spoke to the FBI's main concern: Timothy Bird and the danger he posed to the public and Tick and Brad.

Scanning the report, Mattie was disappointed. There was little new information of value.

She knew that Timothy Bird and a handful of college students at the University of Washington had formed a group describing themselves as the Epilektoi, an ancient name for elite Greek warriors meaning "the chosen ones." She had seen the reports on the astonishing mortality rate of his associates.

What was new and quite troublesome was the supposition that Timothy Bird belonged to a much larger criminal organization and was involved with powerful, dangerous people.

Then there was the mysterious Kask who had visited them in the cave. It was a name known to the FBI, an elusive, mysterious assassin wanted by several agencies worldwide. Could it be the same individual? The thought of another killer in the mix was chilling.

Subsequent folders concerned the many victims found at the ranch along with autopsy information. Mattie picked her way through the folders taking notes on items of particular interest.

The Victims

Thornton and David Bittner

Thornton Bittner, David's father, was a forty-five-year-old accountant who died of multiple stab wounds. What struck Mattie was his arrest record for physically abusing his wife and son. On three occasions, his wife had claimed she had fallen, but her injuries had been suspect.

Thornton's 6'2" sixteen-year-old son David had a reputation for aggressive behavior, being suspended from school on many occasions for fighting. David also showed signs of previous abuse, fractures not on record at the medical facilities he frequented.

Until now, Mattie had not accepted Tick's account of the battle. Even after seeing the scars on Tick's arms, she found it hard to imagine that a normal high school boy would so viciously attack an unarmed child with a knife. Now she believed Tick's account. David was a good subject for Bird, an angry, aggressive child who could be goaded into becoming a killer, especially with his own life at stake. The report was both gratifying and troubling. Tick had not delivered the deathblow. David was too tall and the blow too massive for Tick to have ever delivered. Still, Tick had cut him, small cuts everywhere. It was an ugly story, and one that Brad thought sounded incomplete.

Tammy Rockford

Mattie hadn't felt that Tick had been in any way disingenuous about her account of Tammy; she had only wanted to learn what it was about the girl that had provoked Tick and her mother to revolt against Timothy and Janet openly. The FBI confirmed every assumption Mattie had about the girl. Tammy was a wonderful girl, active in her church, school, and community. The entire town had turned out for her funeral. She had left behind a mother, a father, and two siblings.

Janet Herrington

Janet was forty-nine years old and a National Karate Champion. She had been a fellow student of Timothy Bird. Her cause of death was a stab wound from a sharp object into the heart.

She had been raised in a good family, an overachieving child, close to her mother, father, and two brothers. A family she was close to until her sophomore year in college. Then Bird and his friends managed to isolate her from friends and family, successfully indoctrinating her into their cult. At the time, her family had tried everything to get her back. Unsuccessful in their efforts, they had not heard from her in years.

Mattie was troubled by her death. Bird wasn't the type to stab somebody in the heart; death would come much too quickly and painlessly. Brad was right something was missing from Tick's accounting of this last battle.

⁓

Setting aside a folder on Alissa Morgan, Mattie read through the list of remaining victims found in the cemetery: Marjory Perkins, people from surrounding states, a prostitute from Nevada, two teenage girls from Wyoming, a rancher from Idaho, a truck driver from Arizona, and two victims whose identities were under investigation. All showed evidence of violent deaths, and some bodies showed evidence of extreme torture—all of the reports corresponded with Tick's testimony.

Mattie struggled with the violent images: knife fights, the slaughter of children, Perkins being buried alive, a poor woman burned at the stake. Tick had lived her formative years in an environment saturated in violence.

More to the point, Mattie was now convinced that Hoger was right in his assessment of Tick—she was someone who could kill a person with about any object found in a room. Tick had unquestionably fought two battles against strong opponents, both of whom intended to kill her. Mattie thought, *Tick claims she has never killed, but she clearly won out over impossible odds.*

Mattie knew that, statistically, victims of personal violence and abuse were twice as likely to commit a violent crime within two years after being assaulted. She also knew that violence is as contagious as any disease and that Tick, who had been exposed to violence countless times over during the last seven years, had shown herself to be an example of this pattern on several occasions. Mattie had vouched for Tick to the courts, to Brad, and Brad's family.

Had she made a mistake? she asked herself. Mattie paced the floor before once again settling down at her desk.

THE COMMUNITY, THE CEMETERY, THE RANCH, THE LIBRARY, THE CAVE COMPLEX

Mattie reached for a large separate folder containing pictures and drawings of the ranch site before the explosion, as well as interactions with neighbors.

The Community

Interview transcripts from neighboring ranchers and townsfolk had yielded little in the way of new information. Alissa infrequently went to town, and those who remembered her thought she was friendly but timid. More information was available on Janet Herrington and Marjory Perkins. Reports from residents state that both women were aloof and tightlipped.

Only one neighbor ever recalled meeting Tick, a rancher who recalled an encounter with her during deer season when he met up with Timothy and Tick high in the mountains. When he asked about

Tick, who had continued to walk on ahead, Timothy said she was a niece visiting from Canada. He was teaching her how to hunt. The rancher remembered being impressed by the small girl who carried a heavy deer rifle effortlessly.

The Cemetery

Photos and drawings of the cemetery showed it to be located about five hundred yards from the house, well-hidden in a dry river-bed called a draw.

The pictures of the cemetery showed carefully marked and tagged gravesites. Each grave had been meticulously excavated and examined by the FBI for any shred of evidence it might provide. Two fresh graves contained the remains of Janet Herrington and Alissa Morgan. Forensics indicated that they had both died close to the time Tick made her escape.

Mattie wondered just how many of those graves had Tick and Alissa dug?

The Ranch

The ranch pictures included shots of a rustic but well-designed upscale house similar to what you might find around Park City. The contractors were aware of the cave complex and had made an extension into it. The company's representative said that Bird mentioned something about plans to use the cave as a storage area and a wine cellar.

Other pictures showed a sturdy-looking barn and a large chicken coop. Authorities had rounded up more than forty chickens and distributed them among local ranchers. These chickens had been Tick's responsibility.

There was a large, well-tended vegetable garden to one side of the ranch house, the front landscaped with flowerbeds, ornamental trees, and shrubs. Mattie thought back to her first days with Tick, remembering the rough condition of her hands. She envisioned Alissa and Tick tending the garden as one of their many duties.

Thumbing through pictures of the inside of the ranch house, Mattie noted its immaculate condition. The kitchen looked spotless, with granite countertops, handsome wood cabinetry, and a large, glass-front china cabinet holding an array of porcelain dishware. There was a well-stocked spice rack on the counter next to a commercial-grade cooking range, and wilted remains of what had been fresh vegetables sat in a carved wooden bowl on the kitchen island.

Mattie surmised that Tick and her mother were meticulous caretakers—or as Tick put it, doing their best before God.

The Library

There were numerous close-up shots of shelves holding an impressive collection of books, including an assortment of historical novels on Rome, Greece, and other ancient civilizations. Mattie cringed when she noticed the titles of numerous books devoted to genocide and human manipulation experiments of every genre. There were rows and rows of books covering the horrific medical experimentations practiced by the Nazi regime during World War II and other publications documenting atrocities of human cruelty— books written by the Russian neurophysiologist, Ivan Pavlov, about behavior modification and conditioned reflexes and other books documenting studies on obedience and the impact of torture on the victims.

In her years studying human behavior in medical school and her practice as a psychiatrist, Mattie was familiar with studies of respected scientists and doctors whose names she recognized on some of these books' spines, but Bird's vast collection of illustrated works about appalling and deviant human behavior, written primarily for the vicarious pleasure of sadistic individuals, disturbed Mattie on many levels.

Now there was more for her to consider: Tick's access to Bird's library.

There were no longer any doubts in Mattie's mind. Tick had unrestricted access to the library and had lied about it. Tick, in their conversations, had surprised her with quotations and insights, many of which Mattie realized came from books on those shelves. Mattie had to question what aberrant information Tick had picked up from reading Bird's books and how Tick might apply what she had learned. Tick was undeniably skilled at sizing people up when she would either lash out at them or manipulate events to suit her needs. No question, Tick could be a holy terror.

A spiritual war had been fought at that ranch. Who had won the battle?

The Cave Complex

Tick had never been reluctant to talk about the cave where she spent most of her childhood, describing in detail a childhood home and the arena where she had trained and fought.

Nevertheless, for Mattie, there was another source of terror that had to have impacted Tick. On more than one occasion, Alissa and Tick had been left alone for weeks at a time, carefully rationing their food to survive and grateful for the small stream running through the cave that provided their drinking water.

Even if outsiders had found them, death would have followed for all at the site heavily rigged with explosives. Tick would have been aware of their predicament.

Still, when looking at a picture and close up of the arena, Mattie was shocked to her core, becoming aware of a sight that Tick had neatly blocked from her mind.

Off to the side of the arena was a ten-foot post with iron rings attached at the top.

A close-up picture of the post revealed a whip hanging from a hook. The image was shocking: a whip made of carefully braided ox-hide strips containing small chunks of iron, sharp animal bones, and pieces of lead.

Tick had never talked about the post and was ashamed of her scars, becoming angry if the topic came up.

Mattie felt sick as she pictured Tick's wrists handcuffed to the rings, Timothy shredding her back with blows that should have killed her.

Bird must have planned to finish her. What stopped him?

Alissa Morgan

Feeling energized, Mattie then turned her attention to Alissa Morgan, a woman whom Mattie already had deep feelings for. Ruth Evers had kept her promise; the file was a treasure trove of information.

The autopsy report was hard reading. Like her daughter, Alissa was scarred from beatings with a bullwhip and had several old bone fractures, including a fractured jaw. Her death was painful; defensive knife wounds were on her hands and forearms, and she sustained a fatal stab wound to her abdomen.

Lab results of the blood found on Alissa's dress showed DNA from Timothy Bird, Tick, and Janet Herrington. Alissa's front teeth were missing; healed gums indicated that the tooth loss had occurred well before her death.

Tick has never mentioned anything about her mom's teeth, Mattie realized.

Then it all got fascinating as Mattie dove into Agent Steve Brewer's interview with Sister Agatha, an elderly nun who had raised Alissa Morgan from age nine.

Mattie read that Alissa was born in Columbia, South America. Her father migrated to South America from Wales as a young man with dreams of becoming a cattle rancher in eastern Columbia's grassland plains. He married a lovely, spirited young Columbian woman. Together, they established a ranching operation near Villavicencio, just outside of Bogota's capital city, where they started a family and raised cattle. Alissa's early childhood was blessed but cut short when leftist rebels wanting to cultivate coca on their land murdered her parents. Alissa survived and was sent to the United States to live with her mother's aunt, her only living relative, in Roanoke, Virginia. When Alissa was nine years old, her aunt died of congestive heart failure, and social services placed the girl in the local Catholic orphanage. A childless couple quickly adopted the stunningly beautiful child and took Alissa to their home more than 330 miles away in Lancaster, Pennsylvania.

Several days later, she was reported missing, and three weeks later, she showed up on the orphanage steps, exhausted and in tattered clothes. The soles of her shoes were nearly gone, and her feet were bloody with open blisters. She told the Mother Superior that the man who adopted her drank liquor all day and was always trying to put his hands on her, so she ran away. She told authorities that she wanted to remain in the orphanage, where she spent the remainder of her childhood.

The report on Alissa contained many direct statements by Sister Agatha taken from Brewer's recorded interview:

> "Alissa's life at the orphanage was good, and she thrived beautifully."
>
> "She was a gift from God to all who knew her, tremendously kindhearted and giving, radiating hope and optimism everywhere she went."
>
> "She was an outstanding student and became an exceptional tutor to the younger children who needed extra help with their schoolwork. She was also a marvelous cook and a wiz in our large but outdated kitchen."

In his report, Brewer included the nun's narration about her struggle with the sin of favoring Alissa over other children at the orphanage. Eventually, through prayer, her bias turned into praise for God's wisdom in placing Alissa where she could build up others through faith.

Brewer reported that Alissa had expressed a desire to join their order when she turned eighteen. Still, Agatha, the Mother Superior of the orphanage at that time, persuaded her to wait to defer her decision until after she attended college. Agatha wanted Alissa to have time to grow and gain a broader perspective of life before committing herself to the religious life.

Alissa attended a local junior college and moved into a small apartment. She supported herself by working part-time as a line cook at a local restaurant. After receiving an associate's degree in elementary education, Emmanuel College in Franklin Springs, Georgia, accepted her for admission with a full scholarship. She never enrolled.

Sister Agatha reported that when Alissa was attending junior college, she came by the orphanage quite often to visit and to check on the other children:

> During her final year at the junior college, she couldn't have been happier, confessing that she had met a young man and was in love with him. The last time I saw her was when I attended her graduation. We sat together on a campus bench, and I knew something was wrong. I tried to get her to tell me what was troubling her, but she wouldn't say, only that her plans to attend Emmanuel College had changed. She begged me not to ask her any more questions, saying that she needed to find her way and that she would be leaving. She said she would keep in touch and that her thoughts and prayers would always be with everyone at the orphanage.

Sister Agatha retrieved a stack of envelopes from her desk. From a tattered envelope that showed signs of wear, she pulled out a picture of Alissa and young Esther together on a pier.

"Each year, Alissa would drop us a note," Sister Agatha said in the report, "writing that she was doing well and living with a wonderful older couple. She always asked us to pray for her and her little daughter. They are both so beautiful. Look at their eyes—God's artwork there. I didn't know where she had gone. She never provided a return address."

Mattie had seen the picture before. Tick had a framed copy removed from the Fowlers' home and given to her by Ruth Evers.

Yes, Sister Agatha was right—such beautiful eyes.

Mattie made a mental note to talk with Brad that evening about taking Tick to the orphanage when the time was right. *Tick would undoubtedly benefit from hearing about her mother.*

The FBI report then went on to summarize interviews held in and around Southern California. Alissa had moved to Los Angeles, a young unmarried pregnant woman with two years of college. She rented a studio apartment in a rundown apartment building, working the evening shift at a fast-food restaurant and in a grocery store during the day. One day, Alissa spent her lunch break on a nearby park bench and conversed with Mabel and Henry Fowler.

The Fowlers' only son told the FBI officer that his folks who lived in Sherman Oaks, California, took an instant liking to someone they described as a wonderful, deserving girl, who, as they explained to their concerned son, needed them. They persuaded Alissa to move into their furnished carriage house apartment behind the main house. Weeks later, they would drive Alissa to the hospital, where a one-month premature, five-pound baby girl was born. The infant was a feisty, fussy beauty with oversized green and amber eyes, which, from the beginning, locked onto her adoring mother's face.

The Fowlers cherished Alissa and Esther, and Alissa attempted to repay their kindness by doing all the cooking and the majority of the housework.

The Fowlers' son, who lived in Texas at the time, remembered how upset he was with his parents for taking in a pregnant stranger. However, years before Alissa and Esther's kidnapping, he realized what a godsend Alissa had been for his folks. Visiting his parents for a week, he observed how dependent they had become on Alissa, even relying on her to pay the bills and manage their money. An accountant, he appreciated that Alissa kept impeccable records of every dollar spent. Months after the kidnapping, the Fowlers, unable to manage their household, moved into an assisted living facility. They passed away within one year of each other and two years after Alissa and Esther's disappearance.

The report included Alissa's tax returns, which showed that she worked as a dispatcher for a local cement company while residing at the Fowlers, a job she could do from the carriage house while still caring for her daughter. Highly organized and with a genuine likability, Alissa had been a wiz at her job, ready to cajole even the most obstinate drivers into willingly keeping on their tight schedules. Her company, valuing her work, compensated her well. When Esther was two years old and into everything, Alissa hired a caregiver she knew from her church who could help out with both little Esther and the Fowlers.

Then, following her love of cooking, she quit her job with the trucking company and accepted a prestigious restaurant position. A decision that had disastrous consequences—Timothy Bird was a regular patron.

Alissa and her daughter's disappearance confounded the local police and triggered a long, involved, and ongoing police investigation.

Mattie then came across a photo found at the Fowler residence—new to her—Alissa, with her arms wrapped around a handsome young man. The young couple, sitting by a fountain in a courtyard, looked so happy and carefree, and it was clear they were completely enamored with each other. Mattie had seen the picture before; it was a copy of the picture given to Tick by Evers at the FBI interview. Mattie was convinced that this picture contained an image of Tick's unnamed father, who had so mysteriously died, triggering some crisis between Alissa and his parents.

Mattie recalled her efforts to flush out the details during breakfast with Tick and Brad one morning. She had asked Tick why she didn't know her father's name. Tick refused to respond to the question, turning away, but Brad pressed the issue, and Tick finally wrote, *"Whenever I asked about my father, Momma became tearful. She told me that she had disappointed and angered his family—that it would only cause trouble to contact them. Momma said that they were wealthy and powerful, and she didn't want them in our lives. She promised that when I turned eighteen, she would tell me the whole story. Now I will never know anything about them except how upset my mother became when she talked about them. If they're still alive, I don't want to meet them."*

Looking at the picture again, Mattie wondered why Alissa, a kind, smart, young girl would go to such lengths to hide information about Tick's father and his family.

What happened to force a young pregnant mother to drop everything and flee to another state?

Esther Morgan

Finally, Mattie opened the file on her patient. Esther's preschool and kindergarten records were there. Significant among the papers was a written report by Dr. Albert Thomas, a child psychologist.

Reading through the reports and the comments, Mattie learned that, within the first few days of kindergarten, Esther's teacher recognized that she was not like other children. At times, Esther would overrule the teacher with her clear views on how to run the classroom; at other times, she would drop out entirely, disappearing into a private world of her own. The school referred Alissa to Dr. Thomas, an eminent child developmental psychologist, to evaluate her daughter. He did so without charging the single mother, who was on a tight budget.

Dr. Thomas discovered that Esther's main difficulty at school was "mind-crushing boredom." He determined her IQ in a range that put her well over "Very Superior" on the Wechsler Preschool and Primary Scale of Intelligence. The doctor's solution was for Esther to continue interacting with children her age and place her in a classroom with children with more advanced reading and comprehension levels.

Acting on the doctor's advice and with some financial assistance from the Fowlers and from her church, Alissa enrolled Esther in the Crossgate School for gifted and talented children. She blossomed at the school, an institution that challenged and stimulated her mind. Still, it was clear, even back then, that Tick had been a handful. Sharing his findings of little Miss Morgan in his report for the FBI, Dr. Thomas wrote that Esther had the brightest, most imaginative young mind he had ever come across.

"I'd like to think that in the years since I've worked with her, Esther has modified her approach with her teachers," Thomas wrote. "At Crossgate School, she consistently challenged her teachers, and they learned not to patronize her with simple platitudes. She compelled those teachers to be on their toes and to be direct with her. She was a challenge, as gifted children usually are, but Esther's teachers were extremely fond of her, as was I."

Nowhere in the teachers' reports was there any mention or concern about Tick behaving violently, but several teachers commented about her exceptional physical coordination and how much she enjoyed playing in the schoolyard.

Mattie finished reading the reports and spent the half-hour envisioning the circumstances under which Tick somehow survived. This extraordinarily gifted, assertive child, precociously racing through life, had been suddenly thrust into a cult-like culture where disobedience against a deranged leader's orders was simply not tolerated. Given Tick's strong disposition, she would have been defiant, and based on the physical signs of abuse on her body, she was punished severely for any waywardness.

At some point, Mattie thought, *Tick had adapted, perhaps bonded with Timothy Bird, becoming his little athletic protégé. Under his manipulative, distorted coaching, she may have turned on her mother, rejecting Allisa's values and teachings. This tension could be one aspect of Tick's crushing guilt. But just what had happened between Tick and her mother? What had made her bond so completely with Brad? Why couldn't she bring herself to talk?*

I'm not a practicing psychiatrist anymore, she thought. *I am an emergency care physician with a full schedule. I don't have time for this. I need to let this one go.*

She sat silently, looking out of the window, one question after another swirling around in her head.

Saying Goodbye

The next day, December 10, Brad was at the airport to meet his three sons and two daughters-in-law. The three flights arrived within thirty minutes of each other, and because Brad's jeep couldn't accommodate the whole group with their luggage, they arranged to hook up at the car rental agency near the baggage carousel. Brad's unmarried son, David, rode with his dad, and the other four followed them to the Deer Valley safe house in the rental car. It was late afternoon when the vehicles pulled into the driveway, and the sky had turned all shades of red and orange with the setting sun. There was no denying that Utah was a beautiful state, and the Deer Valley resort area set in the mountains was as scenic as it gets.

Family values dictated that, out of respect for their newly adopted sister, Brad's adult children would make the trip to attend Alissa's funeral, but in truth, they came mainly to meet Tick for the first time. Brad's grandchildren did not make the trip. Brad felt it would be better to meet their new aunt on a happier occasion. As Tick's brothers and sisters-in-law entered the impressive looking house, Tick was in the foyer to receive each one with a cordial, if not shy, smile. Undeterred by neither the wheelchair nor her pink cast, the family ensemble didn't hesitate to encircle Tick with warmhearted hellos and careful hugs, each one kindly offering words of sympathy for the sad circumstance of their gathering.

Brad gave the group a quick tour around the house before assigning bedrooms and allowing everyone time to freshen up. Seemingly disregarding her physical limitations and speechlessness, Tick was determined to make a good impression on the family and adamantly refused to let Brad order take-out food—most certainly not for the family's first meal together. But the time Brad spent assisting her in the kitchen earlier in the day was another warning shot fired regarding Tick's impaired psyche: Tick was particularly apprehensive that the food she was preparing would not be perfect.

Brad told her that she needed to relax. "You're not cooking for the king, you know," he said. On a pad, Tick began sketching a man wielding a sword and wearing a crown with the initials TB. He was pointing to a tearful woman holding a pan, and she was standing next to an angry-looking child who was holding a spoon. The caption read "Off with Their Heads!" Watching this humorous but disturbingly telling production, Brad took the iPad, erased everything except the king, drew devil horns on the crown, and added the caption "Down with the Evil King!"

When it was dinnertime, Tick ushered the family into the dining room, where a delicious buffet supper of meat tarts, salads, and sweet treats awaited them. Later in the kitchen, Tick freely shared some of her recipes and baking secrets with the Hughes's wives. Still, after spending a good part of her day working in the kitchen dealing with an awkward cast and feeling apprehensive about her adopted family, Tick began to fade. Up to that point, Tick masterfully hid any signs of the dread she was feeling about viewing her mother's body the next day or the funeral that would follow, but exhaustion had set in. Tick, now reverting to her cautionary behaviors—intense, studying, and guarded—was quick to nod her head in agreement when Brad suggested that she turn in early.

After saying good night to their adopted sister, the family talked long into the night. Everyone was anxious to learn as much as he or she could about the capable, enigmatic, strikingly beautiful young girl who had become a new member of the Hughes family, forcing Brad to recount story after story.

The next morning—the day of the funeral—Laura and Mattie arrived at the house early. Mattie brought something pretty for Tick to wear, a long, flared blouse with sheer sleeves and a ribbon bow at the neck. Shopping for clothes to suit a girl in a body cast was not easy. Thankfully, in just a few weeks, the cast would become a distant, uncomfortable memory. In Tick's bedroom, Becky and Natalie thought to distract their silent, unhappy-looking adoptee from thinking about her mother's funeral by fussing over her and talking about their kids' activities.

Knowing Tick and recognizing that she needed a reprieve from draining chatter, Laura asked Tick if she would mind baking some breakfast scones for the family. Mattie visited with Becky and Natalie; both women taken with the attractive doctor, fascinated by her undertakings and accomplishments. Brad caught up with his older boys; and David, Brad's youngest son, drifted off to the kitchen doing his best to get to know Laura. Before too long, the aroma of the baking scones heartened the atmosphere.

Quietly enjoying Tick's pastries in the dining room while watching the ski lift carry skiers up the slope, the family managed to avoid talking to their sister about the painful occasion that lay ahead for her. By any account, she was a detached, troubled, and speechless child who was making an effort to pay attention and to be polite but whose thoughts were miles away. Knowing Tick's thoughts was impossible; perhaps she was in a dark cave with her mother, possibly in an arena fighting for her life, maybe on a mountain cliff huddled behind a lone pine tree hiding from the stranger who would later become her father.

Too soon, it was time to depart for the funeral and to the tragic reality of Alissa's death. It was a frigid day without sunshine. Three vehicles formed the convoy—Brad and his single, silent passenger, Tick, led the way in his jeep; the married sons and their wives trailed in the rental car; and Mattie drove alone. Laura and David had taken off earlier on some vague mission for Mattie, but they would be catching up with the rest of the family as soon as possible.

The viewing was in a room adjacent to a small, non-sectarian chapel. Brad's chest tightened as he wheeled Tick up to a beautiful, custom-made casket surrounded by a mass of fragrant pink roses and white lilies. He helped her out of the wheelchair, allowing his tormented daughter one last, parting look at her mother. It was Brad's first look at the woman who had played the lead role in his adopted daughter's life.

The previous day, Alissa started her final journey carefully and secretly in a nondescript van. Security had been tight, with FBI agents transferring the body from the city morgue to the mortuary, alert to anyone following en route.

The mortuary had done an exceptional job—Alissa looked peaceful. Even in death, one could easily match her features with those of her daughter, yet that mysterious gift of life had left her— her soul was now in heaven—leaving behind a cold, marble-like, lifeless statue.

Brad's chest tightened as he watched Tick, her body trembling, gently brush back a strand of hair from her mother's forehead. Then, cupping Alissa's face in her hands, she leaned over and appeared to whisper silently in her ear.

Seeing and touching her mother's lifeless body had somehow magnified Tick's fragility—the pinkish scar on her face had turned a bluish-white. Pronounced veins in her forehead, incongruous to see in one so young, resembled a roadmap of stony anguish, grief nearly extinguishing her fierce spirit.

Thankfully, Mattie was at Brad's side to help, and the two of them quickly bracketed Tick at the casket. Once Tick had finished saying her good-byes, Brad gently gathered her up to wheel her into the chapel.

As they left for the chapel, Brad took a final look at Alissa. He imagined the hard journey she and her daughter had made and then wordlessly promised that he would do everything in his power to take care of her daughter, that Esther would be loved and protected. Unable to process his feelings, he wished that Alissa was aware of him and knew everything that was happening to her child now.

Tick had asked Brad to speak at her mother's service, a task he had obsessed over for days. After the casket was brought in, with "Amazing Grace" playing in the background, he delivered a short but meaningful eulogy based on what he and Mattie had learned about Alissa Morgan from the FBI reports and Tick's few disclosures about her.

During the eulogy, Laura and David escorted an unfamiliar older woman into the chapel. Sister Agatha's appearance, as it happened, was the one exception the FBI made to the highly restricted guest list, per Dr. Barnes's petition.

Brad said a few words of introduction before inviting Sister Agatha to the podium. The aged Mother Superior of the orphanage where Alissa had spent her formative years rose and gingerly walked down the aisle, holding on to her walker with small, bony hands wrapped around the handles, her feet slowly shuffling behind the wheels. Laura and David walked alongside her and then helped her to the podium—a short but seemingly endless walk.

Tick's reaction to the disruption of her carefully planned program was, mercifully for the attendees, without any confrontation. Still, the look on her face was a clear indictment of Laura, who had left the safe house with David without explanation. *Now she has the nerve to show up late to my carefully planned service with a total stranger.*

Tick gave Laura a sharp, nasty look and then turned, eyes and ears fixed on the elderly stranger.

Her anger quickly faded as the nun, speaking in an energetic, clear, and strong voice, gave the most eloquent, loving eulogy imaginable. She described Alissa's life from the day she had entered the orphanage until the night she left, recounting story after story in loving detail.

As Sister Agatha finished her tribute to Alissa, she looked directly at Tick.

"My one regret when I entered God's service was that I would never have children. Then the good Lord answered my prayers and provided me with hundreds of them, all of them so special and so unique in God's eyes. But there was one child who came first in my prayers at night, and that has always been Alissa. Today, I'm blessed to meet her precious daughter, finally. I am so grateful to be here, Esther, and feel such joy seeing you. Looking at you, I see Alissa's every feature and recognize the same courage that made her so special. You come from the purest earthly blood I have ever known. Bless you, my child."

It was snowing heavily when the hearse and the family's cars turned into the cemetery grounds. Brad, his sons, Dr. Brackford, and Nate Hoger carried the casket to the gravesite, under the canopy of a small heated tent. Tick bundled up in a new, hooded winter coat that Laura had picked out for her, held a bouquet of white roses. Mattie wheeled Tick next to Brad as the interment took place.

Mattie observed Tick and Brad, her mind racing as Brad read Isaiah 57:1–2, a verse Tick had requested.

"The righteous perish, and no one takes it to heart; the devout are taken away, and no one understands that the righteous are taken away to be spared from evil. Those who walk uprightly enter peace; they find rest as they lie in death."

Brad had wanted his pastor to speak at the funeral, but the FBI unequivocally nixed his plans. Not even a trusted pastor should know her true identity.

Brad is doing such a splendid job, Mattie thought, *a man totally and wholeheartedly invested in making this service as meaningful as possible for his daughter.*

She looked over at Tick, who stood by her father, her face unreadable.

She has that shield up, Mattie observed. *That damn shield that locks all of us out. The armor that protected you from Timothy Bird, the armor that continues to screen you away from the world.*

A small tremor in Tick's hands, hands that rarely shook, betrayed Tick as she dropped her bouquet of roses onto the casket.

Tick wasn't the only one grieving that day, Mattie observed. Following the interment, Brad and his sons walked a few feet from the tent to place flowers on Catherine's grave, just a row away. Mattie, who had gone outside with them, respectfully stood back and noticed Brad's hands were shaking as well.

As the family prepared to return to the Deer Valley house for some welcomed rest and an early supper, Sister Agatha, tired and saddened by the event that brought her to Utah, went to Tick to say farewell. Tick pulled her slate out from under her coat.

"May I please see you tomorrow to hear some more about my mother?"

Sister Agatha didn't hesitate with her response, and she asked Brad to help reschedule her flight. "My flight tomorrow is at 9:00 a.m., but I really would like to spend some time with Esther, or Tick as you call her."

Laura changed the reservations before driving the sister back to her downtown Salt Lake City hotel.

For Laura, the night was, regrettably, not over. After dropping Sister Agatha off at the Little America Hotel, only minutes from the beckoning peace of her apartment, she received a text from Mattie: "Tick is upset to hear that you won't be back here with us tonight. She wants to see you."

Grudgingly, Laura drove back up to Deer Valley, emotionally and physically wiped out by the day's events. She was too tired to deal with Tick, but Mattie wouldn't have asked her unless she thought it was necessary.

Watching Tick at the funeral had brought Laura's critical, unspoken case against the girl into a better focus.

Maybe I've been too hard on Tick, she thought.

While not easy to admit, Laura was somewhat jealous of Tick's growing close relationship with Mattie. As she drove up the mountain pass, she wondered if the funeral preparations just wore her down, but it shattered her heart to witness Tick's final farewell with her mother.

Walking into the house, Tick was waiting for Laura in the foyer. Together, they made their way to the unoccupied study for some privacy. Mattie and the wives were finishing up dinner preparations when Tick and Laura joined them in the kitchen. Tick offered to help cook, and Laura came in to say a quick hello and good-bye. She needed to get on the road before it started to snow again.

Mattie escorted Laura to the door.

"Is everything okay?" she asked. "Is Tick okay?"

"Well," Laura replied, "Tick just wanted to let me know that she thought the funeral was wonderful. She let me know that it was even better than she had hoped and that she couldn't have done it without me. She said that her mom would have loved the service."

"No kidding… I'm happy to hear this. It's good to know that Tick expressed her appreciation for all you did to make it meaningful to her. So that's it?"

"No. Tick apologized for the dirty look she gave me when I showed up late to the service today with Sister Agatha. She knows the sister being there was your idea, and she's very grateful that we made it happen. Oh, and she apologized for slamming my tattoo and hurting my feelings—even though she still thinks the dragon looks outrageous."

"She simply cannot help herself," Mattie said, amused. "So, Laura, where do you stand with little Miss Hughes now?"

Laura knew what Mattie wanted to hear, feelings she could now honestly express. "All right, you win. I admit it! I do care about her. I care about her very, very much, Mattie. God only knows why. There, I said it. Now, let me go home before I get stuck in a snowdrift!"

Mattie gave Laura a big hug and walked her out to her car.

⁓⟨၀ၬၚ⟩⁓

Walking with a cane this time, Sister Agatha arrived early the next morning for a private visit with Tick. The two could be seen with their heads together—Tick with her iPad and Sister Agatha speaking softly—communicating with each other as seamlessly as age-old friends.

"*Do you believe that a person who has killed another person, regardless of the circumstances, can go to heaven?*" Tick questioned.

Sister Agatha took hold of Tick's hand. "Countless people throughout history have taken the lives of others, in wars or while protecting their family. God knows there are far too many reasons people justify killing. We live in a fallen world, Tick, where sin abounds, but in His mercy, God sent His son, our Savior, who came to forgive us of our sins, including the sin of killing another human."

Sister Agatha stood and tottered over to the picture window, taking in the magnificent wintry scene outside. "Yes, Tick, I believe that many of those individuals have made their way to heaven. God is merciful, and the Gospel teaches that even those whom we call undeserving can find their way into heaven if their faith in the Lord is genuine, without pretense."

"*Even someone who believes in God, knows His commandments, but kills anyway?*" asked Tick.

"Even Moses and David killed, you know. Unfortunately, even the best of us are quite flawed, but God is good and merciful, and He knows what's in our hearts. As the wonderful hymn proclaims, His amazing grace saves even a wretch like me. Was this someone a believer?"

Tick nodded yes.

"Child, do you know what the Bible says in John 3:16?"

Tick was quick to write, "*For God so loved the world that He gave his only Son, that whoever believes in him shall not perish but have eternal life.*"

Sister Agatha smiled. "You have just answered your question, my dear. Your mother would be proud of you."

"*Do you believe that I will see her again?*"

Walking back to sit next to Tick again, the nun took her hand. As she replied, her eyes fastened onto Tick's wide eyes.

"There are very few things in life that I am certain about, child, but about this question, yes, I'm certain that not only will you be reunited with your mother again someday, but I'm quite sure that I will be seeing her again too. At my age, it probably will be fairly soon!"

The quiet, somber tone of Sister's Agatha's voice abruptly changed into a joyful pitch, declaring, "Now, I really must be off to catch my plane. Rest easy, my dear Esther Hughes, your sweet mother is safe now." Then, the nun rose, spoke privately to Brad for a few moments, and, accompanied by an FBI agent, left for the airport.

The boys and their wives stayed for another two days, endeavoring to get to know Tick and make her feel a welcomed member of the Hughes family, but the visit had been a strain on everyone. Privately, Brad's children still questioned their father's decision to take on such an enormous responsibility, concerned over the problems, challenges, and risks he faced because of this complicated, mute child.

Tick was understandably exhausted and grieving, but the family found her exceedingly proper and stiff demeanor quite peculiar. But most disturbing was the way Tick studied them, intently observing everything going on and following conversations without an expression on her face. It was unnerving.

"What on earth is she thinking!" barked Ben to his father one day when they were out walking together.

Brad merely wrapped his arm around Ben's shoulder and, drawing him close, said, "Go easy, son, be kind."

The night before their scheduled departure, the boys herded everyone, including Mattie, into the study for a game of Trivial Pursuit. Reluctantly, Tick joined in, but her participation only added fuel to the unsettling perception Brad's brood held about the girl. Her exceptional intellect emerged unrestrained that night, far surpassing her years, correctly answering nearly every single question asked in the categories of Geography, History, Science and Nature, and Arts and Literature. She could not help her teammates, Ben, Brian, and David, in the Sports and Leisure or Entertainment categories, but she was the most dependable player on her team. Her body of knowledge was mind-bogglingly advanced.

In the end, Tick won the game for her team by correctly naming the Roman emperor who made his horse a senator. "*Caligula*," she wrote, then added, "*Incitatus was the name of his favorite horse.*"

Game over.

Brian was the first to ask her how a twelve-year-old could know so much about ancient history.

Tick coolly typed out, "Caligula: Divine Carnage. *It's a book about the emperor's atrocities. I've also read other books about the Roman emperors, like Commodus and Heliogabalus. They were both as deranged as Caligula.*"

Ben Hughes let out a loud airy whistle before commenting, "Wow, Tick, the books you read sound like real page-turners!"

Becky Hughes couldn't hold her tongue when she sounded off, disapprovingly, "Did your mother know you were reading books like that?"

Seeing the pained expression on Tick's face, Brad redirected the question quickly before Tick could answer, recounting a story of his youth. "I remember this small library in a Peruvian jungle resort where my family often vacationed... On one trip to this place, I pulled a particularly inappropriate book for a young kid off the shelf and read the book in secret. They would have thrown the book away if any adult knew I had found it, so I hid it in a nook behind the bookshelf. I found it, still hidden there, and reread it on our next visit the following year."

The night reconfirmed Mattie's assessment that Tick had unrestricted access to Timothy Bird's library. Her mother would never have allowed her to read much of the literature Tick could so easily recall. Still, there was another book Tick was familiar with: unquestionably the most influential book in history: The Bible, The Word, a book of hope and redemption, but one that also contained stories of atrocious acts, not hiding or glossing over the flaws and imperfection of early Christians or mankind in general.

For Dr. Mattie Barnes, the critical question remained unanswered: *What lessons had Tick taken from all those books?*

There was another topic that arose during the evening. They would not be spending Christmas together in Utah. The boys all liked to ski and every other year held a family reunion in Utah over the holidays. While at the hospital, Brad had canceled that plan, explaining that it wasn't a good year for a family reunion. His decision had disappointed the boys and added to the confusion about what was going on with their father. Nevertheless, they made other plans to fill in the vacuum: Ben and Becky would be on a cruise with her family, Brian and Natalie would be with her parents in Mississippi, and David would be hiking in Junín, Peru, with friends.

Brad and Tick would be alone over the holidays and unable to travel in the foreseeable future. The fact that Brad wouldn't be seeing his grandchildren for months did not make anyone in this close-knit family very happy.

They penciled in a family vacation at the beach in San Diego for the first two weeks in July. Some short weekend trips might be possible before then, but that would depend on how well Tick was getting along.

Standing in the driveway, Brad gave a thumbs-up as his family drove away in their rental car, its tires crunching through the newly fallen snow, making deep furrows as it went. He sensed Tick's eyes on him from where she watched inside the house, and he worried about what she might be thinking. Maybe she thought her adoption had damaged the Hughes family's fabric, or perhaps she was wondering if she would ever find her place in the family? He felt his normal sadness whenever saying good-bye to the boys and their families, but in no way was he second-guessing his decision to adopt Tick. He had a daughter to look after now. Anyway, feeling sorry for himself was not in his nature.

Time doesn't pause for folks to catch their breaths, Brad reflected, remembering the unceasing list of undertakings that lay ahead of them. In less than a month, Tick's big cast comes off, and she would be back in the hospital for ankle surgery. Renovation on his house was weeks from completion, and his contractor was waiting for a final decision on hardware selections, all those tiny decisions that seemed endless. With the holidays approaching, there was the end-of-the-year business to wrap up at the office, Christmas bonuses that needed processing, and holiday cards to send to clients and closest friends. He would cancel having outdoor Christmas lights put out this year, but it wouldn't be Christmas without a tree to decorate. Then, there was Christmas shopping for the family, with lots of gifts to buy, wrap, and send off. Ana would help with it all, and Mattie wanted to shop for Tick's Christmas, so that was a huge break.

Walking into the house, Brad turned into the living room with an idea to present to his daughter:

"It's such a beautiful, clear night, Tick. There's not a cloud in the sky. How would you like to spend some time up in the observatory? We can escape and be entertained by God's late-night show."

Nodding her okay, Tick waited while Brad grabbed their coats and a couple of blankets. He then proceeded to wrap Tick up like a burrito with only her head exposed. Pulling a wool cap down over her ears, he picked her up, carried her up the stairs, and opened the ceiling dome to reveal millions of stars.

Brad's thoughts went to Genesis. "God also made the stars and set them in the expanse of the sky to give light on the earth, to govern the day and the night, and to separate light from the darkness. And God saw that it was good."

That night, God was going for bragging rights, his vault crammed with beautiful twinkling lights. It would have taken endless lifetimes to count them all.

Tick's eyes were the only part of her body exposed to the bitterly cold night air, and Brad wished that she could talk to him about the beautiful night sky. He had hoped that her muteness would disappear, that she would start talking just like that, but that hadn't happened. She was so good at communicating without speech—probably too good. Her eyes and expressions competently conveyed her moods to the people who knew her best; she was an excellent writer and a master at using her iPhone and iPad, using her devices to stream on TV when communicating with a group. Brad worried that she would never feel the need to speak.

Tick's head, like that of a turtle retreating into its shell, suddenly disappeared into the coverlet as she gradually fell asleep. Brad sat with her, gently rubbing her back before carrying her to bed and heading off to bed as well. There was much to do in the morning.

She's Missing

Tick's emancipation day, the day her body cast would be removed, fell on December 29, two days before Tick's ankle surgery, and a few days before Brad would vacate the Deer Valley house. Tick would be staying in long-term care at Children's Hospital; Brad would check into the Little America Hotel until they finished renovations at his home.

When Tick and Brad arrived at the orthopedic center, a few staff members greeted Tick with hoorays and applause. One of her nurses held a pink helium balloon. After an x-ray was taken and analyzed by Dr. Brackford, he gave his technician the go-ahead to remove the ungainly, cumbersome pink cast. Despite all efforts to diminish an unpleasant odor, Tick's sweaty upper body workouts created a stinky shell.

Brad teased Tick about how girls were made of sugar, spice, and everything nice—unless they were carrying around a portable locker room. She dismissed him with a playful swat of her hand and a zany smile on her face.

That same lighthearted smile was not on her face when, cast-free and freshly showered, she was wheeled back to the waiting room by Dr. Brackford and Mattie. Tick looked terrific, healthy, her blond hair shining. She was wearing a sporty new outfit, a gift from Mattie, and she smelled like a rose, but her eyes were red and puffy, and her face looked pinched. Deflecting Brad's move to rush over to her, Tick put her hand up. She did not want to be consoled by him or anyone for that matter.

Dr. Brackford explained that Tick hadn't expected to lose so much of her mobility from the time of her fall; she was understandably upset and disappointed. He discussed that it was important for Tick to take things slowly. The muscles and tendons, dormant under the cast, had atrophied and would require months of careful rehabilitation to regain their former strength. He warned Tick about the risk of falling while her body adjusted to the change, and he cautioned her to move at a slower pace until she regained her balance.

Both Brad and Mattie knew that Dr. Brackford was barking up the wrong tree if he thought Tick was paying a bit of attention to him. She just wanted out of there. Brad thanked Dr. Brackford and his staff as he wheeled Tick and her pink balloon out to the parking lot, where she unceremoniously released the unintended symbol of her injuries and diminished physical freedom into the clouds.

Brad had only one day to spend with his daughter before she would be admitted back into the hospital for ankle surgery, this time as Tick Hughes. Another operation and hospitalization seemed like such a harsh sentence to hand down, but Mattie was firm in her decision. For Tick's overall well-being, her battered ankle needed to be repaired sooner rather than later, and Mattie wanted Tick to recuperate in the hospital, this time with other children and in controlled physical therapy.

Hoping to distract his daughter from the ordeal she was facing, Brad planned a road trip through Provo Canyon and the beautiful drive up to Robert Redford's mountain resort, Sundance, for lunch.

The hour or so that he and Tick spent together at the resort was pleasant enough. They both ordered bison burgers, cooked over a massive grill in one of Sundance's rustically elegant restaurants, and they sat near a window taking in the extraordinary mountain views. Still, Brad realized that this little outing had not been enough to lift his daughter's spirits. From his iPhone, he secretly bought two tickets for the two o'clock tubing session at Soldier Hollow, remembering how much fun he and his sons always had there.

A short distance from Sundance, the winter tubing hill operation at Soldier Hollow offered a motorized rope tow lift system, slowly pulling people nestled in sturdy inner tubes up 1,200 feet to snow-packed sliding lanes. From Brad's perspective, it was a safe activity. He could help Tick get in and out of her tube, and the ride down, while fast, was relatively safe, provided the rider sat still in the tube and didn't move around in it very much. For added security, he would attach his tube to hers.

It took only minutes for Tick, wide-eyed and beaming, and Brad to get into the parkas, caps, gloves, and snow boots stowed in the jeep. With a little help from friendly lift operators, the daring duo spent hours barreling down the snow-covered hill with not a single mishap and lots of laughter.

Mattie spotted the new screensaver on Tick's iPad later that evening—a selfie of Tick and Brad merrily rocketing down a hill in bright orange inner tubes. She dutifully offered up a half-hearted lecture, reminding them of Dr. Brackford's instructions; still, she was glad that Brad had come up with something that made Tick so happy and took her mind off everything she was facing.

"Thank God nothing happened," Mattie muttered inaudibly, feeling comforted that tomorrow Tick would be securely ensconced in the hospital before she could hurt herself.

⁓᪥⁓

A week later, Mattie critically reevaluated the clothes and accessories she had meticulously folded and arranged on her bed, ready to be placed into the suitcase. She was excited and eager to take this trip. At 4:57 p.m., she would be off to Paris to participate in an international symposium and training exercises, dubbed ERP, for Emergency Response Plan, in the event of a catastrophic event. As a Joint Commission expert, Mattie had worked for weeks preparing for her role in this conference; pen drives, handouts, two copies of her presentation—one for the suitcase and one for her briefcase— were safely secured and already packed. She was prepared for any foreseeable contingency and feeling almost giddy about the prospect of spending two weeks in La Ville-Lumiere, the City of Light. Her mind raced back to high school French classes and dear Madame Lassonde, who had long passed, not unlike Mattie's proficiency in the language.

Once Mattie finished packing, the status and treatment strategies for her patients recovering in intensive care invaded her thoughts of France: Candice Martinez, heart transplant; Justin Downs, burn victim resulting from a propane tank explosion; and three other critically ill children presently requiring comprehensive medical management would all be in good hands while she was away. The doctors scheduled to be on call in the ICUs would see to any new admissions.

Soon enough, her thoughts turned to Tick Hughes, as they often did. The corrective ankle surgery Dr. Brackford performed a week earlier was successful, and Tick was now required to brandish a short cast for six to seven weeks.

Troy, or Mr. T, the physical therapist assigned to work with Tick each day, had already transitioned her from the wheelchair to crutches. In the progress report, Mattie found Troy's reference to Tick's muteness bittersweet. "Tick is a textbook example of actions speaking louder than words. Tick's silent determination and desire to work through considerable discomfort is an inspiration and encouragement to all the kids here working through their painful therapy."

From all accounts, Tick was handling herself well at the center. Mattie was aware that, while Tick spent much of her free time working her way through the hospital's library books, she was also participating in most of the group activities, albeit as a silent observer.

Mattie had purposefully placed Tick in the long-term rehabilitation center, a wing to accommodate children who needed longer-term care for a variety of reasons. The patients' rooms with attached bathrooms were small and comfortable, not designed to be more than sleeping quarters.

Strictly speaking, Tick no longer required hospitalization. She still faced months of physical therapy, but with her strong upper body and a remarkable sense of balance, she got around expertly on crutches and easily managed taking showers and using the bathroom without hands-on assistance. Hospital policy dictated that physically independent patients receive care on an outpatient basis, but Mattie had some clout; she insisted that Tick should continue her stay at the center for another week or two, without Brad's constant presence.

Other key issues, however, remained unresolved. Exploring the mind of a patient who was mute and highly secretive was nearly impossible. Mattie was determined to get to the bottom of emotional wounds that had plagued Tick into speechlessness. An extended stay in this ward—populated with other kids experiencing difficulties and lively with activity—was where Mattie wanted Tick to be for now.

Tick's interaction with the other patients at the center was standoffish at first, but she began to make friends, and more importantly, she was helping others. Now, she seemed unconcerned when Brad wasn't there with her, working on his house or at his office, and she had no trouble sleeping alone at night. She tolerated daily visits from various physicians and residents with a relaxed attitude, making fun of them in a playful way if they said or did anything the least bit thickheaded. Tick was proving to be far more independent than most people realized—most people, that is, except Mattie, who knew better.

Mattie had not determined the source of Tick's dramatic, sometimes violent, histrionics when she faced separation from Brad. However, she had long suspected that the behaviors were strategic, not neurotic. To test her theories, she had limited both her and Brad's time with Tick at the center to short visits to observe how Tick adapted to new environments, watching her interactions with strangers and new situations. Mattie was certain that Tick's furious behavior would disappear once losing Brad was no longer an issue. Her initial assessment proved to be spot-on: Tick was a chameleon, an adaptable, strategic thinker, brilliant at both manipulating her environment and at hiding and working around the core emotional issues that held her captive. Tick was going to be a hard nut to crack.

Shortly after noon, Mattie pulled her ringing cell phone from her coat pocket as she was carrying her luggage to the car, well ahead of her departure time. The name that appeared on the screen was that of her head nurse.

"Brenda? What's up?"

"Tick is missing, Mattie. Do you have any idea where she might be? When did you see her last?"

Mattie's heart sank, her knuckles turned white, grasping the phone, hearing the panic and fear in her friend's voice.

"What do you mean she's missing? I saw her this morning during rounds. Where's Brad? Have you talked to him? How long has she been missing?"

"When Brad came to visit, the nurses tried to track her down. She isn't in the ward, and we have searched everywhere."

Mattie's voice was flat, controlled, "Is the hospital locked down? Have they checked the security camera tapes?"

"Yes, we're doing all of that, but she has disappeared. Mattie, I'm worried."

"I'm on my way," replied Mattie.

As she turned into the hospital, her phone rang again. It was Brenda Martin, now breathless but relieved.

"We found her—"

Mattie cut her short. "I'm parking the car now, Brenda. Meet me in the lobby."

Mattie sat frozen in her car for a moment, visions of a madman and Tick's shredded back coming to mind, but she did her best to regain some semblance of control. She felt drained. She pulled down the sun visor to use the mirror, brushed her hair back, and pinched her cheeks for some color before walking into the hospital.

Brenda appeared to be short of breath, taking in short gasps of air as they walked across the lobby to the elevator bank.

"We found her over in the main hospital's gift shop. She went there to buy a gift for her little friend, Brent." Mattie immediately recognized the name. Brent had not responded to conventional treatments and was now in a clinical trial for a new drug that required continual monitoring. Brenda continued, "One of the hospital security guards said he questioned her when he saw her leaving the center; she wrote him a convincing note explaining that you were waiting for her in the cafeteria."

Entering the empty elevator, Brenda reached into her pocket and pulled a scalpel encased in a protective plastic sheath from her pocket. "Look at this. I found it strapped under the armrest of her wheelchair."

Mattie took the scalpel from Brenda's hand, the light from the elevator reflecting on the sharp instrument. "Did you tell anybody about this?"

"No."

As the elevator doors opened, Mattie responded in a voice that brooked no dissent, "Don't."

Brad and Hoger talked outside Tick's room when they saw Mattie making her way down the hall toward them, her face stony, barely acknowledging them.

"Is she in there?" she asked. "Is she alone?"

Brad nodded his head, only to have her walk past him and disappear into the room, slamming the door shut behind her.

"Just *what* did you think you were doing, leaving the center without letting anyone know?" Mattie demanded, hands on her hips. Her words were cold, hard, and angry.

Startled, Tick sat up on the edge of her bed, her back straight as if strapped to an iron bar, her scar crimson red. Grasping her iPad, she typed in bold letters, ***"I just wanted to get something for my friend! I never left this darn hospital! You are all treating me like a prisoner!"***

"What's this?" Mattie asked as she thrust out her hand, palm open, but not empty.

Tick's eyes looked ablaze as she pounded out the note, writing furiously. *"Looks like a sharp knife to me, Dr. Barnes! Please forgive me for wanting to protect myself. Just let me know how I should handle Timothy when he finds me. I'm sure you have a far superior plan, like getting him into therapy!?"*

The two locked eyes.

"I'll tell you what my 'far superior plan' is, young lady… It's to keep you right here where that sicko can't get to you," Mattie said without blinking. "You should know, I have had to ask Brenda to compromise her job to cover this up for you. We can't have armed children wandering around the halls of this hospital… I'm going to miss my plane if I don't leave this minute," Mattie said. "You need to grow up, Tick. I expected more from you!"

Mattie turned in an attempt to leave the room, but just as she reached the door, she stopped to pick up the balled-up wad of paper that rocketed by her head.

"Au revoir. Have fun in Paris!"

Sitting on his bed at the hotel later that night, Brad replayed the day's incident in his head.

What a mess, he thought, *and all she wanted to do was buy a little gift for Brent.*

Brad lay back in his bed and reviewed the entire event in his mind. Tick's bond with her new friend, Brent, had been evolving since the evening a handbell choir came to entertain the children at the hospital. Tick had not been enthusiastic about attending the program. However, her indifference deteriorated into understandable objection when the awkward-looking troupe of bell ringers proved to be agonizingly off tempo, massacring what most would consider standard Christmas songs.

Brad was thinking of ways to inconspicuously bail out of the performance when a small, frail boy with no hair and bright blue eyes appeared, standing directly in front of Tick, holding his arms up wanting to be picked up.

Brad watched with fascination as, without hesitating, Tick reached forward, hoisted the little guy up, and set him down next to her. The five-year-old, suffering from a rare form of leukemia and participating in an experimental drug trial, sat quietly for a few minutes, pretending to listen to the bells before looking up at Tick and asking her what her name was.

Not discouraged when Tick didn't respond, he whispered his name into her ear and told her that he thought she was pretty. From that moment on, Brent and Tick became great pals. Over the next week, Brent demanded that his mother take him to visit Tick. Tick drew pictures for him, raced up and down the hall with him in her wheelchair, sat with him to watch his favorite cartoons on TV, and allowed him to take naps on her bed while she read.

Brent's mother, Melanie, a plainspoken, pleasant woman from a small town not far from Salt Lake City, told Brad that she had run out of ideas to keep her young son entertained when he lobbed onto Tick. "She is so good with him, and she's making him happier than he has been in a very long time."

Brad felt nothing but empathy for the mother, knowing how hard it was for him to keep Tick occupied when she was bedridden not so long ago.

From his own experience of being cooped up for weeks with Tick in the remote hospital wing, Brad also recognized that Melanie was starving for adult conversation. She needed someone to talk to, and Brad found her stories quite interesting.

"My great-grandmother traveled on one of the last wagon trains carrying pioneer Mormons migrating to Utah before they completed the railroad in 1869. You can see one of her quilts in the Pioneer Memorial Museum near the Capital not far from here."

"Really?" Brad said. "I might have seen her quilt when I visited that museum with my wife years ago. I remember all that remarkable handwork. I've always said that the Mormon pioneers, like your great-grandmother, were an impressive lot of strong and determined people. Does your Utah pioneer legacy make you a VIP among Latter-Day Saints, Melanie?"

"Well, yes and no," Melanie said, rolling her eyes. "My family broke with the church many years ago when my great-grandfather announced his decision to enter into a polygamist lifestyle and take on a second wife. It's a long story for another day, but the farm we live on and work has been in the family for a long time ever since my great-grandmother booted her cheating husband out the door."

"Well, good for her! All the jarring she suffered riding in that covered wagon didn't affect her good sense!"

Melanie got a good laugh from Brad's comment, but her story ended on an unhappy note. "The unfortunate thing is that our neighbor is thinking of selling some prime farmland adjacent to ours, but now my husband and I simply can't afford to buy it. Almost all of our financial resources have gone to pay for Brent's treatments and hospitalizations."

That's the least of it, thought Brad that night, recalling Melanie's conversation and trying to sleep with a heavy heart. Brent was failing. *Tick had to know it too.*

⌒∽∞∾∾⌒

Waiting at the gate for her flight, Mattie folded and unfolded the scribbled note Tick had tossed at her feet.

In all the years working with troubled kids who come grudgingly, some with bad, disrespectful attitudes, not one of them has been able to rattle me the way Tick does. Mattie knew that Brent wasn't going to make it, and she wondered why Tick needed to bond so entirely with him. *We can't save him, and it will just be another painful loss for her,* she thought.

Mattie regretted coming down so hard on Tick for venturing out of the rehab center, and she felt horrible about leaving in such a huff. As she looked at the crumpled scrap again, she felt nothing but overriding tenderness for the girl; the thought that Timothy Bird was out to hurt or kill Tick was enough to paralyze this in-control doctor with fear. Mattie would never admit this to Tick, but secretly, she wasn't upset about the hidden scalpel. Once she returned to Utah, she would bring up the subject with Brad. He could handle it.

Settling into her business-class seat on the non-stop 5:00 p.m. flight into Charles De Gaulle airport, Mattie accepted her complimentary glass of champagne but turned down a refill. She would try and get some sleep as soon as possible, considering the eight-hour time difference between Utah and France. It was 1:00 a.m. in Paris as her flight left the ground. Her scheduled arrival time was for 11:15 a.m. The conference registration would begin at noon, and she hoped to avoid extreme jet lag.

Before slipping on the sleep mask that the airlines provided in an amenity kit, she swallowed a sleeping pill—one that wouldn't leave her feeling groggy. Then she flattened her seat and eventually drifted off to sleep.

⌒⟶∞∞∞⟵

We were on the damn brink of issuing an Amber alert, Nate Hoger thought as he lay next to his wife, who was snoring softly. He could see it now—blond, green-eyed teenage girl missing. *They might have just as well rented the Goodyear Blimp to inform Timothy Bird—ESTHER MORGAN IS HERE—in blinking lights as it hovered over the hospital.* Hoger was inordinately fond of Tick, but how was it possible for a teenage girl to cause so much upheaval? His tour of duty in Afghanistan was more stressful, but not by much.

Bird was still out there, and they had to find him. Hoger figured he was probably hiding out in Mexico, just as Tick suspected, but she was far from safe. The more the FBI learned about Bird, the more they realized that he would be coming after her with a vengeance. He had a personality profile that demanded revenge.

A rapid response team was activated when the call that Tick was missing came in. Hoger's men had closed off both exit routes leading from the hospital, creating vehicle checkpoints to search for a missing hospital patient. The night's activities had not escaped the press's attention, activities now represented as a preparedness drill.

Children's Hospital had installed extra security at the main entrances, facial recognition software on all the hospital cameras, and guards that did not allow unidentified people into the children's ward. Security measures were in place to prevent the wrong people from getting in, but no one had considered a scenario where Tick would wander off.

One solution might be to strap a GPS tracking device around her good ankle, Hoger thought, but she would undoubtedly throw a fit, and he wouldn't blame her. He tossed and turned, thinking of how cunning Bird had turned out to be. The bottom line was, no matter what security measures they took, Tick was bait for Timothy, and the thought of it sickened him.

⌒∞∞∞⌒

After registering for the ERP conference, Mattie checked into her hotel room overlooking the Eiffel Tower. She had just sat down to study her lecture schedule when a text from Laura came through:

> *Brent Thomas died around midnight last night. He spent the afternoon with Tick. His mom said that he asked Tick if her mommy could be his mommy in heaven. Tick promised him that Alissa would be there for him. Tick told Brent that she would draw more pictures for him when it was her turn to go to heaven. She was like an angel with him. Sometimes I hate this job!*
>
> *PS. I need to get another Jelly Cat for Tick. She gave hers to Brent. They plan to bury it with him.*

CHAPTER

Final Days in the Hospital

Mattie lifted the window shade on the Airbus A350 as it made its final approach into Salt Lake City. She looked down on the snow-capped Wasatch mountain range. It had been a dreadfully long fourteen-hour flight home, including a connection in Amsterdam, and she was exhausted. Between the intense and often depressing seminars and roundtable discussions—ranging from pandemic outbreaks to events causing massive human catastrophes—her appreciation for life was palpable. Life was so precious.

The time she spent on her own touring Paris was the perfect antidote for gloom and doom scenarios. She strolled down the Champs-Elysees, one of the most famous avenues globally, sipped on expensive espressos and wines throughout the city, and dined on food that was occasionally inspired, sometimes only so-so, and always pricy. At the famous cafe, Laduree, she bought a frilly little gift box filled with a pastel palette of French macaroons, and she walked into Coco Chanel's renowned boutique and purchased a few bottles of the famous perfume.

Her best day by far was spent at the Louvre Museum, walking through many galleries filled with artwork so accomplished and astonishingly beautiful that she could see God's thumbprint on it.

Mattie left the museum at closing time, wishing Tick had been there with her to see the extraordinary, timeless pieces of art that stirred the soul and renewed a person's regard for humanity and the Creator of us all.

In her present travel-weary state, unable to find a seat on the crowded airport shuttle—no man offered to give up his place for her—Mattie's admiration for the human race wilted. Her eyes shifted from traveler to traveler as the shuttle bus made its way ever so slowly from stop to stop, wending its way through the long-term parking lot. She observed a family of five returning from their Hawaiian vacation—the parents wearing glaringly touristy Hawaiian shirts, and two of their younger children looked miserable with blistering sunburns. Mattie felt angry that those dopey parents hadn't protected their kids' tender skin with sunscreen.

The plane had landed just before 2:00 p.m., and at 3:50 p.m., Mattie pulled into her parking space at Children's Hospital and walked to the ICU.

Brenda Martin was seated at the central station outside the patient rooms monitoring the telemetry board when she suddenly noticed Mattie unexpectedly standing next to her. Greeting Brenda with a friendly "Hello," Mattie began scanning the monitors straight-away, simultaneously looking in through the patient room glass walls to get a visual of each patient.

Brenda, surprised to see her good friend and boss, stood up and responded, bemusedly, "What are you doing here, Mattie? I wasn't expecting to see you until tomorrow! How did it go?"

"I arrived a couple of hours ago," Mattie said, now looking over the latest physician entries on the electronic patient data screen. "The conference was worthwhile—extremely well-organized and attended, but it was exhausting. I was thankful when it ended."

"I just read an article about one of the ideas proposed at the conference," Brenda began, "a hospital ship devoted to children, funded by international charities?"

"That news certainly traveled fast!" Mattie responded. "But it's true. A hospital ship for children is in the planning stage. I was nom-inated to be on the design committee for the ship's ICUs."

Brenda's reaction was immediate. "Are you kidding, Mattie? That's wonderful! I hope you agreed to do it."

"Without blinking," Mattie said. "But keep it under your hat. I need to speak to the powers that be here at the hospital. Also they haven't formally announced my appointment."

"Of course! My lips are sealed," assured Brenda. "So tell me, how was Paris?"

"It was marvelous," Mattie answered. "There just wasn't enough time to see all the sites on my list, but I did have time to do a little shopping for a few of my favorite people."

Mattie discreetly pulled out a bag with the recognizable over-lapping double *C* symbol on it from her purse and then handed it to Brenda under the counter. "Here, compliments of Mademoiselle Coco Chanel."

Brenda was delighted and managed to keep her *merci beaucoup* to a whisper.

Then it was down to business, and Mattie requested that Brenda join her on her rounds.

After Mattie saw the last patient, she pulled Brenda aside for a private word. "Were you able to meet with Brad and Tick?"

The day after arriving in Paris, Mattie contacted Brenda by phone and asked her to meet with Brad and Tick to confiscate any unacceptable objects Tick might be harboring. She had also asked the entire affair be kept confidential.

"I did," replied Brenda. "Tick boldly admitted to assembling a nice little armory—a paring knife she appropriated during her tour of the kitchens, a dental pick from her appointment at the dentist, and a screwdriver she pinched from a workman."

"Where had she been hiding these things?"

"She had completely hollowed out Brad's old *Webster's Dictionary* and put everything in there."

"She's a strange little rascal! What did Brad have to say?"

Brenda's answer sounded dryly humorous, and speaking out of one side of her mouth, she said, "He told Tick that if it were up to him, she could wander around the hospital with a howitzer!"

"Oh, brother!" bristled Mattie.

"But," Brenda stepped in right away to soften the blow, "he redeemed himself as a rational parent and reminded her that the security protecting them was extraordinary. He told her that pocketing and concealing weapons for guerilla warfare at Children's Hospital was hardly necessary. He also said that keeping the staff informed of her whereabouts was not negotiable. Not to do so was entirely thoughtless and reckless, especially under circumstances that required the security measures taken to protect her. He said a bit more about showing respect and something about your feelings, but anyway, I'm pretty sure that Tick got the message."

"Is there anything else?" Mattie asked, her face expressionless.

"I think you're up to speed, but remember that I haven't spent any time over at the long-term recovery center. Laura has been keeping close tabs on her, as usual."

Mattie thanked Brenda for keeping the ship afloat while she was away and then made her way to her office. Thirty minutes earlier, Laura had received a text from one of her orderly friends over at the ICU: "The eagle has landed, and she's here making rounds with Brenda." With the cat out of the bag, Laura took off for the gift shop to buy some flowers for Mattie's desk, very happy that her boss was back from Paris.

With the sun setting behind the Oquirrh Mountains, Laura and Mattie reviewed patient admissions, transfers, and discharges that occurred in Mattie's absence. Then Mattie asked the question that had been on her mind all day.

"How has Tick been getting along at the center?"

Laura paused thoughtfully, knowing that the information was important to Mattie. She cited the informal oral reports she had received from the long-term care staff. None of them were knowledgeable about Tick Hughes's background.

"She's doing much better than I anticipated, Mattie. Tick leads the field among independent and strong-willed kids. It's pretty much what you'd expect, only with a new cast of characters. The consensus in rehab is that she likes to do what she wants to do, when and how she wants to do it, with convincing arguments on why she's right."

"The notable difference that I'm hearing is that she hasn't lost her temper once, has been very helpful and considerate of others, and lets Brad come and go without any issues."

"Anything else?" Mattie asked.

"Yeah, but it's nothing new to us. Tick's muteness has been the major stumbling block for normal socializing with the other kids, and it leaves her a bit isolated. Still, the children respect her, are drawn to her, but don't quite know what to make of her. She doesn't back down to anybody, and she nearly owns the place as far as the games are concerned, especially the video games."

"I can only guess what goes on there."

"They say she is unbelievably competitive and takes no prisoners. Tick puts on that face, you know, the one that hides everything? Brad says that's how she looks when she's in her *Star Wars* zone, and then she starts to play and invariably wins—especially if she's had time to practice. It's intimidating and irritating, especially for the older children who would like to win occasionally. She has made one good friend, though, Claire Summers."

"Really?" Mattie asked, quite pleased to hear that Tick and Claire were friends. "How is Claire?" Mattie's thoughts turned to the sixteen-year-old, who was one of the most accomplished athletes that had ever come through the ICU at Children's Hospital. She had been a shoo-in for the Winter Olympics downhill ski racing team before she injured her spinal cord in a terrible fall, leaving her with compromised mobility. Claire Summers was a bright, famous, nationally renowned talent, but she had been grappling with severe depression after her fall.

Laura said that Claire had started to come to terms with her physical limitations, her "new normal," as she explained to Mattie.

"Oh, and," Laura continued, "they both compete like devils in the exercise room, and they've both been kicked out for overexertion. But, and this is so wonderful, they work with the other children every day, encouraging and motivating each one, especially the older ones struggling with physical handicaps. They've been wonderful role models, and Claire has turned a corner since she and Tick joined forces."

"That's terrific news," replied Mattie.

Mattie headed back to her office, her thoughts on Tick and her new father, Brad.

While in Paris, Mattie hadn't opened a single menu without wondering what Tick or Brad might order, and she spent most of her free time shopping for souvenirs for the two of them. Wherever she went, she caught herself wishing that Tick and Brad were there sharing that experience with her. Undeniably, Tick and Brad had been her invisible companions during her entire stay in Paris. The truth was, she had developed deep feelings for both of them, and she suspected that Brad had feelings for her as well.

Unnerved by the notion of a romantic relationship with Brad Hughes, Mattie pushed away from her desk and stood up, waving away her pointless, jet-lagged daydream.

Being involved in a close personal relationship with him or with anyone is out of the question, she held. The decisions she made many years ago concerning her life, what she wanted to do with it, and the sacrifices she had to make to become the best in her field, left no room for love, marriage, or raising a family. Unwelcome thoughts of her life devoid of a loving relationship nagged at her, making her feel foolishly tragic and tangled in a web of her own making.

She summarily blocked out the dissenting voice in her head, the muffled voice that would free her of the commitments she made years earlier. Her choices were ironclad, forged by grief and guilt, and she took stock of the highly problematic doctor-patient relationship that had burgeoned during stressful months with Tick and Brad.

For Mattie, to get back on familiar turf—terrain, where she belonged as an exemplary doctor—a careful and gradual dissolution of emotional ties would have to occur.

Once Tick was home, Mattie would honor her promise to Brad and continue her position as Tick's primary physician and psychiatrist, but that would be it. Their time together would necessarily be limited to regularly scheduled office visits. Given time, Mattie presumed, a far more realistic, workable relationship between her, Tick, and Brad would develop. Above all, Tick's physical and emotional well-being was what mattered.

Mattie arrived at the extended care unit, but Tick, Brad, and several ambulatory patients had gone to a play rehearsal at the University of Utah.

Wanting to let Tick know that she was back, Mattie went to her room, found a loose scrap of paper, and used Tick's large sketchbook as a writing desk:

Hi, Tick!

> *I'm back from France with so much to tell you. They built Paris for the likes of you, my friend, fabulous in so many ways. When you are there to see it for yourself someday, remember that I told you how much you would love it!*
>
> *I want to tell you how amazing you were to take such good care of little Brent before God called him home. We will all miss him, but you were like an angel to him and gave him genuine comfort and assurance.*
>
> *Also, you should know that I have heard nothing but glowing reports about you today. The word out is that you and Claire make a dynamite coaching team, and the staff reports that you two have been inspiring role models for the other kids at the center. Nice job! I'm proud of you!*
>
> *The macaroons are for you and Brad to enjoy—100% Parisian! I have some other goodies for you in my suitcase that I'll drop by tomorrow.*
>
> *—Mattie*
> *PS. I hope you enjoyed the play rehearsal!*

Mattie placed the note along with the macaroons on the bed and then stood up to return Tick's sketchpad, but curiosity drove her to open it and thumb through the drawings.

They are lovely, she thought.

There were sketches of Brent soaring through the sky riding on a unicorn, then under the sea on the back of a giant turtle. Another drawing transposed the images: now, the unicorn was underwater, swimming with the fishes, and the turtle soared in towering clouds along with seagulls. There was also a drawing of Claire, rocketing through downhill ski gates. It was a copy of a photograph tucked between the pages.

The drawings were superb—especially for a twelve-year-old. Tick was a promising artist.

Replacing the sketchpad, Mattie noticed a folded sheet of sketch paper in the back. When she opened it, her heart stopped.

Mattie had seen sketches of events at the Death Ranch, sketches she had encouraged Tick to draw while working with her at the Deer Valley house, drawings of girls with their fingers missing, and even of a woman burning at the stake. But this sketch was different, the perspective complex and disturbing.

The entire background in the illustration was undulating darkness, a product of skilled shading. Mattie could barely make out the details of what looked like a boy or a man, and his head pulled back. A large knife, beautifully drawn down to the small detail of a nick on the blade, was pressed against his throat, terror in his eyes. A bright-red drop of blood, the only color other than shades of black in the drawing, dripped from the knife where it met his neck. There were two hands suspended in the dark background—one hand grasping the hair on the man's head, pulling it back, tendons exposed by the effort. The other hand, relaxed and poised for action, held the knife against his taut neck. Both hands were small and looked like those of a child.

Mattie sank back on the bed, stunned. She contemplated Tick's life and any possible connection she had to this drawing. There was so much Mattie didn't know about what Tick experienced in captivity. She prayed that Timothy Bird would be captured or killed.

What is wrong with the overhyped FBI? Why hadn't they found the monster?

Suddenly feeling inordinately tired and depressed, she replaced the tablet on the bureau and headed for home.

Later that night, as Mattie fell into a troubled sleep, the avalanche hit again—a reoccurring nightmare that haunted her for so many years. It roared off the mountain, snapping large trees like twigs, blocking out the sun, enveloping each man in its wake. Then, like a living creature, the avalanche smashed them all down, shattered them against trees, and buried their broken bodies in mounds of jumbled snow and ice.

But this time, the dream was different. This time, the snow was black.

CHAPTER

Schooling

It was the end of the third week in February, ten days after Mattie's Paris sojourn, and Mattie was in high spirits as she completed her rounds.

Back in her office before noon, Mattie's sunny disposition quickly shifted to dismay when she reached into her pocket and read the text message Brad had sent moments earlier: "Disastrous interview with Professor Turner just now. Tick blew her chance for acceptance, but she did it with style! Call me when you get home."

When Mattie put her phone down, she wanted to scream.

"Why? Why?" She lamented out loud. "Was it too much to hope that any part of this could be easy?"

◆◆◆◆◆◆

Weeks ago, Mattie met with Brad several times in her office to discuss Tick's transition into her soon-to-be-launched new life outside the rehab center. Mattie counseled Brad that homeschooling would be too isolating, but that pinning down the right school, if one even existed, would be the key in helping a highly unconventional girl adjust to a new life. The right school could be a catalyst toward healing and creating a healthy, happy, and productive future for Tick.

Regardless of a school's reputable academic standards, Mattie believed that enrolling Tick in a large school would be disastrous, putting the young, socially isolated girl at a disadvantage among the majority of her peers. Tick's muteness alone set her apart and would prevent her from fitting in, but she was not on the same playing field with the average teenager in any area at this point. And God help anybody who bullied or provoked her because she was different.

Mattie had deferred psychotherapy sessions with Tick until after her scheduled month-long stay at the rehab center following ankle surgery. She wanted Tick to settle into her new home with her father before starting sessions up again. Tick was unquestionably calmer, more patient, and less disruptive since her adoption, but Mattie harbored no illusions concerning her patient's sporadic ferocity.

Copies of two incident reports involving Tick within the past week at the center were on Mattie's desk. The first occurred when a night nurse suffered a badly bruised cheek caused by a hard blow across her face as she attempted to calm Tick out of a frantic night terror. Tick remembered nothing of the incident in the morning and turned away when Mattie told her that the nurse had come running into her room after hearing several loud and very perceptible cries of "*Stop!*" and "*No!*"

The second incident was relatively minor, but it showed poor judgment on Tick's part. Jimmy Gardner, another patient on the ward, had snatched the PlayStation controller away from a much younger boy in the game room, leaving the kid in tears. Tick grabbed it back, returning it to the child, but when Jimmy went after it again, Tick quickly slapped the top of his hand before he could blink and then shoved him out of the room. One of the nurses reported that the slap left an angry purple welt.

Tick respectfully endured the standard series of lectures and apologized to Jimmy, but Mattie was sure that Tick wasn't the least bit remorseful. She needed more time to identify her triggers and then to react appropriately. Tick's mother may have been a candidate for sainthood, but Timothy and his cohorts had been at the opposite end of the scale. These conflicting influences had played a significant role in the formation of Tick's character, and she needed to be clear about which voice to listen to whenever she felt angry.

TICK

Tick's best chance for success would be at a school where the students didn't fit into the stereotypical teenage mold, a school with the highest academic demands that would challenge her. Ideally, this would be a student body of open-minded intellectual types—Laura would call them *"nice nerds"*—and Mattie, after extensive research, had come up with the perfect solution.

It was an experimental enrichment program for the super high-achieving students in Utah, funded by local businesses and private donations in conjunction with the University of Utah and local schools. Brainy, eager-to-learn high school students came together for this advanced level program covering the arts and sciences. The classes were relatively small and taught by university professors for college credit. It was a two-year program, and after graduating, the students advanced into the university's system.

Brad had initially protested. "Are you sure, Mattie? How could she possibly succeed among this all-star team when she's more than three years younger than they are, has spent more than half her life in captivity, and can't or won't speak? I think we could be setting her up for failure."

"You know, Brad," Mattie had replied patiently, "for *your* peace of mind, you could attempt to shield Tick from the world she now lives in, but let's take a minute and review just who we're dealing with here. As I recall, your daughter narrowly escaped a homicidal maniac and then dug her feet into the rocky ground to help the two of you get up a cliff. Then what? Let's see, didn't she deck two adult male orderlies on the helicopter tarmac and then a CPS caseworker. After that, your little snowflake survived a fall that would have killed most people, and oh, yeah, then she ran roughshod over the FBI before they gave up and agreed that you should adopt her. I can see why you would question your daughter's ability to surmount the perils she'd be facing at a school for young brainiacs."

"Tell me, Dr. Barnes," Brad had replied, feeling the heat rise in his face, "are you aware that reverse psychology served up as exaggerated sarcasm is a lousy strategy?"

Mattie stiffened in her chair while Brad's comment lingered.

"You're right, Brad. I'm sorry. What I said was as much for me as it was for you. I'm feeling protective too. We know that the perfect school for Tick doesn't exist, but if I didn't believe that she could manage this program and get along with the students, I wouldn't have suggested it. May I have your permission to call the school?"

First, Mattie spoke with the school's registrar, where she got nowhere. The registrar, hearing about Tick's off-the-grid homeschooling before her parents died in Florida, said Tick would not be eligible as a candidate without complete school records, recommendations, and standardized test scores. Besides, their student population's average age was sixteen years, and Tick wouldn't turn thirteen until April.

Mattie, unabashedly exploiting her impressive title at Children's Hospital, persisted by going over the registrar's head and calling the program director, Sue Ellen Kasch. After a lengthy conversation, Ms. Kasch agreed, dubiously, to allow Tick to take the admissions test, along with conventional IQ and other standardized tests: a hopeful first step.

Throughout the two-day interview and testing process, Tick was relaxed and responsive, delighted for the chance to be out of the rehab center. Using airplay on her computer with a wall-mounted TV monitor, her written communication with the teaching staff was effortless and articulate. She definitely won Sue Ellen's vote for acceptance: "She is a shoo-in for the arts, English literature, and history programs. Her mind grasps complex historical content with more insight than I would ever have imagined for someone so young. She tests at the college level in reading comprehension, AP English, and writing, and it shouldn't surprise you that her IQ test score was extremely high. We designed this program for young scholars such as Tick."

The director of the math and science program, Professor Turner, was a harder sell. He wanted to personally interview both Tick and Brad before considering Tick as a viable candidate in the program. It shouldn't have been necessary; a strategy to shore up the deficiencies found in her math test was already in place. Sue Ellen would allow Tick to audit the math classes during the first year, supported by a private tutor. Then, if her math competency showed enough improvement, they would enroll her in the full program.

Turner's interview disintegrated into a complete disaster when the professor began a boastful discourse about the program, the students, and how fortunate Tick was to be considered a candidate for the program.

"Your test scores indicate that your mother may have been a gifted English tutor, but she failed you when it comes to math. Your scores are not even close to where they should be, and your high IQ can only get you so far. Why was no effort made for your math instruction? Why didn't your mother hire someone qualified to tutor you in mathematics?"

Tick, infuriated by the man's sharp criticism and insensitive questioning about her mother, pointed a finger angrily at Turner, then wrote, "*You are an arrogant, insensitive man, evaluating people unfairly with inadequate knowledge of their circumstances. I can't imagine you could teach mathematics to anyone. That takes logic.*"

Her comments and challenging behavior hadn't gone over well; discipline and comportment were vital components for admission into the program. They rejected Tick's application on the spot, with Turner's declaration that she lacked sufficient maturity.

◦⸻⸻◦

After calling Brad the minute she returned to her apartment later that afternoon and hearing details of the interview, Mattie's first reaction was to call the professor and give him a piece of her mind. But deep sadness and defensiveness for Tick far surpassed any ill will she held for Turner. Mattie knew Tick's maturity wasn't the problem at all. Whatever happened on that mountain was so atrocious that it upended Tick's world, left her mute, and drove those explosive behaviors.

At the center of Tick's torment was one very gifted English tutor, Alissa Morgan, a mother Tick had adored.

The next morning, Mattie spent over an hour on the phone, exercising her superior edge in human psychology with Sue Ellen

Kasch. Dr. Mattie Barnes was able to convince the director to accept Tick into the arts, literature, and history programs—"On probation, mind you." However, Tick would not be able to participate in the math and sciences program until they reevaluated her the following year, and provided that Tick apologized to Professor Turner first. Bringing Tick's math up to speed was not going to be a problem, but getting her to apologize to Turner was not going to be easy.

No matter how disturbing Tick's reactionary behavior was, Mattie's thoughts inevitably turned to the same girl who was as likable and as fascinated with life as anyone she had ever known. Mattie had almost forgotten how magical the Christmas season had been, for example, until she experienced it anew through Tick's eyes.

Tick and her mother typically celebrated Christmas alone in their cave. Bird and his devotees regularly traveled during the holidays. But this last Christmas had been special both for Tick and for Mattie.

Mattie had arrived at the Hughes winter wonderland safe house early, not wanting to miss Brad's famous Christmas breakfast waffles, which the three of them enjoyed while watching a Christmas morning worship service broadcasted on television. Brad wanted Tick to experience a merry, old-fashioned Christmas; in his family, that had always included unwrapping gifts from Santa, listening to every Christmas song ever composed, and savoring the aroma of a turkey roasting in the oven.

Brad, Tick, and Mattie had worked together in the kitchen preparing traditional Christmas dishes that would grace their table later in the day. When Laura drove up to join them for supper, Tick put her on gravy duty, while Brad poured the water and lit the candles on the beautifully arranged table that Mattie had set.

At three place settings, they found an excellent, small charcoal sketch of a Christmas scene. These amazing offerings were Tick's gifts to the most important people in her life.

Then they had driven into the city to see the lights. For Tick, the sight of the city's trees wrapped up and illuminated with glowing lights filled her with joy; Christmas displays in storefront windows and on neighborhood houses and lawns were novel and beautiful wonders. She loved all the eye-catching holiday trimmings, the Christmas carols, bell ringers in Santa suits, and the Christmastime bustle in the city. Most of all, she loved being free to experience this special time of the year.

Mattie would never forget how Tick reacted to hearing a performance of the Hallelujah Chorus from Handel's Messiah for the first time. She was transfixed, listening to the powerful music, tears brimming in those beautiful eyes.

Tick's childhood shaped a multifaceted outcome. She was a child with an adult's understanding of how short and transient life was. A child-adult who viewed new experiences through a young person's eyes, but with a grown-up's appreciation—a child who seemed determined to live her life with her ears and eyes wide open, not about to miss a thing.

Mattie's thoughts returned to the present. Less serious matters were on the table for now; for instance, Tick's request to go shopping for a herringbone blazer she saw in the Nordstrom catalog. While Mattie had chosen a few outfits for Tick before Alissa's funeral and had presented her with a collection of tees, slacks, and blouses brought back from Paris, Tick's wardrobe was still quite limited. She truthfully needed some more clothes.

Driving together to the City Creek shopping center in downtown Salt Lake City, Tick, walking competently on crutches, Mattie and Laura made their way to the stores that carried fashions for petite teenagers. Not surprisingly, Tick was not impressed with any of the clothes hanging on the racks in those teenage dedicated boutiques, scowling at the skimpy looking outfits and the shredded jeans currently popular with the younger crowd.

The three shoppers ended up on the designers' floor at Nordstrom's, where Tick found what she liked: two large bags worth of classic, conservative styles, including several long sleeve tops that hid her scars. The herringbone blazer on the rack was too big, but the saleswoman ordered one in her size that they would deliver to Mattie's apartment within the week. Tick also needed some comfortable flats and sports shoes, and they spent some time in the underwear department before the shopping excursion ended.

Mattie tucked the receipt for the new purchases in her wallet, wondering how high Brad's eyebrows would rise when he saw the charge. He was about to learn that his daughter was a bit of a clotheshorse.

When Laura examined Tick's purchases, she turned to Mattie and said, "No surprises here. She wants to dress just like you."

She's ready, Mattie thought. *It is time to discharge Tick from the hospital and finally send her home. Thank God.*

Transitions

Some four months after her rescue, and two months after her adoption, Tick would be leaving the hospital the following day and finally going to her new home. In preparation, Mattie and Laura drove to Brad's house after work to drop off some personal care items for Tick that Laura had purchased for her. They freely admitted their ulterior motive was to see the house, which had been newly renovated and redecorated for Tick. Brad had invited them for an early supper and a tour of the house.

The Hughes home was located high on Salt Lake's east bench, with a broad view of the city below. The 6,200 square foot house, situated on a five-acre lot, could not be seen from the road. Mattie stopped in front of an imposing iron gate, entered the code that Brad had given her, and waited for admission. Driving slowly up the driveway, beautiful natural landscaping and various stately trees draped in snow guided their way up to the residence.

Brad greeted his guests and helped carry the bundle of packages to the foot of the main stairway leading to the second floor. Later, Brad led Mattie and Laura into the kitchen and introduced them to the family housekeeper, Ana Canasa, who was at the sink polishing some silver. Brad's special guests were here thirty minutes early, Ana thought, displeased.

She turned away from the sink to address Brad in Spanish. "*No es así como quería conocer a la famosa doctora Barnes y su simpatica asistente!*"

Brad laughed. "You look fine, Ana. Don't worry, Mattie and Laura are like family."

Mattie had already learned quite a lot about Ana from Brad.

Roque Canasa, a short, barrel-chested Peruvian, had immigrated to America from Junín, a small town located at 13,474 feet above sea level in central Peru. Two years later, Roque, employed as a sheepherder in Craig, Colorado, returned to Junin to marry Ana, a girl from his village. The two subsequently returned to the USA and worked out on the range in isolated locations in and around Craig. Tragically, Roque died in a lightning strike while exposed on a mountainside tending sheep. Ana, with little formal education and speaking a broken mixture of Quechua, Spanish, and a smattering of English, found employment at a local McDonald's restaurant, where she won awards on more than one occasion for her outstanding work.

Over thirty years ago, Catherine Hughes met Ana Canasa under dire circumstances. Catherine always claimed that meeting Ana that night was a "God thing." Catherine was seven-months pregnant and on a road trip with her two small boys to join Brad for a long week-end together in Steamboat Springs, Colorado. Brad had made the five-hour drive earlier in the week for business and thought a family get-away would be good for his wife, who had been down with a cold and cooped up with their energetic and restless boys. Catherine enjoyed road trips, and she was an excellent driver, but about an hour outside of Steamboat Springs, she felt terrible, lightheaded, and her eyes began to blur.

Ana's shift was just about to end when she saw a woman looking very ill with small children come into the restaurant asking for help. She immediately went into action, driving Catherine to the nearby hospital, where she was diagnosed with pneumonia and admitted as a patient. Ana stayed with the children until Brad could make his way to the hospital, and later that night, Brad drove Ana back to her apartment as both boys cuddled beside her in the car, sound asleep.

Four months later, Ana Canasa lived in the newly constructed guest quarters of Brad's classy barn. She began taking English classes, a mission she never entirely mastered, and assisted Catherine with housework and her ever-so-busy little boys' care. Some thirty-five years later, Ana, while no longer living at the Hughes's place, was still running the household. She now had her own home, an English cottage she shared with her niece, Consuela, her niece's husband, Arturo, and their four-year-old son, Paco, who spent many summer hours in Brad's pool. Brad managed Ana's financial affairs from the start and hired Arturo as a foreman for one of his ready-mix operations. The family was now in excellent shape financially.

Blushing from the embarrassment of meeting Mattie and Laura with silver polish all over her hands and apron, Ana said she was honored to meet them, thinking that Brad was right—Dr. Barnes was *muy hermosa*, very beautiful.

From the kitchen, Brad escorted the women outside to an arbor-covered stone path that led from the back of the house to a spacious back yard.

There, facing east, they saw a large swimming pool with a spectacular view of the Wasatch Mountains. The property, landscaped with elegant garden spaces, held gazebos and water features, where, in January, spikey bluish icicles dripped from natural stone boulders. To the north, about thirty meters from the house stood a handsome two-story barn. The main floor stored outdoor furniture and property maintenance equipment, but the top-level held a guest bedroom suite, a family room, a kitchen, bathroom, and a sleeping porch.

"Did you ever own horses?" Mattie asked.

"That was the original plan," Brad replied, "but after Catherine became ill, caring for horses was not realistic, so I converted the second floor into a living space for Ana."

Laura spoke up, inquiring what Mattie herself was wondering, "You never mentioned that Catherine had been ill, just that she died from a heart condition. What—"

"Cardiomyopathy. She caught pneumonia when she was pregnant with David. It left her heart weakened. She was quite ill for years."

The sad look on Brad's face said everything, and Mattie didn't pursue the subject. He and his family had endured the trial and pain of loss, but Brad was disciplined about keeping his sorrows in check. Mattie had spent hours with Brad, but in some ways, she hardly knew him. She knew that Brad wouldn't withhold information deliberately, but he wasn't one to talk about himself.

Brad keeps his own counsel, she thought. *It's none of my business anyway. Poor Catherine. Poor Brad.*

The house tour continued in the fully finished basement, comprising a large recreation room with access to the front of the pool, three well-appointed bedrooms, three baths, and an exercise room. From there, they walked up a stairway to the main floor and into a large, comfortable living room. A screened-in porch looked out at the pool. There was a spacious family room area just off the kitchen, a separate dining room, and a sitting room with book-lined shelves. The house's flow was outstanding, and Brad's decorator, who had replaced formal antiques with more contemporary pieces and fabrics, had done a professional job; the home had a warm and welcoming feel to it.

Up another flight of stairs led them to the bedrooms and Brad's office, located on a large landing area overlooking the living room. A computer sat upon a beautiful mahogany desk placed against a wall displaying a large metallic sculpture of a horse; pictures of horses and mining scenes bracketed the piece of art. The adjacent wall supported two bookcases framing a large window that peered down on the valley. A cushioned window seat topped with overstuffed throw pillows was an ideal place to sprawl out and read a book. Like the rest of the house, the office was functional and restful, with large leather chairs strategically located under good lighting.

Then, without fanfare, Brad led Mattie and Laura down a hallway toward a handsomely framed arched doorway supporting a heavy oak door. Oddly, the door had no visible doorknob. Brad pressed against the wall just left of the door, and a panel opened, revealing a glass plate. Looking into the plate triggered a soft hissing sound, and the door magically opened. Mattie thought of the automatic doors to the surgical wing at Children's Hospital, doors that helped keep their brand of deadly microorganisms out.

Brad's explanation was brief, and he looked annoyed. "It was the best solution we could devise…that is to fortify this entire wing." Pointing to a brass button on the inside wall, he added, "When you press this once, it locks the doors, twice it sets off alarms, press it three times, and the cavalry comes."

Mattie sighed with the awful knowledge that Tick and Brad would never be at peace—or, for that matter, safe—until Timothy Bird and his followers were behind bars or dead. Tick's security was Brad's top priority, and he had a good reason for making it so.

An investigative team working with the Mexican government was looking for Timothy Bird in and around Puebla. Another group was looking for Bart Madison near Mobile Bay, Alabama. But to date, the searches had been disappointing. And, worse, the more they learned, the more they came to understand the rampant evil perpetrated by these soulless men—men who enjoyed inflicting pain.

Brad's expression reenergized as he opened the door into Tick's room. It was large, fresh, and uncluttered, ready for Tick to create her very own teenage sanctuary. The room was newly carpeted in a neutral cream color; the walls were a soft grayish-green, with the moldings, shutters, and doors painted off-white. Along the longest wall was a queen-sized bed with an upholstered headboard covered in a beautiful fabric of aqua and shimmers of gold. A fluffy duvet, gold with aqua piping, and several decorative pillows in subtle patterns and coordinating colors were at the head of the bed. Other furnishings included two bedside tables, lamps, a large antique desk with a brand new Apple computer resting on it, and a large, empty bookcase ready to be filled with books.

In a tiled bay, next to the window, Brad had set up a proper artist's easel and stool that Mrs. Amori had recommended for Tick to have.

Mattie observed what looked like a large pocketknife or a multiplier tool on the bedside table. She started to ask Brad about it when she noticed the oil painting—a large portrait of Tick and Alissa. It hadn't been hung and rested against the wall next to the end table.

In the painting, Tick was lying on a bed, reading a book, with a light coverlet over her hips. Her arms were exposed, with fine lines marking old wounds on her forearm: the top of the scar across her shoulder visible. Tick, her attention fixed on the pages, appeared to be completely relaxed and safe, her knees drawn up into her chest.

Alissa, her mother, stood next to the bed with her hand resting lightly on her daughter's shoulder. She looked down at her daughter with a fusion of emotions—pure love, pride, and concern. It was, perhaps, the most stunning portrait study Mattie had ever seen—it took her breath away.

"She will love it," Mattie announced. "It's splendid."

"I think so, too," Brad said reticently, "but I don't want the painting to upset or depress her. It's very realistic, don't you think?"

Her eyes locked on the portrait, Laura said, "It's just as Tick has described Alissa. It may bring her some sadness at first, but it will soon become a source of strength. She will treasure it for life."

"Mrs. Amori says it is the best portrait she has ever done," Brad added. "Although she may never forgive me for stipulating that it can never be exhibited or photographed."

"Well, I'm sure she'll get over it," Laura commented as she walked into Tick's bathroom and closet area.

The master bedroom and guest bedroom were much of the same—attractive, well-appointed rooms. But now Mattie felt like an intruder, invading Brad's personal space, so she was thankful when he escorted them downstairs for a glass of wine.

They slipped past Ana, who was hauling Tick's bags up to her room as they started down the stairs.

"I will put these in the *chica*'s bedroom, okay?" Ana asked.

As Brad turned to help her, Mattie stepped in. "Let me help." Mattie snagged a bundle from Ana and instructed Brad and Laura to go ahead. "I'll be down in *un momento*," she said, winking at Ana.

Mattie followed the stocky little woman into Tick's bedroom, where they got busy removing tags, hanging or folding everything, and putting Tick's clothes into her closet.

"These clothes are so nice, Dr. Mattie," Ana said in halting English. "Tick will like them, no? Brad says she is very pretty."

"Tick picked out most of these outfits herself. She likes nice clothes, and yes, she is beautiful."

The women worked quietly together, Mattie stocking the bathroom cabinets with enough products to keep Tick well supplied for months.

As the women began gathering up all the empty bags and packaging trash, Ana said quietly, "*No te preocupes.* Don't worry. We are going to take good care of your Tick. *El pajaro del diablo* won't get her. *El señor* will kill him if he comes here."

Mattie was somewhat startled, but Ana's expression was serious, heartfelt, and determined. *She knows about Timothy. Brad must unequivocally trust her.*

"I know you will take good care of her," Mattie replied. "I can see that. She is lucky to have you and Brad. What has Brad told you about Tick?"

"Many sad things that break my heart, but..." Ana said playfully, "He says she is like you—very smart, brave, and very *mandóna*... uh, bossy." Instantly realizing her mistake and noticing Mattie's eyes widen, Ana attempted a retraction. "You know...she likes things perfect."

Seeing Ana struggle, Mattie laughed and gave the flustered woman an enormous smile. "Señor Brad is right. Both Tick and I can be bossy, but she's going to love you, and you are going to love her."

Mattie and Ana went downstairs, where Brad was showing Laura his mineral collection, a display that he had gathered over the years from different mining sites. Mattie wandered about the house, admiring its charm and imagining that Tick would feel very comfortable and at home. Pausing at the fireplace, she studied family pictures on the mantle.

Photos of Brad and Catherine together made her feel uneasy, like she was once again intruding into Brad's private life. Catherine was a gorgeous, blue-eyed redhead with a giant smile. In early pictures surrounded by her young family, she looked healthy and vibrant, but more recent photos exposed her illness—a wonderful woman betrayed by her body.

Dinner was sumptuous, and fine wine complemented Ana's Peruvian fare: ceviche, Arroz Con Pato, and custard.

Tick will love Ana's cooking, Mattie thought with a tinge of jealousy.

⁓⟡⟡⟡⟡⟡⟢

Mattie was not the only person in the house checking things out that afternoon. Basing her curiosity on the way Señor Brad looked when he spoke of Tick's doctor, Ana was intensely interested in how the beautiful doctor and her boss interacted with each other. Ana could see that the doctor acted a little formal with him, a little stiff, but she noticed Mattie glancing over at the *señor* when he wasn't looking. Also, Ana didn't miss the sadness in her eyes when she was looking at family pictures of Catherine and the boys. Nonetheless, the intuitive housekeeper remained frustrated, unable to get a reliable reading on Dr. Mattie Barnes' feelings for Señor Brad.

Brad looked happier than Ana had seen him in quite some time. His face seemed to soften when he was around the doctor as if he had feelings for her. Maybe it was just the look of a tired man who had been busy with too much on his plate. After all, he had spent the last week pushing the house contractor to finish the last of the renovations and then orchestrating everything required to reassemble the house. On this day, he had spent the entire morning snow blowing all the walkways and putting down salt.

He hasn't worked this hard around the house in years, Ana thought. Perhaps *el señor* wasn't only trying to make everything perfect for *la chica* Tick, but maybe for the doctor, too.

Dinnertime conversation centered on Tick. They talked mostly about her schooling, her physical progress, and her speechlessness. However, from the kitchen, Ana overheard a discussion about Tick that seemed impossible to imagine in one so young: her courage and will to survive under the circumstances too grim to conceive.

Ana had read some terrible things in the papers about *el señor*'s new daughter, but Señor Brad was never wrong about people.

I bet I can get her to talk again, she mused.

Brad had spoken to Ana about Tick: her true identity, how he found her, everything. He had been entirely open with her, and when she thanked him for entrusting her with such a *secreto*, Brad told Ana that he hoped she would help raise his new daughter, just as he and Catherine had trusted her with their boys' lives so many years earlier. Brad warned her about Timothy Bird—*el diablo pájaro*, the "devil bird" as Ana called him—explaining that working at the house put her at some risk. When Brad said that he would understand if she decided to retire instead, Ana felt like giving him a swift kick in the rear for the first time. She wasn't going anywhere!

⁓⚬⚬⚬⚬⚬⟲

Mattie accelerated onto Highway 215, and Brad followed closely behind in his jeep. The three had an early supper because Mattie wanted to get home and pack for her annual trip to her cabin. She and Laura would be leaving the next morning, as soon as Tick checked out of the hospital, and they would stay at the cabin with a few friends. Brad was on his way to the hospital for a short visit with Tick before lights out.

"Cat got your tongue?" Mattie asked Laura. "You're so quiet."

Looking out the window and lost in thought, Laura was slow to reply. "I guess I'm feeling a little sad," she said. "I'm going to miss them. Then, I can't stop thinking about that painting. Do you think Alissa loved Tick that much, or is that just what Tick wants to believe?"

Mattie glanced over at Laura, and for the first time in years, she saw a trace of the alienated young lady who sat next to her on that airplane, alone, filled with disappointment and self-loathing—a girl who had been betrayed by self-centered parents.

"Well, based on everything I know about Tick at this point, I'm quite sure that Alissa was a remarkable mother," Mattie said. "If having children is in your future, Laura, you're going to make a remarkable mother too. As for missing them, they'll be coming by the office at least twice a week. Tick and I still have a lot of work ahead of us."

Mattie paused, focusing on merging into traffic, and then continued in a clipped, professional manner. "But our job is to heal her wounds and then see her off to a happy, healthy life."

Laura didn't say a word but continued to stare out the window, thinking about Tick.

She won't like it, coming in, sitting in a chair for an hour twice a week to face painful issues. She won't like it one bit, and when Tick doesn't like something, she changes it.

Laura glanced over at her friend. It was apparent to her that Brad adored Mattie and that Mattie liked him too. But Laura could see that the closer Brad got, the more Mattie seemed to pull away.

It would be sad if she let this one slip away, she thought.

⁓⁓⁓

Claire Summers sat across from her new friend, Tick Hughes. Tick painstakingly picked her way through the dinner tray in front of her, searching for something she could eat and treating the food as if it had come out of a dumpster.

Claire had never had such a problematic friend: one who constantly challenged her thoughts and opinions about life—who was so driven and was so annoyingly smart and capable. Both girls would be leaving the hospital in the morning: Claire, home to be with her family. Tick, unable to talk, would be going to a home she had never seen, a home without her mom or dad, to a new school, and with an adopted father, she had only known for months. Amazingly, Tick seemed to be at peace and ready to go.

Two months earlier, Claire, the young phenomenon destined for greatness, wanted nothing more than to crawl in a hole and die.

The doctors say I will probably never ski again. I'll never feel my skies under me, the g-forces radiating up my ankles, the muscles in my quadriceps compressing, the feeling of flight and the sensation of time slowing down. It was all over now.

Claire was in physical therapy when Dr. Brackford and Mattie came in with Tick. They introduced her to Mr. T., the physical therapist in charge of post-op rehabilitation.

Mattie pulled her aside to ask her a favor—say hello to Tick and keep an eye on her.

It hadn't gone well at first. Tick, working twice as hard as anyone in the room, was asked by Mr. T. to call it a day. "That's it, Tick, you've done enough for your first day."

At dinner that night, Claire gave Tick a hard time about working out so hard and asked if she was trying to impress Mr. T. Tick, resenting the accusation, began writing on her tablet: "*Whatever you do, work at it with all your heart, as if you are working for the Lord, not for human masters. Why have you become so lazy, Claire? Why have you given up? You should be an example for others. The children here look up to you. I've heard about you—you're a famous skier, a star.*"

Chief Cripple, Claire thought to spit back at Tick. Instead, she pushed herself away from the table and left the mini-sermonizer to polish her halo by herself.

The next day was tense. Claire set out to outlast Tick with competitive juices stirring by doubling down on the regimen that Mr. T had assigned. She pushed herself vigorously, determined to up the ante with her holier-than-thou younger rival. It was an "uncle" competition that might have gone on forever if it hadn't been for Tick, who went up to Claire with a huge smile. "*You win!*" she wrote. "*I've had enough! You did great today! That was an awesome workout.*"

Claire laughed for the first time in weeks. "You're killing me, Tick! Mr. T. was about to kick us out of there!" Grabbing a towel to wipe her face, she asked, "Why do you work out so hard, anyway, Tick? What does it matter to you?"

Tick's odd response only piqued her interest in the girl. "*Have you ever read the Call of the Wild by Jack London?*" Tick wrote. "*It's about a wolf, and there's a part in the novel that reads, 'He was a killer, a thing that preyed, living on the things that lived, unaided, alone, by virtue of his own strength and prowess, surviving triumphantly in a hostile environment where only the strong survive.'*"

Tick paused before she wrote, "*My life requires me to be strong like that wolf.*"

Claire didn't comment, wondering if Tick's intensity came from something real, something significant, or if the girl was just overdramatic. Either way, the curious girl, who trained and competed with the same intensity and focus as Claire's most committed teammates, should be on a cereal box.

They spent more and more time together, Claire enduring a never-ending stream of questions: "*What are your favorite books? What are your parents like? Do you like going to the movies? What kind of music do you enjoy? Do you cook for your family? Do you have a boyfriend? Do you kiss each other?*"

Then came the whys: "*Why don't I ever see you reading? Why do you think God has deserted you? Why don't you prove the doctors wrong and ski again?*"

An encyclopedic knowledge of the Bible backed up Tick's questions, and her immense, overall book smarts was outrageous, Claire had thought. She seemed to have read everything and was quick to quote almost anything verbatim.

Tick's appetite for information was insatiable, bordering on obnoxious, but her questions, while probing and often personal, forced Claire to think more purposefully and to reassess some of her positions. Her striking-eyed competitor had candidly encouraged her to consider placing God, instead of herself, in the center of her life. One of Tick's quotations—from 2 Corinthians 12:9—played over and over again in Claire's mind: "My grace is sufficient for you, for my power is made perfect in weakness." If she just trusted—believed— she could let it all go, her past, the dreams, and her fears—simply trust in God's purpose and move on. She could do it all again, but this time, she'd be playing in a different sandbox.

Still, her new friend puzzled Claire. For all her Christian beliefs and the genuine kindness and gentleness she showed the other children, especially little Brent, Tick had a dark side. She could be cold and unapproachable. There was shrewdness about her, a hardness that wasn't what one would expect from a preacher's daughter. For Claire, it was hard to ignore.

Claire had been in the recreation room when Tick slapped Jimmy Gardner and pushed him away. She had seen real fierceness on Tick's face when the kid snatched the controller for the second time, and when she struck him, her hand moved with such speed and control that, from Claire's athletic perspective, it looked like a technically perfected move.

Days later, when Claire's former ski team members, Carmen and Ben, dropped by the hospital, Claire had felt extremely uncomfortable introducing them to Tick. They were obviously under the influence of alcohol or drugs, possibly both.

It was a disaster from the start. Carmen asked Tick if she wanted to be a big girl and get high on marijuana-infused brownies she had smuggled in for Claire. Ben started coming on to Tick, saying that she was hot and that he would set her up with friends who would show her a good time when she got out.

"Do you know how twisted and disgusting you both are?" Tick wrote on her slate. *"Whatever garbage you're taking is muddling your brains, get ahold of yourselves before it's too late, and get it right with God."*

When Ben read the slate, he grabbed it, erasing Tick's words, and then scribbled his message, making derisive sounds as he wrote, *"What a pious loser! Your brain is muddled with that propaganda and nonsense about God. Forget the fantasy, Tinkerbell, and join the real world before it's too late."*

Tick's reaction was scary. If she had been the wolf in Jack London's book, her fangs would have been showing, and the hackles on her neck standing straight up. But as it happened, Tick's face turned stony as she wiped her slate clean and, still looking at Ben with unmistakable hostility in her eyes, she wrote, *"And what you don't know about the 'real world' will be your bad ending."*

If Ben had said another word—if he had moved to block her as she made for the door—Claire was sure Tick would have gone after him. But the prey had been smart, afraid. Sensing unfavorable odds, Ben froze and then moved aside without uttering a sound.

"Geez, talk about a head case. Who let her out of the psych ward?" Ben mocked once Tick was out of sight.

Claire was beside herself, furious. "Are you insane? She's twelve years old, for god's sake! You don't know a thing about her, and you come in here high, offering her dope? You both need to leave now and do me a favor, don't come back."

She found Tick in her room, waiting. *What is wrong with you, Claire? Why would you have friends like that?*

"They're not my friends," Claire answered. "We were just on the same team." Not wanting Tick to start in with Biblical quotations, she said, "They're not worth getting upset over."

"You're right. They're ungodly idiots. They would drag you down. You can do so much better."

Ha! Claire thought to herself. *The preacher's daughter is not only a little commando, but she is also a little judgmental.* Wisely, Claire changed the subject and announced that it was lunchtime.

"For He satisfies the thirsty and fills the hungry with good things," Tick wrote.

"Okay, Pastor Tick, but I'm off to feed my growling stomach with mac and cheese."

The last weeks at the hospital had almost been fun—fun, that is, for an ex-super athlete whose best friend and mentor had turned out to be a twelve-year-old mute. Claire had enjoyed working with the younger children, reading to them, playing games, listening to music with Tick in the common room, and helping the other children in physical therapy. She was ready to go home, move back to Reno, and see her brothers and sisters again. She and Tick would begin new lives.

But she was going to miss her new friend.

Picking up an apple off of her tray, she pitched it toward Tick, who casually plucked the apple out of the air as it sailed by her ear.

"Eat the apple, Tick! You're going to fade away," Claire blustered.

Her eyes shining, intelligent, and playful, her eyes fixed on Claire, Tick took a big bite out of the apple.

Those eyes, Claire thought, *I would give anything to know what goes on behind those amazing eyes.*

CHAPTER

32

Home Free

The hospital discharged both Tick and Claire on the same day, but their departure was by no means typical. Almost everyone in the Rehab Center, staff and young patients alike, gathered to say farewell to the determined duo, textbook examples of courage for those with physical and emotional struggles, lifting spirits with their upbeat exuberance and encouraging can-do support.

Receiving hugs, high-fives, and stacks of cards expressing best wishes and appreciation, the girls thanked the staff for all the care they received. Tick wrote something on her iPad and held it up for her friends: "*Besides Mr. T., who can you lean on for comfort and strength whenever you feel discouraged?*" Tick hoped that their enthusiastic comeback—"Jesus!"—was more than just a knee-jerk response for her benefit.

Mattie came by to see the girls off, making a point to tell Tick that she would be at her cabin for a few days, but she looked forward to seeing her for their appointment the following week.

Watching as Tick settled into Brad's jeep, Mattie felt her stomach tighten.

Was this day going to end so quickly, without some calamity befalling all of them first? No knockout blows? No injuries? No chaos?

Fortunately, Mattie witnessed smiling faces and two thumbs-up from Brad Hughes and his daughter as they pulled away from the hospital.

⁓

Ana heard the garage door open and made her way down the hallway to help Brad with the luggage. Her heart was racing. "*La chica esta aquí!*" she called out loud to no one, excitedly nervous. Regardless of the uncertainty she felt, Ana would do everything she could to help Señor Brad's new daughter feel welcome and comfortable in her new home.

Ana was a descendant from the ancient Inca civilization in Peru, raised in a village steeped in traditions that maintain that unique culture's legacy. She was a keen observer of nature and the stars, characteristic of her people, thus providing her with great satisfaction through those solitary years when her husband was away in the mountains watching and protecting sheep, and again while watching and protecting Brad's children. It was a life of service. Even as a tiny child, Ana was expected to work hard, wresting potatoes from the ground, taking care of the *cuyes* (guinea pigs), watching her younger siblings, and helping her mother with the daily chores.

She had misgivings about the foundling Brad had adopted—doubts she couldn't dismiss. She wanted to believe that Brad knew what he was doing. But since Catherine's death, and with the boys and their families so far away, his life had become increasingly solitary, drifting away from close friends and spending most of his time working at his office or sitting behind his desk at home.

Ana worried about him, always suggesting things that might perk him up: hosting a small dinner party, playing a round of golf with a friend, grabbing one of his buddies for a beer, or taking a hike to enjoy the fall colors. Adopting a child he found while backpacking alone in the mountains—a girl the newspapers reported as being a suspect in the Death Ranch investigations—seemed uncharacteristically reckless.

Why would such an intelligent, levelheaded man take on such a risk?

With the instincts of a good sheepherder, determined to watch over and protect her main concern and *querido* amigo, Señor Brad, Ana watched as the car door opened. She marveled as the wiry yet delicate-looking girl reached for the grab handle and swung her way out of the car, pivoting like a dancer on one foot before opening the rear door to pull crutches from the back seat.

Such a beautiful child, Ana thought, aware that the girl with eyes streaked with comets was now examining her just as intently. The observer was the observed, and Ana instinctively knew what Tick was seeking. Her caretaker's mind returned to the painting in Tick's bedroom. A captivating painting that pulled her over and over into the bedroom—a portrait of a mother and daughter. So much love. So much heartache!

At that very moment, Ana prayed to God that she could be a blessing in Tick's life, that she could alleviate her pain and grief. Knowing anything more about Tick no longer seemed important.

Ana stepped forward to meet the new Hughes addition and greeted Tick with a welcoming hug. The same hug reserved for Ben, Brian, and David: warm, firm, accepting, loving.

"I know you want to see everything, but while you have your boots and jacket on, let's start with the outside," Brad said, placing Tick's suitcase near the garage door before commencing his grand tour of the place. "I will take the suitcases up later," he added for Ana's benefit.

Tick appeared happy, excited, taking in everything, observing every detail of the property. She was especially curious about Ana's previous living quarters in the barn, asking Brad to help her navigate the oak staircase. *"My mom and I would have thought this was heaven on earth,"* she wrote upon inspection. *"Except we had a stream."*

They walked back to the house, where Ana was waiting to welcome Tick, who was in the process of writing something on her iPad—a request to see her bedroom. "Good idea, Tick," Brad said. "Let's go up right now and add you to the bedroom wing security system."

Tick carefully made her way up the stairs, followed closely by Brad and Ana. Coming to the hall door, Brad guided her through the necessary steps to log her into the security system, explaining how it worked.

As the trio entered Tick's bedroom, Ana and Brad locked their gazes on Tick, who immediately spotted the large painting, now hanging over the bed. At first, she was stunned, standing perfectly still with one hand covering her mouth. Turning to Brad, with a tear running down her cheek, she began typing.

"It is wonderful. It's as if Momma's right here with me. I love it!"

"Amori outdid herself," Brad said after expelling the breath he had been holding in. Tick's response was everything he had hoped it would be.

The three sat on the bed for some time, just looking up at the painting. Brad's arms encircled his daughter, and Ana said, "*Te pareces a tu madre…* You look like your mother."

Brad wanted to promote Tick's relationship with Ana, so he excused himself to make some calls, leaving Ana and Tick alone. There was work to be done. Tick's suitcase needed emptying, the closets, shelves, and drawers—previously stocked by Mattie—needed to be reorganized to suit Tick's preferences. Ana gave Mattie credit for the new purchases. She said, "La Dr. Mattie is a good shopper. She found so many nice things for you." Once they unpacked, Ana led Tick down to the main floor for a tour of the house. The circuit culminated in the dining room, where Ana proudly served a delicious lunch for Tick and Brad: *lomo saltado* (Peruvian beef stir fry), before leaving for the day.

After lunch, Tick and Brad retreated to Brad's office, where Tick sat perched on the window seat with a book while Brad worked at his computer, but neither party could focus on the task at hand.

There's a certain blissfulness—a feeling of accomplishment—about reaching the end of a long, arduous journey. This very moment was a long time coming.

Miraculously, Brad realized Tick was alive and safe in his home, and he was overwhelmed with satisfaction. It was a picture he might have dreamed of: Tick propped up with pillows behind her back, a light blanket over her legs, and the snow-covered valley behind her. She appeared quite relaxed, the warm afternoon sun shining through the window, with all tension drained from her features. He wanted the moment to last forever.

But, of course, time is relentless, and those moments never last.

The next morning, Brad woke up early and checked on Tick. Not finding her in her bedroom, he panicked and grabbed his pistol. Heart racing, he rushed down to the kitchen to find her emptying the dishwasher and putting everything away.

"What are you doing?" he grumpily asked, hiding a new pistol behind his back.

"*I like to get my chores done early,*" Tick wrote, explaining that she always fed the chickens and began working in the garden before the sun was out. Tick raised her hand before Brad could respond, then wrote, "*I'd love to see that handgun you're holding, Dad. Did you just buy it? Is it a G19 Gen 4 Glock?*"

Brad could only muster a grin and a nod as he handed the weapon over to his daughter.

Within two days after her homecoming, Tick had reorganized the entire kitchen. She started the project as soon as Ana had gone home, opening every drawer and cabinet and making copious notes. By four o'clock, she had the contents of every shelf, counter, drawer, and nook in the kitchen spread out all over the dining room table and floor, and she refused to go to bed until well after midnight.

The next morning, Ana walked into the kitchen and found Brad lining shelves. Swearing in Quechua, Ana shooed Brad out of the kitchen and, following *la princesa's* directions, spent the day helping the twelve-year-old reorganize a kitchen that had been Ana's territory for over thirty-five years.

Brad wished that Mattie could witness what was going on in his kitchen, as this underscored Tick's capacity for carrying things to the extreme. As for Ana, Brad was proud of her for helping Tick and tactfully taking a back seat to his daughter's impulsive mission. Before Ana went home that evening, she grudgingly admitted to him that Tick's changes made the kitchen seem more functional.

The next day, Ana was still smarting from the kitchen venture. She walked into the laundry room and found Tick at the ironing board with a stack of Brad's shirts. Ana waved her hands in disapproval and then, speaking a nearly incomprehensible mixture of English and Spanish, let Tick know that the laundry was her domain.

"*No te metas en mi trabajo*," she loudly protested.

Tick obediently put the iron down and left the room, but Ana worried that she would have her hands full with the new Hughes family member.

Ana quickly learned that waiting on Tick would not be easy. Even with the ankle boot, crutches, and her balance still off-kilter, Tick insisted on either doing things for herself or working alongside Ana.

Tick had been reading books about the history of Peru and gathering information about Ana's village. Brad even purchased a text-to-speech computer program that Tick used to build a Spanish working vocabulary, and Tick didn't hesitate to try it out.

One afternoon, Tick was sitting at the kitchen island, flipping through an old cookbook that once belonged to Catherine and playing with her laptop. When Ana heard a strange, mechanical voice, she stopped to listen as the voice thanked her in Spanish for preparing such wonderful custard the previous day. The voice then asked what Ana called the desert. Between the robotic, bizarre-sounding Spanish, and the idea that Tick could have such a strange voice, Ana began giggling so hard that she covered her face behind her dishtowel.

"Flan de caramel, Tick," Ana sputtered, "and I pray that when God returns your voice, it won't sound anything like that horrible machine!"

Later that day, Mattie called Brad to cancel Tick's first therapy session, a session scheduled for the following day, February 7. Her aunt had just died in Helena, Montana, and she needed to go home. Mattie rescheduled for the coming Friday.

Tick seemed disappointed when Brad explained Mattie's situation, particularly upon hearing that Mattie would not be back before school started. When he asked if she was upset, she defensively denied the suggestion.

Disappearing into her room until Ana left at four o'clock that day, Tick slipped into the kitchen and began an all-out baking frenzy—rolls, cookies, loaves of bread—enough to feed a small army. She often prepared a large amount of food for others at Timothy's ranch but rarely ate much herself.

The next morning, Tick asked Brad to drive her to the library. While he was busy signing the parental consent form for his minor's library card, she went about accumulating a stack of books about PTSD behavioral psychology. At the checkout desk, she quickly crammed them into her book bag before Brad could comment or question her reading material choice.

Arriving at home, Tick spent most of the weekend in her bedroom, explaining that she wanted to read up on some subjects. Brad assumed the subjects were school-related and that Tick was feeling anxious about being a bona fide student at her new school.

⌒∽∞∽⌒

Where is Mattie when I need her, Brad lamented, wishing the aunt had not died the past week. He had counted on seeing Mattie Monday morning to dispense moral support for Tick, who would be participating in an actual classroom setting for the first time since kindergarten.

A small floral arrangement was delivered to the house. Addressed to Tick was a generic card with a short note reading, "I know you will do your best.—Mattie" Laura, on the other hand, sent Tick a hilarious text. "Try not to crack open all the eggheads you are about to encounter, at least not on your first day!"

Monday finally arrived, and Brad awakened feeling unprepared to face whatever possible ordeals were in store for him if things didn't go well for Tick. Would there be troubles with the other students who might shun or, worse, bully her? Would her teachers ignore or, worse, talk down to her? Would she retaliate or, worse, deck one of the other students or, worse, a teacher?

Standing at the bathroom sink to shave, Brad relaxed when he remembered the quotation displayed on his office desk: *"Forget all the reasons why it won't work and believe the one reason why it will!"*

Dressed in a white dress shirt, striped tie, navy blazer, gray slacks, and polished black oxfords, Brad made his way down the stairs and caught a whiff of bacon in the air. Ana had come in early to see that *la chica* ate a good breakfast.

Tick was sitting at the kitchen island and reading one of her textbooks. Her hair, which had grown out over the months, was in a neat ponytail, and she looked stunning, dressed in skinny black pants, a silk beige blouse under the herringbone blazer she ordered, and stylish running shoes. Tick didn't want to hide. That was apparent. She would be a standout.

Arriving early at the university, Brad walked with Tick up to Sue Ellen Kasch's office and left his daughter in her care, feeling apprehensive but gratified that she seemed calm.

He should never have worried. Tick thrived in the environment, loving every second of her newfound freedom. Over the coming weeks, Sue Ellen reported that Tick was interacting with her fellow students remarkably well.

The school's curriculum team had tailored Tick's program to meet her special needs. They designed a study program that would enable her to quickly catch up with the other students, and TV monitors allowed her to communicate with the class using her laptop. Two handpicked upper-class students would serve as mentors, happy to help the new girl settle in during her first month.

Tick seemed oblivious to her striking good looks. Still, her beautiful face and classy outfits almost certainly helped soften the student body's initial impression of a strange, mute girl on crutches. Whatever pity anyone felt for her was quickly dispelled during the morning assembly when Mrs. Kasch introduced their new classmate to her fellow students. Tick came across as self-confident, approachable, and composed. There was a directness about her, a no-nonsense, fearless approach that was undeniably disarming. When being introduced to a fellow student, she smiled, looked the student directly in his or her eyes, and conducted herself as if she were the ship's captain meeting her new crew.

Nobody knew quite what to make of her. Some were put off by her assertiveness; others thought that she didn't belong because she was too young, and her muteness, which had to be accommodated, changed the normal class dynamics.

Squelching the faculty's initial concerns, Tick's overall competency in the classroom was nothing short of impressive. Her muteness, for example, was not the hindrance that some teachers anticipated. Her writing skills were so exceptional that the class would fixate on the screen when she wrote something. She communicated through both her writing and her art. Often written in tiny script on the right-hand side of the screen, one could find some biblical reference appropriate to the discussion. Her artwork was ingenious, somewhat outrageous, but mostly hilarious, drawings associated with pertinent academic information, often with a complementary Biblical quotation attached.

One such artful episode involved Catherine of Aragon. Tick had been happily drawing away on her iPad, seemingly not paying attention to the day's English history lecture, when her teacher, Samantha Cumberland, became perturbed by Tick's apparent inattention and asked her to share with the rest of the class.

The laughter in the room was nearly deafening when Tick presented her notes to her classmates—a neat series of drawings with carefully written subscripts attached to them:

- The first sketch showed the newborn baby, Catherine, with the date, December 16, 1485, inscribed on the baby's bottom and proud parents, Isabella I of Castile and Ferdinand II of Aragon, hovering over her.
- Next was a depiction of little three-year-old Catherine sucking her thumb with a perplexed expression on her face and an enormous engagement ring from her betrothed, Arthur, Prince of Wales, heir apparent to the English throne, on her finger.

- Then came skilled drawings of a lavish wedding and a tragic funeral, depicting Catherine's marriage to Arthur in 1501 and his death five months later. Large tears were falling from the widow's face, with the caption, "I knew him since I was three, but I never slept with him."
- A comical drawing titled *Keep It in the Family* followed, depicting Catherine's marriage in 1509 to Henry VIII, Arthur's younger brother. A lecherous smile pictured on Henry's face.
- The final image was a racy bedroom scene showing Henry VIII under the covers with Anne Boleyn, with the same lustful smile on his face. Catherine of Aragon was horrified, sad, and looking betrayed, spying in from behind a curtain. In neat block print below the sketch, Tick added a Bible verse, Proverbs 16:12: "It is an abomination to kings to do evil, for the throne is established by righteousness."

Tick hadn't missed any main points covered in the lecture, all the while thoughtfully amusing herself. Ms. Cumberland apologized for accusing Tick of drifting off.

Recognizing that Tick's learning approach was unique and insightful, the teacher began calling on her to share any sketches she may have made during the day's lectures. The renderings were mostly humorous and perceptive, but sometimes the descriptions were dark and troubling, depicting historical acts of cruelty or disregard for human life. These disquieting sketches often left classmates feeling depressed and left Ms. Cumberland feeling perplexed over a child her age who seemed to have such a profound understanding of the dark side of human nature.

Tick's school acquaintances knew her as a witty, intelligent girl. For the most part, she was accepted and moved easily within all the social subgroups, not affiliating with a particular crowd. She was independent, private, and without a social profile on any of the social media sites. Many would consider Tick as a friend, ready to help with any issue, but not someone who was particularly sympathetic to their teenage problems, having little tolerance or patience for self-pity or victimhood. Still some people weren't so impressed with her, as expressed by one classmate in the lunchroom: "Am I the only one at this table who thinks Tick has become hard to take? I mean, it's not like she's the only smart or talented kid in this world, and I am not about to add more fuel to her hero worship fan club."

Brad would later hear about Tick's adventures in Ms. Cumberland's class from one of her classmates, but not before some very trying days—days that Brad had hoped were far behind him.

Psychoanalysis

The evening before Tick's rescheduled appointment with Mattie, Brad received a short text message. "Possibly coming down with a bug… I canceled all my appointments. If convenient, reschedule Tick for the twentieth, same time. I am looking forward to seeing her then. Happy to hear things are going well for her at school. Mattie."

Brad showed the text to his daughter, who seemed calm about the cancellation, but later, when he referred to something about Mattie, Tick bristled and walked away.

Then two days before her appointment, a wadded up ball of paper suddenly landed on Brad's desk. Tick, perched on her window seat, watched Brad as he unraveled the note to read, "*I won't be going.*"

Brad looked up from the preliminary year-end report he was working on for his company.

"Where aren't you going?" he asked. Tick picked up her iPad and began typing.

"I'm not going to the appointment to see Dr. Barnes. I don't have an emotional illness. I can take care of my problems. I've read enough about psychoanalysis to know that I don't need her. I don't want her in my head. BTW, read James 1:6–8. That's Mattie. Double-minded."

"Okay, sport, I'll look into that later," replied Brad. "But for now, I think it's a good idea to work with someone trained to help you work through feelings that are getting in your way."

"Did you require therapy when Catherine died?"

TICK

"Come on, Tick." Brad sighed. "You're too smart to make such an unfair comparison. Nobody ever kidnapped me. I wasn't abused and tortured, and nobody murdered Catherine. Just the same, it probably would have helped me quite a bit if I had joined a support group to talk about my loss."

"*But you have me now, and I have you,*" Tick replied.

Smiling, hoping he could quickly end the conversation, Brad replied, "Yes, and you always will, but we are not qualified, licensed psychiatrists. Mattie is."

Tick's expression was unreadable, but her reddening scar betrayed her. "*Her qualifications don't impress me. Anyway, she doesn't want to work with me anymore. That's okay because there is nothing wrong with me that I can't handle.*"

"Her qualifications don't impress you?" Brad asked, sitting up taller in his chair. "I'm curious to know what qualifies you to come up with that ludicrous appraisal?" Brad's voice took on a tone of irritated authority. "Besides some misdirected pride, where is all this coming from, Tick? Mattie is a remarkable doctor and has gone way beyond her purview to watch out for you, and the notion that you can manage emotions that still plague you is unrealistic. Understand me, my dear, you know that I think you are remarkable, and there's not much you can't tackle, but you have some pressing issues that need resolution if you are to get the most out of your life—a life your mother wanted you to have. In my book, Mattie is the best there is, and you need to work with her until she and I think you are ready to move on, capisce?"

Tick stood up and charged out of the room, only to be stalled out in the hallway while waiting for the security door to open. She did a respectable job slamming her bedroom door shut once she got there.

Brad grunted as he heard the bang, and perturbed, he turned back to his work.

I didn't sign on to be her best friend, he thought. But Tick had touched on a point that had been bothering him as well. Mattie had been quite distant lately. She had texted many times, but what she communicated lacked any familiarity or warmth. They were cold, professional messages: "Have you found a math and science tutor for

Tick?" "Please keep a record of any night terrors Tick experiences." "Contact Laura or me if Tick's appetite declines."

He worried that perhaps they had done something to push Mattie away.

When the twentieth finally arrived, Brad noticed Tick's scar begin to redden as they drove to the hospital. He knew it was going to be a long day.

The day before, Tick persuaded Brad to take her to the department store to buy a new outfit. When Brad asked if she would prefer to go shopping with Mattie, Tick's answer was an emphatic *"NO THANKS!"*

Arriving at Mattie's office with Brad several steps behind, Tick, dressed in an outfit that Mattie had nothing to do with, went flying in on her crutches, passed through the outer reception room, not acknowledging Laura, and entered Mattie's office with a look intended to wound. When Mattie greeted her and complimented her outfit, Tick hurriedly wrote, "*Yes, I rather like it too, and I chose it without any help from you.*"

Brad had been in Mattie's office on several occasions. It was a good-sized, nicely appointed office with windows that looked out at the ICU. The office held a desk for Mattie and a small table with chairs where she could meet privately with her staff. Mattie's decorations were impeccable, providing a feeling of intimacy in an otherwise sterile environment. Mattie could draw curtains for privacy, and access was through Laura's office, which provided an additional separation of confidentiality.

Turning away from Mattie, Tick began investigating every nook and corner of the office as Brad and Mattie quietly watched. Slowly running her fingers across the spines of the books on the bookshelf, she would pause to write down some of the titles. Then, she began reading Mattie's many diplomas, certifications, and professional award plaques. From there, she checked out all the knickknacks and casual books Mattie had scattered around on coffee tables.

Brad stayed until Mattie signaled that it was time for him to step out. Laura sat with him in the anteroom, happy to see her good friend and catch up on family news.

Finally, Tick stopped to write something on her notepad and slapped it down on Mattie's desk, her face stony. *"I'm so grateful that you could find some time for me, Dr. Barnes. I assume anything I tell you, if I decide to tell you anything, will be protected under the HIPAA law, and that you will not include confidential information in my regular hospital files."*

Looking up from the paper Tick had written on, Mattie replied, "That's correct, I won't share information with my colleagues or authorities unless I feel you are in danger of hurting yourself or others. By law, I must report to the authorities if a patient is a danger to herself or others."

Turning, Tick sat down on at a small worktable that had been set up just for her use. On it sat a computer that transmitted type to the TV monitor on the wall. A drawing pad and a variety of pencils were on the table as well.

Tick turned off the link to the live screen and promptly began typing, her fingers racing over the keys.

Tick typed furiously away as Mattie looked on patiently. She could only guess what the girl was so purposefully trying to convey. Most likely, it was backlash anger from her recent effort to create a professional distance between them. Regardless of Tick's reaction, their relationship needed to be adjusted.

Twenty minutes later, Tick finished with flair. She banged down the computer's cover, stood up, scribbled something on a pad, and disrespectfully slammed the note down on Mattie's desk. *"This is a ridiculous waste of my time... I am not crazy! No more barking for you!"*

Charging out of the room with an angry flip of her crutches, Tick sent an arrangement of flowers crashing to the floor, and the large crystal vase that housed them shattered into a thousand pieces.

Hearing the crash, Brad stood up and stopped Tick as she tried to shoot by. Looking into Mattie's office, he saw the flowers and pieces of crystal scattered across a wet carpet.

He spoke in a steady but angry voice.

"You're not going to act like a wild animal on my watch, Tick. Clean up this mess... Now!"

Mattie stood in the doorway, shook her head at Brad. "Laura, please take Tick down to the cafeteria and get her something to drink. Tick, I'm asking you nicely to please go with Laura."

Tick responded by rapidly making her way down the hall, Laura at her side. Mattie walked back into her office, followed by Brad.

"I'm so sorry, Mattie," Brad uttered. "I don't know what's going on with her, but she will be cleaning up this mess."

Mattie lifted her hand to let Brad know that now wasn't the time to talk, and she moved to the computer to begin reading what Tick had written. Brad was uncomfortable about the mess Tick had made and grabbed a wastepaper basket.

Minutes later, Mattie spoke up. "Did Tick say anything about coming here today?"

Brad, still on his hands and knees, picking up shards from the carpet, repeated Tick's comments about being able to work out her problems for herself.

"Was there anything else?"

Brad paused. He was reluctant to repeat Tick's sentiments, but he knew that Mattie probably should know.

"She called you a liar, Mattie, a fraud. That you were weak, double-minded... Some reference to James 1... I don't know. I have no clue what's behind this."

Mattie turned back to the note, reading it intently, her eyes pinched, focused on the screen, reading Tick's words again and again.

Looking up at the clock on the wall, she announced that she had another appointment, but she told Brad to go down to the cafeteria and give his daughter a big hug.

"Take her to lunch," Mattie said. "Show her that she is loved. Let her know that you disapprove of her actions here today, but don't punish her. Tick is a thousand times harder on herself than you could ever be."

Mattie's day attending to her ICU patients seemed endless before she could get back to her office, where Laura was still working at her desk.

"What went on between you and Tick today?" Laura asked. "She all but ignored me in the cafeteria, just staring out the window until Brad found us, and then they just left without saying goodbye."

"Not now, Laura. I'm sorry, but I need some time to think." And she retreated into her office.

It was five o'clock by the time Mattie looked up from her desk computer. She had read Tick's words many times over.

Written in the third person as if composed by some unknown review board, the note first provided an argumentative essay, covering all the possible diagnoses Tick might face by an outsider. The document went on to specify that Tick Hughes didn't fit any of the criteria, why she was not a candidate for psychoanalysis, and why drug therapy would not be suitable. What was necessary for recovery required privacy, time, and rest. Tick then cited several case studies where young patients were forced into improper treatment programs with disastrous results.

The composition finally focused on Mattie, and in persuasive essay form, Tick set out to disprove Dr. Mattie Barnes' ability to be her therapist.

Tick's conclusion revealed her perspective:

> *While unquestionably a brilliant ICU physician, Dr. Mattie Barns is not a competent child psychiatrist: her personality makeup is geared around short-term, life-or-death situations with outcomes generally settled in a matter of days. Dr. Barnes is not emotionally equipped to engage in longer-term psychoanalysis with uncertain outcomes, and where her patients can challenge her.*
>
> *Dr. Barnes's career choices evidence this inclination. This is a doctor who first trained in psychiatric care but then underwent extensive retraining to become an ICU doctor. The ICU, the hospital unit where Barnes's skills are on display with patients hovering between life and death and dependent upon quick-thinking decisions, is a domain where*

outcomes get resolved in days. Then when Barnes has won or lost the battle, she is free to move on.

Other evidence is clear, pointing to Dr. Barnes's unwillingness or inability to engage in long-term commitments:

(A) Except for her office assistant and immediate colleagues, she has shown no history of establishing long-lasting connections.

(B) The usually scrupulous doctor chose to lie to her patient about her availability at an earlier alternative appointment. She elected to go snowshoeing on February 14, the appointment date she had reserved and then canceled at the very last moment.

The doctor is demonstrably "double-minded" about entering into a long-term counseling relationship.

───∽∾⟡∾∽───

Tick's analysis floored Mattie. She was incensed that Tick questioned her competency and mortified that she kept track of her movements. She felt vulnerable and exposed.

Double-minded... James 1, she thought, and she reached for the Bible to read the passage: "If any of you lacks wisdom, you should ask God, who gives generously to all without finding fault, and it will be given to you. But when you ask, you must believe and not doubt, because the one who doubts is like a wave of the sea, blown and tossed by the wind. That person should not expect to receive anything from the Lord. Such a person is double-minded and unstable in all they do."

What has provoked this tantrum? Mattie was turning possibilities over and over in her mind. Knowing Tick, what she wrote was deliberate and well thought out, but the answers weren't forthcoming.

Fighting for poise and allowing her professionalism to reassert itself, Mattie searched for clues to Tick's behavior in her writing.

Mattie methodically went through each paragraph in the document, making some observations:

- Tick has prepared herself to fight the establishment and her status as a minor, a child subject to authorities. This is an understandable stance given her life experiences and the limited freedom provided to her since her escape from Timothy Bird.
- Any therapist who works with her will be up against a formidable adversary. Tick's fundamental understanding of therapy methods and what analysis is trying to accomplish is counterproductive. She will give all the right answers and not reveal one grain of what is truly behind her problems.
- Tick's defense of her speechlessness is weak and insincere, attributing it to a lesion in Broca's area resulting from a severe blow. Further brain scans are unwarranted, and I ruled this out as a possibility.
- Tick emphatically rejects the idea of taking drugs. She is determined to face her problems without medication. More than anything, she fears being forced to take psychotropic medications.

Even though the paper had Mattie in Tick's gun sights, it wasn't a complete dismissal. Mattie had lost Tick's trust, but not her respect, and there was a cry for help in all of it. Tick had an introspection gift, and she was aware of areas that were apparently beyond her control.

Tick hadn't locked the door, but it could only open on Tick's terms.

Laura poked her head into Mattie's office. "I'm going home. It's almost six, and the weather is terrible. Is there anything I can do for you before I go?"

"Tell me something," Mattie said. "If a colleague told me that I was ill-equipped to treat a troubled patient requiring long-term therapy, how do you think I would react?"

Laura smiled, breaking into a chuckle. "It would be like waving a red cape in front of a bull. You would move heaven and earth to prove that person wrong." Then, for an indelicate emphasis, she added, "You would tell him to shove it where the sun doesn't shine."

The light from the computer screen painted Mattie's face a ghostly gray.

How did Tick know that I went snowshoeing on the fourteenth? Mattie wondered. That's the day she experienced a terrible headache and mild flu-like symptoms the night before, so she sensibly canceled all her appointments. The next afternoon with no signs of a virus and feeling perfectly well, she went snowshoeing with a group of nurses to get some fresh air and exercise.

"How did Tick know I went snowshoeing the other day?" Mattie asked from her desk.

Laura knew the answer. "Abigail posted a picture on Facebook. I thought Tick might see it, so I asked Abigail to pull it down, and she did, but I take it I was too late. Did Tick see it? Is that why she was so angry?"

Mattie moved away from the computer, her face now hidden in the shadows. "I have one more question for you, and I want a truthful yes or no answer. Would you say that I have trouble with long-term relationships?"

"With long term…um… I think you… Maybe you're not—" Laura's stammering was cut short.

"Thank you. I will take that to mean yes. Drive carefully, Laura. The roads are terrible."

As she walked down the poorly lit corridor and into the hospital's parking garage, Mattie knew she had reached a crossroads. She was facing one of Tick's "my way or the highway" decision points. To maintain a beneficial relationship, Mattie would need to go full in— acting not only as a therapist but also as a committed family friend and a surrogate mother to a child who resisted her every affection. It would take a great deal of her time, and she might fail.

Instinctively, Mattie knew finding another therapist would be close to impossible for Brad. Tick would never go for it.

For the long term, she thought.

She and Brad shook hands on that, Mattie vividly recalled, but that agreement had just taken on a chilling dimension, and if she continued down that path, she could be placing her very career in jeopardy.

If Tick turns out to be a threat to society, she thought, *my reckless intervention in advising her to go on a hunger strike could come to light. Perhaps it's time to walk away. Tick is right. Long-term involvement with an uncertain outcome is not my strongest suit. Treating the physical body is a very different challenge from healing the mind and the soul, and feelings of affection should not be part of this equation.*

Stepping into her jeep, Mattie had made her decision.

A Poor Decision?

It was dark outside when Mattie left her office. A strong wind blowing in from the West announced an approaching storm. Stopping at her favorite bakery shop on South Temple Street minutes before closing, she purchased an assortment of Tick's favorite store-bought French pastries—napoleons, éclairs, and petit fours. She then drove directly to Brad's house and, using the security code Brad gave her, opened the gate and drove up to the house.

As she stepped from the car, she was inhospitably caught up in a flurry of wind and pelted with icy snow that made her hunker down and dash for the house. When she reached the front door, she shook off the frozen globules caught in her hair and stamped and brushed off the clinging snow. Shivering, pastry box in hand, she saw Brad pull back the curtain from the bulletproof side window. He quickly moved to open the door.

"Mattie! What in heaven's name? Are you all right?"

"I'm fine, Brad, just wet. I could use a towel."

"Of course…come on in."

"Where's Tick? I'm here to talk to her."

"She is in the kitchen," Brad said, helping Mattie out of her coat as she started down the hall. Out of the corner of her eye, she saw Brad place a large pistol into the entry table's opened drawer, and he quickly closed it.

Mattie found Tick sitting on a barstool in the kitchen, suspiciously watching Mattie as she walked in with wet, dripping hair that had matted against her head.

Mattie took her time as she headed to the seat directly across from Tick, laying the box of French pastries on the counter.

"Here," Mattie said, "I brought you some pastries…and I have a few things to say to you."

Tick remained still, her eyes fixed on Mattie. Brad followed a few seconds later, then grabbed a hand towel from a drawer and handed it to Mattie before discreetly working his way toward the back of the kitchen. The towel could hardly dry her off, and Mattie couldn't help but roll her eyes; still, it was better than nothing.

Then she began. "Well, I think we can both agree that today's appointment went rather poorly. I think the issue was that I let you down by canceling on you—not once, but twice—and I'm very sorry. I certainly couldn't help that my aunt would die when I scheduled our first appointment, and I texted your father as soon as I was feeling sick to postpone the rescheduled appointment. I would never risk your health or that of my other patients with some virus. And yes, I did go snowshoeing later in the day because I felt better. Who knows better than you that fresh air and exercise beats lying around?"

Tick reached for her pad, but Mattie stopped her, placing her hand over it.

"I need to finish what I want to say to you. You're right. I have struggled with my decision to continue working with you. My main practice is in treating critically ill or injured children, and you are well past that point, thank God. But a prevailing emotional roadblock is barring you from speaking, and resolving the issue will take time and effort on both our parts. So, Tick, I have had to consider how to plan my time so that you receive the help you deserve."

Tick wrestled the tablet from Mattie and began to scribble. "*I don't care about how you should properly arrange me into your schedule. I'm not going to your pretentious office where half of the awards on your wall are on display for your inflated ego. Forget thinking that you can experiment on me like some prized lab rat because, frankly, I think you're a fraud.*"

Mattie read the note slowly. She then peered calmly and directly into Tick's eyes.

"I want you to listen very carefully to me now, and please do not interrupt. First of all, you won't be coming to my office anymore, especially now that I know that you don't think much of it. We will be working from your house and from my apartment from time to time. As soon as the weather permits and Dr. Brackford says you're good to go, you and I will be taking some hikes together. Also, I have season tickets at Abravanel Concert Hall, and I would like you to attend some upcoming concerts with me, maybe even see some plays."

Tick gave a slight shake of her head in disapproval; she didn't like being told what to do.

"This is how we are going to be working together," Mattie continued, "on an informal basis until I decide that you don't need to see me anymore."

Mattie's voice grew stronger, more absolute.

"And while your accusation that I'm a fraud is surprisingly harsh, even for you, I won't hold your disparaging estimation of my qualifications as a psychiatrist against you. However, I will be charging you for the Baccarat crystal vase that I bought in Paris—you know, the one you so spitefully knocked over and shattered to smithereens? So I hope I've made myself clear? Do we have an understanding?"

Tick quickly glanced over at Brad, only to have Mattie place her hand firmly over hers, capturing her attention once again.

"Don't look to Brad, Tick," Mattie continued. "He isn't going to rescue you here. He and I have a clear understanding of how your care will continue and for how long. And another thing, the decision I've made to dedicate a healthy portion of my free time for your welfare is right out of Proverbs 16:9."

Brad walked toward Tick with his iPhone and held out for her to see the verse: "The mind of man plans his way, but the Lord directs his steps."

Tick nodded her head toward Mattie, this time with reluctant obedience.

"Okay," replied Mattie, reaching into the pastry box and pulling out an éclair to take home. "I'll be going now, but I'll see you tomorrow. I think I'll cook. Perhaps the two of us should cook dinner together, Tick. Anything special you might like to help me prepare?"

"*Twice-cooked pork*," Tick wrote out on her tablet, a nonchalant expression on her face. "*It's a Chinese dish.*"

"Okay, sure. I've never attempted that one, but I guess we can give it a shot! Do you have a recipe?"

Tick showed Mattie the cover of the book she was reading, an ancient Chinese military treatise attributed to Sun Tzu, a high-ranking military general, strategist, and tactician. It was the definitive work on military strategy and tactics of its time.

"*It's a Chinese specialty*," Tick penciled out.

Perfect, Mattie sarcastically thought to herself.

Mattie found Brad waiting for her down the hall, this time with a large orange beach towel that he had quickly thrown into the dryer to heat. He wrapped the towel around her shoulders, her coat too wet to wear. The storm abated as they walked to the car, and Brad was thankful to have a chance to talk with Mattie alone.

"You warned me about Tick's ability to manipulate outcomes," Brad began, "and I can't help but believe that much of this, your decision to see her—"

Mattie abruptly cut him off. "No, Brad, it was all *my* decision to work out a treatment plan that has a chance to help your daughter."

"But Mattie, you should know that after she misbehaved in your office today, she spent the day tied up in knots in her room looking at her mother's picture and watching the clock. And what do you know, the moment you walked into the house, as soon as you started talking to her, she magically collected herself."

At the car, Brad stopped Mattie from opening her door and turned her gently to face him.

"She was testing you, wasn't she, Mattie? Or gambling that if she turned her back on you, then you would give her the kind of attention she wants from you?"

Brad paused to capture his thoughts. "I couldn't be happier with the idea of you coming here to the house, but not if you feel forced into it. I don't want you resenting us, Mattie. She can go beyond being difficult."

Mattie cautiously searched for the right words. "I don't do anything I don't want to do or believe is right, Brad, and this is no exception. I'll go out of the box with her treatment because I believe it's the right thing to do. After all, her reasons to be difficult trump my time and because she is way beyond being worth it."

Brad slipped his hand on Mattie's and edged his fingers around her palm until he could grip his hand into hers. "You're an amazing woman, Mattie. I do trust you, and I am so grateful for you."

"You do understand, Brad, this can only be about Tick," Mattie replied, gently pulling her hand away from his.

His face went expressionless, shielded. "Of course... I wouldn't expect anything else. Let's let it go at that."

Brad then gave her one of his patented grins. "Drive carefully, Mattie. We'll see you tomorrow."

As Mattie drove away, she looked in her rear-view mirror and saw Brad standing in the driveway, watching as the snow started falling again.

Brad remained in the driveway as the taillights on Mattie's car disappeared. He walked into the house prepared to give Tick a lecture about her behavior, but his heart just wasn't in it. His mind was still on Mattie.

Mattie didn't head straight for home. Instead, she drove to Laura's and, with the orange towel still wrapped around her shoulders, rang the bell. Laura opened the door and saw her boss standing there, looking like a drenched cat.

"Up for a visit?" Mattie asked.

"Absolutely, but first, how do you feel about getting out of those wet clothes and into a dry robe?"

Emerging from Laura's bedroom barefoot and wearing a thick terry robe, Mattie settled down on the couch, pulled her knees up to her chest, and gratefully accepted the mug of hot chocolate with a healthy shot of brandy that Laura handed her.

"Just what the doctor ordered, Laura. Thanks. Oh, there's a Backers Bakery Éclair in my bag over there. Want to split it?"

"Forget the éclair, Mattie. You saw her, didn't you? What happened?"

Mattie proceeded to replay her conversation with Tick, becoming as unguarded as Laura could recall.

"Watching you roll your eyes tells me that you don't agree with my treatment plan, Laura, but Tick refuses to see me in a professional capacity, and I can't bear the idea of giving up on her. Tick experienced a hell few could imagine, now she's here with us, a survivor in an unfamiliar world, being tormented by her past and threatened by a serial killer who wants her dead."

"You don't need to defend your plan with me, Mattie. I'm on your side. It's just that, rational thinking aside, where are you going to find those Bracelets of Submission?"

"Bracelets of Submission?"

"Yeah, you know, the bracelets Wonder Woman wore to absorb the impact of incoming attacks."

Laura timed her comment perfectly. It was the first chuckle she had heard from Mattie since she walked through the door.

"Well, I don't know about those bracelets, but I sure could use her Lasso of Truth on Tick to know what she isn't telling us. I know you think I'm overly involved, but I have to see this case through for Tick's sake and to honor the commitment I made to Brad."

"I understand."

"I know you do, Laura, and there's something else on my mind that involves you."

"What's that?" Laura asked.

"Tick needs a friend who isn't intimidated by her, and you have been that friend. Would you continue to take some time for her—get-together for a movie now and then, go shopping, or try a new restaurant? Something along those lines?"

Laura responded by raising her mug of cocoa and offering a toast. "To fearless, plain-spoken…friendships. May they ever wave! Of course, I'm happy to do that. In case you don't know this, I like the little monster. She got under my skin a long time ago. And anyway, following your progress with Tick and watching you two together is like watching the greatest show on earth."

Then, putting her hand on Mattie's shoulder, Laura changed the subject, her tone solemn, but in a comical way. "Now, let's talk about you-know-who, and I don't mean that nice plumber you're always recommending."

The brandy was already doing its work on Mattie.

"Now, don't go there, Laura. Brad is a complete gentleman, and I'm not a bit uneasy about us, I mean him. Our relationship is purely platonic."

"Right, so how did he react tonight to your new plan of attack," asked Laura.

"Oh, good grief! I appeared at Brad's door completely drenched to the bone and looking pathetic, I'm sure. He seemed happy to see me, but I noticed he had a pistol hidden behind his back, so that's the last time I'll ever show up without calling. Anyway, I went into the kitchen to ask our twelve-year-old fire-breather to forgive me for canceling two appointments. She was sitting on a stool reading and looked me over like I was a naughty child, wet and dripping water all over the floor. Can you guess what she was reading?"

"What?" Laura asked.

"*The Art of War!*" Mattie answered, shaking her head and snickering.

"She is quite the little weirdo, Mattie. You have to admit," Laura retorted, teasingly.

"You said it, not me!" Mattie said, and both women broke into laughter.

Mattie was happy to spend the night at Laura's, and over breakfast the next morning, she couldn't stop thinking about the pistol she saw Brad put away. "You know, I am not sure I want Tick in a house with a loaded gun. I should talk to Brad about it."

"Well, you should know that Tick has gone through a complete gun safety course," said Laura, who stood up to clear the table. "And Brad is licensed to carry a concealed weapon. When I was working on the funeral arrangements at the safe house, Nate came by to pick them up for their firearm safety training session. He told me that they were halfway through the course and that Tick was an exceptional student and knew as much about firearms as he did."

"Why am I only learning about this now?" asked Mattie.

"Brad asked me not to say anything about it," Laura replied, halfway apologetically.

"I see. We certainly don't want to upset the little woman," replied Mattie.

"That's not it, Mattie. He was worried that you would think gun training was inappropriate under the circumstances, but Nate wanted Tick and Brad to receive the training and insisted that Brad get a carry permit before they moved into their house. I do have to agree with you, though. Brad still operates under the assumption that women should be protected. It's old-fashioned, but kind of sexy."

Mattie snickered. *Old-fashioned? Mesozoic is probably more like it.* Mattie couldn't help but feel a tinge of indignation, wondering where she could sign up for firearm training. She would show Brad just who needed protection.

CHAPTER

Professor Becket

Weeks later, with life in the Hughes's household settling in and Tick peacefully complying with the revised therapy plan, Mattie's lunch-time mission one afternoon was to meet Sue Ellen Kasch at the university cafeteria to interview a math and science tutor for Tick. Brad had met the previous candidate, Vasile Petrescu, at the house. The interview lasted only ten minutes. The young man was from Brasov, Transylvania, working toward a master's degree in mathematics at the University of Utah. The interview had gone poorly, as Tick made one of her instant judgments. It was frustrating to Brad, bringing back memories of Tick's winnowing of the hospital's nursing staff.

Mattie spotted Sue Ellen sitting at a table with an impeccably dressed older man she assumed was the potential tutor. His facial disfigurement brought her to the conclusion that he was in a fierce battle with skin cancer.

David Becket stood to introduce himself to Mattie. He was a retired university professor of mathematics, a former recipient of the prestigious Fields Medal, and a well-respected teacher. Sue Ellen explained that David had developed the gifted students' enrichment program and was currently serving as the board's chairman.

After they exchanged pleasantries, Sue Ellen wasted no time getting to the point.

"Mattie, David agrees with me that we should forget trying to find a qualified tutor for Tick, per se, and just go ahead and integrate her fully into the school's program. Accordingly, we have developed a special curriculum to match her needs."

She paused for a response, but none came, so she continued. "The goal of our program is to identify and develop minds such as hers, and we are confident that we can catch Tick up in math and science."

The discussion continued for well over an hour, culminating with a broadly composed strategy for Tick's education and Becket's assurance that he would call Brad Hughes that afternoon.

Brad's morning was swallowed up on the phone with Nate Hoger, who had called to fill Brad in on the search for Timothy Bird. After extensive negotiations, the Mexican Federales had teamed up with the FBI. A task force was actively searching the area south of the volcano, El Popo, where Tick testified that Timothy might have property.

Hoger was unable to provide specific details, but he sounded hopeful, almost excited. The FBI had a lead that confirmed Tick's suggestion.

Finally, they were making progress, Brad thought hopefully.

When the phone rang again, it was Professor Becket. Becket explained who he was. He reported that the board had reevaluated Tick's standing as a provisional student. He was now in charge of designing a specialized curriculum for her as a fully integrated school student.

Tick's acceptance came as a pleasant surprise to Brad. He was aware that the full-scholarship, merit-based program that instituted different teaching approaches and learning yardsticks, was capped at forty students. Tick's admission increased it to forty-one.

Brad was under the impression that Tick wouldn't get a shot at full admission until the following year, just from a policy point of view, and that was before her episode with Professor Turner. He wondered if Mattie hadn't pulled some strings.

But more surprises were in store. Becket stated that he would like to act as Tick's mentor and academic advisor, and if Brad and Tick agreed, he would like the opportunity to meet Tick soon.

Why the personal interest in Tick from the head of the program? Brad wondered. He agreed to a meeting at the house late Friday afternoon.

Brad called Mattie as soon as he hung up with the professor. He wasn't surprised to hear that she was a step ahead of him, having met David Becket and listened to his proposals for Tick's curriculum.

"No, Tick's admission came as big a surprise to me as it has to you," she explained. "As for Becket, he has melanoma. The long-term prognosis is not good, but he's still strong and is hanging in there. He lives to teach, but he's aware that his students have become uncomfortable with his distressing disfigurement. Tick will be able to handle it, and he will challenge her. It will be a good match for both of them."

Friday arrived, at precisely five o'clock, Brad opened the door to see a slightly hunched over older man wearing an immaculately tailored suit, one hand clutching a hand-carved cane and the other carrying a timeworn but refined leather briefcase. His face, as Mattie had warned, was severely disfigured from surgeries to remove the aggressive melanoma.

"Good afternoon, Mr. Hughes. It's nice to meet you. I am here to meet your young protégé. I have heard so much about her."

"Good afternoon, Professor Becket. She's in the dining room," responded Brad. "But please call her Tick. She is enough of a challenge without giving her airs."

Becket scanned the house through thick glasses, and Brad took note of his apparent approval of the surroundings.

Tick was sitting in the dining room, arms resting on the table, fingers intertwined. Her posture was perfect, and her full attention was on the stranger at the door.

As Becket entered the room, Tick rose from her chair and shook his hand. She examined him, looking him squarely in the eye. Her face was neutral, expressionless, showing no fear or revulsion of his disfigurement.

"Tick, this is the professor I told you about, the head of the program in which you are participating. I will leave the two of you to get acquainted. May I offer either of you something to drink?"

Both declined the offer, and Brad politely excused himself.

The pair sat across the table from one another, each cautiously examining one another. The professor broke the ice first.

"Does my face upset you?"

"*No*," wrote Tick. "*I have seen far worse. What happened to you?*"

Becket paused to wonder why a young girl would have seen worse. *What could have been worse?*

He responded with a thin smile. "I had melanoma that went undiagnosed, even though I saw a doctor and asked about a darkening mole. When they caught the cancer, it was quite advanced."

"*Dr. Barnes would have caught it!*" replied Tick.

"Ah, the famous Dr. Mattie Barnes. She seems to be quite fond of you. I have talked with her at length. She is an exceptional doctor, quite knowledgeable."

"*She's my doctor,*" Tick replied, typing rapidly on her iPad. "*I couldn't say if she is fond of me or not, and she wouldn't have shared information about me... She doesn't make that kind of mistake.*"

"Of course, we only spoke about your course of study. You are indeed fortunate to have her in your corner."

They sat quietly for a few minutes, each challenging the other to communicate. Becket finally spoke up.

"I'm relieved that the malady on my face doesn't upset you, and I have no difficulty with your being mute, either. I have to confess that I find quietude a refreshing quality in a girl. I have found that most of my female students are overly loquacious."

Tick studied him carefully, then started typing on her tablet, "*Proverbs 17:28 says, 'Even a fool who keeps silent is considered wise; when he closes his lips, he is deemed intelligent.' It's a shame you just opened yours to bash women.*"

Becket broke into laughter.

"Touché, young lady... And thank you for admonishing me with wise advice that Solomon penned hundreds of years before the birth of Christ. I wasn't serious, just a bit nervous, I suppose, Tick, meeting you for the first time. So what can you tell me about yourself? I read in your school files that Mr. Hughes has recently adopted you. He seems to be a very nice man, but you grew up in Florida?"

Tick was quick to respond, *"This subject comes up ad nauseam. My parents are dead, but I finally have a father. That's it, and I'd prefer not to tell more about it."*

Finally, you have a father? Becket thought. *Was the deceased father not present in her life?*

"Fair enough," he replied. "And pardon me if you think I'm prying. It's called small talk. You know, some silliness people tend to engage in to learn more about each other, presumably to determine the nature of their relationship going forward. Frankly, I don't like talking about myself either, so we can skip it."

Reaching into his briefcase, Becket pulled out an electronic tablet.

"Have you ever played Sudoku?" he asked.

Tick indicated that she had not.

"It's a popular puzzle game that's not at all that complicated to learn. I'll quickly explain the rules and then let you play a few practice rounds. Let's see how fast you can complete some of the puzzles."

Sudoku was just the start of a lively evening, and Tick was in her element. Both avid game players, she and Becket became engrossed in a variety of brain games that he brought with him. Before Ana left for the evening, she set an array of sandwiches, cookies, and a pitcher of iced tea on the dining room sideboard for the pair, muttering something about the fact that Tick hadn't had any supper.

After taking a short break to eat, Becket asked Tick if she knew how to play chess.

Tick's eyes lit up, typing, *"Can you teach me to play? I know something about the rudiments of the game, but I've never actually played. Someone told me I wasn't smart enough to play. He said that the object of chess is to crush the opponent's mind."*

"Absurd," Becket responded. "Whoever said that to you was repeating an unacceptable and unfortunate perspective on chess. The greatest player in the game's history, Bobby Fisher, made that exact comment in an interview, I believe. He was a troubled, quite insane man, a victim of his twisted mind. When Bobby Fisher played, he didn't just beat people. He humiliated them and enjoyed watching them squirm. He once said that he liked the moment when he broke a man's ego. He was a chess genius who became a poster boy for the dark side of human nature, diminishing the value of a game that many great and not-so-great men have played for fifteen hundred years. The person who told you that you aren't smart enough to play must be twisted or resents your intelligence or both."

When Tick didn't respond, the professor continued, saying, "Chess is a great game, and I believe it helps develop the area of the brain responsible for judgment, planning, and self-control. Playing a good game of chess helps young people make better decisions about life, perhaps helping to prevent teenagers from making irresponsible, risky choices. I would like all my students to take up the game, and anyway, what good is being intelligent if you can't have some fun with it. I have already observed your reasoning skills, Tick, and you're a natural, so let's get started!"

Finally, around ten o'clock, Brad came in to see Tick and her new devotee concentrating on Becket's portable chessboard, so he took a seat to watch. Becket won that game, but he was the consummate teacher, clearly explaining each move he made and why, while Tick took notes on her slate.

Mattie was right. They made a good match.

"Say, you two," Brad said, "don't you think you've had enough for the night?"

Professor Becket looked up, smiling, likely having lost track of time and sure that Brad's question was rhetorical. "Of course, it's my fault. We have been having a grand time. Your daughter is on her way to enjoying playing an excellent game of chess."

"No worries," Brad said. "My daughter would happily play games until the sun comes up. I'm impressed that she didn't wear you out!"

Brad helped the professor gather up his chess set. "Have you two discussed working together? Will you help Tick get caught up with the other students in math?

Becket looked over at Tick and then to Brad. "Your daughter is capable of handling my course of study quite well, providing she puts in the effort. It will come down to how motivated she is, but this will not be an issue from what I have seen tonight. When I challenge her with unfamiliar tasks, she controls her emotions, analyzes the data and her errors, and moves on. However, she needs to dial down her perfectionist tendencies—wanting to perfect every game she plays, for example. That's a mindset I often see with highly competitive kids, but it robs them of ever feeling satisfied and fulfilled."

Without Becket noticing, Brad nudged Tick to emphasize Becket's comment.

"She also thinks strategically," Becket continued, "always thinking ahead, and this is an aptitude not many young people possess. She put in a remarkable effort tonight with me, and honestly, I can't remember when I spent such an enjoyable evening. I was particularly impressed with the way she picked up on chess. It is a game that requires numerous calculations, the value of the pieces, movement patterns, and higher-order predictive thinking. She is a quick learner."

Catching his breath, he continued. "We will get Tick caught up in math and science, and yes, I would very much like to work with her. I will structure her a study program with the principal goal of positioning her for any top university program. I will provide you with periodic progress reports, as well as enlisting your support when needed. You should realize she will be under extreme academic pressure, particularly for her age, and parental support is critical."

Then he added, "Dr. Barnes has advised me about your aversion to publicity and explained that I am not to publish or speak on any matters directly identifying your daughter. Of course, I will respect your privacy and be happy to provide a written agreement. We can start next Monday after she gets home from school. I will e-mail her some material that I would like her to review over the weekend."

Brad looked over at Tick. "It's your call. What do you think?"

Tick nodded her head, typing, "*I would like to work with David. He is very, very smart. He's a nice man and has a good sense of humor. I didn't even mind losing a few of the games to him!*"

"That's good," replied Brad, turning to Becket, relieved that the final piece of the puzzle was in place, at least regarding Tick's schooling. "Then it's settled. Of course, we need to work out fair compensation for your time."

Becket replied, "We won't need to be doing that, Mr. Hughes. I will not be accepting compensation. I have been following your daughter's progress since she entered the program, and frankly, I have been looking forward to the opportunity to work directly with her. Your daughter already has quite a reputation at the school. She's told you about Maya Ramirez and Ben Ferguson, hasn't she?"

"Ben? No. Maya? Yes. Maya is the girl from Guatemala who plays the violin so well. Tick took me to one of her recitals, and she has been over to the house many times."

"Yes," replied Becket. "Maya is an accomplished violinist but painfully shy and not sure of herself. Her academic performance had been sinking, and her teachers were unable to reach her. When Tick and Maya became friends, we noticed a real change in Maya's demeanor and self-confidence, and we believe Tick turned things around for Maya through friendship, support, and encouragement.

"As for Ben, he is quite intelligent, but full of himself and quite disruptive. We were at the point of asking him to leave the program when your daughter set him back on his heels by blasting him with some harsh truths and the pathetic reality of his behavior. Ben is still with us, his advisor told me because Tick Hughes got to him. She has a leadership gift and has gained a reputation for her critical thinking."

Becket then looked over at Tick and quietly added, "You are no doubt aware she has an extraordinary ability to express herself when she gets angry."

Brad looked over at his daughter, who would not meet his eyes. "It's something we have been working on."

Becket continued, "Tick, I do need to be on my way, but there is one final issue I need to discuss with you before I go. I believe that you have seriously misjudged Professor Turner. He is an outstanding individual and could help you immeasurably with your math."

Becket watched as the girl stiffened, her face becoming expressionless, inscrutable—just as Dr. Barnes had told him she would react.

Becket continued, "Turner is not the most gifted man when it comes to his social skills, but he is kindhearted and a top-notch teacher. He makes mathematics come alive and understandable for his students, and he goes out of his way to help them. He did not realize that your parents had recently died in a car accident, and he would like to make amends for his poor choice of words. If you want, I can arrange a meeting with him next week and get you going to catch up with the rest of the group. I have one final question for you this evening, Tick. Isn't forgiveness the business of a Christian? Is that in dispute these days?"

Tick, her face still wholly unreadable, shook her head no.

"That's good. I will be texting you a reading list tomorrow. Please get started familiarizing yourself with these textbooks, and I want you to think about meeting with Professor Turner."

Then, after shaking hands with Brad, Professor Becket made his way out the door.

As he opened the door to his car, a text message came in. "*Would you please arrange a meeting with Professor Turner? I'll play nice! PS. You can tell Dr. Barnes she won this round. I'm still barking.*"

Becket laughed aloud as he put down his phone and started the engine.

She is just as Barnes and Kasch said she would be. This will be my pleasure, Becket thought. *My swan song.*

⁓∽⊱⊰∽⁓

As Tick settled into bed, Brad expressed how proud he was of her and how well she conducted herself being tested, in effect, by the professor. "You may be his last scholar. I think he saved the best for his last. By the way, are you going to make peace with Turner?"

Tick was quick to respond on her tablet. "*I've already texted David about Turner... I'm going to apologize.*"

Then she added, "*About the professor, he doesn't miss much, and he's curious about me. He could potentially figure out who I am, but we shouldn't worry. I'm sure he won't be a threat.*"

CHAPTER

36

Fitting Sentiments

APPRECIATIVE

A fitting sentiment to describe how Brad felt when Mattie, Laura, and Ana took it upon themselves to continue nurturing friendships with Tick in traditionally all-girl ways, time-honored female activities that most men avoid like the plague. These first-rate women, with busy lives of their own, frequently included Tick on shopping expeditions, girls' "beauty day" for manicures and pedicures, antique store outings, and Tuesday night half-price movie specials when a chick flick was worth seeing. They baked with Tick, fussed with her hair, and met her at the university for lunch or coffee between classes.

A feeling motivated by the faithful, positive support he received from his sons and their families. Their phone calls, texts, emails, and "Thinking of You" greeting cards for Tick were always the highlight of the day.

PROTECTED

A term describing Brad's feelings about the police officer who checked in with them daily, keeping them informed and up-to-date with developments concerning Timothy Bird. An officer, who weekly, took them to the pistol range to sharpen their firearm skills.

Proud

A word conveying how Brad felt when he walked into a restaurant or a theater with two, sometimes three, strikingly beautiful females and saw heads turn amid looks of admiration.

Words recounting how Brad felt when his daughter rocketed to the top of her class while competing with much older students.

This was the word that explained how he felt when Mattie took his elbow when crossing a street or when she offhandedly brushed a stray hair from his forehead—soft, infrequent touches from a distant, reserved beauty.

Happy

A word portraying Brad when he looked up from his desk to see his daughter perched on her favorite window seat, intently reading a book or working out a math problem.

A word describing how Brad felt watching her spend an evening in the study with a wise old professor who sipped Brad's Louis XIII de Remy Martin Grande Cognac as he and Tick discussed the Great Books or contemplated Tick's next chess move.

The feeling that gripped Brad when he poked his head in her room and found her surrounded by some school friends, listening to music while eating Ana's famous whole wheat artichoke empanadas.

Helpless

The word that identify Brad's inner feelings as he helplessly stood by Tick's bedside when—with eyes wide open, screaming and arms flailing—she underwent yet another night terror. Hard as he tried, Brad was never able to wake her up until the terror ran its course.

The word describing Brad's emotions when Tick sank into one of her depressions (*días de la Cara triste*, as Ana called those days), sitting on the back porch, sometimes for an entire day wanting to be left alone, looking up at the mountains, trapped by thoughts she couldn't share.

The word to express how Brad felt knowing his housekeeper wept from concern for her unhappy *chica*, watching her like a hawk, ready to respond to her every need, and determined to use any excuse possible to stay close by.

HOPE

A word that Brad associated with Mattie's opinion that Tick's need to isolate herself from everyone was similar to that of rebooting a computer: an overactive mind trying to make sense of the world and shutting down periodically to rest and file away overwhelming thoughts and emotions. Still, Mattie believed Tick was making progress; she was healing.

PERPLEXED

A word that portrayed Brad's feeling about Tick's stubborn rejection of a responsive relationship with Mattie—a woman who always had Tick's best interests at heart. This woman had known and fought for Tick almost as long as he had.

A word that explained how Brad felt knowing that Tick could speak but remained mute.

RESIGNED, STOICAL, APPREHENSIVE

Words that formulate Brad's thinking each morning as he reviewed the security camera tapes that recorded any activity in and around the house during the night.

Words that voice his mood each morning when determining which route he would take that day to get Tick to and from school, not wanting to fall into predictable routines or patterns that could set them up and make them vulnerable to Bird.

Words that convey Brad's gut feeling when he realized his relationships with everyone he cared about had put them at risk and placed them in the path of a madman.

APPALLED, FURIOUS, SICKENED

Appropriate words to describe how Brad felt when told that Bart Madison, the sadistic pedophile and death ranch fugitive, had been captured in Fairhope, Alabama, and that a young girl, Leslie Quinton, had been found murdered on his bayside property. Words to express how Brad felt when the FBI found corpses of two other young girls on the same site.

HORRIFIED, WORRIED, FEARFUL

Words signaling Brad's emotions when he learned of a failed raid in Mexico, leaving four FBI agents and six Policía Federal dead, and FBI Agent, Martha Rucker, missing.

No words could adequately describe how Brad felt knowing that his daughter's kidnapper and tormentor had slipped away again, undoubtedly ragingly angry and conceivably aware that Tick was connected to both the raid in Mexico and to Madison's capture.

VENGEFUL, MALIGNANT

These words describe Timothy Birds' reaction after the FBI raid in Mexico and Madisons' capture in Fairhope.

It was Esther, Bird thought, *and if the council ever suspects that she knew anything about Mexico, they will tear me to pieces. Letting a slave, a child, cause so much damage was unforgivable.*

He was on thin ice already. The unwanted attention focused on the Epilektoi following events at the ranch had enraged the council. He had convinced them that she knew nothing.

Luck was on his side; he had captured the FBI agent and cut out her tongue shortly after her capture. Only Alfredo had heard her say that the girl found on the mountain was behind the tip leading to Mexico, and he had solved that problem: Alfredo had gone missing.

He remembered talking to Janet about the ranch in Mexico in front of Esther but had no recollection of ever discussing where Madison lived.

How did she figure it all out? he wondered.

Still, there was no doubt in his mind that she was behind it all. His options were now limited. If he used organization resources to track her down, they might draw a connection between the raid in Mexico and the girl. If he went after Brewer or his family, they would ask why he was going after the FBI. He needed to get to her alone, finish her, and he needed to do it fast. He should have finished her when he had her tied to the post. He wouldn't make the same mistake again.

El Popo

It was a beautiful spring day in late April, the sun just setting, when the security gate buzzer sounded off, indicating that a driver was requesting entry onto the property. The surveillance camera showed trusted friend Nate Hoger sitting at the wheel, and Agent Steve Brewer, who Brad had not seen since they were at the safe house in Deer Valley. In the backseat sat an older man whom Brad and Tick were about to meet.

The stranger was Trenton Wright, a seventy-something retired Navy Seal instructor, now a consultant for the FBI. The stern look on each man's face indicated that something unpleasant was forthcoming.

"Brad… Good evening," Hoger said quickly, adding, "I'd like you to meet Trenton Wright…and, of course, you know Steve. Trenton is working on the Bird case, and part of his responsibilities will be Tick's security."

Brad invited them back to the screened-in porch, grabbed four bottles of Corona from the refrigerator, and followed Tick, who was carrying a plate of her famous brownies. They exchanged pleasantries, and Brad, when Hoger and Wright asked, substituted their beer with soft drinks. Mentally, he kicked himself for assuming the men would drink on duty, *but why has Brewer kept his beer,* he wondered. *Had he been fired?* Brad then took a seat next to Tick on the porch sofa, facing the men.

Agent Brewer started the conversation by talking directly to Tick and in a tone that confirmed Brad's ominous suspicions.

"I'm sorry, Tick," Brewer said. "I wish that you didn't need to be part of this conversation... Normally we wouldn't, we don't disclose case details, but given your connection with our investigation, we have no choice but to include you. The fact is Agent Rucker is no longer missing. She's dead, found heartlessly murdered in the garden at the Convento Agustino in Ocuituco, Mexico, just southeast of El Popo. There was a message from Timothy Bird in the pocket of her jacket, and the message was meant chiefly for you, Tick."

"What does the note say?" Brad asked.

Unfolding a scrap of paper, Brewer read aloud, "*Buenos días*, cowardly pup. Do you miss me as much as you miss your pathetic mother? I haven't forgotten you, or what I said to you the last time I saw you on that cliff, spinelessly huddled behind a tree. Just so we're clear when I find you, and you know that I will, I am going to skin you alive, as promised. Ole, Brewer! Hasta la vista. Timothy."

"Did Agent Rucker know about me or where we live?" Brad asked anxiously.

"No," Brewer replied. "She wasn't privy to any information about you, although she did know about Esther Morgan's testimony. We have no reason to believe that anyone has compromised you on the force. Unfortunately, I'm a problem, Brad. Bird and I go way back, and he hates me. We can correctly assume that he knows that I'm still actively involved in the investigation. Bets are that smart bastard assumes that I have questioned Esther Morgan, who may have given me some clues about his possible whereabouts in Mexico, and it stands to reason that he believes I know where Esther is."

"That's a huge problem, Steve," Brad said, distressed by the likely significance of what he was hearing, and wondering why Steve or his superiors hadn't immediately disclosed the risk to Tick or himself that he posed.

"I think so too now, Brad, and so does the agency. Before the raid in Mexico, extra security precautions were in place to protect me from Bird, in particular. Still, since our second failed attempt, we believe we are dealing with something much larger and better-organized than one or two demented individuals."

"You mean a crime syndicate?" Brad asked.

Taking a long swig of his beer to stall for time before answering, Brewer finally replied. "Sorry, Brad, I can't speculate about that. I'm no longer authorized to comment on anything associated with ongoing cases. That's what I've come to tell you and Miss Amazing here," he said, winking at Tick. "Considering that Bird can link me to you, that makes me a risk to your safety—yours and your dad's—as well as to the safety of my wife and family... So the agency has retired me and has placed the entire Brewer family in a witness protection program. Everyone has been relocated with new identities until Bird is no longer a threat. I leave tomorrow to join my wife at our new home in an active seniors' community, where I plan to learn how to play pickleball!"

Brad couldn't have gotten to his feet faster, and as Brewer also stood, Brad grasped his friend's shoulder and shook his hand with the warmth and affection conveyed to one good friend from another.

"Well, it's high time you retired from this game, Steve, and not too soon, God knows. I'm happy and relieved for you and your family."

Taking Brad's place on the sofa next to Tick, Brewer sounded slightly choked up speaking to her.

"I especially wanted to say goodbye to you, young lady, and to tell you how much I admire you. You drove all of us a bit crazy, but you are the bravest witness and, truthfully, the bravest person I have ever known. I want to believe that I would never divulge information about you under any circumstances. Still, I'm not sure how I would hold up under a monster like Timothy, and then, of course, there's my wife and family to consider. I am going to miss you, Tick, but as you said to me a long time ago, perhaps I should disappear."

Tick began typing on her tablet. "*But I didn't mean it,*" she wrote. "*You know I like you! You are the first one who understood what Timothy is and what he is capable of doing. Sooner or later, he would have found you, and now you'll be safe. I'm very thankful for that, Agent Brewer.*"

"I never took what you said to me to heart, Tick, and you have been right all along. That sick SOB. Sorry, Tick, but that psycho lunatic has always been a step ahead of me."

Under his breath, but not so muffled, he added, "That worthless piece-of…" Steve continued with a string of vulgarities.

"At this point, Nate Hoger cut off his consummately professional but very frustrated friend before the crusty FBI agent could tip the cart with expletives.

"Tick, let me help my buddy here get to the point of our visit. As you know, we are not in the position to provide you and your father with round the clock bodyguards. It would be too expensive and might be counterproductive, given our primary defense is keeping your identity and adoption secret. As a backup measure, we rely on security measures to provide a rapid response if the camera and facial recognition technology recognize him near or in your house.

Current plans are to up that security.

"We will now be providing you with emergency beacon locators. It's a relatively new device that allows us to track you in any terrain, and when activated, it sends out an alarm showing your whereabouts as it's calling in the cavalry. It also acts as a watch, an audio-video recorder, and a phone, if that's any consolation. It is a bit James Bondish, although I guess when compared with the newer cellular phone technology, it's not that big a leap. If activated, we will have a team ready to react immediately."

Still, there may come a time when you need to defend yourselves.

"Steve and I have seen you in action a couple of times, so we're pretty sure that if there is anybody on this planet who could kick Bird to the curb, that is if he ever managed to find you, it's you and your dad. The FBI has decided to provide you with another security level to help you defend yourself—just in case Bird gets through our net, which he won't.

"Trenton here was one of my instructors when I was a Navy Seal and, hands down, the best instructor around with firearms and hand-to-hand combat. One of the mottos this guy made us recite was 'You don't have to like it, you just have to do it.' He prepared us for the times when the best course of action was to put our heads down, grit our teeth, and run into the fray. The point is the FBI has engaged Trenton to prepare you for any possible confrontation with Bird."

"You mean, in self-defense?" asked Brad, looking at Trenton and thinking, *This is absurd. Are they that worried? It sounds like they're panicking and preparing us for battle!*

"Well, yes, self-defense, but not in the sense that you may be thinking," replied Trenton. "My focus will be on the offensive, not defensive survival tactics and skills. I will teach you both how to drop a bad actor without hesitation and how to work as a team. You will be learning how to handle a gun and a knife, how to spot someone trailing you, and how to cover each other. Of course, you will need to learn evasive driving techniques as well. I understand you have a barn that we can convert into a training center. I can modify it, and I would like to begin boot camp there next week."

"I don't think that's going to work," Brad quickly answered. "Tick hasn't fully recovered from her hip and ankle surgery. Mattie says that it will be weeks before she can resume full physical activity. The training will have to wait until she's fully healed."

"Here's the situation, Mr. Hughes," Trenton replied. "Ruth Evers has ordered me to start your training right away, and I will modify my program to meet Tick's restrictions. We'll begin slowly, getting to know each other and working on basic firearm training—the combat training will start as soon as Tick receives the all-clear from her doctor. Much of my early training focuses on human anatomy and mental preparedness, so there won't be a problem."

At this point, Tick began vetting Trenton, peppering him with specific military and combat-related questions, prepared to reject him if she thought he was a poor choice for such an undertaking.

At last satisfied that Trenton had merit and something to teach her, Tick announced that she would call him Grandpa since she didn't have one. She sat next to him for the next hour while the group discussed converting the barn.

Brad knew he had a problem, and that was how Mattie would respond to the news about these plans. Explaining how Tick would be in training again to kill, only this time by a "good" guy, would be like splitting hairs to a child psychiatrist focused on her patient's mental health.

He realized how such combative, lethal training could further entrench his daughter into her past life with Timothy, her fight-to-kill trainer, perhaps intensify the aggressive side of her nature. But in Brad's mind, Tick's physical survival was the obvious, urgent priority now.

Still, keeping the true nature of this training from Mattie would be indefensible, Brad acknowledged. It could severely hamstring Mattie's ongoing therapy with Tick. His loathing of Timothy Bird had never been so great. Finding himself in the position of having to weigh his daughter's physical survival against her emotional survival resulted from pure, unmitigated evil. He elected to take a middle-of-the-road path. He would tell Mattie that they would be receiving enhanced security training, including weapons training, but leave off Trenton's instruction's true emphasis.

Four days later, Tick and Brad began training under a bona fide taskmaster—Trenton was deadly serious about what he wanted to accomplish. The barn was transformed, complete with a firing range and dummies hanging from the ceiling. Trenton's first action was to present Tick and Brad with specialized daggers, along with hand made belt sheaths, allowing them to conceal the blades behind their backs. These weapons were double-edged thrusting daggers, hand-made from Damascus steel, and Trenton would teach Tick and Brad how to draw them in a fraction of a second. One of his anatomy lessons involved learning prime areas to attack, including the heart, the lungs, the liver, the femoral artery near the groin, and the carotid arteries located on either side of the neck.

Trenton firmly held that, without weaponry and subterfuge, neither Tick nor Brad would win out over a highly skilled and seasoned fighter like Timothy Bird.

"No thirteen-year-old girl, or sixty-year-old man for that matter, can expect to win a fight against an experienced martial arts fighter. You will need to shoot him, knife him, or run him down with a car, and I am going to teach you how to accomplish all of that without hesitation."

Three weeks later, Dr. Brackford pronounced that Tick was soundly healed and allowed her to resume her full activity level. Trenton had been eagerly anticipating the doctor's go-ahead, curious to see if this thirteen-year-old with a history of fighting had what it took to handle his "take-no-prisoner" brand of defensive training. He had no idea what to expect.

Fully padded, Tick and Grandpa (Trenton) faced off. Tick started slowly, moving in a combination of offensive and defensive stances, demonstrating extreme grace, but acting more like a cobra than a fighter, captivating Grandpa with her fluidity.

Without warning, she struck, with a flurry of punches, alternate left and right vertical punches thrown in quick succession in a combination that left Grandpa defenseless. It was over in seconds—Grandpa, on the mat, along with his pride, realized that if she had pressed the attack, he would have lost an eye or had his throat torn out. She could be his instructor in Wing-Chun Kung Fu, Timothy Bird's specialty. Still, Trenton knew that she would be no match for Bird. Using a knife and a gun with speed and stealth was Grandpa's specialty, and it would be Tick's best defense.

Nate Hoger was there to watch Trenton and Tick spar, and what he witnessed didn't shock him all that much. He had seen Tick at work on the hospital's tarmac and remembered the fierce look she gave him while being wheeled into the hospital. Then there were the tapes that showed how effortlessly she had taken down the CPS woman. She was every bit as skilled as he thought she might be, perhaps even more so.

That night, Trenton sent a text message to Evers: "Tick picked me off the floor today, literally. I have a black eye, and my jaw is killing me. I deserve combat pay! I still have much to teach her, but not in the martial arts. She should be my teacher."

The text back had read, "What's hurting more, your jaw or your ego? My advice is to use lots of ice. Combat pay for training a thirteen-year-old is not happening. Concentrate on teaching her what you do best. I'll scout out a martial arts instructor who can handle Tick."

Trenton believed in speed and agility drills, and lots of them, which was okay with Tick, who couldn't get enough of them. After being confined for so long in casts and then restricted from physical activities while she healed, she was happier than she had been in months, feeling alive, strong, whole, and free.

As the weeks passed following her full recovery, the barn group expanded when Nate joined the morning training sessions, along with a newcomer, Linn Wong, Tick and Brad's new martial arts instructor. Wong, a Korean expert in the martial arts, was stationed in Denver, Colorado, and was possibly the FBI's top expert in the martial arts. Wong and his wife, Nari, had been lobbying to move to Salt Lake City ever since their daughter began working at the Huntsman Cancer Center. When Ruth Evers learned about this, she readily signed for his immediate transfer, all expenses paid.

In addition to training Tick and Brad, Wong would be training local FBI agents, including Hoger's team.

While the transfer was quite advantageous for Linn, he was obligated to accept two binding requirements that Evers wrote into the transfer agreement. Namely, Linn's residence had to be within a two-mile radius of the Hughes's home, making it possible for him to be on the first responder team in case of a breach. And two, he would commence martial arts instruction for Brad Hughes and his daughter three times a week within the month.

As a trusted FBI agent, Linn was familiar with the Hughes's case and the reasoning behind his selection as their karate instructor. Still, nobody informed him about the level of Tick's fighting ability. He anticipated teaching an older man and his thirteen-year-old daughter some necessary skills and then acting like an overpaid bodyguard. After his first session with Tick, he informed his wife that he would be going on a strict diet and running five miles every day.

Tick Hughes had combat skills and a talent for it far beyond her years, coupled with an intensity that few high-level students would ever achieve in the martial arts. Linn saw a savage streak emerge on occasion, and this gave him pause. He wondered about her captivity and her captor. But Tick was able to keep herself in check, and she took instruction and criticism without objection. Linn, Nate, and Grandpa became Tick's biggest fans, and she thrived under their watch.

Equally important, but more like a game to Tick, was the awareness training—studying different surroundings quickly for anything or anyone suspicious or out of place. Doing it without looking obvious or paranoid was the goal. Tick loved the challenge, ferreting out the traps and decoys Grandpa had set out in the barn. As a result, both Brad and Tick began taking on this inconspicuous activity as they entered public places, work or school buildings, elevators, hallways, and rooms—even their own home—carefully sizing up each environment, always prepared for a confrontation.

Zealously observant, Mattie soon became aware that Tick seemed calmer and less aggressive during their informal therapy sessions together. There were other changes; Tick had begun sporting bruises that peeked out under the sleeves of her blouse and shorts as if someone had been stamping her with an ink pad. Mattie questioned Tick about the injuries, and Tick explained that Trenton and Linn were teaching her some self-defense techniques that were "a little tricky."

Before clamming up on the subject, Tick scribbled down Trenton's opinion that a few bruises were just a normal consequence of defensive exercises and ended her explanation using his unoriginal "no pain, no gain" expression. This off-handed retort provided Mattie with enough fuel to drive her professional curiosity into overdrive.

What other normal consequences can I expect to see? Mattie wanted to know.

The next time she saw Brad, she grilled him for information about the man Tick was calling Grandpa, questioning what this fellow had been teaching her, inquiring about the Korean man and his role with Tick, and pushing Brad for an explanation for all the bruising. Brad assured her that the bruises were the result of Tick acquiring new karate skills but that Trenton thought she was doing great and getting better at defending herself.

When Mattie arrived for her scheduled appointment at the house, she found Tick on the den sofa, her leg elevated with two ice packs that Ana had secured over a mean-looking hematoma extending down her shin. Tick explained that she tripped over a shovel in the barn, but Mattie wasn't buying it.

"We hit the barn on Monday, Wednesday, and Friday at five in the morning," Brad answered after Mattie casually inquired about the training sessions at dinner that evening. "It seems like a ridiculously early call, I know, but Trenton believes in working out on an empty stomach, and the time works well with everyone's busy schedules."

Tick quickly sketched a picture of a bird with a worm dangling from its beak, the top of the sun just peeking out in the background. "*An idiom worth knowing*" written at the bottom.

Between Brad's weak assurances and Tick's brush-offs, gaining an accurate picture of what was going on during these training sessions was not going to happen, so Mattie decided to take a different approach.

On Wednesday morning at five ten, Mattie came walking into the barn, unannounced and unexpected. In a flash, she saw men aiming pistols at her, but they immediately holstered their weapons and acted as though their actions had never occurred.

"I reckon I've walked into the okay corral," she said, nodding hello to Nate before turning to the older gentleman, giving him her most charming, coquettish smile.

"I understand you are Tick's new trainer," she quipped. "Tick and Brad have told me such good things about you. I'm Dr. Barnes, Tick's doctor and friend, but you can call me Mattie. I'm here to observe the training session, that is, if you have no objections?"

Mattie didn't wait for an answer. She smiled toward Brad and said in a stage whisper meant for all to hear, "Why do you and Tick call him Grandpa? He sure doesn't look like any grandpa I've ever seen."

"It's Trenton Wright, ma'am, I mean Doctor...er... Mattie. Please call me Trenton. I would like to introduce you to Linn Wong, our martial arts master."

"Well, Trenton... Linn, just pretend I'm not here, and please don't do anything differently than what you normally do. I understand that you are both amazing trainers, and I'm excited to see you in action."

Mattie was wearing a slim gray pencil skirt and beautiful white silk blouse tucked in, underscoring her attractive figure, with the top two buttons uncharacteristically unbuttoned. She was wearing expensive-looking black, very high heel shoes, and ultra-sheer black stockings that highlighted her slender, shapely legs. Brad and Tick looked utterly puzzled, seeing a side of Mattie they didn't know existed. Trenton and Linn weren't looking at a highly recognized physician and Children's Hospital VIP, but a beautiful and charming woman they were determined to impress.

They proceeded to put Tick and Brad through an exhaustive training session while Mattie, a vision of loveliness, sitting on a bale of hay, watched on.

The session began with hand-to-hand combat and the use of a training knife. Tick was at her best, effortlessly flowing from move to move with quick, lethal-looking thrusts, clearly frustrated with her father, who was repeatedly corrected by Linn for sloppy footwork, lousy posture, and sluggish reaction time.

Mattie mentally compared Tick's performances to the talented athletes she had watched in gymnastic meets, dance competitions, and ballet performances at the university—young women moving with seemingly impossible grace, strength, and beauty. But logic and her medical training told a different story. The intended purpose of every move Tick made was to maim or kill.

Trenton walked over next to Mattie. "Your young friend is superb—better than me, actually—and I was the martial arts trainer for Navy Seal teams for many years."

"She's something else, that's for sure," Mattie replied.

"Linn can still outfox her, though, and he keeps her on her toes. I'll be taking over after Linn, and you'll see how Tick handles a gun. On her best day, she could probably shoot the eyes out of a gnat on the back of a hummingbird, but she's inconsistent. Brad is a very decent shot, by the way."

Trenton was right about the their gun skills; Brad's ego restored after he outshot Tick.

When Trenton talked Mattie into trying her hand at shooting a target, everyone watched with astonishment. She assertively and confidently fired off five rounds, hitting the target dummy in the heart three times, two shots slamming between the dummy's eyes.

Brad was speechless. "Where did you learn to shoot like that?"

"Why are you so surprised?" Mattie quipped. "The subject of my gun skills has never come up in our conversations. I was also the hopscotch champion in grade school, and I play a mean game of badminton, besides."

Mattie handed the gun back to Trenton. Then, following a warm handshake for both Trenton and Linn, she offered a tight smile for Tick and a scowl for Brad as she said her goodbyes.

After the training session, Tick and Brad walked back to the house, where Ana had breakfast waiting.

"*I think we're in trouble with you-know-who,*" Tick wrote on her iPad. "*She's clueless.*"

"Well, I think you're clueless if you believe that," Brad said. "Don't you get it? She's dedicated her life to saving lives, not taking them. She saved your life, and now she is working tirelessly to help you lead a good, wholesome life, one that's not focused on the ability to kill a person with a knife or a gun. She understands the threat that Timothy is to you—to both of us—but she wants something entirely different for you in her mind and heart. She wants you to be free of your past, and the violent girl Timothy Bird was trying to create."

Tick's vague nod of her head left Brad wondering if his message had sunk in.

After Mattie left the barn, Brad dreaded the confrontation he knew was coming when he would see her again that evening. Right on time, Mattie arrived at six-thirty carrying all the ingredients for a chicken curry dinner. She corralled Tick for assistance and led her through each step of the recipe, discussing the pungent, aromatic spices used in a curry dish.

Brad enjoyed seeing Mattie working alongside his daughter. Even when Tick was moody or irritable, Mattie was consistently patient and kind with her, always direct and honest, but also firm. She never allowed Tick to be impertinent, which seldom occurred. Still, Tick rarely provided Mattie with any open signs of warmth or affection, which continued to disturb Brad.

Even Ana was aware of Tick's behavior. She queried Brad about Tick's distant and reserved manner, hoping he could explain why

Tick never demonstrated affection toward *la* Señorita Mattie, who Tick seemed to care for very much. Despite keeping Mattie at arm's-length, Tick couldn't fool Ana, who regularly noticed *la chica complicada* waiting eagerly for the doctor to arrive, sensing the child's discontent when it came time for Mattie to leave.

Tick's standoffishness must have been very hard on Mattie, Brad thought, but Mattie never talked or complained about it. She kept her feelings to herself and focused on helping Tick. The odd thing was that Brad, like Ana, knew Tick was crazy about Mattie. She was happiest when Mattie was around.

As usual, the meal that evening was terrific, but the conversation was forced, never touching on Mattie's surprise appearance at the training session. Brad talked about the cutting-edge entrepreneurial business school at the university and the program's new iconic, copper-clad building funded by a very successful friend of his. Mattie related a story about an unusual case she had handled that day when a toddler came into the ER with a tiny, visible flashlight shining in her stomach.

Tick was annoyingly reserved, contributing little to the dinnertime conversation, focusing mainly on her dinner plate. When she went back to the kitchen for a second helping of curry, Brad said something about her excellent appetite. Mattie responded sarcastically with a comment about how her calorie expenditure during the training sessions must be phenomenal.

After dinner, Brad walked Mattie to her car, but before she opened the door to get in, she took a deep breath to defuse the outrage she felt, the anger that she had been concealing from Tick all night.

"You have let Tick down in so many ways, it's not even believable. I cannot fathom your thinking when you consented to throw your daughter back into a killing environment, just with a different cast of characters now. You have lost your senses, Brad, and you may have tossed Tick's chance for a normal life right out the window."

Brad knew this confrontation was coming, and his insides felt like they were crumbling under pressure. He wanted to do the responsible thing for Tick.

God, he prayed silently, *please help me explain my actions so that Mattie doesn't hate me or, worse, leave us.*

"Mattie, I completely understand your perspective… I do. Her training wasn't an easy decision by any stretch. But he's coming for her. You heard what he did to Agent Rucker and all about the threatening note he left on her body. Tick doesn't know this, but Steve Brewer told me that, in some sick symbolic gesture, Bird punctured her eardrums, gouged out her eyes, and cut out her tongue. I can't sleep anymore just thinking about how he tortured that poor young woman. I know we have a great cover story, and there's no logical reason to believe he will find us, but in my gut, I know we need to be ready. We have to give Tick the right tools to survive if Bird finds her."

He continued, "Besides, combat training empowers Tick. It's something she has mastered. It's like catnip to her. It energizes her and helps relieve her stress and anxiety. She is sleeping better."

Mattie gave him a long, appraising look and then responded in a cold, tightly controlled voice. "Catnip? Is that your opinion as a veterinarian or her loving father? Listen to me, Brad, you okayed these sessions without consulting me, and I'm very concerned for her. I can only hope and pray that you and the mod squad team handle her with the utmost care while respecting that, no matter how amazing you or Grandpa says she is, she's still a very young girl, not some fantasy ninja warrior."

"We're doing our best, Mattie, and I'll always be there training with her and watching out for her."

"Yes, I could see that you were struggling out there today. Tick is so much better than you are. It's not funny," Mattie bluntly critiqued.

Brad chuckled, attempting to disguise his wounded pride. "I appreciate all comments from the peanut gallery, but consider the unfortunate fact that Tick has been doing this most of her young life…with an emphasis on the word *young*—and factor in a sixty-year-old's martial arts learning curve. Well, I think you get the picture."

Brad turned his back on Mattie for a moment but then faced her again with a devilish expression. "Okay, since you mentioned watching me, I think it's only fair I should mention that the outfit you were wearing this morning caught everyone's eye. Killer look, Dr. Barnes!"

"Is that so, Brad?" Mattie snapped back. "The pathetic thing is that a short skirt and high heels worked, didn't it? Call it testosterone, catnip, or whatever. Gramps, let me stay and see the show! You marginalize my work with Tick by downplaying the true nature of Tick's training, and now that I have the picture, Tick won't be working with an ill-informed therapist. I need to go now, but I'll be here for Tick after school tomorrow."

When Brad walked back to the house, Tick was waiting for him in the kitchen with an inquisitive look on her face.

"I'll give you the short version," Brad offered. "All she cares about is you. She has your best welfare at heart, and I believe she would take a bullet for you. She loves you as much as you love her."

"*That's ridiculous,*" Tick scribbled out on a paper towel. "*She is my doctor. That's not even professional. And who says I love her!*"

"That's enough of that, Tick," Brad reacted, becoming short with his daughter. "You know she loves you, and we both know you love her too… Stop playing your stupid games. You need to get ready for bed, and it might be a good idea to ask God to soften your heart."

It was an all-too-familiar night for Brad, lying in bed with his stomach tied up in knots, feeling short of breath. Losing the ability to shut down and fall asleep was miserable. He had never struggled with anxiety before. His unease was painful. The distress that he might fail to protect his daughter was growing with each training session he attended with her.

Tick was a fantastic athlete, rapidly gaining in strength and agility. She was improving day by day, and he couldn't begin to keep up with her. He was feeling his age and felt ineffectual against the likes of Timothy Bird.

Wincing at the thought that Mattie saw his deficiencies and feeling exposed and inadequate, Brad reached for the television remote and began searching for a mind-numbing movie.

CHAPTER

Visit to the Ranch

Something special came in the mail that summer—a letter addressed to "Mr. Brad Hughes" from Melanie Thomas, the mother of the little boy Tick had befriended in the hospital.

Dear Brad,

> *My apologies for taking this long to write to you, but I have had difficulty adjusting to Brent's death. The main thought that has kept me together was what Tick shared with my brave little boy just before he passed away. Brent told me Tick's mommy was in heaven, and, if he ever went there, she would love to take care of him. I don't know why God took Brent from us, but I know he is happy with the Lord and Alissa.*
>
> *Forgive me for unburdening my sorrow in this letter, but I'll never forget how kind you were to me during the countless hours we spent talking in the parents' sitting room at Children's Hospital, and I feel safe expressing these things to you. For the first time since Brent's death, I can at least write about it, and I know you won't mind. So getting to the point of this letter, my husband and daughters have been*

clamoring to invite you and Tick up to our farm, and since we have no travel plans for the summer, we are hoping that you would come for a weekend visit whenever you could make it. We'll put you up in the guestroom, and Tick can sleep with the girls.

Megan and Rachael are anxious to teach Tick how to ride, and we have a wonderful horse for beginners. You mentioned that you grew up riding, and we also have some spirited horses I know you will enjoy. God has blessed us with beautiful trails up into the mountains, and there's a large swimming hole tucked away in the hills—the water feels great this time of year. If you can make it, be sure you and Tick pack riding boots and swimming suits.

Please do come, Brad. You and Tick were islands of hope to me during a difficult time, and I do so much want to see you!

Fondly,
Melanie Thomas

Brad had jumped at the opportunity to get away and see the farm, so he called Melanie and arranged to arrive before noon on Friday, spend two nights, and leave Sunday morning.

The next week, during Mattie's visit to the house, it was impossible not to notice how relaxed Brad seemed.

"On your past road trips when you have driven by one of those neatly maintained farmhouses in the middle of nowhere, have you ever wondered about the people inside and how they live?" he asked.

"I suppose I have," Mattie said. "Why?"

"The Thomas's house fits that picture perfectly. The house is small, built in the 1890s, and set back from the road. It's brick with ivy partially covering the front, and there are two mature shade trees on either side of the house. There's a front porch just big enough for a table and two wooden rocking chairs, and running along one side of the house are roses of all varieties in full bloom. The back looks out over a large plot of irises and a vine-covered trestle with a bench and a small goldfish pond beside it. On the south side of the yard is a large stable, paddock, riding ring, and equipment shed. Beyond are the alfalfa, barley, and oat fields.

"It sounds idyllic, Brad," Mattie said wistfully. "There are fewer and fewer places like that left near Salt Lake City."

"You're right. The Thomas farm is less than fifty miles away, in Morgan County. They own about 1,200 acres of farming property that Jim works. He took a second job with the forestry service because the farm doesn't bring in enough income to support the family, especially in light of the medical expenses that mounted up when Brent was in the hospital."

"I'm sure the bill is steep," Mattie said, looking down at the floor and nodding her head in understanding, "and a heart-wrenching debt considering Brent didn't make it."

"Jim believes he could make the farm profitable if he could purchase the two thousand acres of rich farmland his neighbor has put up for sale," Brad continued. "He told me that he had nearly closed on the sale when Brent got sick—a real shame. The house on the seller's land is only ten years old. It's fairly large and looks quite nice—the Thomases could certainly use more space."

"So is Tick hiding today, Brad? I'm all about getting as many colorful details of this visit as I can!"

"She'll be down in a minute. She and Ana were busy wrapping thank-you gifts to mail to Melanie and the girls."

"That's nice," Mattie said approvingly. "So I take it the visit went well?"

"We had a great time. It's a wonderful family, very warm and friendly, and they couldn't have been more hospitable. The girls, Megan and Rachael, are quite pretty—hardy, I guess one could say, but I'm not sure how to put it. They both have an easygoing, natural way about them. Good pioneer stock. They gave us a quick tour of the house, which is modest but quite comfortable.

"I love hearing about those old houses," Mattie said.

"So when you walk in the front door, you enter a small long living room, which doubles as a dining area. A double doorway leads you into a neat and tidy semi-updated kitchen, not much larger than Tick's closet, and off the kitchen is a covered back porch that serves multiple purposes. It's a laundry, utility, storage room. Melanie had her bread and pies cooling on racks in there, and that's also where she does her canning and where she makes hand and bath soap from scratch. She sent several bars home with us to give to you."

"That's very thoughtful. Did you get to use her soap?"

"I did. I took a bath in the home's original bathtub. People were so much smaller back in the day, weren't they?"

"That's true," Mattie answered. "We're considerably taller than in past generations, but don't get me started on how much heavier Americans have become… I don't mean you, of course. Go on about the house, Brad."

"Sure… Well, three bedrooms and two bathrooms are located on the left side of the house. The whole house couldn't be over 1,600 square feet, not including the root cellar, which was stocked full of canned fruits and vegetables from the garden, as well as bins of onions, potatoes, and yams.

Outside, the stable holds ten stalls and a tack room. The Thomases own four excellent trail horses, and Jim boards six more horses for owners who live here in Salt Lake. Jim and the girls are all capable trainers and riders, and the boarding arrangement involves exercising the horses, permitting Jim and the girls to ride some exceptional horses—'free rein, to ride' as Jim put it."

Mattie chuckled.

"The girls gave Tick a couple of riding lessons before we went out on the trail: they worked with her in the ring, teaching her the basics: how to hold the reins, use her feet and knees, and how to sit properly in the saddle, et cetera. Tick's horse, Toughie, was an even-tempered, older Paint that had been a great barrel racing horse at one time, and the girls had Tick trotting and cantering around the ring in no time before we all took a long trail ride in the mountains. It was a beautiful day to be out riding. I loved hearing the familiar soft grunting sounds the horses make and the leather saddles' rhythmic creaking. The feel of the fresh, cool breeze as we rode through an aspen grove was wonderful. We even had a little race across a sandy riverbed. Tick got drenched, but she stayed in her saddle!"

Tick strolled in to hear Brad talk about the race, and she quickly began writing on her tablet, "*Brad won the race. He's an amazing rider! Rachael and Megan said he looks as natural on a horse as anyone they had ever seen.*"

Brad shook his head. "I'm not sure about that, but they did put me on one heck of a fast horse. I loved it!"

"Did you bring sack lunches along for the ride, or did you just eat hay with the horses?" Mattie asked.

"Some PB&Js," Brad answered, "but when we got back to the ranch at about 5:00 p.m., Tick and the girls worked together to get dinner on while Jim, Melanie, and I took care of the horses. Tick had prepared everything before we left on our ride, and it was ready to go in the oven as soon as we returned."

"And what did young chef Hughes come up with for six hungry people?" Mattie eagerly probed.

Tick drew a cute menu on her tablet, offering "herb-crusted lamb chops, twice-baked potatoes, garden salad with freshly picked lettuces and veggies, and crème brûlée for dessert."

"It was a wonderful meal. Everybody enjoyed every bite," Brad said. "We ate outside while the sun went down. The adults visited while finishing off the bottle of the wine I brought, and then we turned in around nine. I slept in the small guest room. Tick slept in the middle room with the girls, and the four of us shared a bathroom. That part was quite an adventure, I must admit."

"I can only imagine!" Mattie said. "It makes me laugh just thinking about you politely waiting your turn to use it!" She looked over at Tick. "Okay, my friend, your turn. I want you to tell me about the next day."

Tick, turning away with a dismissive expression on her face, rudely wrote, "*Don't ask me. Dad will give you the picture.*"

Straightaway, Brad asked Mattie to excuse him for a moment as he ushered his daughter into the kitchen. "What makes you think you can behave like such a brat?" Brad demanded, boiling mad. "Mattie asked you a simple question, young lady, and your answer was rude and thoughtless." Brad couldn't remember when Tick had made him so angry. "Mattie deserves far better treatment than what she just received, and I won't accept such bad manners from you! Are we clear?"

Returning to the living room only slightly ruffled, Tick picked up her pad and started writing. *"Sorry, Mattie. So we got up early in the morning, around five. The girls had chores, which I helped out with."*

Mattie interrupted. "What did you do?"

"We cleaned out the stalls, fed the horses, pigs, and chickens. We finished up around seven, went in for Melanie's breakfast of waffles with berries and whipped cream. Then we saddled up the horses and took another three-hour ride up into the mountains. We got back around one and had a big lunch—fried chicken, cornbread, baked beans, and potato salad. Then the girls worked on their homework, Dad took a nap, and I went out to see Toughie and check on the chickens. Later, the girls took me swimming."

"Did you go swimming too, Brad?" Mattie asked.

"No, Brad said. "It was an all-girl outing, and I wanted to talk with Jim about the farm. Jim trusted me enough to open his books and give me a feel for his situation. He made some unwise transactions when he bought some farm equipment, and I can help him renegotiate better banking arrangements. I also helped him with some cost analysis, pointing out that boarding horses is a big cash drain for them, and he needs to charge a lot more if he plans to continue training, exercising, and boarding other people's animals."

Tick, playing Miss Innocent now as though her rude brush-off never happened, took out her tablet and wrote, *"I enjoyed riding. Horses are such strong, magnificent animals, and I want to learn how to barrel race as Tammy Rockford did."*

Brad shuddered. Tammy Rockford was the young rodeo star Janet Herrington murdered.

"Do you like the Thomas sisters, Tick?" Mattie asked to change the subject.

"A lot. They work hard around their farm, but they joke around and get along well with each other. When we went swimming, they went in naked and wanted me to try it, but I didn't want them to see my scars."

"I understand," Mattie said.

"Rachael wants to be a veterinarian, and Megan wants to be a farmer. She is planning to major in agricultural science. They are serious about their schooling but worried about not being able to afford to go to college. They also told me that their mom hadn't been the same since Brent died. They think he was her favorite—the only boy in a family—but his death has been hard on all of them. They thanked me for being Brent's good buddy at the hospital. They are also ridiculous at times, teasing each other a lot about boys. And the only music they listen to is country-western. Melanie is so nice, but she talks a lot and wants to mother me. She hasn't recovered from Brent's death, and I feel sorry for her. I get it. Mr. Thomas is a decent, predictable sort of man, a little bit like Brad in some ways, but not as smart. Money is a definite issue with the family, and they watch where every dollar goes. Both of the girls' jeans have patches on them, and they were careful to save any leftovers after each meal."

As Tick finished her "report," Brad was grateful that Tick chose to open up for Mattie.

"Tell Mattie about the drawings on their refrigerator," Brad asked.

"They like the drawings I did for Brent in the hospital. They're on the refrigerator and around the house. I think they look amateurish."

"You realize that you lost your amateur standing when you sold some of your paintings last month." Mattie chuckled, remembering that she had been the beneficiary of Tick's first sale to replace a shattered vase. "Ms. Amori said that you have the gift of capturing the essence of what's in front of you, and I'm sure that artwork provides happy memories of Brent. I am also pleased that you prepared dinner for the group; it was very thoughtful of you."

<hr/>

The Thomases enjoyed the Hughes every bit as much as Tick and Brad enjoyed the visit. Megan, the fifteen-year-old daughter, excitedly wrote her aunt to tell her all about Tick and Brad and how the weekend went.

Dear Aunt Jean,

Our weekend visiting with Mr. Hughes and Tick was so much fun! Tick is as amazing and as beautiful as Mama described. She's weird, though. Her eyes are a little scary. They are green with a brown streak running through one of them, and when she looks at you, it's like she can see right through you, but not in a mean way at all.

Tick is super smart and could solve all my algebra homework in her head, even though she just turned thirteen! She is also a fantastic cook and made us an entire dinner. She also got up with us in the morning and helped with the chores, and she was exceptionally great working with the chickens.

Mama says she's a city girl, but she helped us kill and dress some chickens for lunch, and she acted like she had been doing it all her life.

You know, she doesn't speak, just writes fast on her iPad instead, but I heard her whispering to Toughie when she was in the stable, so I don't know what to think. I didn't tell Tick that I heard her talking, but I told Mama.

Mr. Hughes is so nice, and Mama and Dad like him very much. Dad said he is going to help him with some business hurdles. The only thing Mama didn't like is that he carries a gun, but she decided not to make an issue of it.

The other strange thing is how camera shy they both are, never letting us take their picture. Tick says images are a silly way to remember people. Better to carry them in your head, not your wallet, but that's pretty weird, don't you agree?

Anyway, I have never seen Mama and Dad so happy since Brent died, and now I understand why he loved Tick so much. I hope they come again soon to visit.

I'll write again soon.

Love,
Megan

For Brad, the outing was more than just a wonderful time. It provided him with the information he needed to put a plan in place, a project he had been formulating since Tick's days in the hospital. Rachael and Megan had been fantastic with Tick, warm and friendly, but not intimidated or put off by her distinct peculiarities. Jim Thomas was an honest man who was capable of listening to advice and working with others. Melanie, well, Melanie was still mourning the loss of a child.

Maybe, just maybe, something comforting would come out of it all.

CHAPTER

39

A Family Vacation

With prospects of spending a relaxing summer dashed, Brad added chlorine tablets into the empty chemical dispenser. He hadn't been in the pool once since he opened it up for the season, but Laura, who swam on her high school team, had been coming over to work on Tick's swimming skills. Brad kept the pool in excellent working order. Still, he considered turning the job over to a professional pool service with so much going on now.

Even though Tick was on summer break, Professor Becket hadn't stopped coming to the house for her tutorial sessions, and he seemed to be working her harder than before. Brad found himself dividing his time between his responsibilities at work and the ever-expanding lineup of Tick's needs, pursuits, and schedule of appointments, including their joint training sessions three mornings a week in the barn. He wondered if the topsy-turvy world he now inhabited was payback for keeping such a regimented lifestyle since Catherine's death.

Brad wistfully thought of his past weekly golf game at the country club and the cold draft beer he enjoyed afterward with friends at the nineteenth hole. Spending hours on the golf course was no longer sensible, and he shelved his goal of lowering his handicap.

Before long, the Hughes's annual summer retreat would be upon them, and Brad pushed thoughts of any unpleasant family encounters from his mind. With any luck, his sons and the daughters-in-law would see a healthier, more relaxed Tick this time around; the funeral had been difficult. Also, Brad's five grandchildren would be meeting Tick for the first time, so the gathering held promise for an adventuresome, enjoyable time together.

⁓

In mid-August, Brad and Tick packed the Jeep for their two-day drive to the vacation rental house in San Diego with an overnight stop midway in Las Vegas. The experience was an eye-opener for Tick. "*I think people pulling those levers at the slot machines are in some kind of a trance with all the noise, lights, and free drinks,*" she wrote as they stopped for gas the next morning. "*The casinos have set it up to have a considerable advantage. It seems to me like a waste of time and money. Do you like playing the slots?*"

"No, not really. You're right. The chances are that if you play the slots or any of the gambling games, you will lose money. For some people, it's their idea of having a good time. Still, I'm grateful that I'm free to choose where and how I spend my time and money. Gambling isn't my thing, but I've seen some great shows here in Las Vegas."

Before getting back on the road, Brad read an e-mail that came in from Mattie, expressing some thoughts she wanted to share before they arrived in San Diego:

> This vacation is going to be quite stressful for Tick, who is determined to please your family, but not sure how she should accomplish it. As we both know, Tick's a true non-conformist, Brad, not at all in the people-pleasing business. Striving to be sweet, polite, and "likable" with everyone in the Hughes clan will likely make her feel awkward, insecure, and disingenuous (as it should, I might add).
>
> Nonetheless, I'm sure she will be anxious about winning your family's approval. She knows

how much they mean to you, and she believes she has hurt your relationship with them. I'm working on those guilt issues, but she isn't going to relinquish these matters easily.

Before you arrive in San Diego, you need to have a strategy to help her maintain her equilibrium if any of her actions or communications seem at odds with your family, possibly leading to misunderstandings. Make sure she rooms alone for some privacy and that she gets plenty of rest, and give her space if you think she is struggling and wants to be left alone for a bit. Allow for some one-on-one time just with her, and ask your sons and daughters to try spending some quality time with her as well. Please don't allow Tick to play the role of maid, cook, and bottle-washer! She needs to feel that she is a full-fledged Hughes, no less valued than anyone in the family, and there to enjoy a relaxing vacation, too, whether she knows it or not. Lastly, *have a great time*!

Brad and Tick arrived in San Diego several hours before the rest of the family. The rental proved to be everything they had hoped for and more. Just yards away from the beach, the large, three-story home provided two large family rooms, a big kitchen and eat-in counter, bedrooms and bathrooms for everyone, a sizeable deck overlooking the ocean constructed to accommodate outdoor entertaining, and a pool and a pathway leading down to the beach. The pounding surf's background rumbling and the cawing of the seagulls was music to Brad's ears, and the surroundings enchanted Tick.

The house had been picture-perfect in its prime, but a constant influx of renters had left the place slightly shabby. Its condition was a positive feature, as far as Brad was concerned; the family could relax and not stress over forgetting where all the throw pillows belonged or leaving behind a finger smudge or two.

Brad and Tick took the two main floor bedrooms, saving the larger rooms for his sons' families. Tick's room was small but well-appointed with a window facing the ocean, a gentle breeze stirring the light blue curtains. Brian, Natalie, and their four-year-old daughter, Liz, would take the upstairs rooms. Ben and his wife, Becky, and their three children—ten-year-old Kaitlin and the eight-year-old twins Jerome and Jonathan—could settle in the rooms downstairs, along with their uncle, David.

On her iPad, Tick told Brad to reconsider giving David, the youngest unmarried son, her room, thinking she should sleep downstairs. Brad argued she should have her own space and that David wouldn't care which bedroom he occupied. "He probably will prefer to sleep out on the deck under the stars, anyway, Tick," Brad predicted.

After going through the house and checking out the kitchen cupboards and refrigerator, Brad and Tick made a list of grocery items and supplies. Brad suggested that they should wait and perhaps let her sisters-in-law do the shopping, but Tick persuaded him to go to the nearby Costco before everyone arrived.

They filled up two large shopping carts at the store while systematically crossing items off the shopping list. Back at the rental, they put their load of groceries and paper products away. Next, Tick arranged cut flowers in vases and placed them around the house— Brad tinkered with the grill out on the deck to make sure it was in working order. With the refrigerator and cupboards full and everything looking shipshape, Brad led Tick down the path to the beach, where they took off their shoes for a quick walk along the shoreline before the others arrived. Tick dodged incoming waves, picking up seashells and examining interesting looking seaweed. She was as happy and joyful as Brad suspected she would be. For the first time since age five, she was on a beach at the ocean.

⌒∽⬥⬥∽⌒

When the two cars pulled into the carport, Brad and Tick came out to greet his clan and help with their luggage before ushering everyone into the house. Seeing his family together gave him tremendous pleasure. Tick hung back a bit and braced herself for the rush of hugs she expected to get from everybody. She still felt slightly uncomfortable with the hugging thing but in no way wanted to reject their friendliness.

Becky Hughes spotted Tick when she stepped out of the car, and her misgivings about the girl rose to the surface. She was determined to keep a close watch on Tick, genuinely concerned and skeptical of Brad's decision to adopt a child with such a questionable, troubled history. Becky was a strong-willed girl of Italian parentage, raised in Pittsburgh, Pennsylvania. She was the daughter of an ironworker with old-world family values and a fiercely protective mother.

Just a year earlier, Becky had come close to losing her daughter, Kaitlin, to a virulent strain of flu, an illness Kaitlin had emerged from seemingly unscathed—her mother, not so much. Becky had become an even more overprotective mother, and signs of strain in her relationship with Ben, Brad's first son, were showing up. Ben disapproved of how much his wife indulged the boys, and he felt she was smothering Kaitlin. They constantly fought over their different parenting styles.

Becky had nothing but respect for her father-in-law. Still, after he had gone AWOL for months, later resigning from the presidency of his company, she shared her husband's opinion that his dad was going through some midlife crises, concealing an illness, or perhaps now involved with a new romantic partner. His disappearing act was uncharacteristic. Worse, his e-mails were full of inconsistencies and downright falsehoods, and Ben had lost sleep worrying about him. When Brad eventually scheduled the telephone conference with the family, Becky anticipated the call with a mixture of dread and relief—she dreaded hearing bad news that caused him to drop off the face of the earth but relieved to learn what the mystery was all about, finally.

The revelations that had come out of Brad's conference call had done nothing to relieve Becky's anxieties. Without discussing his intentions with the family, Brad had adopted a twelve-year-old girl who the press speculated was violent and had participated in deadly fight contests. There was no speculation about two violent altercations the family knew had taken place at the hospital before her adoption. To add to Becky's fear, she learned that a ruthless killer, and perhaps his entire criminal organization had targeted the girl. The FBI's discussions about protecting Tick's identity, what to tell friends and family, and restricting family pictures and posts on social media only added to the stress.

The visit with Tick at her mother's funeral did nothing to lessen Becky's apprehensions. She had practically no interaction with Tick because Brad and Dr. Barnes were so protective of the disabled, grief-stricken child during their visit.

Looking over at Tick during the funeral service, Becky had been startled by the unnatural expression of constraint on the young girl's face and how she held her head so rigidly without shedding a tear, never making a sound. Tick's behavior that day unnerved Becky, but she had put on a good face because of her desire to maintain family unity. Concerning the family vacation to San Diego, Becky had secretly been dreading it.

⁓෴⁓

When Becky first saw Tick that August afternoon in San Diego, the girl was standing by her father, happily meeting and greeting all five of the kids. Now the picture of health, Tick was tanned and beautiful with glistening blond hair, a lovely smile, and gorgeous, penetrating eyes. She was tall for her age, with long, lean, muscular legs. She wore red shorts, a long-sleeved white t-shirt, and new, colorful, and trendy tennis shoes.

Becky approached Tick and gave her a quick, cursory hug, then followed Brad and the family for a tour of the house. Both Natalie and Becky quickly spotted the beautiful flowers in each room and assumed that the rental agency had provided the welcoming touch, but Brad explained that Tick had arranged the flowers for them. The tour ended in the kitchen, where Tick went over her checked-off shopping list and meal plan with the wives. Becky mentioned that they needed to buy tater tots, chicken fingers, and pizza for the kids.

Brad announced that Tick had dinner underway, with flank steak being marinated. He waited for one of his sons to volunteer as the meal's grill master. Asparagus and new potatoes were ready to go on the stove, and a mixed green salad was in the fridge. For dessert, Tick had baked cookies and made tapioca pudding. As soon as she unpacked, Natalie volunteered her help with dinner, but Tick quickly wrote out on her pad, *"Thanks anyway, but I have it under control."*

Becky's terse reply, "Well, aren't you just something else!" was voiced out loud as she turned and left the kitchen and headed for her bedroom.

"The last one in is a rotten egg!" shouted one of the boys.

Not about to take a tour of the house, the kids wasted no time getting into their swimsuits, racing to be the first to jump in. Brad's arms were full of grilling tools and a big bag of charcoal, so he asked Tick to watch the kids until a parent appeared, but within minutes, loud wailing caught everyone's attention.

Becky was the first to rush out onto the balcony overlooking the pool to see what was going on. Looking down, she saw Jerome, his leg scraped and bleeding, calling up to his mom and crying because Jonathan had pushed him into the pool.

Becky, Ben, and Brad watched the aftermath of the accident as Tick examined Jerome's leg. Her half-smile and thumbs-up signal indicated that Jerome was fine. But unexpectedly, Tick grabbed Jonathan's wrist in a firm hold, gave him a look that meant serious business, placed his hand on the trickle of blood on his brother's leg, and then lifted his red-streaked hand close to his face. Her message to Jonathan was clear—*You are responsible for this.* Jonathan became completely unnerved and ran off crying.

Becky rushed down to the pool to check on Jerome's injury. She was upset with Jonathan for pushing Jerome into the pool but furious with Tick for manhandling her son so harshly. As she consoled her boys, Tick stood by, disapproving of the undue attention lavished on two oversized crybabies. The family vacation had gotten off on the wrong foot, fueling Becky's misgivings about her adopted sister-in-law.

Dinner was uneventful, served out on the deck, with the children recounting their summer activities for their grandfather. After dinner, Tick and David took the children for a walk on the beach, but not before Becky gave the kids detailed cautionary instructions before letting them out of her sight, instructions that Tick felt were ridiculously excessive.

Before breakfast the following morning, Becky's misgivings about Tick were amplified. Brad and Tick carried their boogie boards down to the beach, followed closely by Kaitlin, who received permission to tag along. A storm was pushing in with overcast skies, but Brad and Tick were anxious to catch a few waves before the surf became too rough.

After a couple of fun rides on their boards, Brad asked Kaitlin if she would like to give it a try, too. In a flash, she waded out into the surf with Tick, following Tick's lead by positioning herself chest down on the board facing the shore, hands gripping the sides for balance, and waiting for a wave to carry her to the beach.

"Woo-hoo! Aawwssoommee!" Kaitlin whooped, laughing as she rode her first wave in, having the time of her life. As she was about to swim out for another go, she heard her name shouted frantically and saw her mother running toward her, holding out a giant beach towel. Becky gave Brad and Tick a look that could kill before wrapping the protesting girl up in the towel and ordering her back to the house. Brad attempted to calm his daughter-in-law down by insisting that Kaitlin had never left his sight. Tick expressed her annoyance with Becky by knitting her brows and shooting a distinctly exasperated look at her.

In Becky's mind, Tick did nothing but create strife between her and Kaitlin, and incidents that confirmed that conviction began piling up. At mealtime, for example, Tick acted as though the kitchen was her domain, and she chased Becky out of it more than once. When Brad once suggested that Tick let someone else take a turn cooking, she left the kitchen in a huff. When Becky stopped Kaitlin from going after her, an argument ensued, and then Kaitlin left the kitchen in a huff.

And there were other maddening goings-on. Tick corrected Kaitlin's grammar, and she critiqued her posture, making her stand with her shoulders pressed up against a wall. Most troubling to Becky,

Kaitlin and Tick began spending time together outside in the small back garden, and when asked what they were doing, Kaitlin told her mother that they were just "chilling out." Kaitlin seemed to idolize Tick, and it galled Becky that her daughter had become so attached to this strange girl.

Then something startling happened before dinner one evening when the boys began mindlessly batting a giant helium balloon around in the main room, unconcerned about all the breakable knick-knacks on the tables and ignoring their parent's requests to take their mischief downstairs. Even after Brad threatened to pop the balloon, the boys, ignoring their grandfather, knocked it into the kitchen where Tick worked at the sink.

As the balloon floated close to Tick's back, she snatched up an eight-inch knife from the counter and, with a fast and furious backhand, stabbed and obliterated the balloon. Setting the blade down, she returned to her work, unaware of the shocked silence in the room, everyone's eyes popping out of their heads. Tick's handling of the knife was like something one might see in a stage act in Las Vegas—it was that amazing and skillful. Brad quickly tried to make light of her action, commenting, "Thank you, Tick. You certainly put an end to that little problem." But the damage was done.

The family found it impossible to put the flashing blade's image and the severed balloon out of their minds, especially the wives. If Tick had looked silly or clumsy in any way, awkwardly swatting and missing the balloon entirely and attempting another shot at it—understandable moves—it might have looked amusing. Instead, her action was perfectly timed, fluid, and precise. She looked lethal, not comical.

Becky's displeasure with Tick's action was planted on her face, and dinnertime stretched out uncomfortably with forced jokes, conversations falling flat, and a noticeable avoidance from the family to engage with her. After dinner, Tick excused herself and disappeared down the hall to her room, giving Becky a chance to take Brad aside and unload her disapproval of Tick to him.

Brad said that her fears were unfounded and that Tick would never dream of hurting a member of her family, but he failed to convince her.

"Well, you may trust her completely," Becky said, "but I have some real concerns, and I don't like knowing that you carry a concealed weapon. What if Tick gets hold of it?"

"The truth is, Becky, that she is the one who should be carrying the gun. She's highly trained, more skilled than I am, and she is extremely responsible when handling any firearm. I carry the gun for her protection, and I pray I never have to use it against anyone who would want to hurt my daughter."

Becky only looked at him as though he had lost his senses.

When Brad checked in on his daughter later that evening, she was standing at the window, gazing out at the ocean with red-rimmed eyes, not wanting to pick up her iPad to let Brad know what she was thinking. Before saying good night, he told her that he loved her, that he was proud of her, and that she should lighten up and not take the family so seriously—that "they just aren't used to so much talent and ability wrapped up in such a beautiful package!"

As he left the room, he thought, *Mattie was right. This is too much for her. Maybe I should take her home. I'll give it another day.*

The next day, the weather was miserable, the beach shrouded in a cold, drizzly fog, and the surf, high, choppy, and congested with seaweed. Brad, Tick, his sons, and the children walked along the beach when Tick suddenly took off running, plunging into the surf. Brad instantly followed her, joined by a lifeguard who had spotted trouble and promptly reacted. The men quickly realized that Tick was clutching the arm of a boy who, as they would later learn, had been surfing when a wave flipped him off his board, crashing down on him and knocking him unconscious. Brad and the lifeguard both powered their way through the chest-high surf to reach Tick and the seemingly lifeless boy. The lifeguard reached them first and took hold of the boy. Getting back to shore was another matter. Tick and Brad struggled against the swells' immense energy, which repeatedly knocked them off their feet, the backwash trying to drag them back out to sea.

Two more lifeguards joined in the rescue, and all six made it out of the surf and onto the beach, where a small crowd had gathered. Brad quickly removed his jacket and handed it to Ben. "Cover Tick's head and shoulders with this," he ordered. "And get the family back to the house immediately. Don't let anyone see her face. Don't give anybody your name or her name. Go now!"

Ben knew that his father meant business in no uncertain terms.

As the Hughes clan headed back to the house, David and Brad turned their attention to the young boy as the lifeguard administered CPR. The boy revived within minutes, so David and Brad quietly left the scene just as the ambulance pulled up. Making their way through the gathering crowd, Brad noticed people taking pictures, and he prayed that Tick had left the scene without being photographed. The emergency vehicle was soon kicking up sand as it motored its way up the beach en route to the nearby hospital.

The children were eating snacks in front of the TV when David and Brad reached the house, the adults sitting silently around the living room.

"Where is Tick?" Brad asked.

"Tick is in her room and wants to be left alone," Becky answered. "She is distraught, Dad. Natalie and I made her take a shower to warm up, and we walked in to check on her without knocking. We saw her terrible scars."

"Oh" was all that Brad could say.

"I'm so sorry, Dad," Becky lamented. "I overreacted. I was horrified and started pressing her to tell me how she got those scars. She just waved me off and shut her door. We decided it would be best to leave her alone until you got back."

"Right," Brad answered, barely audibly, looking in the direction of Tick's room.

Becky was determined to get some answers. "How did she get those scars? Was she in an accident? Did she tear her back up when she fell onto the mountain cliff or when she fell at Children's Hospital?"

Brad's face was flushed, distressed for Tick, and he was angry because nothing seemed to be going right for her on this trip.

"Timothy flogged her, Becky—scourged her. It was one of Timothy Bird's cruel ways of punishing her, and she wants to conceal the ugly remnants of her tormentor from others. I wish you hadn't—"

Brad stopped to collect his thoughts. *It's not Becky's fault,* he thought. *She doesn't know half of it because I've never told them what Timothy did to her. None of them has a clue about Timothy's sadism.*

"It's all right, Becky. I should have told you about the scars, but she doesn't want me to talk about it."

As he started toward Tick's room, Becky called out to him. "Would it be okay if Natalie and I talk to her first?"

Brad nodded yes and let the women walk past him in the hallway leading to Tick's door.

Rapping on the door before poking in their heads, Natalie and Becky found Tick sitting in front of a small vanity table, holding a brush, her Bible open. When they entered, Tick closed the Bible and watched as the woman approached, her posture perfect, her face emotionless, but looking drained.

"Brad's back," Natalie said warmly. "We thought you should know that the boy you rescued is going to be fine. You are a real hero, Tick Hughes."

Tick remained impassive as the ladies stood by her side. "That's a beautiful Bible," Becky said, looking down. "What were you reading?" she asked.

"May I brush your hair?" Natalie spoke up, pointing to the hairbrush. Tick handed her the brush but looked as though she hoped the two of them would just go away. Instead, Becky and Natalie appeared to be settling in for a visit. Tick scribbled down "*Colossians 3:13*" on her iPad for Becky.

Picking up the Bible and finding Colossians, Becky slowly read the verse out loud, "Bearing with one another and, if one has a complaint against another, forgiving each other; as the Lord has forgiven you, so you must also forgive."

Sighing, Becky put the Bible down and met Tick's eyes in the mirror. "We haven't gotten off on the right foot, have we?"

Tick reached for her tablet to respond, "*You don't approve of me, and you're worried for your family and Dad because of me. You have read what was reported about me in the newspapers, right?*"

Becky paused before replying, remembering the e-mail she and Natalie had received from Dr. Barnes. Mattie wrote to say that she hoped the family was having a good time. One paragraph, in particular, stood out:

> If Tick expresses or does something completely at odds with your notion of normal or courteous behavior, please consider that her life, her field of reference for many years was unimaginably harsh, very different from yours or mine. If she upsets you, you should talk to her about it and explain your grievance honestly and openly. Her response will be truthful, and you will find there is almost always a very reasonable explanation, and that she is an exceptionally thoughtful, good girl.

"You may be right about that, Tick," Becky finally said. "I'm sorry, but I find that some of the things you do are extremely hard to swallow."

"Becky," Natalie interjected as she continued brushing Tick's hair, "I hardly think this is the time to get into all of that. Tick just saved a boy's life, for heaven's sake!"

"But I need to know… Why were you so hard on Jonathan the other day? Why on earth did you smear blood all over his hand? That was uncalled for. You upset him."

Tick picked up her stylus. "*You didn't see what happened. I did. And you probably didn't hear Jonathan's laughing over Jerome's wails. If you read Proverbs 15:21 there in my Bible, it says, 'Folly is joy to him that is destitute of wisdom, but a man of understanding walks uprightly.' Jerome's blood was on Jonathan's hand, in every sense, Becky, and he needed to own it. If he doesn't learn to think before he acts foolishly, he will fill his life with one, to use your words, one uncalled for problem after another."*

Natalie snorted, coughing as if something had gone down the wrong throat, catching a severe look from Becky.

Becky continued. "But then you didn't even seem to care that Jerome was hurt!"

"I knew he was fine, and he knew it, too. What I cared about was how ridiculous he was acting, crying for attention like a baby! There were two small scrapes on his leg, Becky, and if you make a big deal every time he gets a scratch, you'll raise him to be a whiny weakling. He won't develop any grit." Pausing, she continued writing, *"And you treat Kaitlin like she has a disability, even though she has fully recovered from her bout with the flu. I can help give her the confidence she has lost in herself."*

Becky glanced over at Natalie, who had read Tick's note and abruptly picked up a nail file, asking Tick if she would like a manicure, hoping a sisterly gesture might ease the tension in the room.

Becky felt her face turning red. Tick had observed what her husband, Ben, had been telling her for years. Arguments about the children had become more and more heated, and the marriage had suffered because of it.

Looking directly at Natalie, Becky asked, "So what do you think? Do you agree with her?"

Natalie was a kindhearted, open-minded farm girl from Mississippi, so she was thoughtful as she replied quietly with her usual Southern charm. "Bless your heart, Becky. I know that nearly losin' Kaitlin tore you apart, but she came through, didn't she? You need to trust that God means for her to grow up and have a wonderful life. As for your twins—oh Lord!—your boys and my Lizzy could make a preacher cuss."

Becky had to agree with her sister-in-law on that point, at least about Lizzy, a "naughty corner" regular. Becky remembered an Easter brunch the two families had together back in April at the Grand Hotel in Point Clear, Alabama. Fidgeting in her highchair, Lizzy began twirling her new stuffed Easter bunny around by its ears so fast that she sent it flying off to another table, landing in a woman's soup bowl and creating quite a commotion. One of Brian's commentaries about his young daughter was that "Lizzy could infuriate Mother Teresa."

Becky was not to be deterred from broaching her more serious concern. "Okay, our kids can be obnoxious sometimes, but they wouldn't be normal if they didn't act up once in a while. It's the *abnormal* stuff going on here that I'm worried about, Natalie. Do you know that both Dad and Tick are training with knives, guns, and who knows what other weaponry? Dad told Ben that Tick is like a self-defense ninja warrior! Didn't you just turn thirteen, Tick? For Pete's sake!"

Natalie laughed as she reached over to hug Tick. "When you murdered that balloon last night... Well I thought I was watching a scene out of a terminator movie! If you're half as good with a gun as you are with a knife, we sure don't have anything to worry about."

"So it sounds like you think I should stop giving my kids vitamins and begin a daily dose of pain and suffering instead to build their strength and character?" Becky didn't appreciate Natalie's unconcerned attitude at all and continued talking, "I get it. Suffering is what's missing in their lives, and must be why they're such losers."

The images of Tick's scars and knowing how she got them immediately flashed through Becky's mind, and she would have given anything to take back such a callous and thoughtless comment, but Tick's response hid any hurt feelings Becky may have caused her.

"You're finally catching on, Becky!" Tick quickly penned with a smile. *"Vitamins are a poor substitute for a well-balanced diet, and a healthy dose of pain and suffering once in a while can't hurt. Suffering produces perseverance, character, and hope. Romans 5: 3–4."*

Becky sat back in her chair to ponder this mute girl with such a grim history behind her yet who was so unusually brave, resilient, and enlightened.

She thought about how Tick was with the children, stern and quick to correct, but ready to acknowledge good behavior with a bright smile and a thumbs-up. The boys straightened up when she was around them, and Kaitlin thought she hung the moon. Tick had always been the first person up in the mornings, greeting the family as they came in with direct eye contact and a big smile. She was the only one in the family who could begin to control Lizzy, an impossible bundle of energy who, from day one, had completely fixated on Tick.

Becky felt like a fool. Yet in most ways, she was a remarkable woman. Despite her sometimes overprotective mollycoddling and suspicious nature, she could admit to being wrong. Tick and Natalie watched Becky wringing her hands and looking out the window as the light-blue curtains fluttered in the ocean breeze.

"All right," Becky said, turning to Tick. "I give up. Dr. Barnes is right. You are a smart, insightful girl, and you're just wonderful with my kids. However… Please don't take this the wrong way. You must promise me that you won't place the kids in any dangerous situation or teach them knife tricks, like, you know, we all know you can do. I want you to be less vigorous with Kaitlin. She isn't as strong as you think."

"*I would never do anything to hurt the kids, and Kaitlin is much stronger than you think.*"

Becky sighed, not about to argue with Tick. "I'm going to trust that you are right. I'm going to start making some adjustments in my parenting."

Tick picked up her iPad again. "*When did you hear from Dr. Barnes? Patient-doctor relationships are confidential, so it wasn't about me, I'm sure.*"

Becky gently replied, now feeling more at peace with Tick. "It's Mattie, right? She just wrote a sweet note, hoping we are all having a good time. I guess you are still seeing her?"

"*We get together four or five times a week. We're working our way through the city's museums and art galleries. She's training me in first aid, giving me piano lessons, and we cook together.*"

Becky and Natalie glanced over at each other with questioning expressions, which didn't escape Tick's notice.

Tossing her head, Tick continued, "*And, yes, she's also my therapist… It's her way of attempting to get into my head. It's sneaky, but I let her think she is getting away with it.*"

Becky's eyebrows rose, wishing that she had someone like Mattie in her life, especially when she and Ben weren't getting along.

"She sounds very nice, but listen, Tick, I want to change the subject and discuss some changes about how things have been running in this house. One issue I have involves all the cooking you've been doing. We will reduce the time you spend preparing everyone's meals each day, and you and Dad won't be doing the dishes anymore. That's going to be Brian, Ben, and David's job. And, please, no more sneaking around to straighten up everybody's room and making the beds. If we're all too messy for your sensibilities, then you'll just have to suck it up."

Tick appeared far more relaxed now. *"I enjoy cooking, you know. Haven't you enjoyed the meals?"*

"Girl, you're the best cook in the house, by far!" said Natalie. "Your cooking is impressive, but you're here on vacation, too, and we want you to enjoy this time before you head back to Utah and have to dig in with schoolwork. What about letting Becky and me help you, and you can give us some of your recipes? We'll call it The Tick Hughes School of Fine Cuisine."

"I can do that," Tick wrote, *"but no frozen pizza, chicken tenders, or tater tots, okay?"*

When the trio emerged from the bedroom to start the evening meal, Brad was confident that he and Tick would not need to go home early.

Texting Mattie that night, Brad let her know about the goings-on. "Relieved to hear things have smoothed out," Mattie replied. "She texted me last night, but no mention of a rescue... Please keep her from drowning herself. It's no surprise that they're getting to know, respect, and like her!"

The message surprised Brad. To his knowledge, Tick had never texted Mattie with a problem. Could this mean that some closeness was developing in their relationship?

The rest of the week went by far too quickly, as vacations do when everyone is having a wonderful time: Days spent at Sea World, the San Diego Zoo, and going on a harbor cruise and visiting Old

San Diego. Then, of course, there was lots of boogie boarding and body surfing.

Becky could only bite her nails as she watched Kaitlin occasionally get lost inside a massive wave, emerging breathless and disoriented. Still, Tick was always close by, urging her to go out again for a better run.

The family also learned how Tick and Kaitlin had been spending their time together in the garden when Jonathan began taunting Lizzy with a dead frog. Kaitlin slammed her brother down onto the lawn with a judo throw and then held the dead frog next to his nose. Jonathan and Jerome were unsuccessful in their attempts to get Tick to teach them that move. "*When you act your age,*" she wrote.

For Brad, his favorite pastime was time spent swimming in the ocean with Tick. She was healing, and when in the water, she was as relaxed as he had ever seen her. The repetitive waves, the seagulls' calls, the powerful and expansive blue Pacific Ocean soothing her nerves, it helped her forget.

"*I think the family likes me, don't you?*" she wrote as they left the house to start the long drive home.

"More than that, they love you, Tick," replied Brad. "They all told me that you won them over. So what route do you want to take home? Should we get on I-15 North and head home, stopping in Mesquite for the night, or do you want to take an extra day to check out the Inyo National Forest and Death Valley? Maybe we can go up to Reno and visit Claire?"

"*I-15 and home,*" she typed. "*Claire has a new boyfriend, and he's all she talks about. Anyway, Mattie promised to come over for dinner when we get back, and I want to see her.*"

"Okay, I-15 it is!" Brad agreed.

Tick pulled a blanket up to her neck, put the seat back, and laid her head on a pillow. It felt good to rest. It was time to head home.

A Morning Briefing

FBI Director Ruth Evers of the National Center for the Analysis of Violent Crime (NCAVC) arrived at her office early and heard that Agent Parker was waiting for her in the surveillance room. She grabbed a cup of coffee and walked down the hall to see him. As she entered the room, Butch Parker, the senior profiler, stood up to begin.

"You might be interested to know what your favorite young witness and her father have been up to lately."

She took a seat across from Agent Parker. "Okay, I'm all ears, Butch."

While Brad and Tick didn't have bodyguards, they were under 24-7 electronic protective surveillance, and Brad had made it known from the beginning that he wasn't entirely happy with such a high-level, invasive stakeout. For that matter, neither was Director Evers, whose workload in staffing and supervising the ongoing Timothy Bird case had doubled in the aftermath of the Death Ranch and Mexican catastrophes.

It isn't all bad, Evers admitted to herself. *Keeping up-to-date with the stupendous progress Tick was making in so many areas of her life was always uplifting and quite entertaining.*

What *did* make things problematic was the media's fascination with the Death Ranch case and its only living survivor, Esther Morgan. Nothing could do more to boost a reporter's standing than to uncover the controversial young girl's identity. Ruth knew that the risk to Tick's life and perhaps the lives of her family might become insurmountable, even for the FBI, if that were to happen.

Previously, because of Brad's belief that Tick should learn how to drive a car sooner rather than later as another survival skill she could use to escape a life-threatening situation, an incident occurred that nearly resulted in FBI intervention. The Carbon County Police pulled Tick over while Brad was teaching her to drive on one of Utah's many backroads. The officer questioned her muteness, why an underage girl was at the wheel, and why she was not in school. He ran a background check on Brad that triggered an alarm at the bureau. Fortunately, the cover story held up, and they expunged the traffic violation.

"What do I need to know now?" Ruth asked. "They're still in Southern California on a family vacation. Don't tell me he let her drive on the freeway, or did she beat the tar out of somebody?"

"No, this is much more interesting," said Parker. "Yesterday, a police officer in San Diego hit the jackpot with his quest to locate the mystery girl who helped rescue a surfer."

"You've lost me. What happened?" Ruth asked incredulously.

"Here, check this out."

Parker grabbed the remote from the table, turned on the monitor, and hit Play. The video showed a segment of a local TV station weatherman running the short video of his son's ocean rescue, followed by his request for the public's help to identify the young girl who helped save his son from drowning. The video's quality was poor, taken on a mobile phone by the excited surfer's friend. However, Ruth could make out the surfboard tumbling in whitewater and people in the surf working their way through the breakers, followed by a lifeguard.

"That's Tick," Butch pointed out. "She spotted the kid and went in after him. That's Brad there behind her. And here come the lifeguards. And there, you can see two more lifeguards closing in."

Butch's voice couldn't hide how impressed he was with what he was watching. The video then showed the group making it to shore with a pretty clear image of Tick.

"The boy's father is that local weatherman, and he wants to acknowledge the girl who helped save his son. A local highway patrolman saw the segment and remembered seeing that same girl and her father at Costco loading groceries into a Jeep Grand Cherokee. He went to Costco, reviewed the store's security tapes, spotted the Jeep in the parking lot, and ran a search of the license plate."

"Give me the bottom line, Butch," requested Ruth. "Will Tick be linked to his search?"

"No. Thankfully, we blocked the inquiry. As you know, police officers are permitted to do two searches that are, by law, programmed into separate systems. The initial search provides the vehicle's year, make, model, and VIN, along with the expiration date of the registration and any flags indicating outstanding warrants attached to the vehicle. That information on the Jeep is accessible. Still, DMV's computer prevents a secondary search on Hughes's Jeep. You can't access the driver's license number, address, date of birth, and Social Security without going through us first.

The DMV told the officer that privacy laws prevented the release of personal information. We flew agent Dresder in from Salt Lake City last night, and she spoke to the head lifeguard. He told her that he had spotted the board with no rider from his tower, grabbed a rescue board, and immediately took off for the surf, but the lifeguard credits the girl for getting to the boy first before another wave took him out."

Evers sighed. "Do we need to pull them out of San Diego? Bear in mind, this is the first family vacation they've taken since Tick came into their lives."

"No, I think we can leave them there," Parker replied. "The incident took place about a mile from their rental house. Dresder tells me that there's little risk of being spotted. They have three cars at the house, and the Jeep is at the end of a long driveway behind a gate. They've been driving the other vehicles. Also the cop works out of Pasadena, California, and he was visiting family. It's highly unlikely he would ever see the Jeep or Tick again. The TV segment has only aired once on local news."

"Okay, let's not bother them now," Evers replied. "I'll call them at the end of the week, but keep Dresder out there for a few more days to follow up on any developments, if there are any. When Brad gets back to Utah, we can help him get rid of that Jeep. I don't ever want it to be a link to Tick."

⸎

Brad and Tick were just leaving the San Diego area when Director Evers picked up her phone and dialed Brad's cellphone.

"Good morning, Brad. It's Ruth Evers calling."

"Good morning, Ruth. What's up?" Brad asked.

"I'm just curious if you and Tick are planning to stop in Vegas for the night, or are you going to drive straight through to Salt Lake?"

Brad, feeling immediately miffed and hating the idea of always being tracked, replied, "Jeez, Ruth, don't your agents have better things to do than follow us, even while we're on the road?"

"Actually, no," replied Ruth. "Your rescue mission has kept my staff earning their pay all week."

"How so?" Brad asked.

"A police officer managed to ID the plates belonging to the heroes of Pacific Beach. You made the local news. Fortunately, the story wasn't quite big enough for the national network news. You need to get a new car ASAP. Please call Agent Parker when you get home."

Evers took the next few minutes explaining to Brad what all had taken place.

"Okay, Ruth. I appreciate your help. Give me a couple of days to replace the Jeep. Is there anything else I need to do?"

"No, we're good, but could you please put Tick on the phone? I want to congratulate her."

"You're on speakerphone, and she is listening," replied Brad.

"Well, in that case... Hello, Tick! I want you to know my team reports that you are quite the hero. The lifeguard doubts that he would have made it to the kid in time, saying that your hold on him made it possible to bring him in minutes sooner. The boy's family is quite grateful."

"Tick is giving you a thumbs-up, Ruth," Brad replied, "and since you asked, we're driving straight through to Salt Lake. Okay?"

"Good enough. Talk to you later, then," Ruth said. "Drive carefully."

It had been a good trip, Brad was thinking, and even though Tick had made significant inroads in winning the family over, her glaring uniqueness, along with her persistent failure to speak, had been the ever-present elephant in the room. It was also a forewarning to Brad that, if anything happened to him, Tick might be more than anyone in his family could handle.

As they drove along, Brad brought up a subject that he had been agonizing over.

"Tick, you know that unexpected things can happen in life, and I want to talk to you about something that's been on my mind. Okay?"

Brad waited for and received a nod from Tick.

"So what I have been thinking about is this, if something were to happen to me, and let me be clear, nothing is going to happen to me, but if something did, it would be irresponsible of me not to make some arrangements for your care in case…you know… It's called insurance."

Tick sat up taller in her seat, looking straight ahead without any expression.

"I talked to Mattie about it, and she said that she would take you into her home in a heartbeat. Mattie is someone who would raise you brilliantly. She's someone I trust. She loves you, Tick. I planned on telling the boys, but I felt I should let you know and allow you some time to think about it."

Brad looked over at her slate to read her response, but suddenly, he jerked the steering wheel sharply, responding to the car alarm warning him that he had veered too close to a large semi-truck in the adjacent lane.

His heart pounding now, he felt a flash of anger, not only because he was so careless for taking his eyes off the road, but also because of Tick's inability to speak.

Why on earth wasn't she talking? he questioned himself for the umpteenth time. *Everyone who has been around Tick for any length of time knows she's able to talk.* The Thomas girls had told him that they heard Tick talking to a horse. Ana reported that she had heard La Chica singing out by the pool. He and Mattie heard Tick enunciate words when she came out of anesthesia after her fall at the hospital. And then there were her verbal "cry outs" for her mom during her night terrors.

What could be holding her back?

If Tick were physically incapable of speech, then he would accept it. He would willingly learn the sign language that she wanted him to use and carry on. Tick had picked up the skill months ago, seemingly without effort—her detailed memory and language skills had made her a natural for it. She had even used the ability to help Mattie communicate with patients at the hospital.

But this inexplicable disorder of hers was exasperating. Without any interest on his end, Tick had begun attempting to teach him to sign, showing him the words in sign before writing them down. What's more, she was working at persuading the rest of the family to learn sign language, too.

In his gut, he felt as if he were being trapped, manipulated into going along with something that she had arbitrarily orchestrated.

He felt like shouting at her, but he knew it would just drive her further underground. Something terrible had happened on that mountain, and whatever it was, it had utterly disrupted the complicated, beautiful wiring in his daughter's head. The fact that she slipped up on occasion and spoke within earshot of people was, in Brad's mind, a subconscious cry for help. She wanted to talk. She wanted a way out, and she needed Brad's help to find the key to unlock her from her prison.

Brad gathered his thoughts and, leaning over again, looked at the response she had written:

"Nothing is going to happen to you... You're too strong. But if it makes you happy, then okay to Mattie. Pay attention to your driving! You almost hit that truck."

Tick's "okay" was Brad's confirmation of the emotional headway she was decidedly making—and hope returned to replace dismay.

False Accusations

A year after Tick's adoption, the press had Tick in their sites once again. The start date for Bart Madison's trial was November 10, and Esther Morgan would be the star witness for the prosecution.

Madison faced charges for the kidnapping and murder of five children: Leslie Quinton, Jane Jennings, and Andrea Stevens—found buried on the Fairhope property—and sisters Sandra and Barbra Hopkins, their remains recovered at the Death Ranch in Utah. Madison was also charged with participation in the murders of Angela Parsons, burned at the stake, and Marjory Perkins, who had been buried alive.

Madison's attorney, Sunder Buckley, could be seen on the news channels daily, expounding on the charges made against his client. Buckley was a well-known defender of the rich and famous gone afoul of the law. Buckley was famous for turning high-profile trials into dramatic stage productions and winning such cases, triggering the distrustful perception for many that Lady Justice was not blind but capricious and able to be swayed.

Buckley declared that Bart Madison had never set foot on the Utah Death Ranch, that Madison had no knowledge or involvement with the victims found on the Fairhope property. He contended that his client was just a proxy for crimes committed by others—crimes in which the key witness to the case, Esther Morgan, could very well have been involved.

Madison freely admitted to visiting the Fairhope property, Buckley conceded, but very infrequently, and only when Timothy Bird had made the house available to him. Madison's residence was in Oregon, Buckley emphasized, and he held no title to the Fairhope property.

Sunder Buckley's statements went much farther afield. He stated that he had evidence that the girls found deceased at the Fairhope property had likely been training fodder for Timothy Bird's trained killers, and he speculated that Esther Morgan was one of them.

Madison contended that he had met the Morgan girl once, at the Fairhope house. Esther, Janet Herrington, and Timothy Bird had stopped there for the night on their way back to Utah. Madison assumed that Esther Morgan had been there before because she knew where to find everything she needed to cook dinner for the group.

Buckley stated that Madison, a former college acquaintance of Timothy Bird, was as horrified as the rest of the world when he learned of the terrible deeds Bird allegedly committed. Buckley asserted that Madison was an innocent man.

⌒⌯∞⌯⌒

Well before the trial date, Tick and Brad agreed to the FBI's carefully planned security procedures for their trip to Mobile, Alabama. First, they flew commercially to Washington DC, just Brad and his daughter taking her first-ever flight on an airplane, sitting in first class on a trip together to visit the nation's capital, if anyone asked.

That day, Director Ruth Evers and Special Agent Butch Parker joined them in DC for the final leg of the journey, the flight to Mobile and Madison's trial, in a Gulfstream G550. The visible vapor trail that the small jet made as it flew through the skies may have looked from the ground like a comet taking people on a fabulous adventure. However, this comet was transporting Tick Hughes, as Esther Morgan, to some of the most challenging days in her life.

Touching down at the Mobile Regional Airport around 4:30 p.m., the small jet taxied into a private hangar. Stepping out of the plane and walking down the craft's stairs, Brad—incognito in a logo-imprinted FBI cap, agency windbreaker, and a pair of dark sunglasses—waited as his daughter and her agent guardians followed.

Tick, feeling the oddly different sensation of the Deep South's humidity on her face and in her lungs, paused for a moment. Brad was sure he had heard her mumble something, but Evers and Parker quickly shepherded them into a heavily armored car with tinted windows. The armored vehicle was one of three cars in convoy, which methodically traversed its way toward their lodgings located across the bay from downtown Mobile and the courthouse.

Driving past Battleship Memorial Park along the way, the knowledgeable FBI driver told his passengers that the historically significant WWII-era battleship, the USS *Alabama*, was docked there. He reported that the ship commenced her shakedown cruise in the Chesapeake Bay on November 11, 1942, and that the forty-five-thousand-ton vessel and its crew served with distinction during the Second World War. As a history buff, Tick would have enjoyed touring the ship, now a military museum. But, as the sole survivor of the Utah Death Ranch, who would soon be testifying against Bart Madison in court, she would not be touring the floating museum on this trip.

The convoy soon passed Daphne and Fairhope's bayside cities, arriving at Point Clear and the beautiful Grand Hotel on Mobile Bay. They settled in a secluded wing of the hotel, with security, to stay during the trial.

⁕

District Attorney Durgan Marshall waited in the hotel's conference room for Esther Morgan's arrival. It was a small, private room with a mahogany table, high ceilings, tasteful drapes, and picture windows looking out at many enormous, decades-old magnolia trees on the frontage property to the bay.

A slightly built man with graying hair, Durgan Marshall was an experienced, hard-hitting criminal prosecutor with a reputation for his strong personal character and his love of the law. His interns joked that he ate nails for breakfast before going into court, but he was quite worried about this case.

Durgan knew that Buckley was preparing to devour his young witness on the stand because, in point of fact, the entire case against the accused killer hinged around her testimony. Esther's interview with the FBI in Deer Valley would provide Madison's defense attorney with plenty of ammunition. Perhaps even worse, Durgan had been warned repeatedly by Agent Butch Parker that Esther Morgan had a way of taking matters into her own hands. An unpredictable or impulsive witness could spell disaster; the outcome of this trial could very quickly be setting a killer free.

Still, expressing such concerns to his travel-weary young witness at this point would serve no purpose, other than to make her more nervous than she undoubtedly was.

On several occasions, Durgan had communicated with Esther Morgan via a closed computer screen and twice with Sunder Buckley who took her deposition. Weeks before, after receiving a compelling petition from the FBI regarding the importance of preserving Esther Morgan's safety and welfare within the Witness Protection Program, the court had issued a pretrial restraining order prohibiting either counsel or their associates from commenting or disclosing verbally or in writing any personal descriptions of Esther. Further, Esther's testimony would be given in the courtroom, closed to the public and the press. The presiding judge would issue a continuing protective "gag" order for all trial participants with the same nondisclosure restraints. Therefore, the media would not be privy to the witness's appearance or her method of testifying.

Durgan and his team had pored over the FBI file on Esther Morgan, concentrating on the statements she had given to the FBI in Deer Valley. He was, at first, skeptical, finding her story highly implausible. Accounts of existing in a dark, drippy cave with her mother for seven years, being witness to unspeakable acts of cruelty by Timothy Bird and Bart Madison, a daring escape with an iron shackle around her ankle, all seemed impossible. If that wasn't enough, reports of her astounding intellect and athleticism seemed to be made-up stories for a gullible, superhero-hungry world.

As fate would have it, once Durgan began communicating with Esther, presumably from an FBI office computer somewhere back East, his skepticism became a possibility, then a real probability, that she was indeed a truth-teller.

From across their computer screens, Durgan Marshall and Esther Morgan covered her life from age five until her rescue. Her intelligent, thorough explanations and willingness to answer everything he asked without hesitating was impressive. Still, it wasn't until he finally met Esther in person, looked into her eyes as she looked back into his that he became a true believer. She had an elusive presence that was difficult to put into words: a matureness, a depth, wisdom, and sadness, like his grandfather who had fought in the Second World War, all mixed in with a youngster's sincerity.

Over dinner served in the conference room, Durgan spent some time working with his leading witness and reviewing her testimony.

"I don't want you to elaborate on your answers. You don't need to. I will respond to Buckley's attacks in my rebuttal arguments. Here's my point, Esther. Your interviews with me make it clear that you are very gifted. Your skill and fluency as a writer is at such an advanced level for someone your age that your intelligence won't help us in court and might even hurt our case. Many of the jurors are farmers and working-class people. They might be puzzled and question how such rapid-fire written testimony is possible coming from a child reportedly cooped up in a cave for seven years. How did you become so scholarly and intellectual? Sure as heck, Sunder Buckley is going to paint Timothy Bird as the intellectual who schooled you all those years."

"Then he'd be lying! My mother was my teacher, not Timothy!" Tick quickly wrote out, with a furious expression on her face.

"I understand, Esther, and you have every right to express your anger with me here tonight, but you cannot lose your temper or look furious in court, even though you have every justification. The defense would like nothing more than for the jury to see you lose your composure and then happily use it as evidence in portraying you as someone you're not—a hostile juvenile with a very short fuse, capable of who knows what?

454

"The jurors are going to be looking at you very, very carefully, and I want them to see only the truth on your face. They need to look at a young victim thrown into a horrific situation beyond her control, finally facing great peril to escape and survive against impossible odds. Express yourself simply and truthfully, Esther, and stay calm. I believe this jury consists of good, solid citizens. They will respond to the truth, and Bart Madison will be found guilty of his terrible crimes. Believe this, Esther."

Durgan Marshall didn't tell Esther his real thoughts. *You are about to go through hell again, child. First by me, since the only chance we have is if I tell your entire story—the good, the bad, and the ungodly—and somehow convince the jury, it's true. Then Buckley will rip into you and your mother, and there will be little I can do to stop him. You won't be in a fighting ring facing hand-to-hand combat, but still, sitting in the witness box could be even tougher on you.*

CHAPTER

42

Opening Statements

Tick was not present in the courtroom when Durgan Marshall delivered his opening statement. She and Brad watched it on a TV monitor set up in a vacant courthouse room:

"Your Honor, Ladies, and Gentlemen of the jury:

"My name is Durgan Marshall, and I represent the State of Alabama and the Federal Government in the case being presented to you today. Over and above that, however, I represent seven lives taken with such unspeakable cruelty that it defies common understanding—the State will be presenting overwhelming evidence that Bart Madison is responsible for their deaths.

"As some of you might remember, the FBI found numerous victims at a death ranch in Utah over a year ago. That man, sitting right over there looking so sharp in his pinstriped suit and shirt and tie, willingly and enthusiastically participated in the deaths of people found at that ranch. One victim, Angela Parsons, was burned on a stake. On another day, he picked up a shovel and buried Marjory Perkins alive.

"If that's not gruesome enough for you to hear, there's more, and it sickens me to say. Mr. Madison has tortured and killed at least five innocent young girls—Sandra Hopkins, age seventeen, and her sister, Barbara, age twelve, murdered at the Death Ranch in Utah. And later, right under our noses here in Fairhope, Bart Madison kidnapped, tortured, and killed Leslie Quinton, age twelve, Angela

Stevens, age nine, and Jane Jennings, age ten. It is difficult—No, it's impossible to adequately verbalize the hideousness or cruelty of Bart Madison's evil deeds. This man abducted these beautiful young girls who had their whole lives ahead of them and proceeded to subject each one to a living hell before sending them to their deaths.

The defense will attempt to convince you that Mr. Madison is not the perpetrator of these unimaginably horrible deeds. They will try to convince you he is a reputable, upright businessman, a retired tax lawyer, and an innocent victim of false accusations—of manipulation and misguided intelligence work orchestrated by anxious bureaucrats motivated to calm a nervous public. But as you hear the facts, you'll learn that his entire career has been one of deception. Mr. Madison was a key player at a law firm based in Panama at the center of a global offshore industry specializing in tax havens. I would say tax evasion. He left that firm four years ago to form a private consultancy and has consulted for none other than the notorious killer, Timothy Bird.

"As jurors, there are questions you will have to ask yourselves. Why, when Esther Morgan escaped, did Bart Madison leave his home in Oregon and hide out on a property in Fairhope, Alabama? A property owned by a faceless Panamanian entity with no linkage to his name. Why did he present a fake ID when an alert trooper in Fairhope questioned him about a broken taillight? Finally, why did cadaver dogs find the bodies of three children on the property?

"You will learn that Bart Madison's close association with Timothy Bird, a suspected murderer still at large, is not at all some random business connection as the defense will claim. Bart Madison roomed with Timothy Bird in college and has maintained a close relationship with this killer throughout the years: Madison has been a frequent guest at the infamous Death Ranch in Utah.

"Timothy Bird—number one on the FBI's Most Wanted List—is a man tied to some forty murders of innocent people, including the deaths of six lawmen. We believe he is a high-ranking member of the Epilektoi, an international crime cabal and the highfalutin name for a gang of psychopathic killers that is currently under investigation by a multinational crime force.

"You will hear direct testimony from Esther Morgan, kidnapped by Timothy Bird when she was only five years old on her way to school. Esther and her mother, Alissa, were transported to Bird's ranch in the Uinta Mountains in Utah and held prisoners as Bird's captives for seven years, imprisoned in a dark cave, and forced to serve as slaves.

"Esther Morgan is a direct witness to Bart Madison's crimes in Utah and the hero responsible for information that led to his capture in Fairhope.

"How was Bart Madison finally tracked down and apprehended? Thankfully, Esther Morgan remembered a conversation between Timothy Bird and his associate, Janet Herrington, related to the kidnapping and murder of young Leslie Quinton. Esther remembered hearing Bird tell Ms. Herrington that he hoped Bart would, and I quote, 'gig himself to death' at one of the jubilees of which he often spoke. One small clue provided by an alert young girl brings us all here today to bring this killer to justice.

"As you will soon learn, Esther is unlike any girl you have ever known, someone who has lived most of her young life confined to a world built and controlled by a madman and lackeys like Bart Madison. She is a remarkable, courageous young lady and a true survivor.

"Esther will provide testimony that is difficult to process because it falls so far outside of our understanding. Esther's testimony describes Timothy Bird, the murderous Svengali leader, and Bart Madison, Bird's depraved lapdog, pitted against Alissa Morgan, her mother, in a battle of good over evil: a desperate struggle between a loving, remarkably righteous woman, and the devil's minions.

"Esther's mother, armed only with a concealed Bible and the determination to teach her daughter good from evil, sacrificed herself to give Esther a chance for a life outside of hell. It is a remarkable story of a child who grew to understand and know evil and then risked everything to oppose and escape from its clutches.

"Esther Morgan's testimony will shock you as you realize the atrocities she witnessed and endured. Still, her story will leave you filled with hope when you grasp the incredible resiliency of the human spirit.

"At considerable risk to herself, Miss Morgan is prepared to testify and tell her story to bring a monster, Bart Madison, to justice.

"Lastly, I need to remind you of the gag order and the nondisclosure agreements you all have signed and that you have all sworn to uphold concerning Miss Morgan. Any divulgence of her physical characteristics would be in contempt of court and subject to hefty fines and possible jail time. Miss Morgan, due to a short-term illness, is also being allowed to type her responses to questions. This fact is also to be held confidential. If you cannot abide by these terms, this is your last opportunity to excuse yourself from this trial. Esther Morgan is a minor and in great danger from Timothy Bird and possibly others. Therefore, we are all obligated to do everything possible to protect her identity.

"Thank you."

⌒⟨⟨⟨∂∂∂⟩⟩⟩⌒

Sunder Buckley, a man with imposing good looks and radiated polish, was in an excellent mood and pleased with himself the morning of the Madison trial. He had a plan of action, a well-thought-out strategy to follow, and he was confident that he could create reasonable doubt about the murder charges his client faced.

In some respects, his hands were tied. The court-ordered gag order prevented Sunder or anyone participating in the trial from discussing information that identified Esther Morgan, and HIPAA laws denied Sunder access to Esther's medical records from the hospital. Sunder also hated the idea that they allowed Esther to respond by typing; it gave her an advantage and time to formulate her answers before the jury read them.

The court did allow the defense counsel to read the reports of two violent episodes involving Esther with hospital personnel and a CPS employee. These incidences were critical to his defense of Madison, even though the courts had heavily redacted those interactions.

Esther Morgan was not on trial officially, but there were many areas of her testimony as a witness that Sunder knew he would mine: the assaults at the hospital, her longevity at the ranch, and her FBI interview. There was a bonanza of implausible information that would lead to his client's acquittal.

Sunder Buckley listened carefully to Durgan Marshall's opening statement while taking notes, and then it was his turn to open. He strode in front of the jury with supreme confidence:

"Your Honor, Counsel Durgan, members of the jury:

"Good morning. My name is Sunder Buckley, and I represent Bart Madison, the wrongfully accused defendant in this trial.

"You are here as jurors to uncover the truth and to reach logical, well-thought-out conclusions. That's your job, and a man's life depends on your attention to the verified evidence presented in this case.

"The prosecution will attempt to convict my client based on guilt by association, making the preposterous leap that because Brad Madison knew and worked for a wanted murderer, he must be guilty himself of kidnap and murder. If that approach were valid, each one of you should feel nothing but alarm because your connection with everyone you know or have ever met makes you a potential target for criminal prosecution!

"The prosecution will then attempt to influence your judgment by telling you about some nefarious organization called the Epilektoi, an organization that may or may not exist. This is an organization that the FBI, as they will admit, has no concrete evidence against, and has only been tied to Timothy Bird through the testimony of a young girl back in college over fifteen years ago.

"Then the prosecution will bring out its star witness, Esther Morgan, a witness given full immunity in exchange for her testimony. The prosecuting attorney has just told you, among other things, to listen very carefully to Esther Morgan's statements. He is right. She will tell you stories—stories of good and evil, tales of depravity, accounts, as you will quickly learn, told by an admitted participant in the very atrocities she will describe.

"If you are to serve justice in this trial, you must use solid reasoning and be very wary of Esther Morgan's accounts of criminal deeds perpetrated by someone other than herself. As you will learn, Miss Morgan has previously admitted to mercilessly tormenting one of her victims using a knife, and I quote, 'with lots of little cuts.' Esther Morgan and her mother, Alissa, will be portrayed as kidnap victims, forced to live in hell for seven years. It is a false claim that opposing counsel will use to elicit sympathy and to divert attention away from the real facts of this case and the guilt of their witness, Esther Morgan."

Buckley paused for a moment, looked at the jury, and then continued in a firm voice.

"So what are the facts as supported by evidence?

"Timothy Bird did not abduct Alissa Morgan, despite what the prosecution tells you. Alissa purposefully joined Timothy Bird's murderous cult and took her five-year-old daughter with her. It is an unfortunate and horrible thing to have done to a child. Still, the evidence will show that Alissa and her daughter, Esther, embraced, thrived, and participated in the lifestyle until its madness turned on them and consumed them.

So let's discuss Esther Morgan in greater detail. As the facts will reveal, when Esther Morgan ran away from the ranch, she carried with her a sordid past as Timothy Bird's one-time young devotee, trained by him to fight and to win in death matches. But without a blameless alibi and some way to gain sympathy and support from the FBI and law enforcement officers, she fabricated or distorted much of her testimony, brilliantly positioning herself into an unfortunate traumatized victim.

"Now, don't misunderstand me—I am not a heartless man. I have a daughter I adore, and I can't begin to wrap my head around the idea of anyone hurting my child. There is no question that Esther Morgan suffered at the hands of Timothy Bird when she lost favor with him, and no child should endure such unbridled wrath. But it was Timothy Bird who harmed her and killed her mother, Timothy Bird, not Bart Madison, a man who had no part in any of that or any of the terrible crimes of which he stands falsely accused.

"Over these past several months, I have learned quite a lot about Esther Morgan. I have spent countless hours reviewing her early school records, examining the testimony she gave to FBI agents, and I have taken her deposition. She is an exceptionally bright young girl, no doubt about that, and quite gifted wielding a knife too, I have learned.

"There is overwhelming evidence to prove that Timothy Bird took Esther under his wing to mold and train her for his perverted purposes and that Esther Morgan embraced his teachings.

"The prosecution has called Esther Morgan a hero, making much ado about the capture of Bart Madison. They have told us that his arrest came about from the recollection of an overheard conversation. I quote Miss Morgan saying, quote, 'I remember Timothy telling Janet that he hoped Madison would gig himself to death at one of those jubilees he always talked about,' end quote.

"Let's look at those words from a different perspective, which will become evident during the trial. What if Esther Morgan had been to Fairhope before? What if Esther Morgan participated in the murders that took place on the Eastern Shore? What if Esther Morgan feared that she could be caught?

"Two different untraceable entities owned both the property in Utah and the property in Fairhope, most likely controlled by Timothy Bird. Esther Morgan had plenty of time and counsel to think up a good story. What better way to deflect blame and gain favor with the authorities than to fabricate a tale leading police to Bart Madison, a man she had met only once. A man who she knew liked to vacation on the Fairhope property, an accountant, a bookish man not prone to violence.

"By the end of this trial, I guarantee that you will be as outraged as I am that Esther Morgan has immunity from criminal prosecution in exchange for throwing stymied law enforcement officials a bone about Timothy Bird and the ranch in Utah. They allowed Esther the opportunity, the liberty to assign her guilt to others—how about that, it worked—until now, that is because now it stops!

"I am here to defend an innocent man. Bart Madison is a surrogate for crimes committed by Timothy Bird and his followers—and Esther Morgan is one of them.

"In summary, the prosecution will present their case implicating an innocent man of kidnap and murder *by association*! They will tell you that Bart Madison is guilty because he knew and had associated with Timothy Bird. Now, this is where justice must step forward to end these unreasonable murder charges based on nothing but a prejudicial link.

"The prosecution will then attempt to strengthen their flimsy case by presenting intelligence reports that are sorely lacking in hard evidence about some secret society. They will tell you that Timothy Bird is a member of this mysterious organization, which may or may not be the controlling operation responsible for malevolent killings in the United States and Mexico. Again, the prosecution will try to hook Mr. Madison with this group ad hominem or guilt by association. Such an organization, if it exists at all, has nothing to do with my client.

"Finally, the prosecution will bring out the star of their case, Esther Morgan, portraying her as an innocent kidnap victim with nothing to gain and everything to lose by testifying against my client. But you will have to ask yourselves what has Miss Morgan obtained from her testimony? You must ask yourselves what if Esther Morgan's involvement in the atrocities we are examining is far greater than even the prosecution knows or wants you to believe?

"Well, I can tell you what she has gained—full, unconditional immunity from prosecution, freedom from prosecution for an admitted participant in death matches.

"Here is the rub, a trial has to be about substantial evidence, and I will show that the evidence, in this case, points the finger away from my client to a very compromised witness, Esther Morgan.

"In Utah, explosions and resulting fires destroyed any trace of evidence that could be used against her. How convenient. In Fairhope, all the prosecution has is a one-line statement about a jubilee. I ask you, just how likely is it for a girl who has never been off a ranch in Utah to know about a jubilee, our celebrated and rare Eastern Shore phenomenon where fish are trapped against the shore by deoxygenated water? My contention is she knows about jubilees because she has been to Fairhope and may very well have experienced one.

"Then you have pages and pages of interviews with FBI agents, where Miss Morgan describes in detail her love of combat training and admits to having fought in death matches. Esther is a violent child whose first acts when rescued off a mountain were to seriously injure two hospital attendants, individuals who were doing their best to help her.

"The courts require proof of guilt beyond a reasonable doubt for conviction of a criminal defendant. A reasonable doubt exists when a fact-finder cannot say with moral certainty that a person is guilty or if a particular fact exists. It must be more than an imaginary doubt, as it is often defined judicially, because such uncertainty would cause a reasonable person to hesitate before deciding on a guilty verdict in a matter of such importance.

"During this trial, I ask you to listen carefully. I ask you to think—and think hard—about what you are hearing. A pattern of deception will make itself known. The prosecution's dead fish will wash up against the shore and start to smell. Horrible crimes have been committed, and the truth as to who the real perpetrators are will become known to you."

⁓෴⁓

Days of testimony from FBI agents and tax authorities began, resulting in a reasoned and robust defense for Bart Madison, and sleepless nights for Durgan Marshall.

Yes, Madison roomed with Timothy Bird in college and associated with him, but the association was not the same as complicity.

Yes, Madison set up tax shelters for Bird in Panama, but he had performed the same service for hundreds of other clients, some of them were quite prominent in government and business.

Were Alissa and Esther Morgan kidnapped? True, they disappeared without a trace, but there was no sign or evidence of their being taken by force. Alissa knew Timothy Bird from the times he frequented the restaurant where she worked. It was just as reasonable to assume that she had made a spur-of-the-moment decision to go off with him. She had nothing significant to keep her grounded where she was, besides the care of two ailing elders.

The prosecution was unable to find any direct evidence that Madison had ever been to the Death Ranch or had even been to Utah. There were no records and nothing to verify that he had ever traveled to or through Salt Lake City. It was a dead end.

Yes, Bart Madison spent a great deal of time at the Fairhope property. Timothy Bird gave him permission to use it as often as he wanted, but he knew nothing about the bodies found on the property.

No, Madison did not have a solid alibi or someone who could attest to his whereabouts the day Leslie Quinton disappeared. As a single retired man, it was not unusual for him to do nothing but stay home and read, but there was no evidence he was even in Atlanta on those days.

Yes, Madison had shown a fake ID, but it had been a stupid mistake. He carried one, as he sometimes had business in both Israel and Iran. It was a deceptive illegal practice, but Madison had clients in both countries, and using the same passport in each jurisdiction would have been impossible. He had not been trying to hide out in Fairhope; he was vacationing there as he did every year.

Both the defense and the prosecution spent a day discussing Timothy Bird—the one topic where they both could agree. Steve Brewer was called to the stand to describe in detail his findings on Timothy Bird, how he had pursued Bird for years while investigating the murder of a college professor, how a nanny who had caught him torturing dogs had characterized Bird. They covered it all—including the Utah Death Ranch and the Mexican massacre.

At the end of day three, Sunder Buckley had accomplished his goals. He was able to establish doubt that aside from questionable accounting services, Bart Madison had not engaged in Timothy Bird's nefarious activities. He had led the jury to consider the idea that Esther Morgan had been at the Fairhope property. The jury now seriously entertained the idea that Esther Morgan was violent and unstable.

Finally, both he and the prosecution had presented the jury with a clear picture of Timothy Bird—a murdering psychopath, intent on killing anyone who crossed him.

Buckley had skillfully set a trap. Esther Morgan would be up next, and Sunder Buckley knew he had the jury eating out of the palm of his hand.

The prosecution had come up with nothing.

CHAPTER 43

Esther Morgan Takes the Stand

Tick spent an hour that morning somewhat distracted by a female FBI special agent who skillfully altered her features using contouring and shading tints commonly used by makeup artists. Fitted with a short, curly black wig, and wearing tinted eyeglasses, she vaguely resembled a well-known actress—Brad thought of a young Elizabeth Taylor. Not surprisingly, Tick enjoyed learning something about the art of makeup magic; she liked the notion of being able to disguise herself.

Durgan Marshall was waiting for Tick and Brad inside the courthouse when they arrived. He was anxious, Brad could tell, as they walked a long corridor together, explaining the setup arranged for Esther's testimony, which included a keyboard linked to a projector and a large screen. Turning down another hall, they arrived at an anteroom, where Tick and Brad took a seat. Durgan asked his witness if she was ready to "give 'em hell," and she gave the man an enthusiastic thumbs-up.

The jury filed in and took their seats in what was now a strangely empty courtroom. Their footsteps and settling-in clatter echoed in the large, stately room devoid of the press and the gallery crowd; the solemnity of the bench, the wood paneling, and the empty witness box imposed an aura of gravity, enormity, and of judgment. Sunder Buckley and Durgan Marshall entered and took their seats.

Bart Madison came in with a uniformed corrections officer. His demeanor was awkward and nervous.

"All rise," the bailiff proclaimed forcefully, irrespective of the near vacant courtroom. "The Honorable Asher Benton residing."

Judge Benton was a slim man who walked with a limp due to a childhood farm accident. A graduate of the University of Alabama Law School, his reputation was impeccable, a lawyer highly respected by prosecutors and defense attorneys alike. His character was forged working long hours on his parent's pecan farm on the Eastern Shore of the Mobile Bay. A hard, flinty man, he would be strictly impartial, rendering no favoritism to the young witness called to the stand. The death penalty was in play, and Benton did not want the decisions of his court overturned. Still, a man of faith, he answered to a higher court, a court above the land, and he would not be swayed by public opinion in fulfilling his duties. Durgan Marshall feared but respected the man.

After clearing through the court preliminaries, the judge instructed Marshall to call in his first witness. The bailiff immediately headed for an imposing door to the side of the courtroom.

"The prosecution calls Esther Morgan."

The bailiff tapped on the door a few times, and then he opened the door and nodded to Tick, indicating that it was time.

Brad turned to Tick as she put on her tinted glasses, and she stood to join the waiting bailiff. Images of the small, horribly wounded girl on the cliff's edge, willing to fight and die for her freedom, flashed through Brad's mind, along with a keen awareness of her miraculous survival throughout the many trials she had endured.

Tick will survive this trial, too, he thought. *She's in the Lord's grip.*

Brad also stood up, gave his daughter an encouraging hug and his customary thumbs-up, and then she was gone.

There wasn't a sound in the courtroom when Esther Morgan, dressed in a black skirt and a black-and-white printed silk blouse that Mattie picked out for her in Paris, made her way toward the witness box, perfectly poised and unmistakably classy, her back ramrod straight.

She stopped just before entering the witness box. With an expressionless gaze, her hands relaxed by her side, she slowly took in her surroundings: the bench, the judge, the court reporter, each juror, Sunder Buckley, and finally, Bart Madison. Her compelling demeanor transfixed nearly everyone, save one.

Tick leaned toward Madison, her eyes fixed on a man who would not, who could not look up from the table, and her hands curled into fists.

"Remain standing and face the clerk. Raise your right hand to be sworn."

The bailiff's voice echoed in the chambers as Tick slowly turned and resolutely stepped up into the witness box, where she raised one hand into the air and placed the other firmly on the Bible as if drawing in guidance from The Word.

"Do you solemnly state that the testimony you will give in this matter will be the truth, the whole truth, and nothing but the truth, so help you God?

Looking at the judge, Tick nodded her head.

The prosecution went first. Durgan Marshall knew that to capture credibility with the jury, Esther would have to disclose everything. He would need to methodically review every aspect of her life at the ranch, leaving out only private details of the whippings she had endured.

He was apprehensive about the trial, but at least it was taking place on familiar ground, held in The John A. Campbell U.S. Courthouse, Mobile, Alabama. The building, built in the relatively austere neo-classical revival style, was constructed in 1934. A new courthouse was under construction; still, Marshall, with years of successes under his belt in the old courthouse, felt strengthened by these comfortable surroundings.

Also heartening to Durgan was seeing the twelve people seated in the jury box. This jury was composed of sensible, down-to-earth, and hardworking Southerners he believed would sniff out hypocrisy or lies. It would be up to him to help them see the truth, a truth he now fervently believed in. He would not try to dramatize his presentation; it would be factual, delivered in a calm, direct manner.

Respecting Esther's request, Marshall would leave out the punishments that caused her disfigurement. HIPAA laws protected her privacy rights. Nevertheless, he would neither sugarcoat what Esther had endured for seven years at the ranch nor whitewash her active participation.

"Good morning, Miss Morgan. I want to ask you about a date, February 10, 2009. Do you remember that day?"

"*I will never forget it,*" Tick wrote.

"And why is that?"

"*It was the day our lives changed forever.*"

"Whose lives, Miss Morgan?"

"*My mother's life and my life.*"

"Can you please tell the jury how your lives changed on that day?"

"*We were taken… Timothy Bird and his friends stole us away from everything we knew, and from everyone who loved or cared about us. It was the last day we would ever see Terrance and Mabel Fowler. It was the day I stopped going to school, playing with my friends, or hearing my mother laugh out loud again. But it was the first day I learned what evil is.*"

Taking a deep breath and finding the strength to continue, Tick described how Timothy pretended to have car trouble, luring her and her mother close to his van, eventually kidnapping them both at gunpoint.

"Where were you taken after Timothy Bird kidnapped you?"

"*His ranch in Utah.*"

"Do you remember what happened when you first arrived at the ranch, after you and your mother were abducted?"

"*When we stopped moving, Timothy Bird was honking the horn and yelled out, 'Home sweet home.' My mom was holding on to me, and I remember the van's back doors opening up all at once and seeing Timothy and another man standing next to him.*"

"Do you know who that other man was?"

"*Yes. I remember very clearly. The other man was Bart Madison.*"

"Miss Morgan, you do see Bart Madison in this courtroom here today?"

"*Yes, I do.*" Tick stared directly at Madison.

"Can you please point him out for the jury?"

With an intense and steely expression, she immediately identified Madison.

"What did Bart Madison do when you and your mother arrived at the ranch?"

"*Madison came into the van to get us out, but because Momma and I were tied up for such a long time, both of us had wet our pants. Madison called us disgusting, and I heard him tell Timothy that he didn't want his early Christmas present to smell like cat pee. Momma screamed at him and said if he did anything to hurt me, they had better kill her right then and there because she would kill them! Timothy laughed at her and told Madison to keep his hands off me—that he could find his own little girl to play with.*"

"What happened next?"

"*They made us take off our clothes, and they sprayed us with the water hose. Madison said terrible things to my momma while he was spraying us—things that were nasty and mean, and I remember how much the cold hard spray hurt my skin and how scared I felt.*"

"Miss Morgan, while you were in captivity at this ranch, did you ever see Bart Madison kill anyone."

"*Yes, I saw him kill two people directly. I also unmistakably heard him murdering two others.*"

"Who was the first person you saw Bart Madison kill at the ranch?"

"*Angela Parsons.*"

"How did he kill her?"

"*Madison poured gasoline on the wood he had piled up around her. My momma was crying and begged Timothy to stop what they were doing. Then Bart lit a match and dropped it on the wood. I closed my eyes, and Momma covered my ears to try to block out Angela's screams, but I could still hear her, and it made me so sick that I threw up. I'll never forget Bart hysterically laughing the whole time.*"

"Who was the next person you witnessed Bart Madison kill?"

"*Marjory Perkins.*"

"What did you witness?"

"*When Timothy Bird shot Marjory's legs, she fell into the grave that Marjory thought was for my mother and me. I watched Bart Madison shovel dirt over her while she screamed. He buried her alive.*"

"Who else do you believe Bart Madison killed?"

"*Sandra and Barbara Hopkins. Bart kidnapped them and brought them to the ranch after their car broke down on the way to school. Timothy was furious, calling him a 'stupid pedophile' and yelling at him for kidnapping the girls so close to the ranch that the police might come around looking for them. A few days later, Timothy ordered Madison to take care of the girls and clear out of his house and never return. The two men argued loudly for some time, but Madison did what he was told and killed Sandra and Barbara. He forced my mother and me to bury them.*"

Tick's testimony caused several jurors to become visibly upset, so the foreman stood to request a ten-minute recess to regroup. It was close to noon by this time, so the judge called for a one-hour lunch break.

Brad stayed with Tick in the anteroom during the break, a detached daughter lost in her memories, and he worried that the pain of reliving her past was causing more emotional damage. Respecting her need for privacy, Brad sat quietly nearby, only suggesting that she eat a bite or two of the sandwich he handed her.

After an hour, the court reconvened, and Marshall resumed his direct examination of Esther Morgan.

It was five o'clock when Durgan Marshall finished questioning his witness, one of the longest and most difficult days he had ever experienced in his career as a prosecutor. He had forced Tick to reveal and relive her horrid existence at the ranch, and though she had held up well, never faltering, he could tell that she was emotionally drained and exhausted. Everyone was.

Tick had conducted herself well on the stand—perhaps too well. Durgan worried that her stoicism might have put off some of the jurors. He was concerned that they would question why not a tear was shed and think that her lack of emotion was very odd, considering so much of her testimony had them gripping the edges of their seats.

⁕

The next morning, jury members, looking very weary, filed into the courtroom. Sunder Buckley's cross-examination was next, and Brad felt anxious. Tick hadn't slept well, tossing and turning throughout the night, but by morning, she had her game face on. It was a face Brad hadn't seen since her early days in the hospital—unreadable and expressionless.

Sunder Buckley's cross-examination started innocently enough but quickly soured.

"Esther, can I call you that, or would you prefer Miss Morgan?"

"Miss Morgan will be fine, Mr. Buckley. Using my first name implies familiarity and suggests friendship, and we both know that is not the case."

Buckley immediately felt relieved. Cross-examining a minor was never an easy proposition. Bullying a child on the stand can often backfire and runs the risk of turning off a jury. However, this was no ordinary child. She was fighting back from the start, and that meant that he could go on the offensive from the start.

Glancing over the jury, he cast a subtle smile.

"Miss Morgan, it will be. You testified that you and your mother were kidnapped in Sherman Oaks, California, correct?"

Tick met his eyes and typed.

"Yes."

"But your mother knew Timothy Bird before your alleged abduction, isn't that right?

"Yes."

"Bird frequently ate at the restaurant where she was a cook?"

"That's what my mother told me."

"They were friends, weren't they?"

"My mom was friendly with everyone."

"Indeed, she was. But she was especially friendly with Timothy Bird, wasn't she?"

473

"I don't know if she was or wasn't. I was five years old."

"Isn't it true that your beautiful, young, and single mother decided to run off with Timothy Bird willingly?"

"Are you talking about the person who locked her in a cave? The man who murdered my mother?"

"Miss Morgan, are you aware the police found absolutely no evidence of a struggle at the scene of the supposed abduction?"

"Does it seem wise to you to struggle with a gun at your head?"

"Your mom wasn't wealthy, was she?"

Tick shook her head, and Buckley reminded her that she must use her keyboard to answer his question.

"No."

"In fact, she was struggling financially, wasn't she?"

"I don't know. Mother would never have burdened me with her worries, but she worked very hard."

"That's right. She held two jobs, didn't she? She worked as a cook, as well as a caregiver for an elderly couple?"

"As I said, she worked hard."

"Miss Morgan, did your mother ever tell you that Timothy Bird was a very wealthy man?"

"No. And even if she knew that, it wouldn't have been important to her."

"Do you think you were important to your mom?"

"She died for me."

"Then don't you think that living a more comfortable life in the home of a wealthy man was a way out—a golden ticket for herself and you?"

"No. That's absurd."

"Now, you also claim that Timothy Bird held your mother against her will at this ranch, correct?"

"That is correct."

"But your mother was free to come and go as she pleased, wasn't she?"

"No. My mother did not have freedom of movement. Timothy always kept us separated when she went shopping, and he made it clear that if she spoke to anyone, he would kill me. I never left the ranch."

"Here are the FBI reports showing that she shopped on several occasions in Evanston, Wyoming. Do you wish to refute these findings?"

"*No… I just gave you an explanation.*"

"No, Miss Morgan, you told me a story… Another of your *stories* involves your mother's alleged *fear*. You claim that your mother *feared* for your life, but if she was as intelligent and capable as you have testified, don't you think she would have found a way to contact the authorities—dropped a note or whispered 'help me' to one of the clerks at one of the stores where she shopped?"

"Objection. Argumentative," asserted Durgan Marshall.

"Sustained," replied the judge.

"Let me rephrase the question. Your mother never made any effort to contact the authorities, either during any of her shopping sprees or during this alleged 'confinement,' did she?"

Tick didn't answer, only glowered at Buckley, who finally turned to the judge and requested that he instruct the witness to answer the question.

"You are required to respond to the questions, Miss Morgan," said the judge.

"*My mother was the strongest person on earth, with one failing. She wouldn't do anything that she believed might endanger me. No, I am not aware of any attempts she made to contact the authorities.*"

"Your mother was an excellent cook and housekeeper, wasn't she?"

"*Yes.*"

"Your mother was quite pretty, as well?"

"*Yes, she was beautiful—inside and out.*"

"A young woman named Marjory Perkins was serving as Timothy Bird's housekeeper when you and your mother first arrived at the ranch, true?"

"*Yes.*"

"And you testified that not long after you and your mother arrived, Ms. Perkins was killed, correct?"

"*Yes. I watched as Bart Madison buried her alive.*"

"Your mom benefited by her death, didn't she? Timothy put your mother in charge of the ranch's upkeep after Marjory's death, true?"

"Timothy put her in charge, but he was the only one who benefited. It just meant more work for her."

"You have claimed that Marjory Perkins abused you and your mother, and told Timothy Bird lies that she made up about the two of you. Do you still stand by those accusations?"

"Yes, she was an extremely abusive, small-minded person."

"And you have testified that Marjory Perkins despised your mother, correct?"

"Yes."

"And your mother knew Marjory Perkins despised her, correct?"

"Yes."

"So neither of you was sorry to see Marjory killed, were you?"

"She didn't deserve to get killed if that's what you mean."

"No, Miss Morgan, what I mean is this. Your mother provoked Timothy Bird to have her killed, isn't that right?"

"That's ludicrous. My mother would never seek to harm anyone. And you have it wrong. It was Madison who covered her up with dirt."

"So you say. So you say," Buckley responded.

"Objection," Marshall interjected. "Argumentative."

"Sustained," replied the judge.

"You didn't like Marjory Perkins, did you?"

"No."

"You hated her, didn't you?"

"Yes. Marjory tried to get us killed."

"And in retaliation, you used your influence with Timothy Bird to get him to turn against Marjory Perkins, didn't you?"

"No."

"Is it your testimony that you or your mother didn't in any way influence Timothy to kill Ms. Perkins?"

"It is. And for the record, nobody at the ranch influenced Timothy Bird, let alone a dispensable woman or her child—nobody! He only did what he wanted to do when he wanted to do it." Looking up at the

judge, she added, *"How many times do I have to repeat that it was Madison who killed her?"*

The question went unanswered.

"Did you make the statement, and I quote, 'Marjory should have run away like a deer, but she was way too fat?'"

"Yes, I did."

"Those were words you used for a woman who you claim was buried alive?"

"Yes. Marjory died a terrible death. My words were sinful and cruel."

Buckley paused and looked at the jury, a jury all eyes now locked on the girl in the witness stand, horror on their faces. *Sinful is right,* he thought, *and genuinely shocking.*

Buckley thought that the girl should be displaying real remorse over her admission, but she was sitting there, staring at him, her face expressionless. He could feel the jury starting to turn against her, and he was just getting started.

"In your testimony, you used the word the 'troubles' to explain the point in time when Timothy Bird began mistreating you and your mother. Is that an accurate statement?"

"Not exactly. We were always in danger, always locked up. I would define our 'troubles' as the time when we both knew Timothy would kill us. It was no longer if, but when. He was always beating us, more harshly each time."

"Did Marjory Perkins die before the troubles started?"

"Yes."

"Have you testified that you loved training with Timothy Bird and Janet Harrington—that they taught you everything about fighting—that you loved being outdoors, hunting for deer and pheasants?"

"Yes."

"Was this before or after Marjory Perkins was murdered?"

"After."

"Was this before or after the death of Angela Parsons?"

"After."

"So you witnessed the most horrific murders possible—a woman buried alive and a woman burned at the stake—but that didn't stop you from enjoying your training and hunting, did it?"

"*It was my only escape, an opportunity not to think about horrible things.*"

For much of Buckley's inquiry of Tick so far, he intentionally stood near the jury box—almost as if he were a member of the jury itself. But as the line of questioning continued, he gradually moved closer and closer to Tick, like a jungle cat moving in for the kill.

"You loved it *so* much that you never attempted to run away, did you?"

"*I didn't run away until the end.*"

"But you had your opportunities, didn't you?"

For the first time in the trial, Tick faltered, pausing in her testimony.

"*Yes.*"

"But you didn't want to?"

"*Not at first.*"

"Not until you had to run like a scared rabbit to save your own life," replied Buckley sarcastically.

Durgan Marshall rose for the first time in the trial, roaring like a lion. "Objection! Your Honor, counsel is maligning the witness!"

"Sustained," replied the judge, reprimanding Buckley. "This court will not tolerate deprecating commentary of this witness. Is that clear?"

"I apologize, Your Honor," Buckley replied, before turning his attention back to Tick. "Miss Morgan, you testify that Bart Madison did all these horrible things at the ranch while you were there."

"*Yes. I have told the court over and over. He stayed at the ranch for a long time.*"

"Don't you find it odd that the FBI has been unable to find any records of Bart Madison ever being in Utah? There are no records of airline flights, no gas receipts, or no rental car arrangements. Nothing."

"Objection!" shouted Marshall. "Speculative. The witness would not know about these records."

"Sustained," replied the judge.

"Let's talk about the FBI. You testified that you warned the FBI about bombs planted at the ranch, is that right?"

"*Yes.*"

"And despite your warnings and the information you supplied, they were all triggered, weren't they?"

"*Yes.*"

"When you warned the FBI, did you deliberately omit your knowledge of the triggering mechanisms?

"*No.*"

"Didn't you deliberately send the FBI into a trap?"

"*No!*"

"And yet, good men died, and any evidence that could be used against you was lost forever."

Durgan Marshall quickly rose to his feet again. "*Argumentative!* Your Honor, are you going to allow this to continue?"

"Sustained," replied the judge.

"Let's talk about Leslie Quinton, Miss Morgan. You say that months before you escaped, you overheard Timothy Bird tell Janet Herrington that Madison had kidnapped a girl in Atlanta and was taking her to his house on the bay."

"*That's right.*"

"You also remember hearing Mr. Bird say that he hoped Madison would gig himself during one of those jubilees he talked about. But, Miss Morgan, didn't this alleged conversation occur after the time you call 'the troubles'?"

"*Yes.*"

"Even before the troubles started, you have testified Timothy Bird didn't trust you, and he was very cautious about revealing business dealings in front of you. Is this correct?"

"*Yes.*"

"After the troubles, did you, in fact, still have access to the house where you could overhear conversations?"

"*Yes. Mom and I worked in and around the house for hours every day.*"

"And yet you want this jury to believe that a cautious man, a man who had become especially paranoid, would have spoken so openly with you around to hear him?"

"Yes," replied Tick, leaning forward, confronting Buckley. *"Perhaps it was like a line in the movie I just saw,* Pirates of the Caribbean... *Maybe you've heard it?* Dead Men Tell No Tales."

Nervous snickers heard coming from the jury drew a stern warning from the judge.

His face turning red, Buckley replied, "This is hardly a joking matter, Miss Morgan. Leslie Quinton, as you well know, is now dead, found here in Fairhope. You say you have never been to Fairhope?"

"That's correct."

"And yet you overheard Bird talking about a jubilee, which happens to be a rare maritime phenomenon?"

"Yes. I overheard a conversation between Janet and Timothy when he used the word jubilee as something Bart talked about."

"And it was this critical, obscure tip that led the authorities to my client, Bart Madison?"

"That's what I understand."

"And that's where Leslie Quinton's body and the other girls' remains were found?"

"Yes."

"Isn't it true that you killed these girls in a death match?"

"No! That is not at all true!"

"But you were in Fairhope training with Timothy Bird to be a killer, weren't you?"

"No, I was never in Fairhope."

"Oh, you have admitted to training to kill people, but just not in Fairhope, is that right?"

"As I have stated, I was never in Fairhope."

"You have testified that you overheard Timothy Bird talking to Janet Herrington about a volcano in Mexico that erupted, scattering ashes on his property southeast of Mexico City."

"Yes."

"And isn't it true that this uncanny recollection of a yet another obscure event led authorities to the site in Mexico?"

"*Yes.*"

"Isn't it true that you had months to think about these two obscure events before your interview with the FBI?"

"*I didn't have to think about them. I remembered the events.*"

"You researched the events to lead authorities to the sites without divulging that you had been to them. You created evidence to be granted immunity?"

"*No. I have a good memory.*"

Durgan Marshall groaned. He had explicitly told Esther not to volunteer information.

Buckley, smelling blood, continued his questioning. "And just how good is your memory?"

"*Ask me about any major news story over the past year. That is after I acquired Internet access to my iPad.*"

Buckley's question was ill-advised and not well thought out. "Okay, I'll play along. What happened on December 5, this past year?"

"*The Army Corps of Engineers stopped construction on the Dakota Access pipeline, and the President announced that Ben Carson would be secretary of the Department of Housing and Urban Development.*"

She waited for the court clerk to confirm her statement and then continued writing.

"*But there is more,*" added Tick. "*It is also the day you settled in court on divorce proceedings with your wife. They awarded her ten million dollars.*" Then in bold type, she added, "**I have studied you as well.**"

The courtroom erupted in laughter, but before Buckley could respond, Tick continued, "*In a* People *Magazine article, your ex-wife said you used to be a good man, but now all you do is destroy lives to defend monsters and entitled rich people, and she couldn't stand it anymore. It sounded like she loved you once. Maybe if you weren't such an ass, you could win her back.*"

"Move to strike!" shouted Buckley enraged.

"Sustained. The jury will disregard the witness's last comments. Young lady, I must ask you to refrain from giving out marital advice."

"*Okay, Your Honor.*"

Buckley was furious, and he turned to the girl and approached the witness box, towering over Tick.

In any other trial, Durgan Marshall would have interrupted, objecting that Sunder Buckley was intimidating his witness, but Marshall sat there, just as entranced by her performance as the jurors. Tick was calm, only a red line appearing on her cheek. The jury had sensed a brewing confrontation between the defense attorney and the young witness, and they didn't appreciate Buckley's tactics. The tables were turning. Durgan would let chips fall.

"This is not a game, young lady, and you are not going to get by with cheap parlor tricks."

"*It's not a parlor trick. Why don't you give me a real test. Ask me forty random words or numbers and see if I can repeat them. Test my memory and see where that leads you.*"

"I will ask the questions, thank you. You have admitted to having fought in two death matches, haven't you?"

"*No.*"

"No? That directly conflicts with your testimony yesterday. Didn't you fight in death matches with young David Bittner and Janet Herrington?"

"*A death match is when two people willingly agree to fight to the death. I was never a willing participant.*"

"Your clever phraseology won't change what you were involved in," Buckley caustically responded, not hiding his antagonism. "You fought in two battles when Timothy Bird instructed you to kill or be killed, isn't that right?"

"*Yes.*"

"One of the matches was against David Bittner, who, along with his father, came to the ranch seeking shelter in a storm?"

"*Yes.*"

"You cut him, didn't you? Lots of little cuts, and then you slashed his forehead, so blood got in his eyes?"

"*Yes, you know all about the fight.*"

"And you also fought Janet Harington. You cut her hamstring, leaving her helpless and perhaps crippled for life?"

"*Yes.*"

"Didn't you say, 'She was finished. I had won!'"

"*Yes.*"

"Isn't it true that Timothy Bird is notorious for murdering people who oppose him or who don't follow his directions? Haven't you testified that your mother would never dare defy him because he might kill her or you?"

"*Yes.*"

"And yet here you are. Why are you alive to tell your tales? What made you so special? How did you get away after not following his instructions?"

"*He had other plans for me, but that doesn't mean he didn't punish me.*"

"Timothy Bird's plans didn't involve hurting or eliminating his pet fighter, did they? He couldn't hurt his best asset, could he?"

"*He hurt me often, I can assure you of that.*"

"Yesterday, were we not told that you broke the nose of an EMT, tore the ligaments on the fingers of another EMT, and attacked a CPS agent, first breaking her finger then knocking her out?"

"*Yes.*"

"And did you make the statement if you find him, you need to kill him and make it slow?"

"*Yes.*"

"You also said, 'I was taught how to win, how to fight dirty, and use a knife and gun.'"

"*Yes.*"

"And you said, 'I loved the training; I was good. I mean, really good.'"

"*Yes.*"

"You said that Timothy said you had a natural talent for mayhem, right?"

"*Yes.*"

"You said you 'took the knife away from him and cut him up— lots of little cuts.'"

"*Yes.*"

"You said, and I quote, 'I should have killed them all when I had the chance.'"

"*Yes.*"

"Yes to all, Miss Morgan," replied Buckley. "You sound positively dangerous."

"Objection!"

"Sustained."

"Timothy Bird has been known to kill people who defy him. Is that a fair statement?"

"*Yes.*"

"But you and your mother survived some seven years at the ranch."

"*Yes.*"

"Didn't you defy him twice by refusing to kill David Bittner and Janet Harrington?"

"*I did.*"

"But here you are, alive."

"*Yes.*"

"So Timothy Bird finished your fights and did the killing for you? Is that correct?"

Tick leaned forward in her chair and was now nearly face-to-face with Sunder Buckley, typing with a furious expression, challenging him.

"*I answered you before, they planned something else for me, but I was unquestionably punished.*"

Durgan Marshall squirmed in his seat. Tick was going off the script again, challenging an experienced trial lawyer, and showing aggressiveness. The case was going up in smoke.

"David Bittner and Janet Herrington are dead. You admit to fighting them in death matches. I'm asking you again, why is it that you are alive?"

"*Are you thick-headed?*" She typed with a defiant expression on her face. "*They all, including your client Bart Madison, had other plans for me, but I was punished.*"

Tick set the trap, the timing was perfect, and Sunder Buckley fell right into it.

"You were punished, Miss Morgan? Clearly, not as harshly as all the victims lying in their graves in Utah, or as grievously as the three girls found brutally killed here in Mobile, right?"

"They were killed. I was not."

"You say they all punished you, but how was that exactly? Were you made to wash windows, scrub the floors, or some other hard-luck chore?"

Buckley watched Tick's immediate reaction, bracing herself as though she had been charged with an unknown power, looking almost exultant. She then settled back into her chair and looked over at the jury. Buckley moved away, waiting for her reply, recognizing the change in her demeanor, and instinctively feeling that something about her had changed.

Durgan Marshall was on his feet, prepared to shout an objection, but a small voice in his head told him to shut up and sit down.

There was a shocked silence in the room. Tick, her face white, stood up, turned her back to the courtroom, unbuttoned her blouse, and slowly removed it, pulling it away from her shoulders.

She showed the hushed jurors her thin, sinewy back and youthful skin crisscrossed with horrific scars. She paused for a minute before putting her blouse back on.

Buckley, realizing he had lost the round, turned to the judge with an outcry, "Objection! Move to strike, Your Honor! The witness is unstable, aggressive, and noncooperative. I ask that she be declared a hostile witness. Further, please instruct the jury to disregard this demonstration. She freely admits that Timothy Bird, not my client, administered her beatings. I also request that Your Honor instruct her to sit down."

Tick quickly typed a question and dangled it out in all-caps for the judge and jury to see.

"I'M SORRY, YOUR HONOR, BUT I THOUGHT MR. BUCKLEY WANTED TO KNOW HOW TIMOTHY BIRD AND BART MADISON PUNISHED ME. HE ASKED THAT QUESTION, AND I GAVE THE COURT MY ANSWER."

"Objection!" shouted Buckley. "The question was about Timothy Bird's punishments. My client was never at the site."

"Overruled," countered the judge. "Your question was made in reference to the witness's statement that they all—including Bart Madison—had other plans for her. It was inclusive of your client. If you don't want answers to your questions, then I would advise you not to ask them."

The judge continued, "Well, Mr. Buckley did ask the question. Yes, the court is interested in learning how you were punished, Esther."

"*You saw how Timothy punished me for not finishing his matches, but Madison was far more sadistic. Timothy killed and tortured as a means to his ends. Madison did it because he loved it.*"

Pointing an accusing finger at Madison, Esther then continued to type. "*I heard Sandra and Barbra screaming all night when that man tortured them. I helped Momma dig their graves, and we even put their cut off fingers in a little box. I saw what happened to Momma when she tried to stop Madison. He struck her so hard that he broke her cheekbone.*"

Then, pausing, she looked directly at the jury and typed, "*Yes, I always fought to win. I wouldn't be alive today if I hadn't. I am not a saint like my mother, but I never killed anyone!*"

Pointing her finger again at Madison, she continued, "*My mother wasn't afraid of Madison or Timothy, and she never joined their evil cult. She said that God would protect her, so she went against those fiends in every way she could. She gave the prisoners her food, washed their wounds, and prayed out loud with them every night. They punished her far more than I ever was. Momma always said that even a slave should do his best, set a good example, as if working for God, and she never gave in!*"

Realizing he was losing control of the case, Buckley stepped back. "Your Honor, I would like to request a recess. Miss Morgan needs time to compose herself."

But it was not to be.

"Do you need a break, Esther?" the judge asked.

"*No,*" typed Tick. "*I wish to stand and defend myself. The Constitution allows me that right.*"

"Judge Benson," Buckley protested, "will Your Honor please remind Miss Morgan that she is not on trial. We all know she is exempt from prosecution. This is about an innocent man, Bart Madison."

"*Not true!*" Tick responded. "*You have put my mother and me on trial. You claim my mother voluntarily joined and supported a monster—that's a lie. You claim I have been in Mexico and here in Alabama—another fabrication. After everything I have experienced, I am not intimidated by your accusations. I know what is true. As far as that weasel you're defending, is there any wonder why he hasn't lifted his head once to look at me? His body language says it all, Mr. Buckley.*"

"Objection!" shouted Buckley once again. "Miss Morgan is not a body language expert, and she must be instructed to answer my questions without embellishment!"

"Sustained. Miss Morgan, I'm going to ask you to try and limit your answers to counsel's questions."

Buckley continued, trying to salvage his examination. "My client did *not* cause those scars, did he? You testified that you were Timothy Bird's property, and my client wasn't even allowed to touch you, isn't that right?"

"*There was an exception to that rule,*" Tick typed out. "*And your client will remember it well, Mr. Buckley.*"

Tick stared at Madison with contempt.

"*May I explain what that was, Your Honor?*"

"Yes, I will hear it. You may continue, Esther," the judge ruled.

"*After I was allowed to work in the kitchen, I added a scoop of chicken droppings into Bart's shepherd's pie. He spent the next week in the bathroom with dysentery. Bart told Timothy how I told him that he deserved to be as sick as a dog and that he should just be taken outside and hosed off. When Timothy figured out that I had something to do with Bart's condition, he allowed the weasel to punish me, as long as it didn't permanently disfigure me.*"

Tick leaned over in her chair, removed her shoes, and then asked the judge permission to show the jury her feet. She then lifted her legs so that the judge and jury could see the soles of her feet pockmarked with round-shaped scars.

"*Madison smokes Panter Blue cigars. He tied me to a chair, tipped it over so he could grip my feet, and then he burned them with his cigar, laughing the whole time. He said that my feet were the perfect size for his small cigars!*"

She peered over at Madison once again, her face triumphant. "*I was nine years old when it happened. Madison burned me eight times before Timothy appeared and put an end to it. You never made me cry, did you Bart?*"

"*Judge Benson,*" Tick persisted, "*no one except Madison smoked at the ranch, and I never saw him without one of those cigars in his mouth. Timothy hated it, and he made my mother pick up all the butts Madison left scattered around the property. If you check the autopsy reports, I think that you'll find that the other girls had similarly shaped burn marks on their bodies. Also I'm sure that the officers searching the house in Fairhope found his Panter Blue cigars and the butts all over the place.*"

Looking at Buckley, she added, "*The odds are good that he has even asked his lawyer to purchase cigars for him.*"

"Objection! Non-responsive, move to strike!" Buckley shouted. "There's been no evidence put forth supporting any claims about these cigars. Further, I am not the one under examination."

"Sustained. Do you have additional questions for the witness, counsel?"

"No. Not at this time, Your Honor."

"I think we have all had enough today. The witness is excused, and the court will resume tomorrow at 9:00 a.m."

Tick, with her shoes back on her feet, head held high, athletically jumped down to the courtroom floor, passing in front of Madison being led away by an officer. The jurors had lingered, captivated by the young witness; they watched as she paused and fearlessly turned to watch Madison's departure. Her face was white, exhaustion, pain etched on her features. She turned to the jury box, removing the tinted eyeglasses she had been wearing, and then looked at each juror in the eye. Then, her back ramrod straight, posture perfect, she left the courtroom.

CHAPTER

44

Repercussions and Deliberations

Sunder Buckley spent a good part of the evening alone, sitting at the bar's far end at The Battle House Renaissance Mobile Hotel. He was in a reflective mood, not an angry one.

Esther Morgan completely nailed it, and nailed me, Buckley acknowledged. She had poked and prodded him throughout the entire trial, but provoking him to anger by quoting his ex-wife's exact words from the *People* Magazine article was the beginning of the end for his case.

"Sunder makes his living destroying lives to defend monsters and entitled rich people. I can't take it anymore…" The words echoed in his head.

Esther Morgan had set him up perfectly; how was he to know that she was a freakish savant? What in the world had prompted him to challenge her by picking the date of his divorce?

She had trounced him like he was a little schoolboy, first getting him angry by goading him about his divorce, then getting in his face, baiting him to ask how they punished her, including Bart Madison in the question.

Had they set him up from the start of the trial, he wondered? No, he believed that Durgan Marshall was agitated when Esther varied from his script. She crushed him on her own.

He wondered why he had asked the question. He never asked a question for which he didn't have an answer. It was a fundamental rule followed by any competent trial lawyer.

In minutes, she had completely turned the case around. Buckley had seen the juror's faces as they left the courtroom; the women on the jury just wanted to hug her, and the men wanted to lynch Madison. They had all spent the last minutes of the trial looking over at him, wondering if he had purchased cigars for Madison.

Buckley knew what was coming. Durgan Marshall would call back witness after witness. Images entered into his mind: pictures of the crime scene, the house in Fairhope, Panter Blue cigar butts everywhere, autopsy reports revealing burn marks on the victims' bodies. Those marks on Esther's feet and those of the other girls would precisely match the size of the cigarillos Madison smokes.

After that, Durgan would call him to the stand to find out if Madison had ever asked him or his staff to purchase Panter Blue cigars, and he would have to claim attorney-client privilege, but they would provide purchase records. The little weasel had begged him to buy him a couple of packs. He had complied, and the purchase had taken place at a shop just a block away from his hotel.

Even worse for the case was the credibility Esther had given her mother. Mobile was in the Bible belt, after all, where children who respected their parents were to be commended. Esther Morgan had utterly won them over, and now it would be far more difficult to explain away information found in Tammy Rockford's brassiere. There would be no damage control once that got out.

In the past, he would have doubled down on his attempts to discredit her. He fancied himself a genius at casting doubt in jurors' minds about the integrity of witnesses, and his ex-wife was right. He had destroyed more than a few sterling reputations defending criminals and entitled stars.

He wouldn't be going after Esther in the morning. If he put her back on the stand, he knew what was coming—or maybe the problem was that he didn't. Esther knew his client backward and forward, and there was no doubt in his mind she was capable of setting other traps. Then Durgan Marshall would put her back on the stand to describe Bart Madison's crimes, and the girl would recall every detail and every blow. He had been warned and now believed that Esther had a near-photographic memory. She would illustrate a picture of horror, and now the jury would believe every word she typed.

He would continue his defense of Madison along the lines he had laid out. Frankly, it wouldn't bother him one bit if the little weasel got the chair. He started this trial believing in his client's innocence—now, not at all. How strange, Buckley thought as he nursed his drink, that he should feel so relieved by his decision not to put Esther on the stand again. He was starting to admire Esther Morgan. Buckley had never encountered a witness who had bested him. She had beaten him fair and square, and he respected her for it.

As he drank his scotch, Esther's comment floated into his thoughts. Could she be right? Was there a chance he could win back Julia?

Dialing his associate's phone number, he braced himself to spend the night working. He still was a lawyer with a client who, by law, required his best efforts.

∽₰₰₰∽

Linda Marshall rushed outside the house to greet her husband when she heard the car pull up into their driveway. She knew that Durgan would be exhausted after a long day in court, and she was worried about him. In truth, the man was tired but couldn't have been happier or more relieved to be home.

"How did it go? I've been praying for you all day."

"Esther went rogue and ignored everything I told her about keeping her cool, hiding her intellect, and not getting angry, and then she went out and won the trial for me," replied Durgan as he hung up his coat. "She ignored me, and starting with her first words, she went right after him. She was superb. Madison is finished."

His wife chuckled and drooped her arms over his shoulders as he turned back toward her from the closet. "Why the long face, then?"

Durgan kissed his wife gently, then walked over to the fireplace hearth, picked up a photograph, and carefully examined it. "How old was Cora when she started to play soccer?"

"I think she was five," said Linda, her mind flashing over to her daughter, captain of the soccer team, now in her third year at LSU, remembering the early days when soccer looked more like a moving rugby scrum, all the children clustered around the ball, making their way up and down the field.

"We've given Cora a good life, haven't we?" Durgan asked reflectively. "Soccer camps, trips to the cabin, the best private schools—Esther Morgan has had none of that. She hasn't had formal schooling since she was five, let alone time on a playground, no camps, no childhood. Her life has been a daily fight for survival, a fight that we have just made riskier by putting her up on the stand. We are all using her. Buckley wants to get his client off, and I want to convict him. Esther is smarter and tougher than I ever could have imagined, but she was so earnest, so distressed when she talked about her mother. I'm sorry, sweetheart. I'm just tired. I should probably try to get some sleep."

Linda knew when her husband was exhausted. It was better to let him work through his thoughts on his own. Yet this was different. Reaching for him, she asked, "You believe her, though? Madison is guilty?"

"Yes. Every word Esther has said is true, heartbreakingly true."

"He won't be killing young girls again."

"No, he won't."

"Then set your mind on that, my dear."

The trial continued for another three days, with two new startling revelations, both of which were particularly welcomed by Brad. The first was that, in a determined overnight search, the FBI found an old security tape taken at the Salt Lake City airport in the smoking lounge. There was a clear shot of Bart Madison smoking a Panter Blue cigar. The video's date coincided perfectly with Tick's timeline for the deaths of Sandra and Barbra Hopkins, the two victims Tick claimed Madison had killed at the ranch. Then other tapes were found. Madison had traveled under a false identity; it explained the lack of ticketing data.

The second revelation was far more emotional, and Tick had openly cried when the prosecution introduced an unexpected piece of evidence. It was a small, stained, badly decomposed piece of paper that had taken forensic specialists at the FBI weeks to decipher. It was a note from Alissa Morgan to Tammy Rockford, the young rodeo star—a note found on Tammy's remains, tucked under her bra, next to her heart.

My dear Tammy,

I know how frightened and panicky you must be feeling, but please know that you have two friends close by who love and care about you. Esther and I are with you always, and you are in our thoughts and prayers. Although we are also powerless and may share a fate difficult to think about, we can all take hope and find strength in God's Word, as found in John 11:25–26.

Jesus said, "I am the resurrection and the life. Whoever believes in me will live, even though they die; and whoever lives by believing in me will never die."

This is God's promise to His children.

I love you, child.

—Alissa Morgan

The trial ended with one of the courthouse's shortest jury deliberations on record for a murder trial: one hour and forty-five minutes. Bart Madison was found guilty on all counts.

Tick was hiding in her own world on the flight from Mobile to Washington. She had drawn her legs up to her chest and was hunched against the window, doing math homework and taking no interest in watching the different landscapes passing beneath them.

Sitting across from Tick, Ruth Evers watched her solve a few math problems before reaching into her briefcase and pulling out an active case file of a wealthy teenager kidnapped in Detroit and being held for ransom. Just before the plane landed in Washington, Evers went to the restroom, leaving the report along with pictures on the table. Tick reached over and picked up the photo of a girl tied to a chair with the day's paper propped up against her legs, confirming that she was still alive.

As Tick was studying the picture, Brad reached over to retrieve the photo, but Evers, who was returning, stopped him.

"So what do you think, Tick? Something doesn't feel right about this case, but I don't know what it is," she probed.

Tick looked at the photo disdainfully, scribbling on her pad, *"She's faking. Look at her face, her eyes. There's no fear there. You should check out all her friends, especially her new ones."*

Then she added, *"She's either stupid or just naïve. She may get killed as soon as her friends get whatever they want."*

Tick passed the photograph back to Agent Evers and then disappeared into her studies again.

⌒⟳⌒

On the drive back to the office, Evers turned to Agent Parker. "She's right. We need to question all of her close friends again, old and new. Find out which families might have a cabin, a second home, or access to an out-of-the-way place. I think this is a staged kidnapping."

"So Tick has gotten under your skin, too. Am I right?"

"Actually," replied Evers, "I think she's a national treasure. She's not only one tough cookie but also the smartest, most intuitive person I have ever run across. I would love to get her into the agency someday. Heck, she could run it if she wanted to."

Parker, seizing an opportunity to express his skepticism about Tick and Evers' glowing evaluation of her, replied, "Right. I guess you're not the least bit uneasy about placing so much trust in her?"

"Meaning?" Evers responded.

"Well, for starters, she baited a seasoned trial lawyer into asking how Madison and Timothy punished her. She set Buckley up and then destroyed Madison's credibility with her testimony about the cigars—talk about a clever piece of strategy! There she was, on the stand, seemingly furious, sucking Buckley in, letting him think he was painting her for the jury as hostile and volatile. Tick led him to ask reckless questions, all the while scheming how to bring him down and, most importantly, aiming to destroy Madison. Did you see how she reacted once he took the bait? Like a wounded angel, it's surreal. How can we be sure she isn't fooling us? Are you 100 percent certain she hasn't ever killed before? We know she is capable of it. Look at the reports on her training. And then, there's the matter of her speechlessness. Every doctor's report I've read says that she is capable of speech. Why isn't she talking?"

"What's gotten into you anyway?" Evers asked. "She isn't a killer, and you know it. Most definitely, she's not a liar. Every autopsy and every lead we follow confirms what she has told us. David Bittner was hit on the top of his head by a shovel—a direct blow so powerful, and at such an angle, that no twelve-year-old girl, not even Tick, could have delivered it. Janet Herrington's knife wounds were just as Tick described. If Tick were the killer, why would she drop her knife and pick up an old screwdriver to finish her? Remember the autopsy report? The cause of death was a screwdriver driven through the heart. It doesn't add up. And, no, she still isn't speaking, but Dr. Barnes feels it's tied to a traumatic event connected to her mother, and I'm not about to question the doctor's judgment. I agree with Dr. Barnes. Tick will start talking again when she is good and ready."

"I suppose," Parker said.

"There is something else you need to consider, Parker. Look at the people who believe in her and support her: Brad Hughes, Dr. Barnes, Hoger, Wright, Wong, to name just a few. These are solid, good people, tops in their fields, all of them highly competent and not the least bit naïve. Do you think Tick could pull the wool over all of their eyes, or mine, for that matter? She has found a safe harbor and is just starting to grow and come out of her shell. I expect wonderful things from her in the future. Until then, we are going to keep her alive and give her every bit of training we can."

Agent Parker didn't reply. He had long ago learned that when his boss was serious about a project, she would stop at nothing to accomplish her goals. No matter what hurdles they would have to jump over, Tick's training would continue, he suspected, even after Timothy Bird's capture.

He agreed with Ruth Evers; she was right, the child was remarkable, and now he felt small.

⁓ↄ⊙ᴑ⊙ↄ⁓

Now disguised as an older man, Timothy Bird checked into a tiny room on State Street in Salt Lake City, a bed, a chest of drawers, and a small table with chairs the only furnishing. He had failed to find her in time, and now the whole world knew about Esther Morgan and the role she had played in leading the FBI to Mexico and Madison. He would be on the run now, hiding from both the FBI and the Epilektoi. He had resources, fake passports, money squirreled away in foreign accounts, and a home on Lake Bariloche in Argentina.

He needed to start his search where it had begun. Someone in Salt Lake City had to know where the FBI had taken her. He would find Esther, kill her, and start a new life. Even if he failed, others would succeed—she was marked now. Still, he wanted to be the one that finished her.

He was hungry; too bad Alissa wasn't around to cook for him.

Joyless Days

For Brad, the days following the Mobile trial had been the most unsettling period he had experienced with Tick since before her adoption. He met with Mattie at her office soon after returning to Utah to review Tick's testimony and discuss how the trial may have emotionally impacted his daughter. Mattie was glad to see Brad, but the warm welcome lasted a short time once she started reading the trial transcript.

As she began leafing through Tick's witness testimony at her desk, she would stop to stick a marker tab on a page, then continue turning the pages until stopping again, reading, and then flagging something that grabbed her attention. Her relaxed expression changed when she got to Buckley's cross-examination of Tick, becoming tense and pinched, and when she had finally turned the last page, she looked up at Brad, poker-faced.

"Tell me how you feel about the trial."

To his ear, Mattie's request sounded like an oral examination, so his response was mindfully measured under her probing eyes, being careful to share helpful information.

"Much as you would have felt, I suspect," Brad said. "It was a brutal trial. Buckley was ruthless with Tick, but he did what you'd expect of a clever defense attorney. The FBI's case was not rock solid, and it came down to her word against Madison's. Tick did what she felt she had to do to get a conviction, and—"

"Brad, I'm sorry to cut you off like this," Mattie interrupted. "Please understand, but I'm going to need some time to go over this transcript very carefully by myself and absorb what happened. It's important for Tick that I study and evaluate this carefully."

Brad nodded at Mattie, truthfully relieved that she had just taken the pressure off of him to give a coherent report on the trial. The image of Edvard Munch's painting, *The Scream*, came to mind as he thought about his daughter's reaction to once again being put through hell.

"Of course, Mattie," Brad said, standing up. "I'm grateful that you'll be doing that. Heaven knows Tick needs you, so I'll leave you to it. That's your transcript to keep, by the way."

"Thanks, Brad," Mattie said, and she stood to walk him out. "And I'll see you tonight, remember? I'll come by the house at six to help Tick with dinner."

"Uh, about that," Brad responded, thankful for the reminder. "Tick asked me to reschedule our dinner tonight for a later date."

"Oh? Why reschedule? What has kept her so busy since you got back?" Mattie asked.

"Not much, actually…just working out in the barn."

Mattie's response was dismissive as she opened the door to usher Brad out. "Hiding out, most likely. Tell her that I will see her at six and that we will be cooking lamb chops together. I'll see you then."

Dinner was delicious but not particularly relaxing. Mattie began pressuring Tick to open up by questioning her trial strategy, a tactic she hoped might elicit some reaction.

"Help me understand," Mattie prodded, "why did you suddenly expose the scars on your back in court when you had strictly prohibited your lawyer from even mentioning them? I'm also confused about why you hadn't told him about your feet and Madison's cigars. The other girls' autopsy reports would have confirmed your testimony if you had given Marshall permission to disclose it. Was all that drama necessary?"

"*Juror 5, the jury foreman,*" Tick began writing, "*she was the tall, stately looking woman who never took her eyes off me. She became my canary in the coal mine, if you understand my meaning. I could see her expressions and get an idea of the opinions she was forming, and I knew the others would follow her lead. I began seeing real distrust in her eyes when she looked at me, so I had to make it real for her—let her know the truth with her own eyes."*

In bolder lettering, Tick then wrote, **"In any case, revealing my back and showing what Bart did to my feet with his disgusting cigars was <u>mine</u> to expose or not."**

"Fair enough, Tick," Mattie answered. "It's okay. That was your call, and I trust your instincts."

Tick continued with a note of self-pity, a trait she rarely displayed. *"Juror 5 seemed like a good person and someone I wish I could get to know. It's unfair and sad that my life prevents that from ever happening."*

Reading that, Brad chimed in, "Delete the word 'ever' in that sentence and add 'right now' at the end if you want to get any sympathy from me. And hold on a second—"

Brad grabbed his phone and scrolled over to his Bible app.

"Here it is: 'For I know the plans I have for you,' declares the Lord. 'Plans to prosper you and not to harm you plans to give you hope and a future.'"

"That's Jeremiah 29:11, Dad, and I appreciate what you're trying to say, but you've taken that scripture out of context, as most people who are looking to feel better about their life do. If you read the verse just before, God says that he will redeem the Jews after seventy years of exile in Babylon. The 'you' in 29:11 is plural, meaning the entire nation of Israel. It happened just as prophesied."

"I stand corrected, Miss Smarty-Pants," Brad replied. "Still I believe the words have meaning for all of us."

Mattie changed the subject. "On a different note, what if Madison appeals his conviction? Are you prepared to testify again?"

"I hope they let him out of jail!" Tick wrote. *"His lifespan would become a matter of days out of prison, you realize. He is nothing but a liability to Timothy and the Epilektoi. They would find him and kill him quickly. Bart knows this better than anyone! You'll see, he'll appeal his death sentence and then strike a plea deal for life imprisonment. He's a coward and is afraid to die."*

The night ended on a tense note when Mattie discussed the coming week's schedule for Tick—a schedule sprinkled with plays, movies, and hikes that would consume much of Tick's free time.

Tick's response was less than grateful.

"I know what your goals are with all these activities, Mattie. You've decided that I'm a dysphoric basket case, and your treatment is to keep me too busy to think."

Mattie paused before answering Tick calmly, but her voice brooked no dissent.

"One, you are not a basket case. Two, you have made a tremendous amount of progress integrating back into society, and I'm not about to let you crawl back into a cave. Further, if you think that going to a performance of *Miss Saigon* is punishment—well, I can live with that, and that's just the way it's going to be until I'm convinced that you have recovered your footing."

"You're not thinking of interfering with my training, are you?" Tick reacted, her scar now bright red. *"You cannot interfere with my training!"*

Mattie's tone remained even but firm. "You can continue with your training and exercise, just as long as you don't overdo it and injure yourself. I will be keeping a close watch on you!"

As the weeks went by, Tick seemed to close down even more. It wasn't that she was rude, disrespectful, or unkind, but all her attention focused on combat training and schoolwork. A call from one of Tick's teachers indicated that things at school were not that great. Her grades were excellent, but the girl everyone had come to know and love had confusingly stopped interacting socially; she seemed blue. The teacher asked if everything was all right at home and if there was anything she could do to help.

Professor Becket was the exception, seemingly understanding what was behind Tick's mood change. He and Tick had earlier established a strong bond, and she continued to enjoy working with him. Tick had never divulged to Becket her true identity, yet he had formed some strong convictions during her recent absence. The professor sensed that she needed some space and adjusted the curriculum accordingly. While he continued the visits, they became less rigorous and included more chess and advanced game playing—activities Tick engaged in enthusiastically.

Her physical training did not fare as well; during the first week back, she badly sprained two fingers in practice, becoming infuriated when Grandpa and Wong stopped the session. Mattie insisted that until her fingers healed, the sessions were canceled, generating a heated confrontation between Brad and Tick about the future of her training. One such outburst left Brad considerably shaken.

"*You know he is going to find me, don't you?*" Tick scrawled. "*Everyone close to me is in danger. I have made you all targets. That's how it works with him, Dad! I need to disappear somewhere far away from here.*"

"Stop this nonsense!" Brad barked as he grabbed her iPad to shut it off, alarmed that she could be serious. "What do you think would happen to me, to all of us, if you left us and disappeared somewhere? That would be so much worse than anything Bird could ever do. It would destroy us. Think about that."

Tick didn't respond, but Brad grabbed her chin, forcing her to look him in the eye. "God put you with me on that cliff for a reason, and He knew what He was doing! I love you more than you could imagine. You are my beloved daughter, and I want you to swear to me right now that you will never leave us and that we will continue to face this together until Bird departs the face of this earth. Swear to me, Tick!"

Tick gently removed her father's grip on her chin, her beautiful eyes flooding with tears, and she crossed her heart and nodded.

Retrieving her iPad, she wrote, "*Okay, but I pray he comes soon. Either we will be going to heaven, or Timothy will be going to hell, but I want it over.*"

Tick's withdrawn behavior also impacted Ana. She tirelessly tried to coax the moody teenager into helping in the kitchen and followed Tick around with one treat after another, doing her best to keep some weight on the girl. Ana began arming herself with an ice pack or two, which Tick often accepted to forestall a bad bruise; the girl was treating her body brutally.

One day, Ruth Evers called to tell Brad that his daughter was about to come into a nice sum of money. Thanks to Tick's insight, they found the girl in the photograph, in perfect health, the kidnapping staged, just as Tick suspected. The mock victim, the spoiled daughter of wealthy parents, and three of her buddies saw their plan as a quick way to get money. In place of the $2 million ransom the delinquents demanded, the girl's parents requested that five hundred thousand dollars be awarded to the person who led the FBI to the vacation condo in Palm Springs, California.

Ruth also reported that Bart Madison had not appealed his conviction. Instead, he struck a plea deal by agreeing to provide Epilektoi members' names, roles in the organization, and two other victims' gravesites.

Lastly, Evers delivered the disturbing news that Susan Messener had been murdered. Timothy Bird was the main suspect. The former CPS administrator's tongue had been cut out and shoved down her throat.

The foolish woman made the mistake of talking to a tabloid reporter in which she made disparaging remarks about Esther and the man who rescued her. After the article hit the street, the FBI interviewed Ms. Messener, and thankfully, she did not know Brad's identity. Messener did believe that he lived in Utah and was not a hiker from back east—part of the FBI's cover story. Her murder was not a positive development.

If Messener had told Bird that she thought Tick's rescuer lived in Utah, what did that mean? Plausibly, it wasn't significant. Utah was a big state, and Timothy wouldn't know about the adoption; he would still believe that Esther was out of state. Further, Utah was probably the last place he would show his face; every law enforcement agent in Utah had seen his picture hundreds of times.

Fortunately, the gag order during Madison's trial had held. Tick's appearance and her muteness never appeared in the press. The jury foreman had put out the only statement made about Tick. She stated that Esther Morgan had acted in self-defense at the ranch and the hospital and that she had taken an extraordinary risk to bring a serial killer to justice. "It's time to stop all this speculation and leave this remarkable girl alone," the juror said.

The juror's compelling comment, Madison's conviction, and Tick's reward were the only positive things to come out of the trial. The impact of the trial on his daughter was far more profound than Brad would ever have imagined.

CHAPTER

Closure

A gust of wind blew flakes of snow off an overhanging branch, and Brad, refreshed by the cold crystals hitting his face, paused to take in the scenery. Tick was leading him and Mattie up a well-grooved deer trail to the side of the rocky ridge that towered over the Death Ranch property. She was wearing a tattered and timeworn John Deere cap, something familiar she spotted an hour ago and reclaimed from the old barn, the only structure left standing on the ranch.

Exploring in the barn, early in her captivity, Tick found the green cap with a yellow logo imprinted above the visor, a forgotten relic from some unknown person. The cap grew to be Tick's prized possession—an unexpected gift from her imaginary kindlier existence, sheltering her from the blistering summer sun and keeping her head warm during cold winter days. Now it was back on her head once again.

Tick had put in a formal request to return to the ranch site months earlier, and Mattie had pushed it through, hoping it would help with Tick's depression. The FBI reluctantly conceded to allow her the chance to go, but not without agents taking specific security measures in advance of her coming. Hoger, Grandpa, and Linn had gone up to the location the day before, touring the property with a local ranger. The ranch property was fenced off and still posted as a crime scene, but the site had become an attraction to the public. Any advance word heralding Tick's impending visit was out of the question because of the possibility that the Epilektoi might have followers in the area.

A ranger had been stationed at the ranch entrance when Tick, Brad, Mattie, and Hoger arrived in an unobtrusive Department of Interior pickup, Tick's face hidden from view. Grandpa and Linn, armed with tactical weapons, had come in an hour earlier and were out of sight, strategically positioned to protect the group. Hoger kept well behind Tick, Mattie, and Brad, and looking back down the trail, Brad spotted him. He knew Linn and Grandpa were ahead. Every possible precaution for their safety was in place.

The pilgrimage had been distressing, and as they hiked up the ridge, Brad hoped that the last leg of this mission would be less painful. The day started when they located the site that had, for a short time, held Alissa Morgan's body. Now just a plot of land, a remnant of a graveyard revealing depressions in the ground: ghastly hollows created by man's cruelty, an obscenity that nature would obliterate in time. Tick, Brad, and Mattie scattered dozens of the white roses they had brought with them around each spot where victims had once lain. Tick shook her head "no" in response to Brad and Mattie's offer to give her some time there by herself, so they went on.

Then they visited the ranch house's site, the structure destroyed—only charred, splintered wood and building debris remained, intermixed with rocks and boulders. The cave where Tick and Alissa lived had collapsed and was completely blocked off by fallen boulders from the overhanging cliff. Weeds and building fragments had plundered the vegetable garden where Tick and her mother had spent endless hours.

The final stop was Tick's secret garden, an oasis located higher up on the mountain and the place where she often retreated whenever Timothy allowed her the freedom to roam—before the "troubles" began. Brad prayed that this wouldn't be just another bitter pill to swallow, that this wistful memory from her fractured childhood would bring some solace.

Fourteen years old now and no longer a child, Tick helped Mattie navigate the rocks and boulders as they hiked, Brad trailing. After the trial, he had felt an abrupt disconnect with his daughter, who became closed off, distant, and uncomfortable with communicating anything on a personal level. She rarely smiled and pushed herself relentlessly in school and her fight training sessions. Ana believed that Tick's soul was in another place, at least for the time being.

Maybe this visit to the ranch would help put her past behind her, Brad hoped, but not with any high degree of optimism. The past weeks had been awful.

Tick continued in the lead, but the path to her secret garden looked as though it had come to an end, enormous boulders blocking the way. Tick nimbly scrambled up a small ledge leading to a gap in the seemingly impassable terrain and motioned for Mattie and Brad to follow.

Yards ahead, to their unbelieving eyes, Brad and Mattie were looking at something that seemed expressly created by God and hidden in a place for Tick to find. It was a secret destination, a page torn out of a child's exquisitely illustrated picture book about a magical garden. A small waterfall filled a crystal clear water pool, shaded by stately pine trees dressed in gowns of crystalline snow. Light, reflecting from their limbs, sparkled like millions of tiny stars, and a smooth sheet of luminous granite was a natural walkway into the pool for use on a hot summer day. Slabs of rock covered in soft green moss protected the entire sanctuary.

Tick's secret garden was breathtaking.

Brad looked around and caught his daughter looking back at him with a smile he hadn't seen in weeks. He felt a surge of optimism, thinking that being there, in this Eden-like garden, was a sign of good things to come.

Unfortunately, he was dead wrong.

CHAPTER

The Devil Pays a Visit

April 18, a few weeks after Tick's trying visit to the death ranch, Tick and Brad rose at four in the morning to drive to the Thomas farm. Jim and Melanie Thomas would be driving to Evanston, Wyoming, to attend a horse auction, and Brad wanted to get to their farm in time to help the Thomas daughters with the morning chores before saddling up a couple of horses and riding out to a neighboring farm that had recently been optioned for purchase by an unknown party. The sisters would not be going along on the ride this time because they had promised to organize the tack room in the stable before their folks returned that evening.

The sunrise that morning found Brad in a more philosophical than annoyed mood as he looked over at his daughter, thankfully sound asleep with her head on a pillow against the Jeep window, a line of drool running down her chin. Sometimes when she slept sitting up, she tended to drool, and while Brad found this picture quite endearing, it was another thing he did not dare mention. He had learned that daughters could be highly sensitive about the silliest things.

Brad could easily justify being irritated with Tick for turning into a prize grouch since the Mobile trial, reflecting on Tick's cantankerous interactions with him on her iPad that morning.

"Was it necessary to shake me awake like that! I told you I would set my alarm clock. You're the grown-up here, so why can't you look at that

farm property by yourself and let me stay to help Rachael and Megan in the stable?"

She would enjoy herself once they arrived, he knew. The Thomas sisters thought the world of Tick, and they had become good friends. Neither girl was the least bit intimidated by Tick's intellect, how well she could do just about everything on the farm, or how she could cook better than anyone they ever knew. Though Tick was not enamored with horses like so many of Megan and Rachael's schoolmates, she became a strong rider and was comfortable helping around the stables.

As predicted, Tick brightened up when the sisters ran out to the car and greeted their mute friend enthusiastically. They assigned Tick to tend the chickens while Brad assisted them in the stables. When Tick went into the house to start breakfast, she was cradling six freshly laid eggs, which she scrambled, along with pork sausage patties and her "over the top" waffles with strawberries and cream. After they wolfed down the meal and washed the dishes, Brad saddled two beautifully spotted Appaloosa mares and brought them around to the house.

Brad and Tick began their ride in the fresh morning air with frost tipping the long grass blades over and puffs of mist billowing out from the horses' nostrils. Their ride to the adjacent farmland was great fun, with Brad pressing his horse into a gallop and Tick following behind, relishing her horse's power, the accelerated pace, and the rhythmic sound the horse hooves made as they hit the ground.

Brad had kept the reason for the ride confidential, eager to survey the acreage he had recently optioned to purchase before losing it to another interested buyer. He had spent over two months working with consultants, and their shared opinion was that expanding the Thomas farm with this acreage could make for a profitable operation. Brad's business plan was still in the works, however. He needed more time to work out the details with his lawyer before approaching the Thomas's with his proposal. Looking over the land again that morning, Brad knew in his heart, his plan was good.

Riding back to the farm at a trot, they rounded the southeast side of the stable, heading for the hitching rails located on the east side. Tick, who was riding outside and slightly in front of Brad, suddenly spurred her horse with such force that it bolted toward Brad's mare. The unexpected movement spooked his mare into an immediate sideways jump, nearly throwing Brad off in its flight toward the walled south side of the stable, around the corner from the stable doors. Confused and angry at Tick's recklessness and busy calming his horse down, Brad saw this daughter leap off her horse. Gripping its mane with her head ducked behind its neck, she was using the animal as a shield until she reached the corner of the stable and the wall's protection.

A look of fury on Tick's face showed that her actions were triggered by something terrible, so Brad quickly dismounted. Before Tick could stop him, he pushed past her to look out around the corner, and in the shadows of the stable's entrance, Brad saw what had caused her concern: Gus, the family's Labrador retriever, was lying dead in a pool of blood just inside the stable door.

Brad quickly retreated, and a voice that had haunted his dreams for far too long erupted from inside the shelter. It was a cold, mad, mocking voice, and Brad realized it belonged to Timothy Bird.

"Brad Hughes! If you want these Thomas sisters to continue breathing with blood still in their veins, you have one minute to get Esther inside this reeking stable. I will allow you and these girls to live. You can be bona fide winners—the only ones who have met me and survived!"

Then, mockingly, Timothy added, "And don't worry about Esther. She has excellent protection, you know, from the one crucified for being an impostor—the legendary Jew who Alissa was always citing to brainwash her daughter's mind. And I know my piglet a lot better than you do. Right now, she's thinking that God will surely bless her for getting in here and saving these poor girls."

He had unraveled, just as the FBI profilers had predicted, Brad realized, keeping one arm around Tick.

"So here's how this goes down," Bird ordered. "I want you to come in with Tick. Hold the barrel of your gun above your head by your fingertips. I know you're packing, Hughes! I'm offering you one sweet deal. Two lives for one—three, counting yours. The count starts now, Hughes, and to prove that I am serious, I'm going to cause some slight damage to one of these piglets right now."

"Don't do it!" Brad shouted. "I've triggered an alarm call to the police. Every road within—"

Bang! A shot rang out, followed by a piercing scream. Reacting with rage, Tick fought unsuccessfully to break free from Brad's hold.

"Stop, Tick!" Brad exclaimed. "Use your head!"

Brad quickly pressed the keys of the car into her hand. "Get out of here now. Help will be here in minutes. Let me handle this."

Tick threw the keys down hard, causing the Jeep's remote alarm to engage in loud honking. She then forcefully grabbed Brad's shoulders, looked at him with an animal-like fierceness, and shook her head furiously.

Beyond confident that Tick would never leave him, and knowing Megan and Rachael were running out of time, Brad fought for composure. Within seconds, he formulated a plan that could have come straight out of Grandpa's "you don't have to like it, you just have to do it" playbook.

They entered the barn together, just as Bird had demanded. Brad, looking frightened, dangling a pistol in his fingertips with a shaky left hand as he held it above his head with a pistol. His right hand gripped Tick's wrist as he pulled her along behind him.

"You don't need to kill the girls," Brad mumbled, unwilling to meet Bird's eyes. "You can have Esther. She's been a lot of trouble for me, and I'm too old to look after her anymore."

Looking at the scene unfolding in front of him, Timothy laughed with crazed amusement as the two slowly approached.

"Well, what a pathetic man you turned out to be, Mr. Hughes. And Esther, I'm completely distressed, looking at you. You're positively disappointing—not nearly as attractive as your mother was with her beautiful auburn hair. Such a pity."

How bizarre, Brad thought, his heart beating through his jacket as he feigned his awkward scuffle. *A monster's face shouldn't look ordinary, even handsome.*

Bird stood tall and motionless in the stable walkway. He had robust, chiseled features deeply set icy blue eyes and neatly styled grayish black hair. He was holding a pistol in his right hand, ignoring the loud sobbing of the girls, now hunkered down in the corner of the otherwise empty stall. Brad couldn't tell which girl Bird had shot, but he prayed for her life.

Tick understood the meaning of what happened next. Brad squeezed her wrist three times rapidly and then took one final vulnerable-looking step forward.

It all began in a split second as Brad quickly threw his gun behind him, hoping it would fall into Tick's waiting hands, and rushed Timothy.

Brad intended to take Bird by surprise with an unexpected move from an older man. If his plan failed, he would take a bullet and hopefully shield Tick long enough for her to start firing his retrieved gun.

As he closed in, it seemed that plan B was imminent—Bird's gun was pointed directly at his chest. But then, unexpectedly, the barrel turned away from Brad, and Bird's sights were now on the more immediate threat, Tick.

Tick had ignored Brad's instructions, bolting past him with a knife in her hand and rage in her eyes. As Bird swung his weapon to take his shot at Tick, Brad lurched forward, grabbed Bird's wrist, and, with his other hand, pressed his palm down hard on the barrel slide, preventing the gun from firing. Brad threw his weight into the pistol and twisted the barrel over with all his strength, hoping to trap Bird's finger in the trigger guard, wrenching the finger's flesh and bone. Bird's attention was fixed on Tick. However, he unexpectedly let go of the gun, throwing Brad off balance and causing him to careen off and down to the ground.

When Tick struck, the thin blade slashed through Bird's forearm to the bone, but it was not the deadly wound she had sought to accomplish. Like Tick, Bird targeted to kill with his furious retaliatory response—a brutal strike to her neck with a rigid right hand—a blow designed to shatter the vertebra supporting her head. Miraculously, Tick somehow propelled her left arm up to her face to absorb most of the impact. Bird hadn't killed her, but his strike fractured her arm and sent her tumbling to the floor.

Brad was now on his hands and knees and reached to get a grip on Bird's gun, but Bird was too quick. The first kick struck his upper arm, sending the pistol skidding off. A second kick smashed into his ribs.

Bird knew that Tick was still a threat, so he jumped over Brad to get to his gun, which had landed across the stable floor.

Oh no, you don't, Brad thought, managing to wrap his arms around Bird's upper leg while he wedged his boot between two slats of a stall door, locking himself down and leveraging a firm hold. Bird grabbed a shovel leaning against the door, and he slammed it into Brad's side. Despite the strike, Brad kept a grip on Bird's leg with one arm as he used his free hand to reach for the sheathed knife concealed on his belt loop—the knife that Grandpa had given him months earlier.

His veins coursing with adrenaline, Brad, unaware of the blows Bird was raining down on him with the shovel, impacts that shattered ribs and drove bone shards into his lungs, thrust the blade up into Timothy's groin. He viciously twisted and turned the blade as deep as he could, and blood began gushing out. It was a mortal wound.

"Bleed out, you bastard!" Brad said. "Off to hell with you!"

Suddenly, Brad's eyes widened as Bird, somehow still standing, raised the shovel above his head one last time, a serial killer's desperate attempt at a final conquest, the blade poised for Brad's neck.

At that instant, rapid-fire blasts rang out—*bang! bang! bang!*—the bullets were smashing into Timothy Bird's chest, Esther Morgan's target.

Bird dropped the shovel to the ground, then stumbled and slammed against the stall door before slumping to the floor. His icy blue eyes were wide open, remorseless, and grossly glaring out without regard for anything or anyone. It was his final salute on his way to eternal damnation.

Timothy Bird was dead.

Attempting to stand, Brad's legs gave way, and he lost consciousness as he sunk back to the stable floor, where his head came to rest on an accommodating pile of straw and manure. He awoke momentarily to cool water on his face, his cheeks being gently slapped by Tick, who was cradling his head. He heard the loud thrum of rotors and was distantly aware of EMTs surrounding him. He felt excruciating pain, and then darkness.

Enough Already!

Mattie had a sandwich to her mouth when the phone rang. Her morning had been horrific, treating three teenagers in an automobile accident. She left the hospital to eat at a local diner before doing some shopping.

"Hello, this is Dr. Barnes."

"Mattie, it's Sam. Tick and Brad have been injured and are on their way to Children's in an air ambulance, along with another injured girl named Rachael Thomas. They had an encounter with Timothy Bird. They're about forty minutes out."

Mattie grabbed her purse and ran to her car. "What's the status of the casualties?"

"From early reports, Tick may have a broken arm, has a badly bruised face, and possibly a broken cheekbone. What they tell me is Tick won't budge from her father's side. She did allow the medics to give her a preliminary examination, and they all think she is stable. Mr. Hughes is in pretty bad shape with fractured ribs, a collapsed lung, and possible additional internal injuries. Rachael Thomas has a bullet hole through her calf muscle and has sustained considerable blood loss. Mattie, you should know the medics think Tick could very well have saved both their lives."

"Where are they taking Brad?" Mattie asked.

"They plan to land at Children's, then hop over to the university hospital with Brad. Ruth Evers has specifically requested your team—the ones who know Tick and Brad and are aware of the security implications—to direct the triage, emergency treatments, and surgeries. They are setting up over at the University Hospital. A separate team is in place at Children's for Rachel."

"I am on my way," replied Mattie.

The helicopter circled the hospital pad and landed as a medical team rushed to extract Rachel, white as a sheet, from a bullet wound in the leg. Mattie watched as they wheeled the girl away, then jumped on the helicopter for the short trip over to the main hospital, her heart sinking when she first saw Brad virtually soaked with blood. Upon closer examination, she realized that the blood belonged to someone else.

Tick was glued to his side, and Mattie permitted her to stay during the preliminary evaluations. Mattie forced her to leave Brad when he entered the surgical suite. Then, she quickly turned her attention to his distraught daughter, who had to be dragged away, examined, and treated for her injuries.

The next twenty-four hours seemed never-ending. Brad remained in critical condition following his surgery, while Tick, her arm in a sling, frantically peppered Mattie with questions and concerns from the minute she was allowed to go in to see her father. When Brad's vital signs had stabilized, Mattie asked Laura to drive Tick to the Hughes's house and have Ana help her pack a bag. Both Tick and Laura would be staying at Mattie's apartment until they could sort things out.

At Children's, Melanie and Jim Thomas sat waiting for news about their daughter. The shocking text Megan sent her parents from the farm, followed up by a call from an FBI agent reporting that Rachel had been shot in the leg, sent Melanie, still grieving her son's death, over the edge and into a full-blown panic attack.

At the hospital ER, the doctor on call gave Melanie a mild tranquilizer, which seemed to help. Still, when Tick and Laura walked into the room to see Rachael, Melanie began screaming at Tick for lying about her true identity and for bringing the devil to their door. Sobbing, she banned both Brad and Tick from having any further contact with anyone in the Thomas family.

Earlier, Megan had provided the FBI with her account of what she and her sister had experienced. Agents and Mattie listened as the younger sister described how a man appeared out of nowhere in the stable and shot Gus, who was trying to protect them—how he tied them up and held them at gunpoint while he taunted and bullied them. She described the moment he shot Rachael after Brad told him not to shoot. From her position in a stall, Megan could see the man and Brad in a terrible fight. She saw Brad holding on to the man's leg to keep him from getting to a gun, and she saw Tick shoot the man just before he brought the shovel down on Brad. Megan said it all happened so fast, and it was hard to recall everything.

She explained that Tick untied her and Rachael and showed her how to apply pressure behind Rachel's knee to control the bleeding. Megan also explained how Tick rolled Brad on his back, elevated his legs, cleared his airways, and used her phone to text someone.

Those texts were placed to Nate Hoger, Steve Brewer, and Ruth Evers, reporting what had happened and the nature of the injuries she was handling. Helicopters were dispatched; roads were blocked off. The emergency summons protocol provided by the FBI had, to some extent, worked.

Tick didn't leave Brad or Rachael's side while constantly communicating with the agents coordinating the rescue. According to Megan, Tick did an amazing job managing the situation until help arrived without ever letting on about her broken arm.

~∽◌◌◌◌∽~

When Brad Hughes opened his eyes, Dr. Mattie Barnes stood by his bed in a glaringly white room that looked and smelled distressfully familiar.

"Don't try to speak, Brad. You've been intubated." Mattie pulled up a chair and took Brad's hand as she spoke. "Just listen for now. Tick, Megan, and Rachael are safe and doing fine. Timothy Bird is dead and will never hurt anyone ever again."

Brad closed his eyes for a moment to take in Mattie's words.

"You have been out for two days, Brad, but you are strong, and you're going to heal. Along with broken ribs, you had a collapsed lung, a lacerated spleen, and a severely sprained ankle. You'll need to recover here in the hospital for a few weeks, but you're an old hand at hospital stays, right? The main thing is that you, Tick, and the Thomas girls are all alive and safe now."

Brad signaled that he wanted to write, so Mattie handed him a tablet and a pencil.

"*Tick?*"

Mattie sighed. "The ulna bone of her right arm is fractured, but it's a clean break and will heal quickly. She does have a very colorful shiner—something about deflecting Timothy's blow that broke her arm—she thinks her fist smashed against her face, but she's not sure. Tick is in good shape, Brad. She and Laura have been staying at my apartment. It isn't the Ritz, but we're all comfortable. I sent them off hiking today because Tick needed some fresh air, and I needed to get Tick away from the hospital and out from under me."

"*Thomas girls?*"

"Well, both girls are traumatized, but they will be receiving some good counseling right away. Physically, Megan is good. She survived the ordeal without much of a scratch. Rachel took a bullet in her calf muscle, but she's going to be fine. She could have bled to death if we hadn't trained Tick in first aid. Your daughter saved both your lives, and from what I understand, you are some kind of a hero, too. For now, I need you to rest, Brad. You can ask more questions later."

"*You?*"

"I'm fine," responded Mattie, "and very thankful that I wasn't able to get away to go to the farm with you and Tick!"

Mattie added a sedative to Brad's IV. "Get some rest now. And by the way, the story is that you have been in a car accident—just you and Tick involved—you remember skidding off the road but nothing else."

The drug was working quickly, but Brad had one more thing to write. "*I'm sorry about all of this, but he had those girls, and he wanted Tick... I can't describe how evil he was!*"

"We'll talk about it later, but please close your eyes and go to sleep."

Mattie sank back into her chair and wondered if she had lost connection with her emotions. She couldn't define what she was feeling. Was it pure relief and happiness, or was it anger, frustration, and resentment? Was she just suffering from stress and exhaustion?

Watching Brad as he drifted off to sleep, Mattie's thoughts began to jump around until, unwittingly and curiously, one of her favorite movies, *Ground Hog Day*, came into her mind. Mattie snickered, remembering how the main character relived the same day over and over and over again. Had she been similarly convicted? Would she relive Tick's and Brad's hospitalizations over and over and over again for who knows how long?

She felt like she was trapped in some roundabout with no end to it, obligated to continue as Tick and Brad's doctor, a spectator to the events in their lives, destined to pick up the pieces as a bit player. She left Brad's room, knowing that his discharge from the hospital was only weeks away, knowing the bogeyman was dead and unsure if she had any part to play in their future lives. What future role did she have in this movie?

Brad's condition improved rapidly from critical to guarded to "get me out of here." Like Tick, Brad proved to be a less-than-ideal patient. He challenged his doctors' instructions, refused to touch any meal that looked distasteful (Tick and Ana had spoiled him), and on one occasion, give a night nurse a piece of his mind for waking him up every hour and disturbing his sleep. As a patient, Brad had taken a page out of Tick's book: *Demanding Behaviors 101*.

Mattie caught some of Brad's flack for calling his family and alerting them to Brad's condition. He was surprised and less than thrilled when his sons appeared at his bedside. The boys explained that Mattie had called to inform them that he was in serious condition, with possible life-threatening injuries, but it didn't help Mattie's case.

"Why did you have to call them, Mattie? All you did was worry them. I wish you hadn't done that."

Mattie's reply was defensive. "First of all, Brad, your survival was not a foregone conclusion... It's hospital policy to notify a family member, never mind that it's the right thing to do when a parent is in a serious or life-threatening condition. Your boys aren't stupid. They knew something was going on. It was headline news about Timothy Bird's death, and they were frantically trying to reach you when I called. How unreasonable do you wish to be? I thought you got your fill deceiving your family for all those weeks after you rescued Tick?"

Feeling foolish, Brad began to apologize, but Mattie had already turned her back and left the room.

Mattie's consideration for Tick's state of mind also demanded her immediate attention. Brad's married sons offered to let their adopted sister stay with them. Still, Mattie diplomatically vetoed the offers, advising the family that Tick would not handle being so far away from Brad while he was in the hospital.

Later, Mattie admitted to Brad that she had never asked Tick about staying with his sons, nor bothered mentioning how hard Ana had lobbied for Tick to come back home and stay with her. She was embarrassed to admit feeling possessive of Tick's company. Despite, or perhaps because of the commotion and overcrowding, Tick and Laura's company had been the best distraction ever. Mattie couldn't bear the thought of Tick and Laura being anywhere else but with her.

Their first night together at the apartment had not been entirely uneventful. Laura flew into Mattie's room, panicked. Tick had disappeared. Rushing out of the bedroom, Mattie felt a sudden breeze coming from the balcony off the living room and saw the curtains rustling. As she and Laura walked to the open sliding glass door, they stopped short when they heard a voice softly murmuring. The instant Tick became aware of someone's presence, she resumed her silence.

Afterward, the three roommates spent a good part of the night on the deck wrapped up in blankets, looking at the city lights and the stars. Tick laid her head in Laura's lap, an expression of trust and affection that Mattie longed for but had never received.

The days shot by, and Brad's condition continued to improve. Mattie found herself relishing the presence of her two young houseg-

uests as they cooked meals together, flipped through fashion magazines, fussed with each other's hair, and took walks around Mattie's
neighborhood. Plenty of good-natured teasing and goofing around
helped keep the purpose for their togetherness less disheartening.
Typically, Tick would pull Laura's chain by writing some cheeky comment and then sit back to watch her reaction. It was always amusing
since Laura, a master at comebacks, proved to be a worthy adversary.

Except for Laura, Mattie hadn't had people stay with her in
years. Her excuse for being so unwelcoming was that her apartment
was too small, with only two bedrooms. However, the open living
and kitchen area was spacious enough, and the large porch and spectacular view of the valley were perfect for entertaining. The truth was
that Mattie had become nearly reclusive; the lively interactions and
constant activities that Laura and Tick ushered into her private life
was something meaningful that had been missing from her life for
years.

Another truth that Mattie couldn't escape from was how
important Tick had become to her. When she and Tick were having
breakfast at the hospital one morning, Brenda Martin, Tick's one-
time favorite nurse who she furiously banished for presumably teaming up with Susan Messener, uneasily approached their table.

"Tick, I know Brad has been hospitalized. Mattie told me what
happened to you both, and it sickens me to think about what you
went through. I am so very sorry. You and Brad will be in my prayers
for healing and God's peace."

"*You will pray for us?*" Tick wrote out on her iPad.

"Of course, Tick. You and Brad have been in my prayers every
day since I began taking care of you. No matter what you think, I will
always care about you."

As Brenda turned to leave, Tick stood and gave her a sincere,
affectionate hug, awkward pink cast on her arm and all.

Ironically, Mattie had been lobbying for Tick to hold out an
olive branch to Brenda for over a year, even arranging for Tick to
view the video of the upsetting incident with the CPS woman, but
watching Tick hug Brenda so warmly and naturally felt decidedly
hurtful. Tick had never once embraced Mattie, nor shown the slight-

est bit of affection toward her. After all this time, she conceded, Tick's feelings for her hadn't deepened at all since the beginning, and she sensed that they never would.

Professionally, Mattie was on solid ground, clear in her responsibility to assist Tick to abandon whatever was keeping her from speaking. Privately, Mattie dreaded the day when neither Tick nor Brad would need her anymore. Now that Timothy Bird was gone, that day seemed even closer.

The FBI added to the stress of the relationship. Needing to deal with their continuing investigation from a detached perspective, agents constantly badgered Dr. Barnes to permit an official interview with Brad and Tick, and she was able to hold them off for two weeks before finally giving in. The whole group showed up: Nate Hoger, Jenny Dresden, Trenton Wright, Linn Wong, and Butch Parker and Ruth Evers from Quantico.

Mattie could not have guessed how stressful the meeting would be for her. For the first time, she learned in detail the FBI's findings at Timothy's ranch in Mexico with several slain victims found at the site; some were quite young. There was no longer any question that Timothy Bird was a bit-player in a much larger organization of unknown philosophy, motivation, or resolve. Tick could feasibly be some zealot member's new target to atone for Timothy's death, although the agents thought that was highly unlikely. Nevertheless, Tick's true identity would have to remain a secret.

The agents reported that Timothy Bird killed the two FBI agents who were found dead weeks before in Nevada, traces of their DNA found on Timothy's knife's leather handle.

The agents speculated that Susan Messener had given Timothy enough information before killing her to start searching for Tick in Salt Lake City. He eventually talked to an unwitting receptionist at the cemetery where they had buried Alissa. The woman remembered taking a call from a man asking if Alissa Morgan was listed in their burial directory. She assisted the caller with specific information, including telling the man that, even though the deceased was not a family member, Mr. Hughes had arranged for her to be interred in the Hughes family plot and had selected a beautiful headstone for her. She had, regrettably, shared information with the wrong person.

Timothy must have had Tick and Brad under surveillance for weeks while planning an abduction and a perfect getaway. Typically, he left no living witnesses to his crimes. His appearance at the Thomas ranch was, true to his nature, meticulously thought out. Agents combing the area around the farm found a mountain bike and a backpack filled with supplies. They found a neatly folded detailed topography map with a well-defined back-road route, a flashlight, two tactical fighting knives, and a wad of hundred-dollar bills. Also included in his preparations were handcuffs, a hood, and a baggie. This bag held locks of auburn hair, a picture of Alissa and her very young daughter, and a very small, tattered Bible.

Timothy's autopsy reported a severed femoral artery in his thigh and three bullets wounds to his heart—the spread of the shots no more extensive than the palm of a small hand. Trenton reminded the group that Tick had fired the heavy pistol with a broken arm from a distance of over four meters, under combat conditions. Tick had finally been forced to kill. However, the agents all agreed that she had merely hastened Timothy's demise.

The group began to assess the fight itself, with Trenton Wright taking the lead in evaluating the overall confrontation.

"I view Brad's plan as smart and insightful," Trenton asserted. "He had a good chance at getting close to Bird without being shot, but failing that, the backup scenario, which would have involved Tick's actions with a gun, was solid."

Turning his attention to Tick, Trenton spoke in the disciplinary manner Mattie had heard him use with Tick during their training sessions in the barn.

"Your job, your responsibility was to stay behind Brad to retrieve his pistol as quickly as possible, using him as a shield. Brad told you to protect yourself and the girls, and you elected not to follow his instruction. Further, using your knife was the last resort you should have reverted to, especially if you had a firearm to use against a much larger, stronger opponent and an expert hand-to-hand fighter. You have proved yourself to be a skilled marksman, and a pistol is an ultimate equalizer. Bird's blow came close to killing you. Your rash actions could have resulted in all of you getting killed."

Having heard enough, Mattie erupted. "Rash actions! Are you out of your mind? Do you realize how outrageous you sound? If you hadn't failed in your mission to protect her, she would never have been in that situation, period! What's more, haven't you learned anything about the girl you've been training all these months? If you did, you'd know that she would sacrifice her life to protect Brad without thinking. You shouldn't be the least bit surprised by her actions. That 'incompetent junior seal' you just berated is only fourteen, and she saved everyone's lives in that barn. Where's the praise she deserves? Doesn't she get a medal for killing the man on the FBI's Most Wanted list?"

Unfazed by Mattie's dressing-down, Trenton stood his ground. "Mattie, I've worked with Tick for over a year, and believe me, I care about her more than you think. You're a doctor, and your job is to save lives. That's my job, too. We both know that Tick can be rash and hardheaded. If God forbid, she finds herself in a similar situation someday, she has to think, not just react. For me to ignore her lack of control and recklessness is not an option."

Tick wrote, "*He's right, Mattie. You don't understand. You don't need to protect me.*"

Too angry to be around any of them for another minute, Mattie left the room, her head spinning with questions that would never be answered satisfactorily. She wanted to know where the FBI agents were when Tick and Brad needed them. Weren't they supposed to be tracking Bird? Wasn't this deadly encounter at the farm evidence that Tick has been used as bait for Bird all along? What kind of person was Brad to endanger his daughter like that? Was he so desperate to save the Thomas girls that involving Tick in his plans was acceptable to him? Why was Tick so damn opposed to her support and her opinions, and why was she always challenging her?

Mattie had had enough—she was fed up with all of them.

Breaking Up

Trained as a child psychiatrist, Dr. Mattie Barnes could sort out and correctly identify emotions that negatively influenced and sometimes controlled a kid's behavior. Getting to the root cause of the problems was where the real work began, and Dr. Barnes's reputation as a competent therapist was impressive. Before specializing in intensive care medicine, she helped scores of children navigate through difficult stretches in their lives.

Nearly as impressive, however, was Mattie's long-standing ability to avoid facing her disturbing past. For many years, she sidestepped her emotional baggage as an obstruction to becoming the best in her field, free of personal attachments. Mattie's protective shell had successfully kept close relationships at bay on her way to achieving demanding objectives, but there was also an emptiness that her work could not fill.

She would never have imagined that a young, physically and emotionally shattered girl—who far surpassed being a complicated patient and whose gifted mind and abilities seemed implausible—could shake up her self-contained world so thoroughly. Beyond that, this guarded woman could never have imagined developing strong feelings for the girl's rescuer and father. Unnerving, ambivalent, and jumbled emotions—about both father and daughter—had left Mattie in an emotional pileup.

On a Wednesday morning, three weeks after Brad had been critically wounded and airlifted to the hospital, Mattie and Tick drove him home. Grateful to be alive and going home, Brad appreciated every pain-free breath he took, even cooperating with Tick and Ana as they helped him settle back into his comfortable bed. At the same time, Mattie went over instructions for his care. She explained to Brad in no uncertain terms that he would still need a great deal of rest, and he agreed to do everything the doctor ordered. Without reservation, he conveyed his gratitude for everything she had done for them, keenly aware of her dedicated involvement with Tick and him since the beginning of their incredible journey together. Brad was genuinely appreciative, and he told her so.

Hearing Brad sing her praises made Mattie so uncomfortable that she could not respond, creating an awkward silence in the room. His eyes looking back at her looked questioning, but Mattie had nothing to say that she was willing to share, too troubled with ambivalent feelings about Brad and his daughter.

Recent events undoubtedly contributed to her unsettling doubts: Brad endangering Tick's life by taking her into the stable, Tick knifing and shooting Timothy Bird and Tick and Brad's continued support of agents who allowed Timothy Bird to slip through their net. Was she flat-out alarmed, appalled, and disappointed in Brad and Tick, or proud, relieved, and enthralled by the courage they demonstrated? Adding to Mattie's confusion were mistakes made at the hospital, errors that would never have occurred before Tick and Brad came into her life. She had missed meetings, had shown a lack of focus that led to an incorrect diagnosis one day, and had levied some unnecessarily harsh criticisms against some student nurses. These were all signs of losing her edge—and for what exactly?

Mattie didn't stay to visit, announcing that she was leaving for her cabin and would be there until the following Monday.

As she drove to the cabin, her only thought was to get away and stay away until she didn't feel like a muddled version of herself. Before her car's motor had time to cool down, she had her walking clothes on and started into the woods. Hiking was Mattie's go-to therapy whenever she felt overloaded or pressured by indecisions and uncertainties—something she had in common with Tick.

Returning to the cabin nearly four hours later, Mattie found a batch of text messages and calls on her phone from Brad, asking if she was all right and if she had arrived safely. Mattie texted back—"Here safely," nothing more, and she didn't bother returning his calls.

Thursday morning, after a sleepless night, she took off hiking again and kept going until the sun dropped behind the tree line. She entered her cabin feeling resolute. It was over. The poor choices she had made for herself could be corrected, and now was the time to turn things around and get back to normal. She couldn't afford to give up her life, career, and everything she had worked for and achieved since leaving Montana just to hang on to a tangled-up notion of a relationship.

Mattie didn't care that it was late or that she hadn't changed her clothes before stuffing a few things into her overnight bag, locking up the cabin, and getting into her car to drive back to Salt Lake City. She arrived at the Hughes gate just before 10:00 p.m. and used her key fob to open the gate. Brad had already turned in when he heard the gate access chime ringing, so he got out of bed and went to the door. Through the door's peephole, he could see Mattie stamping the mud off her boots. When he opened the door, he saw her eyes were red and looked bleary. She appeared disheveled, exhausted, and was wearing hiking clothes and an apologetic look on her face.

"Mattie… Come in! Are you all right? What's going on?"

Mattie didn't respond, looking past Brad to Tick, who was in her pajamas and standing by a small table about ten feet back from the door. Her hand was in an open drawer of the hall console table, and Mattie knew it held a Glock pistol with a laser sight. Brad had several specialty pieces of furniture made and keyed into Brad and Tick's thumbprints.

"It's just me, Tick. You can take your hand out of that drawer now if you don't mind," Mattie requested. "I didn't come here to be shot."

"Mattie, please come inside!" Brad urged. "You look like you could use a stiff drink, but would you like some tea?"

"Sure, some tea sounds good," said Mattie.

Mattie followed Brad and Tick into the kitchen, her boots leaving little bits of dried mud behind on the way to the kitchen counter, where she sat down. As Brad put the kettle on the stove, she fought to come up with words to make her announcement clear.

"Brad...my time, I think my commitment to you and Tick has come to the end of the road. As much as I care about you both, continuing as we have been doing would not be the best course for us to take, especially not for Tick's well-being. Somewhere along the line, I broke doctor-patient protocol by becoming extremely involved in your lives. I knew better than to allow our relationship to go beyond professional boundaries, but that was my choice. And, now, here we are."

Her face stricken, Tick sat down next to Mattie and began writing. "*This is my fault, I know. You're disappointed in me, and I've ruined things between us. This is because I shot Timothy, isn't it?*"

"No, Tick, that's not the reason we need to make some changes, and you haven't ruined a single thing. Yes, I am disturbed that you had to shoot Timothy in a confrontation that should never have taken place, but nothing that happened in the Thomas's stable was your fault, so do not think for a moment that you did anything wrong. Far from it, Tick. I think that you are the bravest, most responsible girl I have ever met."

"*Then, I don't understand,*" Tick probed.

"This is about me, Tick. I believe I have let you down as your doctor. You were right when you told me that I was best at short-term care with short-term outcomes. I've been treating you long-term now, and I realize that much of the time I have spent with you has been about enjoying your company. That's a self-serving position, not the view your therapist should be having."

Standing at the stove, his back to Mattie, Brad followed Mattie's every word but did not contribute to the conversation. Instead, he calmly poured her tea and then spoke.

"Mattie, drink this tea. I added some honey and lemon and a drop or two of rum. Ana fixed some rice pudding for our supper tonight. Would you like some?"

"No, Brad, thank you. We need to talk."

"I agree, but maybe this isn't the best time."

"Listen to me," Mattie replied in a brisk whisper. "There will never be a good time. This just isn't working and—"

"Tick," Brad broke in, "I think Mattie and I need some time alone to talk. Would you mind just saying good night now and scooting on upstairs to bed?"

Tick got off her stool without hesitating but stopped to give Mattie an all-encompassing first-ever hug before leaving the kitchen.

Oh, my gosh, Mattie silently marveled. *I just got a hug!*

"Okay, my dear, I'm all ears," Brad said, and he took a seat on the stool Tick had vacated.

"I'm sorry, Brad. I know it was rash of me to drive out here tonight, but I've made some decisions, and it's only fair I share them with you. I feel confident that Tick is on the verge of speaking again, but someone else will have to take things from here. I'm not the doctor to take her up that hill. It's too difficult for her to relate to me. Her indifference to me could be holding up her progress. This decision is harder for me than you can imagine, but we both have to face reality. My professional and personal association with the two of you is at cross purposes at this point, and it's unethical for me to keep treating Tick."

Brad framed Mattie's face in his hands, forcing her to look him squarely in the eye. "Mattie, you are the strongest person I know, but right now, you can't see the nose in front of your face…"

Brad stood up and walked away from Mattie with his hands clenched behind his head, and he began pacing around the kitchen.

"*Can't relate to you? Indifferent?* That's such nonsense! Tick adores you. She lives to see you. Why do you think she spends so much time getting ready for your visits? She drives Ana and me crazy, making sure that everything around the house is in order whenever you come to see us. The fresh flowers in vases around the house. The magazines scattered on the tables are all for you—they're *your* favorites, not hers or mine. She mopes for hours when you leave. Her feeble attempts to keep you at arms-length may serve some purpose for her, but then you must already know what that is."

"And just what do you think that purpose is?" Mattie asked as she examined her placemat as if it contained the answers to all her problems.

"Maybe she thinks getting close to you is being disloyal to her mother. Perhaps she is still riddled with some unknown guilt that we haven't been able to uncover."

"That's precisely the point I am making," replied Mattie. "I'm—"

"You didn't let me finish," Brad interrupted, now apprehensive, cautious. "I haven't gotten to the one thing about which I am certain. I sensed Tick was putting up a little wall between you as soon as you started to become important to her. That wasn't indifference, Mattie. Remember, Bird savagely murdered her mother. Haven't you drawn the connection? I know for a fact that the fear of Bird possibly hurting you to get at Tick has been very real to both of us until just recently. She had been terrified that Bird would hurt or maybe even kill you. Much of what she does is her way of trying to protect you."

Regaining a semblance of his composure, Brad leaned over, trying to catch her eyes, eyes still fixed on the placemat. "We had a deal that we would be long-term partners in caring for her. Remember? The job is far from over, and I will be damned to let you default on our agreement. I love you too much ever to let you go, and so does Tick. We both need you. You mean everything to both of us."

"What did you say?" replied Mattie, looking up.

"We're partners. That has always been the deal."

"No. What did you say after that?"

"I said I love you, Mattie," Brad said, taking her hand. "But that's no surprise... I thought it was obvious. What happened to the most perceptive person I know? Besides, you made it very clear that you didn't want me to push you. What did you say? 'It needs to be all about Tick.' Maybe it has been all about Tick for you, but never for me. I'm not clueless, Mattie. A man falling for his beautiful doctor is a naive cliché, but how I feel about you is not some schoolboy infatuation. I love you, and it's the real deal."

Mattie's heart felt as if it were turning inside out. Everything she thought she had all figured out no longer held much weight. She began thinking about all the ways Brad and Tick had protected her since the FBI raid in Mexico. Knowing that Timothy was on the loose and looking for Tick, knowing Mattie would be in danger, Brad had a security specialist upgrade the alarm system at her apartment, including FBI camera surveillance. He insisted she needed to change up the route driving to and from her apartment, always staying aware of the car behind her.

If he hadn't received a text from her to say she was home safely, he always called. Whenever Tick and Brad picked her up and dropped her at home, which was most of the time, they still went up with her and checked out every room, and they both texted her multiple times throughout the day when they weren't together just to check on her. Most telling was that, somehow, they had forced the FBI to give her one of their toys to wear, a piece of jewelry that could call in the cavalry.

Tick and Brad's protective behavior had been going on for so long that she became accustomed to it, but she knew it had to have been a strain on both of them, and she felt ashamed for taking that for granted.

She also knew that Brad was right—if he had pushed her, she would have immediately terminated the arrangement. Suddenly, she felt utterly foolish and transparent.

"What are you doing over the weekend?" Brad asked.

"I'll go to my apartment tonight and drive back to the cabin in the morning," Mattie replied.

"What would you think about staying with us this weekend? I understand the guest suite is quite comfortable, and I think we could all use some relaxing time together. If you would rather not stay with people who adore you, then finish drinking your tea before you leave for your apartment. But you must know that you have a home here with the two of us."

Their eyes met, and Mattie handed Brad the keys to her car. "Would you mind going out to my car and bringing in my overnight bag? I think I'd like to stay."

Brad shot out of the kitchen before she could change her mind. Sipping on her tea, Mattie heard the distinctive hiss of cylinders as the upper hall's security door opened and closed.

Had a certain girl spy-snuck down and listened to our conversation? Impossible to sneak around with that security system, she thought with amusement.

For the first time, Mattie found herself spending the night in Brad's house, a crystal pitcher full of water on the nightstand, and the bedspread neatly folded back.

By the time Mattie climbed into bed, she had admitted to herself that she had come looking for some part of herself that was lost. She was thankful that Brad hadn't given up on her.

On the verge of falling asleep, she heard someone enter her room. It was Tick, who silently walked over to the bed and carefully tucked the blanket in around Mattie before leaving the room, closing the door behind her.

As Mattie drifted off to sleep, she said a silent prayer. It was short but to the point.

"Dear Lord, You know that Tick and Brad have been in my prayers since the day I met them. You know how much I love both of them, how complicated the relationship has been for me. I'm all in, but I need your help with Tick. Amen."

The next morning, Mattie woke up close to noon, as though recouping from a hospital's long shift. When she came downstairs, breakfast was waiting for her outside by the pool.

Brad and Tick greeted her cheerfully.

"We thought you might like a drive up to Brighton after breakfast," Brad said. "I think I am up for a short walk around Silver Lake if you're okay with that. I would like to get out of the house."

Somehow Mattie knew her days of being an island unto herself were over, and spending the weekend with the people she loved and cared for the most felt like heaven.

New Lives

Nothing remarkable changed during the following weeks, but everything was changing. Tick had resumed training sessions with Grandpa, Linn, and Hoger, and her studies at the school and home tutorials with Professor Becket continued. She did a bit more hiking in the mountains—sometimes with Brad, sometimes with Mattie, and occasionally alone—preferring to take a different trail each time. Her other extracurricular interests now included fly-fishing with Hoger and his son James, who had invited the Hughes on several of their trips. Tick was always game to go. She wasn't as anxious to catch a trout as she was listening to Hoger quietly share his excellent knowledge about the intricacies of the sport as they waded their way up a creek, casting as they went.

There were some observable changes in Tick's frame of mind. She was seen smiling and even laughing sometimes. Her night terrors had diminished, and she began disclosing her daytime dream with the family: a trip to the Galapagos Islands. Cleverly nudging her father to consent to her wish, she sketched giant tortoises, marine iguanas, blue-footed boobies, and other wildlife found around the Ecuadorian Archipelago and scattered her artwork all around the house.

For the first time in months, Ana felt some peace of mind about Tick. The child's compulsive, bruising workouts in the barn, along with her reclusive behavior and poor appetite, had Ana wringing her hands with worry. Replacing the sullen girl who pushed her eggs around her plate and left the table to withdraw into her world, Tick now came to the breakfast table with a sunny disposition to eat breakfast before going off to school. She also made a point to spend more time with her Peruvian caretaker, insisting that Ana speak only Spanish to her as they cooked or did chores together around the house.

Realizing that it was no longer necessary to keep an eagle eye on Tick, and seeing that *el señor* was doing well, Ana began making plans to take an extended trip to Peru. It had been many years since she had been to her homeland, and understanding how close her employer had come to dying, she felt a need to reconnect with her family in the Andes. She would be away for two months.

Mattie started making an honest effort to curb her need to control every aspect of her life, turning much of it over to the One who holds it all anyway. Never one to believe in the fatalistic "*Que sera, sera*" outlook on life, Dr. Barnes began trusting that God had provided her with the ability and all the information she needed to figure things out. High on her priority list was to stop obsessing over unfamiliar feelings that her relationship with Brad and Tick had ushered in.

Overall, her relationship with Brad was, by mutual agreement, measured, cautious, and privately affectionate. Of course, it wasn't all roses. Tick was a work in progress. Neither Brad nor Mattie wanted to tamper with the girl's overall improvement until she was farther along and until Mattie felt that Tick was on board and willing to accept the committed relationship between her father and herself.

Mattie no longer confined discussions with Brad concerning Tick to her medical point of view. The protective, maternal undercurrents that existed with Tick were rising to the forefront now, notably where the FBI was concerned. The continued FBI presence in Tick's life was a sharp point of contention between Mattie and Brad, and she expressed her outrage when she learned that the FBI had invited Tick to an extensive in-house training seminar on cyber warfare.

"What is the point of this, Brad?" Mattie asked. "Bird is dead. It's over. They need to leave her alone now."

"I guess they think of her as part of their organization," Brad said, casually.

"Well, she isn't part of their organization! That's absurd, Tick is just a young teenager! Why exactly is she continuing to train with these guys, anyway? And why in the world are they asking her to attend special seminars?"

"Relax, sweetheart. These are the good guys, remember? It's all good."

"It isn't all good, and please don't tell me to relax. Where were these 'good guys' when you and Tick faced Timothy alone?"

"We've been through all of that, Mattie. You need to let that go."

"They need to let your daughter go!" Mattie's voice was loud but steady. "Why is Ruth Evers contacting Tick directly? Don't you see the pattern here? They're trying to recruit her! Why can't they just leave her alone?"

Brad's response was cautious. "This is how I see it. Tick likes the training, and the FBI is willing to provide it. In the last update I received, Bird's organization still exists, so we remain slightly at risk from a possible revenge seeker. But, and you're right, Ruth Evers' motivations go beyond that. She is doing her best to build a long-term relationship with Tick. I don't see sufficient grounds to put a stop to it, so we'll wait and see where it leads. It can't hurt Tick to have such a strong advocate in Washington."

Sounding amused, Brad added, "Have I told you that my daughter decided she should charge the Bureau? She sent a text to Evers claiming that since the FBI is depriving her of what was left of her childhood, they should pay her to take these special classes. She demanded fifty dollars an hour, along with expenses, and Evers capitulated! Tick loves the idea of taking these cyberwarfare classes, insisting it's all about solving puzzles. She has also signed up for an additional computer class at the university."

Days later, after she had time to cool down, Mattie explained her place in the Hughes family when Laura asked her boss where things stood.

"How should I put this?" Mattie said with her eyebrows furrowed in thought. "We are on life support, but there's a good chance for survival. I am like a transplanted organ in Brad and Tick's system. I know I'm important to them, but rejection is always a possibility."

"Rejection by you or them?"

"Well, if the relationship doesn't survive, that's a moot point. Anyway, I'm all about keeping things alive, and I'm as hopeful as I can be."

Talking to Mattie one night over dinner, Brad had less-than-encouraging words about Melanie Thomas, who still refused to speak to either Tick or Brad and did not want them to come to the farm for a visit.

"I thought she would come around by now, but she still won't take my calls," he vented. "I don't know what else I can do at this point, and it's been hard on Tick. She misses those girls."

Mattie listened patiently before remarking; "On top of being grief-stricken over Brent's death, Melanie nearly lost both daughters. It might take her some time to recover and stop blaming you and Tick. Let me give it a try. I will call her in the morning."

The following evening, Mattie reported back to Brad. "Melanie has agreed to see you and Tick on Saturday morning. If that works for you, the family will expect to see you around ten o'clock."

"How in the world did you pull that off?"

"Do you want the long or the short version?" Mattie replied.

Brad smiled. "The version that's long enough for me to hear how a miracle worker does her job."

"Well, I reminded her that you and Tick didn't have to go into that stable, that you risked your lives to rescue her daughters, that neither of them would be alive today if it weren't for you and Tick. I told her that Tick is the real victim in every aspect of Timothy Bird's horrific actions."

"Look, in her heart, Melanie wants to reconcile with the two of you. She just doesn't know what to think. You need to be honest and open with her, and please remember, she is hurting and very fragile."

The drive up to the ranch seemed to take forever. When the Hughes arrived, they received big welcoming hugs from the girls, while Jim and Melanie stood quietly at the front door.

The meeting got off to an awkward start. Brad and Tick settled onto the living room couch, and Melanie, Jim, and the girls took seats around the room. Knowing that the family was now aware of Tick's true identity, Brad began by chronicling his involvement with Esther Morgan from the time he met her on the mountain. The family listened to him in silence, taking in every word. While he spoke, Tick's face was unreadable.

At the end of the account, Brad reviewed instructions for keeping Tick's identity secret—instructions the family had already received from the FBI. Jim acknowledged the importance of protecting Tick and everyone around her from possible Bird-related retaliation and, just as importantly, shielding her from the press.

Melanie spoke up and began asking questions that reinforced Brad's awareness of how badly the media had damaged Tick's reputation.

"Are you so sure Tick didn't participate in the killing of David Bittner? If she is innocent, what does she have to hide? Why won't she meet with the Bittner family? I saw them on a TV interview where they claimed you wouldn't meet with them."

Brad choked down his anger. The Bittner family was a painful thorn in his side. Since Madison's trial, the Bittner family seemed to be on some senseless campaign to discredit Esther Morgan's testimony. Still, he responded as civilly as possible.

"Tick did not kill the Bittner boy, Melanie. She said she didn't kill David, and I believe her. The boy's autopsy report is irrefutable proof of that. As for the Bittner family, I can understand their grief. We sincerely tried to reach out to them, but they demanded a public forum with the media present. They don't want to acknowledge the truth. They just want to expose Tick to her enemies out of blind revenge. Their hearts are full of hate. Perhaps things will change over time."

The room was silent, and Brad decided it was time to go when Rachel, her leg in a high therapy boot to protect the healing calf muscle, spoke up angrily.

"How cruel do you wish to be, Mother? You know that Tick is no killer! I think you're punishing them for Brent's death. He loved

Tick! If Brent were alive, you wouldn't be acting like this. You're pushing all of us out of your life. Tick is wonderful! She saved my and Megan's life, and she will always be my friend. That's not ever going to change!"

Rachel rose from her seat and shot out the door, followed by Megan, who was shouting and in tears. "Ever since Brent got sick, you have ignored us! We miss him too!"

"I am so sorry for the troubles we have caused," Brad said, breaking the painful silence that followed. "I think we should go."

Melanie was visibly upset as she spoke. "No, please don't leave. The girls are right. I've made a mess of our lives." Then Melanie turned toward Tick. "Tick, I feel so ashamed. I don't know what to say except that I have acted shamefully, and I am so sorry. Of course, you didn't kill that boy, dear. Brad, Tick, please forgive me. You two saved my girls, and I will be forever grateful. My daughters adore you, Tick, and with good reason."

Melanie asked Tick if she would go out to find the girls and spend some time with them, and Tick happily obliged.

Melanie turned to Brad. "Please tell Dr. Barnes... Mattie that she is right. I could use some help dealing with Brent's death. I will call her in the morning to get the name of someone to call." She then excused herself from the room.

Left alone in the room, Jim and Brad looked at each other self-consciously before Brad suggested they take a walk. Wordlessly, the men walked down a well-worn path to an outlook on the edge of the property—a perspective that oversaw a sizable farmhouse and property that Jim had coveted and dreamed of farming full-time.

"It sold" Jim said. I hate even coming out here and looking at it; all in all, over two thousand acres. From what I hear, it sold about a month ago. I saved up most of my life to get that farm, and it all went up in smoke with Brent's illness. First, Brent, then, losing the land, then Bird and all he did to hurt my girls and Tick. Not to mention that he killed the best dog on the planet and nearly killed you. It's been a lousy year for sure, Brad. Small wonder Melanie is so distraught.

Jim Thomas sighed and then added, "You know, the strange thing is that nobody knows anything about the new owner. The purchase was very secretive. Rumors are it's some wealthy Chinese family. They've hired a caretaker, but so far, it doesn't look like they have any real plans for the property. It's a shame. With those properties, I really could have put together a terrific operation."

Brad looked out at the fields and then gave an absentminded reply. "I'm the one who bought the farm," he said. "I had toyed with the idea of owning land out here for years. When Melanie told me about this property, I decided to look into it. I had intended to talk to you about it before making an offer, hoping that you might manage the property, but then the negotiations got difficult, and well, you know what happened after that. I have given a lot of thought as to what to do with this land. Would you like to hear my ideas?"

Jim looked over at Brad with anger stirring in his heart. He had lost the property to a rich man who had casually *toyed* with owning some land and then ended up buying his dream, a dream he had harbored for as long as he could remember. *And, damn it, Hughes was no farmer!*

"Yes, I would," Jim replied coldly, "but you shouldn't expect me to like much of what you're going to say."

"I thought we could combine both of our properties into one farming/ranching operation," Brad said as he swept his hand across the landscape. "I thought you might consider swapping the houses. You need a larger house for your family, and I like the location of your existing home. With a bit of remodeling, it will make a perfect retreat. I have had all the properties appraised. We can combine all the assets, and I will put up a million in working capital. You will have 35 percent ownership, and as a majority owner, I will be the CEO for the short term.

"As the operating manager, you will get a salary off the top, equivalent to what you are making with the forestry service. I have run the numbers under several different scenarios. Still, if the multicrop operation is half as profitable as I think it will be, you should be able to double your salary within a year, much higher as we get the farm established. I have also included a provision where you can purchase another fifteen percent of the shares at favorable terms, making us equal partners over time. There are, of course, numerous boiler-plate provisions, which you will need to review. The contract and the financial statements are in the car."

They made the walk back to the car in complete silence. Brad handed the documents to Jim and watched the brooding farmer go off by himself and sit on a stump as he read through the proposal.

Over an hour later, Jim found Brad in the barn brushing down a horse.

"Brad, I owe you an apology," the farmer said as he walked into the stall. "Your proposal is more than fair, and I am grateful to you for allowing me to expand as I had always wanted. Are you still willing to work with me?"

Brad put his hands on the man's shoulder and said, "Old dreams are hard to put down, my friend, and both our families have been through hell. I can't think of a better partner, and I know we can build something great."

The two men spent the rest of the afternoon, riding around the properties and reviewing the contract and financial projections. Both men became increasingly excited about the prospect of a partnership. That afternoon, they presented the idea to Melanie and the three girls. Everyone was elated with the plan.

When Tick and Brad returned home that evening, Tick excitedly typed a complete summary of the day's events for Mattie.

"Are you kidding? I had no idea that you were getting into the farming business," Mattie said, surprised. "Those are significant plans. It all sounds very enterprising. I'm surprised that you didn't think that I would be interested."

Realizing Mattie was feeling left out, Brad responded guiltily.

"Oh, you're right, Mattie. I should have discussed this with you. I'm sorry. I had been thinking about the farm for months, tossing around the idea of a partnership with Jim. When I learned there was another interested buyer, I had to act before it sold. Then Bird showed up. Melanie didn't want anything to do with us until today, so a partnership with Jim seemed unlikely. It would have been difficult having them as estranged neighbors, so I had planned to put it all back up on the market."

Despite his explanation, Brad knew he had let Mattie down. He had been doing his own thing for so many years. Consulting with Mattie on a business matter hadn't occurred to him.

"In the future, I promise to keep you in the loop, Mattie."

Always keeping Mattie as an informed partner was a promise he intended to keep.

Breakthrough

The seasonal influenza virus had swept the nation and pushed hospitals to overflow in January through March, but it didn't hit northern Utah until early April. Children's Hospital in Salt Lake City had prepared for the epidemic wave that struck the most vulnerable children in the area, but this strain was especially virulent and had pushed the staff to the limit.

Mattie had been operating on autopilot for nearly three weeks, mainly living at the hospital before her caseload began to ease off when she could get back to her pre-epidemic schedule.

She had planned on taking three days off, exhausted and too drained to do anything except stay home, catch up on some badly needed sleep, and possibly watch some mind-numbing television.

Even though she was symptom-free, having developed a robust immune system from years of being exposed to all kinds of germs, Mattie held Brad and Tick at arm's length for weeks, not wanting to risk exposing either of them to yet another health crisis. Brad called her every night, and she and Tick texted back and forth several times each day, but Mattie felt miserable for not having seen them for such a long stretch.

Flopping down on her sofa back at her apartment, she texted out a short message to Tick: "Back at the apartment but completely beat. Taking some time off to get some rest, but I'll see you soon. Miss you both!"

It seemed that Mattie scarcely had time to change out of her hospital scrubs when Brad and Tick appeared at her door, insisting that she come home with them.

"Look," Brad said, determined to persuade Mattie. "I'll bet the farm you're not contagious—say, I can honestly use that expression now!" he said, amused. "But seriously, Mat, you're on your last leg, and we think you'd be much better off home with us. All you do is take care of others and us. Now it's our turn. Just throw a few things in your bag, and we're off to the Hughes' Resort and Spa, where you won't have to lift a finger."

"Okay, you two," Mattie said with a silly smirk directed toward Brad. "That sounds too inviting to turn down, just as long as there aren't any cows to milk or hay to bale, Farmer Brad!" Moments later, Mattie found herself comfortably installed in Brad's new jeep as they made their way to the house, blankly looking out of the window.

As soon as they arrived, Tick, who seemed stressed, dashed off with Mattie's overnight bag, placed it on the luggage rack in the guest bedroom, closed the drapes, and turned down the bed. When she had finished making the room a welcoming refuge, she hustled down to the kitchen and prepared a light cheese and fruit plate for her long-lost friend.

Mattie struggled to muster as much sociability as she could while nibbling on her snack, grateful for Tick and Brad's thoughtfulness, but wilting fast. She would find out what was bothering Tick in the morning. When Brad suggested that they call it a night and plan to have a late breakfast together in the morning, Mattie nodded in relieved agreement and said her good night. She anticipated nothing but a sound night's sleep and a relaxing weekend.

The next morning, Mattie opened her eyes in the Hughes' guest bedroom and glanced over at the bedside table's digital clock. The clock displayed 10:30 a.m. She had been sleeping for nearly ten hours.

Feeling groggy and hesitant about going downstairs before she had her wits about her, Mattie ran the water in the shower as cold as she could tolerate. She began a mental review of the past weeks at the hospital and why she was now in Brad's home, but her thoughts turned sharply to Tick and what occurred hours earlier in the middle of the night.

Was I just dreaming, Mattie considered, staring into the bathroom mirror after stepping out of the shower? Last night she was exhausted, yes, but delusional? *Not likely,* Mattie assured herself, suspecting instead that her three-week absence from Tick's life triggered the incident.

Recalling what took place that night, Mattie wasn't sure what had awakened her, but she sat up to see Tick sitting in the chair by the bay window. Through open drapes, Tick was staring out at the moon. It was full, bright, and poised just above the mountains behind the house. Its light also betrayed Tick's tears.

"What time is it? Are you all right, Tick?" Mattie asked, dazed and bleary-eyed.

Tick nodded her head, rose from the chair, and started for the door.

"Tick," Mattie called out. "Please don't leave. Stay here with me so we can visit. Do you have something to write on? I'm awake now."

Now fully awake, Mattie propped herself up against the headboard, turned her bedside table lamp on, and patted the space next to her on the bed. "Come back and sit next to me."

Tick had stopped by the door. She was wiping the tears off her cheeks and then turned toward Mattie, but it didn't appear that she was going to stay.

"I have missed you more than you will ever know," Mattie said, "but I couldn't get away. There were too many children fighting to recover from that horrible virus. I hope you don't think for a minute that I was avoiding you. I love you, Tick."

Just outside in the hallway, a barely audible whisper made it to Mattie's ears.

"*I know you love me. I love you, too.*"

Then the door closed, and Tick was gone.

Now, hours later, the kitchen was offering up the aromas of coffee and freshly baked muffins. Brad jumped up from the counter when Mattie walked in.

"Good morning, sleepyhead! Ready for some coffee?" Brad asked.

"Oh, yes, definitely, and please pour it into your largest mug. Where's Tick?"

"She was up early baking these muffins you like," Brad answered, "but I haven't seen her. She left a note on the counter to let us know she's in the barn working out. I'm surprised she's not back to wait on you."

"It's likely she's avoiding me right now," Mattie said.

"Hardly, my darling guru," he huffed. "Why would you say that? She couldn't be happier that you're here!"

"She talked to me last night," Mattie announced. "She was in my room very late last night sitting by the window looking out at the moon. She probably didn't want me to know she was there because she bolted out when I woke up and asked her not to go. But, Brad, just before she closed the door, she spoke to me."

Brad looked at Mattie anxiously. "Are you sure you weren't dreaming? What did she say? She certainly wasn't talking this morning."

"I told her that I love her," Mattie said. "She said that she loves me, too."

"Thank God! Finally! That's fantastic!" Brad could see that Mattie was looking less than pleased. "So what's wrong? Why don't you look happy about it?"

"Well, because I'm not, and this is not the time to celebrate a breakthrough in Tick's mutism. Speaking to me was a red flag she raised. What happened last night was her way of letting me know that she's not doing well. It was a cry for help, Brad."

"But she talked to you! Isn't that a sign that she's getting better?"

"It's more of a sign of emotional overload, Brad, and has little or nothing to do with her speechlessness. Trust me. I'm right about this."

"It's not that I don't trust you, Dr. Barnes, but you've lost me, and I don't know what to think."

"I'm sorry, Brad. It sounds counterintuitive because she did speak directly to someone—to me, but getting into psychiatry mumbo jumbo of mental health complexities could confuse you even more."

"Well, thanks so much for saving me from ambiguous language," Brad returned sarcastically, "so in layman's terms, what the heck is going on with my daughter?"

Mattie began to pace the floor in thought, stopping at a window looking toward the barn. "Brad, I don't want Tick walking into this discussion."

"Then make it quick, Doctor… Please."

"Okay, the big picture is that the emotions that pushed Esther Morgan to stop speaking before you rescued her still exist. So…these feelings that continue to haunt and control much of her thinking have become tangled up with her present life spectrum of thoughts and feelings. As I said, it's emotional overload, and I suspect my absence upset the applecart."

"But she knew what was going on at the hospital. You two texted each other every day."

"A wounded human psyche seeks attention, Brad. If Tick fears being abandoned or hurt on some level in her mind, then separating from her for three weeks may have triggered the incident."

The two of them drank their coffee in silence, apprehensive, waiting for Tick to surface from the barn.

When the sweat-soaked gladiator appeared, she didn't acknowledge either adult as she shot through the kitchen, grabbing an ice pack on her way to the shower. In nothing flat, she was back—with her game face on, only betrayed by a slight reddening of her scar. She informed the two onlookers that she was about to make Denver omelets.

During breakfast, in the dining room, Tick was non-communicative and playing with her food, and before it was time to clear the table, Tick scribbled a note for Brad.

"Dad, please leave the dishes for me to do later. Mattie and I need some time together."

Without hesitating, Brad encouraged the two to go ahead and not to worry about the dishes. He watched as they made their way to the back porch, Tick's favorite spot in the house with an unrestricted view of the mountains.

Mattie sat down on the sofa next to Tick, who had already opened her laptop. Looking over at Tick, Mattie watched as the teenager, sitting ramrod straight, regarded the blank computer screen intently. Her striking, intelligent eyes narrowed, and she bit her lower lip as she began typing.

Mattie interpreted Tick's aggressive body language as a signal to *let the games begin.* She was not surprised that this child, this survivor, looked like she was preparing for some kind of fight.

Not attempting to guess what Tick was writing, Mattie was taken off guard when she read the question that appeared on the screen.

"Why have you never married? I'm sure you have met many suitable prospects throughout the years. I have seen how some of the doctors look at you."

Mattie, feeling perturbed but not about to give Tick the satisfaction of becoming rattled, casually responded with a friendly rebuke. "You've been watching too many adult-rated movies with Laura, my friend!"

Not allowing time for Tick to respond, Mattie continued to answer, offering Tick her pat response to the question that had been asked by many others over the years. "My career choice and marriage have never been compatible, Tick. Anyway, I never met a man who I wanted to marry."

Tick was exasperated with Mattie's answer and reacted with an icy, agitated shudder before purposefully moving further away from Mattie on the couch.

Mattie overlooked the rebuff, but what she read next came as a complete shock:

"I think that you have never gotten over Steve Brooks. Maybe you don't think any man can measure up to him?"

How did she find out about Steve? Mattie marveled, shaken. Her attention hurtled back to the day she lost her father, brother, and Steve in an avalanche—over forty years ago.

Guardedly, Mattie asked, "And just how do you know about Steve?"

"I read all about the avalanche in the Bozeman Daily Chronicle."

Mattie flashed back to something Brad had revealed about Tick in their first conversation together: He said that Tick was insatiably curious about people. If Mattie had known back then what she was feeling now, she would have corrected Brad and described Tick as "an intrusive meddler."

"I see," Mattie said. "The Chronicle must have charged you a pretty penny to get into their archives. That was a very long time ago."

"No charge, Mattie. It took a few e-mails, but the people in Bozeman were quite accommodating. Once I tracked down Sam Rexford, the retired editor, it was an easy search. The snowmobile tragedy made the front page. I'm surprised you have never mentioned it."

"Yes, a tragedy," Mattie repeated, feeling gutted by the memories of that day. "A tragedy where the reported hero was, in reality, an overindulged, thoughtless fool."

"Why would you say that? Tell me what you mean."

With curiosity overcoming her usual detached manner, Tick scooted closer to Mattie on the couch, expectantly waiting for a reply.

Dr. Barnes felt apprehensive about confronting or sharing something she had kept to herself for four decades. Her heart pounded, and she felt a flash of resentment and vulnerability as Tick's eyes focused in on her, undoubtedly aware of the change in the respondent's demeanor.

"Well, I haven't thought about him in a very long time," Mattie said, honestly. "Steve was a wonderful guy and my first serious boyfriend. He was very handsome, popular, and good to his family. He might have made a wonderful husband for somebody, had he lived, but not for me. Steve was a complete adrenaline junkie who lived for thrills and the outdoors. He had no desire to go to college and no interest in thinking about his future or how he would support himself, let alone a family. I was truthfully over Steve and at the point of breaking up with him when the accident occurred. My relationship with him was effectively over before he died, you see, so it's wrong to think that Steve's death is the reason I have never married or even been serious about another man. I only wish it had been that simple."

"Why is that?" Tick's expression had softened, and she was now leaning even closer to Mattie.

Mattie was silent, struggling to answer a question that would reveal the long-standing, self-inflicted penalty that barred her from entering into a close, loving relationship for so long.

"Why wasn't it so simple, Mattie?" Tick pressed. *"Does this have something to do with the Bozeman heroine being a self-indulged, thoughtless fool?"*

Not surprised that Tick had zeroed in on her corrected assessment of the avalanche tragedy, Mattie conceded. "Yes, I'm afraid it does. As they say, the truth hurts. I have never shared this with another person, but the papers got it wrong. The truth is the avalanche happened because of me—it was my fault that three wonderful men died."

"Did someone tell you that you were to blame?"

"No, but only because I was riding quite a distance behind the men. Technically, I didn't trigger the avalanche, but we were on the steeper side of the mountain because of the big fuss I had made. Worried about avalanche danger, my father, brother, and Steve intended us to ride our snowmobiles on the less steep west face—the cold, shady side of the mountain. I hadn't dressed warmly enough, so I began whining and insisted that either we ride on the sunny, east face, or I would turn around and go home. I was the spoiled princess in my family—the apple of my father's eye—and I was good at getting my way. 'My way' ended up killing all three of them. What's more, my mother never recovered from the accident. I turned inward and hid in my books, so she lost her only daughter as well. Mom died three years later. I think it was from a broken heart."

"But you didn't know there would be an avalanche. It wasn't your fault. That's not logical, Mattie."

"We both know logic and feelings are very different things," countered Mattie, sighing. "I was the one responsible for changing their minds. I was only thinking of myself that day."

"So if you truly believe that you are responsible for their deaths, you must hate yourself for it."

"You're right, Tick, I did, along with feeling enormous guilt. I carried that burden all through medical school, virtually isolating myself while working my way to becoming first in my class. I've held on to the notion that the only way I could forgive myself for what happened in Montana was to earn it by working harder than everyone else, by excelling, by saving lives, and by rejecting the idea that I deserved to be happy, ever."

"*But with those perceptions, and considering everything you have achieved, you should be pleased now and feeling absolved from your guilt.*"

Mattie paused to look at Tick. "Is that what you think?"

"*What I think isn't relevant, Dr. Barnes. It's what* you *think that's important,*" Tick wrote, mimicking something Mattie often said during their therapy sessions.

"Ha-ha," Mattie retorted. "Is this where I stomp out of the room in a big huff because you've hit a nerve?"

"*Touché, Mattie. So have you forgiven yourself?*"

"I'll answer that, but first, I'm curious if the biblical scholar sitting here next to me can recall Psalm 103:12?"

"*I have a pretty good idea of that passage. Why?*"

Mattie did a quick search on her iPhone, then began reading. "As far as the east is from the west, so far He removed our transgressions from us."

Tick did not respond, her hands folded in her lap as she looked out at the mountains.

Mattie turned her phone off and stood up to stretch her legs and collect her thoughts. Tick pursued and turned her screen around for Mattie to see.

"*But even though He forgives you…you still did what you did that day. Nothing can ever change that. Don't you still hate yourself for it?*"

"What I hate and will always struggle with is the memory of the lifeless faces of my dad and Steve when I dug them out of the snow, the terrified look in my brother's eyes when he died in my arms. Then there was my mother. I didn't support her, and the loss of dad and my brother destroyed her. But no, Tick, I have stopped hating myself for their deaths."

"*What changed your thinking?*"

"Long story short, when you and Brad came into my life, I made the decision to take God seriously." Mattie sat back and patted

Tick's back before continuing. "I felt motivated to open my Bible again after I met a twelve-year-old who made me feel incredibly foolish with her impressive command of the scriptures. I learned a few Bible verses growing up and always thought of myself as a believer, but I disregarded the message about God's amazing grace after the avalanche. I buried myself in medical textbooks and journals and put my Bible and my relationship with God on a shelf, unable to forgive myself for what I had done to my family.

What did it matter that Jesus died for my sins if I couldn't forgive myself? Without being aware of it, I placed another opinion above God's word, mine. I put another god above Him, me. It was all about me."

"So you never separated yourself from that thoughtless fool on the mountainside."

"Sadly, we were the same. Psychologists call my coping mechanism 'self-handicapping.' It's also separation from God, but then my life started to change. You see, the director of Children's Hospital called me, desperate for my help with a little girl who was near death after taking a terrible fall, a girl who knew what she wanted and was determined to be with the man who rescued her from a cliff in the mountains."

"I guess I've kept Dad rather busy rescuing me."

"When I first saw you, you were still unconscious from your surgery. Then I met your rescuer, who was raging like a lion with concern for you. From the moment I became your doctor and, with a handshake, committed myself to your care *for the long run*, something changed within me—something outside of myself. While I got busy treating your broken body, God got busy healing my broken spirit. He put the three of us together for His purpose and for all our good, Tick, I believe this fervently."

"It sounds like you've figured things out for yourself."

"You have been listening to me, right? It has taken me years to abandon my arrogant ways and accept the Lord's grace and forgiveness. Even now, I don't think I completely understand the fullness of it, but the message throughout the Bible is clear: If we confess our sins and trust him, He is faithful and just and will forgive us our sins and purify us from all unrighteousness."

1 John 1:9 immediately appeared on Tick's screen with a side note.

"Mom prayed for Timothy Bird—for his salvation. I'm sure that would mystify most people."

Mattie reached over to take Tick's hand. "Your mom had a genuine heart for God, Tick. And what's more, she was the most exceptional mother, imaginable. Alissa loved you boundlessly, and your love for her will never end. The circumstances in which your mom found herself—held captive and caged with her little girl—were unimaginable, and yet she not only protected you from perishing, she also transformed that cave into a magical place for you.

"Alissa sparked your imagination and cultivated your natural aptitude and desire to learn. She nurtured your faith in God and gave you hope and the will to survive. With God's help, she did everything she could do to raise you properly, even when it meant self-sacrifice. As much as Brad and I love you, we would turn back the clock in an instant if it meant that you could be with her again and tell her what's in your heart."

Pausing, she squeezed Tick's hand. "We can't turn back the clock, but she will always be with you..."

Tick looked away with a pained expression on her face, and then, Mattie just blurted it out.

"I heard what you said to me last night," Mattie said. "Your words meant everything to me, not only because you spoke, but also because you said the one thing I was longing to know: that you care about me. Even before I met you, you started getting under my skin when I heard how hard you fought to be with Brad, nearly killing yourself in the process. I knew then that you had to be very special, and when you were coming out of anesthesia, when you cried out for Brad, desperate to know how he was—your only thought was about him."

Tick interrupted with a scribbled note. *"Brad didn't want me to go into the stable. I forced his hand."*

Mattie laughed. "Darling girl, do you think for one minute that I didn't know that? It's in your DNA. You are always going to be the first into a burning building. You will always cover for your father, and he will always cover for you. It's part of what makes the two of you so charming and so difficult."

"*We can be big pains, I know,*" Tick admitted.

"I think you're worth it! I thank God for bringing you and your dad into my life. I believe that becoming your doctor and growing to know and love you two was part of His plan. I also think you should know how much I care about your dad."

"*I'm all ears, Mattie, tell me. I want to know how much you love him.*"

"Enough that I want to be his life partner. I want him to be in my life forever. How's that?"

"*I think Dad would like that. I especially like the forever part. It's comforting.*"

"And I want to be here for you to be your best support and help you grow up to be a happy, successful woman. There is no double-mindedness in what I am saying, Tick. I want to be part of your family always.

Another thing, no matter what happened to you or me in the past, there is a part of us that is undamaged and whole, the part that is connected to God who has coded us to be survivors."

Tick sat back, her eyes clouding up with tears as she typed out a confession.

"*I have been so wrong about you, Mattie. I have misunderstood and have judged you unfairly. I didn't know all the details about the avalanche or that you were carrying such a heavy burden. I wasn't sure how you felt about Dad.*"

Mattie stood up, put her arms around Tick, and whispered into her ear, "Young lady, you are the light of my life. Getting to know and love you has freed me, and from the start, you have been one of my greatest joys. Don't you ever forget that."

They left the porch together and found Brad on the phone in his study. The call ended quickly, and when he spun his desk chair around to acknowledge the girls, he could see that something was very different in the way they were interacting. Mattie had her arm affectionately wrapped around Tick's shoulder, and Tick's arm was around Mattie's waist, pulling her close.

Then Tick walked to her dad's desk and wrote a note to ask if she could take a short hike by herself, promising to be home in time to help get dinner started, around four. Brad looked over at Mattie to ask what she thought of the request, but Mattie spoke up first. "I think our girl could use some fresh air and exercise. A little hike sounds like a good idea."

"Is everything all right?" Brad asked Mattie, as Tick left for her trek up the mountain trail behind the house. "What did she want to talk to you about?"

Mattie looked beseechingly into Brad's eyes, not wanting to hurt his feelings. "Please, don't be upset with me, but I have to play the patient-doctor confidentiality card right now, even though I'm not entirely sure who was the patient or who was the doctor."

Standing by his side, she took his hand. "We're okay, Brad. God is good. We've all come such a long way."

CHAPTER

52

Icing on the Cake

The relaxing weekend Brad had promised got off to a slow start, but when Tick left for her hike in buoyant spirits, Brad's attention happily turned to Mattie. He rubbed her tired feet while they watched television, they snacked on cheese and crackers, and best of all, they agreed not to talk about work or anything Tick-related. Neither of them felt apprehensive about Tick, who was now high on the mountain behind the house.

Brad left Mattie's side at one point to check his daughter's progress on the mountain. Her surveillance system was still in place, and Brad's computer screen showed that his mountain goat daughter was charging up the trail quickly. He speculated that she had chosen a brisk cardio workout as a means to sort out whatever she and Mattie had discussed after breakfast. Brad wisely decided not to disturb Mattie with his thoughts. She had fallen sound asleep watching the sports network's coverage of a golf tournament.

Making it home at the agreed-upon time, Tick got busy organizing and starting the evening meal. She shooed Mattie upstairs until dinner was ready and asked her dad if he would grill the steaks, allowing her to concentrate on the dessert—carrot cake with cream cheese frosting, his favorite. When the cake had cooled and the frosting expertly spread, Tick privately took the cake into the pantry for some finishing touches.

Tick also asked Brad to set the table in the formal dining room. Although Brad was the family's grill master, setting an elegant table was not in his province, and he suddenly wished Ana were back from Peru. He didn't even know where they kept the tablecloths. Declaring his cluelessness, he called Tick in for help.

When Tick rushed into the dining room to lend a hand, Brad noticed that her scar was rosy, and she seemed particularly wired and excited. He knew she was up to something, but he could not ascertain what that might be.

Mattie was called down to dinner and found a beautifully set table, complete with candles and a floral centerpiece. She looked rested and, Brad thought, gorgeous in a sky-blue silk blouse and black silk palazzo slacks. Brad—wearing his navy blazer, button-down shirt, and a paisley necktie—stood waiting to seat her, and as he helped move her chair closer to the table, he leaned over and whispered in her ear.

"Thank you, kind sir," responded Mattie, pleased. "What a sweet compliment. You look fabulous too!"

Tick, adorable as ever, strolled in wearing a snazzy new aqua-blue shift and dressy sandals. She began bringing in the dinner plates while Brad poured the water and filled two wine glasses. When all three were seated, Brad said grace before lifting his glass.

"Thank you, Mattie, for spending this weekend with Tick and me. Nothing could make us happier than showing you how much you mean to us. Bon appétit!"

Dinner was delicious, but Brad and Mattie felt distinctly rushed to finish their meal. Tick had begun clearing the table by first taking her plate into the kitchen and then waiting impatiently to clear Brad and Mattie's plates.

"Where's the fire, Tick?" questioned Brad, not expecting an answer but hoping to make a point.

Within a minute, Tick was back with a covered platter, which she set down in front of Brad. Slowly, she lifted the dome, and there it was, the carrot cake, which had been spirited away and decorated far from prying eyes. Brad and Mattie studied the cake, wide-eyed at the confection, as Tick clapped her hands with excitement. Artistically piped out in frosting, the top of the cake pictured a man and woman standing before an altar in front of a preacher. The bride wore green hospital scrubs instead of a bridal gown, the groom donned a leather jacket, like Indiana Jones—complete with a rope coiled around his shoulder and a big shiny knife dangling at his hip.

By any stretch of the imagination, the cake was a masterpiece in creative and whimsical design, and it left no doubt whom the bride and groom represented as they were exchanging marriage vows.

Mattie sputtered "Oh my" several times as she examined the depiction on the cake and cast an embarrassed look at Brad.

"I'm so sorry, Brad," said Mattie. "This is my doing. I'm afraid I unintentionally set her up for this."

Brad did not respond to Mattie's comment but immediately turned to Tick, who looked crestfallen at the unpredicted, less-than-enthusiastic reaction her special cake was receiving.

"Well, Tick, one look at this cake is definitely worth a thousand words," said Brad, clearing his voice. "The thing is, my girl, your words remain frustratingly unspoken, and until you start speaking again, Mattie and I will not be getting married any time soon."

Tick grabbed her iPad. "*Just why should my not speaking prevent you from marrying? That hasn't stopped you from falling in love with each other!*"

Brad was about to answer but stopped when he felt Mattie emphatically squeeze his knee under the table. He saw a look in her eye that was curiously familiar. It said "trust me."

"It's time," she mouthed.

Brad felt a mounting panic in his chest, knowing what Mattie meant by "it's time," and he wished that time would stop long enough for him to get his bearings. He and Mattie had discussed their future together on many occasions, agreeing that they could not marry until Tick faced and broke through the protective wall that she had built and imprisoned herself behind.

When Brad adopted Tick, he put his own needs last, and that wasn't going to change until Tick's emotional problems were no longer the enormous elephant in the room. Mattie had also made it clear that she didn't want Brad to confront his daughter about the inconsistencies in her account of events at the Death Ranch until the time was right. Before Brad could put real pressure on Tick to tell the truth about what happened, Mattie would have to let him know when she thought Tick was ready.

Whichever frequency Mattie was tuned into had escaped Brad's hearing, however, because this frequency sounded off in her ear alone—a signal announcing that the time to lower the boom on Tick had come.

Still, this didn't mean that Brad was okay with Mattie's decision to blindside Tick that night, just when she seemed happier than she had been for months. Carrying out their agreed plan of action at that time seemed almost cruel. Wasn't this the time, instead, to make Tick and, hopefully, Mattie happy by getting down on his knees and proposing to the woman he loved?

Communicating a silent plea of resistance, he mouthed the words "Now?" and received a firm, confirming nod.

Resigned to trust the mental health expert looking back at him, Brad answered Tick's question.

"Your question lacks your usual insight, sweetheart. The fact that you are not speaking and the fact that Mattie and I love each other are two separate matters. As far as the love part is concerned, it's no secret that I adore this lady with all my heart, and I've been told that she loves me too. Unfortunately, our love for each other is secondary to more pressing matters, so marrying this incredible woman will not be possible until…"

Brad stopped talking for a moment and stared at his daughter, who appeared confused and upset. He steeled himself to say things that he knew would precipitate a watershed event in his daughter's life.

"I plan on marrying Mattie when you decide to start talking again, Tick, and when you can open up to us. I know that you have been less than straightforward about what happened with David Bittner and Janet Herrington. But before I say another thing, I want to make this clear. You are my daughter, forever, and my love for you is not contingent on whether or not you talk, nor is it affected by what happened to you in the past, whatever that might be. You have my love forever, and that will never change.

"With that being said, Tick, we both know that life is short, and…" Pausing for a breath, Brad continued, "I am not getting any younger. I'm hoping that you're at the point where you realize it's time to let go of whatever menacing issues you've been holding on to. Tick, you must recognize that Mattie and I both know that you can talk. I understand you *spoke* to Mattie last night, and I have heard you talking to yourself many times, even singing when you don't think anyone is around.

"At some point, before I found you on that cliff, you chose to stop speaking, and for the last two years, I have respected your need for self-protection as your method to survive the hell that few people could imagine. The only way I could relate to your choice to become mute was remembering how I didn't want to talk to anyone after Catherine died. After the funeral, I isolated myself for weeks, only speaking to Ana when I needed to."

"*I'm so sorry, Dad,*" Tick wrote on her iPad. "*That must have been a terrible time for you.*"

"Recovering from grief is a rough road," Brad corroborated, "but if anyone understands that, you do. What puzzles me, Tick is that your continued refusal to speak after all this time seems rather pointless, especially considering how much and how fluently you express yourself in writing. Anyway, I will not enter into a marriage having a daughter who suffers so much that she is unwilling to speak. That is not the picture of the family life I want for the three of us."

They had ambushed Tick. Brad trapped her on a day where she was trying to do her best by him, and he felt terrible. The scar on her face had turned bright red, and Brad's heart ached to see his daughter immobile in her chair like a beautiful butterfly pinned down and set in a display case.

When Tick turned to Mattie for support, none was forthcoming. Mattie only looked back lovingly and spoke to her objectively.

"It's time, darling. You can talk to your dad now. I know that you love and trust him completely, so put your writing tablet away and talk to him."

Tick gazed at Brad intently for a few moments before looking down at her iPad and writing on it.

"I'm sorry that you and Mattie can't accept me the way I am, but I understand. It would be best if I weren't here so that you and Mattie can get married and have a happy life together without me holding you back."

After reading Tick's note, Brad said nothing but turned it over to Mattie to read.

"I completely understand where you are coming from, Tick," Mattie said quietly, "and I can't blame you for feeling betrayed by our decision not to marry until you can speak your truths, as is your God-given right. What kind of happy life do you imagine your dad and I could have without you in it? The notion that I would, or even could come between you and your father is unthinkable, so I think it would be best to take marriage off the table for now, along with that cake. It's pretty fabulous though!"

Brad followed up, "It is, Tick. You are an amazing artist, even on a cake. I especially like the Indiana Jones look since I can't stand wearing a tuxedo. Let's call it a day, Sweetie, and freeze the cake for another time. Mattie and I aren't going anywhere."

The room was dead quiet when Tick finally spoke. It wasn't a whisper, but it had a hollow, slightly mechanical sound.

"It all started when I refused to kill David in the ring," said Tick. "Timothy turned against me that day because I listened to my mom instead of following his orders. He whipped us both. If I did anything that he didn't like after that, he would beat Momma badly and say that it was all my fault."

"Tick!" Brad exclaimed, more alarmed about what she had said than the fact she finally spoke. "Are you saying that you think you were to blame for anything that madman ever did?"

"But I was," she said.

"Oh, my girl, even if you had been some child robot, programmed never to say or do a single thing to invoke Timothy's wrath, he would have devised some other way to hurt you and your mother. Bird was as mentally ill as a human being could be. He was a sociopath without empathy, oblivious to others' needs and feelings. What he did to you showed no imagination whatsoever. He simply took advantage of the close relationship you and your mom had and began going after your mom to control you. You cannot blame yourself for Timothy Bird's sick actions."

Tick looked frantic, barely able to control her limbs.

"But I knew what he was doing! I tried to guard what I said around him, but I failed to keep quiet, and what happened to Momma was my fault."

"What happened?" Brad asked.

"Momma and I were quarreling that morning. She told me that I had done a poor job cleaning the kitchen after breakfast and said that I needed to go over everything again. I got mad at her because I had spent my entire morning in that hot kitchen, and I just wanted to get out of there and check on the new hatchlings outside. Timothy heard us squabbling and came in, furious with both of us. He shouted that he would not tolerate being disturbed by a worthless cook and her useless piglet. I couldn't keep my mouth shut. I asked him why a little noise should matter to him at all since he never did anything worthwhile or decent. I also accused him of being a tyrant and a coward who only fought against weaker opponents.

"He grabbed me around my neck and shoved me so hard against the stove that I lost my breath. Then he went after Momma. He kept hitting and kicking her over and over, even though I begged him to stop. He beat her so savagely that he broke her ribs, her jaw, and knocked out her front teeth. He nearly killed her. I grabbed a kitchen knife and went after him. That's when he kicked me and broke my ribs. I wasn't fast enough, and I didn't have the strength to fight him."

With her eyes cast down, Tick began quoting scripture robotically. "'The tongue is a small part of the body, but it makes great boasts. Consider what a great forest is set on fire by a small spark. The tongue also is a fire, a world of evil among the parts of the body. It corrupts the whole body, sets the whole course of one's life on fire, and is itself set on fire by hell.'"

"Look at me, Tick," Brad urged. "That scripture was written for instruction, not to silence a child. Of course, words can be hurtful and destructive, both spoken and written, but people make thoughtless statements all the time without fear of being savagely beaten. Your decision to stop talking was a self-prescribed penance for feeling responsible for something completely out of your control."

"Momma never fully recovered from her injuries, and she could only speak with great difficulty. What I said that morning caused so much pain and suffering for her. I don't even have the words to tell you or Mattie how horrible it was, but it wasn't right that she couldn't even talk anymore without pain because of me. It wasn't right that I should talk again, either. Timothy never heard my voice again."

Brad felt shattered for his daughter, but he had started this, and he knew it was essential to see it through.

He softly replied, "Your decision to stop talking was a sacrifice made out of love for your mother, Tick, but you need to consider that not speaking now is only self-destructive. Your mother is in heaven, and you are giving a dead monster power over your life."

Crying, her voice barely audible, Tick said that it had infuriated Timothy when she stopped talking to him, so he took his vengeance out on her more than before, which protected her mom from him, at least for a while.

Mattie squeezed Tick's hand reassuringly, her every thought focused on the child.

What an amazing prize you raised, Alissa, Mattie thought. *She loved you so.*

"Bird isn't here anymore," Brad repeated. "We put him down for good, and I can't imagine that your mother wanted to leave you as a mute. She would want to hear you laugh, to hear you defend your ideas, to sing."

"Yes," replied Tick, fatigue seeping into her face. She looked up at Mattie, whose reassuring smile could not hide the pained look in her eyes.

Then Brad began to press again with more questions.

"I know this is difficult for you, Tick, but I want you to tell me what happened when you fought David Bittner."

Tick became more agitated and impatient, her voice hoarse and brittle. "I've already explained what happened. I fought David in the ring, but when I wouldn't kill him, Timothy whipped my mom and me and then killed David."

"But what are you leaving out? I know there's more to that story. What is it, Tick? You can tell me."

Tick began squirming in her chair like an animal desperate to escape the snare that had entrapped it. Finally, the panicky girl responded, "Momma stopped me from killing David!"

"You were going to kill David?"

Becoming perfectly still, as if in a trance, Tick answered, "Yes. When I got into the ring to fight David, he went after me instantly. I wasn't armed, but Timothy had given David a knife and told him to use it. I raised my arm to block his attack, and he slashed it. David began screaming terrible things at me, charging at me, saying that he would make Timothy happy by gutting me like a fish. He was much bigger than I was, but he was slow and clumsy. Timothy knew David was no match for me. I was able to get his knife and go after him with it. I felt nothing but hate for him and Timothy, so it didn't bother me to taunt David with that knife and cut him. I liked doing it. I wanted to do it."

Then, in a flat voice, she added, "I got behind him and pulled his head back to kill him, but when I heard screams, I stopped. I had never heard her scream before, but I knew it was Momma. I would have cut David's throat if I hadn't heard her scream. The truth is, I became the killer Timothy wanted me to be."

Mattie cringed, and her thoughts rocketed back to an image she had seen in the hospital shortly after returning from Paris. She remembered a group of drawings she had looked at while Tick was out, artwork in a folio on her bedside table. One illustration was disturbing, a dark, black-and-white charcoal sketch folded over in the back of the folder of a shadowy, obscure human figure with the head pulled back, chin exposed, with a knife against the throat. The assailant was obscured, hidden in a dark background. The drawing had stayed in the back of Mattie's mind, but she had never pressed the subject, not wanting Tick to know that she had gone through the drawings without permission.

Without a hint of emotion, Mattie said, "Many months ago, when you were in the hospital recovering from your ankle surgery, I flipped through your art portfolio and saw a drawing folded up in the back. Do you know the sketch I'm talking about?"

Tick didn't meet Mattie's eyes when she responded. "Yes, I destroyed it. I didn't want you to hate me."

Looking up, Tick added, "I'm nothing like my mother. Buckley was right about me. At the trial, he told the jury that I am a killer, like Timothy Bird."

Brad spoke up, compellingly. "No, Tick! You are so wrong! God called you to be a warrior that day, like the young David in the Bible who God appointed to kill Goliath. You have the same warrior's spirit that God gave to hundreds of people in the Bible and continues to give people today for His purpose."

Tick looked thoughtful and seemed to relax, hearing what Brad had said. Mattie and Brad both knew that the Bible was the key to Tick's psyche, the touchstone to her world view, and the book that connected her to her mother.

"What does the Bible say about putting on the armor of God?" Brad asked.

"It says to put on the full armor of God so that you can take your stand against the devil's schemes."

Brad leaned forward. "And your mother was a warrior, too, who God used to intercede for Him. You heard Alissa just in time, and you reacted. In the end, you chose not to kill the Bittner boy. You made that choice knowing and prepared to take a whipping, perhaps even to be killed. You have nothing to be ashamed of. God knows that you are nothing like Timothy Bird, and I suspect Sunder Buckley is just as convinced."

Tick remained silent as Brad continued. "Hearing you speak to me tonight is an answer to my prayers, Tick, and I couldn't be happier about it, especially for your sake. Having to ask you tonight to relive this nightmare again is horrible, and I am so sorry. I have never met anyone who comes close to being as brave as you. However, there is still something that doesn't add up about your fight with Janet. What happened?"

Tensing up, Tick evasively replied, "There's nothing to tell. Timothy forced me to fight her. She was winning, but after she cut my face, she looked up at Timothy for his approval, and I got in under her guard. I told you that I cut her hamstring. After that, she could barely move."

"But you didn't kill her, did you?"

"No. I have told you a thousand times, Timothy did."

Brad was nearly whispering now. "I'm pretty sure that Timothy wasn't the one who killed her."

Tick's reaction was instantaneous. She rose, facing him angrily, her face wild as she began shouting in a fractured-sounding voice. "I don't care what you think! That's what happened. I was there!"

"No," replied Brad in a calm voice as he stood facing her. "I believe that your mother killed Janet, trying to protect you. The Mother Superior told me that you asked her if someone could still go to heaven after killing someone to protect another person. At first, I thought you were asking about yourself, but that never made any sense. Why would Timothy whip you so savagely for doing his bidding?

You weren't asking the Sister for yourself; you asked her because of what your mother did. She killed Janet to protect you. Isn't that what happened?"

Brad and Tick locked eyes and were standing toe-to-toe when Tick suddenly sank to her knees. Rocking back and forth and sobbing, she choked out her words.

"When I wouldn't kill Janet, Timothy decided to beat me with his new whip and then chain me to Janet, just like the Romans did, so we could die and rot together. Janet was supposedly his girlfriend, but he was finished with her just as he was finished with me. He wanted us both dead. Everyone in his life was expendable."

"He was the scum of the earth," Brad mumbled.

"Timothy tied Momma's hands behind her back and ordered her to stand where she could see me. She just stood there, praying."

Brad interrupted. "Let me understand. So it was your decision alone not to kill Janet?"

"Yes, I knew Timothy was malicious and evil, and Janet looked helpless and desperate. I couldn't kill her. Janet told Momma once that she came from a Christian home. Momma said that she had lost her way and that Janet was trapped, just like we were."

"So go back to when you knew you weren't going to kill her. What happened then?" Brad asked.

"After I disabled her, I backed away and dropped the knife. Timothy told me he would skin me alive if I didn't kill her—but I didn't care. It was finished. I knew what I was doing was right.

He started shouting at Momma, telling her that he had no use for me any longer. He said that she had ruined me with religious garbage, and he would take my hide off.

"When Timothy started to whip me, Momma begged for him to stop. He told her that if she killed Janet as he had ordered her piglet to do, then he would spare me. The moment Momma agreed to kill Janet, Timothy threw the whip down. He looked up to the sky, shouting that the saint was a sinner after all. He laughed the whole time he was untying her hands. Then he tossed her an old screwdriver and told her to get on with it.

"I watched Momma walk toward Janet, who was still on the ground. She knelt next to Janet, took her hand, and started talking to her. I couldn't hear what she was saying, but Janet stopped crying and listened as Momma spoke to her. They spoke quietly for a few minutes, and then Momma began singing 'Amazing Grace.'"

Tick lapsed into silence to catch her breath.

"Momma ignored Timothy's furious demands to kill Janet, and she just sat there, rubbing Janet's back and singing to her. Then it was over in a second, and Janet was dead. If I had killed Janet, I could have bought enough time for Momma and me to escape. Instead, the one person who never hurt a living thing was willing to kill for me. I should have done it. It was all so ugly, so horrible."

Mattie and Brad had known that a time would have to come when they would be forced to press Tick about the full story of what happened at the Death Ranch. Mattie felt that Brad would have to be the one to confront her. Her role would be that of an objective bystander poised to intervene to protect Brad and Tick's relationship, and an observer determined to learn every scrap of information that might be helpful in future therapy.

Now every instinct was fighting against her professional objectivity. All she wanted to do was push Brad aside and hug and cry with the child she had grown to love.

Now too shaken to speak, Brad took his daughter up into his arms and just rocked her. After some time, Brad helped his heartbroken daughter back into the chair and knelt beside her.

"Oh, my precious child, I have no answers to help you understand why you and your mother had to endure such agony. God gave mankind free will, and I will never understand why some people can do such horrible things. But none of the torment that either of you experienced was your fault. You have to believe that.

"True, your mother took Janet's life to save yours, but she had the presence of mind, and I believe the power of desperate prayer to God for divine guidance. She knew that when Timothy finished with you, Janet's life would soon end brutally at his hands, as well. The real truth is your mom blessed Janet by pointing her back to her faith and renewing her hope that she would be in heaven with the Lord. I read the coroner's reports indicating that Janet died instantly from a strategically located puncture wound through her heart. For someone who never hurt a fly, your mother's hand must have been guided by divine intervention so that you could live.

"Now, you must learn to forgive yourself, to live a life that brings honor to your mother, to trust that God is in control, and to believe that He loves you."

The sound of his daughter's voice still startlingly new, Tick said something to Mattie about forgiveness and avalanches.

Mattie, now moving to hug Tick and crying openly, was quick to reply. "Exactly, darling. That's for me too."

What avalanches? Brad wondered.

No one spoke a word as the three held on to each other for support in a tight, emotionally exhausted bundle. Brad broke away first, saying that he would be right back. He shot out of the room, leaving the girls slightly bewildered.

A few minutes later, he returned wearing his well-worn leather jacket and a wide-brimmed fedora hat. He took Mattie's hands, got down on his knee, and pulled a small felt box from his pocket. Opening the box, Mattie saw a beautifully set three-carat diamond ring.

"I've wanted to give this to you for quite some time now," said Brad. "Will you do me the greatest honor and marry me?"

Mattie started to laugh while wiping away tears. Tick rushed over to hug Mattie, and they both looked down at Brad, still on his knee.

"Yes! Of course, I will marry you! I can't imagine sharing my life with anyone but you, Brad."

Brad slid the ring on her finger and stood to give Mattie a kiss that ended when she lifted her arm high to get another peek at the ring. Examining the sizable rock by twisting and turning her hand, she giggled with schoolgirl delight, saying quietly, "I can always count on you to come through when the chips are down!"

Before Brad could respond, she pulled him close and kissed him passionately to let him know exactly where he stood. Reluctantly pulling away, Mattie asked Brad if he would mind if she stole some time alone with Tick, who had discreetly disappeared into the kitchen.

"Of course not," Brad answered. "Tick needs to be with you."

Brad watched as the two crossed the deck and settled on the double swing under the gazebo opposite from the moonlit pool. They began slowly swinging, comfortably nestled under a blanket that Mattie had grabbed on their way out.

From his seat on the back porch, Brad could hear Mattie's calm, reassuring voice through the open door. The still unfamiliar voice belonging to Tick was strong and clear, reminding him of the tinkling of chimes—distinctly feminine, but with sharp, clipped enunciation. He couldn't hear the conversation, but Tick sounded distressed at first. Then her voice changed, becoming softer, more relaxed. Brad could see Tick cuddled up next to Mattie, her knees tightly drawn up with her head in Mattie's lap. Brad could hear Tick's laughter, along with Mattie's, a welcomed, joyful sound, followed by excited chatter that eventually lapsed into a silence, which accentuated the rhythmic creaking of the swing.

It was slightly past midnight when Mattie signaled Brad over.

"This girl has earned her forty winks," she whispered. "Would you mind taking her up to her bedroom? I'll go on up with you."

After helping Brad get Tick settled, Mattie left the room to give the two some time alone. Brad sat with his daughter for a few moments, rubbing her back and reassuring her that the sky hadn't fallen and what he had learned had only made him prouder of her. Before leaving the room, he uttered a short prayer.

"Tick is so tired, Father. Help her to sleep now, give her peace and watch over her mind. Let her rest in you tonight. And thank you, dear Lord, for her wonderful voice. Amen."

When he came downstairs, he found Mattie back by the pool, sipping something from a champagne glass.

As he sat down, she reached over and handed him a glass. "Here, I think you could use this."

"What's this? Pink champagne? I could use something stronger than pink bubbles right now."

"Hey, pink is Tick's favorite color, and she picked this bottle from your wine cellar, especially for us."

"I gather this was to enjoy with her carrot cake surprise that we spoiled for her?"

"Yes, I believe it was." Mattie sighed. "But no worries, we can have a do-over cake unveiling tomorrow night.

"After what I put her through tonight, it wouldn't surprise me if she didn't want to leave her room tomorrow, poor kid. When I told her that I wouldn't marry you until she started talking again, the look on her face broke my heart. It felt cruel putting her through that kind of pain. What prompted you to know it was time for a breakthrough?"

"Instinct, Brad…backed by this morning's conversation, and my license as a child psychiatrist," Mattie said, teasingly. "The deck was stacked in my favor. Tick will do anything to protect you and make you happy, and she trusts you… This may sound silly, but once she started talking, I was hoping that you had a ring ready."

Brad replied beaming, "It seems as though I've been carrying it around forever."

"It's gorgeous, Brad. Much more than I deserve," replied Mattie, twisting and admiring the ring on her finger once again. "I have just received everything I could ever want—marrying the man I adore and inheriting a daughter whom I treasure. I'm getting an amazing family and a farm to boot! Thank you, Brad. You are the man of my dreams, and today has been the best day of my life."

"Well, hold on to your hat, my darling. I'm sure there are plenty more where this one came from!"

Looking deeper into Mattie's eyes, he declared, "Tick's protective feelings toward me are pretty intense, I agree, but believe me, I'm not the only person she loves. We know the lengths she will go to get what she wants, what she needs. Lucky for me, she wants you in her life forever, too."

Pausing, he shuffled his feet and looked across the pool toward the house. "Still and all, I'm glad it was the two of us here tonight," he said. "It feels like closure, both of us being here when she finally started talking, that she loves both of us so much that she would break through her shell to keep us all together... Am I making any sense? Do you think she will be all right? Is it finally over?"

"You're making a lot of sense, but no, it couldn't possibly be over for her," Mattie admitted. "She has seen and experienced unimaginable horrors, and the anger and guilt she feels will not simply disappear overnight.

"When we were on the swing tonight," Mattie continued, "she told me that Timothy allowed her to read everything in his library, over her mother's strong and repeated objections. Many books contained subject matter that bordered on the fringe of human behavior, but Timothy liked discussing the books with her. Tick loved that he thought she was so intelligent. She feels that she deeply betrayed her mother in many ways. For years, Tick idolized Timothy, and I believe that both she and her mother liked Janet. It's hard to imagine how a young child could survive the mental and physical scars she endured after *seven years* of absolute horror. It's hard to wrap my head around it. Perhaps I never will. Also, I don't think she will rest until she finds out what happened between her mother and her father's parents, whoever they are. Still, feeling free to speak now is a vast improvement to her overall well-being."

"I'd like to think she will feel like a normal girl someday, whatever that means," Brad said.

"Well, we both know she will never be mainstream," Mattie replied. "Raising Tick is going to be an extraordinary adventure and often quite challenging. But, with God's help, I know we're up to it."

Brad was suddenly feeling more relaxed. "What made her laugh, and what were you talking about out there? She sounded quite excited about something."

"Oh, that," replied Mattie. "I agreed that she and Laura could plan our wedding. We could be in for some sticker shock, so don't lose your wallet."

Brad embraced Mattie as she put her head on his shoulder. "Please tell me that you'll set the date soon," he said. "Why don't we just elope? I'm not getting any younger, if you get my drift."

"I think we have some say in setting the date, but your daughter is excited about planning a real wedding for us, and your family would be devastated if we eloped. Speaking of which, we need to call your boys tomorrow."

Squeezing his hand and laughing, she whispered into his ear, "And I am confident that you have many good years ahead of you, if you get my drift. Now, why don't you kiss me and let's drink pink champagne before I fall asleep?

Spread the News

Tick was first to go downstairs around eight o'clock on Sunday morning. When Brad walked into the kitchen, he found his daughter attempting to reach something on a side cabinet's top-shelf.

"Let me give you a hand, Tick. What are you after?" Brad inquired.

Tick pointed to the honey jar.

"You want that honey, honey?" Brad smiled, waiting to hear Tick's reply, but he received only an affirmative shake of her head.

Oh, no, Brad thought, his spirits sinking. *This isn't good.*

"Sure, no problem," he said. "Let me get that for you. The honey should be on a lower shelf, don't you think?"

Not hearing a reply, Brad's chest began tightening. *Has she gone back to being mute?*

Just then, Mattie came in and brushed past him, asking if he would grab a lemon and squeeze half of it into a big mug while she riffled through the spice drawer.

"Tick, I'm going to add some ginger and turmeric to your tea," Mattie declared. "That should relieve some of the tightness in your throat and help with some of that hoarseness. Good morning, Brad! How did you sleep?"

"I'll tell you after you tell me what's up with you two. Are you okay, Tick? Are you going to speak to me this morning?"

Tick reached for a pad of paper on the counter and wrote, "*I'm perfectly fine, thank you, but my voice is so croaky that your fiancée told me I needed to rest it this morning and drink her hot tea concoction.*"

"Oh, sure," Brad responded, thanking the Lord that his fear came down to a scratchy throat. "It's not surprising that your throat would be irritated. What about rinsing with saltwater? That's what I always do when my throat is irritated."

Whether it was the result of a habit that had turned into second nature, or because she was intentionally saving her tender throat, Tick wrote her dad a reply that allowed both Mattie and Brad to enjoy a good laugh:

"*No offense, Dad—It's not that I don't appreciate your advice, but I think one doctor in this house is going to be more than enough. But thanks anyway.*"

"Very sound advice," Mattie said, giving Brad a peck on his cheek. "But your dad is right. You should gargle with warm salt water after breakfast."

Over breakfast, they discussed plans for the day. Brad had arranged a 3:30 mountain-time videoconference call with the entire family. Because Mattie's time away from the hospital would be coming to a screeching halt at "dawn-thirty" the next morning, she asked if they would consider having an early supper somewhere close to her apartment downtown. Tick requested that they place some flowers at her mother's gravesite, and Laura would be joining them at Brad's house for lunch at 1:00 p.m.

A short time later, Brad and Mattie watched as Tick placed a beautiful bouquet of seasonal flowers on Alissa Morgan's grave. A misty summer rain was falling with the sun's rays lighting the raindrops. It was a healthy sprinkle that seemed especially fitting that morning. Tick's emotional pain had given way to some relief and peace. She spoke to her mother as naturally as though Alissa had been standing right there with her.

"I miss you so much, and you are never far from my thoughts. I need to tell you something. I'm so sorry for trampling over your amazing act of love for me by blaming and hating myself. I would never have seen another day without your sacrifice for me, and I promise that I will cherish the life you gave me until I see you again in heaven. Thanks for my life, Momma. I love you."

Brad and Mattie had walked over to Catherine's grave together, where he placed a bouquet. He felt at peace, believing that a loving God planned his decision to adopt Tick and marry Mattie.

He wondered how the boys would react that afternoon when he announced his engagement to Mattie. Catherine had been an amazing mother and a marvelous wife, and the boys adored her. They would all be polite and gracious, he felt confident, but he also knew the news would sting, and he guessed that it would hit David, his youngest, harder than the others.

David felt particularly close to his mother, so the feeling of loss for his mom and his original family would be understandable. Brad had never considered the notion of falling in love and marrying again, but then, he had never contemplated meeting anyone like Mattie. He would go on loving his sons, as always, giving them time to adjust to a new reality—a journey they would have to take on their own.

Fortunately, Brad's daughters-in-law, Becky and Natalie, had bonded with Mattie months ago, with special privileges to call the superstar pediatrician for medical consultation about the kids at any time. They had both contacted Dr. Barnes on several occasions, and they liked her immensely.

Brad put his thoughts aside when Tick approached, smiling. She took his and Mattie's hand as they walked back to the car together. On the way home, they stopped at Tony Caputo's Market and Deli and picked up four signature Caputo sandwiches along with some pasta salad to-go. Laura would be happy with that.

Laura had only just arrived at the house and was getting out of her car when the jeep pulled up.

Tick's door flew open, and she ran to greet her good friend. "Mattie and Brad are getting married! You and I are going to plan the wedding!"

Eyeing Tick wide-eyed, and then over to Mattie and Brad, Laura was speechless for a moment, and then grabbed Tick up in a huge bear hug, hollering enthusiastically, "It's a miracle! It's a miracle! I've lived to witness a true miracle. Praise God!"

"It's a miracle they're getting married?" Tick questioned loudly after Laura finally put her down.

"No, you little freak... Well, maybe that, too, but the miracle is that you're talking! You're talking! Wait, am I being punked? Okay, where's the camera?"

"You are so funny that I forgot to laugh," Tick teased back.

"Praise heaven!" Laura gushed. "It's true, you're finally talking, you little imp! No more hiding away behind your tablet."

"Okay, you two, break it up," Brad said jokingly. "Let's go in and have some lunch. I'm hungry."

Poking a finger at the highly visible tattoo on Laura's back, Tick said, "If we don't feed this dragon pretty soon, I think it is going to eat us for lunch!"

"Hey! Leave my dragon alone," Laura bantered back. "You scared him when you opened your mouth and spoke!"

Walking into the house carrying the deli bags, Mattie handed one to Laura, and with her left hand now freed, Mattie proudly showed Laura what was shiny and new on her finger.

"So I'm guessing you like it," Laura said calmly as her demeanor shifted to a wry smile. "I knew you would. I helped Brad pick it out."

"Really? Well, I'm not surprised. Brad recognizes that your taste has greatly improved," Mattie said, casting a sideways glance at the dragon tattoo. "I love this ring!"

After lunch, Laura and Tick huddled together for nearly two hours, discussing ideas for the wedding. Still, when Mattie noticed that Tick's voice had begun to sound husky, she stepped in and suggested that the wedding planners take a break and get back together in a few days. After Laura said goodbye, Tick ran upstairs to use a saltwater rinse for her throat before the boys called.

At precisely 3:30 p.m., Brad made his third officially scheduled conference call to his boys and their wives. The first of these calls was when he had to tell the boys of their mother's failing health. His second conference call was to introduce their adopted sister. Announcing his engagement to Mattie was now the third such call. This time, Brad had requested that the grandchildren be present.

David, Brad's youngest son, was the first to speak out.

"Hi, Dad! Hello there, Mattie. Hey, Tick! So what's going on out there in Utah? Is everything okay?"

Before Brad could answer, one of the twins broke in, excited to tell Grandpa Brad about the home run he had hit, but his news was cut short by his mother, who was anxious to hear why Brad had called everyone together.

The boys and their families remained quiet as Brad spoke. "Okay, let me cut to the chase and tell you what's up. I know you are all aware of how important Mattie has been to Tick and me over the past two years. We would both be lost without her, no question about it. But the wonderful thing that happened to me along the way is that I fell head over heels in love with Dr. Barnes, and last night I asked her to marry me. Happily for me, she said yes."

Becky managed to get in the first words. "Congratulations, Dad! I'm so happy for you and Mattie. I wish you both great happiness."

Natalie chimed in, saying, "It's high time! We all knew it was coming! What took y'all so long?"

A chorus of congratulations, blessings, and best wishes followed, with Mattie graciously responding to everyone's kind words.

Brad's middle son, Brian, asked the questions that they all wanted to know.

"Have you set a date yet? What are your plans? What can we do to help?"

"Glad you asked, son," replied Brad, "because we can't set a date or make specific plans without everyone's input. Mattie and I would like the wedding to take place as soon as we can get all of you out here at the same time, hopefully, next month. Also, we want all of you to join us for two weeks in Hawaii after the wedding. Tick and Laura have teamed up as our wedding planners, but they need to pin down dates that will work for all of you before they can make any arrangements.

Brad turned to Tick. "Tick, let me hand the floor over to you now."

With performance anxiety pushing her heart rate to climb as though she had been running laps, Tick waved to everyone on the screen, cleared her throat, and spoke, "Hello, everyone, it's wonderful to see all of you…" The family erupted with everybody talking excitedly at the same time, mixed in with some drama. Kaitlin immediately broke into tears, dramatically announcing that she had been praying every night for Tick to talk, and Natalie loudly told everyone to hush and let the precious child speak "for mercy sake!"

Once the commotion had died down, Tick began speaking again, reaffirming Brad and Mattie's wish to be married in a month, and expressing how anxious she and Laura were to start planning the wedding as soon as the family agreed upon their weeks. She wisely made Becky and Natalie feel included in this significant family event by asking if she could call on them for their opinions and advice, and suggested that they start shopping for wedding outfits and beach clothes. "Of course!" Becky said. "We will get started on that right away since Dad is in such a hurry to tie the knot!"

Brad quickly spoke up to say, "I realize that scheduling two weeks together on such short notice is going to be a challenge for you, but the kids will be out of school in four weeks, and it would be wonderful if we could make our plans soon after that."

"Okay, Dad, no worries!" Ben said. "This is all very exciting, and we'll work this out for you and Mattie and let you know right away."

"That's what I wanted to hear, Ben," Brad responded. "When Laura has your dates, I've asked her to make all the flight and hotel reservations we'll need to get you to Utah and all of us to Hawaii, and since Mattie has never been to Kauai, that's where we would like to go."

The family continued to visit back and forth until the conversation ended with lots of good-natured laughing, everyone recalling the vacation in San Diego after Kaitlin called out, "Tick! Just think about those huge waves we'll be catching together in Kauai! Okay with that, Mom?"

Not to be outdone, one of the twin boys called out, "Tick! I'm going to pack one of those big balloons like the one you divided in half with the kitchen knife. That was so cool!"

Tick took that opportunity to shout out the martial arts battle cry that Linn had taught her in training—"Kiai!"

Becky interrupted the jocularity by sharing what was on her mind: "Tick, before we go, I want you to know how thankful we all feel that you and now Mattie are part of our family. I know God has blessed the Hughes clan."

Tick joyfully responded in a cheerful voice. "1 John 5:4 says: 'For whatever is born of God overcomes the world. And this is the victory that has overcome the world—our faith.' We are all blessed for sure, and words can't express how much I love this family."

Angels in Our Midst

Mattie glanced up at the clock. Brad and Tick would be coming for her soon, the two loves of her life, and she wanted to look perfect for them.

Dear God, she thought, *I don't deserve either of them but thank You—thank You.*

She studied her reflection in the mirror, turning to see the back of the short, rhinestone-covered blue jean jacket that Brenda had created for her. Brenda's talents went beyond her nursing skills; the jacket was dazzling, bling meets blasé, and perfect for the occasion. In less than three hours, friends and family would gather together in the Hughes's barn, a barn entirely transformed to play on the shabby chic theme chosen for the rehearsal dinner—diamonds and denim. It was an idea Tick had suggested, remembering when Brad mentioned the fantastic birthday party that his friend from grad school days had thrown when all the women wore glittery denim attire, and the men looked like polished cowboys. Mattie thought it sounded quirky and fun, so Tick ran with it.

As Mattie pulled on a new pair of Levi's that she had washed in salt water to help soften the stiff denim, two thoughts crossed her mind. First, she had no prewedding jitters whatsoever—she had never been happier or more excited. Second, she marveled at the phenomenal job Tick and Laura had done to pull off this wedding event in just a month. The wedding venues that Laura would even consider were all booked for at least a year. Brad's property behind the house was an ideal setting for an open-air wedding ceremony, and it could also comfortably accommodate a large wedding tent for the reception. The barn was the perfect space for the rehearsal dinner.

Aside from the hunt to find a bridal gown that suited her fashion style, the most challenging job asked of Mattie and Brad was to furnish a guest list ASAP. They handed the completed tally to Laura after only two days of deliberation, and one month before the big day, 150 plain, elegant invitations were in the mail.

Fifty-four family members and out-of-town friends planned to attend the rehearsal dinner, and 137 guests would be attending the wedding and reception the following day.

The denim-clad bride-to-be standing in front of the mirror—the same woman who had fought for control most of her life—had willingly allowed Tick and Laura to plan and execute the entire affair. As Brad had teased, the wedding was a perfect excuse to throw a party for all the people he and Mattie owed.

Feeling confident that her intensive care units at the hospital were running smoothly, Mattie felt perfect freedom from work-related concerns. The ICU's infrastructure, which she had been instrumental in developing, and the committed work of highly skilled and competent personnel were leading factors contributing to the units functioning at the highest evaluation level in the country. She knew that her decision to marry would in no way undermine her department, with a plan for her two-week absence in place. Sam Evans, director of Children's Hospital and a personal friend, assured her that the sky would not fall while she was gone. He ordered her to relax and enjoy this once-in-a-lifetime chapter in her life.

Mattie's female co-workers threw a bridal shower for her at an upscale restaurant, where the guest of honor sipped a glass of pink champagne and opened thoughtful and unique gifts, from monogrammed towels and linens to silver candlesticks. She took a round of needling with grace and humor about marrying the handsome father of the hospital's most demanding patient.

The inner circle of nurses Tick was willing to cooperate with had gotten to know Brad quite well, especially when he and Tick were in the Palace Wing. Brenda, Abigail, Leslie, and Beverly Lee began teasing their boss about snatching up one of the richest, best-looking bachelors in Utah.

"Were all those extraordinary gourmet meals you prepared and brought to the hospital all that time actually for Tick?" Abigail asked, jesting. "After all, everybody has heard that the way to a man's heart is through his stomach!"

Brenda couldn't help but recall the day Tick called her a traitor, mistakenly accusing her of teaming up with the CPS woman. The experience had been hard on her, as she had felt terrible about losing Tick's trust. Mattie's bridal shower was probably not the best time to ask Mattie what was scarier—confronting a teenage girl who was smarter and tougher than nearly everyone on the planet or walking into a lion's den. All of Tick's private nurses came to love the girl dearly, but it was no secret that she was more than capable of wreaking havoc and hurting some feelings.

⚬⚬⚬⚬⚬

Brad checked his watch. He had some time to kill before he needed to pick Mattie up for the rehearsal dinner, so he knocked on Tick's bedroom door to get her approval of his clothes. He was wearing blue jeans with a shiny sterling silver belt buckle, a white-collared shirt, light-blue tie, and a denim vest under a tweed sports jacket, and he capped it off with some "classy" alligator cowboy boots. Tick looked him over, quite pleased to see her dad looking handsome and so happy. She gave him two thumbs-up and told him that he was the best-looking cowboy she had ever seen. He then walked to his office to tidy it up while Tick grabbed her wedding planner portfolio and headed outside to check on how things were progressing with the dinner.

⚬⚬⚬⚬⚬

Laura and her friend, an event planner named Sophia, had arrived earlier, and the two women were working on the finishing touches for the wedding the next day. Tick had sensibly agreed to let this stranger help out, knowing that Laura was juggling more than anyone should expect her to manage, even with Becky and Natalie's input. Laura had her full-time work at the hospital while spending most evenings and every weekend working with Tick on the wedding and rehearsal dinner. She was responsible for reserving a picture-perfect honeymoon suite and five other suites and rooms at a resort hotel on Kauai, along with scheduling and booking the family's flights to Utah and the flights to Hawaii. Laura would be included on the trip, sharing a room with Tick.

The three flights she booked for Brad's sons and their families arrived within twenty minutes of each other two days before the wedding. Both Ben and Brian had rented SUVs, and David would ride wherever there was room for him. Still, Brad and Tick were there at the airport to meet everyone, waving as they all came down the escalator. Brad thought of the boys' mother and how proud Catherine would be of her family, and he was grateful for the outstanding job she had done raising her sons.

The entire gang showed genuine pleasure seeing Tick again. They were excited about hearing her speak and being able to carry on regular conversations with her. The family was relieved that Tick had such a pleasant, normal voice—she didn't sound a bit like Minnie Mouse, as four-year-old Lizzy had decided she would.

At the airport, Brad told his family that he had made dinner reservations at Asian Star, a restaurant not far from the house. He chose this place because the family could all sit comfortably around a large round table while helping themselves to platters of tasty Chinese food placed on a lazy Susan turntable.

Mattie joined them for dinner.

Brad's sons had met Mattie in person at Alissa's funeral and had spent a little bit of time with her one evening at the Deer Valley house. At that time, she was Dr. Barnes—Tick and their father's excellent physician. When she walked into the Asian Star restaurant on this night, the boys quickly stood to greet the woman about to marry their dad.

Brad needn't have worried. Mattie was already well-liked by Becky and Natalie, but that night she was achieving rock star status, captivating the boys, their wives and each of the five grandchildren with humorous hospital stories. Tick took in stride being tapped as four-year-old Lizzy's favorite relative, hopping in Tick's lap, and begging her to draw animal pictures on their placemats.

Brad made a point of sitting next to his youngest son, David, who initially didn't react to his father's announcement to remarry with much enthusiasm. However, given some time to adjust to the idea that his dad had found love again and deserved to be happy, David was finally able to express his heartfelt good wishes to his dad for a happy life with Mattie. When the meal was over, everyone piled into their vehicles, still laughing about the fortune Brad had pulled out of his cookie: "You will be hungry again in one hour."

The family would stay at the Snowbird Lodge since the house was ground zero for the wedding preparations; it wasn't a good time for the kids to have the run of the place. The lodge was close by and offered super activities to keep everyone entertained—an alpine slide, climbing wall, mountain rollercoaster, zip line, and beautiful hiking trails.

∽᭬ᝈᣰᣰᣰᣰ᭬ᝈ∼

It was almost time for Brad to leave and pick up Mattie for the rehearsal dinner. From his second-story office window, he could see Tick, who was flipping through the pages of the wedding planner binder she had started compiling the day after Mattie accepted Brad's marriage proposal. Since then, she and Laura, along with a few Hughes Industry workers Brad had recruited to help with numerous projects, had been working tirelessly on the wedding. To the girls' credit, they had managed to keep the expenses as reasonable as possible.

Brad hadn't seen nearly as much of Mattie as he had wanted during the past month. She had been working hard to tie up any loose ends at the hospital, and Tick and Laura had taken up any free time she may have had.

All of that will end tomorrow, Brad reflected. *I will be seeing a lot more of Dr. Barnes, just as I fancied from the moment I laid eyes on her in the hospital two years ago*. He had learned about the avalanche and how Mattie and Tick had found peace together. As he walked out the door on his way downstairs, he knew he was a lucky man.

Professor Becket pulled on a broad-brimmed cowboy hat, tilted on one side to hide the bandages that Mattie and Tick had helped him apply earlier in the day. They were so kind and gentle with him, chatting away gaily while they worked to cover the horrible and painful effects of his skin cancer, unaware of how much he relished the soft touch of two such beautiful ladies. Now, he looked like some sort of dashing cowboy.

The professor hadn't gone to a party in years, but he wasn't about to miss the dinner tonight or the wedding tomorrow. It had been two months since Tick, seemingly just like that, began talking. Beckett had learned that her vocal debut in her classroom at the university had been quite unspectacular. She simply walked to the front of the room before class commenced and announced that computer monitors were no longer needed. Thanking her teacher and her classmates for their tolerance and support, Tick provided no further explanation of the profound alterations made in her life. Her classmates, an accepting bunch who respected Tick's privacy, reacted with affirming nods and one or two "cool" comebacks. They admired Tick Hughes, no matter how she chose to communicate.

The professor needed no explanation, either, but for different reasons. He knew that, with steadfast love and support from Brad Hughes, along with some capable and perceptive therapy, Tick had finally freed herself from the cave that had once held her hostage. Becket wasn't sure what pleased him more: the fact that he had figured out that Tick Hughes was, in fact, Esther Morgan of the Death Ranch, or that Tick privately knew that he knew and trusted him with this knowledge.

Following his first meeting with Tick, Becket and Tick had never discussed her past. His suspicions were confirmed when her absences coincided with the Madison trial, and he had seen profound changes in her behavior when their tutoring sessions resumed.

Your secret is safe with me, Becket thought to himself as he pulled on a well-worn pair of cowboy boots. In addition to being far more gifted than he had initially tagged her, Tick had turned out to be someone much more important to the terminally ill old peda-gogue—it was like Tick was his personal angel. She had renewed his faith in people as well as in a God that cared about him. She seemed to sense his moods, his worries and had a way of challenging him and pulling him out of his low spirits when he felt down.

⎯⎰⎰⎰⎯

Claire Summers rode one of the Thomas's horses into the barn with Megan and Rachael riding in behind her. Claire had flown into Salt Lake City three days before the wedding, and Tick and Brad met her at her baggage carrousel. Each girl had her special surprise to reveal, and as Claire tentatively walked forward, without the aid of a walker, Tick ran to her with big happy tears. "Oh my gosh, you're walking!" Tick said. Flabbergasted, Claire replied, "Oh my gosh, you're talking!"

Claire would be staying with the Thomases rather than con-tending with all the pre-wedding madness at the Hughes' house. Tick and Brad knew that the family would treat Claire like their own, and they were right. They took to Claire immediately, and Megan and Rachael didn't let Claire's handicap stop them from getting her on a horse the day she arrived, then taking Claire to their hidden pool in the mountains, where the three went swimming. Claire felt freer than she had in years.

Over a picnic lunch that Melanie had packed, Claire told sto-ries about Tick's shenanigans when they were in rehab together. She described how Tick would get in trouble rocketing up and down the hallways in a wheelchair, Brent in her lap, nurses chasing after the two of them; how Brent would beg his nurses to take him to Tick's room, where she would read to him, or they would color pictures together, or he would just take a nap with her. It was good for the

Thomas sisters to hear how happy Tick had made their little brother, and they asked Claire if she would share those stories with their mom and dad.

Hanging over the Thomas's fireplace mantel was a fantastic painting, which Claire immediately recognized as Tick's artwork. It was of a little boy floating up into the sky, with angels and all types of whimsical animals soaring around him. It was a joyful scene that undoubtedly brought the family great comfort. Claire knew that some of Tick's paintings were now on display at the Amori Studios in New York City, but what she didn't know was that two of Tick's paintings had recently sold for a hefty price.

As Claire and the Thomases drove to the rehearsal dinner, all decked out and shining in their best western wear, Melanie mentioned that Brad and Jim had formed a farming partnership and that Brad had made it all possible.

An example of something positive coming from something terrible, Claire thought, thinking of Brent's passing.

Still, after Megan commented on Tick's life-saving skills, Rachael's immediate and stern hushing of her sister not to "go there" was odd. Claire couldn't shake the feeling that there was more to that story than she would learn. It was the same feeling she felt after spending so many weeks with Tick at the center, but she could never identify her suspicion that there was more to her friend's story than she was willing to divulge. Claire somehow knew that their friendship could be spoiled if she pressed the issue, so she didn't pry. Claire believed that God placed her and Tick together for a good reason. Tick gave her the will to fight for her recovery and to get strong again, and Tick needed a friend she could trust.

One thing was certain: Tick and Claire would be friends for life.

⌒⦚⦚⦚⌒

Ruth Evers and Butch Parker headed for the hotel elevator to join Grandpa Wright, Wong, Brewer, Dresder, Judge Thornton, and Hoger for a drink at the Little America lounge before they all left for the dinner party at the Hughes' place. Parker had gotten into the spirit of the party's theme and was wearing faded blue jeans and a black western-style shirt with a rhinestone bolo tie.

Agent Evers, looking attractive in a long blue jean skirt and a sparkly beige pullover was lost in thought as Butch pressed the main floor's button. *Tick's story is so improbable,* the seasoned FBI agent silently considered. *A battered, orphaned, and mute child, rising from the ashes like the phoenix to eradicate two of the most sadistic criminals on record, now, joyfully celebrating the marriage of two people she loved the most.* Evers was eager to see Tick and to hear her voice for the first time. She would make a point of telling this exceptional girl how proud she was of her.

But Ruth's anticipation seeing Tick again was not without a troublesome feeling of guilt for enrolling the girl in the Bureau's computer class. Because of her nimble, gifted mind, Tick was a natural with code, able to grasp it as if she had known the language all her life. One assignment given to the students was to recreate a previously solved case identifying an overseas hacker who had stolen funds from a government account. The task was an object lesson on cybercrime, with the students provided the same information available to the experts.

The case had taken a crack investigation team six months to solve, but Tick figured it out by herself in less than half that time. Her instructors were astounded and reported their high opinion about the teenage girl to their superiors. How Miss Hughes' talents could be utilized and "handled" was on the drawing board, and Ruth was uneasy about the possible outcome. She was no stranger to ambition, greed, and power, and she knew that there would be influential people stopping at nothing to gain access to the girl's gifts, with no regard for the consequences to Tick.

I'm guilty of doing the same thing to her, Ruth admitted to herself, thinking back to Madison's trial. *Didn't I use Tick to help convict a killer? Didn't I use her to make the Bureau, and myself, look good?*

Tick was fourteen and expected to graduate from college in two years. Ruth hoped that she would continue at the University of Utah, hopefully pursuing additional degrees and broadening her interests until she was eighteen. Then, who knew what she would decide to do. For now, Agent Evers would be strongly allied with Dr. Barnes and Brad Hughes to protect their daughter. The Epilektoi were still out there. Tick's life was still in danger.

It was no secret that Dr. Barnes was more than a little disillusioned with the FBI, so she was flattered and surprised to receive an invitation to both the rehearsal dinner and the wedding. Undoubtedly, Brad and Tick were behind the invitation, and Ruth wondered if Tick and Brad overruled Mattie when her name went into the wedding guest 'sorting hat.'

When the elevator reached the lobby floor, Ruth and Butch stepped out to meet up with the others. They weren't hard to spot, looking like a bunch of rodeo promoters sitting around small lounge tables pushed together to accommodate the group. The thought crossed Ruth's mind that the Hughes' friends and family would soon be eyewitnesses to a ceremony that was a product of divine intervention—one of the miraculous consequences of a little girl's escape from hell. Special Agent Ruth Evers felt encouraged to think that there was a force for good at work that dwarfed anything the Bureau could hope to embody.

<hr />

In charge of looking after the children, Ben ordered them out of the Snowbird Lodge pool. It was time to get dressed for the wedding rehearsal. He and his brother, Brian, had spent the afternoon by the pool relaxing, catching up, and watching their kids swim while Becky and Natalie had their nails done and went shopping for hair ribbons for Kaitlin and Lizzy. The brothers found themselves on the same page regarding their dad. The fact that he was about to be married to someone besides their mother was hard to grasp, but they thought Mattie was terrific, and Tick certainly needed a mother figure in her life. They believed that their father and Mattie made a good match, and the two boys were happy for them and Tick.

Ben shook his head in disbelief as he recalled the first time he saw Tick and Dr. Barnes two years earlier when his dad resurfaced after disappearing without a word for months. The conference call his father had set up seemed surreal. Here was this strange, mute girl sitting in a wheelchair next to his dad, and a woman wearing a white lab coat sitting on his other side. Mad as hell with his father for his mysterious absences, Ben now realized that he missed the first hint of a much deeper attachment to come between his father and this doctor. He had been focused on his dad's adoption of a twelve-year-old girl. Then, once he heard the shocking complications attached to the girl, the former Esther Morgan, he thought that his dad had utterly lost his mind.

But when Dr. Barnes spoke to the family the following day, she turned Ben's thinking around. She was impressively professional, informed, and composed as she talked at length about Tick, patiently answering every question the family had about the girl. The conversation ended with Ben feeling proud of his father and with the resolve to make his new sister feel safe, comfortable, and wanted in the family.

Ben's wife, Becky, took longer to get on the "Tick train," as she put it. Still, the little dynamo became Wonder Woman to her daughter, Kaitlin, and encouraged an overprotected mother to allow her now vigorous daughter to venture out and test her wings.

Thanks to Tick, Ben and Becky were more unified in their role as parents, and Kaitlin was enjoying a healthier, happier life.

⎯⎯⎯∾∾∾⎯⎯⎯

It was a familiar picture for Brian, watching as Natalie tried to capture Lizzy long enough to throw a dress on her. Neither parent wanted their child to be a nuisance or hang on Tick for the next two days, so they arranged for a babysitter to watch their daughter. They figured that an experienced and entertaining sitter would be the best solution to keep their high-spirited child out of mischief and out of Tick's hair.

Natalie's predictions about a possible marriage between Brad and Mattie had been right on target. "Your dad loves her, you know," she commented one day after Brad called to check-in.

"I should hope so," Brian answered. "He did adopt her, after all."

Natalie's reply had surprised him. "I'm not talking about Tick! I meant Dr. Barnes. Don't you notice how his voice softens every time he speaks of her? That's a man in love!"

Brian did not know Dr. Barnes well, but he knew that she had already become a big part of the family, so it was about time to make it official. He knew that his pregnant wife had called Mattie on at least three occasions to receive advice that turned out to be extremely helpful. Tomorrow, the Hughes would have an excellent doctor in the family. *Pretty special,* he thought.

Brian hadn't taken a real vacation in years, and the prospect of a Hawaiian vacation left him almost light-headed with excitement. Unbelievably, his caseload for once accommodated their unexpected vacation plans. He enjoyed going over every detail of the trip to Kauai. He had texted Tick multiple times over the past weeks with ideas for island excursions and activities that they should consider. Not surprisingly, she had already scoped out every possible outing. She could be so funny, Brian thought, so irreverent, scolding him whenever he said something that sounded ridiculous to her, but she was smart, thoughtful, and loads of fun.

Brian was crazy about his new sister.

～⚬⚬⚬～

David sat nursing a beer on the balcony of his room. His thoughts were on his mother. He missed her as much now as ever, and he remembered how naïve he was to believe that her failing health was something he could have prevented with positive thoughts and fervent prayers. He had come to discover just how few things he had any control over, and his father's wedding tomorrow was a looming case in point.

Intellectually, David understood why his father had adopted Tick and why he was marrying Mattie. He liked both of them more than he cared to admit. Still, childhood memories haunted him: ski outings, Christmas mornings, family dinners, and memories too firmly imprinted in his mind to ignore the mother he cherished.

David had met Laura at Alissa's funeral many months ago, and the attractive young woman came to his mind quite often. He didn't know exactly why. Maybe it was because he noticed how protective and sure-footed Laura had been with Tick at her mother's funeral—how appropriately and responsibly she had acted when Tick became emotional, and how at ease she seemed with everyone.

And there was something else—another side to her that he detected and also quite liked. Sure, she was smart, but she had a kind of wisdom about her and a bit of a worldly and wild side. He even thought that he had spotted the top of a tattoo on her back.

Laura was a beautiful young woman with dark hair, dark eyes, and a perfect figure. When David asked his dad about her, Brad's response was evasive, but he could discern that Laura was like a daughter to Mattie. David heard the message behind his dad's response loud and clear: *Better not mess with that one, son.*

Perhaps Brad had good reason to put a lid on his son's inquiry. Even David wasn't proud of his track record with women. He had dated many wonderful young women who had pursued a more meaningful, long-term relationship with him, but he was more inter-ested in traveling the world than in settling down. His relationships rarely lasted very long, and his brothers joked that he was working his way through the United Nations.

Taking one last swallow of his beer before rising to dress for the dinner, David chuckled as he imagined his brothers' reaction if they knew that he hadn't dated anyone since Alissa's funeral.

⚬⚬⚬

Walking into the kitchen, Laura greeted Consuelo, Ana's niece, who looked like she was on her last legs. The girl had been wash-ing and preparing a massive mound of vegetables since dawn. Tick had successfully orchestrated how Consuelo and a handful of others would be spending their time helping with wedding preparations. But this was nothing new to Laura, who had worked with an older version of Tick for years. Truth be known, bossy Miss Hughes was

590

just a younger variation of Mattie, but Tick's clout with people always seemed bizarre coming from someone so young.

Laura's deep affection for Tick was undeniable, and their sisterly relationship permitted lots of good-natured bantering. Laura was not above dishing out a little payback for Tick's cheekiness, however, and she left the hot kitchen to go outside to join Tick and present her with a surprise.

A month earlier, Tick had asked Laura to design a sparkly unicorn applique to put on the back of her blue jean jacket for the Diamonds and Denim dinner. Laura agreed but insisted that Tick could not see it until the day of the party. Laura secretly overturned Tick's request for a unicorn, designing instead a fantastic, glittering variation of the identical dragon tattooed on her back.

⎯⎯⎯⎯⎯⎯⎯

Looking out of the kitchen window to see who was laughing, Ana saw Laura and Tick hugging and laughing up a storm. She also noticed that Tick's blue jean jacket looked too big for her, and she tried to remember the last time she had checked her *chica's* weight.

Ana had been Tick's weigh-in commander in the past, making her young charge stand on a scale every Monday morning, then carefully recording her weight for the doctor. Ana had learned that the weight loss wasn't intentional. Tick would just get so busy that she would forget to eat. If food were in front of her, she would eat it.

The faithful caretaker wondered how her work would change when Señora Mattie came to live at the house. Things might get more manageable, she guessed. Keeping up with *la chica* and worrying about her could be very tiring—the girl never seemed to stop, always overdoing.

Señor Brad bent to her will too much, she thought, and Tick needed a much firmer hand.

Upon returning from Peru, Ana's heart jumped out of her chest when Tick spoke to her for the first time at the airport. To hear her voice was like a gift from Jesus. Then in nearly perfect Spanish, Tick began asking her about the trip and a thousand other questions about

Peru and her family. It was hard for Ana to believe that anyone could learn a language so quickly and so well, but she had always known that Señorita Tick was not just anyone. Not very much about Brad's new daughter surprised Ana anymore.

Considered to be a member of the Hughes family, Ana would be in the wedding as one of Mattie's attendants. Señor Brad and Señorita Tick made it impossible for her to say no. Mattie had found a beautifully designed long skirt and jacket at a Park City boutique that carried high-end Peruvian garments. Still, the outfit did little to calm Ana's insecurity. She thought she would feel silly standing alongside such tall and beautiful women: Laura, Becky, Natalie, and Mattie. Even Tick was now at least a foot taller than she was.

Ana drew the line on her involvement, however, when it came to the family trip to Hawaii. She certainly didn't need to go on another vacation, and she believed that only the immediate family should spend time together weaving beautiful new "threads" into the Hughes's family tapestry.

Ana was mostly concerned for Catherine's youngest, David. He was so sensitive, and she knew that he still suffered over his mother's illness and death.

David needs to leave his sorrow behind him tonight and have a good time, Ana thought. Perhaps she would nudge David to sit with Laura at the dinner. Laura would be perfect for him: practical, beautiful, and kind, like Catherine and like Mattie.

As Laura started back to the kitchen, a contented Ana made her way to the refrigerator, where she would search for a nutritious snack to take to Tick before dinner.

Alone now, Tick sat on the swing by the pool, her knees drawn up, looking through the wedding binder. The wedding was less than twenty-four hours away, and everything had to be perfect.

The beautiful flower arrangements were in cold storage, ready to enhance the outdoor wedding site and complete the tent's table decorations. All the attendants' dresses were pressed and upstairs in the closet. The caterer's wagons had arrived to begin the wedding dinner preparations. A four-tiered cake that Tick had slaved over for days was in a giant rented refrigerator. Welcome baskets were in the rooms of all the out-of-town guests. The brothers were all settled with their families at Snowbird, their tuxes waiting for them in Brad's study. And all the flights and hotel reservations in Kauai had been booked and confirmed.

For that night's rehearsal dinner, Ana, Arturo, and Consuela prepared a special surprise, planned mostly for Brad—a pachamanca, the age-old Peruvian feast that Brad enjoyed during his years living in South America. Large quantities of corn, potatoes, onions, lamb, pork, and chicken roasted for hours in an earthen oven that Arturo built behind the barn, and Tick had baked cornbread and made a massive pot of baked beans, cowboy style. The large beer keg that Laura ordered had arrived, and the country and western singer and his band were setting up their equipment.

It seemed unlikely that there was anything left to plan, organize, or order. All the checklists were complete, and the time had arrived. Had they pulled it off? Was this wedding going to be as enjoyable and as unique as she and Laura hoped it would be—as beautiful as she had envisioned for her father and Mattie? Could she and Laura and everyone who had helped them all these weeks rest assured that they had accomplished something suitable, something memorable for the two most important people in her life?

Unexpectedly, she felt a sense of dread, almost fear, as she pored over the list.

What if things didn't go well? What if she had forgotten something big and there was no time to do anything about it? What if Brad and Mattie didn't look very pleased but stressed by all the preparations? On top of that, what if the family could never accept Mattie in their hearts as Brad's wife—just another outsider like herself?

Tick's chest tightened as she fought for breath. In her mind cursed with perfect recall, Tick launched into the dark places of her past. She remembered Tammy Rockford's last confused sideways glance at her, unable to process the reality of her impending death in the ring. She pictured the sneering look of triumph on David

Bittner's face when he slashed her, and the rage she felt when a long, thin red line blossomed and spilled out red across her forearm. She recaptured Timothy Bird's crazed look as he beat her mother; she saw the dazed and pained look on her mother's face when Timothy left her lying broken and bleeding. She recalled the last glimpse she had of her mother—an unearthly, fierce, and unyielding expression on her face as she ordered her daughter to run.

A strong, cold gust of wind blew down the mountain, striking Tick's face chastening her like one of Grandpa's "wakeup" cuffs when she lost focus while training. It was like receiving a sharp reprimand from her mother, Brad, Mattie, or the Bible.

She noticed the leaves dancing on the quaking aspen, small ripples in the pool glistening in the setting sun, and two enormous white clouds playfully mimicking a poodle and a giant whale. She took a deep, calming breath and squinted up at the rocky peaks towering majestically behind the house. Just then, she began silently reciting the Psalm that she and her mother prayed together every night:

> *He maketh me to lie down in green pastures;*
> *He leadeth me beside the still waters. He restoreth*
> *my soul.*

Her mother's face flashed through her mind. She missed her so much, but she knew she was safe now, with God.

Closing her eyes, she heard Ana, Consuelo, and Laura laughing in the kitchen, and happy images came into her mind: the bear hugs from Brad that left her feeling safe and loved and Mattie's laughter when they cooked together and that ever-so-serious expression she had when they talked, as though there could never be a conversation that mattered more. Tick thought of Ana's grumpy but loving expressions and her determination to make her eat something—the lectures she sputtered out in blisteringly fast Spanish when she felt Brad's *chica* was doing something foolish. Finally, she thought of her friends—Claire, Megan, Rachael, Laura, the professor, and even Laura's tattoo. Friends that always had her back.

Tick opened her eyes to see the contrails of a jet streaming across the sky. She remembered watching a similar display on the cliff when she believed all was lost. The day after tomorrow, she would be on one of those jets with her new family, flying off to an island paradise and a fantastic adventure, with more experiences to follow and a life to live.

"You tried to beat me down and destroy me, but you failed. God has my back and has given me a wonderful life, with a family that loves me."

She noticed Brad exiting the house and heading in her direction, and a joyous expression came over her face. She thought back to the sketch she had drawn two years earlier when she was in the hospital. It pictured Brad, standing on a cliff, with enormous, fiery eagle wings extending from his back. He had told her then that he would never forget that eagle or how it appeared like an incoming aircraft that stalled for a second before abruptly aborting its landing. They studied the sketch together for a long time that day, their thoughts privately held.

Tick couldn't help but smile as her father marched toward her, and she whispered, "Thank you, God, for sending me an angel to rescue me."

And as Brad leaned down to give Tick yet another hug, he thanked God for guiding him to her.

Who's Who

Brad Hughes: Family and Friends

Brad Hughes: Successful businessman, father
                                and grandfather, widowed four
                                years (age 58)

Catherine Hughes: Deceased wife of Brad Hughes

Brad Hughes
family:

                Oldest son: Ben Hughes (age 33)
                Ben's wife: Becky Hughes (age 32)
                Their children: Kaitlin (age 10)
                                Jerome (twin, age 5)
                                Jonathan (twin, age 5)

                Middle son: Brian Hughes (age 32)
                Brian's wife: Natalie Houghes (age 30)
                Children: Lizzy (age 2)
                Youngest son: David Hughes (age 30)

Whitney Heldar: Brad Hughes's executive
                                secretary

Ana Canasa: Brad's housekeeper

Alissa Morgan: Family and Friends

Alissa Morgan:	Tick's mother
Esther Morgan:	Tick's given name (age 12)
Tick Esther Hughes:	Brad's adopted name for Esther Morgan
Mable and Terrance Fowler:	Couple that housed Esther and Alissa

Children's Primary Hospital Staff and Support

Sam Evans:	Director of Children's Primary Hospital
Vince Dogart:	Assistant director, Children's Primary Hospital
Andrew Therber	Senior council, Children's Primary Hospital
Dr. Mattie Barnes:	Director of the Intensive Care Unit at the Children's Primary Hospital
Laura Shelby:	Mattie Barnes' assistant (age 28)
Brenda Martin:	Head nurse, Pediatric Care
Abigale Jones:	Nurse, Pediatric ICU
Leslie Thomas:	Nurse, Pediatric ICU
Beverly Lee:	Nurse, Pediatric ICU
Dr. Joseph Weinstein:	Plastic surgeon, Children's Primary Hospital
Dr. Oliver Brackford:	Orthopedic surgeon, Children's Primary Hospital
Dr. Joseph Stobel:	Vascular surgeon, Children's Primary Hospital

Childhood Protective Services

Diane Mansfield:	Director of Child Protective Services
Susan Messener:	Childcare Protective Services
Kenneth Enloe:	Susan Messener's Attorney

FBI and Law Enforcement

Judge Thornton:	Juvenile Court, Third District
Nate Hoger:	Deputy chief of the Special Operations Bureau, SLC
Steve Brewer:	FBI field agent, Seattle
Jenny Dresder:	FBI field officer, SLC
Martha Rucker:	FBI field agent—killed in Mexico
Mrs. Ruth Evers:	Head of National Center for the Analysis of Violent Crime NCAVC Quantico, Virginia
Butch Parker:	Senior FBI profiler at (NCAVC)
Trenton Wright (Grandpa):	Ex-Navy Seal trainer (FBI)
Linn Wong:	Martial arts trainer (FBI)
Durgan Marshall:	Prosecutor at Bart Madison's trial
Dr. Gifford Palmore	FBI Consultant

Tick Hughes: Friends and Supporters

Brent Thomas:	Age 4, cancer patient
Melanie and Jim Thomas:	Brent's parents
Megan and Rachael Thomas:	Thomas's daughters (ages 15 and 17)
Claire Summers:	Injured Olympic skier (age 16)

Tick Hughes Schooling

Professor Becket: Tick's tutor and chairman of the University of Utah's Special Program for Gifted Students

Sue Ellen Kasch: Directory of U. of U. Gifted Program

Timothy Bird: Associates

Timothy Bird: Psychopath who kidnaps Tick and Alissa Morgan

Janet Herrington: Timothy Bird's associate

Marjory Perkins: Timothy Bird's associate

Bart Madison: Timothy Bird's associate

Sunder Buckley: Bart Madison's defense attorney

Timothy Bird and Bart Madison Victims

- Jessica Milford University of Washington professor murdered by Timothy Bird
- Marjory Perkins (age 49)—Timothy follower
- Janet Herrington (age 49)—Timothy follower
- Angela Parsons (age 25)—Nevada prostitute
- Tom Ford (age 49)—rancher
- John Harbor (age 52)—trucker
- Tammy Rockford (age 17)—rodeo star
- Thornton Bittner (age 45) and his son David Bittner (age 16)
- Alissa Morgan (age 32)
- Two graves, victims unknown
- FBI agents killed (2 in Uinta Mountain, 5 including agent Rucker in Mexico)

<u>Bart Madison—Fairhope and Ranch Victims</u>

- Leslie Quinton (age 12)
- Andrea Stevens (age 9)
- Jane Jennings (age 10)
- Sandra Hopkins (age17)
- Barbra Hopkins (age12)

About the Author

The storyteller, a graduate in civil engineering from Tufts University with an MBA from the University of Utah, grew up in an isolated Peruvian mining camp located at 12,000 feet elevation. His childhood pastimes included exploring the mountains and jungles of Peru, reading, riding horses, and hunting. Following a family tradition, Mr. Higgs went into the mining business, participating in operations in Minnesota, Nova Scotia, the Bahamas, Peru, Chile, Alberta (Fort McMurray), and Utah. The book would not be possible without his wife Kathryn, who poured over every paragraph, adding life and color to the dialogue.

CPSIA information can be obtained
at www.ICGtesting.com
Printed in the USA
JSHW022250190622
27191JS00001B/1

9 781638 746744